Agatha Christie is known th............................Crime. Her books have sold over a billion copies in ....billion in foreign languages. She is the most widely published author of all time and in any language, outsold only by the Bible and Shakespeare. She is the author of 80 crime novels and short story collections, 19 plays, and six novels written under the name of Mary Westmacott.

Agatha Christie's first novel, *The Mysterious Affair at Styles*, was written towards the end of the First World War, in which she served as a VAD. In it she created Hercule Poirot, the little Belgian detective who was destined to become the most popular detective in crime fiction since Sherlock Holmes. It was eventually published by The Bodley Head in 1920.

In 1926, after averaging a book a year, Agatha Christie wrote her masterpiece. *The Murder of Roger Ackroyd* was the first of her books to be published by Collins and marked the beginning of an author–publisher relationship which lasted for 50 years and well over 70 books. *The Murder of Roger Ackroyd* was also the first of Agatha Christie's books to be dramatized – under the name *Alibi* – and to have a successful run in London's West End. *The Mousetrap*, her most famous play of all, opened in 1952 and is the longest-running play in history.

Agatha Christie was made a Dame in 1971. She died in 1976, since when a number of books have been published posthumously: the bestselling novel *Sleeping Murder* appeared later that year, followed by her autobiography and the short story collections *Miss Marple's Final Cases*, *Problem at Pollensa Bay* and *While the Light Lasts*. In 1998 *Black Coffee* was the first of her plays to be novelized by another author, Charles Osborne.

THE AGATHA CHRISTIE COLLECTION

Agatha Christie

POIROT

THE COMPLETE BATTLES OF
HASTINGS

VOLUME I

•

THE MYSTERIOUS AFFAIR AT STYLES

•

THE MURDER ON THE LINKS

•

THE BIG FOUR

•

PERIL AT END HOUSE

•

HarperCollins*Publishers*

HarperCollins*Publishers*
77–85 Fulham Palace Road,
Hammersmith, London W6 8JB
www.harpercollins.co.uk

This edition first published 2003
1 3 5 7 9 8 6 4 2

This collection copyright © Agatha Christie Limited 2004
www.agathachristie.com

The Mysterious Affair At Styles © Agatha Christie Limited 1920
The Murder on the Links © Agatha Christie Limited 1923
The Big Four © Agatha Christie Limited 1927
Peril At End House © Agatha Christie Limited 1932

ISBN 0 00 717117 X

Typeset in Plantin Light and Gill Sans by
Palimpsest Book Production Limited,
Polmont, Stirlingshire

Printed and bound in Great Britain by
Clays Ltd, St Ives plc

CONTENTS

THE MYSTERIOUS AFFAIR
AT STYLES

To my mother

CONTENTS

I GO TO STYLES

The intense interest aroused in the public by what was known at the time as 'The Styles Case' has now somewhat subsided. Nevertheless, in view of the world-wide notoriety which attended it, I have been asked, both by my friend Poirot and the family themselves, to write an account of the whole story. This, we trust, will effectually silence the sensational rumours which still persist.

I will therefore briefly set down the circumstances which led to my being connected with the affair.

I had been invalided home from the Front; and, after spending some months in a rather depressing Convalescent Home, was given a month's sick leave. Having no near relations or friends, I was trying to make up my mind what to do, when I ran across John Cavendish. I had seen very little of him for some years. Indeed, I had never known him particularly well. He was a good fifteen years my senior, for one thing, though he hardly looked his forty-five years. As a boy, though, I had often stayed at Styles, his mother's place in Essex.

We had a good yarn about old times, and it ended in his inviting me down to Styles to spend my leave there.

'The mater will be delighted to see you again – after all those years,' he added.

'Your mother keeps well?' I asked.

'Oh, yes. I suppose you know that she has married again?'

I am afraid I showed my surprise rather plainly. Mrs Cavendish, who had married John's father when he was a widower with two sons, had been a handsome woman of middle-age as I remembered her. She certainly could not be a day less than seventy now. I recalled her as an energetic, autocratic personality, somewhat inclined to charitable and social notoriety, with a fondness for opening bazaars and playing the Lady Bountiful. She was a most generous woman, and possessed a considerable fortune of her own.

Their country-place, Styles Court, had been purchased by Mr Cavendish early in their married life. He had been completely under his wife's ascendancy, so much so that, on dying, he left the place to her for her lifetime, as well as the larger part of his income; an arrangement that was distinctly unfair to his two sons. Their stepmother, however, had always been most generous to them; indeed, they were so young at the time of their father's remarriage that they always thought of her as their own mother.

Lawrence, the younger, had been a delicate youth. He had qualified as a doctor but early relinquished the profession of medicine, and lived at home while pursuing literary ambitions; though his verses never had any marked success.

John practised for some time as a barrister, but had finally settled down to the more congenial life of a country squire. He had married two years ago, and had taken his wife to live at Styles, though I entertained a shrewd suspicion that he would have preferred his mother to increase his allowance, which would have enabled him to have a home of his own. Mrs Cavendish, however, was a lady who liked to make her own plans, and expected other people to fall in with them, and in this case she certainly had the whip hand, namely: the purse strings.

John noticed my surprise at the news of his mother's remarriage and smiled rather ruefully.

'Rotten little bounder too!' he said savagely. 'I can tell you, Hastings, it's making life jolly difficult for us. As for Evie – you remember Evie?'

'No.'

'Oh, I suppose she was after your time. She's the mater's factotum, companion, Jack of all trades! A great sport – old Evie! Not precisely young and beautiful, but as game as they make them.'

'You were going to say –'

'Oh, this fellow! He turned up from nowhere, on the pretext of being a second cousin or something of Evie's, though she didn't seem particularly keen to acknowledge the relationship. The fellow is an absolute outsider, anyone can see that. He's got a great black beard, and wears patent leather boots in all weathers!

But the mater cottoned to him at once, took him on as secretary – you know how she's always running a hundred societies?'

I nodded.

'Well, of course, the war has turned the hundreds into thousands. No doubt the fellow was very useful to her. But you could have knocked us all down with a feather when, three months ago, she suddenly announced that she and Alfred were engaged! The fellow must be at least twenty years younger than she is! It's simply bare-faced fortune hunting; but there you are – she is her own mistress, and she's married him.'

'It must be a difficult situation for you all.'

'Difficult! It's damnable!'

Thus it came about that, three days later, I descended from the train at Styles St Mary, an absurd little station, with no apparent reason for existence, perched up in the midst of green fields and country lanes. John Cavendish was waiting on the platform, and piloted me out to the car.

'Got a drop or two of petrol still, you see,' he remarked. 'Mainly owing to the mater's activities.'

The village of Styles St Mary was situated about two miles from the little station, and Styles Court lay a mile the other side of it. It was a still, warm day in early July. As one looked out over the flat Essex country, lying so green and peaceful under the afternoon sun, it seemed almost impossible to believe that, not so very far away, a great war was running its appointed course. I felt I had suddenly strayed into another world. As we turned in at the lodge gates, John said:

'I'm afraid you'll find it very quiet down here, Hastings.'

'My dear fellow, that's just what I want.'

'Oh, it's pleasant enough if you want to lead the idle life. I drill with the volunteers twice a week, and lend a hand at the farms. My wife works regularly "on the land". She is up at five every morning to milk, and keeps at it steadily until lunch-time. It's a jolly good life taking it all round – if it weren't for that fellow Alfred Inglethorp!' He checked the car suddenly, and glanced at his watch. 'I wonder if we've time to pick up Cynthia. No, she'll have started from the hospital by now.'

'Cynthia! That's not your wife?'

'No, Cynthia is a protégée of my mother's, the daughter of

an old schoolfellow of hers, who married a rascally solicitor. He came a cropper, and the girl was left an orphan and penniless. My mother came to the rescue, and Cynthia has been with us nearly two years now. She works in the Red Cross Hospital at Tadminster, seven miles away.'

As he spoke the last words, we drew up in front of the fine old house. A lady in a stout tweed skirt, who was bending over a flower bed, straightened herself at our approach.

'Hullo, Evie, here's our wounded hero! Mr Hastings – Miss Howard.'

Miss Howard shook hands with a hearty, almost painful, grip. I had an impression of very blue eyes in a sunburnt face. She was a pleasant-looking woman of about forty, with a deep voice, almost manly in its stentorian tones, and had a large sensible square body, with feet to match – these last encased in good thick boots. Her conversation, I soon found, was couched in the telegraphic style.

'Weeds grow like house afire. Can't keep even with 'em. Shall press you in. Better be careful!'

'I'm sure I shall be only too delighted to make myself useful,' I responded.

'Don't say it. Never does. Wish you hadn't later.'

'You're a cynic, Evie,' said John, laughing. 'Where's tea today – inside or out?'

'Out. Too fine a day to be cooped up in the house.'

'Come on then, you've done enough gardening for today. "The labourer is worthy of his hire," you know. Come and be refreshed.'

'Well,' said Miss Howard, drawing off her gardening gloves, 'I'm inclined to agree with you.'

She led the way round the house to where tea was spread under the shade of a large sycamore.

A figure rose from one of the basket chairs, and came a few steps to meet us.

'My wife, Hastings,' said John.

I shall never forget my first sight of Mary Cavendish. Her tall, slender form, outlined against the bright light; the vivid sense of slumbering fire that seemed to find expression only in those wonderful tawny eyes of hers, remarkable eyes, different from any other woman's that I have ever known; the intense power of stillness she possessed, which nevertheless conveyed the impression of a wild untamed spirit in an exquisitely civilized body – all these things are burnt into my memory. I shall never forget them.

She greeted me with a few words of pleasant welcome in a low clear voice, and I sank into a basket chair feeling distinctly glad that I had accepted John's invitation. Mrs Cavendish gave me some tea, and her few quiet remarks heightened my first impression of her as a thoroughly fascinating woman. An appreciative listener is always stimulating, and I described, in a humorous manner, certain incidents of my Convalescent Home, in a way which, I flatter myself, greatly amused my hostess. John, of course, good fellow though he is, could hardly be called a brilliant conversationalist.

At that moment a well remembered voice floated through the open french window near at hand:

'Then you'll write to the Princess after tea, Alfred? I'll write to Lady Tadminster for the second day, myself. Or shall we wait until we hear from the Princess? In case of a refusal, Lady Tadminster might open it the first day, and Mrs Crosbie the second. Then there's the Duchess – about the school fête.'

There was the murmur of a man's voice, and then Mrs Inglethorp's rose in reply:

'Yes, certainly. After tea will do quite well. You are so thoughtful, Alfred dear.'

The french window swung open a little wider, and a handsome white-haired old lady, with a somewhat masterful cast of features, stepped out of it on to the lawn. A man followed her, a suggestion of deference in his manner.

Mrs Inglethorp greeted me with effusion.

'Why, if it isn't too delightful to see you again, Mr Hastings, after all these years. Alfred, darling, Mr Hastings – my husband.'

I looked with some curiosity at 'Alfred darling'. He certainly struck a rather alien note. I did not wonder at John objecting to his beard. It was one of the longest and blackest I have ever seen. He wore gold-rimmed pince-nez, and had a curious impassivity of feature. It struck me that he might look natural on a stage, but was strangely out of place in real life. His voice was rather deep and unctuous. He placed a wooden hand in mine and said:

'This is a pleasure, Mr Hastings.' Then, turning to his wife: 'Emily dearest, I think that cushion is a little damp.'

She beamed fondly at him, as he substituted another with every demonstration of the tenderest care. Strange infatuation of an otherwise sensible woman!

With the presence of Mr Inglethorp, a sense of constraint and veiled hostility seemed to settle down upon the company. Miss Howard, in particular, took no pains to conceal her feelings. Mrs Inglethorp, however, seemed to notice nothing unusual. Her volubility, which I remembered of old, had lost nothing in the intervening years, and she poured out a steady flood of conversation, mainly on the subject of the forthcoming bazaar which she was organizing and which was to take place shortly. Occasionally she referred to her husband over a question of days or dates. His watchful and attentive manner never varied. From the very first I took a firm and rooted dislike to him, and I flatter myself that my first judgements are usually fairly shrewd.

Presently Mrs Inglethorp turned to give some instructions about letters to Evelyn Howard, and her husband addressed me in his painstaking voice:

'Is soldiering your regular profession, Mr Hastings?'

'No, before the war I was in Lloyd's.'

'And you will return there after it is over?'

'Perhaps. Either that or a fresh start altogether.'

Mary Cavendish leant forward.

'What would you really choose as a profession, if you could just consult your inclination?'

'Well, that depends.'

'No secret hobby?' she asked. 'Tell me – you're drawn to something? Everyone is – usually something absurd.'

'You'll laugh at me.'

She smiled.

'Perhaps.'

'Well, I've always had a secret hankering to be a detective!'

'The real thing – Scotland Yard? Or Sherlock Holmes?'

'Oh, Sherlock Holmes by all means. But really, seriously, I am awfully drawn to it. I came across a man in Belgium once, a very famous detective, and he quite inflamed me. He was a marvellous little fellow. He used to say that all good detective work was a mere matter of method. My system is based on his – though of course I have progressed rather further. He was a funny little man, a great dandy, but wonderfully clever.'

'Like a good detective story myself,' remarked Miss Howard. 'Lots of nonsense written, though. Criminal discovered in last chapter. Every one dumbfounded. Real crime – you'd know at once.'

'There have been a great number of undiscovered crimes,' I argued.

'Don't mean the police, but the people that are right in it. The family. You couldn't really hoodwink them. They'd know.'

'Then,' I said, much amused, 'you think that if you were mixed up in a crime, say a murder, you'd be able to spot the murderer right off?'

'Of course I should. Mightn't be able to prove it to a pack of lawyers. But I'm certain I'd know. I'd feel it in my finger-tips if he came near me.'

'It might be a "she",' I suggested.

'Might. But murder's a violent crime. Associate it more with a man.'

'Not in a case of poisoning.' Mrs Cavendish's clear voice startled me. 'Dr Bauerstein was saying yesterday that, owing to the general ignorance of the more uncommon poisons among the medical profession, there were probably countless cases of poisoning quite unsuspected.'

'Why, Mary, what a gruesome conversation!' cried Mrs Inglethorp. 'It makes me feel as if a goose were walking over my grave. Oh, there's Cynthia!'

A young girl in VAD uniform ran lightly across the lawn.

'Why, Cynthia, you are late today. This is Mr Hastings – Miss Murdoch.'

Cynthia Murdoch was a fresh-looking young creature, full of life and vigour. She tossed off her little VAD cap, and I admired the great loose waves of her auburn hair, and the smallness and whiteness of the hand she held out to claim her tea. With dark eyes and eyelashes she would have been a beauty.

She flung herself down on the ground beside John, and as I handed her a plate of sandwiches she smiled up at me.

'Sit down here on the grass, do. It's ever so much nicer.'

I dropped down obediently.

'You work at Tadminster, don't you, Miss Murdoch?'

She nodded.

'For my sins.'

'Do they bully you, then?' I asked, smiling.

'I should like to see them!' cried Cynthia with dignity.

'I have got a cousin who is nursing,' I remarked. 'And she is terrified of "Sisters".'

'I don't wonder. Sisters *are*, you know, Mr Hastings. They simp-ly *are*! You've no idea! But I'm not a nurse, thank heaven, I work in the dispensary.'

'How many people do you poison?' I asked, smiling.

Cynthia smiled too.

'Oh, hundreds!' she said.

'Cynthia,' called Mrs Inglethorp, 'do you think you could write a few notes for me?'

'Certainly, Aunt Emily.'

She jumped up promptly, and something in her manner reminded me that her position was a dependent one, and that Mrs Inglethorp, kind as she might be in the main, did not allow her to forget it.

My hostess turned to me.

'John will show you your room. Supper is at half-past seven. We have given up late dinner for some time now. Lady Tadminster, our Member's wife – she was the late Lord Abbotsbury's daughter – does the same. She agrees with me that one must set an example of economy. We are quite a war household; nothing is wasted here – every scrap of waste paper, even, is saved and sent away in sacks.'

I expressed my appreciation, and John took me into the house and up the broad staircase, which forked right and left half-way to different wings of the building. My room was in the left wing, and looked out over the park.

John left me, and a few minutes later I saw him from my window walking slowly across the grass arm in arm with Cynthia Murdoch. I heard Mrs Inglethorp call 'Cynthia' impatiently, and the girl started and ran back to the house. At the same moment, a man stepped out from the shadow of a tree and walked slowly in the same direction. He looked about forty, very dark with a melancholy clean-shaven face. Some violent emotion seemed to be mastering him. He looked up at my window as he passed, and I recognized him, though he had changed much in the fifteen years that had elapsed since we last met. It was John's younger brother, Lawrence Cavendish. I wondered what it was that had brought that singular expression to his face.

Then I dismissed him from my mind, and returned to the contemplation of my own affairs.

The evening passed pleasantly enough; and I dreamed that night of that enigmatical woman, Mary Cavendish.

The next morning dawned bright and sunny, and I was full of the anticipation of a delightful visit.

I did not see Mrs Cavendish until lunch-time, when she volunteered to take me for a walk, and we spent a charming afternoon roaming in the woods, returning to the house about five.

As we entered the large hall, John beckoned us both into the smoking-room. I saw at once by his face that something disturbing had occurred. We followed him in, and he shut the door after us.

'Look here, Mary, there's the deuce of a mess. Evie's had a row with Alfred Inglethorp, and she's off.'

'Evie? Off?'

John nodded gloomily.

'Yes; you see she went to the mater, and – oh, here's Evie herself.'

Miss Howard entered. Her lips were set grimly together, and she carried a small suit-case. She looked excited and determined, and slightly on the defensive.

'At any rate,' she burst out, 'I've spoken my mind!'

'My dear Evelyn,' cried Mrs Cavendish, 'this can't be true!'

Miss Howard nodded grimly.

'True enough! Afraid I said some things to Emily she won't forget or forgive in a hurry. Don't mind if they've only sunk in a bit. Probably water off a duck's back, though. I said right out: "You're an old woman, Emily, and there's no fool like an old fool. The man's twenty years younger than you, and don't you fool yourself as to what he married you for. Money! Well, don't let him have too much of it. Farmer Raikes has got a very pretty young wife. Just ask your Alfred how much time he spends over there." She was very angry. Natural! I went on: "I'm going to warn you, whether you like it or not. That man would as soon murder you in your bed as look at you. He's a bad lot. You can say what you like to me, but remember what I've told you. He's a bad lot!"'

'What did she say?'

Miss Howard made an extremely expressive grimace.

'"Darling Alfred" – "dearest Alfred" – "wicked calumnies" – "wicked lies" – "wicked woman" – to accuse her "dear husband"! The sooner I left her house the better. So I'm off.'

'But not now?'

'This minute!'

For a moment we sat and stared at her. Finally John Cavendish, finding his persuasions of no avail, went off to look up the trains. His wife followed him, murmuring something about persuading Mrs Inglethorp to think better of it.

As she left the room, Miss Howard's face changed. She leant towards me eagerly.

'Mr Hastings, you're honest. I can trust you?'

I was a little startled. She laid her hand on my arm, and sank her voice to a whisper.

'Look after her, Mr Hastings. My poor Emily. They're a lot of sharks – all of them. Oh, I know what I'm talking about. There isn't one of them that's not hard up and trying to get money out of her. I've protected her as much as I could. Now I'm out of the way, they'll impose upon her.'

'Of course, Miss Howard,' I said, 'I'll do everything I can, but I'm sure you're excited and overwrought.'

She interrupted me by slowly shaking her forefinger.

'Young man, trust me. I've lived in the world rather longer than you have. All I ask you is to keep your eyes open. You'll see what I mean.'

The throb of the motor came through the open window, and Miss Howard rose and moved to the door. John's voice sounded outside. With her hand on the handle, she turned her head over her shoulder, and beckoned to me.

'Above all, Mr Hastings, watch that devil – her husband!'

There was no time for more. Miss Howard was swallowed up in an eager chorus of protests and goodbyes. The Inglethorps did not appear.

As the motor drove away, Mrs Cavendish suddenly detached herself from the group, and moved across the drive to the lawn to meet a tall bearded man who had been evidently making for the house. The colour rose in her cheeks as she held out her hand to him.

'Who is that?' I asked sharply, for instinctively I distrusted the man.

'That's Dr Bauerstein,' said John shortly.

'And who is Dr Bauerstein?'

'He's staying in the village doing a rest cure, after a bad nervous breakdown. He's a London specialist; a very clever man – one of the greatest living experts on poisons, I believe.'

'And he's a great friend of Mary's,' put in Cynthia, the irrepressible.

John Cavendish frowned and changed the subject.

'Come for a stroll, Hastings. This has been a most rotten business. She always had a rough tongue, but there is no stauncher friend in England than Evelyn Howard.'

He took the path through the plantation, and we walked down to the village through the woods which bordered one side of the estate.

As we passed through one of the gates on our way home again, a pretty young woman of gipsy type coming in the opposite direction bowed and smiled.

'That's a pretty girl,' I remarked appreciatively.

John's face hardened.

'That is Mrs Raikes.'

'The one that Miss Howard –'

'Exactly,' said John, with rather unnecessary abruptness.

I thought of the white-haired old lady in the big house, and that vivid wicked little face that had just smiled into ours, and a vague chill of foreboding crept over me. I brushed it aside.

'Styles is really a glorious old place,' I said to John.

He nodded rather gloomily.

'Yes, it's a fine property. It'll be mine some day – should be mine now by rights, if my father had only made a decent will. And then I shouldn't be so damned hard up as I am now.'

'Hard up, are you?'

'My dear Hastings, I don't mind telling you that I'm at my wits' end for money.'

'Couldn't your brother help you?'

'Lawrence? He's gone through every penny he ever had, publishing rotten verses in fancy bindings. No, we're an impecunious lot. My mother's always been awfully good to us, I must say. That is, up to now. Since her marriage, of course –' He broke off, frowning.

For the first time I felt that, with Evelyn Howard, something indefinable had gone from the atmosphere. Her presence had spelt security. Now that security was removed – and the air seemed rife with suspicion. The sinister face of Dr Bauerstein recurred to me unpleasantly. A vague suspicion of everyone and everything filled my mind. Just for a moment I had a premonition of approaching evil.

CHAPTER 2

THE 16TH AND 17TH OF JULY

I had arrived at Styles on the 5th of July. I come now to the events of the 16th and 17th of that month. For the convenience of the reader I will recapitulate the incidents of those days in as exact a manner as possible. They were elicited subsequently at the trial by a process of long and tedious cross-examinations.

I received a letter from Evelyn Howard a couple of days after her departure, telling me she was working as a nurse at the big hospital in Middlingham, a manufacturing town some fifteen miles away, and begging me to let her know if Mrs Inglethorp should show any wish to be reconciled.

The only fly in the ointment of my peaceful days was Mrs Cavendish's extraordinary and, for my part, unaccountable preference for the society of Dr Bauerstein. What she saw in the man

I cannot imagine, but she was always asking him up to the house, and often went off for long expeditions with him. I confess that I was quite unable to see his attraction.

The 16th of July fell on a Monday. It was a day of turmoil. The famous bazaar had taken place on Saturday, and an entertainment, in connection with the same charity, at which Mrs Inglethorp was to recite a War poem, was to be held that night. We were all busy during the morning arranging and decorating the Hall in the village where it was to take place. We had a late luncheon and spent the afternoon resting in the garden. I noticed that John's manner was somewhat unusual. He seemed very excited and restless.

After tea, Mrs Inglethorp went to lie down to rest before her efforts in the evening and I challenged Mary Cavendish to a single at tennis.

About a quarter to seven, Mrs Inglethorp called to us that we should be late as supper was early that night. We had rather a scramble to get ready in time; and before the meal was over the motor was waiting at the door.

The entertainment was a great success, Mrs Inglethorp's recitation receiving tremendous applause. There were also some tableaux in which Cynthia took part. She did not return with us, having been asked to a supper party, and to remain the night with some friends who had been acting with her in the tableaux.

The following morning, Mrs Inglethorp stayed in bed to breakfast, as she was rather over-tired; but she appeared in her briskest mood about 12.30, and swept Lawrence and myself off to a luncheon party.

'Such a charming invitation from Mrs Rolleston. Lady Tadminster's sister, you know. The Rollestons came over with the Conqueror – one of our oldest families.'

Mary had excused herself on the plea of an engagement with Dr Bauerstein.

We had a pleasant luncheon, and as we drove away Lawrence suggested that we should return by Tadminster, which was barely a mile out of our way, and pay a visit to Cynthia in her dispensary. Mrs Inglethorp replied that this was an excellent idea, but as she had several letters to write she would drop us there, and we could come back with Cynthia in the pony-trap.

We were detained under suspicion by the hospital porter, until Cynthia appeared to vouch for us, looking very cool and sweet in her long white overall. She took us up to her sanctum, and introduced us to her fellow dispenser, a rather awe-inspiring individual, whom Cynthia cheerily addressed as 'Nibs'.

'What a lot of bottles!' I exclaimed, as my eye travelled round the small room. 'Do you really know what's in them all?'

'Say something original,' groaned Cynthia. 'Every single person who comes up here says that. We are really thinking of bestowing a prize on the first individual who does *not* say: "What a lot of bottles!" And I know the next thing you're going to say is: "How many people have you poisoned?"'

I pleaded guilty with a laugh.

'If you people only knew how fatally easy it is to poison someone by mistake, you wouldn't joke about it. Come on, let's have tea. We've got all sorts of secret stores in that cupboard. No, Lawrence – that's the poison cupboard. The big cupboard – that's right.'

We had a very cheery tea, and assisted Cynthia to wash up afterwards. We had just put away the last teaspoon when a knock came at the door. The countenances of Cynthia and Nibs were suddenly petrified into a stern and forbidding expression.

'Come in,' said Cynthia, in a sharp professional tone.

A young and rather scared-looking nurse appeared with a bottle which she proffered to Nibs, who waved her towards Cynthia with the somewhat enigmatical remark:

'*I'*m not really here today.'

Cynthia took the bottle and examined it with the severity of a judge.

'This should have been sent up this morning.'

'Sister is very sorry. She forgot.'

'Sister should read the rules outside the door.'

I gathered from the little nurse's expression that there was not the least likelihood of her having the hardihood to retail this message to the dreaded 'Sister'.

'So now it can't be done until tomorrow,' finished Cynthia.

'Don't you think you could possibly let us have it tonight?'

'Well,' said Cynthia graciously, 'we are very busy, but if we have time it shall be done.'

The little nurse withdrew, and Cynthia promptly took a jar from the shelf, refilled the bottle and placed it on the table outside the door.

I laughed.

'Discipline must be maintained?'

'Exactly. Come out on our little balcony. You can see all the outside wards there.'

I followed Cynthia and her friend and they pointed out the different wards to me. Lawrence remained behind, but after a few moments Cynthia called to him over her shoulder to come and join us. Then she looked at her watch.

'Nothing more to do, Nibs?'

'No.'

'All right. Then we can lock up and go.'

I had seen Lawrence in quite a different light that afternoon. Compared to John, he was an astoundingly difficult person to get to know. He was the opposite of his brother in almost every respect, being unusually shy and reserved. Yet he had a certain charm of manner, and I fancied that, if one really knew him well, one could have a deep affection for him. I had always fancied that his manner to Cynthia was rather constrained, and that she on her side was inclined to be shy of him. But they were both gay enough this afternoon, and chatted together like a couple of children.

As we drove through the village, I remembered that I wanted some stamps, so accordingly we pulled up at the post office.

As I came out again, I cannoned into a little man who was just entering. I drew aside and apologized, when suddenly, with a loud exclamation, he clasped me in his arms and kissed me warmly.

'*Mon ami* Hastings!' he cried. 'It is indeed *mon ami* Hastings!'

'Poirot!' I exclaimed.

I turned to the pony-trap.

'This is a very pleasant meeting for me, Miss Cynthia. This is my old friend, Monsieur Poirot, whom I have not seen for years.'

'Oh, we know Monsieur Poirot,' said Cynthia gaily. 'But I had no idea he was a friend of yours.'

'Yes, indeed,' said Poirot seriously. 'I know Mademoiselle Cynthia. It is by the charity of that good Mrs Inglethorp that I am here.' Then, as I looked at him inquiringly: 'Yes, my friend, she had kindly extended hospitality to seven of my country-people who, alas, are refugees from their native land. We Belgians will always remember her with gratitude.'

Poirot was an extraordinary-looking little man. He was hardly more than five feet four inches, but carried himself with great dignity. His head was exactly the shape of an egg, and he always perched it a little on one side. His moustache was very stiff and military. The neatness of his attire was almost incredible; I believe a speck of dust would have caused him more pain than a bullet wound. Yet this quaint dandified little man who, I was sorry to see, now limped badly, had been in his time one of the most celebrated members of the Belgian police. As a detective, his *flair* had been extraordinary, and he had achieved triumphs by unravelling some of the most baffling cases of the day.

He pointed out to me the little house inhabited by him and his fellow Belgians, and I promised to go and see him at an early date. Then he raised his hat with a flourish to Cynthia and we drove away.

'He's a dear little man,' said Cynthia. 'I'd no idea you knew him.'

'You've been entertaining a celebrity unawares,' I replied.

And, for the rest of the way home, I recited to them the various exploits and triumphs of Hercule Poirot.

We arrived back in a very cheerful mood. As we entered the hall, Mrs Inglethorp came out of her boudoir. She looked flushed and upset.

'Oh, it's you,' she said.

'Is there anything the matter, Aunt Emily?' asked Cynthia.

'Certainly not,' said Mrs Inglethorp sharply. 'What should there be?' Then catching sight of Dorcas, the parlourmaid, going into the dining-room, she called to her to bring some stamps into the boudoir.

'Yes, m'm.' The old servant hesitated, then added diffidently:

'Don't you think, m'm, you'd better get to bed? You're looking very tired.'

'Perhaps you're right, Dorcas – yes – no – not now. I've some letters I must finish by post-time. Have you lighted the fire in my room as I told you?'

'Yes, m'm.'

'Then I'll go to bed directly after supper.'

She went into her boudoir again, and Cynthia stared after her.

'Goodness gracious! I wonder what's up?' she said to Lawrence.

He did not seem to have heard her, for without a word he turned on his heel and went out of the house.

I suggested a quick game of tennis before supper and, Cynthia agreeing, I ran upstairs to fetch my racquet.

Mrs Cavendish was coming down the stairs. It may have been my fancy, but she, too, was looking odd and disturbed.

'Had a good walk with Dr Bauerstein?' I asked, trying to appear as indifferent as I could.

'I didn't go,' she replied abruptly. 'Where is Mrs Inglethorp?'

'In the boudoir.'

Her hand clenched itself on the banisters, then she seemed to nerve herself for some encounter, and went rapidly past me down the stairs across the hall to the boudoir, the door of which she shut behind her.

As I ran out to the tennis court a few moments later, I had to pass the open boudoir window, and was unable to help overhearing the following scrap of dialogue. Mary Cavendish was saying in the voice of a woman desperately controlling herself: 'Then you won't show it to me?'

To which Mrs Inglethorp replied:

'My dear Mary, it has nothing to do with that matter.'

'Then show it to me.'

'I tell you it is not what you imagine. It does not concern you in the least.'

To which Mary Cavendish replied, with a rising bitterness: 'Of course, I might have known you would shield him.'

Cynthia was waiting for me, and greeted me eagerly with:

'I say! There's been the most awful row! I've got it all out of Dorcas.'

'What kind of row?'

'Between Aunt Emily and *him*. I do hope she's found him out at last!'

'Was Dorcas there, then?'

'Of course not. She "happened to be near the door". It was a real old bust-up. I do wish I knew what it was all about.'

I thought of Mrs Raikes's gipsy face, and Evelyn Howard's warnings, but wisely decided to hold my peace, whilst Cynthia exhausted every possible hypothesis, and cheerfully hoped, 'Aunt Emily will send him away, and will never speak to him again.'

I was anxious to get hold of John, but he was nowhere to be seen. Evidently something very momentous had occurred that afternoon. I tried to forget the few words I had overheard; but, do what I would, I could not dismiss them altogether from my mind. What was Mary Cavendish's concern in the matter?

Mr Inglethorp was in the drawing-room when I came down to supper. His face was impassive as ever, and the strange unreality of the man struck me afresh.

Mrs Inglethorp came down at last. She still looked agitated, and during the meal there was a somewhat constrained silence. Inglethorp was unusually quiet. As a rule, he surrounded his wife with little attentions, placing a cushion at her back, and altogether playing the part of the devoted husband. Immediately after supper, Mrs Inglethorp retired to her boudoir again.

'Send my coffee in here, Mary,' she called. 'I've just five minutes to catch the post.'

Cynthia and I went and sat by the open window in the drawing-room. Mary Cavendish brought our coffee to us. She seemed excited.

'Do you young people want lights, or do you enjoy the twilight?' she asked. 'Will you take Mrs Inglethorp her coffee, Cynthia? I will pour it out.'

'Do not trouble, Mary,' said Inglethorp. 'I will take it to Emily.' He poured it out, and went out of the room carrying it carefully.

Lawrence followed him, and Mrs Cavendish sat down by us.

We three sat for some time in silence. It was a glorious

night, hot and still. Mrs Cavendish fanned herself gently with a palm leaf.

'It's almost too hot,' she murmured. 'We shall have a thunderstorm.'

Alas, that these harmonious moments can never endure! My paradise was rudely shattered by the sound of a well-known, and heartily disliked, voice in the hall.

'Dr Bauerstein!' exclaimed Cynthia. 'What a funny time to come.'

I glanced jealously at Mary Cavendish, but she seemed quite undisturbed, the delicate pallor of her cheeks did not vary.

In a few moments, Alfred Inglethorp had ushered the doctor in, the latter laughing, and protesting that he was in no fit state for a drawing-room. In truth, he presented a sorry spectacle, being literally plastered with mud.

'What have you been doing, doctor?' cried Mrs Cavendish.

'I must make my apologies,' said the doctor. 'I did not really mean to come in, but Mr Inglethorp insisted.'

'Well, Bauerstein, you are in a plight,' said John, strolling in from the hall. 'Have some coffee, and tell us what you have been up to.'

'Thank you, I will.' He laughed rather ruefully, as he described how he had discovered a very rare species of fern in an inaccessible place, and in his efforts to obtain it had lost his footing, and slipped ignominiously into a neighbouring pond.

'The sun soon dried me off,' he added, 'but I'm afraid my appearance is very disreputable.'

At this juncture, Mrs Inglethorp called to Cynthia from the hall, and the girl ran out.

'Just carry up my despatch-case, will you, dear? I'm going to bed.'

The door into the hall was a wide one. I had risen when Cynthia did, John was close by me. There were, therefore, three witnesses who could swear that Mrs Inglethorp was carrying her coffee, as yet untasted, in her hand. My evening was utterly and entirely spoilt by the presence of Dr Bauerstein. It seemed to me the man would never go. He rose at last, however, and I breathed a sigh of relief.

'I'll walk down to the village with you,' said Mr Inglethorp.

'I must see our agent over those estate accounts.' He turned to John. 'No one need sit up. I will take the latch-key.'

CHAPTER 3

THE NIGHT OF THE TRAGEDY

To make this part of my story clear, I append the following plan of the first floor of Styles. The servants' rooms are reached through the door B. They have no communication with the right wing, where the Inglethorps' rooms were situated.

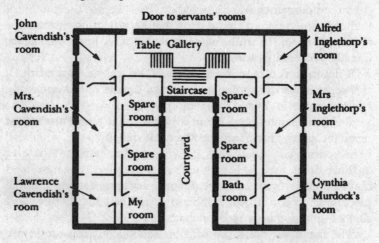

It seemed to be the middle of the night when I was awakened by Lawrence Cavendish. He had a candle in his hand, and the agitation of his face told me at once that something was seriously wrong.

'What's the matter?' I asked, sitting up in bed, and trying to collect my scattered thoughts.

'We are afraid my mother is very ill. She seems to be having some kind of fit. Unfortunately she has locked herself in.'

'I'll come at once.'

I sprang out of bed, and pulling on a dressing-gown, followed Lawrence along the passage and the gallery to the right wing of the house.

John Cavendish joined us, and one or two of the servants were standing round in a state of awe-stricken excitement. Lawrence turned to his brother.

'What do you think we had better do?'

Never, I thought, had his indecision of character been more apparent.

John rattled the handle of Mrs Inglethorp's door violently, but with no effect. It was obviously locked or bolted on the inside. The whole household was aroused by now. The most alarming sounds were audible from the interior of the room. Clearly something must be done.

'Try going through Mr Inglethorp's room, sir,' cried Dorcas. 'Oh, the poor mistress!'

Suddenly I realized that Alfred Inglethorp was not with us – that he alone had given no sign of his presence. John opened the door of his room. It was pitch dark, but Lawrence was following with the candle, and by its feeble light we saw that the bed had not been slept in, and that there was no sign of the room having been occupied.

We went straight to the connecting door. That, too, was locked or bolted on the inside. What was to be done?

'Oh, dear, sir,' cried Dorcas, wringing her hands, 'whatever shall we do?'

'We must try and break the door in, I suppose. It'll be a tough job, though. Here, let one of the maids go down and wake Baily and tell him to go for Dr Wilkins at once. Now then, we'll have a try at the door. Half a moment, though, isn't there a door into Miss Cynthia's room?'

'Yes, sir, but that's always bolted. It's never been undone.'

'Well, we might just see.'

He ran rapidly down the corridor to Cynthia's room. Mary Cavendish was there, shaking the girl – who must have been an unusually sound sleeper – and trying to wake her.

In a moment or two he was back.

'No good. That's bolted too. We must break in the door. I think this one is a shade less solid than the one in the passage.'

We strained and heaved together. The framework of the door was solid, and for a long time it resisted our efforts, but at last we felt it give beneath our weight, and finally, with a resounding crash, it was burst open.

We stumbled in together, Lawrence still holding his candle. Mrs Inglethorp was lying on the bed, her whole form agitated by violent convulsions, in one of which she must have overturned the table beside her. As we entered, however, her limbs relaxed, and she fell back upon the pillows.

John strode across the room and lit the gas. Turning to Annie, one of the housemaids, he sent her downstairs to the dining-room for brandy. Then he went across to his mother whilst I unbolted the door that gave on the corridor.

I turned to Lawrence, to suggest that I had better leave them now that there was no further need of my services, but the words were frozen on my lips. Never have I seen such a ghastly look on any man's face. He was white as chalk, the candle he held in his shaking hand was sputtering on to the carpet, and his eyes, petrified with terror, or some such kindred emotion, stared fixedly over my head at a point on the further wall. It was as though he had seen something that turned him to stone. I instinctively followed the direction of his eyes, but I could see nothing unusual. The still feebly flickering ashes in the grate, and the row of prim ornaments on the mantelpiece, were surely harmless enough.

The violence of Mrs Inglethorp's attack seemed to be passing. She was able to speak in short gasps.

'Better now – very sudden – stupid of me – to lock myself in.'

A shadow fell on the bed and, looking up, I saw Mary Cavendish standing near the door with her arm around Cynthia. She seemed to be supporting the girl, who looked utterly dazed and unlike herself. Her face was heavily flushed, and she yawned repeatedly.

'Poor Cynthia is quite frightened,' said Mrs Cavendish in a low clear voice. She herself, I noticed, was dressed in her white land smock. Then it must be later than I thought. I saw that a faint streak of daylight was showing through the curtains of the windows, and that the clock on the mantelpiece pointed to close upon five o'clock.

A strangled cry from the bed startled me. A fresh access of pain seized the unfortunate old lady. The convulsions were of a violence terrible to behold. Everything was confusion. We thronged round her, powerless to help or alleviate. A final convulsion lifted her from the bed, until she appeared to rest upon her head and her heels, with her body arched in an extraordinary manner. In vain Mary and John tried to administer more brandy. The moments flew. Again the body arched itself in that peculiar fashion.

At that moment, Dr Bauerstein pushed his way authoritatively into the room. For one instant he stopped dead, staring at the figure on the bed, and, at the same instant, Mrs Inglethorp cried out in a strangled voice, her eyes fixed on the doctor:

'Alfred – Alfred –' Then she fell back motionless on the pillows.

With a stride, the doctor reached the bed, and seizing her arms worked them energetically, applying what I knew to be artificial respiration. He issued a few short sharp orders to the servants. An imperious wave of his hand drove us all to the door. We watched him, fascinated, though I think we all knew in our hearts that it was too late, and that nothing could be done now. I could see by the expression on his face that he himself had little hope.

Finally he abandoned his task, shaking his head gravely. At that moment, we heard footsteps outside, and Dr Wilkins, Mrs Inglethorp's own doctor, a portly, fussy little man, came bustling in.

In a few words Dr Bauerstein explained how he had happened to be passing the lodge gates as the car came out, and had run up to the house as fast as he could, whilst the car went on to fetch Dr Wilkins. With a faint gesture of the hand, he indicated the figure on the bed.

'Ve – ry sad. Ve – ry sad,' murmured Dr Wilkins. 'Poor dear lady. Always did far too much – far too much – against my advice. I warned her, "Take – it – easy." But no – her zeal for good works was too great. Nature rebelled. Na – ture – re – belled.'

Dr Bauerstein, I noticed, was watching the local doctor narrowly. He still kept his eyes fixed on him as he spoke.

'The convulsions were of a peculiar violence, Dr Wilkins. I am sorry you were not here in time to witness them. They were quite – tetanic in character.'

'Ah!' said Dr Wilkins wisely.

'I should like to speak to you in private,' said Dr Bauerstein. He turned to John. 'You do not object?'

'Certainly not.'

We all trooped out into the corridor, leaving the two doctors alone, and I heard the key turned in the lock behind us.

We went slowly down the stairs. I was violently excited. I have a certain talent for deduction, and Dr Bauerstein's manner had started a flock of wild surmises in my mind. Mary Cavendish laid her hand upon my arm.

'What is it? Why did Dr Bauerstein seem so – peculiar?'

I looked at her.

'Do you know what I think?'

'What?'

'Listen!' I looked round, the others were out of earshot. I lowered my voice to a whisper. 'I believe she has been poisoned! I'm certain Dr Bauerstein suspects it.'

'*What?*' She shrank against the wall, the pupils of her eyes dilating wildly. Then, with a sudden cry that startled me, she cried out: 'No, no – not that – not that!' And breaking from me, fled up the stairs. I followed her, afraid that she was going to faint. I found her leaning against the banisters, deadly pale. She waved me away impatiently.

'No, no – leave me. I'd rather be alone. Let me just be quiet for a minute or two. Go down to the others.'

I obeyed her reluctantly. John and Lawrence were in the dining-room. I joined them. We were all silent, but I suppose I voiced the thoughts of us all when I at last broke it by saying:

'Where is Mr Inglethorp?'

John shook his head.

'He's not in the house.'

Our eyes met. Where *was* Alfred Inglethorp? His absence was strange and inexplicable. I remembered Mrs Inglethorp's dying words. What lay beneath them? What more could she have told us, if she had had time?

At last we heard the doctors descending the stairs. Dr Wilkins was looking important and excited, and trying to conceal an inward exultation under a manner of decorous calm. Dr Bauerstein remained in the background, his grave bearded face unchanged. Dr Wilkins was the spokesman for the two. He addressed himself to John:

'Mr Cavendish, I should like your consent to a post-mortem.'

'Is that necessary?' asked John gravely. A spasm of pain crossed his face.

'Absolutely,' said Dr Bauerstein.

'You mean by that –?'

'That neither Dr Wilkins nor myself could give a death certificate under the circumstances.'

John bent his head.

'In that case, I have no alternative but to agree.'

'Thank you,' said Dr Wilkins briskly. 'We propose that it should take place tomorrow night – or rather tonight.' And he glanced at the daylight. 'Under the circumstances, I am afraid an inquest can hardly be avoided – these formalities are necessary, but I beg that you won't distress yourselves.'

There was a pause, and then Dr Bauerstein drew two keys from his pocket, and handed them to John.

'These are the keys of the two rooms. I have locked them and, in my opinion, they would be better kept locked for the present.'

The doctors then departed.

I had been turning over an idea in my head, and I felt that the moment had now come to broach it. Yet I was a little chary of doing so. John, I knew, had a horror of any kind of publicity, and was an easy-going optimist, who preferred never to meet trouble half-way. It might be difficult to convince him of the soundness of my plan. Lawrence, on the other hand, being less conventional, and having more imagination, I felt I might count upon as an ally. There was no doubt that the moment had come for me to take the lead.

'John,' I said, 'I am going to ask you something.'

'Well?'

'You remember my speaking of my friend Poirot? The Belgian who is here? He has been a most famous detective.'

'Yes.'

'I want you to let me call him in – to investigate this matter.'

'What – now? Before the post-mortem?'

'Yes, time is an advantage if – if – there has been foul play.'

'Rubbish!' cried Lawrence angrily. 'In my opinion the whole thing is a mare's nest of Bauerstein's! Wilkins hadn't an idea of such a thing, until Bauerstein put it into his head. But, like all specialists, Bauerstein's got a bee in his bonnet. Poisons are his hobby, so, of course, he sees them everywhere.'

I confess that I was surprised by Lawrence's attitude. He was so seldom vehement about anything.

John hesitated.

'I can't feel as you do, Lawrence,' he said at last, 'I'm inclined to give Hastings a free hand, though I should prefer to wait a bit. We don't want any unnecessary scandal.'

'No, no,' I cried eagerly, 'you need have no fear of that. Poirot is discretion itself.'

'Very well then, have it your own way. I leave it in your hands. Though, if it is as we suspect, it seems a clear enough case. God forgive me if I am wronging him!'

I looked at my watch. It was six o'clock. I determined to lose no time.

Five minutes' delay, however, I allowed myself. I spent it in ransacking the library until I discovered a medical book which gave a description of strychnine poisoning.

CHAPTER 4

POIROT INVESTIGATES

The house which the Belgians occupied in the village was quite close to the park gates. One could save time by taking a narrow path through the long grass, which cut off the detours of the winding drive. So I, accordingly, went that way. I had nearly reached the lodge, when my attention was arrested by the running figure of a man approaching me. It was Mr Inglethorp. Where had he been? How did he intend to explain his absence?

He accosted me eagerly.

'My God! This is terrible! My poor wife! I have only just heard.'

'Where have you been?' I asked.

'Denby kept me late last night. It was one o'clock before we'd finished. Then I found that I'd forgotten the latch-key after all. I didn't want to arouse the household, so Denby gave me a bed.'

'How did you hear the news?' I asked.

'Wilkins knocked Denby up to tell him. My poor Emily! She

was so self-sacrificing – such a noble character. She overtaxed her strength.'

A wave of revulsion swept over me. What a consummate hypocrite the man was!

'I must hurry on,' I said, thankful that he did not ask me whither I was bound.

In a few minutes I was knocking at the door of Leastways Cottage.

Getting no answer, I repeated my summons impatiently. A window above me was cautiously opened, and Poirot himself looked out.

He gave an exclamation of surprise at seeing me. In a few brief words, I explained the tragedy that had occurred, and that I wanted his help.

'Wait, my friend, I will let you in, and you shall recount to me the affairs whilst I dress.'

In a few moments he had unbarred the door, and I followed him up to his room. There he installed me in a chair, and I related the whole story, keeping back nothing, and omitting no circumstance, however insignificant, whilst he himself made a careful and deliberate toilet.

I told him of my awakening, of Mrs Inglethorp's dying words, of her husband's absence, of the quarrel the day before, of the scrap of conversation between Mary and her mother-in-law that I had overheard, of the former quarrel between Mrs Inglethorp and Evelyn Howard, and of the latter's innuendoes.

I was hardly as clear as I could wish. I repeated myself several times, and occasionally had to go back to some detail that I had forgotten. Poirot smiled kindly on me.

'The mind is confused? Is it not so? Take time, *mon ami*. You are agitated; you are excited – it is but natural. Presently, when we are calmer, we will arrange the facts, neatly, each in his proper place. We will examine – and reject. Those of importance we will put on one side; those of no importance, pouf!' – he screwed up his cherub-like face, and puffed comically enough – 'blow them away!'

'That's all very well,' I objected, 'but how are you going to decide what is important, and what isn't? That always seems the difficulty to me.'

Poirot shook his head energetically. He was now arranging his moustache with exquisite care.

'Not so. *Voyons*! One fact leads to another – so we continue. Does the next fit in with that? *A merveille*! Good! We can proceed. This next little fact – no! Ah, that is curious! There is something missing – a link in the chain that is not there. We examine. We search. And that little curious fact, that possibly paltry little detail that will not tally, we put it here!' He made an extravagant gesture with his hand. 'It is significant! It is tremendous!'

'Y – es –'

'Ah!' Poirot shook his forefinger so fiercely at me that I quailed before it. 'Beware! Peril to the detective who says: "It is so small – it does not matter. It will not agree. I will forget it." That way lies confusion! Everything matters.'

'I know. You always told me that. That's why I have gone into all the details of this thing whether they seemed to me relevant or not.'

'And I am pleased with you. You have a good memory, and you have given me the facts faithfully. Of the order in which you present them, I say nothing – truly, it is deplorable! But I make allowances – you are upset. To that I attribute the circumstance that you have omitted one fact of paramount importance.'

'What is that?' I asked.

'You have not told me if Mrs Inglethorp ate well last night.'

I stared at him. Surely the war had affected the little man's brain. He was carefully engaged in brushing his coat before putting it on, and seemed wholly engrossed in the task.

'I don't remember,' I said. 'And, anyway, I don't see –'

'You do not see? But it is of the first importance.'

'I can't see why,' I said, rather nettled. 'As far as I can remember, she didn't eat much. She was obviously upset, and it had taken her appetite away. That was only natural.'

'Yes,' said Poirot thoughtfully, 'it was only natural.'

He opened a drawer, and took out a small despatch-case, then turned to me.

'Now I am ready. We will proceed to the château, and study matters on the spot. Excuse me, *mon ami*, you dressed in haste, and your tie is on one side. Permit me.' With a deft gesture, he rearranged it.

'*Ça y est*! Now, shall we start?'

We hurried up the village, and turned in at the lodge gates. Poirot stopped for a moment, and gazed sorrowfully over the beautiful expanse of park, still glittering with morning dew.

'So beautiful, so beautiful, and yet, the poor family, plunged in sorrow, prostrated with grief.'

He looked at me keenly as he spoke, and I was aware that I reddened under his prolonged gaze.

Was the family prostrated by grief? Was the sorrow at Mrs Inglethorp's death so great? I realized that there was an emotional lack in the atmosphere. The dead woman had not the gift of commanding love. Her death was a shock and a distress, but she would not be passionately regretted.

Poirot seemed to follow my thoughts. He nodded his head gravely.

'No, you are right,' he said, 'it is not as though there was a blood tie. She has been kind and generous to these Cavendishes, but she was not their own mother. Blood tells – always remember that – blood tells.'

'Poirot,' I said, 'I wish you would tell me why you wanted to know if Mrs Inglethorp ate well last night? I have been turning it over in my mind, but I can't see how it has anything to do with the matter.'

He was silent for a minute or two as we walked along, but finally he said:

'I do not mind telling you – though, as you know, it is not my habit to explain until the end is reached. The present contention is that Mrs Inglethorp died of strychnine poisoning, presumably administered in her coffee.'

'Yes?'

'Well, what time was the coffee served?'

'About eight o'clock.'

'Therefore she drank it between then and half-past eight – certainly not much later. Well, strychnine is a fairly rapid poison. Its effects would be felt very soon, probably in about an hour. Yet, in Mrs Inglethorp's case, the symptoms do not manifest themselves until five o'clock the next morning: nine hours! But a heavy meal, taken at about the same time as the poison, might retard its effects, though hardly to that extent. Still, it is a possibility to be taken into account. But, according to you, she ate very little for supper, and yet the symptoms do not develop until early the next morning! Now that is a curious circumstance, my friend. Something may arise at the autopsy to explain it. In the meantime, remember it.'

As we neared the house, John came out and met us. His face looked weary and haggard.

'This is a very dreadful business, Monsieur Poirot,' he said. 'Hastings has explained to you that we are anxious for no publicity?'

'I comprehend perfectly.'

'You see, it is only suspicion so far. We have nothing to go upon.'

'Precisely. It is a matter of precaution only.'

John turned to me, taking out his cigarette-case, and lighting a cigarette as he did so.

'You know that fellow Inglethorp is back?'

'Yes. I met him.'

John flung the match into an adjacent flower bed, a proceeding which was too much for Poirot's feelings. He retrieved it, and buried it neatly.

'It's jolly difficult to know how to treat him.'

'That difficulty will not exist long,' pronounced Poirot quietly.

John looked puzzled, not quite understanding the portent of this cryptic saying. He handed the two keys which Dr Bauerstein had given him to me.

'Show Monsieur Poirot everything he wants to see.'

'The rooms are locked?' asked Poirot.

'Dr Bauerstein considered it advisable.'

Poirot nodded thoughtfully.

'Then he is very sure. Well, that simplifies matters for us.'

We went up together to the room of the tragedy. For convenience I append a plan of the room and the principal articles of furniture in it.

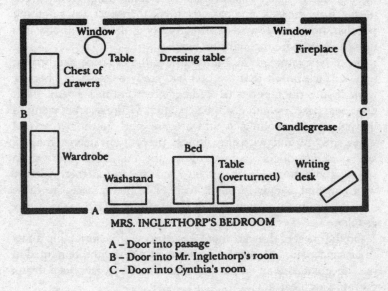

MRS. INGLETHORP'S BEDROOM

A – Door into passage
B – Door into Mr. Inglethorp's room
C – Door into Cynthia's room

Poirot locked the door on the inside, and proceeded to a minute inspection of the room. He darted from one object to the other with the agility of a grasshopper. I remained by the door, fearing to obliterate any clues. Poirot, however, did not seem grateful to me for my forbearance.

'What have you, my friend?' he cried, 'that you remain there like – how do you say it? – ah, yes, the stuck pig?'

I explained that I was afraid of obliterating any footmarks.

'Footmarks? But what an idea! There has already been practically an army in the room! What footmarks are we likely to find? No, come here and aid me in my search. I will put down my little case until I need it.'

He did so, on the round table by the window, but it was an ill-advised proceeding; for, the top of it being loose, it tilted up, and precipitated the despatch-case on to the floor.

'*En voilà une table!*' cried Poirot. 'Ah, my friend, one may live in a big house and yet have no comfort.'

After which piece of moralizing, he resumed his search.

A small purple despatch-case, with a key in the lock, on the writing-table, engaged his attention for some time. He took out the key from the lock, and passed it to me to inspect. I saw nothing peculiar, however. It was an ordinary key of the Yale type, with a bit of twisted wire through the handle.

Next, he examined the framework of the door we had broken in, assuring himself that the bolt had really been shot. Then he went to the door opposite leading into Cynthia's room. That door was also bolted, as I had stated. However, he went to the length of unbolting it, and opening and shutting it several times; this he did with the utmost precaution against making any noise. Suddenly something in the bolt itself seemed to rivet his attention. He examined it carefully, and then, nimbly whipping out a pair of small forceps from his case, he drew out some minute particle which he carefully sealed up in a tiny envelope.

On the chest of drawers there was a tray with a spirit lamp and a small saucepan on it. A small quantity of a dark fluid remained in the saucepan, and an empty cup and saucer that had been drunk out of stood near it.

I wondered how I could have been so unobservant as to overlook this. Here was a clue worth having. Poirot delicately dipped his finger into the liquid, and tasted it gingerly. He made a grimace.

'Cocoa – with – I think – rum in it.'

He passed on to the debris on the floor, where the table by the bed had been overturned. A reading-lamp, some books, matches, a bunch of keys, and the crushed fragments of a coffee-cup lay scattered about.

'Ah, this is curious,' said Poirot.

'I must confess that I see nothing particularly curious about it.'

'You do not? Observe the lamp – the chimney is broken in two places; they lie there as they fell. But see, the coffee-cup is absolutely smashed to powder.'

'Well,' I said wearily. 'I suppose someone must have stepped on it.'

'Exactly,' said Poirot, in an odd voice. 'Someone stepped on it.'

He rose from his knees, and walked slowly across to the

mantelpiece, where he stood abstractedly fingering the ornaments, and straightening them – a trick of his when he was agitated.

'*Mon ami*,' he said, turning to me, 'somebody stepped on that cup, grinding it to powder, and the reason they did so was either because it contained strychnine or – which is far more serious – because it did not contain strychnine!'

I made no reply. I was bewildered, but I knew that it was no good asking him to explain. In a moment or two he roused himself, and went on with his investigations. He picked up the bunch of keys from the floor, and twirling them round in his fingers finally selected one, very bright and shining, which he tried in the lock of the purple despatch-case. It fitted, and he opened the box, but after a moment's hesitation, closed and relocked it, and slipped the bunch of keys, as well as the key that had originally stood in the lock, into his own pocket.

'I have no authority to go through these papers. But it should be done – at once!'

He then made a very careful examination of the drawers of the wash-stand. Crossing the room to the left-hand window, a round stain, hardly visible on the dark brown carpet, seemed to interest him particularly. He went down on his knees, examining it minutely – even going so far as to smell it.

Finally, he poured a few drops of the cocoa into a test tube, sealing it up carefully. His next proceeding was to take out a little notebook.

'We have found in this room,' he said, writing busily, 'six points of interest. Shall I enumerate them, or will you?'

'Oh, you,' I replied hastily.

'Very well, then. One, a coffee-cup that has been ground into powder; two, a despatch-case with a key in the lock; three, a stain on the floor.'

'That may have been done some time ago,' I interrupted.

'No, for it is still perceptibly damp and smells of coffee. Four, a fragment of some dark green fabric – only a thread or two, but recognizable.'

'Ah!' I cried. 'That was what you sealed up in the envelope.'

'Yes. It may turn out to be a piece of one of Mrs Inglethorp's own dresses, and quite unimportant. We shall see. Five, *this!*'

With a dramatic gesture, he pointed to a large splash of candle grease on the floor by the writing-table. 'It must have been done since yesterday, otherwise a good housemaid would have at once removed it with blotting-paper and a hot iron. One of my best hats once – but that is not to the point.'

'It was very likely done last night. We were very agitated. Or perhaps Mrs Inglethorp herself dropped her candle.'

'You brought only one candle into the room?'

'Yes. Lawrence Cavendish was carrying it. But he was very upset. He seemed to see something over here' – I indicated the mantelpiece – 'that absolutely paralysed him.'

'That is interesting,' said Poirot quickly. 'Yes, it is suggestive' – his eye sweeping the whole length of the wall – 'But it was not his candle that made this great patch, for you perceive that this is white grease; whereas Monsieur Lawrence's candle, which is still on the dressing-table, is pink. On the other hand, Mrs Inglethorp had no candlestick in the room, only a reading lamp.'

'Then,' I said, 'what do you deduce?'

To which my friend only made a rather irritating reply, urging me to use my own natural faculties.

'And the sixth point?' I asked. 'I suppose it is the sample of cocoa.'

'No,' said Poirot thoughtfully, 'I might have included that in the six, but I did not. No, the sixth point I will keep to myself for the present.'

He looked quickly round the room. 'There is nothing more to be done here, I think, unless' – he stared earnestly and long at the dead ashes in the grate. 'The fire burns – and it destroys. But by chance – there might be – let us see!'

Deftly, on hands and knees, he began to sort the ashes from the grate into the fender, handling them with the greatest caution. Suddenly, he gave a faint exclamation.

'The forceps, Hastings!'

I quickly handed them to him, and with skill he extracted a small piece of half-charred paper.

'There, *mon ami!*' he cried. 'What do you think of that?'

I scrutinized the fragment. This is an exact reproduction of it:

I was puzzled. It was unusually thick, quite unlike ordinary notepaper. Suddenly an idea struck me.

'Poirot!' I cried. 'This is a fragment of a will!'

'Exactly.'

I looked at him sharply.

'You are not surprised?'

'No,' he said gravely, 'I expected it.'

I relinquished the piece of paper, and watched him put it away in his case, with the same methodical care that he bestowed on everything. My brain was in a whirl. What was this complication of a will? Who had destroyed it? The person who had left the candle grease on the floor? Obviously. But how had anyone gained admission? All the doors had been bolted on the inside.

'Now, my friend,' said Poirot briskly, 'we will go. I should like to ask a few questions of the parlourmaid – Dorcas, her name is, is it not?'

We passed through Alfred Inglethorp's room, and Poirot delayed long enough to make a brief but fairly comprehensive examination of it. We went out through that door, locking both it and that of Mrs Inglethorp's room as before.

I took him down to the boudoir which he had expressed a wish to see, and went myself in search of Dorcas.

When I returned with her, however, the boudoir was empty.

'Poirot,' I cried, 'where are you?'

'I am here, my friend.'

He had stepped outside the french window, and was standing, apparently lost in admiration, before the various shaped flower beds.

'Admirable!' he murmured. 'Admirable! What symmetry! Observe that crescent; and those diamonds – their neatness rejoices the eye. The spacing of the plants, also, is perfect. It has been recently done; is it not so?'

'Yes, I believe they were at it yesterday afternoon. But come in – Dorcas is here.'

'*Eh bien, eh bien!* Do not grudge me a moment's satisfaction of the eye.'

'Yes, but this affair is more important.'

'And how do you know that these fine begonias are not of equal importance?'

I shrugged my shoulders. There was really no arguing with him if he chose to take that line.

'You do not agree? But such things have been. Well, we will come in and interview the brave Dorcas.'

Dorcas was standing in the boudoir, her hands folded in front of her, and her grey hair rose in stiff waves under her white cap. She was the very model and picture of a good old-fashioned servant.

In her attitude towards Poirot, she was inclined to be suspicious, but he soon broke down her defences. He drew forward a chair.

'Pray be seated mademoiselle.'

'Thank you, sir.'

'You have been with your mistress many years, is it not so?'

'Ten years, sir.'

'That is a long time, and very faithful service. You were much attached to her, were you not?'

'She was a very good mistress to me, sir.'

'Then you will not object to answering a few questions. I put them to you with Mr Cavendish's full approval.'

'Oh, certainly, sir.'

'Then I will begin by asking you about the events of yesterday afternoon. Your mistress had a quarrel?'

'Yes, sir. But I don't know that I ought –' Dorcas hesitated.

Poirot looked at her keenly.

'My good Dorcas, it is necessary that I should know every detail of that quarrel as fully as possible. Do not think you are betraying your mistress's secrets. Your mistress lies dead, and it is necessary that we should know all – if we are to avenge her. Nothing can bring her back to life, but we do hope, if there has been foul play, to bring the murderer to justice.'

'Amen to that,' said Dorcas fiercely. 'And, naming no names, there's *one* in this house that none of us could ever abide! And an ill day it was when first *he* darkened the threshold.'

Poirot waited for her indignation to subside, and then, resuming his business-like tone, he asked:

'Now, as to this quarrel? What is the first you heard of it?'

'Well, sir, I happened to be going along the hall outside yesterday –'

'What time was that?'

'I couldn't say exactly, sir, but it wasn't teatime by a long way. Perhaps four o'clock – or it may have been a bit later. Well, sir, as I said, I happened to be passing along, when I heard voices very loud and angry in here. I didn't exactly mean to listen, but – well, there it is. I stopped. The door was shut, but the mistress was speaking very sharp and clear, and I heard what she said quite plainly. "You have lied to me, and deceived me," she said. I didn't hear what Mr Inglethorp replied. He spoke a good bit lower than she did – but she answered: "How dare you? I have kept you and clothed you and fed you! You owe everything to me! And this is how you repay me! By bringing disgrace upon our name!" Again I didn't hear what he said, but she went on: "Nothing that you can say will make any difference. I see my duty clearly. My mind is made up. You need not think that any fear of publicity, or scandal between husband and wife will deter me." Then I thought I heard them coming out, so I went off quickly.'

'You are sure it was Mr Inglethorp's voice you heard?'

'Oh, yes, sir, whose else's could it be?'

'Well, what happened next?'

'Later, I came back to the hall; but it was all quiet. At five o'clock, Mrs Inglethorp rang the bell and told me to bring her a cup of tea – nothing to eat – to the boudoir. She was looking dreadful – so white and upset. "Dorcas," she says, "I've had a great shock." "I'm sorry for that, m'm," I says. "You'll feel better after a nice hot cup of tea, m'm." She had something in her hand. I don't know if it was a letter, or just a piece of paper, but it had writing on it, and she kept staring at it, almost as if she couldn't believe what was written there. She whispered to herself, as though she had forgotten I was there: "These few words – and everything's changed." And then she says to me: "Never trust a man, Dorcas, they're not worth it!" I hurried off, and got her a good strong cup of tea, and she thanked me, and said she'd feel better when she'd drunk it. "I don't know what to do," she says. "Scandal between husband and wife is a dreadful thing, Dorcas. I'd rather hush it up if I could." Mrs Cavendish came in just then, so she didn't say any more.'

'She still had the letter, or whatever it was, in her hand?'

'Yes, sir.'

'What would she be likely to do with it afterwards?'

'Well, I don't know, sir, I expect she would lock it up in that purple case of hers.'

'Is that where she usually kept important papers?'

'Yes, sir. She brought it down with her every morning, and took it up every night.'

'When did she lose the key of it?'

'She missed it yesterday at lunch-time, sir, and told me to look carefully for it. She was very much put out about it.'

'But she had a duplicate key?'

'Oh, yes, sir.'

Dorcas was looking very curiously at him and, to tell the truth, so was I. What was all this about a lost key? Poirot smiled.

'Never mind, Dorcas, it is my business to know things. Is this the key that was lost?' He drew from his pocket the key that he had found in the lock of the despatch-case upstairs.

Dorcas's eyes looked as though they would pop out of her head.

'That's it, sir, right enough. But where did you find it? I looked everywhere for it.'

'Ah, but you see it was not in the same place yesterday as it was today. Now, to pass to another subject, had your mistress a dark green dress in her wardrobe?'

Dorcas was rather startled by the unexpected question.

'No, sir.'

'Are you quite sure?'

'Oh, yes, sir.'

'Has anyone else in the house got a green dress?'

Dorcas reflected.

'Miss Cynthia has a green evening dress.'

'Light or dark green?'

'A light green, sir; a sort of chiffon, they call it.'

'Ah, that is not what I want. And nobody else has anything green?'

'No, sir – not that I know of.'

Poirot's face did not betray a trace of whether he was disappointed or otherwise. He merely remarked:

'Good, we will leave that and pass on. Have you any reason to believe that your mistress was likely to take a sleeping powder last night?'

'Not *last* night, sir, I know she didn't.'

'Why do you know so positively?'

'Because the box was empty. She took the last one two days ago, and she didn't have any more made up.'

'You are quite sure of that?'

'Positive, sir.'

'Then that is cleared up! By the way, your mistress didn't ask you to sign any paper yesterday?'

'To sign a paper? No, sir.'

'When Mr Hastings and Mr Lawrence came in yesterday evening, they found your mistress busy writing letters. I suppose you can give me no idea to whom these letters were addressed?'

'I'm afraid I couldn't, sir. I was out in the evening. Perhaps Annie could tell you, though she's a careless girl. Never cleared the coffee-cups away last night. That's what happens when I'm not here to look after things.'

Poirot lifted his hand.

'Since they have been left, Dorcas, leave them a little longer, I pray you. I should like to examine them.'

'Very well, sir.'

'What time did you go out last evening?'

'About six o'clock, sir.'

'Thank you, Dorcas, that is all I have to ask you.' He rose and strolled to the window. 'I have been admiring these flower beds. How many gardeners are employed here, by the way?'

'Only three now, sir. Five, we had, before the war, when it was kept as a gentleman's place should be. I wish you could have seen it then, sir. A fair sight it was. But now there's only old Manning, and young William, and a new-fashioned woman gardener in breeches and such-like. Ah, these are dreadful times!'

'The good times will come again, Dorcas. At least, we hope so. Now, will you send Annie to me here?'

'Yes, sir. Thank you, sir.'

'How did you know that Mrs Inglethorp took sleeping powders?' I asked, in lively curiosity, as Dorcas left the room. 'And about the lost key and the duplicate?'

'One thing at a time. As to the sleeping powders, I knew by this.' He suddenly produced a small cardboard box, such as chemists use for powders.

'Where did you find it?'

'In the wash-stand drawer in Mrs Inglethorp's bedroom. It was Number Six of my catalogue.'

'But I suppose, as the last powder was taken two days ago, it is not of much importance?'

'Probably not, but do you notice anything that strikes you as peculiar about this box?'

I examined it closely.

'No, I can't say that I do.'

'Look at the label.'

I read the label carefully: One powder to be taken at bedtime, if required. Mrs Inglethorp. 'No, I see nothing unusual.'

'Not the fact that there is no chemist's name?'

'Ah!' I exclaimed. 'To be sure, that is odd!'

'Have you ever known a chemist to send out a box like that, without his printed name?'

'No, I can't say that I have.'

I was becoming quite excited, but Poirot damped my ardour by remarking:

'Yet the explanation is quite simple. So do not intrigue yourself, my friend.'

An audible creaking proclaimed the approach of Annie, so I had no time to reply.

Annie was a fine, strapping girl, and was evidently labouring under intense excitement, mingled with a certain ghoulish enjoyment of the tragedy.

Poirot came to the point at once, with a business-like briskness.

'I sent for you, Annie, because I thought you might be able to tell me something about the letters Mrs Inglethorp wrote last night. How many were there? And can you tell me any of the names and addresses?'

Annie considered.

'There were four letters, sir. One was to Miss Howard, and one was to Mr Wells, the lawyer, and the other two I don't think I remember, sir – oh, yes, one was to Ross's, the caterers in Tadminster. The other one, I don't remember.'

'Think,' urged Poirot.

Annie racked her brains in vain.

'I'm sorry, sir, but it's clean gone. I don't think I can have noticed it.'

'It does not matter,' said Poirot, not betraying any sign of disappointment. 'Now I want to ask you about something else. There is a saucepan in Mrs Inglethorp's room with some cocoa in it. Did she have that every night?'

'Yes, sir, it was put in her room every evening, and she warmed it up in the night – whenever she fancied it.'

'What was it? Plain cocoa?'

'Yes, sir, made with milk, with a teaspoonful of sugar, and two teaspoonfuls of rum in it.'

'Who took it to her room?'

'I did, sir.'

'Always?'

'Yes, sir.'

'At what time?'

'When I went to draw the curtains, as a rule, sir.'

'Did you bring it straight up from the kitchen then?'

'No, sir, you see there's not much room on the gas stove, so Cook used to make it early, before putting the vegetables on for supper. Then I used to bring it up, and put it on the table by the swing door, and take it into her room later.'

'The swing door is in the left wing, is it not?'

'Yes, sir.'

'And the table, is it on this side of the door, or on the farther – servants' side?'

'It's this side, sir.'

'What time did you bring it up last night?'

'About quarter-past seven, I should say, sir.'

'And when did you take it into Mrs Inglethorp's room?'

'When I went to shut up, sir. About eight o'clock. Mrs Inglethorp came up to bed before I'd finished.'

'Then, between seven-fifteen and eight o'clock, the cocoa was standing on the table in the left wing?'

'Yes, sir.' Annie had been growing redder and redder in the face, and now she blurted out unexpectedly:

'And if there *was* salt in it, sir, it wasn't me. I never took the salt near it.'

'What makes you think there was salt in it?' asked Poirot.

'Seeing it on the tray, sir.'

'You saw some salt on the tray?'

'Yes. Coarse kitchen salt, it looked. I never noticed it when I took the tray up, but when I came to take it into the mistress's room I saw it at once, and I suppose I ought to have taken it down again, and asked Cook to make some fresh. But I was in a hurry, because Dorcas was out, and I thought maybe the cocoa itself was all right, and the salt had only gone on the tray. So I dusted it off with my apron, and took it in.'

I had the utmost difficulty in controlling my excitement. Unknown to herself, Annie had provided us with an important piece of evidence. How she would have gaped if she had realized that her 'coarse kitchen salt' was strychnine, one of the most deadly poisons known to mankind. I marvelled at Poirot's calm. His self-control was astonishing. I awaited his next question with impatience, but it disappointed me.

'When you went into Mrs Inglethorp's room, was the door leading into Miss Cynthia's room bolted?'

'Oh! Yes, sir; it always was. It had never been opened.'

'And the door into Mr Inglethorp's room? Did you notice if that was bolted too?'

Annie hesitated.

'I couldn't rightly say, sir; it was shut but I couldn't say whether it was bolted or not.'

'When you finally left the room, did Mrs Inglethorp bolt the door after you?'

'No, sir, not then, but I expect she did later. She usually did lock it at night. The door into the passage, that is.'

'Did you notice any candle grease on the floor when you did the room yesterday?'

'Candle grease? Oh, no, sir. Mrs Inglethorp didn't have a candle, only a reading-lamp.'

'Then, if there had been a large patch of candle grease on the floor, you think you would have been sure to have seen it?'

'Yes, sir, and I would have taken it out with a piece of blotting-paper and a hot iron.'

Then Poirot repeated the question he had put to Dorcas:

'Did your mistress ever have a green dress?'

'No, sir.'

'Nor a mantle, nor a cape, nor a – how do you call it? – a sports coat?'

'Not green, sir.'

'Nor anyone else in the house?'

Annie reflected.

'No, sir.'

'You are sure of that?'

'Quite sure.'

'*Bien!* That is all I want to know. Thank you very much.'

With a nervous giggle, Annie took herself creakingly out of the room. My pent-up excitement burst forth.

'Poirot,' I cried, 'I congratulate you! This is a great discovery.'

'What is a great discovery?'

'Why, that it was the cocoa and not the coffee that was poisoned. That explains everything! Of course, it did not take effect until the early morning, since the cocoa was only drunk in the middle of the night.'

'So you think that the cocoa – mark well what I say, Hastings, the *cocoa* – contained strychnine?'

'Of course! That salt on the tray, what else could it have been?'

'It might have been salt,' replied Poirot placidly.

I shrugged my shoulders. If he was going to take the matter that way, it was no good arguing with him. The idea crossed my mind, not for the first time, that poor old Poirot was growing old. Privately I thought it lucky that he had associated with him someone of a more receptive type of mind.

Poirot was surveying me with quietly twinkling eyes.

'You are not pleased with me, *mon ami*?'

'My dear Poirot,' I said coldly, 'it is not for me to dictate to you. You have a right to your own opinion, just as I have to mine.'

'A most admirable sentiment,' remarked Poirot, rising briskly to his feet. 'Now I have finished with this room. By the way, whose is the smaller desk in the corner?'

'Mr Inglethorp's.'

'Ah!' He tried the roll top tentatively. 'Locked. But perhaps one of Mrs Inglethorp's keys would open it.' He tried several, twisting and turning them with a practised hand, and finally uttering an ejaculation of satisfaction. '*Voila!* It is not the key, but it will open it at a pinch.' He slid back the roll top, and ran a rapid eye over the neatly filed papers. To my surprise, he did not examine them, merely remarking approvingly as he relocked the desk: 'Decidedly, he is a man of method, this Mr Inglethorp!'

A 'man of method' was, in Poirot's estimation, the highest praise that could be bestowed on any individual.

I felt that my friend was not what he had been as he rambled on disconnectedly:

'There were no stamps in his desk, but there might have been, eh, *mon ami*? There might have been? Yes' – his eyes wandered round the room – 'this boudoir has nothing more to tell us. It did not yield much. Only this.'

He pulled a crumpled envelope out of his pocket, and tossed it over to me. It was rather a curious document. A plain, dirty-looking old envelope with a few words scrawled across it, apparently at random. The following is a facsimile of it:

posessed

I am posessed

He is possessed

I am possessed

possessed

CHAPTER 5

'IT ISN'T STRYCHNINE, IS IT?'

'Where did you find this?' I asked Poirot, in lively curiosity.

'In the waste-paper basket. You recognize the handwriting?'

'Yes, it is Mrs Inglethorp's. But what does it mean?'

Poirot shrugged his shoulders.

'I cannot say – but it is suggestive.'

A wild idea flashed across me. Was it possible that Mrs Inglethorp's mind was deranged? Had she some fantastic idea of demoniacal possession? And, if that were so, was it not also possible that she might have taken her own life?

I was about to expound these theories to Poirot, when his own words distracted me.

'Come,' he said, 'now to examine the coffee-cups!'

'My dear Poirot! What on earth is the good of that, now that we know about the cocoa?'

'Oh, *là là!* That miserable cocoa!' cried Poirot flippantly.

He laughed with apparent enjoyment, raising his arms to

heaven in mock despair, in what I could not but consider the worst possible taste.

'And, anyway,' I said, with increasing coldness, 'as Mrs Inglethorp took her coffee upstairs with her, I do not see what you expect to find, unless you consider it likely that we shall discover a packet of strychnine on the coffee tray!'

Poirot was sobered at once.

'Come, come, my friend,' he said, slipping his arm through mine. '*Ne vous fâchez pas!* Allow me to interest myself in my coffee-cups, and I will respect your cocoa. There! Is it a bargain?'

He was so quaintly humorous that I was forced to laugh; and we went together to the drawing-room, where the coffee-cups and tray remained undisturbed as we had left them.

Poirot made me recapitulate the scene of the night before, listening very carefully, and verifying the position of the various cups.

'So Mrs Cavendish stood by the tray – and poured out. Yes. Then she came across to the window where you sat with Mademoiselle Cynthia. Yes. Here are the three cups. And the cup on the mantelpiece, half drunk, that would be Mr Lawrence Cavendish's. And the one on the tray?'

'John Cavendish's. I saw him put it down there.'

'Good. One, two, three, four, five – but where, then, is the cup of Mr Inglethorp?'

'He does not take coffee.'

'Then all are accounted for. One moment, my friend.'

With infinite care, he took a drop or two from the grounds in each cup, sealing them up in separate test tubes, tasting each in turn as he did so. His physiognomy underwent a curious change. An expression gathered there that I can only describe as half puzzled, and half relieved.

'*Bien!*' he said at last. 'It is evident! I had an idea – but clearly I was mistaken. Yes, altogether I was mistaken. Yet it is strange. But no matter!'

And, with a characteristic shrug, he dismissed whatever it was that was worrying him from his mind. I could have told him from the beginning that this obsession of his over the coffee was bound to end in a blind alley, but I restrained my tongue. After all, though he was old, Poirot had been a great man in his day.

'Breakfast is ready,' said John Cavendish, coming in from the hall. 'You will breakfast with us, Monsieur Poirot?'

Poirot acquiesced. I observed John. Already he was almost restored to his normal self. The shock of the events of the last night had upset him temporarily, but his equable poise soon swung back to the normal. He was a man of very little imagination, in sharp contrast with his brother, who had, perhaps, too much.

Ever since the early hours of the morning, John had been hard at work, sending telegrams – one of the first had gone to Evelyn Howard – writing notices for the papers, and generally occupying himself with the melancholy duties that a death entails.

'May I ask how things are proceeding?' he said. 'Do your investigations point to my mother having died a natural death – or – or must we prepare ourselves for the worst?'

'I think, Mr Cavendish,' said Poirot gravely, 'that you would do well not to buoy yourself up with any false hopes. Can you tell me the views of the other members of the family?'

'My brother Lawrence is convinced that we are making a fuss over nothing. He says that everything points to its being a simple case of heart failure.'

'He does, does he? That is very interesting – very interesting,' murmured Poirot softly. 'And Mrs Cavendish?'

A faint cloud passed over John's face.

'I have not the least idea what my wife's views on the subject are.'

The answer brought a momentary stiffness in its train. John broke the rather awkward silence by saying with a slight effort:

'I told you, didn't I, that Mr Inglethorp has returned?'

Poirot bent his head.

'It's an awkward position for all of us. Of course, one has to treat him as usual – but, hang it all, one's gorge does rise at sitting down to eat with a possible murderer!'

Poirot nodded sympathetically.

'I quite understand. It is a very difficult situation for you, Mr Cavendish. I would like to ask you one question. Mr Inglethorp's reason for not returning last night was, I believe, that he had forgotten the latch-key. Is not that so?'

'Yes.'

'I suppose you are quite sure that the latch-key *was* forgotten – that he did not take it after all?'

'I have no idea. I never thought of looking. We always keep it in the hall drawer. I'll go and see if it's there now.'

Poirot held up his hand with a faint smile.

'No, no, Mr Cavendish, it is too late now. I am certain that you will find it. If Mr Inglethorp did take it, he has had ample time to replace it by now.'

'But do you think –'

'I think nothing. If anyone had chanced to look this morning before his return, and seen it there, it would have been a valuable point in his favour. That is all.'

John looked perplexed.

'Do not worry,' said Poirot smoothly. 'I assure you that you need not let it trouble you. Since you are so kind, let us go and have some breakfast.'

Everyone was assembled in the dining-room. Under the circumstances, we were naturally not a cheerful party. The reaction after a shock is always trying, and I think we were suffering from it. Decorum and good breeding naturally enjoined that our demeanour should be much as usual, yet I could not help wondering if this self-control were really a matter of great difficulty. There were no red eyes, no signs of secretly indulged grief. I felt that I was right in my opinion that Dorcas was the person most affected by the personal side of the tragedy.

I pass over Alfred Inglethorp, who acted the bereaved widower in a manner that I felt to be disgusting in its hypocrisy. Did he know that we suspected him, I wondered. Surely he could not be unaware of the fact, conceal it as we would. Did he feel some secret stirring of fear, or was he confident that his crime would go unpunished? Surely the suspicion in the atmosphere must warn him that he was already a marked man.

But did everyone suspect him? What about Mrs Cavendish? I watched her as she sat at the head of the table, graceful, composed, enigmatic. In her soft grey frock, with white ruffles at the wrists falling over her slender hands, she looked very beautiful. When she chose, however, her face could be sphinx-like in its inscrutability. She was very silent, hardly opening her lips, and yet in some queer way I felt that the great strength of her personality was dominating us all.

And little Cynthia? Did she suspect? She looked very tired and ill, I thought. The heaviness and languor of her manner were very marked. I asked her if she were feeling ill, and she answered frankly:

'Yes, I've got the most beastly headache.'

'Have another cup of coffee, mademoiselle?' said Poirot solicitously. 'It will revive you. It is unparalleled for the *mal de tête.*' He jumped up and took her cup.

'No sugar,' said Cynthia, watching him, as he picked up the sugar-tongs.

'No sugar? You abandon it in the war-time, eh?'

'No, I never take it in coffee.'

'*Sacré!*' murmured Poirot to himself, as he brought back the replenished cup.

Only I heard him, and glancing up curiously at the little man I saw that his face was working with suppressed excitement, and his eyes were as green as a cat's. He had heard or seen something that had affected him strongly – but what was it? I do not usually label myself as dense, but I must confess that nothing out of the ordinary had attracted *my* attention.

In another moment, the door opened and Dorcas appeared. 'Mr Wells to see you, sir,' she said to John.

I remembered the name as being that of the lawyer to whom Mrs Inglethorp had written the night before.

John rose immediately.

'Show him into my study.' Then he turned to us. 'My mother's lawyer,' he explained. And in a lower voice: 'He is also Coroner – you understand. Perhaps you would like to come with me?'

We acquiesced and followed him out of the room. John strode on ahead and I took the opportunity of whispering to Poirot:

'There will be an inquest then?'

Poirot nodded absently. He seemed absorbed in thought; so much so that my curiosity was aroused.

'What is it? You are not attending to what I say.'

'It is true, my friend. I am much worried.'

'Why?'

'Because Mademoiselle Cynthia does not take sugar in her coffee.'

'What? You cannot be serious?'

'But I am most serious. Ah, there is something there that I do not understand. My instinct was right.'

'What instinct?'

'The instinct that led me to insist on examining those coffee-cups. *Chut!* no more now!'

We followed John into his study, and he closed the door behind us.

Mr Wells was a pleasant man of middle-age, with keen eyes, and the typical lawyer's mouth. John introduced us both, and explained the reason of our presence.

'You will understand, Wells,' he added, 'that this is all strictly private. We are still hoping that there will turn out to be no need for investigation of any kind.'

'Quite so, quite so,' said Mr Wells soothingly. 'I wish we could have spared you the pain and publicity of an inquest, but, of course, it's quite unavoidable in the absence of a doctor's certificate.'

'Yes, I suppose so.'

'Clever man, Bauerstein. Great authority on toxicology, I believe.'

'Indeed,' said John with a certain stiffness in his manner. Then he added rather hesitatingly: 'Shall we have to appear as witnesses – all of us, I mean?'

'You, of course – and ah – er – Mr – er – Inglethorp.'

A slight pause ensued before the lawyer went on in his soothing manner:

'Any other evidence will be simply confirmatory, a mere matter of form.'

'I see.'

A faint expression of relief swept over John's face. It puzzled me, for I saw no occasion for it.

'If you know of nothing to the contrary,' pursued Mr Wells, 'I had thought of Friday. That will give us plenty of time for the doctor's report. The post-mortem is to take place tonight, I believe?'

'Yes.'

'Then the arrangement will suit you?'

'Perfectly.'

'I need not tell you, my dear Cavendish, how distressed I am at this most tragic affair.'

'Can you give us no help in solving it, monsieur?' interposed Poirot, speaking for the first time since we had entered the room.

'I?'

'Yes, we heard that Mrs Inglethorp wrote to you last night. You should have received the letter this morning.'

'I did, but it contains no information. It is merely a note asking me to call upon her this morning, as she wanted my advice on a matter of great importance.'

'She gave you no hint as to what that matter might be?'

'Unfortunately, no.'

'That is a pity,' said John.

'A great pity,' agreed Poirot gravely.

There was a silence. Poirot remained lost in thought for a few minutes. Finally he turned to the lawyer again.

'Mr Wells, there is one thing I should like to ask you – that is, if it is not against professional etiquette. In the event of Mrs Inglethorp's death, who would inherit her money?'

The lawyer hesitated a moment, and then replied:

'The knowledge will be public property very soon, so if Mr Cavendish does not object –'

'Not at all,' interpolated John.

'I do not see any reason why I should not answer your question. By her last will, dated August of last year, after various unimportant legacies to servants, etc., she gave her entire fortune to her stepson, Mr John Cavendish.'

'Was not that – pardon the question, Mr Cavendish – rather unfair to her other stepson, Mr Lawrence Cavendish?'

'No, I do not think so. You see, under the terms of their father's will, while John inherited the property, Lawrence, at his stepmother's death, would come into a considerable sum of money. Mrs Inglethorp left her money to her elder stepson, knowing that he would have to keep up Styles. It was, to my mind, a very fair and equitable distribution.'

Poirot nodded thoughtfully.

'I see. But I am right in saying, am I not, that by your English law that will was automatically revoked when Mrs Inglethorp remarried?'

Mr Wells bowed his head.

'As I was about to proceed, Monsieur Poirot, that document is now null and void.'

'*Hein!*' said Poirot. He reflected for a moment, and then asked: 'Was Mrs Inglethorp herself aware of that fact?'

'I do not know. She may have been.'

'She was,' said John unexpectedly. 'We were discussing the matter of wills being revoked by marriage only yesterday.'

'Ah! One more question, Mr Wells. You say "her last will". Had Mrs Inglethorp, then, made several former wills?'

'On an average, she made a new will at least once a year,' said Mr Wells imperturbably. 'She was given to changing her mind as to her testamentary dispositions, now benefiting one, now another member of her family.'

'Suppose,' suggested Poirot, 'that, unknown to you, she had made a new will in favour of someone who was not, in any sense of the word, a member of the family – we will say Miss Howard, for instance – would you be surprised?'

'Not in the least.'

'Ah!' Poirot seemed to have exhausted his questions.

I drew close to him, while John and the lawyer were debating the question of going through Mrs Inglethorp's papers.

'Do you think Mrs Inglethorp made a will leaving all her money to Miss Howard?' I asked in a low voice, with some curiosity.

Poirot smiled.

'No.'

'Then why did you ask?'

'Hush!'

John Cavendish had turned to Poirot.

'Will you come with us, Monsieur Poirot? We are going through my mother's papers. Mr Inglethorp is quite willing to leave it entirely to Mr Wells and myself.'

'Which simplifies matters very much,' murmured the lawyer. 'As technically, of course, he was entitled –' He did not finish the sentence.

'We will look through the desk in the boudoir first,' explained

John, 'and go up to her bedroom afterwards. She kept her most important papers in a purple despatch-case, which we must look through carefully.'

'Yes,' said the lawyer, 'it is quite possible that there may be a later will than the one in my possession.'

'There *is* a later will.' It was Poirot who spoke.

'What?' John and the lawyer looked at him startled.

'Or rather,' pursued my friend imperturbably, 'there *was* one.'

'What do you mean – there was one? Where is it now?'

'Burnt!'

'Burnt?'

'Yes. See here.' He took out the charred fragment we had found in the grate in Mrs Inglethorp's room, and handed it to the lawyer with a brief explanation of when and where he had found it.

'But possibly this is an old will?'

'I do not think so. In fact I am almost certain that it was made no earlier than yesterday afternoon.'

'What?' 'Impossible!' broke simultaneously from both men.

Poirot turned to John.

'If you will allow me to send for your gardener, I will prove it to you.'

'Oh, of course – but I don't see –'

Poirot raised his hand.

'Do as I ask you. Afterwards you shall question as much as you please.'

'Very well.' He rang the bell.

Dorcas answered it in due course.

'Dorcas, will you tell Manning to come round and speak to me here.'

'Yes, sir.'

Dorcas withdrew.

We waited in a tense silence. Poirot alone seemed perfectly at his ease, and dusted a forgotten corner of the bookcase.

The clumping of hobnailed boots on the gravel outside proclaimed the approach of Manning. John looked questioningly at Poirot. The latter nodded.

'Come inside, Manning,' said John, 'I want to speak to you.'

Manning came slowly and hesitatingly through the french window, and stood as near it as he could. He held his cap in his hands, twisting it very carefully round and round. His back was much bent, though he was probably not as old as he looked, but his eyes were sharp and intelligent, and belied his slow and rather cautious speech.

'Manning,' said John, 'this gentleman will put some questions to you which I want you to answer.'

'Yessir,' mumbled Manning.

Poirot stepped forward briskly. Manning's eye swept over him with a faint contempt.

'You were planting a bed of begonias round by the south side of the house yesterday afternoon, were you not, Manning?'

'Yes, sir, me and Willum.'

'And Mrs Inglethorp came to the window and called you, did she not?'

'Yes, sir, she did.'

'Tell me in your own words exactly what happened after that.'

'Well, sir, nothing much. She just told Willum to go on his bicycle down to the village, and bring back a form of will, or such-like – I don't know what exactly – she wrote it down for him.'

'Well?'

'Well, he did, sir.'

'And what happened next?'

'We went on with the begonias, sir.'

'Did not Mrs Inglethorp call you again?'

'Yes, sir, both me and Willum, she called.'

'And then?'

'She made us come right in, and sign our names at the bottom of a long paper – under where she'd signed.'

'Did you see anything of what was written above her signature?' asked Poirot sharply.

'No, sir, there was a bit of blotting paper over that part.'

'And you signed where she told you?'

'Yes, sir, first me and then Willum.'

'What did she do with it afterwards?'

'Well, sir, she slipped it into a long envelope, and put it inside a sort of purple box that was standing on the desk.'

'What time was it when she first called you?'

'About four, I should say, sir.'

'Not earlier? Couldn't it have been about half-past three?'

'No, I shouldn't say so, sir. It would be more likely to be a bit after four – not before it.'

'Thank you, Manning, that will do,' said Poirot pleasantly.

The gardener glanced at his master, who nodded, where-upon Manning lifted a finger to his forehead with a low mumble, and backed cautiously out of the window.

We all looked at each other.

'Good heavens!' murmured John. 'What an extraordinary coincidence.'

'How – a coincidence?'

'That my mother should have made a will on the very day of her death!'

Mr Wells cleared his throat and remarked drily:

'Are you so sure it is a coincidence, Cavendish?'

'What do you mean?'

'Your mother, you tell me, had a violent quarrel with – someone yesterday afternoon –'

'What do you mean?' cried John again. There was a tremor in his voice, and he had gone very pale.

'In consequence of that quarrel, your mother very suddenly and hurriedly makes a new will. The contents of that will we shall never know. She told no one of its provisions. This morning, no doubt, she would have consulted me on the subject – but she had no chance. The will disappears, and she takes its secret with her to her grave. Cavendish, I much fear there is no coincidence there. Monsieur Poirot, I am sure you agree with me that the facts are very suggestive.'

'Suggestive, or not,' interrupted John, 'we are most grateful to Monsieur Poirot for elucidating the matter. But for him, we should never have known of this will. I suppose I may not ask you, monsieur, what first led you to suspect the fact?'

Poirot smiled and answered:

'A scribbled-over old envelope, and a freshly planted bed of begonias.'

John, I think, would have pressed his questions further, but at that moment the loud purr of a motor was audible, and we all turned to the window as it swept past.

'Evie!' cried John. 'Excuse me, Wells.' He went hurriedly out into the hall.

Poirot looked inquiringly at me.

'Miss Howard,' I explained.

'Ah, I am glad she has come. There is a woman with a head and a heart too, Hastings. Though the good God gave her no beauty!'

I followed John's example, and went out into the hall, where Miss Howard was endeavouring to extricate herself from the voluminous mass of veils that enveloped her head. As her eyes fell on me, a sudden pang of guilt shot through me. This was the woman who had warned me so earnestly, and to whose warning I had, alas, paid no heed! How soon, and how contemptuously, I had dismissed it from my mind. Now that she had been proved justified in so tragic a manner, I felt ashamed. She had known Alfred Inglethorp only too well. I wondered whether, if she had remained at Styles, the tragedy would have taken place, or would the man have feared her watchful eyes?

I was relieved when she shook me by the hand, with her well remembered painful grip. The eyes that met mine were sad, but not reproachful; that she had been crying, bitterly, I could tell by the redness of her eyelids, but her manner was unchanged from its old blunt gruffness.

'Started the moment I got the wire. Just come off night duty. Hired car. Quickest way to get here.'

'Have you had anything to eat this morning, Evie?' asked John.

'No.'

'I thought not. Come along, breakfast's not cleared away yet, and they'll make you some fresh tea.' He turned to me. 'Look after her, Hastings, will you? Wells is waiting for me. Oh, here's Monsieur Poirot. He's helping us, you know, Evie.'

Miss Howard shook hands with Poirot, but glanced suspiciously over her shoulder at John.

'What do you mean – helping us?'

'Helping us to investigate.'

'Nothing to investigate. Have they taken him to prison yet?'

'Taken who to prison?'

'Who? Alfred Inglethorp, of course!'

'My dear Evie, do be careful. Lawrence is of the opinion that my mother died from heart seizure.'

'More fool, Lawrence!' retorted Miss Howard. 'Of course Alfred Inglethorp murdered poor Emily – as I always told you he would.'

'My dear Evie, don't shout so. Whatever we may think or suspect, it is better to say as little as possible for the present. The inquest isn't until Friday.'

'Not until fiddlesticks!' The snort Miss Howard gave was truly magnificent. 'You're all off your heads. The man will be out of the country by then. If he's any sense, he won't stay here tamely and wait to be hanged.'

John Cavendish looked at her helplessly.

'I know what it is,' she accused him, 'you've been listening to the doctors. Never should. What do they know? Nothing at all – or just enough to make them dangerous. I ought to know – my own father was a doctor. That little Wilkins is about the greatest fool that even I have ever seen. Heart seizure! Sort of thing he would say. Anyone with any sense could see at once that her husband had poisoned her. I always said he'd murder her in her bed, poor soul. Now he's done it. And all you can do is to murmur silly things about "heart seizure" and "inquest on Friday". You ought to be ashamed of yourself, John Cavendish.'

'What do you want me to do?' asked John, unable to help a faint smile. 'Dash it all, Evie, I can't haul him down to the local police station by the scruff of his neck.'

'Well, you might do something. Find out how he did it. He's a crafty beggar. Dare say he soaked fly papers. Ask Cook if she's missed any.'

It occurred to me very forcibly at that moment that to harbour Miss Howard and Alfred Inglethorp under the same roof, and keep the peace between them, was likely to prove a Herculean task, and I did not envy John. I could see by the expression of his face that he fully appreciated the difficulty of the position. For the moment, he sought refuge in retreat, and left the room precipitately.

Dorcas brought in fresh tea. As she left the room, Poirot came over from the window where he had been standing, and sat down facing Miss Howard.

'Mademoiselle,' he said gravely, 'I want to ask you something.'

'Ask away,' said the lady, eyeing him with some disfavour.

'I want to be able to count upon your help.'

'I'll help you to hang Alfred with pleasure,' she replied gruffly. 'Hanging's too good for him. Ought to be drawn and quartered, like in good old times.'

'We are at one then,' said Poirot, 'for I, too, want to hang the criminal.'

'Alfred Inglethorp?'

'Him, or another.'

'No question of another. Poor Emily was never murdered until *he* came along. I don't say she wasn't surrounded by sharks – she was. But it was only her purse they were after. Her life was safe enough. But along comes Mr Alfred Inglethorp – and within two months – hey presto!'

'Believe me, Miss Howard,' said Poirot very earnestly, 'if Mr Inglethorp is the man, he shall not escape me. On my honour, I will hang him as high as Haman!'

'That's better,' said Miss Howard more enthusiastically.

'But I must ask you to trust me. Now your help may be very valuable to me. I will tell you why. Because, in all this house of mourning, yours are the only eyes that have wept.'

Miss Howard blinked, and a new note crept into the gruffness of her voice.

'If you mean that I was fond of her – yes, I was. You know, Emily was a selfish old woman in her way. She was very generous, but she always wanted a return. She never let people forget what she had done for them – and, that way, she missed love. Don't think she ever realized it, though, or felt the lack of it. Hope not, anyway. I was on a different footing. I took my stand from the first. "So many pounds a year I'm worth to you. Well and good. But not a penny piece besides – not a pair of gloves, nor a theatre ticket." She didn't understand – was very offended sometimes. Said I was foolishly proud. It wasn't that – but I couldn't explain. Anyway, I kept my self-respect. And so, out of the whole bunch, I was the only one who could allow myself to be fond of her. I watched over her. I guarded her from the lot of them. And then a glib-tongued scoundrel comes along, and pooh! all my years of devotion go for nothing.'

Poirot nodded sympathetically.

'I understand, mademoiselle, I understand all you feel. It is most natural. You think that we are lukewarm – that we lack fire and energy – but trust me, it is not so.'

John stuck his head in at this juncture, and invited us both to come up to Mrs Inglethorp's room, as he and Mr Wells had finished looking through the desk in the boudoir.

As we went up the stairs, John looked back to the dining-room, and lowered his voice confidentially:

'Look here, what's going to happen when these two meet?'

I shook my head helplessly.

'I've told Mary to keep them apart if she can.'

'Will she be able to do so?'

'The Lord only knows. There's one thing, Inglethorp himself won't be too keen on meeting her.'

'You've got the keys still, haven't you, Poirot?' I asked, as we reached the door of the locked room.

Taking the keys from Poirot, John unlocked it, and we all passed in. The lawyer went straight to the desk, and John followed him.

'My mother kept most of her important papers in this despatch-case, I believe,' he said.

Poirot drew out the small bunch of keys.

'Permit me. I locked it, out of precaution, this morning.'

'But it's not locked now.'

'Impossible!'

'See.' And John lifted the lid as he spoke.

'*Mille tonnerres!*' cried Poirot, dumbfounded. 'And I – who have both the keys in my pocket!' He flung himself upon the case. Suddenly he stiffened. '*En voilà une affaire!* This lock has been forced!'

'What?'

Poirot laid down the case again.

'But who forced it? Why should they? When? But the door was locked!' These exclamations burst from us disjointedly.

Poirot answered them categorically – almost mechanically.

'Who? That is the question. Why? Ah, if I only knew. When? Since I was here an hour ago. As to the door being locked, it is a very ordinary lock. Probably any other of the doorkeys in this passage would fit it.'

We stared at one another blankly. Poirot had walked over to the mantelpiece. He was outwardly calm, but I noticed his hands, which from long force of habit were mechanically straightening the spill vases on the mantelpiece, were shaking violently.

'See here, it was like this,' he said at last. 'There was something in that case – some piece of evidence, slight in itself perhaps, but still enough of a clue to connect the murderer with the crime. It was vital to him that it should be destroyed before it was discovered and its significance appreciated. Therefore, he took the risk, the great risk, of coming in here. Finding the case locked, he was obliged to force it, thus betraying his presence. For him to take that risk, it must have been something of great importance.'

'But what was it?'

'Ah!' cried Poirot, with a gesture of anger. 'That, I do not know! A document of some kind, without doubt, possibly the scrap of paper Dorcas saw in her hand yesterday afternoon. And I' – his anger burst forth freely – 'miserable animal that I am! I guessed nothing! I have behaved like an imbecile! I should never have left that case here. I should have carried it away with me. Ah, triple pig! And now it is gone. It is destroyed – but is it destroyed? Is there not yet a chance – we must leave no stone unturned –'

He rushed like a madman from the room, and I followed him as soon as I had sufficiently recovered my wits. But, by the time I had reached the top of the stairs, he was out of sight.

Mary Cavendish was standing where the staircase branched, staring down into the hall in the direction in which he had disappeared.

'What has happened to your extraordinary little friend, Mr Hastings? He has just rushed past me like a mad bull.'

'He's rather upset about something,' I remarked feebly. I really did not know how much Poirot would wish me to disclose. As I saw a faint smile gather on Mrs Cavendish's expressive mouth, I endeavoured to try and turn the conversation by saying: 'They haven't met yet, have they?'

'Who?'

'Mr Inglethorp and Miss Howard.'

She looked at me in rather a disconcerting manner.

'Do you think it would be such a disaster if they did meet?'

'Well, don't you?' I said, rather taken aback.

'No.' She was smiling in her quiet way. 'I should like to see a good flare up. It would clear the air. At present we are all thinking so much, and saying so little.'

'John doesn't think so,' I remarked. 'He's anxious to keep them apart.'

'Oh, John!'

Something in her tone fired me, and I blurted out:

'Old John's an awfully good sort.'

She studied me curiously for a minute or two, and then said, to my great surprise:

'You are loyal to your friend. I like you for that.'

'Aren't you my friend, too?'

'I am a very bad friend.'

'Why do you say that?'

'Because it is true. I am charming to my friends one day, and forget all about them the next.'

I don't know what impelled me, but I was nettled, and I said foolishly and not in the best of taste:

'Yet you seem to be invariably charming to Dr Bauerstein!'

Instantly I regretted my words. Her face stiffened. I had the impression of a steel curtain coming down and blotting out the real woman. Without a word, she turned and went swiftly up the stairs, whilst I stood like an idiot gaping after her.

I was recalled to other matters by a frightful row going on below. I could hear Poirot shouting and expounding. I was vexed to think that my diplomacy had been in vain. The little man appeared to be taking the whole house into his confidence, a proceeding of which I, for one, doubted the wisdom. Once again I could not help regretting that my friend was so prone to lose his head in moments of excitement. I stepped briskly down the stairs. The sight of me calmed Poirot almost immediately. I drew him aside.

'My dear fellow,' I said, 'is this wise? Surely you don't want the whole house to know of this occurrence? You are actually playing into the criminal's hands.'

'You think so, Hastings?'

'I am sure of it.'

'Well, well, my friend, I will be guided by you.'

'Good. Although, unfortunately, it is a little too late now.'

'True.'

He looked so crestfallen and abashed that I felt quite sorry, though I still thought my rebuke a just and wise one.

'Well,' he said at last, 'let us go, *mon ami*.'

'You have finished here?'

'For the moment, yes. You will walk back with me to the village?'

'Willingly.'

He picked up his little suitcase, and we went out through the open window in the drawing-room. Cynthia Murdoch was just coming in, and Poirot stood aside to let her pass.

'Excuse me, mademoiselle, one minute.'

'Yes?' she turned inquiringly.

'Did you ever make up Mrs Inglethorp's medicines?'

A slight flush rose in her face, as she answered rather constrainedly:

'No.'

'Only her powders?'

The flush deepened as Cynthia replied:

'Oh, yes, I did make up some sleeping powders for her once.'

'These?'

Poirot produced the empty box which had contained powders. She nodded.

'Can you tell me what they were? Sulphonal? Veronal?'

'No, they were bromide powders.'

'Ah! Thank you, mademoiselle; good morning.'

As we walked briskly away from the house, I glanced at him more than once. I had often before noticed that, if anything excited him, his eyes turned green like a cat's. They were shining like emeralds now.

'My friend,' he broke out at last, 'I have a little idea, a very strange, and probably utterly impossible idea. And yet – it fits in.'

I shrugged my shoulders. I privately thought that Poirot was rather too much given to these fantastic ideas. In this case, surely, the truth was only too plain and apparent.

'So that is the explanation of the blank label on the box,' I remarked. 'Very simple, as you said. I really wonder that I did not think of it myself.'

Poirot did not appear to be listening to me.

'They have made one more discovery, *là-bas*,' he observed, jerking his thumb over his shoulder in the direction of Styles. 'Mr Wells told me as we were going upstairs.'

'What was it?'

'Locked up in the desk in the boudoir, they found a will of Mrs Inglethorp's, dated before her marriage, leaving her fortune to Alfred Inglethorp. It must have been made just at the time they were engaged. It came quite as a surprise to Wells – and to John Cavendish also. It was written on one of those printed will forms, and witnessed by two of the servants – not Dorcas.'

'Did Mr Inglethorp know of it?'

'He says not.'

'One might take that with a grain of salt,' I remarked sceptically. 'All these wills are very confusing. Tell me, how did those scribbled words on the envelope help you to discover that a will was made yesterday afternoon?'

Poirot smiled.

'*Mon ami*, have you ever, when writing a letter, been arrested by the fact that you did not know how to spell a certain word?'

'Yes, often. I suppose everyone has.'

'Exactly. And have you not, in such a case, tried the word once or twice on the edge of the blotting-paper, or a spare scrap of paper, to see if it looked right? Well, that is what Mrs Inglethorp did. You will notice that the word "possessed" is spelt first with one "s" and subsequently with two – correctly. To make sure, she had further tried it in a sentence, thus: "I am possessed." Now, what did that tell me? It told me that Mrs Inglethorp had been writing the word "possessed" that afternoon, and, having the fragment of paper found in the grate fresh in my mind, the possibility of a will – a document almost certain to contain that word – occurred to me at once. This possibility was confirmed by a further circumstance. In the general confusion, the boudoir had not been swept that morning, and near the desk were several traces of brown mould and earth. The weather had been perfectly fine for some days, and no ordinary boots would have left such a heavy deposit.

'I strolled to the window, and saw at once that the begonia beds had been newly planted. The mould in the beds was exactly similar to that on the floor of the boudoir, and also I learnt from you that they *had* been planted yesterday afternoon. I was now sure that one, or possibly both of the gardeners – for there were two sets of footprints in the bed – had entered the boudoir, for if Mrs Inglethorp had merely wished to speak to them she would in all probability have stood at the window, and they would not have come into the room at all. I was now quite convinced that she had made a fresh will, and had called the two gardeners in to witness her signature. Events proved that I was right in my supposition.'

'That was very ingenious,' I could not help admitting. 'I must confess that the conclusions I drew from those few scribbled words were quite erroneous.'

He smiled.

'You gave too much rein to your imagination. Imagination is a good servant, and a bad master. The simplest explanation is always the most likely.'

'Another point – how did you know that the key of the despatch-case had been lost?'

'I did not know it. It was a guess that turned out to be correct. You observed that it had a piece of twisted wire through the handle. That suggested to me at once that it had possibly been wrenched off a flimsy key-ring. Now, if it had been lost and recovered, Mrs Inglethorp would at once have replaced it on her bunch; but on her bunch I found what was obviously the duplicate key, very new and bright, which led me to the hypothesis that somebody else had inserted the original key in the lock of the despatch-case.'

'Yes,' I said, 'Alfred Inglethorp, without a doubt.'

Poirot looked at me curiously.

'You are very sure of his guilt?'

'Well, naturally. Every fresh circumstance seems to establish it more clearly.'

'On the contrary,' said Poirot quietly, 'there are several points in his favour.'

'Oh, come now!'

'Yes.'

'I see only one.'

'And that?'

'That he was not in the house last night.'

'"Bad shot!" as you English say! You have chosen the one point that to my mind tells against him.'

'How is that?'

'Because if Mr Inglethorp knew that his wife would be poisoned last night, he would certainly have arranged to be away from the house. His excuse was an obviously trumped up one. That leaves us two possibilities: either he knew what was going to happen or he had a reason of his own for his absence.'

'And that reason?' I asked sceptically.

Poirot shrugged his shoulders.

'How should I know? Discreditable, without doubt. This Mr Inglethorp, I should say, is somewhat of a scoundrel – but that does not of necessity make him a murderer.'

I shook my head, unconvinced.

'We do not agree, eh?' said Poirot. 'Well, let us leave it. Time will show which of us is right. Now let us turn to other aspects of the case. What do you make of the fact that all the doors of the bedroom were bolted on the inside?'

'Well –' I considered. 'One must look at it logically.'

'True.'

'I should put it this way. The doors *were* bolted – our own eyes have told us that – yet the presence of the candle grease on the floor, and the destruction of the will, prove that during the night someone entered the room. You agree so far?'

'Perfectly. Put with admirable clearness. Proceed.'

'Well,' I said, encouraged, 'as the person who entered did not do so by the window, nor by miraculous means, it follows that the door must have been opened from inside by Mrs Inglethorp herself. That strengthens the conviction that the person in question was her husband. She would naturally open the door to her own husband.'

Poirot shook his head.

'Why should she? She had bolted the door leading into his room – a most unusual proceeding on her part – she had had a most violent quarrel with him that very afternoon. No, he was the last person she would admit.'

'But you agree with me that the door must have been opened by Mrs Inglethorp herself?'

'There is another possibility. She may have forgotten to bolt the door into the passage when she went up to bed, and have got up later, towards morning, and bolted it then.'

'Poirot, is that seriously your opinion?'

'No, I do not say it is so, but it might be. Now, turn to another feature, what do you make of the scrap of conversation you overheard between Mrs Cavendish and her mother-in-law?'

'I had forgotten that,' I said thoughtfully. 'That is as enigmatical as ever. It seems incredible that a woman like Mrs Cavendish, proud and reticent to the last degree, should interfere so violently in what was certainly not her affair.'

'Precisely. It was an astonishing thing for a woman of her breeding to do.'

'It is certainly curious,' I agreed. 'Still, it is unimportant, and need not be taken into account.'

A groan burst from Poirot.

'What have I always told you? Everything must be taken into account. If the fact will not fit the theory – let the theory go.'

'Well, we shall see,' I said, nettled.

'Yes, we shall see.'

We had reached Leastways Cottage, and Poirot ushered me upstairs to his own room. He offered me one of the tiny Russian cigarettes he himself occasionally smoked. I was amused to notice that he stowed away the used matches most carefully in a little china pot. My momentary annoyance vanished.

Poirot had placed our two chairs in front of the open window which commanded a view of the village street. The fresh air blew in warm and pleasant. It was going to be a hot day.

Suddenly my attention was arrested by a weedy-looking young man rushing down the street at a great pace. It was the expression on his face that was extraordinary – a curious mingling of terror and agitation.

'Look, Poirot!' I said.

He leant forward. '*Tiens!*' he said. 'It is Mr Mace, from the chemist's shop. He is coming here.'

The young man came to a halt before Leastways Cottage, and, after hesitating a moment, pounded vigorously at the door.

'A little minute,' cried Poirot from the window. 'I come.'

Motioning to me to follow him, he ran swiftly down the stairs and opened the door. Mr Mace began at once.

'Oh, Mr Poirot, I'm sorry for the inconvenience, but I heard that you'd just come back from the Hall?'

'Yes, we have.'

The young man moistened his dry lips. His face was working curiously.

'It's all over the village about old Mrs Inglethorp dying so suddenly. They do say –' he lowered his voice cautiously – 'that it's poison?'

Poirot's face remained quite impassive.

'Only the doctors can tell us that, Mr Mace.'

'Yes, exactly – of course –' The young man hesitated, and then his agitation was too much for him. He clutched Poirot by the arm, and sank his voice to a whisper: 'Just tell me this, Mr Poirot, it isn't – it isn't strychnine, is it?'

I hardly heard what Poirot replied. Something evidently of a non-committal nature. The young man departed, and as he closed the door Poirot's eyes met mine.

'Yes,' he said, nodding gravely. 'He will have evidence to give at the inquest.'

We went slowly upstairs again. I was opening my lips, when Poirot stopped me with a gesture of his hand.

'Not now, not now, *mon ami*. I have need of reflection. My mind is in some disorder – which is not well.'

For about ten minutes he sat in dead silence, perfectly still, except for several expressive motions of his eyebrows, and all the time his eyes grew steadily greener. At last he heaved a deep sigh.

'It is well. The bad moment has passed. Now all is arranged and classified. One must never permit confusion. The case is not clear yet – no. For it is of the most complicated! It puzzles *me*. Me, Hercule Poirot! There are two facts of significance.'

'And what are they?'

'The first is the state of the weather yesterday. That is very important.'

'But it was a glorious day!' I interrupted. 'Poirot, you're pulling my leg!'

'Not at all. The thermometer registered 80° in the shade. Do not forget that, my friend. It is the key to the whole riddle!'

'And the second point?' I asked.

'The important fact that Monsieur Inglethorp wears very peculiar clothes, has a black beard, and uses glasses.'

'Poirot, I cannot believe you are serious.'

'I am absolutely serious, my friend.'

'But this is childish!'

'No, it is very momentous.'

'And supposing the Coroner's jury returns a verdict of Wilful Murder against Alfred Inglethorp. What becomes of your theories, then?'

'They would not be shaken because twelve stupid men had happened to make a mistake! But that will not occur. For one thing, a country jury is not anxious to take responsibility upon itself, and Mr Inglethorp stands practically in the position of local squire. Also,' he added placidly, '*I* should not allow it!'

'*You* would not allow it?'

'No.'

I looked at the extraordinary little man, divided between annoyance and amusement. He was so tremendously sure of himself. As though he read my thoughts, he nodded gently.

'Oh, yes, *mon ami*, I would do what I say.' He got up and laid his hand on my shoulder. His physiognomy underwent a complete change. Tears came into his eyes. 'In all this, you see, I think of the poor Mrs Inglethorp who is dead. She was not extravagantly loved – no. But she was very good to us Belgians – I owe her a debt.'

I endeavoured to interrupt, but Poirot swept on.

'Let me tell you this, Hastings. She would never forgive me if I let Alfred Inglethorp, her husband, be arrested *now* – when a word from me could save him!'

CHAPTER 6

THE INQUEST

In the interval before the inquest, Poirot was unfailing in his activity. Twice he was closeted with Mr Wells. He also took long walks into the country. I rather resented his not taking me into his confidence, the more so as I could not in the least guess what he was driving at.

It occurred to me that he might have been making inquiries at Raikes's farm; so, finding him out when I called at Leastways Cottage on Wednesday evening, I walked over there by the fields, hoping to meet him. But there was no sign of him, and I hesitated to go right up to the farm itself. As I walked away, I met an aged rustic, who leered at me cunningly.

'You'm from the Hall, bain't you?' he asked.

'Yes. I'm looking for a friend of mine whom I thought might have walked this way.'

'A little chap? As waves his hands when he talks? One of them Belgies from the village?'

'Yes,' I said eagerly. 'He has been here, then?'

'Oh, ay, he's been here, right enough. More'n once too. Friend of yours, is he? Ah, you gentlemen from the Hall – you'm a pretty lot!' And he leered more jocosely than ever.

'Why, do the gentlemen from the Hall come here often?' I asked, as carelessly as I could.

He winked at me knowingly.

'*One* does, mister. Naming no names, mind. And a very liberal gentleman too! Oh, thank you, sir, I'm sure.'

I walked on sharply. Evelyn Howard had been right then, and I experienced a sharp twinge of disgust, as I thought of Alfred Inglethorp's liberality with another woman's money. Had that piquant gipsy face been at the bottom of the crime, or was it the base mainspring of money? Probably a judicious mixture of both.

On one point, Poirot seemed to have a curious obsession. He once or twice observed to me that he thought Dorcas must have made an error fixing the time of the quarrel. He suggested to her repeatedly that it was four-thirty, and not four o'clock when she heard the voices.

But Dorcas was unshaken. Quite an hour, or even more, had elapsed between the time when she had heard the voices and five o'clock, when she had taken tea to her mistress.

The inquest was held on Friday at the Stylites Arms in the village. Poirot and I sat together, not being required to give evidence.

The preliminaries were gone through. The jury viewed the body, and John Cavendish gave evidence of identification.

Further questioned, he described his awakening in the early hours of the morning, and the circumstances of his mother's death.

The medical evidence was next taken. There was a breathless hush, and every eye was fixed on the famous London specialist, who was known to be one of the greatest authorities of the day on the subject of toxicology.

In a few brief words, he summed up the result of the post-mortem. Shorn of its medical phraseology and technicalities, it amounted to the fact that Mrs Inglethorp had met her death as a result of strychnine poisoning. Judging from the quantity recovered, she must have taken not less than three-quarters of a grain of strychnine, but probably one grain or slightly over.

'Is it possible that she could have swallowed the poison by accident?' asked the Coroner.

'I should consider it very unlikely. Strychnine is not used for domestic purposes, as some poisons are, and there are restrictions placed on its sale.'

'Does anything in your examination lead you to determine how the poison was administered?'

'No.'

'You arrived at Styles before Dr Wilkins, I believe?'

'That is so. The motor met me just outside the lodge gates, and I hurried there as fast as I could.'

'Will you relate to us exactly what happened next?'

'I entered Mrs Inglethorp's room. She was at that moment in a typical tetanic convulsion. She turned towards me, and gasped out: "Alfred – Alfred –"'

'Could the strychnine have been administered in Mrs Inglethorp's after-dinner coffee which was taken to her by her husband?'

'Possibly, but strychnine is a fairly rapid drug in its action. The symptoms appear from one to two hours after it has been swallowed. It is retarded under certain conditions, none of which, however, appear to have been present in this case. I presume Mrs Inglethorp took the coffee after dinner about eight o'clock, whereas the symptoms did not manifest themselves until the early hours of the morning, which, on the face of it, points to the drug having been taken much later in the evening.'

'Mrs Inglethorp was in the habit of drinking a cup of cocoa in the middle of the night. Could the strychnine have been administered in that?'

'No, I myself took a sample of the cocoa remaining in the saucepan and had it analysed. There was no strychnine present.'

I heard Poirot chuckle softly beside me.

'How did you know?' I whispered.

'Listen.'

'I should say' – the doctor was continuing – 'that I would have been considerably surprised at any other result.'

'Why?'

'Simply because strychnine has an unusually bitter taste. It can be detected in a solution of 1 in 70,000, and can only be disguised by some strongly flavoured substance. Cocoa would be quite powerless to mask it.'

One of the jury wanted to know if the same objection applied to coffee.

'No. Coffee has a bitter taste of its own which would probably cover the taste of the strychnine.'

'Then you consider it more likely that the drug was administered in the coffee, but that for some unknown reason its action was delayed?'

'Yes, but, the cup being completely smashed, there is no possibility of analysing its contents.'

This concluded Dr Bauerstein's evidence. Dr Wilkins corroborated it on all points. Sounded as to the possibility of suicide, he repudiated it utterly. The deceased, he said, suffered from a weak heart, but otherwise enjoyed perfect health, and was of a cheerful and well-balanced disposition. She would be one of the last people to take her own life.

Lawrence Cavendish was next called. His evidence was quite unimportant, being a mere repetition of that of his brother. Just as he was about to step down, he paused, and said rather hestitatingly:

'I should like to make a suggestion if I may?'

He glanced deprecatingly at the Coroner, who replied briskly:

'Certainly, Mr Cavendish, we are here to arrive at the truth of this matter, and welcome anything that may lead to further elucidation.'

'It is just an idea of mine,' explained Lawrence. 'Of course I may be quite wrong, but it still seems to me that my mother's death might be accounted for by natural means.'

'How do you make that out, Mr Cavendish?'

'My mother, at the time of her death, and for some time before it, was taking a tonic containing strychnine.'

'Ah!' said the Coroner.

The jury looked up, interested.

'I believe,' continued Lawrence, 'that there have been cases where the cumulative effect of the drug, administered for some time, has ended by causing death. Also, is it not possible that she may have taken an overdose of her medicine by accident?'

'This is the first we have heard of the deceased taking strychnine at the time of her death. We are much obliged to you, Mr Cavendish.'

Dr Wilkins was recalled and ridiculed the idea.

'What Mr Cavendish suggests is quite impossible. Any doctor would tell you the same. Strychnine is, in a certain sense, a cumulative poison, but it would be quite impossible for it to result in sudden death in this way. There would have to be a long period of chronic symptoms which would at once have attracted my attention. The whole thing is absurd.'

'And the second suggestion? That Mrs Inglethorp may have inadvertently taken an overdose?'

'Three, or even four doses, would not have resulted in death. Mrs Inglethorp always had an extra large amount of medicine made up at a time, as she dealt with Coot's, the Cash Chemists in Tadminster. She would have had to take very nearly the whole bottle to account for the amount of strychnine found at the post-mortem.'

'Then you consider that we may dismiss the tonic as not being in any way instrumental in causing her death?'

'Certainly. The supposition is ridiculous.'

The same juryman who had interrupted before here suggested that the chemist who made up the medicine might have committed an error.

'That, of course, is always possible,' replied the doctor.

But Dorcas, who was the next witness called, dispelled even that possibility. The medicine had not been newly made up. On the contrary, Mrs Inglethorp had taken the last dose on the day of her death.

So the question of the tonic was finally abandoned, and the Coroner proceeded with his task. Having elicited from Dorcas how she had been awakened by the violent ringing of her mistress's bell, and had subsequently roused the household, he passed to the subject of the quarrel on the preceding afternoon.

Dorcas's evidence on this point was substantially what Poirot and I had already heard, so I will not repeat it here.

The next witness was Mary Cavendish. She stood very upright, and spoke in a low, clear, and perfectly composed voice. In answer to the Coroner's question, she told how, her alarm clock having aroused her at four-thirty as usual, she was dressing, when she was startled by the sound of something heavy falling.

'That would have been the table by the bed?' commented the Coroner.

'I opened my door,' continued Mary, 'and listened. In a few minutes a bell rang violently, Dorcas came running down and woke my husband, and we all went to my mother-in-law's room, but it was locked –'

The Coroner interrupted her.

'I really do not think we need trouble you further on that point. We know all that can be known of the subsequent happenings. But I should be obliged if you would tell us all you overheard of the quarrel the day before.'

'I?'

There was a faint insolence in her voice. She raised her hand and adjusted the ruffle of lace at her neck, turning her head a little as she did so. And quite spontaneously the thought flashed across my mind: 'She is gaining time!'

'Yes. I understand,' continued the Coroner deliberately, 'that you were sitting reading on the bench just outside the long window of the boudoir. That is so, is it not?'

This was news to me and glancing sideways at Poirot, I fancied that it was news to him as well.

There was the faintest pause, the mere hesitation of a moment, before she answered:

'Yes, that is so.'

'And the boudoir window was open, was it not?'

Surely her face grew a little paler as she answered:

'Yes.'

'Then you cannot have failed to hear the voices inside, especially as they were raised in anger. In fact, they would be more audible where you were than in the hall.'

'Possibly.'

'Will you repeat to us what you overheard of the quarrel?'

'I really do not remember hearing anything.'

'Do you mean to say you did not hear voices?'

'Oh, yes, I heard the voices, but I did not hear what they said.' A faint spot of colour came into her cheek. 'I am not in the habit of listening to private conversations.'

The Coroner persisted.

'And you remember nothing at all? *Nothing*, Mrs Cavendish? Not one stray word or phrase to make you realize that it *was* a private conversation?'

She paused, and seemed to reflect, still outwardly as calm as ever.

'Yes; I remember, Mrs Inglethorp said something – I do not remember exactly what – about causing scandal between husband and wife.'

'Ah!' The Coroner leant back satisfied. 'That corresponds with what Dorcas heard. But excuse me, Mrs Cavendish, although you realized it was a private conversation, you did not move away? You remained where you were?'

I caught the momentary gleam of her tawny eyes as she raised them. I felt certain that at that moment she would willingly have torn the little lawyer, with his insinuations, into pieces, but she replied quietly enough:

'No. I was very comfortable where I was. I fixed my mind on my book.'

'And that is all you can tell us?'

'That is all.'

The examination was over, though I doubted if the Coroner was entirely satisfied with it. I think he suspected that Mary Cavendish could tell more if she chose.

Amy Hill, shop assistant, was next called, and deposed to

having sold a will form on the afternoon of the 17th to William Earl, under-gardener at Styles.

William Earl and Manning succeeded her, and testified to witnessing a document. Manning fixed the time at about four-thirty, William was of the opinion that it was rather earlier.

Cynthia Murdoch came next. She had, however, little to tell. She had known nothing of the tragedy, until awakened by Mrs Cavendish.

'You did not hear the table fall?'

'No. I was fast asleep.'

The Coroner smiled.

'A good conscience makes a sound sleeper,' he observed. 'Thank you, Miss Murdoch, that is all.'

'Miss Howard.'

Miss Howard produced the letter written to her by Mrs Inglethorp on the evening of the 17th. Poirot and I had, of course, already seen it. It added nothing to our knowledge of the tragedy. The following is a facsimile:

July 17th

Styles Court
Essex

My dear Evelyn
    Can we not bury
the hatchet? I have
found it hard to forget
the things you said
against my dear husband
but I am an old woman
    very fond of you
        Yours affectionately
            Emily Inglethorp

It was handed to the jury who scrutinized it attentively.

'I fear it does not help us much,' said the Coroner, with a

sigh. 'There is no mention of any of the events of that afternoon.'

'Plain as a pikestaff to me,' said Miss Howard shortly. 'It shows clearly enough that my poor old friend had just found out she'd been made a fool of!'

'It says nothing of the kind in the letter,' the Coroner pointed out.

'No, because Emily never could bear to put herself in the wrong. But *I* know her. She wanted me back. But she wasn't going to own that I'd been right. She went round about. Most people do. Don't believe in it myself.'

Mr Wells smiled faintly. So, I noticed, did several of the jury. Miss Howard was obviously quite a public character.

'Anyway, all this tomfoolery is a great waste of time,' continued the lady, glancing up and down the jury disparagingly. 'Talk – talk – talk! When all the time we know perfectly well –'

The Coroner interrupted her in an agony of apprehension:

'Thank you, Miss Howard, that is all.'

I fancy he breathed a sigh of relief when she complied.

Then came the sensation of the day. The Coroner called Albert Mace, chemist's assistant.

It was our agitated young man of the pale face. In answer to the Coroner's questions, he explained that he was a qualified pharmacist, but had only recently come to this particular shop, as the assistant formerly there had just been called up for the army.

These preliminaries completed, the Coroner proceeded to business.

'Mr Mace, have you lately sold strychnine to any unauthorized person?'

'Yes, sir.'

'When was this?'

'Last Monday night.'

'Monday? Not Tuesday?'

'No, sir, Monday, the 16th.'

'Will you tell us to whom you sold it?'

You could have heard a pin drop.

'Yes, sir. It was Mr Inglethorp.'

Every eye turned simultaneously to where Alfred Inglethorp was sitting, impassive and wooden. He started slightly, as the damning words fell from the young man's lips. I half thought he was going to rise from his chair, but he remained seated, although a remarkably well acted expression of astonishment rose on his face.

'You are sure of what you say?' asked the Coroner sternly.

'Quite sure, sir.'

'Are you in the habit of selling strychnine indiscriminately over the counter?'

The wretched young man wilted visibly under the Coroner's frown.

'Oh, no, sir – of course not. But, seeing it was Mr Inglethorp of the Hall, I thought there was no harm in it. He said it was to poison a dog.'

Inwardly I sympathized. It was only human nature to endeavour to please 'The Hall' – especially when it might result in custom being transferred from Coot's to the local establishment.

'Is it not customary for anyone purchasing poison to sign a book?'

'Yes, sir, Mr Inglethorp did so.'

'Have you got the book here?'

'Yes, sir.'

It was produced; and, with a few words of stern censure, the Coroner dismissed the wretched Mr Mace.

Then, amidst a breathless silence, Alfred Inglethorp was called. Did he realize, I wondered, how closely the halter was being drawn around his neck?

The Coroner went straight to the point.

'On Monday evening last, did you purchase strychnine for the purpose of poisoning a dog?'

Inglethorp replied with perfect calmness:

'No, I did not. There is no dog at Styles, except an outdoor sheepdog, which is in perfect health.'

'You deny absolutely having purchased strychnine from Albert Mace on Monday last?'

'I do.'

'Do you also deny *this*?'

The Coroner handed him the register in which his signature was inscribed.

'Certainly I do. The handwriting is quite different from mine. I will show you.'

He took an old envelope out of his pocket, and wrote his name on it, handing it to the jury. It was certainly utterly dissimilar.

'Then what is your explanation of Mr Mace's statement?'

Alfred Inglethorp replied imperturbably:

'Mr Mace must have been mistaken.'

The Coroner hesitated for a moment, and then said:

'Mr Inglethorp, as a mere matter of form, would you mind telling us where you were on the evening of Monday, July 16th?'

'Really – I cannot remember.'

'That is absurd, Mr Inglethorp,' said the Coroner sharply. 'Think again.'

Inglethorp shook his head.

'I cannot tell you. I have an idea that I was out walking.'

'In what direction?'

'I really can't remember.'

The Coroner's face grew graver.

'Were you in company with anyone?'

'No.'

'Did you meet anyone on your walk?'

'No.'

'That is a pity,' said the Coroner dryly. 'I am to take it then that you decline to say where you were at the time that Mr Mace positively recognized you as entering the shop to purchase strychnine?'

'If you like to take it that way, yes.'

'Be careful, Mr Inglethorp.'

Poirot was fidgeting nervously.

'*Sacré!*' he murmured. 'Does this imbecile of a man *want* to be arrested?'

Inglethorp was indeed creating a bad impression. His futile denials would not have convinced a child. The Coroner, however, passed briskly to the next point, and Poirot drew a deep breath of relief.

'You had a discussion with your wife on Tuesday afternoon?'

'Pardon me,' interrupted Alfred Inglethorp, 'you have been misinformed. I had no quarrel with my dear wife. The whole story is absolutely untrue. I was absent from the house the entire afternoon.'

'Have you anyone who can testify to that?'

'You have my word,' said Inglethorp haughtily.

The Coroner did not trouble to reply.

'There are two witnesses who will swear to having heard your disagreement with Mrs Inglethorp.'

'Those witnesses were mistaken.'

I was puzzled. The man spoke with such quiet assurance that I was staggered. I looked at Poirot. There was an expression of exultation on his face which I could not understand. Was he at last convinced of Alfred Inglethorp's guilt?

'Mr Inglethorp,' said the Coroner, 'you have heard your wife's dying words repeated here. Can you explain them in any way?'

'Certainly I can.'

'You can?'

'It seems very simple. The room was dimly lighted. Dr Bauerstein is much of my height and build, and, like me, wears a beard. In the dim light, and suffering as she was, my poor wife mistook him for me.'

'Ah!' murmured Poirot to himself. 'But it is an idea, that!'

'You think it is true?' I whispered.

'I do not say that. But it is truly an ingenious supposition.'

'You read my wife's last words as an accusation' – Inglethorp was continuing – 'they were, on the contrary, an appeal to me.'

The Coroner reflected a moment, then he said:

'I believe, Mr Inglethorp, that you yourself poured out the coffee, and took it to your wife that evening?'

'I poured it out, yes. But I did not take it to her. I meant to do so, but I was told that a friend was at the hall door, so I laid down the coffee on the hall table. When I came through the hall again a few minutes later, it was gone.'

This statement might, or might not, be true, but it did not seem to me to improve matters much for Inglethorp. In any case, he had had ample time to introduce the poison.

At that point, Poirot nudged me gently, indicating two men who were sitting together near the door. One was a little, sharp, dark, ferret-faced man, the other was tall and fair.

I questioned Poirot mutely. He put his lips to my ear.

'Do you know who that little man is?'

I shook my head.

'That is Detective-Inspector James Japp of Scotland Yard – Jimmy Japp. The other man is from Scotland Yard, too. Things are moving quickly, my friend.'

I stared at the two men intently. There was certainly nothing of the policeman about them. I should never have suspected them of being official personages.

I was still staring, when I was startled and recalled by the verdict being given:

'Wilful Murder against some person or persons unknown.'

CHAPTER 7

POIROT PAYS HIS DEBTS

As we came out of the Stylites Arms, Poirot drew me aside by a gentle pressure of the arm. I understood his object. He was waiting for the Scotland Yard men.

In a few moments, they emerged, and Poirot at once stepped forward, and accosted the shorter of the two.

'I fear you do not remember me, Inspector Japp.'

'Why, if it isn't Mr Poirot!' cried the Inspector. He turned to the other man. 'You've heard me speak of Mr Poirot? It was in 1904 he and I worked together – the Abercrombie forgery case – you remember, he was run down in Brussels. Ah, those were great days, Moosier. Then, do you remember "Baron" Altara? There was a pretty rogue for you! He eluded the clutches of half the police in Europe. But we nailed him in Antwerp – thanks to Mr Poirot here.'

As these friendly reminiscences were being indulged in, I drew nearer, and was introduced to Detective-Inspector Japp, who in his turn introduced us both to his companion, Superintendent Summerhaye.

'I need hardly ask what you are doing here, gentlemen,' remarked Poirot.

Japp closed one eye knowingly.

'No, indeed. Pretty clear case I should say.'

But Poirot answered gravely:

'There I differ from you.'

'Oh, come!' said Summerhaye, opening his lips for the first time. 'Surely the whole thing is clear as daylight. The man's caught red-handed. How he could be such a fool beats me!'

But Japp was looking attentively at Poirot.

'Hold your fire, Summerhaye,' he remarked jocularly.

'Me and Moosier here have met before – and there's no man's judgement I'd sooner take than his. If I'm not greatly mistaken, he's got something up his sleeve. Isn't that so, Moosier?'

Poirot smiled.

'I have drawn certain conclusions – yes.'

Summerhaye was still looking rather sceptical, but Japp continued his scrutiny of Poirot.

'It's this way,' he said, 'so far, we've only seen the case from the outside. That's where the Yard's at a disadvantage in a case of this kind, where the murder's only out, so to speak, after the inquest. A lot depends on being on the spot first thing, and that's where Mr Poirot's had the start of us. We shouldn't have been here as soon as this even, if it hadn't been for the fact that there was a smart doctor on the spot, who gave us the tip through the Coroner. But you've been on the spot from the first, and you may have picked up some little hints. From the evidence at the inquest, Mr Inglethorp murdered his wife as sure as I stand here, and if anyone but you hinted the contrary I'd laugh in his face. I must say I was surprised the jury didn't bring it in Wilful Murder against him right off. I think they would have, if it hadn't been for the Coroner – he seemed to be holding them back.'

'Perhaps, though, you have a warrant for his arrest in your pocket now,' suggested Poirot.

A kind of wooden shutter of officialdom came down over Japp's expressive countenance.

'Perhaps I have, and perhaps I haven't,' he remarked dryly.

Poirot looked at him thoughtfully.

'I am very anxious, Messieurs, that he should not be arrested.'

'I dare say,' observed Summerhaye sarcastically.

Japp was regarding Poirot with comical perplexity.

'Can't you go a little further, Mr Poirot? A wink's as good as a nod – from you. You've been on the spot – and the Yard doesn't want to make any mistakes, you know.'

Poirot nodded gravely.

'That is exactly what I thought. Well, I will tell you this. Use your warrant: Arrest Mr Inglethorp. But it will bring you no kudos – the case against him will be dismissed at once! *Comme ça!*' And he snapped his fingers expressively.

Japp's face grew grave, though Summerhaye gave an incredulous snort.

As for me, I was literally dumb with astonishment. I could only conclude that Poirot was mad.

Japp had taken out a handkerchief, and was gently dabbing his brow.

'I daren't do it, Mr Poirot. I'd take your word, but there's others over me who'll be asking what the devil I mean by it. Can't you give me a little more to go on?'

Poirot reflected a moment.

'It can be done,' he said at last. 'I admit I do not wish it. It forces my hand. I would have preferred to work in the dark just for the present, but what you say is very just – the word of a Belgian policeman, whose day is past, is not enough! And Alfred Inglethorp must not be arrested. That I have sworn, as my friend Hastings here knows. See, then, my good Japp, you go at once to Styles?'

'Well, in about half an hour. We're seeing the Coroner and the doctor first.'

'Good. Call for me in passing – the last house in the village. I will go with you. At Styles, Mr Inglethorp will give you, or if he refuses – as is probable – I will give you such proofs that shall satisfy you that the case against him could not possibly be sustained. Is that a bargain?'

'That's a bargain,' said Japp heartily. 'And, on behalf of the Yard, I'm much obliged to you, though I'm bound to confess I can't at present see the faintest possible loophole in the evidence, but you always were a marvel! So long, then, Moosier.'

The two detectives strode away, Summerhaye with an incredulous grin on his face.

'Well, my friend,' cried Poirot, before I could get in a word, 'what do you think? *Mon dieu!* I had some warm moments in that court; I did not figure to myself that the man would be so pig-headed as to refuse to say anything at all. Decidedly, it was the policy of an imbecile.'

'H'm! There are other explanations besides that of imbecility,' I remarked. 'For, if the case against him is true, how could he defend himself except by silence?'

'Why, in a thousand ingenious ways,' cried Poirot. 'See; say that it is I who have committed this murder, I can think of seven most plausible stories! Far more convincing than Mr Inglethorp's stony denials!'

I could not help laughing.

'My dear Poirot, I am sure you are capable of thinking of seventy! But, seriously, in spite of what I heard you say to the detectives, you surely cannot still believe in the possibility of Alfred Inglethorp's innocence?'

'Why not now as much as before? Nothing has changed.'

'But the evidence is so conclusive.'

'Yes, too conclusive.'

We turned in at the gate of Leastways Cottage, and proceeded up the now familiar stairs.

'Yes, yes, too conclusive,' continued Poirot, almost to himself. 'Real evidence is usually vague and unsatisfactory. It has to be examined – sifted. But here the whole thing is cut and dried. No, my friend, this evidence has been very cleverly manufactured – so cleverly that it has defeated its own ends.'

'How do you make that out?'

'Because, so long as the evidence against him was vague and intangible, it was very hard to disprove. But, in his anxiety, the criminal has drawn the net so closely that one cut will set Inglethorp free.'

I was silent. And in a minute or two, Poirot continued:

'Let us look at the matter like this. Here is a man, let us say, who sets out to poison his wife. He has lived by his wits as the saying goes. Presumably, therefore, he has some wits. He is not altogether a fool. Well, how does he set about it? He goes boldly to the village chemist's and purchases strychnine under his own name, with a trumped-up story about a dog which is bound to be proved absurd. He does not employ the poison that night. No, he waits until he has had a violent quarrel with her, of which the whole household is cognizant, and which naturally directs their suspicions upon him. He prepares no defence – no shadow of an alibi, yet he knows the chemist's assistant must necessarily come forward with the facts. Bah! Do not ask me to believe that any man could be so idiotic! Only a lunatic, who wished to commit suicide by causing himself to be hanged, would act so!'

'Still – I do not see –' I began.

'Neither do I see. I tell you, *mon ami*, it puzzles me. *Me* – Hercule Poirot!'

'But if you believe him innocent, how do you explain his buying the strychnine?'

'Very simply. He did *not* buy it.'

'But Mace recognized him!'

'I beg your pardon, he saw a man with a black beard like Mr Inglethorp's, and wearing glasses like Mr Inglethorp, and dressed in Mr Inglethorp's rather noticeable clothes. He could not recognize a man whom he had probably only seen in the distance, since, you remember, he himself had only been in the village a fortnight, and Mrs Inglethorp dealt principally with Coot's in Tadminster.'

'Then you think –'

'*Mon ami*, do you remember the two points I laid stress upon? Leave the first one for the moment, what was the second?'

'The important fact that Alfred Inglethorp wears peculiar clothes, has a black beard, and uses glasses,' I quoted.

'Exactly. Now suppose anyone wished to pass himself off as John or Lawrence Cavendish. Would it be easy?'

'No,' I said thoughtfully. 'Of course an actor –'

But Poirot cut me short ruthlessly.

'And why would it not be easy? I will tell you, my friend: Because they are both clean-shaven men. To make up successfully as one of these two in broad daylight, it would need an actor of genius, and a certain initial facial resemblance. But in the case of Alfred Inglethorp, all that is changed. His clothes, his beard, the glasses which hide his eyes – those are the salient points about his personal appearance. Now, what is the first instinct of the criminal? To divert suspicion from himself, is it not so? And how can he best do that? By throwing it on someone else. In this instance, there was a man ready to his hand. Everybody was predisposed to believe in Mr Inglethorp's guilt. It was a foregone conclusion that he would be suspected; but, to make it a sure thing there must be tangible proof – such as the actual buying of the poison, and that, with a man of the peculiar appearance of Mr Inglethorp, was not difficult. Remember, this young Mace had never actually spoken to Mr Inglethorp. How should he doubt that the man in his clothes, with his beard and his glasses, was not Alfred Inglethorp?'

'It may be so,' I said, fascinated by Poirot's eloquence. 'But, if that was the case, why does he not say where he was at six o'clock on Monday evening?'

'Ah, why indeed?' said Poirot, calming down. 'If he were arrested, he probably would speak, but I do not want it to come to that. I must make him see the gravity of his position. There is, of course, something discreditable behind his silence. If he did not murder his wife, he is, nevertheless, a scoundrel, and has something of his own to conceal, quite apart from the murder.'

'What can it be?' I mused, won over to Poirot's views for the moment, although still retaining a faint conviction that the obvious deduction was the correct one.

'Can you not guess?' asked Poirot, smiling.

'No, can you?'

'Oh, yes, I had a little idea some time ago – and it has turned out to be correct.'

'You never told me,' I said reproachfully.

Poirot spread out his hands apologetically.

'Pardon me, *mon ami*, you were not precisely *sympathique*.' He turned to me earnestly. 'Tell me – you see now that he must not be arrested?'

'Perhaps,' I said doubtfully, for I was really indifferent to the fate of Alfred Inglethorp, and thought that a good fright would do him no harm.

Poirot, who was watching me intently, gave a sigh.

'Come, my friend,' he said changing the subject, 'apart from Mr Inglethorp, how did the evidence at the inquest strike you?'

'Oh, pretty much what I expected.'

'Did nothing strike you as peculiar about it?'

My thoughts flew to Mary Cavendish, and I hedged:

'In what way?'

'Well, Mr Lawrence Cavendish's evidence for instance?'

I was relieved.

'Oh, Lawrence! No, I don't think so. He's always a nervous chap.'

'His suggestion that his mother might have been poisoned accidentally by means of the tonic she was taking, that did not strike you as strange – *hein?*'

'No, I can't say it did. The doctors ridiculed it of course. But it was quite a natural suggestion for a layman to make.'

'But Monsieur Lawrence is not a layman. You told me yourself that he had started by studying medicine, and that he had taken his degree.'

'Yes, that's true. I never thought of that.' I was rather startled. 'It *is* odd.'

Poirot nodded.

'From the first, his behaviour has been peculiar. Of all the household, he alone would be likely to recognize the symptoms of strychnine poisoning, and yet we find him the only member of the family to uphold strenuously the theory of death from natural causes. If it had been Monsieur John, I could have understood it. He has no technical knowledge, and is by nature unimaginative. But Monsieur Lawrence – no! And now, today, he puts forward a suggestion that he himself must have known was ridiculous. There is food for thought in this, *mon ami!*'

'It's very confusing,' I agreed.

'Then there is Mrs Cavendish,' continued Poirot. 'That is another who is not telling all she knows! What do you make of her attitude?'

'I don't know what to make of it. It seems inconceivable that she should be shielding Alfred Inglethorp. Yet that is what it looks like.'

Poirot nodded reflectively.

'Yes, it is queer. One thing is certain, she overheard a good deal more of that "private conversation" than she was willing to admit.'

'And yet she is the last person one would accuse of stooping to eavesdrop!'

'Exactly. One thing her evidence *has* shown me. I made a

mistake. Dorcas was quite right. The quarrel did take place earlier in the afternoon, about four o'clock, as she said.'

I looked at him curiously. I had never understood his insistence on that point.

'Yes, a good deal that was peculiar came out today,' continued Poirot. 'Dr Bauerstein, now, what was *he* doing up and dressed at that hour in the morning? It is astonishing to me that no one commented on the fact.'

'He has insomnia, I believe,' I said doubtfully.

'Which is a very good, or a very bad explanation,' remarked Poirot. 'It covers everything, and explains nothing. I shall keep my eye on our clever Dr Bauerstein.'

'Any more faults to find with the evidence?' I inquired satirically.

'*Mon ami*,' replied Poirot gravely, 'when you find that people are not telling you the truth – look out! Now, unless I am much mistaken, at this inquest today only one – at most, two persons were speaking the truth without reservation or subterfuge.'

'Oh, come now, Poirot! I won't cite Lawrence, or Mrs Cavendish. But there's John – and Miss Howard, surely they were speaking the truth?'

'Both of them, my friend? One, I grant you, but both –!'

His words gave me an unpleasant shock. Miss Howard's evidence, unimportant as it was, had been given in such a downright straightforward manner that it had never occurred to me to doubt her sincerity. Still, I had a great respect for Poirot's sagacity – except on the occasions when he was what I described to myself as 'foolishly pig-headed'.

'Do you really think so?' I asked. 'Miss Howard had always seemed to me so essentially honest – almost uncomfortably so.'

Poirot gave me a curious look, which I could not quite fathom. He seemed about to speak, and then checked himself.

'Miss Murdoch too,' I continued, 'there's nothing untruthful about *her*.'

'No. But it was strange that she never heard a sound, sleeping next door; whereas Mrs Cavendish, in the other wing of the building, distinctly heard the table fall.'

'Well, she's young. And she sleeps soundly.'

'Ah, yes, indeed! She must be a famous sleeper, that one!'

I did not quite like the tone of his voice, but at that moment a smart knock reached our ears, and looking out of the window we perceived the two detectives waiting for us below.

Poirot seized his hat, gave a ferocious twist to his moustache, and, carefully brushing an imaginary speck of dust from his sleeve, motioned me to precede him down the stairs; there we joined the detectives and set out for Styles.

I think the appearance of the two Scotland Yard men was rather a shock – especially to John, though, of course, after the verdict, he had realized that it was only a matter of time. Still, the presence of the detectives brought the truth home to him more than anything else could have done.

Poirot had conferred with Japp in a low tone on the way up, and it was the latter functionary who requested that the household, with the exception of the servants, should be assembled together in the drawing-room. I realized the significance of this. It was up to Poirot to make his boast good.

Personally, I was not sanguine. Poirot might have excellent reasons for his belief in Inglethorp's innocence, but a man of the type of Summerhaye would require tangible proofs, and these I doubted if Poirot could supply.

Before very long we had all trooped into the drawing-room, the door of which Japp closed. Poirot politely set chairs for everyone. The Scotland Yard men were the cynosure of all eyes. I think that for the first time we realized that the thing was not a bad dream, but a tangible reality. We had read of such things – now we ourselves were actors in the drama. Tomorrow the daily papers, all over England, would blazon out the news in staring headlines:

MYSTERIOUS TRAGEDY IN ESSEX
WEALTHY LADY POISONED

There would be pictures of Styles, snap-shots of 'The family leaving the Inquest' – the village photographer had not been idle! All the things that one had read a hundred times – things that happen to other people, not to oneself. And now, in this house, a murder had been committed. In front of us were 'the detectives in charge of the case'. The well-known glib phraseology passed rapidly through my mind in the interval before Poirot opened the proceedings.

I think everyone was a little surprised that it should be he and not one of the official detectives who took the initiative.

'*Mesdames* and *messieurs*,' said Poirot, bowing as though he were a celebrity about to deliver a lecture, 'I have asked you to come here all together, for a certain object. That object, it concerns Mr Alfred Inglethorp.'

Inglethorp was sitting a little by himself – I think, unconsciously, everyone had drawn his chair slightly away from him – and he gave a faint start as Poirot pronounced his name.

'Mr Inglethorp,' said Poirot, addressing him directly, 'a very dark shadow is resting on this house – the shadow of murder.'

Inglethorp shook his head sadly.

'My poor wife,' he murmured. 'Poor Emily! It is terrible.'

'I do not think, monsieur,' said Poirot pointedly, 'that you quite realize how terrible it may be – for you.' And as Inglethorp did not appear to understand, he added: 'Mr Inglethorp, you are standing in very grave danger.'

The two detectives fidgeted. I saw the official caution 'Anything you say will be used in evidence against you,' actually hovering on Summerhaye's lips. Poirot went on:

'Do you understand now, monsieur?'

'No. What do you mean?'

'I mean,' said Poirot deliberately, 'that you are suspected of poisoning your wife.'

A little gasp ran round the circle at this plain speaking.

'Good heavens!' cried Inglethorp, starting up. 'What a monstrous idea! I – poison my dearest Emily!'

'I do not think' – Poirot watched him narrowly – 'that you quite realize the unfavourable nature of your evidence at the inquest. Mr Inglethorp, knowing what I have now told you, do you still refuse to say where you were at six o'clock on Monday afternoon?'

With a groan, Alfred Inglethorp sank down again and buried his face in his hands. Poirot approached and stood over him.

'Speak!' he cried menacingly.

With an effort, Inglethorp raised his face from his hands. Then, slowly and deliberately, he shook his head.

'You will not speak?'

'No. I do not believe that anyone could be so monstrous as to accuse me of what you say.'

Poirot nodded thoughtfully, like a man whose mind is made. '*Soit!*' he said. 'Then I must speak for you.'

Alfred Inglethorp sprang up again.

'You? How can you speak? You do not know –' he broke off abruptly.

Poirot turned to face us. '*Mesdames* and *messieurs!* I speak! Listen! I, Hercule Poirot, affirm that the man who entered the chemist's shop, and purchased strychnine at six o'clock on Monday last, was not Mr Inglethorp, for at six o'clock on that day Mr Inglethorp was escorting Mrs Raikes back to her home from a neighbouring farm. I can produce no less than five witnesses to swear to having seen them together, either at six or just after and, as you may know, the Abbey Farm, Mrs Raikes's home, is at least two and a half miles distant from the village. There is absolutely no question as to the alibi!'

CHAPTER 8

FRESH SUSPICIONS

There was a moment's stupefied silence. Japp, who was the least surprised of any of us, was the first to speak.

'My word,' he cried, 'you're the goods! And no mistake, Mr Poirot! These witnesses of yours are all right, I suppose?'

'*Voilà!* I have prepared a list of them – names and addresses. You must see them, of course. But you will find it all right.'

'I'm sure of that.' Japp lowered his voice. 'I'm much obliged to you. A pretty mare's nest arresting him would have been.' He turned to Inglethorp. 'But, if you'll excuse me, sir, why couldn't you say all this at the inquest?'

'I will tell you why,' interrupted Poirot. 'There was a certain rumour –'

'A most malicious and utterly untrue one,' interrupted Alfred Inglethorp in an agitated voice.

'And Mr Inglethorp was anxious to have no scandal revived just at present. Am I right?'

'Quite right.' Inglethorp nodded. 'With my poor Emily not yet buried, can you wonder I was anxious that no more lying rumours should be started?'

'Between you and me, sir,' remarked Japp, 'I'd sooner have any amount of rumours than be arrested for murder. And I venture to think that your poor lady would have felt the same. And, if it hadn't been for Mr Poirot here, arrested you would have been, as sure as eggs is eggs!'

'I was foolish, no doubt,' murmured Inglethorp. 'But you do not know, inspector, how I have been persecuted and maligned.' And he shot a baleful glance at Evelyn Howard.

'Now, sir,' said Japp, turning briskly to John, 'I should like to see the lady's bedroom, please, and after that I'll have a little chat with the servants. Don't you bother about anything. Mr Poirot, here, will show me the way.'

As they all went out of the room, Poirot turned and made me a sign to follow him upstairs. There he caught me by the arm, and drew me aside.

'Quick, go to the other wing. Stand there – just this side of the baize door. Do not move till I come.' Then, turning rapidly, he rejoined the two detectives.

I followed his instructions, taking up my position by the baize door, and wondering what on earth lay behind the request. Why was I to stand in this particular spot on guard? I looked thoughtfully down the corridor in front of me. An idea struck me. With the exception of Cynthia Murdoch's, every room was in this left wing. Had that anything to do with it? Was I to report who came or went? I stood faithfully at my post. The minutes passed. Nobody came. Nothing happened.

It must have been quite twenty minutes before Poirot rejoined me.

'You have not stirred?'

'No, I've stuck here like a rock. Nothing's happened.'

'Ah!' Was he pleased, or disappointed? 'You've seen nothing at all?'

'No.'

'But you have probably heard something? A big bump – eh, *mon ami*?'

'No.'

'Is it possible? Ah, but I am vexed with myself! I am not usually clumsy. I made but a slight gesture' – I know Poirot's gestures – 'with the left hand, and over went the table by the bed!'

He looked so childishly vexed and crestfallen that I hastened to console him.

'Never mind, old chap. What does it matter? Your triumph downstairs excited you. I can tell you, that was a surprise to us all. There must be more in this affair of Inglethorp's with Mrs Raikes than we thought, to make him hold his tongue so persistently. What are you going to do now? Where are the Scotland Yard fellows?'

'Gone down to interview the servants. I showed them all our exhibits. I am disappointed in Japp. He has no method!'

'Hullo!' I said, looking out of the window. 'Here's Dr Bauerstein. I believe you're right about that man, Poirot. I don't like him.'

'He is clever,' observed Poirot meditatively.

'Oh, clever as the devil! I must say I was overjoyed to see him in the plight he was in on Tuesday. You never saw such a spectacle!' And I described the doctor's adventure. 'He looked a regular scarecrow! Plastered with mud from head to foot.'

'You saw him, then?'

'Yes. Of course, he didn't want to come in – it was just after dinner – but Mr Inglethorp insisted.'

'What?' Poirot caught me violently by the shoulders.

'Was Dr Bauerstein here on Tuesday evening? Here? And you never told me? Why did you not tell me? Why? Why?'

He appeared to be in an absolute frenzy.

'My dear Poirot,' I expostulated, 'I never thought it would interest you. I didn't know it was of any importance.'

'Importance? It is of the first importance! So Dr Bauerstein was here on Tuesday night – the night of the murder. Hastings, do you not see? That alters everything – everything!'

I had never seen him so upset. Loosening his hold of me, he mechanically straightened a pair of candlesticks, still murmuring to himself: 'Yes, that alters everything – everything.'

Suddenly he seemed to come to a decision.

'*Allons!*' he said. 'We must act at once. Where is Mr Cavendish?'

John was in the smoking-room. Poirot went straight to him.

'Mr Cavendish, I have some important business in Tadminster. A new clue. May I take your motor?'

'Why, of course. Do you mean at once?'

'If you please.'

John rang the bell, and ordered round the car. In another ten minutes, we were racing down the park and along the high road to Tadminster.

'Now, Poirot,' I remarked resignedly, 'perhaps you will tell me what all this is about?'

'Well, *mon ami*, a good deal you can guess for yourself. Of course, you realize that, now Mr Inglethorp is out of it, the whole position is greatly changed. We are face to face with an entirely new problem. We know now that there is one person who did not buy the poison. We have cleared away the manufactured clues. Now for the real ones. I have ascertained that anyone in the household, with the exception of Mrs Cavendish, who was playing tennis with you, could have personated Mr Inglethorp on Monday evening. In the same way, we have his statement that he put the coffee down in the hall. No one took much notice of that at the inquest – but now it has a very different significance. We must find out who did take that coffee to Mrs Inglethorp eventually, or who passed through the hall whilst it was standing there. From your account, there are only two people whom we can positively say did not go near the coffee – Mrs Cavendish, and Mademoiselle Cynthia.'

'Yes, that is so.' I felt an inexpressible lightening of the heart. Mary Cavendish could certainly not rest under suspicion.

'In clearing Alfred Inglethorp,' continued Poirot, 'I have been obliged to show my hand sooner than I intended. As long as I might be thought to be pursuing him, the criminal would be off his guard. Now, he will be doubly careful. Yes – doubly careful.' He turned to me abruptly. 'Tell me, Hastings, you yourself – have you no suspicions of anybody?'

I hesitated. To tell the truth, an idea, wild and extravagant in itself, had once or twice that morning flashed through my brain. I had rejected it as absurd, nevertheless it persisted.

'You couldn't call it a suspicion,' I murmured. 'It's so utterly foolish.'

'Come now,' urged Poirot encouragingly. 'Do not fear. Speak your mind. You should always pay attention to your instincts.'

'Well then,' I blurted out, 'it's absurd – but I suspect Miss Howard of not telling all she knows!'

'Miss Howard?'

'Yes – you'll laugh at me –'

'Not at all. Why should I?'

'I can't help feeling,' I continued blunderingly, 'that we've rather left her out of the possible suspects, simply on the strength of her having been away from the place. But, after all, she was only fifteen miles away. A car would do it in half an hour. Can we say positively that she was away from Styles on the night of the murder?'

'Yes, my friend,' said Poirot unexpectedly, 'we can. One of my first actions was to ring up the hospital where she was working.'

'Well?'

'Well, I learnt that Miss Howard had been on afternoon duty on Tuesday, and that – a convoy coming in unexpectedly – she had kindly offered to remain on night duty, which offer was gratefully accepted. That disposes of that.'

'Oh!' I said, rather nonplussed. 'Really,' I continued, 'it's her extraordinary vehemence against Inglethorp that started me off suspecting her. I can't help feeling she'd do anything against him. And I had an idea she might know something about the destroying of the will. She might have burnt the new one, mistaking it for the earlier one in his favour. She is so terribly bitter against him.'

'You consider her vehemence unnatural?'

'Y – es. She is so very violent. I wonder really whether she is quite sane on that point.'

Poirot shook his head energetically.

'No, no, you are on a wrong track there. There is nothing weak-minded or degenerate about Miss Howard. She is an excellent specimen of well balanced English beef and brawn. She is sanity itself.'

'Yet her hatred of Inglethorp seems almost a mania. My idea was – a very ridiculous one, no doubt – that she had intended to poison him – and that, in some way, Mrs Inglethorp got hold of it by mistake. But I don't at all see how it could have been done. The whole thing is absurd and ridiculous to the last degree.'

'Still you are right in one thing. It is always wise to suspect everybody until you can prove logically, and to your own satisfaction, that they are innocent. Now, what reasons are there against Miss Howard's having deliberately poisoned Mrs Inglethorp?'

'Why, she was devoted to her!' I exclaimed.

'Tcha! Tcha!' cried Poirot irritably. 'You argue like a child. If Miss Howard were capable of poisoning the old lady, she would be quite equally capable of simulating devotion. No, we must look elsewhere. You are perfectly correct in your assumption that her vehemence against Alfred Inglethorp is too violent to be natural; but you are quite wrong in the deduction you draw from it. I have drawn my own deductions, which I believe to be correct, but I will not speak of them at present.' He paused a minute, then went on. 'Now, to my way of thinking, there is one insuperable objection to Miss Howard's being the murderess.'

'And that is?'

'That in no possible way could Mrs Inglethorp's death benefit Miss Howard. Now there is no murder without a motive.'

I reflected.

'Could not Mrs Inglethorp have made a will in her favour?' Poirot shook his head.

'But you yourself suggested that possibility to Mr Wells?' Poirot smiled.

'That was for a reason. I did not want to mention the name of the person who was actually in my mind. Miss Howard occupied very much the same position, so I used her name instead.'

'Still, Mrs Inglethorp might have done so. Why, that will made on the afternoon of her death may –'

But Poirot's shake of the head was so energetic that I stopped.

'No, my friend. I have certain little ideas of my own about that will. But I can tell you this much – it was not in Miss Howard's favour.'

I accepted his assurance, though I did not really see how he could be so positive about the matter.

'Well,' I said, with a sigh, 'we will acquit Miss Howard, then. It is partly your fault that I ever came to suspect her. It was what you said about her evidence at the inquest that set me off.'

Poirot looked puzzled.

'What did I say about her evidence at the inquest?'

'Don't you remember? When I cited her and John Cavendish as being above suspicion?'

'Oh – ah – yes.' He seemed a little confused, but recovered himself. 'By the way, Hastings, there is something I want you to do for me.'

'Certainly. What is it?'

'Next time you happen to be alone with Lawrence Cavendish, I want you to say this to him. "I have a message for you from Poirot. He says: 'Find the extra coffee-cup, and you can rest in peace!'" Nothing more. Nothing less.'

'"Find the extra coffee-cup, and you can rest in peace!" Is that right?' I asked, much mystified.

'Excellent.'

'But what does it mean?'

'Ah, that I will leave you to find out. You have access to the facts. Just say that to him, and see what he says.'

'Very well – but it's all extremely mysterious.'

We were running into Tadminster now, and Poirot directed the car to the 'Analytical Chemist'.

Poirot hopped down briskly, and went inside. In a few minutes he was back again.

'There,' he said. 'That is all my business.'

'What were you doing there?' I asked in lively curiosity.

'I left something to be analysed.'

'Yes, but what?'

'The sample of cocoa I took from the saucepan in the bedroom.'

'But that has already been tested!' I cried, stupefied. 'Dr Bauerstein had it tested, and you yourself laughed at the possibility of there being strychnine in it.'

'I know Dr Bauerstein had it tested,' replied Poirot quietly.

'Well, then?'

'Well, I have a fancy for having it analysed again, that is all.'

And not another word on the subject could I drag out of him.

This proceeding of Poirot's, in respect of the cocoa, puzzled me intensely. I could see neither rhyme nor reason in it. However, my confidence in him, which at one time had rather waned, was fully restored since his belief in Alfred Inglethorp's innocence had been so triumphantly vindicated.

The funeral of Mrs Inglethorp took place the following day, and on Monday, as I came down to a late breakfast, John drew me aside, and informed me that Mr Inglethorp was leaving that morning, to take up his quarters at the Stylites Arms, until he should have completed his plans.

'And really it's a great relief to think he's going, Hastings,' continued my honest friend. 'It was bad enough before, when we thought he'd done it, but I'm hanged if it isn't worse now, when we all feel guilty for having been so down on the fellow. The fact is, we've treated him abominably. Of course, things did look black against him. I don't see how anyone could blame us for jumping to the conclusions we did. Still, there it is, we were in the wrong, and now there's a beastly feeling that one ought to make amends; which is difficult, when one doesn't like the fellow a bit better than one did before. The whole thing's damned awkward! And I'm thankful he's had the tact to take himself off. It's a good thing Styles wasn't the mater's to leave to him. Couldn't bear to think of the fellow lording it here. He's welcome to her money.'

'You'll be able to keep up the place all right?' I asked.

'Oh, yes. There are the death duties, of course, but half my father's money goes with the place, and Lawrence will stay with us for the present, so there is his share as well. We shall be pinched at first, of course, because, as I once told you, I am in a bit of a hole financially myself. Still, the Johnnies will wait now.'

In the general relief at Inglethorp's approaching departure, we had the most genial breakfast we had experienced since the tragedy. Cynthia, whose young spirits were naturally buoyant, was looking quite her pretty self again, and we all, with the exception of Lawrence, who seemed unalterably gloomy and nervous, were quietly cheerful, at the opening of a new and hopeful future.

The papers, of course, had been full of the tragedy. Glaring headlines, sandwiched biographies of every member of the household, subtle innuendoes, the usual familiar tag about the police having a clue. Nothing was spared us. It was a slack time. The war was momentarily inactive, and the newspapers seized with avidity on this crime in fashionable life: 'The Mysterious Affair at Styles' was the topic of the moment.

Naturally it was very annoying for the Cavendishes. The house was constantly besieged by reporters, who were consistently denied admission, but who continued to haunt the village and the grounds, where they lay in wait with cameras, for any unwary members of the household. We all lived in a blast of publicity. The Scotland Yard men came and went, examining, questioning, lynx-eyed and reserved of tongue. Towards what end they were working, we did not know. Had they any clue, or would the whole thing remain in the category of undiscovered crimes?

After breakfast, Dorcas came up to me rather mysteriously, and asked if she might have a few words with me.

'Certainly. What is it, Dorcas?'

'Well, it's just this, sir. You'll be seeing the Belgian gentleman today perhaps?' I nodded. 'Well, sir, you know how he asked me so particular if the mistress, or anyone else, had a green dress?'

'Yes, yes. You have found one?' My interest was aroused.

'No, not that, sir. But since then I've remembered what the young gentlemen' – John and Lawrence were still the 'young gentlemen' to Dorcas – 'call the "dressing-up box". It's up in the front attic, sir. A great chest, full of old clothes and fancy dresses, and what not. And it came to me sudden like that there might be a green dress amongst them. So, if you'd tell the Belgian gentleman –'

'I will tell him, Dorcas,' I promised.

'Thank you very much, sir. A very nice gentleman he is, sir. And quite a different class from them two detectives from London, what goes prying about, and asking questions. I don't hold with foreigners as a rule, but from what the newspapers says I make out as how these brave Belgies isn't the ordinary run of foreigners and certainly he's a most polite spoken gentleman.'

Dear old Dorcas! As she stood there, with her honest face upturned to mine, I thought what a fine specimen she was of the old-fashioned servant that is so fast dying out.

I thought I might as well go down to the village at once, and look up Poirot; but I met him half-way, coming up to the house, and at once gave him Dorcas's message.

'Ah, the brave Dorcas! We will look at the chest, although – but no matter – we will examine it all the same.'

We entered the house by one of the windows. There was no one in the hall, and we went straight up to the attic.

Sure enough, there was the chest, a fine old piece, all studded with brass nails, and full to overflowing with every imaginable type of garment.

Poirot bundled everything out on the floor with scant ceremony. There were one or two green fabrics of varying shades; but Poirot shook his head over them all. He seemed somewhat apathetic in the search, as though he expected no great results from it. Suddenly he gave an exclamation.

'What is it?'

'Look!'

The chest was nearly empty, and there, reposing right at the bottom, was a magnificent black beard.

'*Ohó!*' said Poirot. '*Ohó!*' He turned it over in his hands, examining it closely. 'New,' he remarked. 'Yes, quite new.'

After a moment's hesitation, he replaced it in the chest, heaped all the other things on top of it as before, and made his way briskly downstairs. He went straight to the pantry, where we found Dorcas busily polishing her silver.

Poirot wished her good morning with Gallic politeness, and went on:

'We have been looking through that chest, Dorcas. I'm much obliged to you for mentioning it. There is, indeed, a fine collection there. Are they often used, may I ask?'

'Well, sir, not very often nowadays, though from time to time we do have what the young gentlemen call "a dress-up night". And very funny it is sometimes, sir. Mr Lawrence, he's wonderful. Most comic! I shall never forget the night he came down as the Char of Persia, I think he called it – a sort of Eastern King it was. He had the big paper knife in his hand, and "Mind, Dorcas," he says, "you'll have to be very respectful. This is my specially sharpened scimitar, and it's off with your head if I'm at all displeased with you!" Miss Cynthia, she was what they call an Apache, or some such name – a Frenchified sort of cut-throat, I take it to be. A real sight she looked. You'd never have believed a pretty young lady like that could have made herself into such a ruffian. Nobody would have known her.'

'These evenings must have been great fun,' said Poirot genially. 'I suppose Mr Lawrence wore that fine black beard in the chest upstairs, when he was Shah of Persia?'

'He did have a beard, sir,' replied Dorcas, smiling. 'And well I know it, for he borrowed two skeins of my black wool to make it with! And I'm sure it looked wonderfully natural at a distance. I didn't know as there was a beard up there at all. It must have been got quite lately, I think. There was a red wig, I know, but nothing else in the way of hair. Burnt corks they use mostly – though 'tis messy getting it off again. Miss Cynthia was a Negress once, and, oh, the trouble she had.'

'So Dorcas knows nothing about that black beard,' said Poirot thoughtfully, as we walked out into the hall again.

'Do you think it is *the* one?' I whispered eagerly.

Poirot nodded.

'I do. You noticed it had been trimmed?'

'No.'

'Yes. It was cut exactly the shape of Mr Inglethorp's and I found one or two snipped hairs. Hastings, this affair is very deep.'

'Who put it in the chest, I wonder?'

'Someone with a good deal of intelligence,' remarked Poirot drily. 'You realize that he chose the one place in the house to hide it where its presence would not be remarked? Yes, he is intelligent. But we must be more intelligent. We must be so intelligent that he does not suspect us of being intelligent at all.'

I acquiesced.

'There, *mon ami*, you will be of great assistance to me.'

I was pleased with the compliment. There had been times when I hardly thought that Poirot appreciated me at my true worth.

'Yes,' he continued, staring at me thoughtfully, 'you will be invaluable.'

This was naturally gratifying, but Poirot's next words were not so welcome.

'I must have an ally in the house,' he observed reflectively.

'You have me,' I protested.

'True, but you are not sufficient.'

I was hurt, and showed it. Poirot hurried to explain himself.

'You do not quite take my meaning. You are known to be working with me. I want somebody who is not associated with us in any way.'

'Oh, I see. How about John?'

'No, I think not.'

'The dear fellow isn't perhaps very bright,' I said thought-fully.

'Here comes Miss Howard,' said Poirot suddenly. 'She is the very person. But I am in her black books, since I cleared Mr Inglethorp. Still, we can but try.'

With a nod that was barely civil, Miss Howard assented to Poirot's request for a few minutes' conversation.

We went into the little morning-room, and Poirot closed the door.

'Well, Monsieur Poirot,' said Miss Howard impatiently, 'what is it? Out with it. I'm busy.'

'Do you remember, mademoiselle, that I once asked you to help me?'

'Yes, I do.' The lady nodded. 'And I told you I'd help you with pleasure – to hang Alfred Inglethorp.'

'Ah!' Poirot studied her seriously. 'Miss Howard, I will ask you one question. I beg of you to reply to it truthfully.'

'Never tell lies,' replied Miss Howard.

'It is this. Do you still believe that Mrs Inglethorp was poisoned by her husband?'

'What do you mean?' she asked sharply. 'You needn't think your pretty explanations influence me in the slightest. I'll admit that it wasn't he who bought strychnine at the chemist's shop. What of that? I dare say he soaked fly paper, as I told you at the beginning.'

'That is arsenic – not strychnine,' said Poirot mildly.

'What does that matter? Arsenic would put poor Emily out of the way just as well as strychnine. If I'm convinced he did it, it doesn't matter a jot to me *how* he did it.'

'Exactly. If you are convinced he did it,' said Poirot quietly. 'I will put my question in another form. Did you ever in your heart of hearts believe that Mrs Inglethorp was poisoned by her husband?'

'Good heavens!' cried Miss Howard. 'Haven't I always told you the man is a villain? Haven't I always told you he would murder her in her bed? Haven't I always hated him like poison?'

'Exactly,' said Poirot. 'That bears out my little idea entirely.'

'What little idea?'

'Miss Howard, do you remember a conversation that took place on the day of my friend's arrival here? He repeated it to me, and there is a sentence of yours that has impressed me very much. Do you remember affirming that if a crime had been committed, and anyone you loved had been murdered, you felt certain that you would know by instinct who the criminal was, even if you were quite unable to prove it?'

'Yes, I remember saying that. I believe it, too. I suppose you think it nonsense?'

'Not at all.'

'And yet you will pay no attention to my instinct against Alfred Inglethorp?'

'No,' said Poirot curtly. 'Because your instinct is not against Mr Inglethorp.'

'What?'

'No. You wish to believe he committed the crime. You believe him capable of committing it. But your instinct tells you he did not commit it. It tells you more – shall I go on?'

She was staring at him, fascinated, and made a slight affirmative movement of the hand.

'Shall I tell you why you have been so vehement against Mr Inglethorp? It is because you have been trying to believe what you wish to believe. It is because you are trying to drown and stifle your instinct, which tells you another name –'

'No, no, no!' cried Miss Howard, wildly, flinging up her hands. 'Don't say it! Oh, don't say it! It isn't true! It can't be true. I don't know what put such a wild – such a dreadful – idea into my head!'

'I am right, am I not?' asked Poirot.

'Yes, yes; you must be a wizard to have guessed. But it can't be so – it's so monstrous, too impossible. It *must* be Alfred Inglethorp.'

Poirot shook his head gravely.

'Don't ask me about it,' continued Miss Howard, 'because I shan't tell you. I won't admit it, even to myself. I must be mad to think of such a thing.'

Poirot nodded, as if satisfied.

'I will ask you nothing. It is enough for me that it is as I thought. And I – I, too, have an instinct. We are working together towards a common end.'

'Don't ask me to help you, because I won't. I wouldn't lift a finger to – to –' She faltered.

'You will help me in spite of yourself. I ask you nothing – but you will be my ally. You will not be able to help yourself. You will do the only thing that I want of you.'

'And that is?'

'You will watch!'

Evelyn Howard bowed her head.

'Yes, I can't help doing that. I am always watching – always hoping I shall be proved wrong.'

'If we are wrong, well and good,' said Poirot. 'No one will be more pleased than I shall. But, if we are right? If we are right, Miss Howard, on whose side are you then?'

'I don't know, I don't know –'

'Come now.'

'It could be hushed up.'

'There must be no hushing up.'

'But Emily herself –' She broke off.

'Miss Howard,' said Poirot gravely, 'this is unworthy of you.'

Suddenly she took her face from her hands.

'Yes,' she said quietly, 'that was not Evelyn Howard who spoke!' She flung her head up proudly. '*This* is Evelyn Howard! And she is on the side of Justice! Let the cost be what it may.' And with these words, she walked firmly out of the room.

'There,' said Poirot, looking after her, 'goes a very valuable ally. That woman, Hastings, has got brains as well as a heart.'

I did not reply.

'Instinct is a marvellous thing,' mused Poirot. 'It can neither be explained nor ignored.'

'You and Miss Howard seem to know what you are talking about,' I observed coldly. 'Perhaps you don't realize that I am still in the dark.'

'Really? Is that so, *mon ami?*'

'Yes. Enlighten me, will you?'

Poirot studied me attentively for a moment or two. Then, to my intense surprise, he shook his head decidedly.

'No, my friend.'

'Oh, look here, why not?'

'Two is enough for a secret.'

'Well, I think it is very unfair to keep back facts from me.'

'I am not keeping back facts. Every fact that I know is in your possession. You can draw your own deductions from them. This time it is a question of ideas.'

'Still, it would be interesting to know.'

Poirot looked at me very earnestly, and again shook his head.

'You see,' he said sadly, '*you* have no instincts.'

'It was intelligence you were requiring just now,' I pointed out.

'The two often go together,' said Poirot enigmatically.

The remark seemed so utterly irrelevant that I did not even take the trouble to answer it. But I decided that if I made any interesting and important discoveries – as no doubt I should – I would keep them to myself, and surprise Poirot with the ultimate result.

There are times when it is one's duty to assert oneself.

CHAPTER 9

DR BAUERSTEIN

I had no opportunity as yet of passing on Poirot's message to Lawrence. But now, as I strolled out on the lawn, still nursing a grudge against my friend's high-handedness, I saw Lawrence on the croquet lawn, aimlessly knocking a couple of very ancient balls about, with a still more ancient mallet.

It struck me that it would be a good opportunity to deliver my message. Otherwise, Poirot himself might relieve me of it. It was true that I did not quite gather its purport, but I flattered myself that by Lawrence's reply, and perhaps a little skilful cross-examination on my part, I should soon perceive its significance. Accordingly I accosted him.

'I've been looking for you,' I remarked untruthfully.

'Have you?'

'Yes. The truth is, I've got a message for you – from Poirot.'

'Yes?'

'He told me to wait until I was alone with you,' I said, dropping my voice significantly, and watching him intently out of the corner of my eye. I have always been rather good at what is called, I believe, creating an atmosphere.

'Well?'

There was no change of expression in the dark melancholic face. Had he any idea of what I was about to say?

'This is the message.' I dropped my voice still lower. '"Find the extra coffee-cup, and you can rest in peace."'

'What on earth does he mean?' Lawrence stared at me in quite unaffected astonishment.

'Don't you know?'

'Not in the least. Do you?'

I was compelled to shake my head.

'What extra coffee-cup?'

'I don't know.'

'He'd better ask Dorcas, or one of the maids, if he wants to know about coffee-cups. It's their business, not mine. I don't know anything about the coffee-cups, except that we've got some that are never used, which are a perfect dream! Old Worcester. You're not a connoisseur, are you, Hastings?'

I shook my head.

'You miss a lot. A really perfect bit of old china – it's pure delight to handle it, or even to look at it.'

'Well, what am I to tell Poirot?'

'Tell him I don't know what he's talking about. It's double Dutch to me.'

'All right.'

I was moving off towards the house again when he suddenly called me back.

'I say, what was the end of that message? Say it over again, will you?'

'"Find the extra coffee-cup, and you can rest in peace." Are you sure you don't know what it means?' I asked him earnestly.

He shook his head.

'No,' he said musingly, 'I don't. I – I wish I did.'

The boom of the gong sounded from the house, and we went in together. Poirot had been asked by John to remain to lunch, and was already seated at the table.

By tacit consent, all mention of the tragedy was barred. We conversed on the war, and other outside topics. But after the cheese and biscuits had been handed round, and Dorcas had left the room, Poirot suddenly leant forward to Mrs Cavendish.

'Pardon me, madame, for recalling unpleasant memories, but I have a little idea' – Poirot's 'little ideas' were becoming a perfect byword – 'and would like to ask one or two questions.'

'Of me? Certainly.'

'You are too aimable, madame. What I want to ask is this: the door leading into Mrs Inglethorp's room from that of Mademoiselle Cynthia, it was bolted, you say?'

'Certainly it was bolted,' replied Mary Cavendish, rather surprised. 'I said so at the inquest.'

'Bolted?'

'Yes.' She looked perplexed.

'I mean,' explained Poirot, 'you are sure it was bolted, and not merely locked?'

'Oh, I see what you mean. No, I don't know. I said bolted, meaning that it was fastened, and I could not open it, but I believe all the doors were found bolted on the inside.'

'Still, as far as you are concerned, the door might equally well have been locked?'

'Oh, yes.'

'You yourself did not happen to notice, madame, when you entered Mrs Inglethorp's room, whether that door was bolted or not?'

'I – I believe it was.'

'But you did not see it?'

'No. I – never looked.'

'But I did,' interrupted Lawrence suddenly. 'I happened to notice that it *was* bolted.'

'Ah, that settles it.' And Poirot looked crestfallen.

I could not help rejoicing that, for once, one of his 'little ideas' had come to naught.

After lunch Poirot begged me to accompany him home. I consented rather stiffly.

'You are annoyed, is it not so?' he asked anxiously, as we walked through the park.

'Not at all,' I said coldly.

'That is well. That lifts a great load from my mind.'

This was not quite what I had intended. I had hoped that he would have observed the stiffness of my manner. Still, the fervour of his words went towards the appeasing of my just displeasure. I thawed.

'I gave Lawrence your message,' I said.

'And what did he say? He was entirely puzzled?'

'Yes. I am quite sure he had no idea of what you meant.'

I had expected Poirot to be disappointed; but, to my surprise, he replied that that was as he had thought, and that he was very glad. My pride forbade me to ask any questions.

Poirot switched off on another tack.

'Mademoiselle Cynthia was not at lunch today? How was that?'

'She is at the hospital again. She resumed work today.'

'Ah, she is an industrious little demoiselle. And pretty too. She is like pictures I have seen in Italy. I would rather like to see that dispensary of hers. Do you think she would show it to me?'

'I am sure she would be delighted. It's an interesting little place.'

'Does she go there every day?'

'She has all Wednesdays off, and comes back to lunch on Saturdays. Those are her only times off.'

'I will remember. Women are doing great work nowadays, and Mademoiselle Cynthia is clever – oh, yes, she has brains, that little one.'

'Yes. I believe she has passed quite a stiff exam.'

'Without doubt. After all, it is very responsible work. I suppose they have very strong poisons there?'

'Yes, she showed them to us. They are kept locked up in a little cupboard. I believe they have to be very careful. They always take out the key before leaving the room.'

'Indeed. It is near the window, this cupboard?'

'No, right the other side of the room. Why?'

Poirot shrugged his shoulders.

'I wondered. That is all. Will you come in?'

We had reached the cottage.

'No. I think I'll be getting back. I shall go round the long way through the woods.'

The woods round Styles were very beautiful. After the walk across the open park, it was pleasant to saunter lazily through the cool glades. There was hardly a breath of wind, the very chirp of the birds was faint and subdued. I strolled on a little way, and finally flung myself down at the foot of a grand old beech-tree. My thoughts of mankind were kindly and charitable. I even forgave Poirot for his absurd secrecy. In fact, I was at peace with the world. Then I yawned.

I thought about the crime, and it struck me as being very unreal and far off.

I yawned again.

Probably, I thought, it really never happened. Of course, it was all a bad dream. The truth of the matter was that it was Lawrence who had murdered Alfred Inglethorp with a croquet mallet. But it was absurd of John to make such a fuss about it, and to go shouting out: 'I tell you I won't have it!'

I woke up with a start.

At once I realized that I was in a very awkward predicament. For, about twelve feet away from me, John and Mary Cavendish were standing facing each other, and they were evidently quarrelling. And, quite as evidently, they were unaware of my vicinity, for before I could move or speak John repeated the words which had aroused me from my dream.

'I tell you, Mary, I won't have it.'

Mary's voice came, cool and liquid:

'Have *you* any right to criticize my actions?'

'It will be the talk of the village! My mother was only buried on Saturday, and here you are gadding about with the fellow.'

'Oh,' she shrugged her shoulders, 'if it is only village gossip that you mind!'

'But it isn't. I've had enough of the fellow hanging about. He's a Polish Jew, anyway.'

'A tinge of Jewish blood is not a bad thing. It leavens the' – she looked at him – 'stolid stupidity of the ordinary Englishman.'

Fire in her eyes, ice in her voice. I did not wonder that the blood rose to John's face in a crimson tide.

'Mary!'

'Well?' Her tone did not change.

The pleading died out of his voice.

'Am I to understand that you will continue to see Bauerstein against my express wishes?'

'If I choose.'

'You defy me?'

'No, but I deny your right to criticize my actions. Have *you* no friends of whom I should disapprove?'

John fell back a pace. The colour ebbed slowly from his face.

'What do you mean?' he said, in an unsteady voice.

'You see!' said Mary quietly. 'You *do* see, don't you, that *you* have no right to dictate to *me* as to the choice of my friends?'

John glanced at her pleadingly, a stricken look in his face.

'No right? Have I *no* right, Mary?' he said unsteadily. He stretched out his hands. 'Mary –'

For a moment, I thought she wavered. A softer expression came over her face, then suddenly she turned almost fiercely away.

'None!'

She was walking away when John sprang after her, and caught her by the arm.

'Mary' – his voice was very quiet now – 'are you in love with this fellow Bauerstein?'

She hesitated, and suddenly there swept across her face a strange expression, old as the hills, yet with something eternally young about it. So might some Egyptian sphinx have smiled.

She freed herself quietly from his arm, and spoke over her shoulder.

'Perhaps,' she said; and then swiftly passed out of the little glade, leaving John standing there as though he had been turned to stone.

Rather ostentatiously, I stepped forward, crackling some dead branches with my feet as I did so. John turned. Luckily, he took it for granted that I had only just come upon the scene.

'Hullo, Hastings. Have you seen the little fellow safely back to his cottage? Quaint little chap! Is he any good, though, really?'

'He was considered one of the finest detectives of his day.'

'Oh, well, I suppose there must be something in it, then. What a rotten world it is, though!'

'You find it so?' I asked.

'Good Lord, yes! There's this terrible business to start with. Scotland Yard men in and out of the house like a jack-in-the-box! Never know where they won't turn up next. Screaming headlines in every paper in the country – damn all journalists, I say! Do you know there was a whole crowd staring in at the lodge gates this

morning. Sort of Madame Tussaud's chamber of horrors business
that can be seen for nothing. Pretty thick, isn't it?'

'Cheer up, John!' I said soothingly. 'It can't last for ever.'

'Can't it, though? It can last long enough for us never to be
able to hold up our heads again.'

'No, no, you're getting morbid on the subject.'

'Enough to make a man morbid, to be stalked by beastly
journalists and stared at by gaping moon-faced idiots, wherever
he goes! But there's worse than that.'

'What?'

John lowered his voice:

'Have you ever thought, Hastings – it's a nightmare to me –
who did it? I can't help feeling sometimes it must have been an
accident. Because – because – who could have done it? Now
Inglethorp's out of the way, there's no one else; no one, I mean,
except – one of us.'

Yes, indeed, that was nightmare enough for any man! One of
us? Yes, surely it must be so, unless –

A new idea suggested itself to my mind. Rapidly, I considered
it. The light increased. Poirot's mysterious doings, his hints – they
all fitted in. Fool that I was not to have thought of this possibility
before, and what a relief for us all.

'No, John,' I said, 'it isn't one of us. How could it be?'

'I know, but, still, who else is there?'

'Can't you guess?'

'No.'

I looked cautiously round, and lowered my voice.

'Dr Bauerstein!' I whispered.

'Impossible!'

'Not at all.'

'But what earthly interest could he have in mother's death?'

'That I don't see,' I confessed, 'but I'll tell you this: Poirot
thinks so.'

'Poirot? Does he? How do you know?'

I told him of Poirot's intense excitement on hearing that Dr
Bauerstein had been at Styles on the fatal night, and added:

'He said twice: "That alters everything." And I've been thinking. You know Inglethorp said he had put down the coffee in
the hall? Well, it was just then that Bauerstein arrived. Isn't it

possible that, as Inglethorp brought him through the hall, the doctor dropped something into the coffee in passing?'

'H'm,' said John. 'It would have been very risky.'

'Yes, but it was possible.'

'And then, how could he know it was her coffee? No, old fellow, I don't think that will wash.'

But I had remembered something else.

'You're quite right. That wasn't how it was done. Listen.' And then I told him of the cocoa sample which Poirot had taken to be analysed.

John interrupted just as I had done.

'But, look here, Bauerstein had had it analysed already?'

'Yes, yes, that's the point. I didn't see it either until now. Don't you understand? Bauerstein had it analysed – that's just it! If Bauerstein's the murderer, nothing could be simpler than for him to substitute some ordinary cocoa for his sample, and send that to be tested. And of course they would find no strychnine! But no one would dream of suspecting Bauerstein, or think of taking another sample – except Poirot,' I added, with belated recognition.

'Yes, but what about the bitter taste that cocoa won't disguise?'

'Well, we've only his word for that. And there are other possibilities. He's admittedly one of the world's greatest toxicologists –'

'One of the world's greatest what? Say it again.'

'He knows more about poisons than almost anybody,' I explained. 'Well, my idea is, that perhaps he's found some way of making strychnine tasteless. Or it may not have been strychnine at all, but some obscure drug no one has ever heard of, which produces much the same symptoms.'

'H'm, yes, that might be,' said John. 'But look here, how could he have got at the cocoa? That wasn't downstairs?'

'No, it wasn't,' I admitted reluctantly.

And then, suddenly, a dreadful possibility flashed through my mind. I hoped and prayed it would not occur to John also. I glanced sideways at him. He was frowning perplexedly, and I drew a deep breath of relief, for the terrible thought that had flashed across my mind was this: that Dr Bauerstein might have had an accomplice.

Yet surely it could not be! Surely no woman as beautiful as Mary Cavendish could be a murderess. Yet beautiful women had been known to poison.

And suddenly I remembered that first conversation at tea on the day of my arrival, and the gleam in her eyes as she had said that poison was a woman's weapon. How agitated she had been on that fatal Tuesday evening! Had Mrs Inglethorp discovered something between her and Bauerstein, and threatened to tell her husband? Was it to stop that denunciation that the crime had been committed?

Then I remembered that enigmatical conversation between Poirot and Evelyn Howard. Was this what they had meant? Was this the monstrous possibility that Evelyn had tried not to believe?

Yes, it all fitted in.

No wonder Miss Howard had suggested 'hushing it up'. Now I understood that unfinished sentence of hers: 'Emily herself –' And in my heart I agreed with her. Would not Mrs Inglethorp have preferred to go unavenged rather than have such terrible dishonour fall upon the name of Cavendish?

'There's another thing,' said John suddenly, and the unexpected sound of his voice made me start guiltily. 'Something which makes me doubt if what you say can be true.'

'What's that?' I asked, thankful that he had gone away from the subject of how the poison could have been introduced into the cocoa.

'Why, the fact that Bauerstein demanded a post-mortem. He needn't have done so. Little Wilkins would have been quite content to let it go at heart disease.'

'Yes,' I said doubtfully. 'But we don't know. Perhaps he thought it safer in the long run. Someone might have talked afterwards. Then the Home Office might have ordered exhumation. The whole thing would have come out, then, and he would have been in an awkward position, for no one would have believed that a man of his reputation could have been deceived into calling it heart disease.'

'Yes, that's possible,' admitted John. 'Still,' he added, 'I'm blest if I can see what his motive could have been.'

I trembled.

'Look here,' I said, 'I may be altogether wrong. And, remember, all this is in confidence.'

'Oh, of course – that goes without saying.'

We had walked, as we talked, and now we passed through the little gate into the garden. Voices rose near at hand, for tea was spread out under the sycamore-tree, as it had been on the day of my arrival.

Cynthia was back from the hospital, and I placed my chair beside her, and told her of Poirot's wish to visit the dispensary.

'Of course! I'd love him to see it. He'd better come to tea there one day. I must fix it up with him. He's such a dear little man! But he *is* funny. He made me take the brooch out of my tie the other day, and put it in again, because he said it wasn't straight.'

I laughed.

'It's quite a mania with him.'

'Yes, isn't it?'

We were silent for a minute or two, and then, glancing in the direction of Mary Cavendish, and dropping her voice, Cynthia said:

'Mr Hastings.'

'Yes?'

'After tea, I want to talk to you.'

Her glance at Mary had set me thinking. I fancied that between these two there existed very little sympathy. For the first time, it occurred to me to wonder about the girl's future. Mrs Inglethorp had made no provision of any kind for her, but I imagined that John and Mary would probably insist on her making her home with them – at any rate until the end of the war. John, I knew, was very fond of her, and would be sorry to let her go.

John, who had gone into the house, now reappeared. His good-natured face wore an unaccustomed frown of anger.

'Confound those detectives! I can't think what they're after! They've been in every room in the house – turning things inside out, and upside down. It really is too bad! I suppose they took advantage of our all being out. I shall go for that fellow Japp, when I next see him!'

'Lot of Paul Prys,' grunted Miss Howard.

Lawrence opined that they had to make a show of doing something.

Mary Cavendish said nothing.

After tea, I invited Cynthia to come for a walk, and we sauntered off into the woods together.

'Well?' I inquired, as soon as we were protected from prying eyes by the leafy screen.

With a sigh, Cynthia flung herself down, and tossed off her hat. The sunlight, piercing through the branches, turned the auburn of her hair to quivering gold.

'Mr Hastings – you are always so kind, and you know such a lot.'

It struck me at this moment that Cynthia was really a very charming girl! Much more charming than Mary, who never said things of that kind.

'Well?' I asked benignantly, as she hesitated.

'I want to ask your advice. What shall I do?'

'Do?'

'Yes. You see, Aunt Emily always told me I should be provided for. I suppose she forgot, or didn't think she was likely to die – anyway, I am *not* provided for! And I don't know what to do. Do you think I ought to go away from here at once?'

'Good heavens, no! They don't want to part with you, I'm sure.'

Cynthia hesitated a moment, plucking up the grass with her tiny hands. Then she said: 'Mrs Cavendish does. She hates me.'

'Hates you?' I cried, astonished.

Cynthia nodded.

'Yes. I don't know why, but she can't bear me and *he* can't either.'

'There I know you're wrong,' I said warmly. 'On the contrary, John is very fond of you.'

'Oh, yes – *John*. I meant Lawrence. Not, of course, that I care whether Lawrence hates me or not. Still, it's rather horrid when no one loves you, isn't it?'

'But they do, Cynthia dear,' I said earnestly. 'I'm sure you are mistaken. Look, there is John – and Miss Howard –'

Cynthia nodded rather gloomily. 'Yes, John likes me, I think, and of course Evie, for all her gruff ways, wouldn't be unkind to a fly. But Lawrence never speaks to me if he can help it, and Mary can hardly bring herself to be civil to me. She wants Evie to stay on, is begging her to, but she doesn't want me, and – and – I don't know what to do.' Suddenly the poor child burst out crying.

I don't know what possessed me. Her beauty, perhaps, as she sat there, with the sunlight glinting down on her head; perhaps the sense of relief at encountering someone who so obviously could have no connection with the tragedy; perhaps honest pity for her youth and loneliness. Anyway, I leant forward, and taking her little hand, I said awkwardly:

'Marry me, Cynthia.'

Unwittingly, I had hit upon a sovereign remedy for her tears. She sat up at once, drew her hand away, and said, with some asperity:

'Don't be silly!'

I was a little annoyed.

'I'm not being silly. I am asking you to do me the honour of becoming my wife.'

To my intense surprise, Cynthia burst out laughing, and called me a 'funny dear'.

'It's perfectly sweet of you,' she said, 'but you know you don't want to!'

'Yes, I do. I've got –'

'Never mind what you've got. You don't really want to – and I don't either.'

'Well, of course, that settles it,' I said stiffly. 'But I don't see anything to laugh at. There's nothing funny about a proposal.'

'No, indeed,' said Cynthia. 'Somebody might accept you next time. Good-bye, you've cheered me up *very* much.'

And, with a final uncontrollable burst of merriment, she vanished through the trees.

Thinking over the interview, it struck me as being profoundly unsatisfactory.

It occurred to me suddenly that I would go down to the village, and look up Bauerstein. Somebody ought to be keeping an eye on the fellow. At the same time, it would be wise to allay any suspicions he might have as to his being suspected. I remembered how Poirot had relied on my diplomacy. Accordingly, I went to the little house with the 'Apartments' card inserted in the window, where I knew he lodged, and tapped on the door.

An old woman came and opened it.

'Good afternoon,' I said pleasantly. 'Is Dr Bauerstein in?'

She stared at me.

'Haven't you heard?'

'Heard what?'

'About him.'

'What about him?'

'He's took.'

'Took? Dead?'

'No, took by the perlice.'

'By the police!' I gasped. 'Do you mean they've arrested him?'

'Yes, that's it, and –'

I waited to hear no more, but tore up the village to find Poirot.

CHAPTER 10

THE ARREST

To my extreme annoyance, Poirot was not in, and the old Belgian who answered my knock informed me that he believed he had gone to London.

I was dumbfounded. What on earth could Poirot be doing in London? Was it a sudden decision on his part, or had he already made up his mind when he parted from me a few hours earlier?

I retraced my steps to Styles in some annoyance. With Poirot away, I was uncertain how to act. Had he foreseen this arrest? Had he not, in all probability, been the cause of it? Those questions I could not resolve. But in the meantime what was I to do? Should I announce the arrest openly at Styles, or not? Though I did not acknowledge it to myself, the thought of Mary Cavendish was weighing on me. Would it not be a terrible shock to her? For the moment, I set aside utterly any suspicions of her. She could not be implicated – otherwise I should have heard some hint of it.

Of course, there was no possibility of being able permanently to conceal Dr Bauerstein's arrest from her. It would be announced in every newspaper on the morrow. Still, I shrank from blurting it out. If only Poirot had been accessible, I could have asked his advice. What possessed him to go posting off to London in this unaccountable way?

In spite of myself, my opinion of his sagacity was immeasurably heightened. I would never have dreamt of suspecting the doctor, had not Poirot put it into my head. Yes, decidedly, the little man was clever.

After some reflecting, I decided to take John into my confidence, and leave him to make the matter public or not, as he thought fit.

He gave vent to a prodigious whistle, as I imparted the news.

'Great Scot! You *were* right, then. I couldn't believe it at the time.'

'No, it is astonishing until you get used to the idea, and see how it makes everything fit in. Now, what are we to do? Of course, it will be generally known tomorrow.'

John reflected.

'Never mind,' he said at last, 'we won't say anything at present. There is no need. As you say, it will be known soon enough.'

But to my intense surprise, on getting down early the next morning, and eagerly opening the newspapers, there was not a word about the arrest! There was a column of mere padding about 'The Styles Poisoning Case', but nothing further. It was rather inexplicable, but I supposed that, for some reason or other, Japp wished to keep it out of the papers. It worried me just a little, for it suggested the possibility that there might be further arrests to come.

After breakfast, I decided to go down to the village, and see if Poirot had returned yet; but, before I could start, a well-known face blocked one of the windows, and the well-known voice said:

'*Bonjour, mon ami!*'

'Poirot,' I exclaimed, with relief, and seizing him by both hands I dragged him into the room. 'I was never so glad to see anyone. Listen, I have said nothing to anybody but John. Is that right?'

'My friend,' replied Poirot, 'I do not know what you are talking about.'

'Dr Bauerstein's arrest, of course,' I answered impatiently.

'Is Bauerstein arrested, then?'

'Did you not know it?'

'Not the least in the world.' But, pausing a moment, he added: 'Still, it does not surprise me. After all, we are only four miles from the coast.'

'The coast?' I asked, puzzled. 'What has that got to do with it?'

Poirot shrugged his shoulders.

'Surely, it is obvious!'

'Not to me. No doubt I am very dense, but I cannot see what the proximity of the coast has got to do with the murder of Mrs Inglethorp.'

'Nothing at all, of course,' replied Poirot, smiling. 'But we were speaking of the arrest of Dr Bauerstein.'

'Well, he is arrested for the murder of Mrs Inglethorp –'

'What?' cried Poirot, in apparently lively astonishment. 'Dr Bauerstein arrested for the murder of Mrs Inglethorp?'

'Yes.'

'Impossible! That would be too good a farce! Who told you that, my friend?'

'Well no one exactly told me,' I confessed. 'But he is arrested.'

'Oh, yes, very likely. But for espionage, *mon ami*.'

'Espionage?' I gasped.

'Precisely.'

'Not for poisoning Mrs Inglethorp?'

'Not unless our friend Japp has taken leave of his senses,' replied Poirot placidly.

'But – but I thought you thought so too?'

Poirot gave me one look, which conveyed a wondering pity, and his full sense of the utter absurdity of such an idea.

'Do you mean to say,' I asked, slowly adapting myself to the new idea, 'that Dr Bauerstein is a spy?'

Poirot nodded.

'Have you never suspected it?'

'It never entered my head.'

'It did not strike you as peculiar that a famous London doctor should bury himself in a little village like this, and should be in the habit of walking about at all hours of the night, fully dressed?'

'No,' I confessed, 'I never thought of such a thing.'

'He is, of course, a German by birth,' said Poirot thoughtfully, 'though he has practised so long in this country that nobody thinks of him as anything but an Englishman. He was naturalized about fifteen years ago. A very clever man – a Jew of course.'

'The blackguard!' I cried indignantly.

'Not at all. He is, on the contrary, a patriot. Think what he stands to lose. I admire the man myself.'

But I could not look at it in Poirot's philosophical way.

'And this is the man with whom Mrs Cavendish has been wandering about all over the country!' I cried indignantly.

'Yes. I should fancy he had found her very useful,' remarked Poirot. 'So long as gossip busied itself in coupling their names together, any other vagaries of the doctor's passed unobserved.'

'Then you think he never really cared for her?' I asked eagerly – rather too eagerly, perhaps, under the circumstances.

'That, of course, I cannot say, but – shall I tell you my own private opinion, Hastings?'

'Yes.'

'Well, it is this: that Mrs Cavendish does not care, and never has cared one little jot about Dr Bauerstein!'

'Do you really think so?' I could not disguise my pleasure.

'I am quite sure of it. And I will tell you why.'

'Yes?'

'Because she cares for someone else, *mon ami.*'

'Oh!' What did he mean? In spite of myself, an agreeable warmth spread over me. I am not a vain man where women are concerned, but I remembered certain evidences, too lightly thought of at the time, perhaps, but which certainly seemed to indicate –

My pleasing thoughts were interrupted by the sudden entrance of Miss Howard. She glanced round hastily to make sure there was no one else in the room, and quickly produced an old sheet of brown paper. This she handed to Poirot, murmuring as she did so the cryptic words:

'On top of the wardrobe.' Then she hurriedly left the room.

Poirot unfolded the sheet of paper eagerly, and uttered an exclamation of satisfaction. He spread it out on the table.

'Come here, Hastings. Now tell me, what is that initial – J. Or L.?'

It was a medium-sized sheet of paper, rather dusty, as though it had lain by for some time. But it was the label that was attracting Poirot's attention. At the top, it bore the printed stamp of Messrs Parkson's, the well-known theatrical costumiers, and it was addressed to '– (the debatable initial) Cavendish, Esq., Styles Court, Styles St Mary, Essex.'

'It might be T. Or it might be L.,' I said, after studying the thing for a minute or two. 'It certainly isn't a J.'

'Good,' replied Poirot, folding up the paper again. 'I, also, am of your way of thinking. It is an L., depend upon it!'

'Where did it come from?' I asked curiously. 'Is it important?'

'Moderately so. It confirms a surmise of mine. Having deduced its existence, I set Miss Howard to search for it, and, as you see, she has been successful.'

'What did she mean by "On top of the wardrobe"?'

'She meant,' replied Poirot promptly, 'that she found it on top of a wardrobe.'

'A funny place for a piece of brown paper,' I mused.

'Not at all. The top of a wardrobe is an excellent place for brown paper and cardboard boxes. I have kept them there myself. Neatly arranged, there is nothing to offend the eye.'

'Poirot,' I asked earnestly, 'have you made up your mind about this crime?'

'Yes – that is to say, I believe I know how it was committed.'

'Ah!'

'Unfortunately, I have no proof beyond my surmise, unless –' With sudden energy, he caught me by the arm, and whirled me down the hall, calling out in French in his excitement: 'Mademoiselle Dorcas, Mademoiselle Dorcas, *un moment, s'il vous plaît!'*

Dorcas, quite flurried by the noise, came hurrying out of the pantry.

'My good Dorcas, I have an idea – a little idea – if it should prove justified, what magnificent chance! Tell me, on Monday, not Tuesday, Dorcas, but Monday, the day before the tragedy, did anything go wrong with Mrs Inglethorp's bell?'

Dorcas looked very surprised.

'Yes, sir, now you mention it, it did; though I don't know how you came to hear of it. A mouse, or some such, must have nibbled the wire through. The man came and put it right on Tuesday morning.'

With a long-drawn exclamation of ecstasy, Poirot led the way back to the morning-room.

'See you, one should not ask for outside proof – no, reason should be enough. But the flesh is weak, it is consolation to find that one is on the right track. Ah, my friend, I am like a giant refreshed. I run! I leap!'

And, in very truth, run and leap he did, gambolling wildly down the stretch of lawn outside the long window.

'What is your remarkable little friend doing?' asked a voice behind me, and I turned to find Mary Cavendish at my elbow.

She smiled, and so did I. 'What is it all about?'

'Really, I can't tell you. He asked Dorcas some question about a bell, and appeared so delighted with her answer that he is capering about as you see!'

Mary laughed.

'How ridiculous! He's going out of the gate. Isn't he coming back today?'

'I don't know. I've given up trying to guess what he'll do next.'

'Is he quite mad, Mr Hastings?'

'I honestly don't know. Sometimes, I feel sure he is as mad as a hatter; and then, just as he is at his maddest, I find there is method in his madness.'

'I see.'

In spite of her laugh, Mary was looking thoughtful this morning. She seemed grave, almost sad.

It occurred to me that it would be a good opportunity to tackle her on the subject of Cynthia. I began rather tactfully, I thought, but I had not gone far before she stopped me authoritatively.

'You are an excellent advocate, I have no doubt, Mr Hastings, but in this case your talents are quite thrown away. Cynthia will run no risk of encountering any unkindness from me.'

I began to stammer feebly that I hoped she hadn't thought – But again she stopped me, and her words were so unexpected that they quite drove Cynthia, and her troubles, out of my mind.

'Mr Hastings,' she said, 'do you think I and my husband are happy together?'

I was considerably taken aback, and murmured something about it not being my business to think anything of the sort.

'Well,' she said quietly, 'whether it is your business or not, I will tell you that we are *not* happy.'

I said nothing, for I saw that she had not finished.

She began slowly, walking up and down the room, her head a little bent, and that slim, supple figure of hers swaying gently as she walked. She stopped suddenly, and looked up at me.

'You don't know anything about me, do you?' she asked. 'Where I come from, who I was before I married John – anything, in fact? Well, I will tell you. I will make a father confessor of you. You are kind, I think – yes, I am sure you are kind.'

Somehow, I was not quite as elated as I might have been. I remembered that Cynthia had begun her confidences in much the same way. Besides, a father confessor should be elderly, it is not at all the rôle for a young man.

'My father was English,' said Mrs Cavendish, 'but my mother was a Russian.'

'Ah,' I said, 'now I understand –'

'Understand what?'

'A hint of something foreign – different – that there has always been about you.'

'My mother was very beautiful, I believe. I don't know, because I never saw her. She died when I was quite a little child. I believe there was some tragedy connected with her death – she took an overdose of some sleeping draught by mistake. However that may be, my father was broken-hearted. Shortly afterwards, he went into the Consular Service. Everywhere he went, I went with him. When I was twenty-three, I had been nearly all over the world. It was a splendid life – I loved it.'

There was a smile on her face, and her head was thrown back. She seemed living in the memory of those old glad days.

'Then my father died. He left me very badly off. I had to go and live with some old aunts in Yorkshire.' She shuddered. 'You will understand me when I say that it was a deadly life for a girl brought up as I had been. The narrowness, the deadly monotony of it, almost drove me mad.' She paused a minute, and added in a different tone: 'And then I met John Cavendish.'

'Yes?'

'You can imagine that, from my aunts' point of view, it was a very good match for me. But I can honestly say it was not this fact which weighed with me. No, he was simply a way of escape from the insufferable monotony of my life.'

I said nothing, and after a moment, she went on:

'Don't misunderstand me. I was quite honest with him. I told him, what was true, that I liked him very much, that I hoped to come to like him more, but that I was not in any way what the world calls "in love" with him. He declared that that satisfied him, and so – we were married.'

She waited a long time, a little frown had gathered on her forehead. She seemed to be looking back earnestly into those past days.

'I think – I am sure – he cared for me at first. But I suppose we were not well matched. Almost at once, we drifted apart. He – it is not a pleasant thing for my pride, but it is the truth – tired of me very soon.' I must have made some murmur of dissent, for she went on quickly: 'Oh, yes, he did! Not that it matters now – now that we've come to the parting of the ways.'

'What do you mean?'

She answered quietly:

'I mean that I am not going to remain at Styles.'

'You and John are not going to live here?'

'John may live here, but I shall not.'

'You are going to leave him?'

'Yes.'

'But why?'

She paused a long time, and said at last:

'Perhaps – because I want to be – free!'

And, as she spoke, I had a sudden vision of broad spaces, virgin tracts of forests, untrodden lands – and a realization of what freedom would mean to such a nature as Mary Cavendish. I seemed to see her for a moment as she was, a proud wild creature, as untamed by civilization as some shy bird of the hills. A little cry broke from her lips:

'You don't know, you don't know, how this hateful place has been prison to me!'

'I understand,' I said, 'but – but don't do anything rash.'

'Oh, rash!' Her voice mocked at my prudence.

Then suddenly I said a thing I could have bitten out my tongue for:

'You know that Dr Bauerstein has been arrested?'

An instant coldness passed like a mask over her face, blotting out all expression.

'John was so kind as to break that to me this morning.'

'Well, what do you think?' I asked feebly.

'Of what?'

'Of the arrest?'

'What should I think? Apparently he is a German spy; so the gardener had told John.'

Her face and voice were absolutely cold and expressionless. Did she care, or did she not?

She moved away a step or two, and fingered one of the flower vases. 'These are quite dead. I must do them again. Would you mind moving – thank you, Mr Hastings.' And she walked quietly past me out of the window, with a cool little nod of dismissal.

No, surely she could not care for Bauerstein. No woman could act her part with that icy unconcern.

Poirot did not make his appearance the following morning, and there was no sign of the Scotland Yard men.

But, at lunch-time, there arrived a new piece of evidence – or rather lack of evidence. We had vainly tried to trace the fourth letter which Mrs Inglethorp had written on the evening preceding her death. Our efforts having been in vain, we had abandoned the matter, hoping that it might turn up of itself one day. And this is just what did happen, in the shape of a communication, which arrived by the second post from a firm of French music publishers, acknowledging Mrs Inglethorp's cheque, and regretting they had been unable to trace a certain series of Russian folk-songs. So the last hope of solving the mystery, by means of Mrs Inglethorp's correspondence on the fatal evening, had to be abandoned.

Just before tea, I strolled down to tell Poirot of the new disappointment, but found, to my annoyance, that he was once more out.

'Gone to London again?'

'Oh, no, monsieur, he has but taken the train to Tadminster. "To see a young lady's dispensary," he said.'

'Silly ass!' I ejaculated. 'I told him Wednesday was the one day she wasn't there! Well, tell him to look us up tomorrow morning, will you?'

'Certainly, monsieur.'

But, on the following day, no sign of Poirot. I was getting angry. He was really treating us in the most cavalier fashion.

After lunch, Lawrence drew me aside, and asked if I was going down to see him.

'No, I don't think I shall. He can come up here if he wants to see us.'

'Oh!' Lawrence looked indeterminate. Something unusually nervous and excited in his manner roused my curiosity.

'What is it?' I asked. 'I could go if there's anything special.'

'It's nothing much, but – well, if you are going, will you tell him' – he dropped his voice to a whisper – 'I think I've found the extra coffee-cup!'

I had almost forgotten that enigmatical message of Poirot's but now my curiosity was aroused afresh.

Lawrence would say no more, so I decided that I would descend from my high horse, and once more seek out Poirot at Leastways Cottage.

This time I was received with a smile. Monsieur Poirot was within. Would I mount? I mounted accordingly.

Poirot was sitting by the table, his head buried in his hands. He sprang up at my entrance.

'What is it?' I asked solicitously. 'You are not ill, I trust?'

'No, no, not ill. But I decide an affair of great moment.'

'Whether to catch the criminal or not?' I asked facetiously.

But to my great surprise, Poirot nodded gravely.

'"To speak or not to speak," as your so great Shakespeare says, "that is the question".'

I did not trouble to correct the quotation.

'You are not serious, Poirot?'

'I am of the most serious. For the most serious of all things hangs in the balance.'

'And that is?'

'A woman's happiness, *mon ami*,' he said gravely.

I did not quite know what to say.

'The moment has come,' said Poirot thoughtfully, 'and I do not know what to do. For, see you, it is a big stake for which I play.

No one but I, Hercule Poirot, would attempt it!' And he tapped himself proudly on the breast.

After pausing a few minutes respectfully, so as not to spoil his effect, I gave him Lawrence's message.

'Aha!' he cried. 'So he has found the extra coffee-cup. That is good. He has more intelligence than would appear, this long-faced Monsieur Lawrence of yours!'

I did not myself think very highly of Lawrence's intelligence; but I forbore to contradict Poirot, and gently took him to task for forgetting my instructions as to which were Cynthia's days off.

'It is true. I have the head of a sieve. However, the other young lady was most kind. She was sorry for my disappointment, and showed me everything in the kindest way.'

'Oh, well, that's all right, then, and you must go to tea with Cynthia another day.'

I told him about the letter.

'I am sorry for that,' he said. 'I always had hopes of that letter. But, no, it was not to be. This affair must all be unravelled from within.' He tapped his forehead. 'These little grey cells. It is "up to them" – as you say over here.' Then, suddenly, he asked: 'Are you a judge of finger-marks, my friend?'

'No,' I said, rather surprised, 'I know that there are no two finger-marks alike, but that's as far as my science goes.'

'Exactly.'

He unlocked a little drawer, and took out some photographs which he laid on the table.

'I have numbered them, 1, 2, 3. Will you describe them to me?'

I studied the proofs attentively.

'All greatly magnified, I see. No. 1, I should say, are a man's finger-prints; thumb and first finger. No. 2 are a lady's; they are much smaller, and quite different in every way. No. 3' – I paused for some time – 'there seems to be a lot of confused finger-marks, but here, very distinctly, are No. 1's.'

'Overlapping the others?'

'Yes.'

'You recognize them beyond fail?'

'Oh, yes; they are identical.'

Poirot nodded, and gently taking the photographs from me locked them up again.

'I suppose,' I said, 'that as usual, you are not going to explain?'

'On the contrary. No. 1 were the finger-prints of Monsieur Lawrence. No. 2 were those of Mademoiselle Cynthia. They are not important. I merely obtained them for comparison. No. 3 is a little more complicated.'

'Yes?'

'It is, as you see, highly magnified. You may have noticed a sort of blur extending all across the picture. I will not describe to you the special apparatus, dusting powder, etc., which I used. It is a well-known process to the police, and by means of it you can obtain a photograph of the finger-prints on any object in a very short space of time. Well, my friend, you have seen the finger-marks – it remains to tell you the particular object on which they had been left.'

'Go on – I am really excited.'

'*Eh bien!* Photo No. 3 represents the highly magnified surface of a tiny bottle in the top poison cupboard of the dispensary in the Red Cross Hospital at Tadminster – which sounds like the house that Jack built!'

'Good heavens!' I exclaimed. 'But what were Lawrence Cavendish's finger-marks doing on it? He never went near the poison cupboard the day we were there?'

'Oh, yes, he did!'

'Impossible! We were all together the whole time.'

Poirot shook his head.

'No, my friend, there was a moment when you were not all together. There was a moment when you could not have been all together, or it would not have been necessary to call to Monsieur Lawrence to come and join you on the balcony.'

'I'd forgotten that,' I admitted. 'But it was only for a moment.'

'Long enough.'

'Long enough for what?'

Poirot's smile became rather enigmatical.

'Long enough for a gentleman who had once studied medicine to gratify a very natural interest and curiosity.'

Our eyes met. Poirot's were pleasantly vague. He got up and hummed a little tune. I watched him suspiciously.

'Poirot,' I said, 'what was in this particular little bottle?'

Poirot looked out of the window.

'Hydro-chloride of strychnine,' he said, over his shoulder, continuing to hum.

'Good heavens!' I said it quite quietly. I was not surprised. I had expected that answer.

'They use the pure hydro-chloride of strychnine very little – only occasionally for pills. It is the official solution, Liq. Strychnine Hydro-clor. that is used in most medicines. That is why the finger-marks have remained undisturbed since then.'

'How did you manage to take this photograph?'

'I dropped my hat from the balcony,' explained Poirot simply. 'Visitors were not permitted below at that hour, so, in spite of my many apologies, Mademoiselle Cynthia's colleague had to go down and fetch it for me.'

'Then you knew what you were going to find?'

'No, not at all. I merely realized that it was possible, from your story, for Monsieur Lawrence to go to the poison cupboard. The possibility had to be confirmed, or eliminated.'

'Poirot,' I said, 'your gaiety does not deceive me. This is a very important discovery.'

'I do not know,' said Poirot. 'But one thing does strike me. No doubt it has struck you too.'

'What is that?'

'Why, that there is altogether too much strychnine about this case. This is the third time we run up against it. There was strychnine in Mrs Inglethorp's tonic. There is the strychnine sold across the counter at Styles St Mary by Mace. Now we have more strychnine, handled by one of the household. It is confusing; and, as you know, I do not like confusion.'

Before I could reply, one of the other Belgians opened the door and stuck his head in.

'There is a lady below, asking for Mr Hastings.'

'A lady?'

I jumped up. Poirot followed me down the stairs. Mary Cavendish was standing in the doorway.

'I have been visiting an old woman in the village,' she explained, 'and as Lawrence told me you were with Monsieur Poirot I thought I would call for you.'

'Alas, madame,' said Poirot, 'I thought you had come to honour me with a visit!'

'I will some day, if you ask me,' she promised him, smiling.

'That is well. If you should need a father confessor, madame' – she started ever so slightly – 'remember, Papa Poirot is always at your service.'

She stared at him for a few minutes, as though seeking to read some deeper meaning into his words. Then she turned abruptly away.

'Come, will you not walk back with us too, Monsieur Poirot?'

'Enchanted, madame.'

All the way to Styles, Mary talked fast and feverishly. It struck me that in some way she was nervous of Poirot's eyes.

The weather had broken, and the sharp wind was almost autumnal in its shrewishness. Mary shivered a little, and buttoned her black sports coat closer. The wind through the trees made a mournful noise, like some giant sighing.

We walked up to the great door of Styles, and at once the knowledge came to us that something was wrong.

Dorcas came running out to meet us. She was crying and wringing her hands. I was aware of other servants huddled together in the background, all eyes and ears.

'Oh, m'am! Oh, m'am! I don't know how to tell you –'

'What is it, Dorcas?' I asked impatiently. 'Tell us at once.'

'It's those wicked detectives. They've arrested him – they've arrested Mr Cavendish!'

'Arrested Lawrence?' I gasped.

I saw a strange look come into Dorcas's eyes.

'No, sir. Not Mr Lawrence – Mr John.'

Behind me, with a wild cry, Mary Cavendish fell heavily against me, and as I turned to catch her I met the quiet triumph in Poirot's eyes.

CHAPTER 11

THE CASE FOR THE PROSECUTION

The trial of John Cavendish for the murder of his stepmother took place two months later.

Of the intervening weeks I will say little, but my admiration and sympathy went out unfeignedly to Mary Cavendish. She ranged herself passionately on her husband's side, scorning the mere idea of his guilt, and fought for him tooth and nail.

I expressed my admiration to Poirot, and he nodded thoughtfully. 'Yes, she is of those women who show at their best in adversity. It brings out all that is sweetest and truest in them. Her pride and her jealousy have –'

'Jealousy?' I queried.

'Yes. Have you not realized that she is an unusually jealous woman? As I was saying, her pride and jealousy have been laid aside. She thinks of nothing but her husband, and the terrible fate that is hanging over him.'

He spoke very feelingly, and I looked at him earnestly, remembering that last afternoon, when he had been deliberating whether or no to speak. With his tenderness for 'a woman's happiness', I felt glad that the decision had been taken out of his hands.

'Even now,' I said, 'I can hardly believe it. You see, up to the very last minute, I thought it was Lawrence!'

Poirot grinned.

'I know you did.'

'But John! My old friend John!'

'Every murderer is probably somebody's old friend,' observed Poirot philosophically. 'You cannot mix up sentiment and reason.'

'I must say I think you might have given me a hint.'

'Perhaps, *mon ami*, I did not do so, just because he *was* your old friend.'

I was rather disconcerted by this, remembering how I had busily passed on to John what I believed to be Poirot's views concerning Bauerstein. He, by the way, had been acquitted of the charge brought against him. Nevertheless, although he had been too clever for them this time, and the charge of espionage could not be brought home to him, his wings were pretty well clipped for the future.

I asked Poirot whether he thought John would be condemned. To my intense surprise, he replied that, on the contrary, he was extremely likely to be acquitted.

'But Poirot –' I protested.

'Oh, my friend, have I not said to you all along that I have no proofs. It is one thing to know that a man is guilty, it is quite another matter to prove him so. And, in this case, there is terribly little evidence. That is the whole trouble. I, Hercule Poirot, know, but I lack the last link in my chain. And unless I can find that missing link –' He shook his head gravely.

'When did you first suspect John Cavendish?' I asked, after a minute or two.

'Did you not suspect him at all?'

'No, indeed.'

'Not after that fragment of conversation you overheard between Mrs Cavendish and her mother-in-law, and her subsequent lack of frankness at the inquest?'

'No.'

'Did you not put two and two together, and reflect that if it was not Alfred Inglethorp who was quarrelling with his wife – and you remember, he strenuously denied it at the inquest – it must be either Lawrence or John? Now, if it was Lawrence, Mary Cavendish's conduct was just as inexplicable. But if, on the other hand, it was John, the whole thing was explained quite naturally.'

'So,' I cried, a light breaking in upon me, 'it was John who quarrelled with his mother that afternoon?'

'Exactly.'

'And you have known this all along?'

'Certainly. Mrs Cavendish's behaviour could only be explained that way.'

'And yet you say he may be acquitted?'

Poirot shrugged his shoulders.

'Certainly I do. At the police court proceedings, we shall hear the case for the prosecution, but in all probability his solicitors will advise him to reserve his defence. That will be sprung upon us at the trial. And – ah, by the way, I have a word of caution to give you, my friend. I must not appear in the case.'

'What?'

'No. Officially, I have nothing to do with it. Until I have found that last link in my chain, I must remain behind the scenes. Mrs Cavendish must think I am working for her husband, not against him.'

'I say, that's playing it a bit low down,' I protested.

'Not at all. We have to deal with a most clever and unscrupulous man, and we must use any means in our power – otherwise he will slip through our fingers. That is why I have been careful to remain in the background. All the discoveries have been made by Japp, and Japp will take all the credit. If I am called upon to give evidence at all' – he smiled broadly – 'it will probably be as witness for the defence.'

I could hardly believe my ears.

'It is quite *en règle*,' continued Poirot. 'Strangely enough, I can give evidence that will demolish one contention of the prosecution.'

'Which one?'

'The one that relates to the destruction of the will. John Cavendish did not destroy that will.'

Poirot was a true prophet. I will not go into the details of the police court proceedings, as it involves many tiresome repetitions. I will merely state baldly that John Cavendish reserved his defence, and was duly committed for trial.

September found us all in London. Mary took a house in Kensington, Poirot being included in the family party.

I myself had been given a job at the War Office, so was able to see them continually.

As the weeks went by, the state of Poirot's nerves grew worse and worse. That 'last link' he talked about was still lacking. Privately, I hoped it might remain so, for what happiness could there be for Mary, if John were not acquitted?

On September 15th John Cavendish appeared in the dock of the Old Bailey, charged with 'The Wilful Murder of Emily Agnes Inglethorp', and pleaded 'Not Guilty'.

Sir Ernest Heavywether, the famous K.C., had been engaged to defend him.

Mr Philips, K.C., opened the case for the Crown.

The murder, he said, was a most premeditated and cold-blooded one. It was neither more nor less than the deliberate poisoning of a fond and trusting woman by the stepson to whom she had been more than a mother. Ever since his boyhood, she had supported him. He and his wife had lived at Styles Court in every luxury, surrounded by her care and attention. She had been their kind and generous benefactress.

He proposed to call witnesses to show how the prisoner, a

profligate and spendthrift, had been at the end of his financial tether, and had also been carrying on an intrigue with a certain Mrs Raikes, a neighbouring farmer's wife. This having come to his stepmother's ears, she taxed him with it on the afternoon before her death, and a quarrel ensued, part of which was overheard. On the previous day, the prisoner had purchased strychnine at the village chemist's shop, wearing a disguise by means of which he hoped to throw the onus of the crime upon another man – to wit, Mrs Inglethorp's husband, of whom he had been bitterly jealous. Luckily for Mr Inglethorp, he had been able to produce an unimpeachable alibi.

On the afternoon of July 17th, continued Counsel, immediately after the quarrel with her son, Mrs Inglethorp made a new will. This will was found destroyed in the grate of her bedroom the following morning, but evidence had come to light which showed that it had been drawn up in favour of her husband. Deceased had already made a will in his favour before her marriage, but – and Mr Philips wagged an expressive forefinger – the prisoner was not aware of that. What had induced the deceased to make a fresh will, with the old one still extant, he could not say. She was an old lady, and might possibly have forgotten the former one; or – this seemed to him more likely – she may have had an idea that it was revoked by her marriage, as there had been some conversation on the subject. Ladies were not always very well versed in legal knowledge. She had, about a year before, executed a will in favour of the prisoner. He would call evidence to show that it was the prisoner who ultimately handed his stepmother her coffee on the fatal night. Later in the evening, he had sought admission to her room, on which occasion, no doubt, he found an opportunity of destroying the will which, as far as he knew, would render the one in his favour valid.

The prisoner had been arrested in consequence of the discovery, in his room, by Detective-Inspector Japp – a most brilliant officer – of the identical phial of strychnine which had been sold at the village chemist's to the supposed Mr Inglethorp on the day before the murder. It would be for the jury to decide whether or no these damning facts constituted an overwhelming proof of the prisoner's guilt.

And, subtly implying that a jury which did not so decide was quite unthinkable, Mr Philips sat down and wiped his fore-head.

The first witnesses for the prosecution were mostly those who had been called at the inquest, the medical evidence being again taken first.

Sir Ernest Heavywether, who was famous all over England for the unscrupulous manner in which he bullied witnesses, only asked two questions.

'I take it, Dr Bauerstein, that strychnine, as a drug, acts quickly?'

'Yes.'

'And that you are unable to account for the delay in this case?'

'Yes.'

'Thank you.'

Mr Mace identified the phial handed him by Counsel as that sold by him to 'Mr Inglethorp'. Pressed, he admitted that he only knew Mr Inglethorp by sight. He had never spoken to him. The witness was not cross-examined.

Alfred Inglethorp was called, and denied having purchased the poison. He also denied having quarrelled with his wife. Various witnesses testified to the accuracy of these statements.

The gardeners' evidence as to the witnessing of the will was taken, and then Dorcas was called.

Dorcas, faithful to her 'young gentlemen', denied strenuously that it could have been John's voice she heard, and resolutely declared, in the teeth of everything, that it was Mr Inglethorp who had been in the boudoir with her mistress. A rather wistful smile passed across the face of the prisoner in the dock. He knew only too well how useless her gallant defiance was, since it was not the object of the defence to deny this point. Mrs Cavendish, of course, could not be called upon to give evidence against her husband.

After various questions on other matters, Mr Philips asked:

'In the month of June last, do you remember a parcel arriving for Mr Lawrence Cavendish from Parkson's?'

Dorcas shook her head.

'I don't remember, sir. It may have done, but Mr Lawrence was away from home part of June.'

'In the event of a parcel arriving for him whilst he was away, what would be done with it?'

'It would either be put in his room or sent on after him.'

'By you?'

'No, sir, I should leave it on the hall table. It would be Miss Howard who would attend to anything like that.'

Evelyn Howard was called and, after being examined on other points, was questioned as to the parcel.

'Don't remember. Lots of parcels come. Can't remember one special one.'

'You do not know if it was sent after Mr Lawrence Cavendish to Wales, or whether it was put in his room?'

'Don't think it was sent after him. Should have remembered if it was.'

'Supposing a parcel arrived addressed to Mr Lawrence Cavendish, and afterwards it disappeared, should you remark its absence?'

'No, don't think so. I should think someone had taken charge of it.'

'I believe, Miss Howard, that it was you who found this sheet of brown paper?' He held up the same dusty piece which Poirot and I had examined in the morning room at Styles.

'Yes, I did.'

'How did you come to look for it.'

'The Belgian detective who was employed on the case asked me to search for it.'

'Where did you eventually discover it?'

'On the top of – of – a wardrobe.'

'On the top of the prisoner's wardrobe?'

'I believe so.'

'Did you not find it yourself?'

'Yes.'

'Then you must know where you found it?'

'Yes, it was on the prisoner's wardrobe.'

'That is better.'

An assistant from Parkson's, Theatrical Costumiers, testified that on June 29th they had supplied a black beard to Mr L. Cavendish, as requested. It was ordered by letter, and a postal order was enclosed. No, they had not kept the letter. All transactions were entered in their books. They had sent the beard, as directed, to 'L. Cavendish, Esq., Styles Court.'

Sir Ernest Heavywether rose ponderously.

'Where was the letter written from?'

'From Styles Court.'

'The same address to which you sent the parcel?'

'Yes.'

Like a beast of prey, Heavywether fell upon him:

'How do you know?'

'I – I don't understand.'

'How do you know that letter came from Styles? Did you notice the postmark?'

'No – but –'

'Ah, you did *not* notice the postmark! And yet you affirm so confidently that it came from Styles. It might, in fact, have been any postmark?'

'Y – es.'

'In fact, the letter, though written on stamped notepaper, might have been posted from anywhere? From Wales, for instance?'

The witness admitted that such might be the case, and Sir Ernest signified that he was satisfied.

Elizabeth Wells, second housemaid at Styles, stated that after she had gone to bed she remembered that she had bolted the front door, instead of leaving it on the latch as Mr Inglethorp had requested. She had accordingly gone downstairs again to rectify her error. Hearing a slight noise in the West wing, she had peeped along the passage, and had seen Mr John Cavendish knocking at Mrs Inglethorp's door.

Sir Ernest Heavywether made short work of her, and under his unmerciful bullying she contradicted herself hopelessly, and Sir Ernest sat down again with a satisfied smile on his face.

With the evidence of Annie, as to the candle grease on the floor, and as to seeing the prisoner take the coffee into the boudoir, the proceedings were adjourned until the following day.

As we went home, Mary Cavendish spoke bitterly against the prosecuting counsel.

'That hateful man! What a net he has drawn around my poor John! How he twisted every little fact until he made it seem what it wasn't!'

'Well,' I said consolingly, 'it will be the other way about tomorrow.'

'Yes,' she said meditatively; then suddenly dropped her voice.

'Mr Hastings, you do not think – surely it could not have been Lawrence – oh, no, that could not be!'

But I myself was puzzled, and as soon as I was alone with Poirot I asked him what he thought Sir Ernest was driving at.

'Ah!' said Poirot appreciatively. 'He is a clever man, that Sir Ernest.'

'Do you think he believes Lawrence guilty?'

'I do not think he believes or cares anything! No, what he is trying for is to create such confusion in the minds of the jury that they are divided in their opinion as to which brother did it. He is endeavouring to make out that there is quite as much evidence against Lawrence as against John – and I am not at all sure that he will not succeed.'

Detective-Inspector Japp was the first witness called when the trial was reopened, and gave his evidence succinctly and briefly. After relating the earlier events, he proceeded:

'Acting on information received, Superintendent Summerhaye and myself searched the prisoner's room, during his temporary absence from the house. In his chest of drawers, hidden beneath some underclothing, we found: first, a pair of gold-rimmed pince-nez similar to those worn by Mr Inglethorp' – these were exhibited – 'secondly, this phial.'

The phial was that already recognized by the chemist's assistant, a tiny bottle of blue glass, containing a few grains of a white crystalline powder, and labelled: 'Strychnine Hydro-chloride. POISON.'

A fresh piece of evidence discovered by the detectives since the police court proceedings was a long, almost new piece of blotting-paper. It had been found in Mrs Inglethorp's cheque book, and on being reversed at a mirror, showed clearly the words: '. . . everything of which I die possessed I leave to my beloved husband Alfred Ing . . .' This placed beyond question the fact that the destroyed will had been in favour of the deceased lady's husband. Japp then produced the charred fragment of paper recovered from the grate, and this, with the discovery of the beard in the attic, completed his evidence.

But Sir Ernest's cross-examination was yet to come.

'What day was it when you searched the prisoner's room?'

'Tuesday, the 24th of July.'

'Exactly a week after the tragedy?'

'Yes.'

'You found these two objects, you say, in the chest of drawers. Was the drawer unlocked?'

'Yes.'

'Does it not strike you as unlikely that a man who had committed a crime should keep the evidence of it in an unlocked drawer for anyone to find?'

'He might have stowed them there in a hurry.'

'But you have just said it was a whole week since the crime. He would have had ample time to remove them and destroy them.'

'Perhaps.'

'There is no perhaps about it. Would he, or would he not have had plenty of time to remove and destroy them?'

'Yes.'

'Was the pile of underclothes under which the things were hidden heavy or light?'

'Heavyish.'

'In other words, it was winter underclothing. Obviously, the prisoner would not be likely to go to that drawer?'

'Perhaps not.'

'Kindly answer my question. Would the prisoner, in the hottest week of a hot summer, be likely to go to a drawer containing winter underclothing? Yes, or no?'

'No.'

'In that case, is it not possible that the articles in question might have been put there by a third person, and that the prisoner was quite unaware of their presence?'

'I should not think it likely.'

'But it is possible?'

'Yes.'

'That is all.'

More evidence followed. Evidence as to the financial difficulties in which the prisoner had found himself at the end of July. Evidence as to his intrigue with Mrs Raikes – poor Mary, that must have been bitter hearing for a woman of her pride. Evelyn Howard had been right in her facts, though her animosity against Alfred Inglethorp had caused her to jump to the conclusion that he was the person concerned.

Lawrence Cavendish was then put into the box. In a low voice, in answer to Mr Philips' questions, he denied having ordered anything from Parkson's in June. In fact, on June 29th, he had been staying away, in Wales.

Instantly, Sir Ernest's chin was shooting pugnaciously forward.

'You deny having ordered a black beard from Parkson's on June 29th?'

'I do.'

'Ah! In the event of anything happening to your brother, who will inherit Styles Court?'

The brutality of the question called a flush to Lawrence's pale face. The Judge gave vent to a faint murmur of disapprobation, and the prisoner in the dock leant forward angrily.

Heavywether cared nothing for his client's anger.

'Answer my question, if you please.'

'I suppose,' said Lawrence quietly, 'that I should.'

'What do you mean by you "suppose"? Your brother has no children. You *would* inherit it, wouldn't you?'

'Yes.'

'Ah, that's better,' said Heavywether, with ferocious geniality. 'And you'd inherit a good slice of money too, wouldn't you?'

'Really, Sir Ernest,' protested the Judge, 'these questions are not relevant.'

Sir Ernest bowed, and having shot his arrow proceeded.

'On Tuesday, the 17th July, you went, I believe, with another guest, to visit the dispensary at the Red Cross Hospital in Tadminster?'

'Yes.'

'Did you – while you happened to be alone for a few seconds – unlock the poison cupboard, and examine some of the bottles?'

'I – I – may have done so.'

'I put it to you that you did so?'

'Yes.'

Sir Ernest fairly shot the next question at him.

'Did you examine one bottle in particular?'

'No, I do not think so.'

'Be careful, Mr Cavendish, I am referring to a little bottle of Hydro-chloride of Strychnine.'

Lawrence was turning a sickly greenish colour.

'N – o – I am sure I didn't.'

'Then how do you account for the fact that you left the unmistakable impress of your finger-prints on it?'

The bullying manner was highly efficacious with a nervous disposition.

'I – I suppose I must have taken up the bottle.'

'I suppose so too! Did you abstract any of the contents of the bottle?'

'Certainly not.'

'Then why did you take it up?'

'I once studied to be a doctor. Such things naturally interest me.'

'Ah! So poisons "naturally interest" you, do they? Still, you waited to be alone before gratifying that "interest" of yours?'

'That was pure chance. If the others had been there, I should have done just the same.'

'Still, as it happens, the others were not there?'

'No, but –'

'In fact, during the whole afternoon, you were only alone for a couple of minutes, and it happened – I say, it happened – to be during those two minutes that you displayed your "natural interest" in Hydro-chloride of Strychnine?'

Lawrence stammered pitiably.

'I – I –'

With a satisfied and expressive countenance, Sir Ernest observed:

'I have nothing more to ask you, Mr Cavendish.'

This bit of cross-examination had caused great excitement in court. The heads of the many fashionably attired women present were busily laid together, and their whispers became so loud that the Judge angrily threatened to have the court cleared if there was not immediate silence.

There was little more evidence. The handwriting experts were called upon for their opinion of the signature of 'Alfred Inglethorp' in the chemist's poison register. They all declared unanimously that it was certainly not his handwriting, and gave it as their view that it might be that of the prisoner disguised. Cross-examined, they admitted that it might be the prisoner's handwriting cleverly counterfeited.

Sir Ernest Heavywether's speech in opening the case for the defence was not a long one, but it was backed by the full force of his emphatic manner. Never, he said, in the course of his long experience, had he known a charge of murder rest on slighter evidence. Not only was it entirely circumstantial, but the greater part of it was practically unproved. Let them take the testimony they had heard and sift it impartially. The strychnine had been found in a drawer in the prisoner's room. That drawer was an unlocked one, as he had pointed out, and he submitted that there was no evidence to prove that it was the prisoner who had concealed the poison there. It was, in fact, a wicked and malicious attempt on the part of some third person to fix the crime on the prisoner. The prosecution had been unable to produce a shred of evidence in support of their contention that it was the prisoner who ordered the black beard from Parkson's. The quarrel which had taken place between the prisoner and his stepmother was freely admitted, but both it and his financial embarrassments had been grossly exaggerated.

His learned friend – Sir Ernest nodded carelessly at Mr Philips – had stated that if prisoner were an innocent man, he would have come forward at the inquest to explain that it was he, and not Mr Inglethorp, who had been the participator in the quarrel. He thought the facts had been misrepresented. What had actually occurred was this. The prisoner, returning to the house on Tuesday evening, had been authoritatively told that there had been a violent quarrel between Mr and Mrs Inglethorp. No suspicion had entered the prisoner's head that anyone could possibly have mistaken his voice for that of Mr Inglethorp. He naturally concluded that his stepmother had had two quarrels.

The prosecution averred that on Monday, July 16th, the prisoner had entered the chemist's shop in the village, disguised as Mr Inglethorp. The prisoner, on the contrary, was at that time at a lonely spot called Marston's Spinney, where he had been summoned by an anonymous note, couched in blackmailing terms, and threatening to reveal certain matters to his wife unless he complied with its demands. The prisoner had, accordingly, gone to the appointed spot, and after waiting there vainly for half an hour had returned home. Unfortunately, he had met with no one on the way there or back who could vouch for the truth of his story, but luckily he had kept the note, and it would be produced as evidence.

As for the statement relating to the destruction of the will, the prisoner had formerly practised at the Bar, and was perfectly well aware that the will made in his favour a year before was automatically revoked by his stepmother's re-marriage. He would call evidence to show who did destroy the will, and it was possible that that might open up quite a new view of the case.

Finally, he would point out to the jury that there was evidence against other people besides John Cavendish. He would direct their attention to the fact that the evidence against Mr Lawrence Cavendish was quite as strong, if not stronger than that against his brother.

He would now call the prisoner.

John acquitted himself well in the witness-box. Under Sir Ernest's skilful handling, he told his tale credibly and well. The anonymous note received by him was produced, and handed to the jury to examine. The readiness with which he admitted his financial difficulties, and the disagreement with his stepmother, lent value to his denials.

At the close of his examination, he paused, and said:

'I should like to make one thing clear. I utterly reject and disapprove of Sir Ernest Heavywether's insinuations against my brother. My brother, I am convinced, had no more to do with the crime than I have.'

Sir Ernest merely smiled, and noted with a sharp eye that John's protest had produced a very favourable impression on the jury.

Then the cross-examination began.

'I understand you to say that it never entered your head that the witnesses at the inquest could possibly have mistaken your voice for that of Mr Inglethorp. Is not that very surprising?'

'No, I don't think so. I was told there had been a quarrel between my mother and Mr Inglethorp, and it never occurred to me that such was not really the case.'

'Not when the servant Dorcas repeated certain fragments of the conversation – fragments which you must have recognized?'

'I did not recognize them.'

'Your memory must be unusually short!'

'No, but we were both angry, and, I think, said more than

we meant. I paid very little attention to my mother's actual words.'

Mr Philips' incredulous sniff was a triumph of forensic skill. He passed on to the subject of the note.

'You have produced this note very opportunely. Tell me, is there nothing familiar about the handwriting of it?'

'Not that I know of.'

'Do you not think that it bears a marked resemblance to your own handwriting – carelessly disguised?'

'No, I do not think so.'

'I put it to you that it is your handwriting!'

'No.'

'I put it to you that, anxious to prove an alibi, you conceived the idea of a fictitious and rather incredible appointment, and wrote this note yourself in order to bear out your statement!'

'No.'

'Is it not a fact that, at the time you claim to have been waiting about at a solitary and unfrequented spot, you were really in the chemist's shop in Styles St Mary, where you purchased strychnine in the name of Alfred Inglethorp?'

'No, that is a lie.'

'I put it to you that, wearing a suit of Mr Inglethorp's clothes, with a black beard trimmed to resemble his, you were there – and signed the register in his name!'

'That is absolutely untrue.'

'Then I will leave the remarkable similarity of handwriting between the note, the register, and your own, to the consideration of the jury,' said Mr Philips, and sat down with the air of a man who had done his duty, but who was nevertheless horrified by such deliberate perjury.

After this, as it was growing late, the case was adjourned till Monday.

Poirot, I noticed, was looking profoundly discouraged. He had that little frown between the eyes that I knew so well.

'What is it, Poirot?' I inquired.

'Ah, *mon ami*, things are going badly, badly.'

In spite of myself, my heart gave a leap of relief. Evidently there was a likelihood of John Cavendish being acquitted.

When we reached the house, my little friend waved aside Mary's offer of tea.

'No, I thank you, madame. I will mount to my room.'

I followed him. Still frowning, he went across to the desk and took out a small pack of patience cards. Then he drew up a chair to the table, and to my utter amazement, began solemnly to build card houses!

My jaw dropped involuntarily, and he said at once:

'No, *mon ami*, I am not in my second childhood! I steady my nerves, that is all. This employment requires precision of the fingers. With precision of the fingers goes precision of the brain. And never have I needed that more than now!'

'What is the trouble?' I asked.

With a great thump on the table, Poirot demolished his carefully built-up edifice.

'It is this, *mon ami!* That I can build card houses seven storeys high, but I cannot' – thump – 'find' – thump – 'that last link of which I spoke to you.'

I could not quite tell what to say, so I held my peace, and he began slowly building up the cards again, speaking in jerks as he did so.

'It is done – so! By placing – one card – on another – with mathematical – precision!'

I watched the card house rising under his hands, storey by storey. He never hesitated or faltered. It was really almost like a conjuring trick.

'What a steady hand you've got,' I remarked. 'I believe I've only seen your hand shake once.'

'On an occasion when I was enraged, without doubt,' observed Poirot, with great placidity.

'Yes, indeed! You were in a towering rage. Do you remember? It was when you discovered that the lock of the despatch-case in Mrs Inglethorp's bedroom had been forced. You stood by the mantelpiece, twiddling the things on it in your usual fashion, and your hand shook like a leaf! I must say –'

But I stopped suddenly. For Poirot, uttering a hoarse and inarticulate cry, again annihilated his masterpiece of cards, and putting his hands over his eyes swayed backwards, and forwards, apparently suffering the keenest agony.

'Good heavens, Poirot!' I cried. 'What is the matter? Are you taken ill?'

'No, no,' he gasped. 'It is – it is – that I have an idea!'

'Oh!' I exclaimed, much relieved. 'One of your "little ideas"?'

'Ah, *ma foi*, no!' replied Poirot frankly. 'This time it is an idea gigantic! Stupendous! And you – *you*, my friend, have given it to me!'

Suddenly clasping me in his arms, he kissed me warmly on both cheeks, and before I had recovered from my surprise ran headlong from the room.

Mary Cavendish entered at that moment.

'What *is* the matter with Monsieur Poirot? He rushed past me crying out: "A garage! For the love of Heaven, direct me to a garage, madame!" And, before I could answer, he had dashed out into the street.'

I hurried to the window. True enough, there he was, tearing down the street, hatless, and gesticulating as he went. I turned to Mary with a gesture of despair.

'He'll be stopped by a policeman in another minute. There he goes, round the corner!'

Our eyes met, and we stared helplessly at one another.

'What can be the matter?'

I shook my head.

'I don't know. He was building card houses, when suddenly he said he had an idea, and rushed off as you saw.'

'Well,' said Mary, 'I expect he will be back before dinner.'

But night fell, and Poirot had not returned.

CHAPTER 12

THE LAST LINK

Poirot's abrupt departure had intrigued us all greatly. Sunday morning wore away, and still he did not reappear. But about three o'clock a ferocious and prolonged hooting outside drove us to the window, to see Poirot alighting from a car, accompanied by Japp and Summerhaye. The little man was transformed. He radiated an absurd complacency. He bowed with exaggerated respect to Mary Cavendish.

'Madame, I have your permission to hold a little *réunion* in the *salon?* It is necessary for every one to attend.'

Mary smiled sadly.

'You know, Monsieur Poirot, that you have *carte blanche* in every way.'

'You are too amiable, madame.'

Still beaming, Poirot marshalled us all into the drawing-room, bringing forward chairs as he did so.

'Miss Howard – here. Mademoiselle Cynthia. Monsieur Lawrence. The good Dorcas. And Annie. *Bien!* We must delay our proceedings a few minutes more until Mr Inglethorp arrives. I have sent him a note.'

Miss Howard rose immediately from her seat.

'If that man comes into the house, I leave it!'

'No, no!' Poirot went up to her and pleaded in a low voice.

Finally Miss Howard consented to return to her chair. A few minutes later Alfred Inglethorp entered the room.

The company once assembled, Poirot rose from his seat with the air of a popular lecturer, and bowed politely to his audience.

'*Messieurs, mesdames,* as you all know, I was called in by Monsieur John Cavendish to investigate this case. I at once examined the bedroom of the deceased which, by the advice of the doctors, had been kept locked, and was consequently exactly as it had been when the tragedy occurred. I found: first, a fragment of green material; secondly, a stain on the carpet near the window, still damp; thirdly, an empty box of bromide powders.

'To take the fragment of green material first, I found it caught in the bolt of the communicating door between that room and the adjoining one occupied by Mademoiselle Cynthia. I handed the fragment over to the police who did not consider it of much importance. Nor did they recognize it for what it was – a piece torn from a green land armlet.'

There was a little stir of excitement.

'Now there was only one person at Styles who worked on the land – Mrs Cavendish. Therefore it must have been Mrs Cavendish who entered deceased's room through the door communicating with Mademoiselle Cynthia's room.'

'But that door was bolted on the inside!' I cried.

'When I examined the room, yes. But in the first place we have only her word for it, since it was she who tried that particular door and reported it fastened. In the ensuing confusion she would have had ample opportunity to shoot the bolt across. I took an early opportunity of verifying my conjectures. To begin with, the fragment corresponds exactly with a tear in Mrs Cavendish's armlet. Also, at the inquest, Mrs Cavendish declared that she had heard, from her own room, the fall of the table by the bed. I took an early opportunity of testing that statement by stationing my friend Monsieur Hastings, in the left wing of the building, just outside Mrs Cavendish's door. I myself, in company with the police, went to the deceased's room, and whilst there I, apparently accidentally, knocked over the table in question, but found that, as I had expected, Monsieur Hastings had heard no sound at all. This confirmed my belief that Mrs Cavendish was not speaking the truth when she declared that she had been dressing in her room at the time of the tragedy. In fact, I was convinced that, far from having been in her own room, Mrs Cavendish was actually in the deceased's room when the alarm was given.'

I shot a quick glance at Mary. She was very pale, but smiling.

'I proceeded to reason on that assumption. Mrs Cavendish is in her mother-in-law's room. We will say that she is seeking for something and has not yet found it. Suddenly Mrs Inglethorp awakens and is seized with an alarming paroxysm. She flings out her arm, overturning the bed table, and then pulls desperately at the bell. Mrs Cavendish, startled, drops her candle, scattering the grease on the carpet. She picks it up, and retreats quickly to Mademoiselle Cynthia's room, closing the door behind her. She hurries out into the passage, for the servants must not find her where she is. But it is too late! Already footsteps are echoing along the gallery which connects the two wings. What can she do? Quick as thought, she hurries back to the young girl's room, and starts shaking her awake. The hastily aroused household come trooping down the passage. They are all busily battering at Mrs Inglethorp's door. It occurs to nobody that Mrs Cavendish has not arrived with the rest, but – and this is significant – I can find no one who saw her come from the other wing.' He looked at Mary Cavendish. 'Am I right, madame?'

She bowed her head.

'Quite right, monsieur. You understand that, if I had thought I would do my husband any good by revealing these facts, I would have done so. But it did not seem to me to bear upon the question of his guilt or innocence.'

'In a sense, that is correct, madame. But it cleared my mind of many misconceptions, and left me free to see other facts in their true significance.'

'The will!' cried Lawrence. 'Then it was you, Mary, who destroyed the will?'

She shook her head, and Poirot shook his also.

'No,' she said quietly. 'There is only one person who could possibly have destroyed that will – Mrs Inglethorp herself!'

'Impossible!' I exclaimed. 'She had only made it out that very afternoon!'

'Nevertheless, *mon ami*, it was Mrs Inglethorp. Because, in no other way can you account for the fact that, on one of the hottest days of the year, Mrs Inglethorp ordered a fire to be lighted in her room.'

I gave a gasp. What idiots we had been never to think of that fire as being incongruous! Poirot was continuing.

'The temperature on that day, messieurs, was 80° in the shade. Yet Mrs Inglethorp ordered a fire! Why? Because she wished to destroy something, and could think of no other way. You will remember that, in consequence of the War economies practised at Styles, no waste paper was thrown away. There was, therefore, no means of destroying a thick document such as a will. The moment I heard of a fire being lighted in Mrs Inglethorp's room, I leaped to the conclusion that it was to destroy some important document – possibly a will. So the discovery of the charred fragment in the grate was no surprise to me. I did not, of course, know at the time that the will in question had only been made that afternoon, and I will admit that, when I learnt that fact, I fell into a grievous error. I came to the conclusion that Mrs Inglethorp's determination to destroy her will arose as a direct consequence of the quarrel she had that afternoon, and that therefore the quarrel took place after, and not before, the making of the will.

'Here, as we know, I was wrong, and I was forced to abandon the idea. I faced the problem from a new standpoint. Now, at four o'clock, Dorcas overheard her mistress saying angrily: "You need not think that any fear of publicity, or scandal between husband

and wife will deter me." I conjectured, and conjectured rightly, that these words were addressed, not to her husband, but to Mr John Cavendish. At five o'clock, an hour later, she uses almost the same words, but the standpoint is different. She admits to Dorcas, "I don't know what to do; scandal between husband and wife is a dreadful thing." At four o'clock she has been angry, but completely mistress of herself. At five o'clock she is in violent distress, and speaks of having had "a great shock".

'Looking at the matter psychologically, I drew one deduction which I was convinced was correct. The second "scandal" she spoke of was not the same as the first – and it concerned herself!

'Let us reconstruct. At four o'clock, Mrs Inglethorp quarrels with her son, and threatens to denounce him to his wife – who, by the way, overheard the greater part of the conversation. At four-thirty, Mrs Inglethorp, in consequence of a conversation on the validity of wills, makes a will in favour of her husband, which the two gardeners witness. At five o'clock, Dorcas finds her mistress in a state of considerable agitation, with a slip of paper – "a letter", Dorcas thinks – in her hand, and it is then that she orders the fire in her room to be lighted. Presumably, then, between four-thirty and five o'clock, something has occurred to occasion a complete revolution of feeling, since she is now as anxious to destroy the will, as she was before to make it. What was that something?

'As far as we know, she was quite alone during that half-hour. Nobody entered or left that boudoir. What then occasioned this sudden change of sentiment?

'One can only guess, but I believe my guess to be correct. Mrs Inglethorp had no stamps in her desk. We know this, because later she asked Dorcas to bring her some. Now in the opposite corner of the room stood her husband's desk – locked. She was anxious to find some stamps, and, according to my theory, she tried her own keys in the desk. That one of them fitted I know. She therefore opened the desk, and in searching for the stamps she came across something else – that slip of paper which Dorcas saw in her hand, and which assuredly was never meant for Mrs Inglethorp's eyes. On the other hand, Mrs Cavendish believed that the slip of paper to which her mother-in-law clung so tenaciously was a written proof of her own husband's infidelity. She demanded it from Mrs Inglethorp who assured her, quite truly, that it had nothing to do with that matter. Mrs Cavendish did not believe her. She thought that Mrs Inglethorp was shielding her stepson. Now Mrs Cavendish is a very resolute woman, and, behind her mask of reserve, she was madly jealous of her husband. She determined to get hold of that paper at all costs, and in this resolution chance came to her aid. She happened to pick up the key of Mrs Inglethorp's despatch-case, which had been lost that morning. She knew that her mother-in-law invariably kept all important papers in this particular case.

'Mrs Cavendish, therefore, made her plans as only a woman driven desperate through jealousy could have done. Some time in the evening she unbolted the door leading into Mademoiselle Cynthia's room. Possibly she applied oil to the hinges, for I found that it opened quite noiselessly when I tried it. She put off her project until the early hours of the morning as being safer, since the servants were accustomed to hearing her move about her room at that time. She dressed completely in her land kit, and made her way quietly through Mademoiselle Cynthia's room into that of Mrs Inglethorp.'

He paused a moment, and Cynthia interrupted:

'But I should have woken up if anyone had come through my room?'

'Not if you were drugged, mademoiselle.'

'Drugged?'

'*Mais, oui!*'

'You remember' – he addressed us collectively again – 'that through all the tumult and noise next door Mademoiselle Cynthia slept. That admitted of two possibilities. Either her sleep was feigned – which I did not believe – or her unconsciousness was induced by artificial means.

'With this latter idea in my mind, I examined all the coffee-cups most carefully, remembering that it was Mrs Cavendish who had brought Mademoiselle Cynthia her coffee the night before. I took a sample from each cup, and had them analysed – with no result. I had counted the cups carefully, in the event of one having been removed. Six persons had taken coffee, and six cups were duly found. I had to confess myself mistaken.

'Then I discovered that I had been guilty of a very grave oversight. Coffee had been brought in for seven persons, not six, for Dr Bauerstein had been there that evening. This changed the face of the whole affair, for there was now one cup missing. The servants noticed nothing, since Annie, the housemaid, who took in the coffee, brought in seven cups, not knowing that Mr Inglethorp never drank it, whereas Dorcas, who cleared them away the following morning, found six as usual – or strictly speaking she found five, the sixth being the one found broken in Mrs Inglethorp's room.

'I was confident that the missing cup was that of Mademoiselle Cynthia. I had an additional reason for that belief in the fact that all the cups found contained sugar, which Mademoiselle Cynthia never took in her coffee. My attention was attracted by the story of Annie about some "salt" on the tray of cocoa which she took every night to Mrs Inglethorp's room. I accordingly secured a sample of that cocoa, and sent it to be analysed.'

'But that had already been done by Dr Bauerstein,' said Lawrence quickly.

'Not exactly. The analyst was asked by him to report whether strychnine was, or was not, present. He did not have it tested, as I did, for a narcotic.'

'For a narcotic?'

'Yes. Here is the analyst's report. Mrs Cavendish administered a safe, but effectual, narcotic to both Mrs Inglethorp and Mademoiselle Cynthia. And it is possible that she had a *mauvais quart d'heure* in consequence! Imagine her feelings when her mother-in-law is suddenly taken ill and dies, and immediately after she hears the word "Poison"! She has believed that the sleeping draught she administered was perfectly harmless, but there is no doubt that for one terrible moment she must have feared that Mrs Inglethorp's death lay at her door. She is seized with panic, and under its influence she hurries downstairs, and quickly drops the coffee-cup and saucer used by Mademoiselle Cynthia into a large brass vase, where it is discovered later by Monsieur Lawrence. The remains of the cocoa she dare not touch. Too many eyes are upon her. Guess at her relief when strychnine is mentioned, and she discovers that after all the tragedy is not her doing.

'We are now able to account for the symptoms of strychnine

poisoning being so long in making their appearance. A narcotic taken with strychnine will delay the action of the poison for some hours.'

Poirot paused. Mary looked up at him, the colour slowly rising in her face.

'All you have said is quite true, Monsieur Poirot. It was the most awful hour of my life. I shall never forget it. But you are wonderful. I understand now –'

'What I meant when I told you that you could safely confess to Papa Poirot, eh? But you would not trust me.'

'I see everything now,' said Lawrence. 'The drugged cocoa, taken on top of the poisoned coffee, amply accounts for the delay.'

'Exactly. But was the coffee poisoned, or was it not? We come to a little difficulty here, since Mrs Inglethorp never drank it.'

'What?' The cry of surprise was universal.

'No. You will remember my speaking of a stain on the carpet in Mrs Inglethorp's room? There were some peculiar points about that stain. It was still damp, it exhaled a strong odour of coffee, and imbedded in the nap of the carpet I found some little splinters of china. What had happened was plain to me, for not two minutes before I had placed my little case on the table near the window, and the table, tilting up, had deposited it upon the floor on precisely the identical spot. In exactly the same way, Mrs Inglethorp had laid down her cup of coffee on reaching her room the night before, and the treacherous table had played her the same trick.

'What happened next is mere guesswork on my part, but I should say that Mrs Inglethorp picked up the broken cup and placed it on the table by the bed. Feeling in need of a stimulant of some kind, she heated up her cocoa, and drank it off then and there. Now we are faced with a new problem. We know the cocoa contained no strychnine. The coffee was never drunk. Yet the strychnine must have been administered between seven and nine o'clock that evening. What third medium was there – a medium so suitable for disguising the taste of strychnine that it is extraordinary no one has thought of it?' Poirot looked around the room, and then answered himself impressively. 'Her medicine!'

'Do you mean that the murderer introduced the strychnine into her tonic?' I cried.

'There was no need to introduce it. It was already there – in the mixture. The strychnine that killed Mrs Inglethorp was the identical strychnine prescribed by Dr Wilkins. To make that clear to you, I will read you an extract from a book on dispensing which I found in the Dispensary of the Red Cross Hospital at Tadminster:

'The following prescription has become famous in textbooks:

Strychninae Sulph	gr. 1
Potass Bromide	3vi
Aqua ad	3viii
Fiat Mistura	

This solution deposits in a few hours the greater part of the strychnine salt as an insoluble bromide in transparent crystals. A lady in England lost her life by taking a similar mixture: the precipitated strychnine collected at the bottom, and in taking the last dose she swallowed nearly all of it!

'Now there was, of course, no bromide in Dr Wilkins' prescription, but you will remember that I mentioned an empty box of bromide powders. One or two of those powders introduced into the full bottle of medicine would effectually precipitate the strychnine, as the book describes, and cause it to be taken in the last dose. You will learn later that the person who usually poured out Mrs Inglethorp's medicine was always extremely careful not to shake the bottle, but to leave the sediment at the bottom of it undisturbed.

'Throughout the case, there have been evidences that the tragedy was intended to take place on Monday evening. On that day, Mrs Inglethorp's bell wire was neatly cut, and on Monday evening Mademoiselle Cynthia was spending the night with friends, so that Mrs Inglethorp would have been quite alone in the right wing, completely shut off from help of any kind, and would have died, in all probability, before medical aid could have been summoned. But in her hurry to be in time for the village entertainment Mrs Inglethorp forgot to take her medicine, and the next day she lunched away from home, so that the last – and fatal – dose was actually taken twenty-four hours later than had been anticipated by the murderer; and it is owing to that delay that the final proof – the last link of the chain – is now in my hands.'

Amid breathless excitement, he held out three thin strips of paper.

'A letter in the murderer's own handwriting, *mes amis!* Had it been a little clearer in its terms, it is possible that Mrs Inglethorp, warned in time, would have escaped. As it was, she realized her danger, but not the manner of it.'

In the deathly silence, Poirot pieced together the slips of paper and, clearing his throat, read:

Dearest Evelyn,

You will be anxious at hearing nothing. It is all right – only it will be tonight instead of last night. You understand. There's a good time coming once the old woman is dead and out of the way. No one can possibly bring home the crime to me. That idea of yours about the bromides was a stroke of genius! But we must be very circumspect. A false step –

'Here, my friends, the letter breaks off. Doubtless the writer was interrupted; but there can be no question as to his identity. We all know his handwriting and –'

A howl that was almost a scream broke the silence.

'You devil! How did you get it?'

A chair was overturned. Poirot skipped nimbly aside. A quick movement on his part, and his assailant fell with a crash.

'*Messieurs, mesdames,*' said Poirot, with a flourish, 'let me introduce you to the murderer, Mr Alfred Inglethorp!'

CHAPTER 13

···

POIROT EXPLAINS

'Poirot, you old villain,' I said, 'I've half a mind to strangle you! What do you mean by deceiving me as you have done?'

We were sitting in the library. Several hectic days lay behind us. In the room below, John and Mary were together once more, while Alfred Inglethorp and Miss Howard were in custody. Now at last, I had Poirot to myself, and could relieve my still burning curiosity.

Poirot did not answer me for a moment, but at last he said:

'I did not deceive you, *mon ami*. At most, I permitted you to deceive yourself.'

'Yes, but why?'

'Well, it is difficult to explain. You see, my friend, you have a nature so honest, and a countenance so transparent, that – *enfin*, to conceal your feelings is impossible! If I had told you my ideas, the very first time you saw Mr Alfred Inglethorp that astute gentleman would have – in your so expressive idiom – "smelt a rat"! And then, *bonjour* to our chances of catching him!'

'I think that I have more diplomacy than you give me credit for.'

'My friend,' besought Poirot, 'I implore you, do not enrage yourself! Your help has been of the most invaluable. It is but the extremely beautiful nature that you have which made me pause.'

'Well,' I grumbled, a little mollified, 'I still think you might have given me a hint.'

'But I did, my friend. Several hints. You would not take them. Think now, did I ever say to you that I believed John Cavendish guilty? Did I not, on the contrary, tell you that he would almost certainly be acquitted?'

'Yes, but –'

'And did I not immediately afterwards speak of the difficulty of bringing the murderer to justice? Was it not plain to you that I was speaking of two entirely different persons?'

'No,' I said, 'it was not plain to me!'

'Then again,' continued Poirot, 'at the beginning, did I not repeat to you several times that I didn't want Mr Inglethorp arrested *now*? That should have conveyed something to you.'

'Do you mean to say you suspected him as long ago as that?'

'Yes. To begin with, whoever else might benefit by Mrs Inglethorp's death, her husband would benefit the most. There was no getting away from that. When I went up to Styles with you that first day, I had no idea as to how the crime had been committed, but from what I knew of Mr Inglethorp I fancied that it would be very hard to find anything to connect him with it. When I arrived at the château, I realized at once that it was Mrs Inglethorp who had burnt the will; and there, by the way, you cannot complain, my friend, for I tried my best to force on you the significance of that bedroom fire in midsummer.'

'Yes, yes,' I said impatiently. 'Go on.'

'Well, my friend, as I say, my views as to Mr Inglethorp's guilt were very much shaken. There was, in fact, so much evidence against him that I was inclined to believe that he had not done it.'

'When did you change your mind?'

'When I found that the more efforts I made to clear him, the more efforts he made to get himself arrested. Then, when I discovered that Inglethorp had nothing to do with Mrs Raikes, and that in fact it was John Cavendish who was interested in that quarter, I was quite sure.'

'But why?'

'Simply this. If it had been Inglethorp who was carrying on an intrigue with Mrs Raikes, his silence was perfectly comprehensible. But, when I discovered that it was known all over the village that it was John who was attracted by the farmer's pretty wife, his silence bore quite a different interpretation. It was nonsense to pretend that he was afraid of the scandal, as no possible scandal could attach to him. This attitude of his gave me furiously to think, and I was slowly forced to the conclusion that Alfred Inglethorp wanted to be arrested. *Eh bien!* from that moment, I was equally determined that he should not be arrested.'

'Wait a moment. I don't see why he wished to be arrested?'

'Because, *mon ami*, it is the law of your country that a man once acquitted can never be tried again for the same offence. Aha! but it was clever – his idea! Assuredly, he is a man of method. See here, he knew that in his position he was bound to be suspected, so he conceived the exceedingly clever idea of preparing a lot of manufactured evidence against himself. He wished to be suspected. He wished to be arrested. He would then produce his irreproachable alibi – and, hey presto, he was safe for life!'

'But I still don't see how he managed to prove his alibi, and yet go to the chemist's shop?'

Poirot stared at me in surprise.

'Is it possible? My poor friend! You have not yet realized that it was Miss Howard who went to the chemist's shop?'

'Miss Howard?'

'But, certainly. Who else? It was most easy for her. She is of a good height, her voice is deep and manly; moreover, remember, she and Inglethorp are cousins, and there is a distinct resemblance between them, especially in their gait and bearing. It was simplicity itself. They are a clever pair!'

'I am still a little fogged as to how exactly the bromide business was done,' I remarked.

'*Bon!* I will reconstruct for you as far as possible. I am inclined to think that Miss Howard was the master mind in that affair. You remember her once mentioning that her father was a doctor? Possibly she dispensed his medicines for him, or she may have taken the idea from one of the many books lying about when Mademoiselle Cynthia was studying for her exam. Anyway, she was familiar with the fact that the addition of a bromide to a mixture containing strychnine would cause the precipitation of the latter. Probably the idea came to her quite suddenly. Mrs Inglethorp had a box of bromide powders, which she occasionally took at night. What could be more easier than quietly to dissolve one or more of those powders in Mrs Inglethorp's large-sized bottle of medicine when it came from Coot's? The risk is practically nil. The tragedy will not take place until nearly a fortnight later. If anyone has seen either of them touching the medicine, they will have forgotten it by that time. Miss Howard will have engineered her quarrel, and departed from the house. The lapse of time, and her absence, will defeat all suspicion. Yes, it was a clever idea! If they had left it alone, it is possible the crime might never have been brought home to them. But they were not satisfied. They tried to be too clever – and that was their undoing.'

Poirot puffed at his tiny cigarette, his eyes fixed on the ceiling.

'They arranged a plan to throw suspicion on John Cavendish, by buying strychnine at the village chemist's, and signing the register in his handwriting.

'On Monday Mrs Inglethorp will take the last dose of her medicine. On Monday, therefore, at six o'clock, Alfred Inglethorp arranges to be seen by a number of people at a spot far removed from the village. Miss Howard has previously made up a cock-and-bull story about him and Mrs Raikes to account for his holding his tongue afterwards. At six o'clock, Miss Howard, disguised as Alfred Inglethorp, enters the chemist's shop, with her story about a dog, obtains the strychnine, and writes the name of Alfred Inglethorp in John's handwriting, which she had previously studied carefully.

'But, as it will never do if John, too, can prove an alibi, she writes him an anonymous note – still copying his handwriting – which takes him to a remote spot where it is exceedingly unlikely that anyone will see him.

'So far, all goes well. Miss Howard goes back to Middlingham. Alfred Inglethorp returns to Styles. There is nothing that can compromise him in any way, since it is Miss Howard who has the strychnine, which, after all, is only wanted as a blind to throw suspicion on John Cavendish.

'But now a hitch occurs. Mrs Inglethorp does not take her medicine that night. The broken bell, Cynthia's absence – arranged by Inglethorp through his wife – all these are wasted. And then – he makes his slip.

'Mrs Inglethorp is out, and he sits down to write to his accomplice, who, he fears, may be in a panic at the non-success of their plan. It is probable that Mrs Inglethorp returned earlier than he expected. Caught in the act, and somewhat flurried, he hastily shuts and locks his desk. He fears that if he remains in the room he may have to open it again, and that Mrs Inglethorp might catch sight of the letter before he could snatch it up. So he goes out and walks in the woods, little dreaming that Mrs Inglethorp will open his desk, and discover the incriminating document.

'But this, as we know, is what happened. Mrs Inglethorp reads it, and becomes aware of the perfidy of her husband and Evelyn Howard, though, unfortunately, the sentence about the bromide conveys no warning to her mind. She knows that she is in danger – but is ignorant of where the danger lies. She decides to say nothing to her husband, but sits down and writes to her solicitor, asking him to come on the morrow, and she also determines to destroy immediately the will which she has just made. She keeps the fatal letter.'

'It was to discover that letter, then, that her husband forced the lock of the despatch-case?'

'Yes, and from the enormous risk he ran we can see how fully he realized its importance. That letter excepted, there was absolutely nothing to connect him with the crime.'

'There's only one thing I can't make out, why didn't he destroy it at once when he got hold of it?'

'Because he did not dare take the biggest risk of all – that of keeping it on his own person.'

'I don't understand.'

'Look at it from his point of view. I have discovered that there were only five short minutes in which he could have taken it – the five minutes immediately before our own arrival on the scene, for before that time Annie was brushing the stairs, and would have seen anyone who passed going to the right wing. Figure to yourself the scene! He enters the room, unlocking the door by means of one of the other door-keys – they were all much alike. He hurries to the despatch-case – it is locked, and the keys are nowhere to be seen. That is a terrible blow to him, for it means that his presence in the room cannot be concealed as he had hoped. But he sees clearly that everything must be risked for the sake of that damning piece of evidence. Quickly, he forces the lock with a penknife, and turns over the papers until he finds what he is looking for.

'But now a fresh dilemma arises: he dare not keep that piece of paper on him. He may be seen leaving the room – he may be searched. If the paper is found on him, it is certain doom. Probably, at this minute, too, he hears the sounds below of Mr Wells and John leaving the boudoir. He must act quickly. Where can he hide this terrible slip of paper? The contents of the waste-paper basket are kept and, in any case, are sure to be examined. There are no means of destroying it; and he dare not keep it. He looks round, and he sees – what do you think, *mon ami?*'

I shook my head.

'In a moment he has torn the letter into long thin strips, and rolling them up into spills he thrusts them hurriedly in amongst the other spills in the vase on the mantelpiece.'

I uttered an exclamation.

'No one would think of looking there,' Poirot continued. 'And he will be able, at his leisure, to come back and destroy this solitary piece of evidence against him.'

'Then, all the time, it was in the spill vase in Mrs Inglethorp's bedroom, under our very noses?' I cried.

Poirot nodded.

'Yes, my friend. That is where I discovered my "last link", and I owe that very fortunate discovery to you.'

'To me?'

'Yes. Do you remember telling me that my hand shook as I was straightening the ornaments on the mantelpiece?'

'Yes, but I don't see –'

'No, but I saw. Do you know, my friend, I remembered that earlier in the morning, when we had been there together, I had straightened all the objects on the mantelpiece. And, if they were already straightened, there would be no need to straighten them again, unless, in the meantime, someone else had touched them.'

'Dear me,' I murmured, 'so that is the explanation of your extraordinary behaviour. You rushed down to Styles, and found it still there?'

'Yes, and it was a race for time.'

'But I still can't understand why Inglethorp was such a fool to leave it there when he had plenty of opportunity to destroy it.'

'Ah, but he had no opportunity. I saw to that.'

'You?'

'Yes. Do you remember reproving me for taking the household into my confidence on the subject?'

'Yes.'

'Well, my friend, I saw there was just one chance. I was not sure then if Inglethorp was the criminal or not, but if he was I reasoned that he would not have the paper on him, but would have hidden it somewhere, and by enlisting the sympathy of the household I could effectually prevent his destroying it. He was already under suspicion, and by making the matter public I secured the services of about ten amateur detectives, who would be watching him unceasingly, and being himself aware of their watchfulness he would not dare seek further to destroy the document. He was, therefore, forced to depart from the house, leaving it in the spill vase.'

'But surely Miss Howard had ample opportunities of aiding him.'

'Yes, but Miss Howard did not know of the paper's existence. In accordance with their pre-arranged plan, she never spoke to Alfred Inglethorp. They were supposed to be deadly enemies, and until John Cavendish was safely convicted they neither of them dared risk a meeting. Of course, I had a watch kept on Mr Inglethorp, hoping that sooner or later he would lead me to the hiding-place. But he was too clever to take any chances. The paper was safe where it was; since no one had thought of looking there in the first week, it was not likely they would do so afterwards. But for your lucky remark, we might never have been able to bring him to justice.'

'I understand that now; but when did you first begin to suspect Miss Howard?'

'When I discovered that she had told a lie at the inquest about the letter she had received from Mrs Inglethorp.'

'Why, what was there to lie about?'

'You saw that letter? Do you recall its general appearance?'

'Yes – more or less.'

'You will recollect, then, that Mrs Inglethorp wrote a very distinctive hand, and left large clear spaces between her words. But if you look at the date at the top of the letter you will notice that "July 17th" is quite different in this respect. Do you see what I mean?'

'No,' I confessed, 'I don't.'

'You do not see that that letter was not written on the 17th, but on the 7th – the day after Miss Howard's departure? The "1" was written in before the "7" to turn it into the "17th".'

'But why?'

'That is exactly what I asked myself. Why does Miss Howard suppress the letter written on the 17th, and produce this faked one instead? Because she did not wish to show the letter of the 17th. Why, again? And at once a suspicion dawned in my mind. You will remember my saying that it was wise to beware of people who were not telling the truth.'

'And yet,' I cried indignantly, 'after that, you gave me two reasons why Miss Howard could not have committed the crime!'

'And very good reasons too,' replied Poirot. 'For a long time they were a stumbling-block to me until I remembered a very significant fact: that she and Alfred Inglethorp were cousins. She could not have committed the crime single-handed, but the reasons against that did not debar her from being an accomplice. And, then, there was that rather overvehement hatred of hers! It concealed a very opposite emotion. There was, undoubtedly, a tie of passion between them long before he came to Styles. They had already arranged their infamous plot – that he should marry this rich, but rather foolish old lady, induce her to make a will leaving her money to him, and then gain their ends by a very cleverly conceived crime. If all had gone as they planned, they would probably have left England, and lived together on their poor victim's money.

'They are a very astute and unscrupulous pair. While suspicion was to be directed against him, she would be making quiet preparations for a very different *dénouement*. She arrives from Middlingham with all the compromising items in her possession. No suspicion attaches to her. No notice is paid to her coming and going in the house. She hides the strychnine and glasses in John's room. She puts the beard in the attic. She will see to it that sooner or later they are duly discovered.'

'I don't quite see why they tried to fix the blame on John,' I remarked. 'It would have been much easier for them to bring the crime home to Lawrence.'

'Yes, but that was mere chance. All the evidence against him arose out of pure accident. It must, in fact, have been distinctly annoying to the pair of schemers.'

'His manner was unfortunate,' I observed thoughtfully.

'Yes. You realize, of course, what was the back of that?'

'No.'

'You did not understand that he believed Mademoiselle Cynthia guilty of the crime?'

'No,' I exclaimed, astonished. 'Impossible!'

'Not at all. I myself nearly had the same idea. It was in my mind when I asked Mr Wells that first question about the will. Then there were the bromide powders which she had made up, and her clever male impersonations, as Dorcas recounted them to us. There was really more evidence against her than anyone else.'

'You are joking, Poirot!'

'No. Shall I tell you what made Monsieur Lawrence turn so pale when he first entered his mother's room on the fatal night? It was because, whilst his mother lay there, obviously poisoned, he saw, over your shoulder, that the door into Mademoiselle Cynthia's room was unbolted.'

'But he declared that he saw it bolted!' I cried.

'Exactly,' said Poirot dryly. 'And that was just what confirmed my suspicion that it was not. He was shielding Mademoiselle Cynthia.'

'But why should he shield her?'

'Because he is in love with her.'

I laughed.

'There, Poirot, you are quite wrong! I happen to know for a fact that, far from being in love with her, he positively dislikes her.'

'Who told you that, *mon ami*?'

'Cynthia herself.'

'*La pauvre petite!* And she was concerned?'

'She said that she did not mind at all.'

'Then she certainly did mind very much,' remarked Poirot. 'They are like that – *les femmes!*'

'What you say about Lawrence is a great surprise to me,' I said.

'But why? It was most obvious. Did not Monsieur Lawrence make the sour face every time Mademoiselle Cynthia spoke and laughed with his brother? He had taken it into his long head that Mademoiselle Cynthia was in love with Monsieur John. When he entered his mother's room and saw her obviously poisoned, he jumped to the conclusion that Mademoiselle Cynthia knew something about the matter. He was nearly driven desperate. First he crushed the coffee-cup to powder under his feet, remembering that *she* had gone up with his mother the night before, and he determined that there should be no chance of testing its contents. Thenceforward, he strenuously, and quite uselessly, upheld the theory of "Death from natural causes".'

'And what about the "extra coffee-cup"?'

'I was fairly certain that it was Mrs Cavendish who had hidden it, but I had to make sure. Monsieur Lawrence did not know at all what I meant; but, on reflection, he came to the conclusion that if he could find an extra coffee-cup anywhere his lady love would be cleared of suspicion. And he was perfectly right.'

'One thing more. What did Mrs Inglethorp mean by her dying words?'

'They were, of course, an accusation against her husband.'

'Dear me, Poirot,' I said with a sigh, 'I think you have explained everything. I am glad it has all ended so happily. Even John and his wife are reconciled.'

'Thanks to me.'

'How do you mean – thanks to you?'

'My dear friend, do you realize that it was simply and solely the trial which has brought them together again? That John Cavendish still loved his wife, I was convinced. Also, that she was equally in love with him. But they had drifted very far apart. It all arose from a misunderstanding. She married him without love. He knew it. He is a sensitive man in his way, he would not force himself upon her if she did not want him. And, as he withdrew, her love awoke. But they are both unusually proud, and their pride held them inexorably apart. He drifted into an entanglement with Mrs Raikes, and she deliberately cultivated the friendship of Dr Bauerstein. Do you remember the day of John Cavendish's arrest, when you found me deliberating over a big decision?'

'Yes, I quite understood your distress.'

'Pardon me, *mon ami*, but you did not understand it in the least. I was trying to decide whether or not I would clear John Cavendish at once. I could have cleared him – though it might have meant a failure to convict the real criminals. They were entirely in the dark as to my real attitude up to the very last moment – which partly accounts for my success.'

'Do you mean that you could have saved John Cavendish from being brought to trial?'

'Yes, my friend. But I eventually decided in favour of "a woman's happiness". Nothing but the great danger through which they have passed could have brought these two proud souls together again.'

I looked at Poirot in silent amazement. The colossal cheek of the little man! Who on earth but Poirot would have thought of a trial for murder as a restorer of conjugal happiness!

'I perceive your thoughts, *mon ami*,' said Poirot, smiling at me. 'No one but Hercule Poirot would have attempted such a thing! And you are wrong in condemning it. The happiness of one man and woman is the greatest thing in all the world.'

His words took me back to earlier events. I remembered Mary as she lay white and exhausted on the sofa, listening, listening. There had come the sound of the bell below. She had started up. Poirot had opened the door, and meeting her agonized eyes had nodded gently. 'Yes, madame,' he said. 'I have brought him back to you.' He had stood aside, and as I went out I had seen the look in Mary's eyes, as John Cavendish had caught his wife in his arms.

'Perhaps you are right, Poirot,' I said gently. 'Yes, it is the greatest thing in the world.'

Suddenly, there was a tap at the door, and Cynthia peeped in.

'I – I – only –'

'Come in,' I said, springing up.

She came in, but did not sit down.

'I – only wanted to tell you something –'

'Yes?'

Cynthia fidgeted with a little tassel for some moments, then, suddenly exclaiming: 'You dears!' kissed first me and then Poirot, and rushed out of the room again.

'What on earth does this mean?' I asked, surprised.

It was very nice to be kissed by Cynthia, but the publicity of the salute rather impaired the pleasure.

'It means that she has discovered Monsieur Lawrence does not dislike her as much as she thought,' replied Poirot philosophically.

'But –'

'Here he is.'

Lawrence at that moment passed the door.

'Eh! Monsieur Lawrence,' called Poirot. 'We must congratulate you, is it not so?'

Lawrence blushed, and then smiled awkwardly. A man in love is a sorry spectacle. Now Cynthia had looked charming.

I sighed.

'What is it, *mon ami?*'

'Nothing,' I said sadly. 'They are two delightful women!'

'And neither of them is for you?' finished Poirot. 'Never mind. Console yourself, my friend. We may hunt together again, who knows? And then –'

THE MURDER ON THE LINKS

To My Husband
a fellow enthusiast for detective stories
and to whom I am indebted for much
helpful advice and criticism

CONTENTS

A FELLOW-TRAVELLER

I believe that a well-known anecdote exists to the effect that a young writer, determined to make the commencement of his story forcible and original enough to catch and rivet the attention of the most blasé of editors, penned the following sentence:

'"Hell!" said the Duchess.'

Strangely enough, this tale of mine opens in much the same fashion. Only the lady who gave utterance to the exclamation was not a duchess.

It was a day in early June. I had been transacting some business in Paris and was returning by the morning service to London, where I was still sharing rooms with my old friend, the Belgian ex-detective, Hercule Poirot.

The Calais express was singularly empty – in fact, my own compartment held only one other traveller. I had made a somewhat hurried departure from the hotel and was busy assuring myself that I had duly collected all my traps, when the train started. Up till then I had hardly noticed my companion, but I was now violently recalled to the fact of her existence. Jumping up from her seat, she let down the window and stuck her head out, withdrawing it a moment later with the brief and forcible ejaculation 'Hell!'

Now I am old-fashioned. A woman, I consider, should be womanly. I have no patience with the modern neurotic girl who jazzes from morning to night, smokes like a chimney, and uses language which would make a Billingsgate fishwoman blush!

I looked up, frowning slightly, into a pretty, impudent face, surmounted by a rakish little red hat. A thick cluster of black curls hid each ear. I judged that she was little more than seventeen, but her face was covered with powder, and her lips were quite impossibly scarlet.

Nothing abashed, she returned my glance, and executed an expressive grimace.

'Dear me, we've shocked the kind gentleman!' she observed to an imaginary audience. 'I apologize for my language! Most unladylike, and all that, but, oh, Lord, there's reason enough for it! Do you know I've lost my only sister?'

'Really?' I said politely. 'How unfortunate.'

'He disapproves!' remarked the lady. 'He disapproves utterly – of me, and my sister – which last is unfair, because he hasn't seen her!'

I opened my mouth, but she forestalled me.

'Say no more! Nobody loves me! I shall go into the garden and eat worms! Boohoo. I am crushed!'

She buried herself behind a large comic French paper. In a minute or two I saw her eyes stealthily peeping at me over the top. In spite of myself I could not help smiling, and in a minute she had tossed the paper aside, and had burst into a merry peal of laughter.

'I knew you weren't such a mutt as you looked,' she cried.

Her laughter was so infectious that I could not help joining in, though I hardly cared for the word 'mutt'.

'There! Now we're friends!' declared the minx. 'Say you're sorry about my sister –'

'I am desolated!'

'That's a good boy!'

'Let me finish. I was going to add that, although I am desolated, I can manage to put up with her absence very well.' I made a little bow.

But this most unaccountable of damsels frowned and shook her head.

'Cut it out. I prefer the "dignified disapproval" stunt. Oh, your face! "Not one of us", it said. And you were right there – though, mind you, it's pretty hard to tell nowadays. It's not everyone who can distinguish between a demi and a duchess. There now, I believe I've shocked you again! You've been dug out of the backwoods, you have. Not that I mind that. We could do with a few more of your sort. I just hate a fellow who gets fresh. It makes me mad.'

She shook her head vigorously.

'What are you like when you're mad?' I inquired with a smile.

'A regular little devil! Don't care what I say, or what I do, either! I nearly did a chap in once. Yes, really. He'd have deserved it too.'

'Well,' I begged, 'don't get mad with me.'

'I shan't. I like you – did the first moment I set eyes on you. But you looked so disapproving that I never thought we should make friends.'

'Well, we have. Tell me something about yourself.'

'I'm an actress. No – not the kind you're thinking of. I've been on the boards since I was a kid of six – tumbling.'

'I beg your pardon,' I said, puzzled.

'Haven't you ever seen child acrobats?'

'Oh, I understand!'

'I'm American born, but I've spent most of my life in England. We've got a new show now –'

'We?'

'My sister and I. Sort of song and dance, and a bit of patter, and a dash of the old business thrown in. It's quite a new idea, and it hits them every time. There's going to be money in it –'

My new acquaintance leaned forward, and discoursed volubly, a great many of her terms being quite unintelligible to me. Yet I found myself evincing an increasing interest in her. She seemed such a curious mixture of child and woman. Though perfectly worldly-wise, and able, as she expressed it, to take care of herself, there was yet something curiously ingenuous in her single-minded attitude towards life, and her wholehearted determination to 'make good'.

We passed through Amiens. The name awakened many memories. My companion seemed to have an intuitive knowledge of what was in my mind.

'Thinking of the War?'

I nodded.

'You were through it, I suppose?'

'Pretty well. I was wounded once, and after the Somme they invalided me out altogether. I'm a sort of private secretary now to an MP.'

'My! That's brainy!'

'No, it isn't. There's really awfully little to do. Usually a couple of hours every day sees me through. It's dull work too. In fact,

I don't know what I should do if I hadn't got something to fall back upon.'

'Don't say you collect bugs!'

'No. I share rooms with a very interesting man. He's a Belgian – an ex-detective. He's set up as a private detective in London, and he's doing extraordinarily well. He's really a very marvellous little man. Time and again he has proved to be right where the official police have failed.'

My companion listened with widening eyes.

'Isn't that interesting now? I just adore crime. I go to all the mysteries on the movies. And when there's a murder on I just devour the papers.'

'Do you remember the Styles Case?' I asked.

'Let me see, was that the old lady who was poisoned? Somewhere down in Essex?'

I nodded.

'That was Poirot's first big case. Undoubtedly, but for him the murderer would have escaped scot-free. It was a most wonderful bit of detective work.'

Warming to my subject, I ran over the heads of the affair, working up to the triumphant and unexpected dénouement.

The girl listened spellbound. In fact, we were so absorbed that the train drew into Calais station before we realized it.

I secured a couple of porters, and we alighted on the platform. My companion held out her hand.

'Goodbye, and I'll mind my language better in future.'

'Oh, but surely you'll let me look after you on the boat?'

'Mayn't be on the boat. I've got to see whether that sister of mine got aboard after all anywhere. But thanks, all the same.'

'Oh, but we're going to meet again, surely? Aren't you even going to tell me your name?' I cried, as she turned away.

She looked over her shoulder.

'Cinderella,' she said, and laughed.

But little did I think when and how I should see Cinderella again.

CHAPTER 2

AN APPEAL FOR HELP

It was five minutes past nine when I entered our joint sitting-room for breakfast on the following morning. My friend Poirot, exact to the minute as usual, was just tapping the shell of his second egg.

He beamed upon me as I entered.

'You have slept well, yes? You have recovered from the crossing so terrible? It is a marvel, almost you are exact this morning. *Pardon*, but your tie is not symmetrical. Permit that I rearrange him.'

Elsewhere, I have described Hercule Poirot. An extraordinary little man! Height, five feet four inches, egg-shaped head carried a little to one side, eyes that shone green when he was excited, stiff military moustache, air of dignity immense! He was neat and dandified in appearance. For neatness of any kind he had an absolute passion. To see an ornament set crookedly, or a speck of dust, or a slight disarray in one's attire, was torture to the little man until he could ease his feelings by remedying the matter. 'Order' and 'Method' were his gods. He had a certain disdain for tangible evidence, such as footprints and cigarette ash, and would maintain that, taken by themselves, they would never enable a detective to solve a problem. Then he would tap his egg-shaped head with absurd complacency, and remark with great satisfaction: 'The true work, it is done from *within*. *The little grey cells* – remember always the little grey cells, *mon ami*.'

I slipped into my seat, and remarked idly, in answer to Poirot's greeting, that an hour's sea passage from Calais to Dover could hardly be dignified by the epithet 'terrible'.

'Anything interesting come by the post?' I asked.

Poirot shook his head with a dissatisfied air.

'I have not yet examined my letters, but nothing of interest arrives nowadays. The great criminals, the criminals of method, they do not exist.'

He shook his head despondently, and I roared with laughter.

'Cheer up, Poirot, the luck will change. Open your letters. For all you know, there may be a great case looming on the horizon.'

Poirot smiled, and taking up the neat little letter opener with which he opened his correspondence he slit the tops of the several envelopes that lay by his plate.

'A bill. Another bill. It is that I grow extravagant in my old age. Aha! a note from Japp.'

'Yes?' I pricked up my ears. The Scotland Yard Inspector had more than once introduced us to an interesting case.

'He merely thanks me (in his fashion) for a little point in the Aberystwyth Case on which I was able to set him right. I am delighted to have been of service to him.'

Poirot continued to read his correspondence placidly.

'A suggestion that I should give a lecture to our local Boy Scouts. The Countess of Forfanock will be obliged if I will call and see her. Another lap-dog without doubt! And now for the last. Ah –'

I looked up, quick to notice the change of tone. Poirot was reading attentively. In a minute he tossed the sheet over to me.

'This is out of the ordinary, *mon ami*. Read for yourself.'

The letter was written on a foreign type of paper, in a bold characteristic hand:

Villa Geneviève,
Merlinville-sur-Mer,
France.

Dear Sir, – I am in need of the services of a detective and, for reasons which I will give you later, do not wish to call in the official police. I have heard of you from several quarters, and all reports go to show that you are not only a man of decided ability, but one who also knows how to be discreet. I do not wish to trust details to the post, but, on account of a secret I possess, I go in daily fear of my life. I am convinced that the danger is imminent, and therefore I beg that you will lose no time in crossing to France, I will send a car to meet you at Calais, if you will wire me when you are arriving. I shall be obliged if you will drop all cases you have on hand, and devote yourself solely to my interests. I am prepared to pay any compensation necessary. I shall probably need your services for a considerable period of time, as it may be

necessary for you to go out to Santiago, where I spent several years
of my life. I shall be content for you to name your own fee.
   Assuring you once more that the matter is urgent.
   Yours faithfully,
   P. T. Renauld.

Below the signature was a hastily scrawled line, almost il-
legible:

'For God's sake, come!'

I handed the letter back with quickened pulses.

'At last!' I said. 'Here is something distinctly out of the ordinary.'

'Yes, indeed,' said Poirot meditatively.

'You will go of course,' I continued.

Poirot nodded. He was thinking deeply. Finally he seemed to
make up his mind, and glanced up at the clock. His face was
very grave.

'See you, my friend, there is no time to lose. The Continental
express leaves Victoria at 11 o'clock. Do not agitate yourself.
There is plenty of time. We can allow ten minutes for discussion.
You accompany me, *n'est-ce pas?*'

'Well –'

'You told me yourself that your employer needed you not for
the next few weeks.'

'Oh, that's all right. But this Mr Renauld hints strongly that his
business is private.'

'Ta-ta-ta! I will manage M. Renauld. By the way, I seem to
know the name?'

'There's a well-known South American millionaire fellow. His
name's Renauld. I don't know whether it could be the same.'

'But without doubt. That explains the mention of Santiago.
Santiago is in Chile, and Chile it is in South America! Ah; but
we progress finely! You remarked the postscript? How did it
strike you?'

I considered.

'Clearly he wrote the letter keeping himself well in hand, but
at the end his self-control snapped and, on the impulse of the
moment, he scrawled those four desperate words.'

But my friend shook his head energetically.

'You are in error. See you not that while the ink of the signature is nearly black, that of the postscript is quite pale?'

'Well?' I said, puzzled.

'*Mon Dieu, mon ami*, but use your little grey cells. Is it not obvious? Mr Renault wrote his letter. Without blotting it, he re-read it carefully. Then, not on impulse, but deliberately, he added those last words, and blotted the sheet.'

'But why?'

'*Parbleu!* so that it should produce the effect upon me that it has upon you.'

'What?'

'*Mais oui* – to make sure of my coming! He re-read the letter and was dissatisfied. It was not strong enough!'

He paused, and then added softly, his eyes shining with that green light that always betokened inward excitement:

'And so, *mon ami*, since that postscript was added, not on impulse, but soberly, in cold blood, the urgency is very great, and we must reach him as soon as possible.'

'Merlinville,' I murmured thoughtfully. 'I've heard of it, I think.'

Poirot nodded.

'It is a quiet little place – but chic! It lies about midway between Boulogne and Calais. Mr Renauld has a house in England, I suppose?'

'Yes, in Rutland Gate, as far as I remember. Also a big place in the country, somewhere in Hertfordshire. But I really know very little about him, he doesn't do much in a social way. I believe he has large South American interests in the City, and has spent most of his life out in Chile and the Argentine.'

'Well, we shall hear all the details from the man himself. Come, let us pack. A small suit-case each, and then a taxi to Victoria.'

Eleven o'clock saw our departure from Victoria on our way to Dover. Before starting Poirot had dispatched a telegram to Mr Renauld giving the time of our arrival at Calais.

'I'm surprised you haven't invested in a few bottles of some sea sick remedy, Poirot,' I observed maliciously, as I recalled our conversation at breakfast.

My friend, who was anxiously scanning the weather, turned a reproachful face upon me.

'Is it that you have forgotten the method most excellent of Laverguier? His system, I practise it always. One balances oneself, if you remember, turning the head from left to right, breathing in and out, counting six between each breath.'

'H'm,' I demurred. 'You'll be rather tired of balancing yourself and counting six by the time you get to Santiago, or Buenos Aires, or wherever it is you land.'

'*Quelle idée!* You do not figure to yourself that I shall go to Santiago?'

'Mr Renauld suggests it in his letter.'

'He did not know the methods of Hercule Poirot. I do not run to and fro, making journeys, and agitating myself. My work is done from within – *here* –' he tapped his forehead significantly.

As usual, this remark roused my argumentative faculty.

'It's all very well, Poirot, but I think you are falling into the habit of despising certain things too much. A fingerprint has led sometimes to the arrest and conviction of a murderer.'

'And has, without doubt, hanged more than one innocent man,' remarked Poirot dryly.

'But surely the study of fingerprints and footprints, cigarette ash, different kinds of mud, and other clues that comprise the minute observation of details – all these are of vital importance?'

'But certainly. I have never said otherwise. The trained observer, the expert, without doubt he is useful! But the others, the Hercules Poirots, they are above the experts! To them the experts bring the facts, their business is the method of the crime, its logical deduction, the proper sequence and order of the facts; above all, the true psychology of the case. You have hunted the fox, yes?'

'I have hunted a bit, now and again,' I said, rather bewildered by this abrupt change of subject. 'Why?'

'*Eh bien*, this hunting of the fox, you need the dogs, no?'

'Hounds,' I corrected gently. 'Yes, of course.'

'But yet,' Poirot wagged his finger at me. 'You did not descend from your horse and run along the ground smelling with your nose and uttering loud Ow Ows?'

In spite of myself I laughed immoderately. Poirot nodded in a satisfied manner.

'So. You leave the work of the d— hounds to the hounds. Yet you demand that I, Hercule Poirot, should make myself ridiculous by lying down (possibly on damp grass) to study hypothetical footprints, and should scoop up cigarette ash when I do not know one kind from the other. Remember the Plymouth Express mystery. The good Japp departed to make a survey of the railway line. When he returned, I, without having moved from my apartments, was able to tell him exactly what he had found.'

'So you are of the opinion that Japp wasted his time.'

'Not at all, since his evidence confirmed my theory. But *I* should have wasted my time if *I* had gone. It is the same with so called "experts". Remember the handwriting testimony in the Cavendish Case. One counsel's questioning brings out testimony as to the resemblances, the defence brings evidence to show dissimilarity. All the language is very technical. And the result? What we all knew in the first place. The writing was very like that of John Cavendish. And the psychological mind is faced with the question "Why?" Because it was actually his? Or because some one wished us to think it was his? I answered that question, *mon ami*, and answered it correctly.'

And Poirot, having effectually silenced, if not convinced me, leaned back with a satisfied air.

On the boat, I knew better than to disturb my friend's solitude. The weather was gorgeous, and the sea as smooth as the proverbial mill-pond, so I was hardly surprised when a smiling Poirot joined me on disembarking at Calais. A disappointment was in store for us, as no car had been sent to meet us, but Poirot put this down to his telegram having been delayed in transit.

'We will hire a car,' he said cheerfully. And a few minutes later saw us creaking and jolting along, in the most ramshackle of automobiles that ever plied for hire, in the direction of Merlinville.

My spirits were at their highest, but my little friend was observing me gravely.

'You are what the Scotch people call "fey", Hastings. It presages disaster.'

'Nonsense. At any rate, you do not share my feelings.'

'No, but I am afraid.'

'Afraid of what?'

'I do not know. But I have a premonition – a *je ne sais quoi!*'

He spoke so gravely that I was impressed in spite of myself.

'I have a feeling,' he said slowly, 'that this is going to be a big affair – a long, troublesome problem that will not be easy to work out.'

I would have questioned him further, but we were just coming into the little town of Merlinville, and we slowed up to inquire the way to the Villa Geneviève.

'Straight on, monsieur, through the town. The Villa Geneviève is about half a mile the other side. You cannot miss it. A big villa, overlooking the sea.'

We thanked our informant, and drove on, leaving the town behind. A fork in the road brought us to a second halt. A peasant was trudging towards us, and we waited for him to come up to us in order to ask the way again. There was a tiny villa standing right by the road, but it was too small and dilapidated to be the one we wanted. As we waited, the gate of it swung open and a girl came out.

The peasant was passing us now, and the driver leaned forward from his seat and asked for direction.

'The Villa Geneviève? Just a few steps up this road to the right, monsieur. You could see it if it were not for the curve.'

The chauffeur thanked him, and started the car again. My eyes were fascinated by the girl who still stood, with one hand on the gate, watching us. I am an admirer of beauty, and here was one whom nobody could have passed without remark. Very tall, with the proportions of a young goddess, her uncovered golden head gleaming in the sunlight, I swore to myself that she was one of the most beautiful girls I had ever seen. As we swung up the rough road, I turned my head to look after her.

'By Jove, Poirot,' I exclaimed, 'did you see that young goddess?'

Poirot raised his eyebrows.

'*Ça commence!*' he murmured. 'Already you have seen a goddess!'

'But, hang it all, wasn't she?'

'Possibly, I did not remark the fact.'

'Surely you noticed her?'

'*Mon ami*, two people rarely see the same thing. You, for instance, saw a goddess. I –' He hesitated.

'Yes?'

'I saw only a girl with anxious eyes,' said Poirot gravely.

But at that moment we drew up at a big green gate, and, simultaneously, we both uttered an exclamation. Before it stood an imposing *sergent de ville*. He held up his hand to bar our way.

'You cannot pass, messieurs.'

'But we wish to see Mr Renauld,' I cried. 'We have an appointment. This is his villa, isn't it?'

'Yes, monsieur, but –'

Poirot leaned forward.

'But what?'

'Monsieur Renauld was murdered this morning.'

CHAPTER 3

AT THE VILLA GENEVIÈVE

In a moment Poirot had leapt from the car, his eyes blazing with excitement.

'What is that you say? Murdered? When? How?'

The *sergent de ville* drew himself up.

'I cannot answer any questions, monsieur.'

'True. I comprehend.' Poirot reflected for a minute. 'The Commissary of Police, he is without doubt within?'

'Yes, monsieur.'

Poirot took out a card, and scribbled a few words on it.

'*Voilà!* Will you have the goodness to see that this card is sent in to the commissary at once?'

The man took it and, turning his head over his shoulder, whistled. In a few seconds a comrade joined him, and was handed Poirot's message. There was a wait of some minutes, and then a short, stout man with a huge moustache came bustling down to the gate. The *sergent de ville* saluted and stood aside.

'My dear Monsieur Poirot,' cried the newcomer, 'I am delighted to see you. Your arrival is most opportune.'

Poirot's face had lighted up.

'Monsieur Bex! This is indeed a pleasure.' He turned to me. 'This is an English friend of mine, Captain Hastings – Monsieur Lucien Bex.'

The commissary and I bowed to each other ceremoniously, and M. Bex turned once more to Poirot.

'*Mon vieux*, I have not seen you since 1909, that time in Ostend. You have information to give which may assist us?'

'Possibly you know it already. You were aware that I had been sent for?'

'No. By whom?'

'The dead man. It seems that he knew an attempt was going to be made on his life. Unfortunately he sent for me too late.'

'*Sacré tonnerre!*' ejaculated the Frenchman. 'So he foresaw his own murder. That upsets our theories considerably! But come inside.'

He held the gate open, and we commenced walking towards the house. M. Bex continued to talk:

'The examining magistrate, Monsieur Hautet, must hear of this at once. He has just finished examining the scene of the crime and is about to begin his interrogations.'

'When was the crime committed?' asked Poirot.

'The body was discovered this morning about nine o'clock. Madame Renauld's evidence and that of the doctors goes to show that death must have occurred about 2 am. But enter, I pray of you.'

We had arrived at the steps which led up to the front door of the villa. In the hall another *sergent de ville* was sitting. He rose at sight of the commissary.

'Where is Monsieur Hautet now?' inquired the latter.

'In the *salon*, monsieur.'

M. Bex opened a door to the left of the hall, and we passed in. M. Hautet and his clerk were sitting at a big round table. They looked up as we entered. The commissary introduced us, and explained our presence.

M. Hautet, the Juge d'Instruction, was a tall gaunt man, with piercing dark eyes, and a neatly cut grey beard, which he had a habit of caressing as he talked. Standing by the mantelpiece was an elderly man, with slightly stooping shoulders, who was introduced to us as Dr Durand.

'Most extraordinary,' remarked M. Hautet as the commissary finished speaking. 'You have the letter here, monsieur?'

Poirot handed it to him, and the magistrate read it.

'H'm! He speaks of a secret. What a pity he was not more explicit. We are much indebted to you, Monsieur Poirot. I hope you will do us the honour of assisting us in our investigations. Or are you obliged to return to London?'

'Monsieur le juge, I propose to remain. I did not arrive in time to prevent my client's death, but I feel myself bound in honour to discover the assassin.'

The magistrate bowed.

'These sentiments do you honour. Also, without doubt, Madame Renauld will wish to retain your services. We are expecting M. Giraud from the Sûreté in Paris any moment, and I am sure that you and he will be able to give each other mutual assistance in your investigations. In the meantime, I hope that you will do me the honour to be present at my interrogations, and I need hardly say that if there is any assistance you require it is at your disposal.'

'I thank you, monsieur. You will comprehend that at present I am completely in the dark. I know nothing whatever.'

M. Hautet nodded to the commissary, and the latter took up the tale:

'This morning, the old servant Françoise, on descending to start her work, found the front door ajar. Feeling a momentary alarm as to burglars, she looked into the dining-room, but seeing the silver was safe she thought no more about it, concluding that her master had, without doubt, risen early, and gone for a stroll.'

'Pardon, monsieur, for interrupting, but was that a common practice of his?'

'No, it was not, but old Françoise has the common idea as regards the English – that they are mad, and liable to do the most unaccountable things at any moment! Going to call her mistress as usual, a young maid, Léonie, was horrified to discover her gagged and bound, and almost at the same moment news was brought that Monsieur Renauld's body had been discovered, stone dead, stabbed in the back.'

'Where?'

'That is one of the most extraordinary features of the case. Monsieur Poirot, the body was lying face downwards, *in an open grave*.'

'What?'

'Yes. The pit was freshly dug – just a few yards outside the boundary of the villa grounds.'

'And it had been dead – how long?'

Dr Durand answered this.

'I examined the body this morning at ten o'clock. Death must have taken place at least seven, and possibly ten hours previously.'

'H'm! that fixes it at between midnight and 3 am.'

'Exactly, and Mrs Renauld's evidence places it at after 2 am, which narrows the field still farther. Death must have been instantaneous, and naturally could not have been self-inflicted.'

Poirot nodded, and the commissary resumed:

'Madame Renauld was hastily freed from the cords that bound her by the horrified servants. She was in a terrible condition of weakness, almost unconscious from the pain of her bonds. It appears that two masked men entered the bedroom, gagged and bound her, while forcibly abducting her husband. This we know at second hand from the servants. On hearing the tragic news, she fell at once into an alarming state of agitation. On arrival, Dr Durand immediately prescribed a sedative, and we have not yet been able to question her. But without doubt she will awake more calm, and be equal to bearing the strain of the interrogation.'

The commissary paused.

'And the inmates of the house, monsieur?'

'There is old Françoise, the housekeeper, she lived for many years with the former owners of the Villa Geneviève. Then there are two young girls, sisters, Denise and Léonie Oulard. Their home is in Merlinville, and they come of most respectable parents. Then there is the chauffeur whom Monsieur Renauld brought over from England with him, but he is away on a holiday. Finally there are Madame Renauld and her son, Monsieur Jack Renauld. He, too, is away from home at present.'

Poirot bowed his head. M. Hautet spoke:

'Marchaud!'

The *sergent de ville* appeared.

'Bring in the woman Françoise.'

The man saluted, and disappeared. In a moment or two he returned, escorting the frightened Françoise.

'Your name is Françoise Arrichet?'

'Yes, monsieur.'

'You have been a long time in service at the Villa Geneviève?'

'Eleven years with Madame la Vicomtesse. Then when she sold the Villa this spring, I consented to remain on with the English milor'. Never did I imagine –'

The magistrate cut her short.

'Without doubt, without doubt. Now, Françoise, in this matter of the front door, whose business was it to fasten it at night?'

'Mine, monsieur. Always I saw to it myself.'

'And last night?'

'I fastened it as usual.'

'You are sure of that?'

'I swear it by the blessed saints, monsieur.'

'What time would that be?'

'The same time as usual, half past ten, monsieur.'

'What about the rest of the household, had they gone up to bed?'

'Madame had retired some time before. Denise and Léonie went up with me. Monsieur was still in his study.'

'Then, if anyone unfastened the door afterwards, it must have been Monsieur Renauld himself?'

Françoise shrugged her broad shoulders.

'What should he do that for? With robbers and assassins passing every minute! A nice idea! Monsieur was not an imbecile. It is not as though he had had to let the lady out –'

The magistrate interrupted sharply:

'The lady? What lady do you mean?'

'Why, the lady who came to see him.'

'Had a lady been to see him that evening?'

'But yes, monsieur – and many other evenings as well.'

'Who was she? Did you know her?'

A rather cunning look spread over the woman's face.

'How should I know who it was?' she grumbled. 'I did not let her in last night.'

'Aha!' roared the examining magistrate, bringing his hand down with a bang on the table. 'You would trifle with the police, would you? I demand that you tell me at once the name of this woman who came to visit Monsieur Renauld in the evenings.'

'The police – the police,' grumbled Françoise. 'Never did I think that I should be mixed up with the police. But I know well enough who she was. It was Madame Daubreuil.'

The commissary uttered an exclamation, and leaned forward as though in utter astonishment.

'Madame Daubreuil – from the Villa Marguerite just down the road?'

'That is what I said, monsieur. Oh, she is a pretty one.'

The old woman tossed her head scornfully.

'Madame Daubreuil,' murmured the commissary. 'Impossible.'

'*Voilà*,' grumbled Françoise. 'That is all you get for telling the truth.'

'Not at all,' said the examining magistrate soothingly. 'We were surprised, that is all. Madame Daubreuil then, and Monsieur Renauld, they were –?' He paused delicately. 'Eh? It was that without doubt?'

'How should I know? But what will you? Monsieur, he was *milord anglais* – *très riche* – and Madame Daubreuil, she was poor, that one – and *très chic*, for all that she lives so quietly with her daughter. Not a doubt of it, she has had her history! She is no longer young, but *ma foi!* I who speak to you have seen the men's heads turn after her as she goes down the street. Besides lately, she had had more money to spend – all the town knows it. The little economies, they are at an end.' And Françoise shook her head with an air of unalterable certainty.

M. Hautet stroked his beard reflectively.

'And Madame Renauld?' he asked at length. 'How did she take this – friendship?'

Françoise shrugged her shoulders.

'She was always most amiable – most polite. One would say that she suspected nothing. But all the same, is it not so, the heart suffers, monsieur? Day by day, I have watched Madame grow paler and thinner. She was not the same woman who arrived here a month ago. Monsieur, too, has changed. He also has had his worries. One could see that he was on the brink of a crisis of the nerves. And who could wonder, with an affair conducted in such a fashion? No reticence, no discretion. *Style anglais*, without doubt!'

I bounded indignantly in my seat, but the examining magistrate was continuing his questions, undistracted by side issues.

'You say that Monsieur Renauld had not to let Madame Daubreuil out? Had she left, then?'

'Yes, monsieur. I heard them come out of the study and go to the door. Monsieur said goodnight, and shut the door after her.'

'What time was that?'

'About twenty-five minutes after ten, monsieur.'

'Do you know when Monsieur Renauld went to bed?'

'I heard him come up about ten minutes after we did. The stair creaks so that one hears everyone who goes up and down.'

'And that is all? You heard no sound of disturbance during the night?'

'Nothing whatever, monsieur.'

'Which of the servants came down the first in the morning?'

'I did, monsieur. At once I saw the door swinging open.'

'What about the other downstairs windows, were they all fastened?'

'Every one of them. There was nothing suspicious or out of place anywhere.'

'Good. Françoise, you can go.'

The old woman shuffled towards the door. On the threshold she looked back.

'I will tell you one thing, monsieur. That Madame Daubreuil she is a bad one! Oh, yes, one woman knows about another. She is a bad one, remember that.' And, shaking her head sagely, Françoise left the room.

'Léonie Oulard,' called the magistrate.

Léonie appeared dissolved in tears, and inclined to be hysterical. M. Hautet dealt with her adroitly. Her evidence was mainly concerned with the discovery of her mistress gagged and bound, of which she gave rather an exaggerated account. She, like Françoise, had heard nothing during the night.

Her sister, Denise, succeeded her. She agreed that her master had changed greatly of late.

'Every day he became more and more morose. He ate less. He was always depressed.' But Denise had her own theory. 'Without doubt it was the Mafia he had on his track! Two masked men – who else could it be? A terrible society that!'

'It is, of course, possible,' said the magistrate smoothly. 'Now, my girl, was it you who admitted Madame Daubreuil to the house last night?'

'Not *last* night, monsieur, the night before.'

'But Françoise has just told us that Madame Daubreuil was here last night?'

'No, monsieur. A lady *did* come to see Monsieur Renauld last night, but it was not Madame Daubreuil.'

Surprised, the magistrate insisted, but the girl held firm. She knew Madame Daubreuil perfectly by sight. This lady was dark also, but shorter, and much younger. Nothing could shake her statement.

'Had you ever seen this lady before?'

'Never, monsieur.' And then the girl added diffidently: 'But I think she was English.'

'English?'

'Yes, monsieur. She asked for Monsieur Renauld in quite good French, but the accent – however slight one can always tell it. Besides, when they came out of the study they were speaking in English.'

'Did you hear what they said? Could you understand it, I mean?'

'Me, I speak the English very well,' said Denise with pride. 'The lady was speaking too fast for me to catch what she said, but I heard Monsieur's last words as he opened the door for her.' She paused, and then repeated carefully and laboriously: '"Yeas – yeas – but for Gaud's saike go nauw!"'

'Yes, yes, but for God's sake go now!' repeated the magistrate.

He dismissed Denise and, after a moment or two for consideration, recalled Françoise. To her he propounded the question as to whether she had not made a mistake in fixing the night of Madame Daubreuil's visit. Françoise, however, proved unexpectedly obstinate. It was last night that Madame Daubreuil had come. Without doubt it was she. Denise wished to make herself interesting, *voilà tout!* So she had cooked up this fine tale about a strange lady. Airing her knowledge of English, too! Probably Monsieur had never spoken that sentence in English at all, and, even if he had, it proved nothing, for Madame Daubreuil spoke English perfectly, and generally used that language when talking to Monsieur and Madame Renauld. 'You see, Monsieur Jack, the son of Monsieur, was usually here, and he spoke the French very badly.'

The magistrate did not insist. Instead, he inquired about the chauffeur, and learned that only yesterday Monsieur Renauld had declared that he was not likely to use the car, and that Masters might just as well take a holiday.

A perplexed frown was beginning to gather between Poirot's eyes.

'What is it?' I whispered.

He shook his head impatiently, and asked a question:

'Pardon, Monsieur Bex, but without doubt Monsieur Renauld could drive the car himself?'

The commissary looked over at Françoise, and the old woman replied promptly:

'No, Monsieur did not drive himself.'

Poirot's frown deepened.

'I wish you would tell me what is worrying you,' I said impatiently.

'See you not? In his letter Monsieur Renauld speaks of sending the car for me to Calais.'

'Perhaps he meant a hired car,' I suggested.

'Doubtless, that is so. But why hire a car when you have one of your own? Why choose yesterday to send away the chauffeur on a holiday – suddenly, at a moment's notice? Was it that for some reason he wanted him out of the way before we arrived?'

CHAPTER 4

THE LETTER SIGNED 'BELLA'

Françoise had left the room. The magistrate was drumming thoughtfully on the table.

'Monsieur Bex,' he said at length, 'here we have directly conflicting testimony. Which are we to believe, Françoise or Denise?'

'Denise,' said the commissary decidedly. 'It was she who let the visitor in. Françoise is old and obstinate, and has evidently taken a dislike to Madame Daubreuil. Besides, our own knowledge tends to show that Renauld was entangled with another woman.'

'*Tiens!*' cried M. Hautet. 'We have forgotten to inform Monsieur Poirot of that.' He searched among the papers on the table, and finally handed the one he was in search of to my friend. 'This letter, Monsieur Poirot, we found in the pocket of the dead man's overcoat.'

Poirot took it and unfolded it. It was somewhat worn and crumpled, and was written in English in a rather unformed hand:

> *My Dearest One, – Why have you not written for so long? You do love me still, don't you? Your letters lately have been so different, cold, and strange, and now this long silence. It makes me afraid. If you were to stop loving me! But that's impossible – what a silly kid I am – always imagining things! But if you did stop loving me, I don't know what I should do – kill myself perhaps! I couldn't live without you. Sometimes I fancy another woman is coming between us. Let her look out, that's all – and you too! I'd as soon kill you as let her have you! I mean it.*
>
> *But there, I'm writing high-flown nonsense. You love me, and I love you – yes, love you, love you, love you!*
>
> *Your own adoring*
> *Bella.*

There was no address or date. Poirot handed it back with a grave face.

'And the assumption is –?'

The examining magistrate shrugged his shoulders.

'Obviously Monsieur Renauld was entangled with this English-woman – Bella! He comes over here, meets Madame Daubreuil, and starts an intrigue with her. He cools off to the other, and she instantly suspects something. This letter contains a distinct threat. Monsieur Poirot, at first sight the case seemed simplicity itself. Jealousy! The fact that Monsieur Renauld was stabbed in the back seemed to point distinctly to its being a woman's crime.'

Poirot nodded.

'The stab in the back, yes – but not the grave! That was

laborious work, hard work – no woman dug that grave, Monsieur. That was a man's doing.'

The commissary exclaimed excitedly:

'Yes, yes, you are right. We did not think of that.'

'As I said,' continued M. Hautet, 'at first sight the case seemed simple, but the masked men, and the letter you received from Monsieur Renauld, complicate matters. Here we seem to have an entirely different set of circumstances, with no relationship between the two. As regards the letter written to yourself, do you think it is possible that it referred in any way to this "Bella" and her threats?'

Poirot shook his head.

'Hardly. A man like Monsieur Renauld, who had led an adventurous life in out-of-the-way places, would not be likely to ask for protection against a woman.'

The examining magistrate nodded his head emphatically.

'My view exactly. Then we must look for the explanation of the letter –'

'In Santiago,' finished the commissary. 'I shall cable without delay to the police in that city, requesting full details of the murdered man's life out there, his love affairs, his business transactions, his friendships, and any enmities he may have incurred. It will be strange if, after that, we do not hold a clue to his mysterious murder.'

The commissary looked around for approval.

'Excellent!' said Poirot appreciatively.

'You have found no other letters from this Bella among Monsieur Renauld's effects?' asked Poirot.

'No. Of course one of our first proceedings was to search through his private papers in the study. We found nothing of interest, however. All seemed square and above-board. The only thing at all out of the ordinary was his will. Here it is.'

Poirot ran through the document.

'So. A legacy of a thousand pounds to Mr Stonor – who is he, by the way?'

'Monsieur Renauld's secretary. He remained in England, but was over here once or twice for a weekend.'

'And everything else left unconditionally to his beloved wife, Eloise. Simply drawn up, but perfectly legal. Witnessed by the two servants, Denise and Françoise. Nothing so very unusual about that.' He handed it back.

'Perhaps,' began Bex, 'you did not notice –'

'The date?' twinkled Poirot. 'But, yes, I noticed it. A fortnight ago. Possibly it marks his first intimation of danger. Many rich men die intestate through never considering the likelihood of their demise. But it is dangerous to draw conclusions prematurely. It points, however, to his having a real liking and fondness for his wife, in spite of his amorous intrigues.'

'Yes,' said M. Hautet doubtfully. 'But it is possibly a little unfair on his son, since it leaves him entirely dependent on his mother. If she were to marry again, and her second husband obtained an ascendancy over her, this boy might never touch a penny of his father's money.'

Poirot shrugged his shoulders.

'Man is a vain animal. Monsieur Renauld figured to himself, without doubt, that his widow would never marry again. As to the son, it may have been a wise precaution to leave the money in his mother's hands. The sons of rich men are proverbially wild.'

'It may be as you say. Now, Monsieur Poirot, you would without doubt like to visit the scene of the crime. I am sorry that the body has been removed, but of course photographs have been taken from every conceivable angle, and will be at your disposal as soon as they are available.'

'I thank you, monsieur, for all your courtesy.'

The commissary rose.

'Come with me, messieurs.'

He opened the door, and bowed ceremoniously to Poirot to precede him. Poirot, with equal politeness, drew back and bowed to the commissary.

'Monsieur.'

'Monsieur.'

At last they got out into the hall.

'That room there, it is the study, *hein*?' asked Poirot suddenly, nodding towards the door opposite.

'Yes. You would like to see it?' He threw open the door as he spoke, and we entered.

The room which M. Renauld had chosen for his own particular use was small, but furnished with great taste and comfort.

A business-like writing-desk, with many pigeon-holes, stood in the window. Two large leather-covered armchairs faced the fireplace, and between them was a round table covered with the latest books and magazines.

Poirot stood a moment taking in the room, then he stepped forward, passed his hand lightly over the backs of the leather chairs, picked up a magazine from the table, and drew a finger gingerly over the surface of the oak sideboard. His face expressed complete approval.

'No dust?' I asked, with a smile.

He beamed on me, appreciative of my knowledge of his peculiarities.

'Not a particle, *mon ami!* And for once, perhaps, it is a pity.'

His sharp, birdlike eyes darted here and there.

'Ah!' he remarked suddenly, with an intonation of relief. 'The hearth-rug is crooked,' and he bent down to straighten it.

Suddenly he uttered an exclamation and rose. In his hand he held a small fragment of pink paper.

'In France, as in England,' he remarked, 'the domestics omit to sweep under the mats?'

Bex took the fragment from him, and I came close to examine it.

'You recognize it – eh, Hastings?'

I shook my head, puzzled – and yet that particular shade of pink paper was very familiar.

The commissary's mental processes were quicker than mine.

'A fragment of a cheque,' he exclaimed.

The piece of paper was roughly about two inches square. On it was written in ink the word 'Duveen'.

'*Bien!*' said Bex. 'This cheque was payable to, or drawn by, someone named Duveen.'

'The former, I fancy,' said Poirot. 'For, if I am not mistaken, the handwriting is that of Monsieur Renauld.'

That was soon established, by comparing it with a memorandum from the desk.

'Dear me,' murmured the commissary, with a crestfallen air, 'I really cannot imagine how I came to overlook this.'

Poirot laughed.

'The moral of that is, always look under the mats! My friend

Hastings here will tell you that anything in the least crooked is a torment to me. As soon as I saw that the hearthrug was out of the straight, I said to myself: "*Tiens!* The legs of the chair caught it in being pushed back. Possibly there may be something beneath it which the good Françoise overlooked."'

'Françoise?'

'Or Denise, or Léonie. Whoever did this room. Since there is no dust, the room *must* have been done this morning. I reconstruct the incident like this. Yesterday, possibly last night, Monsieur Renauld drew a cheque to the order of some one named Duveen. Afterwards it was torn up, and scattered on the floor. This morning –'

But M. Bex was already pulling impatiently at the bell.

Françoise answered it. Yes, there had been a lot of pieces of paper on the floor. What had she done with them? Put them in the kitchen stove of course! What else?

With a gesture of despair, Bex dismissed her. Then, his face lightening, he ran to the desk. In a minute he was hunting through the dead man's cheque book. Then he repeated his former gesture. The last counterfoil was blank.

'Courage!' cried Poirot, clapping him on the back. 'Without doubt, Madame Renauld will be able to tell us all about this mysterious person named Duveen.'

The commissary's face cleared. 'That is true. Let us proceed.'

As we turned to leave the room, Poirot remarked casually: 'It was here that Monsieur Renauld received his guest last night, eh?'

'It was – but how did you know?'

'By *this*. I found it on the back of the leather chair.' And he held up between his finger and thumb a long black hair – a woman's hair!

M. Bex took us out by the back of the house to where there was a small shed leaning against the house. He produced a key from his pocket and unlocked it.

'The body is here. We moved it from the scene of the crime just before you arrived, as the photographers had done with it.'

He opened the door and we passed in. The murdered man lay on the ground, with a sheet over him. M. Bex dexterously whipped off the covering. Renauld was a man of medium height, slender, and lithe in figure. He looked about fifty years of age, and his dark hair was plentifully streaked with grey. He was clean-shaven with a long, thin nose, and eyes set rather close together, and his skin was deeply bronzed, as that of a man who had spent most of his life beneath tropical skies. His lips were drawn back from his teeth and an expression of absolute amazement and terror was stamped on the livid features.

'One can see by his face that he was stabbed in the back,' remarked Poirot.

Very gently, he turned the dead man over. There, between the shoulder-blades, staining the light fawn overcoat, was a round dark patch. In the middle of it there was a slit in the cloth. Poirot examined it narrowly.

'Have you any idea with what weapon the crime was committed?'

'It was left in the wound.' The commissary reached down a large glass jar. In it was a small object that looked to me more like a paper-knife than anything else. It had a black handle and a narrow shining blade. The whole thing was not more than ten inches long. Poirot tested the discoloured point gingerly with his finger-tip.

'*Ma foi!* but it is sharp! A nice easy little tool for murder!'

'Unfortunately, we could find no trace of fingerprints on it,' remarked Bex regretfully. 'The murderer must have worn gloves.'

'Of course he did,' said Poirot contemptuously. 'Even in Santiago they know enough for that. The veriest amateur of an English Mees knows it – thanks to the publicity the Bertillon system has been given in the Press. All the same, it interests me very much that there were no fingerprints. It is so amazingly simple to leave the fingerprints of someone else! And then the police are happy.' He shook his head. 'I very much fear our criminal is not a man of method – either that or he was pressed for time. But we shall see.'

He let the body fall back into its original position.

'He wore only underclothes under his overcoat, I see,' he remarked.

'Yes, the examining magistrate thinks that is rather a curious point.'

At this minute there was a tap on the door which Bex had closed after him. He strode forward and opened it. Françoise was there. She endeavoured to peep in with ghoulish curiosity.

'Well, what is it?' demanded Bex impatiently.

'Madame. She sends a message that she is much recovered and is quite ready to receive the examining magistrate.'

'Good,' said M. Bex briskly. 'Tell Monsieur Hautet and say that we will come at once.'

Poirot lingered a moment, looking back towards the body. I thought for a moment that he was going to apostrophize it, to declare aloud his determination never to rest till he had discovered the murderer. But when he spoke, it was tamely and awkwardly, and his comment was ludicrously inappropriate to the solemnity of the moment.

'He wore his overcoat very long,' he said constrainedly.

CHAPTER 5

MRS RENAULD'S STORY

We found M. Hautet awaiting us in the hall, and we all proceeded upstairs together, Françoise marching ahead to show us the way. Poirot went up in a zigzag fashion which puzzled me, until he whispered with a grimace:

'No wonder the servants heard M. Renauld mounting the stairs, not a board of them but creaks fit to awake the dead!'

At the head of the staircase, a small passage branched off.

'The servants' quarters,' explained Bex.

We continued along a corridor, and Françoise tapped on the last door to the right of it.

A faint voice bade us enter, and we passed into a large, sunny apartment looking out towards the sea, which showed blue and sparkling about a quarter of a mile distant.

On a couch, propped up with cushions, and attended by Dr Durand, lay a tall, striking-looking woman. She was middle-aged, and her once dark hair was now almost entirely silvered, but the intense vitality, and strength of her personality would have made itself felt anywhere. You knew at once that you were in the presence of what the French call *une maîtresse femme*.

She greeted us with a dignified inclination of the head.

'Pray be seated, messieurs.'

We took chairs, and the magistrate's clerk established himself at a round table.

'I hope, madame,' began M. Hautet, 'that it will not distress you unduly to relate to us what occurred last night?'

'Not at all, monsieur. I know the value of time, if these scoundrelly assassins are to be caught and punished.'

'Very well, madame. It will fatigue you less, I think, if I ask you questions and you confine yourself to answering them. At what time did you go to bed last night?'

'At half past nine, monsieur. I was tired.'

'And your husband?'

'About an hour later, I fancy.'

'Did he seem disturbed – upset in any way?'

'No, not more than usual.'

'What happened then?'

'We slept. I was awakened by a hand pressed over my mouth. I tried to scream out, but the hand prevented me. There were two men in the room. They were both masked.'

'Can you describe them at all, madame?'

'One was very tall, and had a long black beard, the other was short and stout. His beard was reddish. They both wore hats pulled down over their eyes.'

'H'm!' said the magistrate thoughtfully. 'Too much beard, I fear.'

'You mean they were false?'

'Yes, madame. But continue your story.'

'It was the short man who was holding me. He forced a gag into my mouth, and then bound me with rope hand and foot. The other man was standing over my husband. He had caught up my little dagger paper-knife from the dressing-table and was holding it with the point just over his heart. When the short man had finished with me, he joined the other, and they forced my husband to get up and accompany them into the dressing-room next door. I was nearly fainting with terror, nevertheless I listened desperately.

'They were speaking in too low a tone for me to hear what they said. But I recognized the language, a bastard Spanish such as is spoken in some parts of South America. They seemed to be demanding something from my husband, and presently they grew angry, and their voices rose a little. I think the tall man was speaking. "You know what we want?" he said. "*The secret!* Where is it?" I do not know what my husband answered, but the other replied fiercely: "You lie! We know you have it. Where are your keys?"

'Then I heard sounds of drawers being pulled out. There is a safe on the wall of my husband's dressing-room in which he always keeps a fairly large amount of ready money. Léonie tells me this has been rifled and the money taken, but evidently what they were looking for was not there, for presently I heard the tall man, with an oath, command my husband to dress himself. Soon after that, I think some noise in the house must have disturbed them, for they hustled my husband out into my room only half dressed.'

'*Pardon*,' interrupted Poirot, 'but is there then no other egress from the dressing-room?'

'No, monsieur, there is only the communicating door into my room. They hurried my husband through, the short man in front, and the tall man behind him with the dagger still in his hand. Paul tried to break away to come to me. I saw his agonized eyes. He turned to his captors. "I must speak to her," he said. Then, coming to the side of the bed, "It is all right, Eloise," he said. "Do not be afraid. I shall return before morning." But, although he tried to make his voice confident, I could see the terror in his eyes. Then they hustled him out of the door, the tall man saying: "One sound – and you are a dead man, remember."

'After that,' continued Mrs Renauld, 'I must have fainted. The next thing I recollect is Léonie rubbing my wrists and giving me brandy.'

'Madame Renauld,' said the magistrate, 'had you any idea what it was for which the assassins were searching?'

'None whatever, monsieur.'

'Had you any knowledge that your husband feared something?'

'Yes. I had seen the change in him.'

'How long ago was that?'

Mrs Renauld reflected.

'Ten days, perhaps.'

'Not longer?'

'Possibly. I only noticed it then.'

'Did you question your husband at all as to the cause?'

'Once. He put me off evasively. Nevertheless, I was convinced that he was suffering some terrible anxiety. However, since he evidently wished to conceal the fact from me, I tried to pretend that I had noticed nothing.'

'Were you aware that he had called in the services of a detective?'

'A detective?' exclaimed Mrs Renauld, very much surprised.

'Yes, this gentleman – Monsieur Hercule Poirot.' Poirot bowed. 'He arrived today in response to a summons from your husband.' And taking the letter written by M. Renauld from his pocket he handed it to the lady.

She read it with apparently genuine astonishment.

'I had no idea of this. Evidently he was fully cognizant of the danger.'

'Now, madame, I will beg of you to be frank with me. Is there any incident in your husband's past life in South America which might throw light on his murder?'

Mrs Renauld reflected deeply, but at last shook her head.

'I can think of none. Certainly my husband had many enemies, people he had got the better of in some way or another, but I can think of no one distinctive case. I do not say there is no such incident – only that I am not aware of it.'

The examining magistrate stroked his beard disconsolately.

'And you can fix the time of this outrage?'

'Yes, I distinctly remember hearing the clock on the mantel-piece strike two.' She nodded towards an eight-day travelling clock in a leather case which stood in the centre of the chimney-piece.

Poirot rose from his seat, scrutinized the clock carefully, and nodded, satisfied.

'And here too,' exclaimed M. Bex, 'is a wristwatch, knocked off the dressing-table by the assassins, without doubt, and smashed to atoms. Little did they know it would testify against them.'

Gently he picked away the fragments of broken glass. Suddenly his face changed to one of utter stupefaction.

'*Mon Dieu!*' he ejaculated.

'What is it?'

'The hands of the watch point to seven o'clock!'

'What?' cried the examining magistrate, astonished.

But Poirot, deft as ever, took the broken trinket from the startled commissary, and held it to his ear. Then he smiled.

'The glass is broken, yes, but the watch itself is still going.'

The explanation of the mystery was greeted with a relieved smile. But the magistrate bethought him of another point.

'But surely it is not seven o'clock now?'

'No,' said Poirot gently, 'it is a few minutes after five. Possibly the watch gains, is that so, madame?'

Mrs Renauld was frowning perplexedly.

'It does gain,' she admitted. 'But I've never known it gain quite so much as that.'

With a gesture of impatience the magistrate left the matter of the watch and proceeded with his interrogatory.

'Madame, the front door was found ajar. It seems almost certain that the murderers entered that way, yet it has not been forced at all. Can you suggest any explanation?'

'Possibly my husband went out for a stroll the last thing, and forgot to latch it when he came in.'

'Is that a likely thing to happen?'

'Very. My husband was the most absent-minded of men.'

There was a slight frown on her brow as she spoke, as though this trait in the dead man's character had at times vexed her.

'There is one inference I think we might draw,' remarked the commissary suddenly. 'Since the men insisted on Monsieur Renauld dressing himself, it looks as though the place they were taking him to, the place where "the secret" was concealed, lay some distance away.'

The magistrate nodded.

'Yes, far, and yet not too far, since he spoke of being back by morning.'

'What time does the last train leave the station of Merlinville?' asked Poirot.

'11.50 one way, and 12.17 the other, but it is more probable that they had a motor waiting.'

'Of course,' agreed Poirot, looking somewhat crestfallen.

'Indeed, that might be one way of tracing them,' continued the magistrate, brightening. 'A motor containing two foreigners is quite likely to have been noticed. That is an excellent point, Monsieur Bex.'

He smiled to himself, and then, becoming grave once more, he said to Mrs Renauld:

'There is another question. Do you know anyone of the name of "Duveen"?'

'Duveen?' Mrs Renauld repeated thoughtfully. 'No, for the moment, I cannot say I do.'

'You have never heard your husband mention anyone of that name.'

'Never.'

'Do you know anyone whose Christian name is Bella?'

He watched Mrs Renauld narrowly as he spoke, seeking to surprise any signs of anger or consciousness, but she merely shook her head in quite a natural manner. He continued his questions.

'Are you aware that your husband had a visitor last night?'

Now he saw the red mount slightly in her cheeks, but she replied composedly:

'No, who was that?'

'A lady.'

'Indeed?'

But for the moment the magistrate was content to say no more. It seemed unlikely that Madame Daubreuil had any connexion with the crime, and he was anxious not to upset Mrs Renauld more than necessary.

He made a sign to the commissary, and the latter replied with a nod. Then rising, he went across the room, and returned with the glass jar we had seen in the outhouse in his hand. From this he took the dagger.

'Madame,' he said gently, 'do you recognize this?'

She gave a little cry.

'Yes, that is my little dagger.' Then she saw the stained point, and she drew back, her eyes widening with horror. 'Is that – blood?'

'Yes, madame. Your husband was killed with this weapon.' He removed it hastily from sight. 'You are quite sure about its being the one that was on your dressing-table last night?'

'Oh, yes. It was a present from my son. He was in the Air Force during the War. He gave his age as older than it was.' There was a touch of the proud mother in her voice. 'This was made from a streamline aeroplane wire, and was given to me by my son as a souvenir of the War.'

'I see, madame. That brings us to another matter. Your son, where is he now? It is necessary that he should be telegraphed to without delay.'

'Jack? He is on his way to Buenos Aires.'

'What?'

'Yes. My husband telegraphed to him yesterday. He had sent him on business to Paris, but yesterday he discovered that it would be necessary for him to proceed without delay to South America. There was a boat leaving Cherbourg for Buenos Aires last night, and he wired him to catch it.'

'Have you any knowledge of what the business in Buenos Aires was?'

'No, monsieur, I know nothing of its nature, but Buenos Aires is not my son's final destination. He was going overland from there to Santiago.'

And, in unison, the magistrate and the commissary exclaimed:

'Santiago! Again Santiago!'

It was at this moment, when we were all stunned by the mention of that word, that Poirot approached Mrs Renauld. He had been standing by the window like a man lost in a dream, and I doubt if he had fully taken in what had passed. He paused by the lady's side with a bow.

'*Pardon*, madame, but may I examine your wrists?'

Though slightly surprised at the request, Mrs Renauld held them out to him. Round each of them was a cruel red mark where the cords had bitten into the flesh. As he examined them, I fancied that a momentary flicker of excitement I had seen in his eyes disappeared.

'They must cause you great pain,' he said, and once more he looked puzzled.

But the magistrate was speaking excitedly.

'Young Monsieur Renauld must be communicated with at once by wireless. It is vital that we should know anything he can tell us about this trip to Santiago.' He hesitated. 'I hoped he might have been near at hand, so that we could have saved you pain, madame.' He paused.

'You mean,' she said in a low voice, 'the identification of my husband's body?'

The magistrate bowed his head.

'I am a strong woman, monsieur. I can bear all that is required of me. I am ready – now.'

'Oh, tomorrow will be quite soon enough, I assure you –'

'I prefer to get it over,' she said in a low tone, a spasm of pain crossing her face. 'If you will be so good as to give me your arm, doctor?'

The doctor hastened forward, a cloak was thrown over Mrs Renauld's shoulders, and a slow procession went down the stairs. M. Bex hurried on ahead to open the door of the shed. In a minute or two Mrs Renauld appeared in the doorway. She was very pale, but resolute. She raised her hand to her face.

'A moment, messieurs, while I steel myself.'

She took her hand away and looked down at the dead man. Then the marvellous self-control which had upheld her so far deserted her.

'Paul!' she cried. 'Husband! Oh, God!' And pitching forward she fell unconscious to the ground.

Instantly Poirot was beside her, he raised the lid of her eye, felt her pulse. When he had satisfied himself that she had really fainted, he drew aside. He caught me by the arm.

'I am an imbecile, my friend! If ever there was love and grief in a woman's voice, I heard it then. My little idea was all wrong. *Eh bien!* I must start again!'

CHAPTER 6

THE SCENE OF THE CRIME

Between them, the doctor and M. Hautet carried the unconscious woman into the house. The commissary looked after them, shaking his head.

'*Pauvre femme*,' he murmured to himself. 'The shock was too much for her. Well, well, we can do nothing. Now, Monsieur Poirot, shall we visit the place where the crime was committed?'

'If you please, Monsieur Bex.'

We passed through the house, and out by the front door. Poirot had looked up at the staircase in passing, and shook his head in a dissatisfied manner.

'It is to me incredible that the servants heard nothing. The creaking of that staircase, with *three* people descending it, would awaken the dead!'

'It was the middle of the night, remember. They were sound asleep by then.'

But Poirot continued to shake his head as though not fully accepting the explanation. On the sweep of the drive he paused, looking up at the house.

'What moved them in the first place to try if the front door were open? It was a most unlikely thing that it should be. It was far more probable that they should at once try to force a window.'

'But all the windows on the ground floor are barred with iron shutters,' objected the commissary.

Poirot pointed to a window on the first floor.

'That is the window of the bedroom we have just come from, is it not? And see – there is a tree by which it would be the easiest thing in the world to mount.'

'Possibly,' admitted the other. 'But they could not have done so without leaving footprints in the flower-bed.'

I saw the justice of his words. There were two large oval flower-beds planted with scarlet geraniums, one each side of the steps leading up to the front door. The tree in question had its roots actually at the back of the bed itself, and it would have been impossible to reach it without stepping on the bed.

'You see,' continued the commissary, 'owing to the dry weather no prints would show on the drive or paths; but, on the soft mould of the flower-bed, it would have been a very different affair.'

Poirot went close to the bed and studied it attentively. As Bex had said, the mould was perfectly smooth. There was not an indentation on it anywhere.

Poirot nodded, as though convinced, and we turned away, but he suddenly darted off and began examining the other flower-bed.

'Monsieur Bex!' he called. 'See here. Here are plenty of traces for you.'

The commissary joined him – and smiled.

'My dear Monsieur Poirot, those are without doubt the footprints of the gardener's large hobnailed boots. In any case, it would have no importance, since this side we have no tree, and consequently no means of gaining access to the upper storey.'

'True,' said Poirot, evidently crestfallen. 'So you think these footprints are of no importance?'

'Not the least in the world.'

Then, to my utter astonishment, Poirot pronounced these words:

'I do not agree with you. I have a little idea that these footprints are the most important things we have seen yet.'

M. Bex said nothing, merely shrugged his shoulders. He was far too courteous to utter his real opinion.

'Shall we proceed?' he asked, instead.

'Certainly. I can investigate this matter of the footprints later,' said Poirot cheerfully.

Instead of following the drive down to the gate, M. Bex turned up a path that branched off at right angles. It led, up a slight incline, round to the right of the house, and was bordered on either side by a kind of shrubbery. Suddenly it emerged into a little clearing from which one obtained a view of the sea. A seat had been placed here, and not far from it was a rather ramshackle shed. A few steps farther on, a neat line of small bushes marked the boundary of the Villa grounds. M. Bex pushed his way through these, and we found ourselves on a wide stretch of open downs. I looked round, and saw something that filled me with astonishment.

'Why, this is a Golf Course,' I cried.

Bex nodded.

'The links are not completed yet,' he explained. 'It is hoped to be able to open them some time next month. It was some of the men working on them who discovered the body early this morning.'

I gave a gasp. A little to my left, where for the moment I had overlooked it, was a long narrow pit and by it, face downwards, was the body of a man! For a moment my heart gave a terrible leap, and I had a wild fancy that the tragedy had been duplicated.

But the commissary dispelled my illusion by moving forward with a sharp exclamation of annoyance:

'What have my police been about? They had strict orders to allow no one near the place without proper credentials!'

The man on the ground turned his head over his shoulder.

'But I have proper credentials,' he remarked, and rose slowly to his feet.

'My dear Monsieur Giraud,' cried the commissary. 'I had no idea that you had arrived, even. The examining magistrate has been awaiting you with the utmost impatience.'

As he spoke, I was scanning the newcomer with the keenest curiosity. The famous detective from the Paris Sûreté was familiar to me by name, and I was extremely interested to see him in the flesh. He was very tall, perhaps about thirty years of age, with auburn hair and moustache, and a military carriage. There was a trace of arrogance in his manner which showed that he was fully alive to his own importance. Bex introduced us, presenting Poirot as a colleague. A flicker of interest came into the detective's eye.

'I know you by name, Monsieur Poirot,' he said. 'You cut quite a figure in the old days, didn't you? But methods are very different now.'

'Crimes, though, are very much the same,' remarked Poirot gently.

I saw at once that Giraud was prepared to be hostile. He resented the other being associated with him, and I felt that if he came across any clue of importance he would be more than likely to keep it to himself.

'The examining magistrate –' began Bex again.

But Giraud interrupted rudely:

'A fig for the examining magistrate! The light is the important thing. For all practical purposes it will be gone in another half hour or so. I know all about the case, and the people at the house will do very well until tomorrow; but, if we're going to find a clue to the murderers, here is the spot we shall find it. Is it your police who have been trampling all over the place? I thought they knew better nowadays.'

'Assuredly they do. The marks you complain of were made by the workmen who discovered the body.'

The other grunted disgustedly.

'I can see the tracks where the three of them came through the hedge – but they were cunning. You can just recognize the centre footmarks as those of Monsieur Renauld, but those on either side have been carefully obliterated. Not that there would really be much to see anyway on this hard ground, but they weren't taking any chances.'

'The external sign,' said Poirot. 'That is what you seek, eh?'

The other detective stared.

'Of course.'

A very faint smile came to Poirot's lips. He seemed about to speak, but checked himself. He bent down to where a spade was lying.

'That's what the grave was dug with, right enough,' said Giraud. 'But you'll get nothing from it. It was Renauld's own spade, and the man who used it wore gloves. Here they are.' He gesticulated with his foot to where two soil-stained gloves were lying. 'And they're Renauld's too – or at least his gardener's. I tell you, the men who carried out this crime were taking no chances. The man was stabbed with his own dagger, and would have been buried with his own spade. They counted on leaving no traces! But I'll beat them. There's always *something!* And I mean to find it.'

But Poirot was now apparently interested in something else, a short, discoloured piece of lead-piping which lay beside the spade. He touched it delicately with his finger.

'And does this, too, belong to the murdered man?' he asked, and I thought I detected a subtle flavour of irony in the question.

Giraud shrugged his shoulders to indicate that he neither knew nor cared.

'May have been lying around here for weeks. Anyway, it doesn't interest me.'

'I, on the contrary, find it very interesting,' said Poirot sweetly.

I guessed that he was merely bent on annoying the Paris detective and, if so, he succeeded. The other turned away rudely, remarking that he had no time to waste, and bending down he resumed his minute search of the ground.

Meanwhile, Poirot, as though struck by a sudden idea, stepped back over the boundary, and tried the door of the little shed.

'That's locked,' said Giraud over his shoulder. 'But it's only a place where the gardener keeps his rubbish. The spade didn't come from there, but from the tool-shed up by the house.'

'Marvellous,' murmured M. Bex ecstatically to me. 'He has been here but half an hour, and he already knows everything! What a man! Undoubtedly Giraud is the greatest detective alive today.'

Although I disliked the detective heartily, I nevertheless was secretly impressed. Efficiency seemed to radiate from the man. I could not help feeling that, so far, Poirot had not greatly distinguished himself, and it vexed me. He seemed to be direct-ing his attention to all sorts of silly puerile points that had nothing to do with the case. Indeed, at this juncture, he sud-denly asked:

'Monsieur Bex, tell me, I pray you, the meaning of this white-washed line that extends all round the grave. Is it a device of the police?'

'No, Monsieur Poirot, it is an affair of the golf course. It shows that there is here to be a "bunkair", as you call it.'

'A bunkair?' Poirot turned to me. 'That is the irregular hole filled with sand and a bank at one side, is it not?'

I concurred.

'Monsieur Renauld, without doubt he played the golf?'

'Yes, he was a keen golfer. It's mainly owing to him, and to his large subscriptions, that this work is being carried forward. He even had a say in the designing of it.'

Poirot nodded thoughtfully. Then he remarked:

'It was not a very good choice they made – of a spot to bury the body? When the men began to dig up the ground, all would have been discovered.'

'Exactly,' cried Giraud triumphantly. 'And that *proves* that they were strangers to the place. It's an excellent piece of indirect evidence.'

'Yes,' said Poirot doubtfully. 'No one who knew would bury a body there – unless they *wanted* it to be discovered. And that is clearly absurd, is it not?'

Giraud did not even trouble to reply.

'Yes,' said Poirot, in a somewhat dissatisfied voice. 'Yes – undoubtedly – absurd!'

CHAPTER 7

THE MYSTERIOUS MADAME DAUBREUIL

As we retraced our steps to the house, M. Bex excused himself for leaving us, explaining that he must immediately acquaint the examining magistrate with the fact of Giraud's arrival. Giraud himself had been obviously delighted when Poirot declared that he had seen all he wanted. The last thing we observed, as we left the spot, was Giraud, crawling about on all fours, with a thoroughness in his search that I could not but admire. Poirot guessed my thoughts, for as soon as we were alone he remarked ironically:

'At last you have seen the detective you admire – the human foxhound! Is it not so, my friend?'

'At any rate, he's *doing* something,' I said, with asperity. 'If there's anything to find he'll find it. Now you –'

'*Eh bien!* I also have found something! A piece of lead-piping.'

'Nonsense, Poirot. You know very well that's got nothing to do with it. I meant *little* things – traces that may lead us infallibly to the murderers.'

'*Mon ami*, a clue of two feet long is every bit as valuable as one measuring two millimetres! But it is the romantic idea that all important clues must be infinitesimal. As to the piece of lead-piping having nothing to do with the crime, you say that because Giraud told you so. No' – as I was about to interpose a question – 'we will say no more. Leave Giraud to his search, and me to my ideas. The case seems straightforward enough – and yet – and yet, *mon ami*, I am not satisfied! And do you know why? Because of the wristwatch that is two hours fast. And then there are several curious little points that do not seem to fit in. For instance, if the object of the murderers was revenge, why did they not stab Renauld in his sleep and have done with it?'

'They wanted the "secret",' I reminded him.

Poirot brushed a speck of dust from his sleeve with a dissatisfied air.

'Well, where is this "secret"? Presumably some distance away, since they wish him to dress himself. Yet he is found murdered close at hand, almost within ear-shot of the house. Then again, it is pure chance that a weapon such as the dagger should be lying about casually, ready to hand.'

He paused, frowning, and then went on:

'Why did the servants hear nothing? Were they drugged? Was there an accomplice, and did that accomplice see to it that the front door should remain open? I wonder if –'

He stopped abruptly. We had reached the drive in front of the house. Suddenly he turned to me.

'My friend, I am about to surprise you – to please you! I have taken your reproaches to heart! We will examine some footprints!'

'Where?'

'In that right-hand bed yonder. Monsieur Bex says that they are the footmarks of the gardener. Let us see if this is so. See, he approaches with his wheelbarrow.'

Indeed an elderly man was just crossing the drive with a barrowful of seedlings. Poirot called to him, and he set down the barrow and came hobbling towards us.

'You are going to ask him for one of his boots to compare with the footmarks?' I asked breathlessly. My faith in Poirot revived a little. Since he said the footprints in this right-hand bed were important, presumably they *were*.

'Exactly,' said Poirot.

'But won't he think it very odd?'

'He will not think about it at all.'

We could say no more, for the old man had joined us.

'You want me for something, monsieur?'

'Yes. You have been gardener here a long time, haven't you?'

'Twenty-four years, monsieur.'

'And your name is –?'

'Auguste, monsieur.'

'I was admiring these magnificent geraniums. They are truly superb. They have been planted long?'

'Some time, monsieur. But of course, to keep the beds looking smart, one must keep bedding out a few new plants, and remove those that are over, besides keeping the old blooms well picked off.'

'You put in some new plants yesterday, didn't you? Those in the middle there, and in the other bed also.'

'Monsieur has a sharp eye. It takes always a day or so for them to "pick up". Yes, I put ten new plants in each bed last night. As monsieur doubtless knows, one should not put in plants when the sun is hot.' Auguste was charmed with Poirot's interest, and was quite inclined to be garrulous.

'That is a splendid specimen there,' said Poirot, pointing. 'Might I perhaps have a cutting of it?'

'But certainly, monsieur.' The old fellow stepped into the bed, and carefully took a slip from the plant Poirot had admired.

Poirot was profuse in his thanks, and Auguste departed to his barrow.

'You see?' said Poirot with a smile, as he bent over the bed to examine the indentation of the gardener's hobnailed boot. 'It is quite simple.'

'I did not realize –'

'That the foot would be inside the boot? You do not use your excellent mental capacities sufficiently. Well, what of the footmark?'

I examined the bed carefully.

'All the footmarks in the bed were made by the same boot,' I said at length after a careful study.

'You think so? *Eh bien!* I agree with you,' said Poirot.

He seemed quite uninterested, and as though he were thinking of something else.

'At any rate,' I remarked, 'you will have one bee less in your bonnet now.'

'*Mon Dieu!* But what an idiom! What does it mean?'

'What I meant was that now you will give up your interest in these footmarks.'

But to my surprise Poirot shook his head.

'No, no, *mon ami*. At last I am on the right track. I am still in the dark, but, as I hinted just now to Monsieur Bex, these footmarks are the most important and interesting things in the case! That poor Giraud – I should not be surprised if he took no notice of them whatever.'

At that moment the front door opened, and M. Hautet and the commissary came down the steps.

'Ah, Monsieur Poirot, we were coming to look for you,' said the magistrate. 'It is getting late, but I wish to pay a visit to Madame Daubreuil. Without doubt she will be very much upset by Monsieur Renauld's death, and we may be fortunate enough to get a clue from her. The secret that he did not confide to his wife, it is possible that he may have told it to the woman whose love held him enslaved. We know where our Samsons are weak, don't we?'

We said no more, but fell into line. Poirot walked with the examining magistrate, and the commissary and I followed a few paces behind.

'There is no doubt that Françoise's story is substantially correct,' he remarked to me in a confidential tone. 'I have been telephoning headquarters. It seems that three times in the last six weeks – that is to say since the arrival of Monsieur Renauld at Merlinville – Madame Daubreuil has paid a large sum in notes into her banking account. Altogether the sum totals two hundred thousand francs!'

'Dear me,' I said, considering, 'that must be something like four thousand pounds!'

'Precisely. Yes, there can be no doubt that he was absolutely infatuated. But it remains to be seen whether he confided his secret to her. The examining magistrate is hopeful, but I hardly share his views.'

During this conversation we were walking down the lane towards the fork in the road where our car had halted earlier in the afternoon, and in another moment I realized that the Villa Marguerite, the home of the mysterious Madame Daubreuil, was the small house from which the beautiful girl had emerged.

'She has lived here for many years,' said the commissary nodding his head towards the house. 'Very quietly, very unobtrusively. She seems to have no friends or relations other than the acquaintances she has made in Merlinville. She never refers to the past, nor to her husband. One does not even know if he is alive or dead. There is a mystery about her, you comprehend.'

I nodded, my interest growing.

'And – the daughter?' I ventured.

'A truly beautiful young girl – modest, devout, all that she should be. One pities her, for, though she may know nothing of the past, a man who wants to ask her hand in marriage must necessarily inform himself, and then –' The commissary shrugged his shoulders cynically.

'But it would not be her fault!' I cried, with rising indignation.

'No. But what will you? A man is particular about his wife's antecedents.'

I was prevented from further argument by our arrival at the door. M. Hautet rang the bell. A few minutes elapsed, and then we heard a footfall within, and the door was opened. On the threshold stood my young goddess of that afternoon. When she saw us, the colour left her cheeks, leaving her deathly white, and her eyes widened with apprehension. There was no doubt about it, she was afraid!

'Mademoiselle Daubreuil,' said M. Hautet, sweeping off his hat, 'we regret infinitely to disturb you, but the exigencies of the Law, you comprehend? My compliments to madame your mother, and will she have the goodness to grant me a few moments' interview?'

For a moment the girl stood motionless. Her left hand was pressed to her side, as though to still the sudden unconquerable agitation of her heart. But she mastered herself, and said in a low voice:

'I will go and see. Please come inside.'

She entered a room on the left of the hall, and we heard the low murmur of her voice. And then another voice, much the same in timbre, but with a slightly harder inflection behind its mellow roundness, said:

'But certainly. Ask them to enter.'

In another minute we were face to face with the mysterious Madame Daubreuil.

She was not nearly so tall as her daughter, and the rounded curves of her figure had all the grace of full maturity. Her hair, again unlike her daughter's, was dark, and parted in the middle in the Madonna style. Her eyes, half hidden by the drooping lids, were blue. Though very well preserved, she was certainly no longer young, but her charm was of the quality which is independent of age.

'You wished to see me, monsieur?' she asked.

'Yes, madame.' M. Hautet cleared his throat. 'I am investigating the death of Monsieur Renauld. You have heard of it, no doubt?'

She bowed her head without speaking. Her expression did not change.

'We came to ask you whether you can – er – throw any light upon the circumstances surrounding it?'

'I?' The surprise of her tone was excellent.

'Yes, madame. We have reason to believe that you were in the habit of visiting the dead man at his villa in the evenings. Is that so?'

The colour rose in the lady's pale cheeks, but she replied quietly:

'I deny your right to ask me such a question!'

'Madame, we are investigating a murder.'

'Well, what of it? I had nothing to do with the murder.'

'Madame, we do not say that for a moment. But you knew the dead man well. Did he ever confide in you as to any danger that threatened him?'

'Never.'

'Did he ever mention his life in Santiago, and any enemies he may have made there?'

'No.'

'Then you can give us no help at all?'

'I fear not. I really do not see why you should come to me. Cannot his wife tell you what you want to know?' Her voice held a slender inflection of irony.

'Mrs Renauld has told us all she can.'

'Ah!' said Madame Daubreuil. 'I wonder –'

'You wonder what, madame?'

'Nothing.'

The examining magistrate looked at her. He was aware that he was fighting a duel, and that he had no mean antagonist.

'You persist in your statement that Monsieur Renauld confided nothing to you?'

'Why should you think it likely that he should confide in me?'

'Because, madame,' said M. Hautet, with calculated brutality, 'a man tells to his mistress what he does not always tell to his wife.'

'Ah!' She sprang forward. Her eyes flashed fire. 'Monsieur, you insult me! And before my daughter! I can tell you nothing. Have the goodness to leave my house!'

The honours undoubtedly rested with the lady. We left the Villa Marguerite like a shamefaced pack of schoolboys. The magistrate muttered angry ejaculations to himself. Poirot seemed lost in thought. Suddenly he came out of his reverie with a start, and inquired of M. Hautet if there was a good hotel near at hand.

'There is a small place, the Hôtel des Bains, on this side of the town. A few hundred yards down the road. It will be handy for your investigations. We shall see you in the morning, then, I presume?'

'Yes, I thank you, Monsieur Hautet.'

With mutual civilities we parted company, Poirot and I going towards Merlinville, and the others returning to the Villa Geneviève.

'The French police system is very marvellous,' said Poirot, looking after them. 'The information they possess about every-one's life, down to the most commonplace detail, is extraordinary. Though he has only been here a little over six weeks, they are perfectly well acquainted with Monsieur Renauld's tastes and pursuits, and at a moment's notice they can produce information as to Madame Daubreuil's banking account, and the sums that have lately been paid in! Undoubtedly the dossier is a great institution. But what is that?' He turned sharply.

A figure was running hatless down the road after us. It was Marthe Daubreuil.

'I beg your pardon,' she cried breathlessly, as she reached us. 'I – I should not do this, I know. You must not tell my mother. But is it true, what the people say, that Monsieur Renauld called in a detective before he died, and – and that you are he?'

'Yes, mademoiselle,' said Poirot gently. 'It is quite true. But how did you learn it?'

'Françoise told our Amélie,' explained Marthe with a blush.

Poirot made a grimace.

'The secrecy, it is impossible in an affair of this kind! Not that it matters. Well, mademoiselle, what is it you want to know?'

The girl hesitated. She seemed longing, yet fearing, to speak. At last, almost in a whisper, she asked:

'Is – anyone suspected?'

Poirot eyed her keenly.

Then he replied evasively:

'Suspicion is in the air at present, mademoiselle.'

'Yes, I know – but – anyone in particular?'

'Why do you want to know?'

The girl seemed frightened by the question. All at once Poirot's words about her earlier in the day occurred to me. The 'girl with the anxious eyes'.

'Monsieur Renauld was always very kind to me,' she replied at last. 'It is natural that I should be interested.'

'I see,' said Poirot. 'Well, mademoiselle, suspicion at present is hovering round two persons.'

'Two?'

I could have sworn there was a note of surprise and relief in her voice.

'Their names are unknown, but they are presumed to be Chileans from Santiago. And now, mademoiselle, you see what comes of being young and beautiful! I have betrayed professional secrets for you!'

The girl laughed merrily, and then, rather shyly, she thanked him.'

'I must run back now. *Maman* will miss me.'

And she turned and ran back up the road, looking like a modern Atalanta. I stared after her.

'*Mon ami*,' said Poirot, in his gentle ironical voice, 'is it that we are to remain planted here all night – just because you have seen a beautiful young woman, and your head is in a whirl.'

I laughed and apologized.

'But she *is* beautiful, Poirot. Anyone might be excused for being bowled over by her.'

But to my surprise Poirot shook his head very earnestly.

'Ah, *mon ami*, do not set your heart on Marthe Daubreuil. She is not for you, that one! Take it from Papa Poirot!'

'Why,' I cried, 'the commissary assured me that she was as good as she is beautiful! A perfect angel!'

'Some of the greatest criminals I have known had the faces of angels,' remarked Poirot cheerfully. 'A malformation of the grey cells may coincide quite easily with the face of a Madonna.'

'Poirot,' I cried, horrified, 'you cannot mean that you suspect an innocent child like this!'

'Ta-ta-ta! Do not excite yourself! I have not said that I suspected her. But you must admit that her anxiety to know about the case is somewhat unusual.'

'For once I see farther than you do,' I said. 'Her anxiety is not for herself – but for her mother.'

'My friend,' said Poirot, 'as usual, you see nothing at all. Madame Daubreuil is very well able to look after herself without her daughter worrying about her. I admit I was teasing you just now, but all the same I repeat what I said before. Do not set your heart on that girl. She is not for you! I, Hercule Poirot, know it. *Sacré!* if only I could remember where I had seen that face?'

'What face?' I asked, surprised. 'The daughter's?'

'No. The mother's.'

Noting my surprise, he nodded emphatically.

'But yes – it is as I tell you. It was a long time ago, when I was still with the police in Belgium. I have never actually seen the woman before, but I have seen her picture – and in connexion with some case. I rather fancy –'

'Yes?'

'I may be mistaken, but I rather fancy that it was a murder case!'

CHAPTER 8
AN UNEXPECTED MEETING

We were up at the villa betimes next morning. The man on guard at the gate did not bar our way this time. Instead, he respectfully saluted us, and we passed on to the house. The maid Léonie was just coming down the stairs, and seemed not averse to the prospect of a little conversation.

Poirot inquired after the health of Mrs Renauld.

Léonie shook her head.

'She is terribly upset, the poor lady! She will eat nothing – but nothing! And she is as pale as a ghost. It is heartrending to see her. Ah, it is not I who would grieve like that for a man who had deceived me with another woman!'

Poirot nodded sympathetically.

'What you say is very just, but what will you? The heart of

a woman who loves will forgive many blows. Still undoubtedly there must have been many scenes of recrimination between them in the last few months?'

Again Léonie shook her head.

'Never, monsieur. Never have I heard madame utter a word of protest – of reproach, even! She had the temper and disposition of an angel – quite different to monsieur.'

'Monsieur Renauld had not the temper of an angel?'

'Far from it. When he enraged himself, the whole house knew of it. The day that he quarrelled with Monsieur Jack – *ma foi!* they might have been heard in the market-place, they shouted so loud!'

'Indeed,' said Poirot. 'And when did this quarrel take place?'

'Oh, it was just before Monsieur Jack went to Paris. Almost he missed his train. He came out of the library, and caught up his bag which he had left in the hall. The automobile, it was being repaired, and he had to run for the station. I was dusting the *salon*, and I saw him pass, and his face was white – white – with two burning spots of red. Ah, but he was angry!'

Léonie was enjoying her narrative thoroughly.

'And the dispute, what was it about?'

'Ah, that I do not know,' confessed Léonie. 'It is true that they shouted, but their voices were so loud and high, and they spoke so fast, that only one well acquainted with English could have comprehended. But monsieur, he was like a thundercloud all day! Impossible to please him!'

The sound of a door shutting upstairs cut short Léonie's loquacity.

'And Françoise who awaits me!' she exclaimed, awakening to a tardy remembrance of her duties. 'That old one, she always scolds.'

'One moment, mademoiselle. The examining magistrate, where is he?'

'They have gone out to look at the automobile in the garage. Monsieur the commissary had some idea that it might have been used on the night of the murder.'

'*Quelle idée,*' murmured Poirot, as the girl disappeared.

'You will go out and join them?'

'No, I shall await their return in the *salon*. It is cool there on this hot morning.'

This placid way of taking things did not quite commend itself to me.

'If you don't mind –' I said, and hesitated.

'Not in the least. You wish to investigate on your own account, eh?'

'Well, I'd rather like to have a look at Giraud, if he's anywhere about, and see what he's up to.'

'The human foxhound,' murmured Poirot, as he leaned back in a comfortable chair, and closed his eyes. 'By all means, my friend. Au revoir.'

I strolled out of the front door. It was certainly hot. I turned up the path we had taken the day before. I had a mind to study the scene of the crime myself. I did not go directly to the spot, however, but turned aside into the bushes, so as to come out on the links some hundred yards or so farther to the right. The shrubbery here was much denser, and I had quite a struggle to force my way through. When I emerged at last on the course, it was quite unexpectedly and with such vigour that I cannoned heavily into a young lady who had been standing with her back to the plantation.

She not unnaturally gave a suppressed shriek, but I, too, uttered an exclamation of surprise. For it was my friend of the train, Cinderella!

The surprise was mutual.

'You!' we both exclaimed simultaneously.

The young lady recovered herself first.

'My only aunt!' she exclaimed. 'What are you doing here?'

'For the matter of that, what are you?' I retorted.

'When last I saw you, the day before yesterday, you were trotting home to England like a good little boy.'

'When last I saw *you*,' I said, 'you were trotting home with your sister, like a good little girl. By the way, how is your sister?'

A flash of white teeth rewarded me.

'How kind of you to ask! My sister is well, I thank you.'

'She is here with you?'

'She remained in town,' said the minx with dignity.

'I don't believe you've got a sister,' I laughed. 'If you have, her name is Harris!'

'Do you remember mine?' she asked with a smile.

'Cinderella. But you're going to tell me the real one now aren't you?'

She shook her head with a wicked look.

'Not even why you're here?'

'Oh, *that!* I suppose you've heard of members of my profession "resting".'

'At expensive French watering-places?'

'Dirt cheap if you know where to go.'

I eyed her keenly.

'Still, you'd no intention of coming here when I met you two days ago?'

'We all have our disappointments,' said Miss Cinderella sententiously. 'There now, I've told you quite as much as is good for you. Little boys should not be inquisitive. You've not yet told me what *you're* doing here?'

'You remember my telling you that my great friend was a detective?'

'Yes?'

'And perhaps you've heard about this crime – at the Villa Geneviève –?'

She stared at me. Her breast heaved, and her eyes grew wide and round.

'You don't mean – that you're in on *that*?'

I nodded. There was no doubt that I had scored heavily. Her emotion, as she regarded me, was only too evident. For some few seconds she remained silent, staring at me. Then she nodded her head emphatically.

'Well, if that doesn't beat the band! Tote me round. I want to see all the horrors.'

'What do you mean?'

'What I say. Bless the boy, didn't I tell you I doted on crimes? I've been nosing round for hours. It's a real piece of luck happening on you this way. Come on, show me all the sights.'

'But look here – wait a minute – I can't. Nobody's allowed in. They're awfully strict.'

'Aren't you and your friends the big bugs?'

I was loath to relinquish my position of importance.

'Why are you so keen?' I asked weakly. 'And what is it you want to see?'

'Oh, everything! The place where it happened, and the weapon, and the body, and any fingerprints or interesting things like that. I've never had a chance before of being right in on a murder like this. It'll last me all my life.'

I turned away, sickened. What were women coming to nowadays? The girl's ghoulish excitement nauseated me.

'Come off your high horse,' said the lady suddenly. 'And don't give yourself airs. When you got called to this job, did you put your nose in the air and say it was a nasty business, and you wouldn't be mixed up in it?'

'No, but –'

'If you'd been here on a holiday, wouldn't you be nosing round just the same as I am? Of course you would.'

'I'm a man. You're a woman.'

'Your idea of a woman is someone who gets on a chair and shrieks if she sees a mouse. That's all prehistoric. But you *will* show me round, won't you? You see, it might make a big difference to me.'

'In what way?'

'They're keeping all the reporters out. I might make a big scoop with one of the papers. You don't know how much they pay for a bit of inside stuff.'

I hesitated. She slipped a small soft hand into mine.

'*Please* – there's a dear.'

I capitulated. Secretly, I knew that I should rather enjoy the part of showman.

We repaired first to the spot where the body had been discovered. A man was on guard there, who saluted respectfully, knowing me by sight, and raised no questions as to my companion. Presumably he regarded her as vouched for by me. I explained to Cinderella just how the discovery had been made, and she listened attentively, sometimes putting an intelligent question. Then we turned our steps in the direction of the villa. I proceeded rather cautiously, for, truth to tell, I was not at all anxious to meet anyone. I took the girl through the shrubbery round to the back of the house where the small shed was. I recollected that yesterday evening, after relocking the door, M. Bex had left the key with the *sergent de ville*, Marchaud, 'In case Monsieur Giraud should require it while we are upstairs.' I thought it quite likely that the Sûreté detective, after using it, had returned it to Marchaud again. Leaving the girl out of sight in the shrubbery, I entered the house. Marchaud was on duty outside the door of the *salon*. From within came the murmur of voices.

'Monsieur desires Monsieur Hautet? He is within. He is again interrogating Françoise.'

'No,' I said hastily, 'I don't want him. But I should very much like the key of the shed outside if it is not against regulations.'

'But certainly, monsieur.' He produced it. 'Here it is. Monsieur Hautet gave orders that all facilities were to be placed at your disposal. You will return it to me when you have finished out there, that is all.'

'Of course.'

I felt a thrill of satisfaction as I realized that in Marchaud's eyes, at least, I ranked equally in importance with Poirot. The girl was waiting for me. She gave an exclamation of delight as she saw the key in my hand.

'You've got it then?'

'Of course,' I said coolly. 'All the same, you know, what I'm doing is highly irregular.'

'You've been a perfect duck, and I shan't forget it. Come along. They can't see us from the house, can they?'

'Wait a minute.' I arrested her eager advance. 'I won't stop you if you really wish to go in. But do you? You've seen the grave, and the grounds, and you've heard all the details of the affair. Isn't that enough for you? This is going to be gruesome, you know, and – unpleasant.'

She looked at me for a moment with an expression that I could not quite fathom. Then she laughed.

'Me for the horrors,' she said. 'Come along.'

In silence we arrived at the door of the shed. I opened it and we passed in. I walked over to the body, and gently pulled down the sheet as Bex had done the preceding afternoon. A little gasping sound escaped from the girl's lips, and I turned and looked at her. There was horror on her face now, and those debonair high spirits of hers were quenched utterly. She had not chosen to listen to my advice, and she was punished now for her disregard of it. I felt singularly merciless towards her. She should go through with it now. I turned the corpse over gently.

'You see,' I said. 'He was stabbed in the back.'

Her voice was almost soundless.

'With what?'

I nodded towards the glass jar.

'That dagger.'

Suddenly the girl reeled, and then sank down in a heap. I sprang to her assistance.

'You are faint. Come out of here. It has been too much for you.'

'Water,' she murmured. 'Quick. Water.'

I left her, and rushed into the house. Fortunately none of the servants were about, and I was able to secure a glass of water unobserved and add a few drops of brandy from a pocket flask. In a few minutes I was back again. The girl was lying as I had left her, but a few sips of the brandy and water revived her in a marvellous manner.

'Take me out of here – oh, quickly, quickly!' she cried, shuddering.

Supporting her with my arm, I led her out into the air, and she pulled the door to behind her. Then she drew a deep breath.

'That's better. Oh, it was horrible! Why did you ever let me go in?'

I felt this to be so feminine that I could not forbear a smile. Secretly, I was not dissatisfied with her collapse. It proved that she was not quite so callous as I had thought her. After all she was little more than a child, and her curiosity had probably been of the unthinking order.

'I did my best to stop you, you know,' I said gently.

'I suppose you did. Well, goodbye.'

'Look here, you can't start off like that – all alone. You're not fit for it. I insist on accompanying you back to Merlinville.'

'Nonsense. I'm quite all right now.'

'Supposing you felt faint again? No, I shall come with you.'

But this she combated with a good deal of energy. In the end, however, I prevailed so far as to be allowed to accompany her to the outskirts of the town. We retraced our steps over our former route, passing the grave again, and making a detour on to the road. Where the first straggling line of shops began, she stopped and held out her hand.

'Goodbye, and thank you ever so much for coming with me.'

'Are you sure you're all right now?'

'Quite, thanks. I hope you don't get into any trouble over showing me things.'

I disclaimed the idea lightly.

'Well, goodbye.'

'Au revoir,' I corrected. 'If you're staying here, we shall meet again.'

She flashed a smile at me.

'That's so. Au revoir, then.'

'Wait a second, you haven't told me your address.'

'Oh, I'm staying at the Hôtel du Phare. It's a little place, but quite good. Come and look me up tomorrow.'

'I will,' I said, with perhaps rather unnecessary *empressement*.

I watched her out of sight, then turned and retraced my steps to the villa. I remembered that I had not relocked the door of the shed. Fortunately no one had noticed the oversight, and turning the key I removed it and returned it to the *sergent de ville*. And, as I did so, it came upon me suddenly that though Cinderella had given me her address I still did not know her name.

CHAPTER 9

M. GIRAUD FINDS SOME CLUES

In the *salon* I found the examining magistrate busily interrogating the old gardener, Auguste. Poirot and the commissary, who were both present, greeted me respectively with a smile and a polite bow. I slipped quietly into a seat. M. Hautet was painstaking and meticulous in the extreme, but did not succeed in eliciting anything of importance.

The gardening gloves Auguste admitted to be his. He wore them when handling a certain species of primula plant which was poisonous to some people. He could not say when he had worn them last. Certainly he had not missed them. Where were they kept? Sometimes in one place, sometimes in another. The spade was usually to be found in the small tool-shed. Was it locked? Of course it was locked. Where was the key kept? *Parbleu*, it was in the door of course. There was nothing of value to steal. Who would have expected a party of bandits, or assassins? Such things did not happen in Madame la Vicomtesse's time.

M. Hautet signifying that he had finished with him, the old man withdrew, grumbling to the last. Remembering Poirot's unaccountable insistence on the footprints in the flower-beds, I scrutinized him narrowly as he gave his evidence. Either he had nothing to do with the crime or he was a consummate actor. Suddenly, just as he was going out of the door, an idea struck me.

'*Pardon*, Monsieur Hautet,' I cried, 'but will you permit me to ask him one question?'

'But certainly, monsieur.'

Thus encouraged, I turned to Auguste.

'Where do you keep your boots?'

'On my feet,' growled the old man. 'Where else?'

'But when you go to bed at night?'

'Under my bed.'

'But who cleans them?'

'Nobody. Why should they be cleaned? Is it that I promenade myself on the front like a young man? On Sunday I wear the Sunday boots, but otherwise –' He shrugged his shoulders.

I shook my head, discouraged.

'Well, well,' said the magistrate, 'we do not advance very much. Undoubtedly we are held up until we get the return cable from Santiago. Has anyone seen Giraud? In verity that one lacks politeness! I have a very good mind to send for him and –'

'You will not have to send far.'

The quiet voice startled us. Giraud was standing outside looking in through the open window.

He leapt lightly into the room and advanced to the table.

'Here I am, at your service. Accept my excuses for not presenting myself sooner.'

'Not at all – not at all!' said the magistrate, rather confused.

'Of course I am only a detective,' continued the other. 'I know nothing of interrogatories. Were I conducting one, I should be inclined to do so without an open window. Anyone standing outside can so easily hear all that passes. But no matter.'

M. Hautet flushed angrily. There was evidently going to be no love lost between the examining magistrate and the detective in charge of the case. They had fallen foul of each other at the start. Perhaps in any event it would have been much the same. To Giraud, all examining magistrates were fools, and to M. Hautet, who took himself seriously, the casual manner of the Paris detective could not fail to give offence.

'*Eh bien*, Monsieur Giraud,' said the magistrate rather sharply. 'Without doubt you have been employing your time to a marvel! You have the names of the assassins for us, have you not? And also the precise spot where they find themselves now?'

Unmoved by this irony, M. Giraud replied:

'I know at least where they have come from.'

Giraud took two small objects from his pocket and laid them down on the table. We crowded round. The objects were very simple ones: the stub of a cigarette and an unlighted match. The detective wheeled round on Poirot.

'What do you see there?' he asked.

There was something almost brutal in his tone. It made my cheeks flush. But Poirot remained unmoved. He shrugged his shoulders.

'A cigarette end and a match.'

'And what does that tell you?'

Poirot spread out his hands.

'It tells me – nothing.'

'Ah!' said Giraud, in a satisfied voice. 'You haven't made a study of these things. That's not an ordinary match – not in this country at least. It's common enough in South America. Luckily it's unlighted. I mightn't have recognized it otherwise. Evidently one of the men threw away his cigarette and lit another, spilling one match out of the box as he did so.'

'And the other match?' asked Poirot.

'Which match?'

'The one he *did* light his cigarette with. You have found that also?'

'No.'

'Perhaps you didn't search very thoroughly.'

'Not search thoroughly –' For a moment it seemed as though the detective was going to break out angrily, but with an effort he controlled himself. 'I see you love a joke, Monsieur Poirot. But in any case, match or no match, the cigarette end would be sufficient. It is a South American cigarette with liquorice pectoral paper.'

Poirot bowed. The commissary spoke:

'The cigarette end and match might have belonged to Monsieur Renauld. Remember, it is only two years since he returned from South America.'

'No,' replied the other confidently. 'I have already searched among the effects of Monsieur Renauld. The cigarettes he smoked and the matches he used are quite different.'

'You do not think it odd,' asked Poirot, 'that these strangers should come unprovided with a weapon, with gloves, with a spade, and that they should so conveniently find all these things?'

Giraud smiled in a rather superior manner.

'Undoubtedly it is strange. Indeed, without the theory that I hold, it would be inexplicable.'

'Aha!' said M. Hautet. 'An accomplice within the house!'

'Or outside it,' said Giraud, with a peculiar smile.

'But someone must have admitted them. We cannot allow that, by an unparalleled piece of good fortune, they found the door ajar for them to walk in?'

'The door was opened for them; but it could just as easily be opened from outside – by someone who possessed a key.'

'But who *did* possess a key?'

Giraud shrugged his shoulders.

'As for that, no one who possesses one is going to admit the fact if he can help it. But several people *might* have had one. Monsieur Jack Renauld, the son, for instance. It is true that he is on his way to South America, but he might have lost the key or had it stolen from him. Then there is the gardener – he has been here many years. One of the younger servants may have a lover. It is easy to take an impression of a key and have one cut. There are many possibilities. Then there is another person who, I should judge, is exceedingly likely to have such a thing.'

'Who is that?'

'Madame Daubreuil,' said the detective.

'Eh, eh!' said the magistrate. 'So you have heard about that, have you?'

'I hear everything,' said Giraud imperturbably.

'There is one thing I could swear you have not heard,' said M. Hautet, delighted to be able to show superior knowledge, and without more ado he retailed the story of the mysterious visitor the night before. He also touched on the cheque made out to 'Duveen', and finally handed Giraud the letter signed 'Bella'.

'All very interesting. But my theory remains unaffected.'

'And your theory is?'

'For the moment I prefer not to say. Remember, I am only just beginning my investigations.'

'Tell me one thing, Monsieur Giraud,' said Poirot suddenly. 'Your theory allows for the door being opened. It does not explain why it was *left* open. When they departed, would it not have been natural for them to close it behind them? If a *sergent de ville* had chanced to come up to the house, as is sometimes done to see that all is well, they might have been discovered and overtaken almost at once.'

'Bah! They forgot it. A mistake, I grant you.'

Then, to my surprise, Poirot uttered almost the same words as he had uttered to Bex the previous evening:

'*I do not agree with you.* The door being left open was the result of either design or necessity, and any theory that does not admit that fact is bound to prove vain.'

We all regarded the little man with a good deal of astonishment. The confession of ignorance drawn from him over the match end had, I thought, been bound to humiliate him, but here he was self-satisfied as ever, laying down the law to Giraud without a tremor.

The detective twisted his moustache, eyeing my friend in a somewhat bantering fashion.

'You don't agree with me, eh? Well, what strikes you particularly about the case? Let's hear your views.'

'One thing presents itself to me as being significant. Tell me, Monsieur Giraud, does nothing strike you as familiar about this case? Is there nothing it reminds you of?'

'Familiar? Reminds me of? I can't say off-hand. I don't think so, though.'

'You are wrong,' said Poirot quietly. 'A crime almost precisely similar has been committed before.'

'When? And where?'

'Ah, that, unfortunately, I cannot for the moment remember, but I shall do so. I had hoped *you* might be able to assist me.'

Giraud snorted incredulously.

'There have been many affairs of masked men. I cannot remember the details of them all. The crimes all resemble each other more or less.'

'There is such a thing as the individual touch.' Poirot suddenly assumed his lecturing manner, and addressed us collectively. 'I am speaking to you now of the psychology of crime. Monsieur Giraud knows quite well that each criminal has his particular method, and that the police, when called in to investigate, say, a case of burglary, can often make a shrewd guess at the offender, simply by the peculiar methods he has employed. (Japp would tell you the same, Hastings.) Man is an unoriginal animal. Unoriginal within the law in his daily respectable life, equally unoriginal outside the law. If a man commits a crime, any other crime he commits will resemble it closely. The English murderer who disposed of his wives in succession by drowning them in their baths was a case in point. Had he varied his methods, he might have escaped detection to this day. But he obeyed the common dictates of human nature, arguing that what had once succeeded would succeed again, and he paid the penalty of his lack of originality.'

'And the point of all this?' sneered Giraud.

'That, when you have two crimes precisely similar in design and execution, you find the same brain behind them both. I am looking for that brain, Monsieur Giraud, and I shall find it. Here we have a true clue – a psychological clue. You may know all about cigarettes and match ends, Monsieur Giraud, but I, Hercule Poirot, know the mind of man.'

Giraud remained singularly unimpressed.

'For your guidance,' continued Poirot, 'I will also advise you of one fact which might fail to be brought to your notice. The wristwatch of Madame Renauld, on the day following the tragedy, had gained two hours.'

Giraud stared.

'Perhaps it was in the habit of gaining?'

'As a matter of fact, I am told it did.'

'Very well, then.'

'All the same, two hours is a good deal,' said Poirot softly. 'Then there is the matter of the footprints in the flower-bed.'

He nodded his head towards the open window. Giraud took two eager strides, and looked out.

'But I see no footprints?'

'No,' said Poirot, straightening a little pile of books on a table. 'There are none.'

For a moment an almost murderous rage obscured Giraud's face. He took two strides towards his tormentor, but at that moment the salon door was opened, and Marchaud announced:

'Monsieur Stonor, the secretary, has just arrived from England. May he enter?'

CHAPTER 10

···

GABRIEL STONOR

The man who now entered the room was a striking figure. Very tall, with a well-knit, athletic frame, and a deeply bronzed face and neck, he dominated the assembly. Even Giraud seemed anaemic beside him. When I knew him better I realized that Gabriel Stonor was quite an unusual personality. English by birth, he had knocked about all over the world. He had shot big game in Africa, travelled in Korea, ranched in California, and traded in the South Sea islands.

His unerring eye picked out M. Hautet.

'The examining magistrate in charge of the case? Pleased to meet you, sir. This is a terrible business. How's Mrs Renauld? Is she bearing up fairly well? It must have been an awful shock to her.'

'Terrible, terrible,' said M. Hautet. 'Permit me to introduce Monsieur Bex, our commissary of police, Monsieur Giraud of the Sûreté. This gentleman is Monsieur Hercule Poirot. Mr Renauld sent for him, but he arrived too late to do anything to avert the tragedy. A friend of Monsieur Poirot's, Captain Hastings.'

Stonor looked at Poirot with some interest.

'Sent for you, did he?'

'You did not know, then, that Monsieur Renauld contemplated calling a detective?' interposed M. Bex.

'No, I didn't. But it doesn't surprise me a bit.'

'Why?'

'Because the old man was rattled. I don't know what it was all about. He didn't confide in me. We weren't on those terms. But rattled he was – and badly.'

'H'm!' said M. Hautet. 'But you have no notion of the cause?'

'That's what I said, sir.'

'You will pardon me, Monsieur Stonor, but we must begin with a few formalities. Your name?'

'Gabriel Stonor.'

'How long ago was it that you became secretary to Monsieur Renauld?'

'About two years ago, when he first arrived from South America. I met him through a mutual friend, and he offered me the post. A thundering good boss he was too.'

'Did he talk to you much about his life in South America?'

'Yes, a good bit.'

'Do you know if he was ever in Santiago?'

'Several times, I believe.'

'He never mentioned any special incident that occurred there – anything that might have provoked some vendetta against him?'

'Never.'

'Did he speak of any secret that he had acquired while sojourning there?'

'Not that I can remember. But, for all that, there *was* a mystery about him. I've never heard him speak of his boyhood, for instance, or of any incident prior to his arrival in South America. He was a French-Canadian by birth, I believe, but I've never heard him speak of his life in Canada. He could shut up like a clam if he liked.'

'So, as far as you know, he had no enemies, and you can give us no clue as to any secret to obtain possession of which he might have been murdered?'

'That's so.'

'Monsieur Stonor, have you ever heard the name of Duveen in connexion with Monsieur Renauld?'

'Duveen. Duveen.' He tried the name over thoughtfully. 'I don't think I have. And yet it seems familiar.'

'Do you know a lady, a friend of Monsieur Renauld's, whose Christian name is Bella?'

Again Mr Stonor shook his head.

'Bella Duveen? Is that the full name? It's curious. I'm sure I know it. But for the moment I can't remember in what connexion.'

The magistrate coughed.

'You understand, Monsieur Stonor – the case is like this. *There must be no reservations.* You might, perhaps, through a feeling of consideration for Madame Renauld – for whom, I gather, you have a great esteem and affection – you might – in fact!' said M. Hautet, getting rather tied up in his sentence, 'there must absolutely be no reservations.'

Stonor stared at him, a dawning light of comprehension in his eyes.

'I don't quite get you,' he said gently. 'Where does Mrs Renauld come in? I've an immense respect and affection for that lady; she's a very wonderful and unusual type, but I don't quite see how my reservations, or otherwise, could affect her.'

'Not if this Bella Duveen should prove to have been something more than a friend to her husband?'

'Ah!' said Stonor. 'I get you now. But I'll bet my bottom dollar that you're wrong. The old man never so much as looked at a petticoat. He just adored his own wife. They were the most devoted couple I know.'

M. Hautet shook his head gently.

'Monsieur Stonor, we hold absolute proof – a love-letter written by this Bella to Monsieur Renauld, accusing him of having tired of her. Moreover, we have further proof that, at the time of his death, he was carrying on an intrigue with a Frenchwoman, a Madame Daubreuil, who rents the adjoining villa.'

The secretary's eyes narrowed.

'Hold on, sir. You're barking up the wrong tree. I knew Paul Renauld. What you've just been saying is plumb impossible. There's some other explanation.'

The magistrate shrugged his shoulders.

'What other explanation could there be?'

'What leads you to think it was a love affair?'

'Madame Daubreuil was in the habit of visiting him here in the evenings. Also, since Monsieur Renauld came to the Villa Geneviève, Madame Daubreuil has paid large sums of money into the bank in notes. In all, the amount totals four thousand pounds of your English money.'

'I guess that's right,' said Stonor quietly. 'I transmitted him those sums in notes at his request. But it wasn't an intrigue.'

'What else could it be?'

'*Blackmail*,' said Stonor sharply, bringing down his hand with a slam on the table. 'That's what it was.'

'Ah!' cried the magistrate, shaken in spite of himself.

'Blackmail,' repeated Stonor. 'The old man was being bled – and at a good rate too. Four thousand in a couple of months. Whew! I told you just now there was a mystery about Renauld. Evidently this Madame Daubreuil knew enough of it to put the screw on.'

'It is possible,' the commissary cried excitedly. 'Decidedly it is possible.'

'Possible?' roared Stonor. 'It's certain. Tell me, have you asked Mrs Renauld about this love-affair stunt of yours?'

'No, monsieur. We did not wish to occasion her any distress if it could reasonably be avoided.'

'Distress? Why, she'd laugh in your face. I tell you, she and Renauld were a couple in a hundred.'

'Ah, that reminds me of another point,' said M. Hautet. 'Did Monsieur Renauld take you into his confidence at all as to the dispositions of his will?'

'I know all about it – took it to the lawyers for him after he'd drawn it out. I can give you the name of his solicitors if you want to see it. They've got it there. Quite simple. Half in trust to his wife for her lifetime, the other half to his son. A few legacies. I rather think he left me a thousand.'

'When was this will drawn up?'

'Oh, about a year and a half ago.'

'Would it surprise you very much, Monsieur Stonor, to hear that Monsieur Renauld had made another will, less than a fortnight ago?'

Stonor was obviously very much surprised.

'I'd no idea of it. What's it like?'

'The whole of his vast fortune is left unreservedly to his wife. There is no mention of his son.'

Mr Stonor gave vent to a prolonged whistle.

'I call that rather rough on the lad. His mother adores him of course, but to the world at large it looks rather like a want of confidence on his father's part. It will be rather galling to his pride. Still, it all goes to prove what I told you, that Renauld and his wife were on first-rate terms.'

'Quite so, quite so,' said M. Hautet. 'It is possible we shall have to revise our ideas on several points. We have, of course, cabled to Santiago, and are expecting a reply from there any minute. In all probability, everything will then be perfectly clear and straightforward. On the other hand, if your suggestion of blackmail is true, Madame Daubreuil ought to be able to give us valuable information.'

Poirot interjected a remark:

'Monsieur Stonor, the English chauffeur, Masters, had he been long with Monsieur Renauld?'

'Over a year.'

'Have you any idea whether he has ever been in South America?'

'I'm quite sure he hasn't. Before coming to M. Renauld he had been for many years with some people in Gloucestershire whom I know well.'

'In fact, you can answer for him as being above suspicion?'

'Absolutely.'

Poirot seemed somewhat crestfallen.

Meanwhile the magistrate had summoned Marchaud.

'My compliments to Madame Renauld, and I should be glad to speak to her for a few minutes. Beg her not to disturb herself. I will wait upon her upstairs.'

Marchaud saluted and disappeared.

We waited some minutes, and then, to our surprise, the door opened, and Mrs Renauld, deathly pale in her heavy mourning, entered the room.

M. Hautet brought forward a chair, uttering vigorous protestations, and she thanked him with a smile. Stonor was holding one hand of hers in his with an eloquent sympathy. Words evidently failed him. Mrs Renauld turned to M. Hautet.

'You wish to ask me something?'

'With your permission, madame. I understand your husband was a French-Canadian by birth. Can you tell me anything of his youth or upbringing?'

She shook her head.

'My husband was always very reticent about himself, monsieur. He came from the North-West, I know, but I fancy that he had an unhappy childhood, for he never cared to speak of that time. Our life was lived entirely in the present and the future.'

'Was there any mystery in his past life?'

Mrs Renauld smiled a little and shook her head.

'Nothing so romantic, I am sure, monsieur.'

M. Hautet also smiled.

'True, we must not permit ourselves to get melodramatic. There is one thing more –' He hesitated.

Stonor broke in impetuously:

'They've got an extraordinary idea into their heads, Mrs Renauld. They actually fancy that Mr Renauld was carrying on an intrigue with a Madame Daubreuil who, it seems, lives next door.'

The scarlet colour flamed into Mrs Renauld's cheeks. She flung her head up, then bit her lip, her face quivering. Stonor stood looking at her in astonishment, but M. Bex leaned forward and said gently:

'We regret to cause you pain, madame, but have you any reason to believe that Madame Daubreuil was your husband's mistress?'

With a sob of anguish, Mrs Renauld buried her face in her hands. Her shoulders heaved convulsively. At last she lifted her head and said brokenly:

'She may have been.'

Never, in all my life, have I seen anything to equal the blank amazement on Stonor's face. He was thoroughly taken aback.

CHAPTER 11

JACK RENAULD

What the next development of the conversation would have been I cannot say, for at that moment the door was thrown open violently and a tall young man strode into the room.

Just for a moment I had the uncanny sensation that the dead man had come to life again. Then I realized that this dark head was untouched with grey, and that, in point of fact, it was a mere boy who now burst in among us with so little ceremony. He went straight to Mrs Renauld with an impetuosity that took no heed of the presence of others.

'Mother!'

'Jack!' With a cry she folded him in her arms. 'My dearest! But what brings you here? You were to sail on the *Anzora* from Cherbourg two days ago?' Then, suddenly recalling to herself the presence of others, she turned with a certain dignity: 'My son, messieurs.'

'Aha!' said M. Hautet, acknowledging the young man's bow. 'So you did not sail on the *Anzora*?'

'No, monsieur. As I was about to explain, the *Anzora* was detained twenty-four hours through engine trouble. I should have sailed last night instead of the night before, but, happening to buy an evening paper, I saw in it an account of the – the awful tragedy that had befallen us –' His voice broke and the tears came into his eyes. 'My poor father – my poor, poor father.'

Staring at him like one in a dream, Mrs Renauld repeated:

'So you did not sail?' And then, with a gesture of infinite weariness, she murmured as though to herself: 'After all, it does not matter – now.'

'Sit down, Monsieur Renauld, I beg of you,' said M. Hautet, indicating a chair. 'My sympathy for you is profound. It must have been a terrible shock to you to learn the news as you did. However, it is most fortunate that you were prevented from sailing. I am in hopes that you may be able to give us just the information we need to clear up this mystery.'

'I am at your disposal, monsieur. Ask me any questions you please.'

'To begin with, I understand that this journey was being undertaken at your father's request?'

'Quite so, monsieur. I received a telegram bidding me to proceed without delay to Buenos Aires, and from thence *via* the Andes to Valparaiso, and on to Santiago.'

'Ah! And the object of this journey?'

'I have no idea.'

'What?'

'No. See, here in the telegram.'

The magistrate took it and read it aloud:

'"Proceed immediately Cherbourg embark *Anzora* sailing tonight Buenos Aires. Ultimate destination Santiago. Further instructions will await you Buenos Aires. Do not fail. Matter is of utmost importance. RENAULD." And there had been no previous correspondence on the matter?'

Jack Renauld shook his head.

'That is the only intimation of any kind. I knew, of course, that my father, having lived so long out there, had necessarily many interests in South America. But he had never mooted any suggestion of sending me out.'

'You have, of course, been a good deal in South America, M. Renauld?'

'I was there as a child. But I was educated in England, and spent most of my holidays in that country, so I really know far less of South America than might be supposed. You see, the War broke out when I was seventeen.'

'You served in the English Flying Corps, did you not?'

'Yes, monsieur.'

M. Hautet nodded his head and proceeded with his inquiries along the, by now, well-known lines. In response, Jack Renauld declared definitely that he knew nothing of any enmity his father might have incurred in the city of Santiago or elsewhere in the South American continent, that he had noticed no change in his father's manner of late, and that he had never heard him refer to a secret. He had regarded the mission to South America as connected with business interests.

As M. Hautet paused for a minute, the quiet voice of Giraud broke in:

'I should like to put a few questions of my own, Monsieur le juge.'

'By all means, Monsieur Giraud, if you wish,' said the magistrate coldly.

Giraud edged his chair a little nearer to the table.

'Were you on good terms with your father, Monsieur Renauld?'

'Certainly I was,' returned the lad haughtily.

'You assert that positively?'

'Yes.'

'No little disputes, eh?'

Jack shrugged his shoulders. 'Everyone may have a difference of opinion now and then.'

'Quite so, quite so. But, if anyone were to assert that you had a violent quarrel with your father on the eve of your departure for Paris, that person, without doubt, would be lying?'

I could not but admire the ingenuity of Giraud. His boast, 'I know everything,' had been no idle one. Jack Renauld was clearly disconcerted by the question.

'We – we did have an argument,' he admitted.

'Ah, an argument! In the course of that argument, did you use this phrase: "When you are dead I can do as I please"?'

'I may have done,' muttered the other. 'I don't know.'

'In response to that, did your father say: "But I am not dead yet!"? To which you responded: "I wish you were!"'

The boy made no answer. His hands fiddled nervously with the things on the table in front of him.

'I must request an answer, please, Monsieur Renauld,' said Giraud sharply.

With an angry exclamation, the boy swept a heavy paper-knife to the floor.

'What does it matter? You might as well know. Yes, I did quarrel with my father. I dare say I said all those things – I was so angry I cannot even remember what I said! I was furious – I could almost have killed him at that moment – there, make the most of that!' He leant back in his chair, flushed and defiant.

Giraud smiled, then, moving his chair back a little, said:

'That is all. You would, without doubt, prefer to continue the interrogatory, Monsieur Hautet.'

'Ah, yes, exactly,' said M. Hautet. 'And what was the subject of your quarrel?'

'That I decline to state.'

M. Hautet sat up in his chair.

'Monsieur Renauld, it is not permitted to trifle with the law!' he thundered. 'What was the subject of the quarrel?'

Young Renauld remained silent, his boyish face sullen and

overcast. But another voice spoke, imperturbable and calm, the voice of Hercule Poirot:

'I will inform you, if you like, monsieur.'

'You know?'

'Certainly I know. The subject of the quarrel was Mademoiselle Marthe Daubreuil.'

Renauld sprang round, startled. The magistrate leaned forward.

'Is that so, monsieur?'

Jack Renauld bowed his head.

'Yes,' he admitted. 'I love Mademoiselle Daubreuil, and I wish to marry her. When I informed my father of the fact he flew at once into a violent rage. Naturally, I could not stand hearing the girl I loved insulted, and I, too, lost my temper.'

M. Hautet looked across at Mrs Renauld.

'You were aware of this – attachment, madame?'

'I feared it,' she replied simply.

'Mother,' cried the boy. 'You too! Marthe is as good as she is beautiful. What can you have against her?'

'I have nothing against Mademoiselle Daubreuil in any way. But I should prefer you to marry an Englishwoman, or if a Frenchwoman, not one who has a mother of doubtful antecedents!'

Her rancour against the older woman showed plainly in her voice, and I could well understand that it must have been a bitter blow to her when her only son showed signs of falling in love with the daughter of her rival.

Mrs Renauld continued, addressing the magistrate:

'I ought, perhaps, to have spoken to my husband on the subject, but I hoped that it was only a boy and girl flirtation which would blow over all the quicker if no notice was taken of it. I blame myself now for my silence, but my husband, as I told you, had seemed so anxious and careworn, different altogether from his normal self, that I was chiefly concerned not to give him any additional worry.'

M. Hautet nodded.

'When you informed your father of your intentions towards Mademoiselle Daubreuil,' he resumed, 'he was surprised?'

'He seemed completely taken aback. Then he ordered me peremptorily to dismiss any such idea from my mind. He would never give his consent to such a marriage. Nettled, I demanded what he had against Mademoiselle Daubreuil. To that he could give no satisfactory reply, but spoke in slighting terms of the mystery surrounding the lives of the mother and daughter. I answered that I was marrying Marthe and not her antecedents, but he shouted me down with a peremptory refusal to discuss the matter in any way. The whole thing must be given up. The injustice and high-handedness of it all maddened me – especially since he himself always seemed to go out of his way to be attentive to the Daubreuils and was always suggesting that they should be asked to the house. I lost my head, and we quarrelled in earnest. My father reminded me that I was entirely dependent on him, and it must have been in answer to that that I made the remark about doing as I pleased after his death –'

Poirot interrupted with a quick question:

'You were aware, then, of the terms of your father's will?'

'I knew that he had left half his fortune to me, the other half in trust for my mother, to come to me at her death,' replied the lad.

'Proceed with your story,' said the magistrate.

'After that we shouted at each other in sheer rage, until I suddenly realized that I was in danger of missing my train to Paris. I had to run for the station, still in a white heat of fury. However, once well away, I calmed down. I wrote to Marthe, telling her what had happened, and her reply soothed me still further. She pointed out to me that we had only to be steadfast, and any opposition was bound to give way at last. Our affection for each other must be tried and proved, and when my parents realized that it was no light infatuation on my part they would doubtless relent towards us. Of course, to her, I had not dwelt on my father's principal objection to the match. I soon saw that I should do my cause no good by violence.'

'To pass to another matter, are you acquainted with the name of Duveen, Monsieur Renauld?'

'Duveen?' said Jack. 'Duveen?' He leant forward and slowly picked up the paper-knife he had swept from the table. As he lifted his head his eyes met the watching ones of Giraud. 'Duveen? No, I can't say I do.'

'Will you read this letter, Monsieur Renauld? And tell me if you have any idea as to who the person was who addressed it to your father.'

Jack Renauld took the letter and read it through, the colour mounting in his face as he did so.

'Addressed to my father?' The emotion and indignation in his tones were evident.

'Yes. We found it in the pocket of his coat.'

'Does –' He hesitated, throwing the merest fraction of a glance towards his mother.

The magistrate understood.

'As yet – no. Can you give us any clue as to the writer?'

'I have no idea whatsoever.'

M. Hautet sighed.

'A most mysterious case. Ah, well, I suppose we can now rule out the letter altogether. Let me see, where were we? Oh, the weapon. I fear this may give you pain, Monsieur Renauld. I understand it was a present from you to your mother. Very sad – very distressing –'

Jack Renauld leaned forward. His face, which had flushed during the perusal of the letter, was now deadly white.

'Do you mean – that it was with an aeroplane wire paper-cutter that my father was – was killed? But it's impossible! A little thing like that!'

'Alas, Monsieur Renauld, it is only too true! An ideal little tool, I fear. Sharp and easy to handle.'

'Where is it? Can I see it? Is it still in the – the body?'

'Oh no, it has been removed. You would like to see it? To make sure? It would be as well, perhaps, though madame has already identified it. Still – Monsieur Bex, might I trouble you?'

'Certainly. I will fetch it immediately.'

'Would it not be better to take Monsieur Renauld to the shed?' suggested Giraud smoothly. 'Without doubt he would wish to see his father's body.'

The boy made a shivering gesture of negation, and the magistrate, always disposed to cross Giraud whenever possible, replied:

'But no – not at present. Monsieur Bex will be so kind as to bring it to us here.'

The commissary left the room. Stonor crossed to Jack and wrung him by the hand. Poirot had risen, and was adjusting a pair of candlesticks that struck his trained eye as being a shade askew. The magistrate was reading the mysterious love-letter through a last time, clinging desperately to his first theory of jealousy and a stab in the back.

Suddenly the door burst open and the commissary rushed in.

'Monsieur le juge! Monsieur le juge!'

'But yes. What is it?'

'The dagger! It is gone!'

'What – gone?'

'Vanished. Disappeared. The glass jar that contained it is empty!'

'What?' I cried. 'Impossible. Why, only this morning I saw –' The words died on my tongue.

But the attention of the entire room was diverted to me.

'What is that you say?' cried the commissary. 'This morning?'

'I saw it there this morning,' I said slowly. 'About an hour and a half ago, to be accurate.'

'You went to the shed, then? How did you get the key?'

'I asked the *sergent de ville* for it.'

'And you went there? Why?'

I hesitated, but in the end I decided that the only thing to do was to make a clean breast of it.

'Monsieur Hautet,' I said, 'I have committed a grave fault, for which I must crave your indulgence.'

'Proceed, monsieur.'

'The fact of the matter is,' I said, wishing myself anywhere else but where I was, 'that I met a young lady, an acquaintance of mine. She displayed a great desire to see everything that was to be seen, and I – well, in short, I took the key to show her the body.'

'Ah!' cried the magistrate indignantly. 'But it is a grave fault you have committed there, Captain Hastings. It is altogether most irregular. You should not have permitted yourself this folly.'

'I know,' I said meekly. 'Nothing that you can say could be too severe, monsieur.'

'You did not invite this lady to come here?'

'Certainly not. I met her quite by accident. She is an English lady who happens to be staying in Merlinville, though I was not aware of that until my unexpected meeting with her.'

'Well, well,' said the magistrate, softening. 'It was most irregular, but the lady is without doubt young and beautiful. What it is to be young!' And he sighed sentimentally.

But the commissary, less romantic and more practical, took up the tale:

'But did you not reclose and lock the door when you departed?'

'That's just it,' I said slowly. 'That's what I blame myself for so terribly. My friend was upset at the sight. She nearly fainted. I got her some brandy and water, and afterwards insisted on accompanying her back to the town. In the excitement I forgot to relock the door. I only did so when I got back to the villa.'

'Then for twenty minutes at least –' said the commissary slowly. He stopped.

'Exactly,' I said.

'Twenty minutes,' mused the commissary.

'It is deplorable,' said M. Hautet, his sternness of manner returning. 'Without precedent.'

Suddenly another voice spoke.

'You find it deplorable?' asked Giraud.

'Certainly I do.'

'I find it admirable!' said the other imperturbably.

This unexpected ally quite bewildered me.

'Admirable, Monsieur Giraud?' asked the magistrate, studying him cautiously out of the corner of his eye.

'Precisely.'

'And why?'

'Because we know now that the assassin, or an accomplice of the assassin, has been near the villa only an hour ago. It will be strange if, with that knowledge, we do not shortly lay hands upon him.' There was a note of menace in his voice. He continued: 'He risked a good deal to gain possession of that dagger. Perhaps he feared that fingerprints might be discovered on it.'

Poirot turned to Bex.

'You said there were none?'

Giraud shrugged his shoulders.

'Perhaps he could not be sure.'

Poirot looked at him.

'You are wrong, Monsieur Giraud. The assassin wore gloves. So he must have been sure.'

'I do not say it was the assassin himself. It may have been an accomplice who was not aware of that fact.'

The magistrate's clerk was gathering up the papers on the table. M. Hautet addressed us:

'Our work here is finished. Perhaps, Monsieur Renauld, you will listen while your evidence is read over to you. I have purposely kept all the proceedings as informal as possible. I have been called original in my methods, but I maintain that there is much to be said for originality. The case is now in the clever hands of the renowned Monsieur Giraud. He will without doubt distinguish himself. Indeed, I wonder that he has not already laid his hands upon the murderers! Madame, again let me assure you of my heartfelt sympathy. Messieurs, I wish you all good day.' And, accompanied by his clerk and the commissary, he took his departure.

Poirot tugged out that large turnip of a watch of his and observed the time.

'Let us return to the hotel for lunch, my friend,' he said. 'And you shall recount to me in full the indiscretions of this morning. No one is observing us. We need make no adieux.'

We went quietly out of the room. The examining magistrate had just driven off in his car. I was going down the steps when Poirot's voice arrested me:

'One little moment, my friend.' Dexterously he whipped out his yard measure and proceeded, quite solemnly, to measure an overcoat hanging in the hall, from the collar to the hem. I had not seen it hanging there before, and guessed that it belonged to either Mr Stonor or Jack Renauld.

Then, with a little satisfied grunt, Poirot returned the measure to his pocket and followed me out into the open air.

CHAPTER 12

POIROT ELUCIDATES CERTAIN POINTS

'Why did you measure that overcoat?' I asked, with some curiosity, as we walked down the hot white road at a leisurely pace.

'*Parbleu!* to see how long it was,' replied my friend imperturbably.

I was vexed. Poirot's incurable habit of making a mystery out of nothing never failed to irritate me. I relapsed into silence, and followed a train of thought of my own. Although I had not noticed them specially at the time, certain words Mrs Renauld had addressed to her son now recurred to me, fraught with a new significance. 'So you did not sail?' she had said, and then had added: '*After all, it does not matter – now.*'

What had she meant by that? The words were enigmatical – significant. Was it possible that she knew more than we supposed? She had denied all knowledge of the mysterious mission with which her husband was to have entrusted his son. But was she really less ignorant than she pretended? Could she enlighten us if she chose, and was her silence part of a carefully thought out and preconceived plan?

The more I thought about it, the more I was convinced that I was right. Mrs Renauld knew more than she chose to tell. In her surprise at seeing her son, she had momentarily betrayed herself. I felt convinced that she knew, if not the assassins, at least the motive for the assassination. But some very powerful considerations must keep her silent.

'You think profoundly, my friend,' remarked Poirot, breaking in upon my reflections. 'What is it that intrigues you so?'

I told him, sure of my ground, though feeling expectant that he would ridicule my suspicions. But to my surprise he nodded thoughtfully.

'You are quite right, Hastings. From the beginning I have been sure that she was keeping something back. At first I suspected her, if not of inspiring, at least of conniving at the crime.'

'You suspected *her*?' I cried.

'But certainly. She benefits enormously – in fact, by this new will, she is the only person to benefit. So, from the start, she was singled out for attention. You may have noticed that I took an early opportunity of examining her wrists. I wished to see whether there was any possibility that she had gagged and bound herself. *Eh bien*, I saw at once that there was no fake, the cords had actually been drawn so tight as to cut into the flesh. That ruled out the possibility of her having committed the crime single-handed. But it was still possible for her to have connived at it, or to have been the instigator with an accomplice. Moreover, the story, as she told it, was singularly familiar to me – the masked men that she could not recognize, the mention of "the secret" – I had heard, or read, all these things before. Another little detail confirmed my belief that she was not speaking the truth. *The wristwatch, Hastings, the wristwatch!*'

Again that wristwatch! Poirot was eyeing me curiously.

'You see, *mon ami*? You comprehend?'

'No,' I replied with some ill humour. 'I neither see nor comprehend. You make all these confounded mysteries, and it's useless asking you to explain. You always like keeping something up your sleeve to the last minute.'

'Do not enrage yourself, my friend,' said Poirot, with a smile. 'I will explain if you wish. But not a word to Giraud, *c'est entendu*? He treats me as an old one of no importance! *We shall see!* In common fairness I gave him a hint. If he does not choose to act upon it, that is his own lookout.'

I assured Poirot that he could rely upon my discretion.

'*C'est bien!* Let us then employ our little grey cells. Tell me, my friend, at what time, according to you, did the tragedy take place?'

'Why, at two o'clock or thereabouts,' I said, astonished. 'You remember, Mrs Renauld told us that she heard the clock strike while the men were in the room.'

'Exactly, and on the strength of that, you, the examining magistrate, Bex, and everyone else, accept the time without further question. But I, Hercule Poirot, say that Madame Renauld lied. *The crime took place at least two hours earlier.*'

'But the doctors –'

'They declared, after examination of the body, that death had taken place between ten and seven hours previously. *Mon ami*, for some reason it was imperative that the crime should seem to have taken place later than it actually did. You have read of a smashed watch or clock recording the exact hour of a crime? So that the time should not rest on Madame Renauld's testimony alone, someone moved on the hands of that wristwatch to two o'clock, and then dashed it violently to the ground. But, as is often the case, they defeated their own object. The glass was smashed, but the mechanism of the watch was uninjured. It was a most disastrous manœuvre on their part, for it at once drew my attention to two points – first, that Madame Renauld was lying; secondly, that there must be some vital reason for the postponement of the time.'

'But what reason could there be?'

'Ah, that is the question! There we have the whole mystery. As yet, I cannot explain it. There is only one idea that presents itself to me as having a possible connexion.'

'And that is?'

'The last train left Merlinville at seventeen minutes past twelve.' I followed it out slowly.

'So that, the crime apparently taking place some two hours later, anyone leaving by that train would have an unimpeachable alibi!'

'Perfect, Hastings! You have it!'

I sprang up.

'But we must inquire at the station! Surely they cannot have failed to notice two foreigners who left by that train! We must go there at once!'

'You think so, Hastings?'

'Of course. Let us go there now.'

Poirot restrained my ardour with a light touch upon the arm.

'Go by all means if you wish, *mon ami* – but if you go, I should not ask for particulars of two foreigners.'

I stared and he said rather impatiently:

'*Là, là*, you do not believe all that rigmarole, do you? The masked men and all the rest of *cette histoire-là!*'

His words took me so much aback, that I hardly knew how to respond. He went on serenely:

'You heard me say to Giraud, did you not, that all the details of this crime were familiar to me? *Eh bien*, that presupposes one of two things, either the brain that planned the first crime also planned this one, or else an account read of a *cause célèbre* unconsciously remained in our assassin's memory and prompted the details. I shall be able to pronounce definitely on that after –' He broke off.

I was revolving sundry matters in my mind.

'But Mr Renauld's letter? It distinctly mentions a secret and Santiago!'

'Undoubtedly there was a secret in Monsieur Renauld's life

– there can be no doubt of that. On the other hand, the word Santiago, to my mind, is a red herring, dragged continually across the track to put us off the scent. It is possible that it was used in the same way on Monsieur Renauld, to keep him from directing his suspicions to a quarter nearer at hand. Oh, be assured, Hastings, the danger that threatened him was not in Santiago, it was near at hand, in France.'

He spoke so gravely, and with such assurance, that I could not fail to be convinced. But I essayed one final objection:

'And the match and cigarette end found near the body? What of them?'

A light of pure enjoyment lit up Poirot's face.

'Planted! Deliberately planted there for Giraud or one of his tribe to find! Ah, he is smart, Giraud, he can do his tricks! So can a good retriever dog. He comes in so pleased with himself. For hours he has crawled on his stomach. "See what I have found," he says. And then again to me: "What do you see here?" Me, I answer, with profound and deep truth, "Nothing." And Giraud, the great Giraud, he laughs, he thinks to himself, "Oh, he is imbecile, this old one!" *But we shall see . . .*'

But my mind had reverted to the main facts.

'Then all this story of the masked men –?'

'Is false.'

'What really happened?'

Poirot shrugged his shoulders.

'One person could tell us – Madame Renauld. But she will not speak. Threats and entreaties would not move her. A remarkable woman that, Hastings. I recognized as soon as I saw her that I had to deal with a woman of unusual character. At first, as I told you, I was inclined to suspect her of being concerned in the crime. Afterwards I altered my opinion.'

'What made you do that?'

'Her spontaneous and genuine grief at the sight of her husband's body. I could swear that the agony in that cry of hers was genuine.'

'Yes,' I said thoughtfully, 'one cannot mistake these things.'

'I beg your pardon, my friend – one can always be mistaken. Regard a great actress, does not her acting of grief carry you away and impress you with its reality? No, however strong my own impression and belief, I needed other evidence before I allowed myself to be satisfied. The great criminal can be a great actor. I base my certainty in this case not upon my own impression, but upon the undeniable fact that Madame Renauld actually fainted. I turned up her eyelids and felt her pulse. There was no deception – the swoon was genuine. Therefore I was satisfied that her anguish was real and not assumed. Besides, a small additional point without interest, it was unnecessary for Madame Renauld to exhibit unrestrained grief. She had had one paroxysm on learning of her husband's death, and there would be no need for her to simulate another such a violent one on beholding his body. No, Madame Renauld was not her husband's murderess. But why has she lied? She lied about the wristwatch, she lied about the masked men – she lied about a third thing. Tell me, Hastings, what is your explanation of the open door?'

'Well,' I said, rather embarrassed, 'I suppose it was an oversight. They forgot to shut it.'

Poirot shook his head, and sighed.

'That is the explanation of Giraud. It does not satisfy me. There is a meaning behind that open door which for the moment I cannot fathom. One thing I am fairly sure of – they did not leave through the door. They left by the window.'

'What?'

'Precisely.'

'But there were no footmarks in the flower-bed underneath.'

'No – and there ought to have been. Listen, Hastings. The gardener, Auguste, as you heard him say, planted both those beds the preceding afternoon. In the one there are plentiful impressions of his big hobnailed boots – in the other, *none!* You see? Someone had passed that way, someone who, to obliterate their footprints, smoothed over the surface of the bed with a rake.'

'Where did they get a rake?'

'Where they got the spade and the gardening gloves,' said Poirot impatiently. 'There is no difficulty about that.'

'What makes you think that they left that way, though? Surely it is more probable that they entered by the window, and left by the door?'

'That is possible, of course. Yet I have a strong idea that they left by the window.'

'I think you are wrong.'

'Perhaps, *mon ami*.'

I mused, thinking over the new field of conjecture that Poirot's deductions had opened up to me. I recalled my wonder at his cryptic allusion to the flower-bed and the wristwatch. His remarks had seemed so meaningless at the moment, and now, for the first time, I realized how remarkably, from a few slight incidents, he had unravelled much of the mystery that surrounded the case. I paid a belated homage to my friend.

'In the meantime,' I said, considering, 'although we know a great deal more than we did, we are no nearer to solving the mystery of who killed Mr Renauld.'

'No,' said Poirot cheerfully. 'In fact we are a great deal farther off.'

The fact seemed to afford him such peculiar satisfaction that I gazed at him in wonder. He met my eye and smiled.

Suddenly a light burst upon me.

'Poirot! Mrs Renauld! I see it now. She must be shielding somebody.'

From the quietness with which Poirot received my remark, I could see that the idea had already occurred to him.

'Yes,' he said thoughtfully. 'Shielding someone – or screening someone. One of the two.'

Then, as we entered our hotel, he enjoined silence on me with a gesture.

CHAPTER 13
....
THE GIRL WITH THE ANXIOUS EYES

We lunched with an excellent appetite. For a while we ate in silence, and then Poirot observed maliciously: '*Eh bien!* And your indiscretions! You recount them not?'

I felt myself blushing.

'Oh, you mean this morning?' I endeavoured to adopt a tone of absolute nonchalance.

But I was no match for Poirot. In a very few minutes he had extracted the whole story from me, his eyes twinkling as he did so.

'*Tiens!* A story of the most romantic. What is her name, this charming young lady?'

I had to confess that I did not know.

'Still more romantic! The first *rencontre* in the train from Paris, the second here. Journeys end in lovers' meetings, is not that the saying?'

'Don't be an ass, Poirot.'

'Yesterday it was Mademoiselle Daubreuil, today it is Mademoiselle – Cinderella! Decidedly you have the heart of a Turk, Hastings! You should establish a harem!'

'It's all very well to rag me. Mademoiselle Daubreuil is a very beautiful girl, and I do admire her immensely – I don't mind admitting it. The other's nothing – I don't suppose I shall ever see her again.'

'You do not propose to see the lady again?'

His last words were almost a question, and I was aware of the sharpness with which he darted a glance at me. And before my eyes, writ large in letters of fire, I saw the words 'Hôtel du Phare', and I heard again her voice saying, 'Come and look me up', and my own answering with *empressement* 'I will.'

I answered Poirot lightly enough:

'She asked me to look her up, but, of course, I shan't.'

'Why "of course"?'

'Well, I don't want to.'

'Mademoiselle Cinderella is staying at the Hôtel d'Angleterre you told me, did you not?'

'No. Hôtel du Phare.'

'True, I forgot.'

A moment's misgiving shot across my mind. Surely I had never mentioned any hotel to Poirot. I looked across at him and felt reassured. He was cutting his bread into neat little squares, completely absorbed in his task. He must have fancied I had told him where the girl was staying.

We had coffee outside facing the sea. Poirot smoked one of his tiny cigarettes, and then drew his watch from his pocket.

'The train to Paris leaves at 2.25,' he observed. 'I should be starting.'

'Paris?' I cried.

'That is what I said, *mon ami.*'

'You are going to Paris? But why?'

He replied very seriously:

'To look for the murderer of Monsieur Renauld.'

'You think he is in Paris?'

'I am quite certain that he is not. Nevertheless, it is there that I must look for him. You do not understand, but I will explain it all to you in good time. Believe me, this journey to Paris is necessary. I shall not be away long. In all probability I shall return tomorrow. I do not propose that you should accompany me. Remain here and keep an eye on Giraud. Also cultivate the society of Monsieur Renauld *fils*.'

'That reminds me,' I said. 'I meant to ask you how you knew about those two?'

'*Mon ami* – I know human nature. Throw together a boy like young Renauld and a beautiful girl like Mademoiselle Marthe and the result is almost inevitable. Then, the quarrel! It was money, or a woman, and, remembering Léonie's description of the lad's anger, I decided on the latter. So I made my guess – and I was right.'

'You already suspected that she loved young Renauld?' Poirot smiled.

'At any rate, *I saw that she had anxious eyes*. That is how I always think of Mademoiselle Daubreuil – *as the girl with the anxious eyes*.'

His voice was so grave that it impressed me uncomfortably.

'What do you mean by that, Poirot?'

'I fancy, my friend, that we shall see before very long. But I must start.'

'I will come and see you off,' I said, rising.

'You will do nothing of the sort. I forbid it.'

He was so peremptory that I stared at him in surprise. He nodded emphatically.

'I mean it, *mon ami*. Au revoir.'

I felt rather at a loose end after Poirot had left me. I strolled down to the beach and watched the bathers, without feeling energetic enough to join them. I rather fancied that Cinderella might be disporting herself among them in some wonderful costume, but I saw no signs of her. I strolled aimlessly along the sands towards the farther end of the town. It occurred to me that, after all, it would only be decent feeling on my part to inquire after the girl. And it would save trouble in the end. The matter would then be finished with. There would be no need for me to trouble about her any further. But if I did not go at all, she might quite possibly come and look me up at the villa.

Accordingly, I left the beach, and walked inland. I soon found the Hôtel du Phare, a very unpretentious building. It was annoying in the extreme not to know the lady's name and, to save my dignity, I decided to stroll inside and look around. Probably I should find her in the lounge. I went in, but there was no sign of her. I waited for some time, till my impatience got the better of me. I took the concierge aside and slipped five francs into his hand.

'I wish to see a lady who is staying here. A young English lady, small and dark. I am not sure of her name.'

The man shook his head and seemed to be suppressing a grin.

'There is no such lady as you describe staying here.'

'But the lady told me she was staying here.'

'Monsieur must have made a mistake – or it is more likely the lady did, since there has been another gentleman here inquiring for her.'

'What is that you say?' I cried, surprised.

'But yes, monsieur. A gentleman who described her just as you have done.'

'What was he like?'

'He was a small gentleman, well dressed, very neat, very spotless, the moustache very stiff, the head of a peculiar shape, and the eyes green.'

Poirot! So that was why he refused to let me accompany him to the station. The impertinence of it! I would thank him not to meddle in my concerns. Did he fancy I needed a nurse to look after me?

Thanking the man, I departed, somewhat at a loss, and still much incensed with my meddlesome friend.

But where was the lady? I set aside my wrath and tried to puzzle it out. Evidently, through inadvertence, she had named the wrong hotel. Then another thought struck me. Was it inadvertence? Or had she deliberately withheld her name and given me the wrong address?

The more I thought about it, the more I felt convinced that this last surmise of mine was right. For some reason or other she did not wish to let the acquaintance ripen into friendship. And, though half an hour earlier this had been precisely my own view, I did not enjoy having the tables turned upon me. The whole affair was profoundly unsatisfactory, and I went up to the Villa Geneviève in a condition of distinct ill humour. I did not go to the house, but went up the path to the little bench by the shed, and sat there moodily enough.

I was distracted from my thoughts by the sound of voices close at hand. In a second or two I realized that they came, not from the garden I was in, but from the adjoining garden of the Villa Marguerite, and that they were approaching rapidly. A girl's voice was speaking, a voice that I recognized as that of the beautiful Marthe.

'*Chéri*,' she was saying, 'is it really true? Are all our troubles over?'

'You know it, Marthe,' Jack Renauld replied. 'Nothing can part us now, beloved. The last obstacle to our union is removed. Nothing can take you from me.'

'Nothing?' the girl murmured. 'Oh Jack, Jack – I am afraid.'

I had moved to depart, realizing that I was quite unintentionally eavesdropping. As I rose to my feet, I caught sight of them through a gap in the hedge. They stood together facing me, the man's arm round the girl, his eyes looking into hers. They were a splendid-looking couple, the dark, well-knit boy, and the fair young goddess. They seemed made for each other as they stood there, happy in spite of the terrible tragedy that overshadowed their young lives.

But the girl's face was troubled, and Jack Renauld seemed to recognize it, as he held her closer to him and asked:

'But what are you afraid of, darling? What is there to fear – now?'

And then I saw the look in her eyes, the look Poirot had spoken of, as she murmured, so that I almost guessed at the words:

'I am afraid – for *you*.'

I did not hear young Renauld's answer, for my attention was distracted by an unusual appearance a little farther down the hedge. There appeared to be a brown bush there, which seemed odd, to say the least of it, so early in the summer. I stepped along to investigate, but, at my advance, the brown bush withdrew itself precipitately, and faced me with a finger to its lips. It was Giraud.

Enjoining caution, he led the way round the shed until we were out of ear-shot.

'What were you doing there?' I asked.

'Exactly what you were doing – listening.'

'But I was not there on purpose!'

'Ah!' said Giraud. 'I was.'

As always, I admired the man while disliking him. He looked me up and down with a sort of contemptuous disfavour.

'You didn't help matters by butting in. I might have heard something useful in a minute. What have you done with your old fossil?'

'Monsieur Poirot has gone to Paris,' I replied coldly.

Giraud snapped his fingers disdainfully. 'So he has gone to Paris, has he? Well, a good thing. The longer he stays there the better. But what does he think he will find there?'

I thought I read in the question a tinge of uneasiness. I drew myself up.

'That I am not at liberty to say,' I said quietly.

Giraud subjected me to a piercing stare.

'He has probably enough sense not to tell *you*,' he remarked rudely. 'Good afternoon. I'm busy.' And with that he turned on his heel, and left me without ceremony.

Matters seemed at a standstill at the Villa Geneviève. Giraud evidently did not desire my company and, from what I had seen, it seemed fairly certain that Jack Renauld did not either.

I went back to the town, had an enjoyable bathe, and returned to the hotel. I turned in early, wondering whether the following day would bring forth anything of interest.

I was wholly unprepared for what it did bring forth. I was eating my *petit déjeuner* in the dining-room, when the waiter, who had been talking to someone outside, came back in obvious excitement. He hesitated for a minute, fidgeting with his napkin, and then burst out:

'Monsieur will pardon me, but he is connected, is he not, with the affair at the Villa Geneviève?'

'Yes,' I said eagerly. 'Why?'

'Monsieur has not heard the news, though?'

'What news?'

'That there has been another murder there last night!'

'*What?*'

Leaving my breakfast, I caught up my hat and ran as fast as I could. Another murder – and Poirot away! What fatality. But who had been murdered?

I dashed in at the gate. A group of servants were in the drive, talking and gesticulating. I caught hold of Françoise.

'What has happened?'

'Oh, monsieur! monsieur! Another death! It is terrible. There is a curse upon the house. But yes, I say it, a curse! They should send for Monsieur le Curé to bring some holy water. Never will I sleep another night under that roof. It might be my turn, who knows?'

She crossed herself.

'Yes,' I cried, 'but who has been killed?'

'Do I know – me? A man – a stranger. They found him up there – in the shed – not a hundred yards from where they found poor Monsieur. And that is not all. He is stabbed – stabbed to the heart *with the same dagger!*'

CHAPTER 14
THE SECOND BODY

Waiting for no more, I turned and ran up the path to the shed. The two men on guard there stood aside to let me pass and, filled with excitement, I entered.

The light was dim, the place was a mere rough wooden erection to keep old pots and tools in. I had entered impetuously, but on the threshold I checked myself, fascinated by the spectacle before me.

Giraud was on his hands and knees, a pocket torch in his hand with which he was examining every inch of the ground. He looked up with a frown at my entrance, then his face relaxed a little in a sort of good-humoured contempt.

'There he is,' said Giraud, flashing his torch to the far corner.

I stepped across.

The dead man lay straight upon his back. He was of medium height, swarthy of complexion, and possibly about fifty years of age. He was neatly dressed in a dark blue suit, well cut, and probably made by an expensive tailor, but not new. His face was terribly convulsed, and on his left side, just over the heart, the hilt of a dagger stood up, black and shining. I recognized it. It was the same dagger I had seen reposing in the glass jar the preceding morning!

'I'm expecting the doctor any minute,' explained Giraud. 'Although we hardly need him. There's no doubt what the man died of. He was stabbed to the heart, and death must have been pretty well instantaneous.'

'When was it done? Last night?'

Giraud shook his head.

'Hardly. I don't lay down the law on medical evidence, but the man's been dead well over twelve hours. When do you say you last saw that dagger?'

'About ten o'clock yesterday morning.'

'Then I should be inclined to fix the crime as being done not long after that.'

'But people were passing and repassing this shed continually.'

Giraud laughed disagreeably.

'You progress to a marvel! Who told you he was killed in this shed?'

'Well –' I felt flustered. 'I – I assumed it.'

'Oh, what a fine detective! Look at him. Does a man stabbed to the heart fall like that – neatly with his feet together, and his arms to his sides? No. Again, does a man lie down on his back and permit himself to be stabbed without raising a hand to defend himself? It is absurd, is it not? But see here – and here –' He flashed the torch along the ground. I saw curious irregular marks in the soft dirt. 'He was dragged here after he was dead. Half dragged, half carried by two people. Their tracks do not show on the hard ground outside, and here they have been careful to obliterate them; but one of the two was a woman, my young friend.'

'A woman?'

'Yes.'

'But if the tracks are obliterated, how do you know?'

'Because, blurred as they are, the prints of the woman's shoe are unmistakable. Also, by *this*.' And, leaning forward, he drew something from the handle of the dagger and held it up for me to see. It was a woman's long black hair, similar to the one Poirot had taken from the armchair in the library.

With a slightly ironic smile he wound it round the dagger again.

'We will leave things as they are as much as possible,' he explained. 'It pleases the examining magistrate. Well, do you notice anything else?'

I was forced to shake my head.

'Look at his hands.'

I did. The nails were broken and discoloured and the skin was hard. It hardly enlightened me as much as I should have liked it to have done. I looked up at Giraud.

'They are not the hands of a gentleman,' he said, answering my look. 'On the contrary, his clothes are those of a well-to-do man. That is curious, is it not?'

'Very curious,' I agreed.

'And none of his clothing is marked. What do we learn from that? This man was trying to pass himself off as other than he was. He was masquerading. Why? Did he fear something? Was he trying to escape by disguising himself? As yet we do not know, but one thing we do know – he was as anxious to conceal his identity as we are to discover it.'

He looked down at the body again.

'As before, there are no fingerprints on the handle of the dagger. The murderer again wore gloves.'

'You think, then, that the murderer was the same in both cases?' I asked eagerly.

Giraud became inscrutable.

'Never mind what I think. We shall see. Marchaud!'

The *sergent de ville* appeared at the door.

'Monsieur?'

'Why is Madame Renauld not here? I sent for her a quarter of an hour ago.'

'She is coming up the path now, monsieur, and her son with her.'

'Good. I only want one at a time, though.'

Marchaud saluted and disappeared again. A moment later he reappeared with Mrs Renauld.

'Here is Madame.'

Giraud came forward with a curt bow.

'This way, madame.' He led her across, and then, standing suddenly aside, 'Here is the man. Do you know him?'

And as he spoke, his eyes, gimlet-like, bored into her face, seeking to read her mind, noting every indication of her manner.

But Mrs Renauld remained perfectly calm – too calm, I felt. She looked down at the corpse almost without interest, certainly without any sign of agitation or recognition.

'No,' she said. 'I have never seen him in my life. He is quite a stranger to me.'

'You are sure?'

'Quite sure.'

'You do not recognize in him one of your assailants, for instance?'

'No.' She seemed to hesitate, as though struck by the idea. 'No, I do not think so. Of course they wore beards – false ones the examining magistrate thought – but still, no.' Now she seemed to make her mind up definitely. 'I am sure neither of the two was this man.'

'Very well, madame. That is all, then.'

She stepped out with head erect, the sun flashing on the silver threads in her hair. Jack Renauld succeeded her. He, too, failed to identify the man in a completely natural manner.

Giraud merely grunted. Whether he was pleased or chagrined I could not tell. He called to Marchaud.

'You have got the other there?'

'Yes, monsieur.'

'Bring her in, then.'

'The other' was Madame Daubreuil. She came indignantly, protesting with vehemence.

'I object, monsieur! This is an outrage! What have I to do with all this?'

'Madame,' said Giraud brutally, 'I am investigating not one murder, but two murders! For all I know you may have committed them both.'

'How dare you?' she cried. 'How dare you insult me by such a wild accusation! It is infamous!'

'Infamous, is it? What about this?' Stooping, he again detached the hair, and held it up. 'Do you see this, madame?' He advanced towards her. 'You permit that I see whether it matches?'

With a cry she started backwards, white to the lips.

'It is false, I swear it. I know nothing of the crime – of either crime. Anyone who says I do lies! Ah, *mon Dieu*, what shall I do?'

'Calm yourself, madame,' said Giraud coldly. 'No one has accused you as yet. But you will do well to answer my questions without more ado.'

'Anything you wish, monsieur.'

'Look at the dead man. Have you ever seen him before?'

Drawing nearer, a little of the colour creeping back to her face, Madame Daubreuil looked down at the victim with a certain amount of interest and curiosity. Then she shook her head.

'I do not know him.'

It seemed impossible to doubt her, the words came so naturally. Giraud dismissed her with a nod of the head.

'You are letting her go?' I asked in a low voice. 'Is that wise? Surely that black hair is from her head.'

'I do not need teaching my business,' said Giraud dryly. 'She is under surveillance. I have no wish to arrest her as yet.'

Then, frowning, he gazed down at the body.

'Should you say that was a Spanish type at all?' he asked suddenly.

I considered the face carefully.

'No,' I said at last. 'I should put him down as a Frenchman most decidedly.'

Giraud gave a grunt of dissatisfaction.

'Same here.'

He stood there for a moment, then with an imperative gesture he waved me aside, and once more, on hands and knees, he continued his search of the floor of the shed. He was marvellous. Nothing escaped him. Inch by inch he went over the floor, turning over pots, examining old sacks. He pounced on a bundle by the door, but it proved to be only a ragged coat and trousers, and he flung it down again with a snarl. Two pairs of old gloves interested him, but in the end he shook his head and laid them aside. Then he went back to the pots, methodically turning them over one by one. In the end he rose to his feet, and shook his head thoughtfully. He seemed baffled and perplexed. I think he had forgotten my presence.

But at that moment a stir and bustle was heard outside, and our old friend, the examining magistrate, accompanied by his clerk and M. Bex, with the doctor behind them, came bustling in.

'But this is extraordinary, Monsieur Giraud,' cried M. Hautet. 'Another crime! Ah, we have not got to the bottom of this case. There is some deep mystery here. But who is the victim this time?'

'That is just what nobody can tell us, monsieur. He has not been identified.'

'Where is the body?' asked the doctor.

Giraud moved aside a little.

'There in the corner. He has been stabbed to the heart, as you see. And with the dagger that was stolen yesterday morning. I fancy that the murder followed hard upon the theft – but that is for you to say. You can handle the dagger freely – there are no fingerprints on it.'

The doctor knelt down by the dead man, and Giraud turned to the examining magistrate.

'A pretty little problem, is it not? But I shall solve it.'

'And so no one can identify him,' mused the magistrate. 'Could it possibly be one of the assassins? They may have fallen out among themselves.'

Giraud shook his head.

'The man is a Frenchman – I would take my oath on that –'

But at that moment they were interrupted by the doctor, who was sitting back on his heels with a perplexed expression.

'You say he was killed yesterday morning?'

'I fix it by the theft of the dagger,' explained Giraud. 'He may, of course, have been killed later in the day.'

'Later in the day? Fiddlesticks! This man has been dead at least forty-eight hours, and probably longer.'

We stared at each other in blank amazement.

CHAPTER 15
A PHOTOGRAPH

The doctor's words were so surprising that we were all momentarily taken aback. Here was a man stabbed with a dagger which we knew to have been stolen only twenty-four hours previously, and yet Dr Durand asserted positively that he had been dead at least forty-eight hours! The whole thing was fantastic to the last extreme.

We were still recovering from the surprise of the doctor's announcement, when a telegram was brought to me. It had been sent up from the hotel to the villa. I tore it open. It was from Poirot, and announced his return by the train arriving at Merlinville at 12.28.

I looked at my watch and saw that I had just time to get comfortably to the station and meet him there. I felt that it was of the utmost importance that he should know at once of the new and startling developments in the case.

Evidently, I reflected, Poirot had had no difficulty in finding what he wanted in Paris. The quickness of his return proved that. Very few hours had sufficed. I wondered how he would take the exciting news I had to impart.

The train was some minutes late, and I strolled aimlessly up and down the platform, until it occurred to me that I might pass the time by asking a few questions as to who had left Merlinville by the last train on the evening of the tragedy.

I approached the chief porter, an intelligent-looking man, and had little difficulty in persuading him to enter upon the subject. It was a disgrace to the police, he hotly affirmed, that such brigands or assassins should be allowed to go about unpunished. I hinted that there was some possibility they might have left by the midnight train, but he negatived the idea decidedly. He would have noticed two foreigners – he was sure of it. Only about twenty people had left by the train, and he could not have failed to observe them.

I do not know what put the idea into my head – possibly it was the deep anxiety underlying Marthe Daubreuil's tones – but I asked suddenly:

'Young Monsieur Renauld – he did not leave by that train, did he?'

'Ah, no, monsieur. To arrive and start off again within half an hour, it would not be amusing, that!'

I stared at the man, the significance of his words almost escaping me. Then I saw.

'You mean,' I said, my heart beating a little, 'that Monsieur Jack Renauld arrived at Merlinville that evening?'

'But yes, monsieur. By the last train arriving the other way, the 11.40.'

My brain whirled. That, then, was the reason of Marthe's poignant anxiety. Jack Renauld had been in Merlinville on the night of the crime. But why had he not said so? Why, on the contrary, had he led us to believe that he had remained in Cherbourg? Remembering his frank boyish countenance, I could hardly bring myself to believe that he had any connexion with the crime. Yet why this silence on his part about so vital a matter? One thing was certain, Marthe had known all along. Hence her anxiety, and her eager questioning of Poirot as to whether anyone was suspected.

My cogitations were interrupted by the arrival of the train, and in another moment I was greeting Poirot. The little man was radiant. He beamed and vociferated and, forgetting my English reluctance, embraced me warmly on the platform.

'*Mon cher ami*, I have succeeded – but succeeded to a marvel!'

'Indeed? I'm delighted to hear it. Have you heard the latest here?'

'How would you that I should hear anything? There have been some developments, eh? The brave Giraud, he has made an arrest? Or even arrests, perhaps? Ah, but I will make him look foolish, that one! But where are you taking me, my friend? Do we not go to the hotel? It is necessary that I attend to my moustaches – they are deplorably limp from the heat of travelling. Also, without doubt, there is dust on my coat. And my tie, that I must rearrange.'

I cut short his remonstrances.

'My dear Poirot – never mind all that. We must go to the villa at once. *There has been another murder!*'

Never have I seen a man so flabbergasted. His jaw dropped. All the jauntiness went out of his bearing. He stared at me open-mouthed.

'What is that you say? Another murder? Ah, then, but I am all wrong. I have failed. Giraud may mock himself at me – he will have reason!'

'You did not expect it, then?'

'I? Not the least in the world. It demolishes my theory – it ruins everything – it – Ah, no!' He stopped dead, thumping himself on the chest. 'It is impossible. I *cannot* be wrong! The facts, taken methodically, and in their proper order, admit of only one explanation. I must be right! I *am* right!'

'But then –'

He interrupted me.

'Wait, my friend. I must be right, therefore this new murder is impossible unless – unless – Oh, wait, I implore you. Say no word.'

He was silent for a moment or two, then resuming his normal manner, he said in a quiet assured voice:

'The victim is a man of middle age. His body was found in the locked shed near the scene of the crime and had been dead at least forty-eight hours. And it is most probable that he was stabbed in a similar manner to Mr Renauld, though not necessarily in the back.'

It was my turn to gape – and gape I did. In all my knowledge of Poirot he had never done anything so amazing as this. And, almost inevitably, a doubt crossed my mind.

'Poirot,' I cried, 'you're pulling my leg. You've heard all about it already.'

He turned his earnest gaze upon me reproachfully.

'Would I do such a thing? I assure you that I have heard nothing whatsoever. Did you not observe the shock your news was to me?'

'But how on earth could you know all that?'

'I was right, then? But I knew it. The little grey cells, my friend, the little grey cells! They told me. Thus, and in no other way, could there have been a second death. Now tell me all. If we go round to the left here, we can take a short cut across the golf links which will bring us to the back of the Villa Geneviève much more quickly.'

As we walked, taking the way he had indicated, I recounted all I knew. Poirot listened attentively.

'The dagger was in the wound, you say? That is curious. You are sure it was the same one?'

'Absolutely certain. That's what makes it so impossible.'

'Nothing is impossible. There may have been two daggers.'

I raised my eyebrows.

'Surely that is in the highest degree unlikely? It would be a most extraordinary coincidence.'

'You speak as usual, without reflection, Hastings. In some cases two identical weapons *would* be highly improbable. But not here. This particular weapon was a war souvenir which was made to Jack Renauld's orders. It is really highly unlikely, when you come to think of it, that he should have had only one made. Very probably he would have another for his own use.'

'But nobody has mentioned such a thing,' I objected.

A hint of the lecturer crept into Poirot's tone.

'My friend, in working upon a case, one does not take into account only the things that are "mentioned". There is no reason to mention many things which may be important. Equally, there is often an excellent reason for *not* mentioning them. You can take your choice of the two motives.'

I was silent, impressed in spite of myself. Another few minutes brought us to the famous shed. We found all our friends there, and after an interchange of polite amenities, Poirot began his task.

Having watched Giraud at work, I was keenly interested. Poirot bestowed but a cursory glance on the surroundings. The only thing he examined was the ragged coat and trousers by the door. A disdainful smile rose to Giraud's lips, and, as though noting it, Poirot flung the bundle down again.

'Old clothes of the gardener's?' he queried.

'Exactly,' said Giraud.

Poirot knelt down by the body. His fingers were rapid but methodical. He examined the texture of the clothes, and satisfied himself that there were no marks on them. The boots he subjected to special care, also the dirty and broken fingernails. While examining the latter he threw a quick question at Giraud.

'You saw them?'

'Yes, I saw them,' replied the other. His face remained inscrutable.

Suddenly Poirot stiffened.

'Dr Durand!'

'Yes?' The doctor came forward.

'There is foam on the lips. You observed it?'

'I didn't notice it, I must admit.'

'But you observe it now?'

'Oh, certainly.'

Poirot again shot a question at Giraud.

'You noticed it without doubt?'

The other did not reply. Poirot proceeded. The dagger had been withdrawn from the wound. It reposed in a glass jar by the side of the body. Poirot examined it, then he studied the wound closely. When he looked up, his eyes were excited and shone with the green light I knew so well.

'It is a strange wound, this! It has not bled. There is no stain on the clothes. The blade of the dagger is slightly discoloured, that is all. What do you think, *monsieur le docteur*?'

'I can only say that it is most abnormal.'

'It is not abnormal at all. It is most simple. The man was stabbed *after he was dead*.' And, stilling the clamour of voices that arose with a wave of his hand, Poirot turned to Giraud and added: 'M. Giraud agrees with me, do you not, monsieur?'

Whatever Giraud's real belief, he accepted the position without moving a muscle. Calmly and almost scornfully he replied:

'Certainly I agree.'

The murmur of surprise and interest broke out again.

'But what an idea!' cried M. Hautet. 'To stab a man after he is dead! Barbaric! Unheard of! Some unappeasable hate perhaps.'

'No,' said Poirot. 'I should fancy it was done quite cold-bloodedly – to create an impression.'

'What impression?'

'The impression it nearly did create,' returned Poirot oracularly.

M. Bex had been thinking.

'How, then, was the man killed?'

'He was not killed. He died. He died, if I am not much mistaken, of an epileptic fit!'

This statement of Poirot's again aroused considerable excitement. Dr Durand knelt down again, and made a searching examination. At last he rose to his feet.

'Monsieur Poirot, I am inclined to believe that you are correct in your assertion. I was misled to begin with. The incontrovertible fact that the man had been stabbed distracted my attention from any other indications.'

Poirot was the hero of the hour. The examining magistrate was profuse in compliments. Poirot responded gracefully, and then excused himself on the pretext that neither he nor I had yet lunched, and that he wished to repair the ravages of the journey. As we were about to leave the shed, Giraud approached us.

'One other thing, Monsieur Poirot,' he said, in his suave mocking voice. 'We found this coiled round the handle of the dagger – a woman's hair.'

'Ah!' said Poirot. 'A woman's hair? What woman's, I wonder?'

'I wonder also,' said Giraud. Then, with a bow, he left us.

'He was insistent, the good Giraud,' said Poirot thoughtfully, as we walked towards the hotel. 'I wonder in what direction he hopes to mislead me? A woman's hair – h'm!'

We lunched heartily, but I found Poirot somewhat distrait and inattentive. Afterwards we went up to our sitting-room, and there I begged him to tell me something of his mysterious journey to Paris.

'Willingly, my friend. I went to Paris to find *this*.'

He took from his pocket a small faded newspaper cutting. It was the reproduction of a woman's photograph. He handed it to me. I uttered an exclamation.

'You recognize it, my friend?'

I nodded. Although the photo obviously dated from very many years back, and the hair was dressed in a different style, the likeness was unmistakable.

'Madame Daubreuil!' I exclaimed.

Poirot shook his head with a smile.

'Not quite correct, my friend. She did not call herself by that name in those days. That is a picture of the notorious Madame Beroldy!'

Madame Beroldy! In a flash the whole thing came back to

me. The murder trial that had evoked such world-wide interest.

The Beroldy Case.

CHAPTER 16
THE BEROLDY CASE

Some twenty years or so before the opening of the present story, Monsieur Arnold Beroldy, a native of Lyons, arrived in Paris accompanied by his pretty wife and their little daughter, a mere babe. Monsieur Beroldy was a junior partner in a firm of wine merchants, a stout middle-aged man, fond of the good things of life, devoted to his charming wife, and altogether unremarkable in every way. The firm in which Monsieur Beroldy was a partner was a small one and, although doing well, it did not yield a large income to the junior partner. The Beroldys had a small apartment and lived in a very modest fashion to begin with.

But, unremarkable though Monsieur Beroldy might be, his wife was plentifully gilded with the brush of Romance. Young and good-looking, and gifted withal with a singular charm of manner, Madame Beroldy at once created a stir in the quarter, especially when it began to be whispered that some interesting mystery surrounded her birth. It was rumoured that she was the illegitimate daughter of a Russian Grand Duke. Others asserted that it was an Austrian Arch-duke, and that the union was legal, though morganatic. But all stories agreed upon one point, that Jeanne Beroldy was the centre of an interesting mystery.

Among the friends and acquaintances of the Beroldys was a young lawyer, Georges Conneau. It was soon evident that the fascinating Jeanne had completely enslaved his heart. Madame Beroldy encouraged the young man in a discreet fashion, but always being careful to affirm her complete devotion to her middle-aged husband. Nevertheless, many spiteful persons did not hesitate to declare that young Conneau was her lover – and not the only one!

When the Beroldys had been in Paris about three months, another personage came upon the scene. This was Mr Hiram P. Trapp, a native of the United States, and extremely wealthy.

Introduced to the charming and mysterious Madame Beroldy, he fell a prompt victim to her fascinations. His admiration was obvious, though strictly respectful.

About this time, Madame Beroldy became more outspoken in her confidences. To several friends, she declared herself greatly worried on her husband's behalf. She explained that he had been drawn into several schemes of a political nature, and also referred to some important papers that had been entrusted to him for safe-keeping and which concerned a 'secret' of far-reaching European importance. They had been entrusted to his custody to throw pursuers off the track, but Madame Beroldy was nervous, having recognized several important members of the Revolutionary Circle in Paris.

On the 28th day of November the blow fell. The woman who came daily to clean and cook for the Beroldys was surprised to find the door of the apartment standing wide open. Hearing faint moans issuing from the bedroom, she went in. A terrible sight met her eyes. Madame Beroldy lay on the floor bound hand and foot, uttering feeble moans, having managed to free her mouth from a gag. On the bed was Monsieur Beroldy, lying in a pool of blood, with a knife driven through his heart.

Madame Beroldy's story was clear enough. Suddenly awakened from sleep, she had discerned two masked men bending over her. Stifling her cries, they had bound and gagged her. They had then demanded of Monsieur Beroldy the famous 'secret'.

But the intrepid wine merchant refused point-blank to accede to their request. Angered by his refusal, one of the men incontinently stabbed him through the heart. With the dead man's keys, they had opened the safe in the corner, and had carried away with them a mass of papers. Both men were heavily bearded, and had worn masks, but Madame Beroldy declared positively that they were Russians.

The affair created an immense sensation. Time went on, and the mysterious bearded men were never traced. And then, just as public interest was beginning to die down, a startling development occurred: Madame Beroldy was arrested and charged with the murder of her husband.

The trial, when it came on, aroused widespread interest. The youth and beauty of the accused, and her mysterious history, were sufficient to make of it a *cause célèbre*.

It was proved beyond doubt that Jeanne Beroldy's parents were a highly respectable and prosaic couple, fruit merchants, who lived on the outskirts of Lyons. The Russian Grand Duke, the court intrigues, and the political schemes – all the stories current were traced back to the lady herself! Remorselessly, the whole story of her life was laid bare. The motive for the murder was found in Mr Hiram P. Trapp. Mr Trapp did his best, but, relentlessly and agilely cross-questioned, he was forced to admit that he loved the lady, and that, had she been free, he would have asked her to be his wife. The fact that the relations between them were admittedly platonic strengthened the case against the accused. Debarred from becoming his mistress by the simple honourable nature of the man, Jeanne Beroldy had conceived the monstrous project of ridding herself of her elderly, undistinguished husband and becoming the wife of the rich American.

Throughout, Madame Beroldy confronted her accusers with complete sang-froid and self-possession. Her story never varied. She continued to declare strenuously that she was of royal birth and that she had been substituted for the daughter of the fruit-seller at an early age. Absurd and completely unsubstantiated as these statements were, a great number of people believed implicitly in their truth.

But the prosecution was implacable. It denounced the masked 'Russians' as a myth, and asserted that the crime had been committed by Madame Beroldy and her lover, Georges Conneau. A warrant was issued for the arrest of the latter, but he had wisely disappeared. Evidence showed that the bonds which secured Madame Beroldy were so loose that she could easily have freed herself.

And then, towards the close of the trial, a letter, posted in Paris, was sent to the Public Prosecutor. It was from Georges Conneau and, without revealing his whereabouts, it contained a full confession of the crime. He declared that he had indeed struck the fatal blow at Madame Beroldy's instigation. The crime had been planned between them. Believing that her husband ill-treated her, and maddened by his own passion for her, a passion which he believed her to return, he had planned the crime and struck the fatal blow that should free the woman he loved from a hateful bondage. Now, for the first time, he learnt of Mr Hiram P. Trapp, and realized that the woman he loved had betrayed him! Not for his sake did she wish to be free, but in order to marry the wealthy American. She had used him as a cat's paw, and now, in his jealous rage, he turned and denounced her, declaring that throughout he had acted at her instigation.

And then Madame Beroldy proved herself the remarkable woman she undoubtedly was. Without hesitation, she dropped her previous defence, and admitted that the 'Russians' were a pure invention on her part. The real murderer was Georges Conneau. Maddened by passion, he had committed the crime, vowing that if she did not keep silence he would exact a terrible vengeance from her. Terrified by his threats, she had consented – also fearing it likely that if she told the truth she might be accused of conniving at the crime. But she had steadfastly refused to have anything more to do with her husband's murderer, and it was in revenge for this attitude on her part that he had written this letter accusing her. She swore solemnly that she had had nothing to do with the planning of the crime, that she had awoke on that memorable night to find Georges Conneau standing over her, the blood-stained knife in his hand.

It was a touch-and-go affair. Madame Beroldy's story was hardly credible. But her address to the jury was a masterpiece. The tears streaming down her face, she spoke of her child, of her woman's honour – of her desire to keep her reputation untarnished for the child's sake. She admitted that, Georges Conneau having been her lover, she might perhaps be held morally responsible for the crime – but, before God, nothing more! She knew that she had committed a grave fault in not denouncing Conneau to the law, but she declared in a broken voice that that was a thing no woman could have done. She had loved him! Could she let her hand be the one to send him to the guillotine? She had been guilty of much, but she was innocent of the terrible crime imputed to her.

However that may have been, her eloquence and personality won the day. Madame Beroldy, amidst a scene of unparalleled excitement, was acquitted.

Despite the utmost endeavours of the police, Georges Conneau was never traced. As for Madame Beroldy, nothing more was heard of her. Taking the child with her, she left Paris to begin a new life.

CHAPTER 17

WE MAKE FURTHER INVESTIGATIONS

I have set down the Beroldy case in full. Of course all the details did not present themselves to my memory as I have recounted them here. Nevertheless, I recalled the case fairly accurately. It had attracted a great deal of interest at the time, and had been fully reported by the English papers, so that it did not need much effort of memory on my part to recollect the salient details.

Just for the moment, in my excitement, it seemed to clear up the whole matter. I admit that I am impulsive, and Poirot deplores my custom of jumping to conclusions, but I think I had some excuse in this instance. The remarkable way in which this discovery justified Poirot's point of view struck me at once.

'Poirot,' I said, 'I congratulate you. I see everything now.'

Poirot lit one of his little cigarettes with his usual precision. Then he looked up.

'And since you see everything now, *mon ami*, what exactly is it that you see?'

'Why, that it was Madame Daubreuil – Beroldy – who murdered Mr Renauld. The similarity of the two cases proves that beyond a doubt.'

'Then you consider that Madame Beroldy was wrongly acquitted? That in actual fact she was guilty of connivance in her husband's murder?'

I opened my eyes wide.

'Of course! Don't you?'

Poirot walked to the end of the room, absent-mindedly straightened a chair, and then said thoughtfully:

'Yes, that is my opinion. But there is no "of course" about it, my friend. Technically speaking, Madame Beroldy is innocent.'

'Of that crime, perhaps. But not of this.'

Poirot sat down again, and regarded me, his thoughtful air more marked than ever.

'So it is definitely your opinion, Hastings, that Madame Daubreuil murdered Monsieur Renauld?'

'Yes.'

'Why?'

He shot the question at me with such suddenness that I was taken aback.

'Why?' I stammered. 'Why? Oh, because –' I came to a stop. Poirot nodded his head at me.

'You see, you come to a stumbling-block at once. Why should Madame Daubreuil (I shall call her that for clearness' sake) murder Monsieur Renauld? We can find no shadow of a motive. She does not benefit by his death; considered as either mistress or blackmailer she stands to lose. You cannot have a murder without motive. The first crime was different – there we had a rich lover waiting to step into her husband's shoes.'

'Money is not the only motive for murder,' I objected.

'True,' agreed Poirot placidly. 'There are two others, the *crime passionnel* is one. And there is the third rare motive, murder for an idea, which implies some form of mental derangement on the part of the murderer. Homicidal mania and religious fanaticism belong to that class. We can rule it out here.'

'But what about the *crime passionnel*? Can you rule that out? If Madame Daubreuil was Renauld's mistress, if she found that his affection was cooling, or if her jealousy was aroused in any way, might she not have struck him down in a moment of anger?'

Poirot shook his head.

'If – I say *if*, you note – Madame Daubreuil was Renauld's mistress, he had not had time to tire of her. And in any case you mistake her character. She is a woman who can simulate great emotional stress. She is a magnificent actress. But, looked at dispassionately, her life disproves her appearance. Throughout, if we examine it, she has been cold-blooded and calculating in her motives and actions. It was not to link her life with that of her young lover that she connived at her husband's murder. The rich American, for whom she probably did not care a button, was her objective. If she committed a crime, she would always do so for gain. Here there was no gain. Besides, how do you account for the digging of the grave? That was a man's work.'

'She might have had an accomplice,' I suggested, unwilling to relinquish my belief.

'I pass to another objection. You have spoken of the similarity between the two crimes. Wherein does that lie, my friend?'

I stared at him in astonishment.

'Why, Poirot, it was you who remarked on that! The story of the masked men, the "secret", the papers!'

Poirot smiled a little.

'Do not be so indignant, I beg of you. I repudiate nothing. The similarity of the two stories links the two cases together inevitably. But reflect now on something very curious. It is not Madame Daubreuil who tells us this tale – if it were, all would indeed be plain sailing – it is Madame Renauld. Is she then in league with the other?'

'I can't believe that,' I said slowly. 'If she is, she must be the most consummate actress the world has ever known.'

'Ta-ta-ta!' said Poirot impatiently. 'Again you have the sentiment and not the logic! If it is necessary for a criminal to be a consummate actress, then by all means assume her to be one. But is it necessary? I do not believe Mrs Renauld to be in league with Madame Daubreuil for several reasons, some of which I have already enumerated to you. The others are self-evident. Therefore, that possibility eliminated, we draw very near to the truth, which is, as always, very curious and interesting.'

'Poirot,' I cried, 'what more do you know?'

'*Mon ami*, you must make your own deductions. You have "access to the facts". Concentrate your grey cells. Reason – not like Giraud – but like Hercule Poirot!'

'But are you *sure*?'

'My friend, in many ways I have been an imbecile. But at last I see clearly.'

'You know everything?'

'I have discovered what Monsieur Renauld sent for me to discover.'

'And you know the murderer?'

'I know one murderer.'

'What do you mean?'

'We talk a little at cross-purposes. There are here not one crime, but two. The first I have solved, the second – *eh bien*, I will confess, I am not sure!'

'But, Poirot, I thought you said the man in the shed had died a natural death?'

'Ta-ta-ta!' Poirot made his favourite ejaculation of impatience. 'Still you do not understand. One may have a crime without a murderer, but for two crimes it is essential to have two bodies.'

His remark struck me as so peculiarly lacking in lucidity that I looked at him in some anxiety. But he appeared perfectly normal. Suddenly he rose and strolled to the window.

'Here he is,' he observed.

'Who?'

'Monsieur Jack Renauld. I sent a note up to the Villa to ask him to come here.'

That changed the course of my ideas, and I asked Poirot if he knew that Jack Renauld had been in Merlinville on the night of the crime. I had hoped to catch my astute little friend napping, but as usual he was omniscient. He, too, had inquired at the station.

'And without doubt we are not original in the idea, Hastings. The excellent Giraud, he also has probably made his inquiries.'

'You don't think –' I said, and then stopped. 'Ah, no, it would be too horrible!'

Poirot looked inquiringly at me, but I said no more. It had just occurred to me that though there were seven women, directly and indirectly connected with the case – Mrs Renauld, Madame Daubreuil and her daughter, the mysterious visitor, and the three servants – there was, with the exception of old Auguste, who could hardly count, only one man – Jack Renauld. *And a man must have dug the grave.*

I had no time to develop farther the appalling idea that had occurred to me, for Jack Renauld was ushered into the room.

Poirot greeted him in business-like manner.

'Take a seat, monsieur. I regret infinitely to derange you, but you will perhaps understand that the atmosphere of the villa is not too congenial to me. Monsieur Giraud and I do not see eye to eye about everything. His politeness to me has not been striking, and you will comprehend that I do not intend any little discoveries I may make to benefit him in any way.'

'Exactly, Monsieur Poirot,' said the lad. 'That fellow Giraud is an ill-conditioned brute, and I'd be delighted to see someone score at his expense.'

'Then I may ask a little favour of you?'

'Certainly.'

'I will ask you to go to the railway station and take a train to the next station along the line, Abbalac. Ask at the cloakroom whether two foreigners deposited a valise there on the night of the murder. It is a small station, and they are almost certain to remember. Will you do this?'

'Of course I will,' said the boy, mystified, though ready for the task.

'I and my friend, you comprehend, have business elsewhere,' explained Poirot. 'There is a train in a quarter of an hour, and I will ask you not to return to the villa, as I have no wish for Giraud to get an inkling of your errand.'

'Very well, I will go straight to the station.'

He rose to his feet. Poirot's voice stopped him:

'One moment, Monsieur Renauld, there is one little matter that puzzles me. Why did you not mention to Monsieur Hautet this morning that you were in Merlinville on the night of the crime?'

Jack Renauld's face went crimson. With an effort he controlled himself.

'You have made a mistake. I was in Cherbourg as I told the examining magistrate this morning.'

Poirot looked at him, his eyes narrowed, cat-like, until they only showed a gleam of green.

'Then it is a singular mistake that I have made there – for it is shared by the station staff. They say you arrived by the 11.40 train.'

For a moment Jack Renauld hesitated, then he made up his mind.

'And if I did? I suppose you do not mean to accuse me of participating in my father's murder?' He asked the question haughtily, his head thrown back.

'I should like an explanation of the reason that brought you here.'

'That is simple enough. I came to see my fiancée, Mademoiselle Daubreuil. I was on the eve of a long voyage, uncertain as to when

I should return. I wished to see her before I went, to assure her of my unchanging devotion.'

'And did you see her?' Poirot's eyes never left the other's face.

There was an appreciable pause before Renauld replied. Then he said:

'Yes.'

'And afterwards?'

'I found I had missed the last train. I walked to St Beauvais, where I knocked up a garage and got a car to take me back to Cherbourg.'

'St Beauvais? That is fifteen kilometres. A long walk, M. Renauld.'

'I – I felt like walking.'

Poirot bowed his head as a sign that he accepted the explanation. Jack Renauld took up his hat and cane and departed. In a trice Poirot jumped to his feet.

'Quick, Hastings. We will go after him.'

Keeping a discreet distance behind our quarry, we followed him through the streets of Merlinville. But when Poirot saw that he took the turning to the station he checked himself.

'All is well. He has taken the bait. He will go to Abbalac, and will inquire for the mythical valise left by the mythical foreigners. Yes, *mon ami*, all that was a little invention of my own.'

'You wanted him out of the way!' I exclaimed.

'Your penetration is amazing, Hastings! Now, if you please, we will go up to the Villa Geneviève.'

CHAPTER 18

GIRAUD ACTS

Arrived at the villa, Poirot led the way up to the shed where the second body had been discovered. He did not, however, go in, but paused by the bench which I have mentioned before as being set some few yards away from it. After contemplating it for a moment or two, he paced carefully from it to the hedge which marked the boundary between the Villa Geneviève and the Villa Marguerite. Then he paced back again, nodding his head as he did so. Returning again to the hedge, he parted the bushes with his hands.

'With good fortune,' he remarked to me over his shoulder, 'Mademoiselle Marthe may find herself in the garden. I desire to speak to her and would prefer not to call formally at the Villa Marguerite. Ah, all is well, there she is. Pst, Mademoiselle! Pst! *Un moment, s'il vous plaît.*'

I joined him at the moment that Marthe Daubreuil, looking slightly startled, came running up to the hedge at his call.

'A little word with you, mademoiselle, if it is permitted?'

'Certainly, Monsieur Poirot.'

Despite her acquiescence, her eyes looked troubled and afraid.

'Mademoiselle, do you remember running after me on the road the day that I came to your house with the examining magistrate? You asked me if anyone were suspected of the crime.'

'And you told me two Chileans.' Her voice sounded rather breathless, and her left hand stole to her breast.

'Will you ask me the same question again, mademoiselle?'

'What do you mean?'

'This. If you were to ask me that question again, I should give you a different answer. Someone is suspected – but not a Chilean.'

'Who?' The word came faintly between her parted lips.

'Monsieur Jack Renauld.'

'What?' It was a cry. 'Jack? Impossible. Who dares to suspect him?'

'Giraud.'

'Giraud!' The girl's face was ashy. 'I am afraid of that man. He is cruel. He will – he will –' She broke off. There was courage gathering in her face, and determination. I realized in that moment that she was a fighter. Poirot, too, watched her intently.

'You know, of course, that he was here on the night of the murder?' he asked.

'Yes,' she replied mechanically. 'He told me.'

'It was unwise to have tried to conceal the fact,' ventured Poirot.

'Yes, yes,' she replied impatiently. 'But we cannot waste time on regrets. We must find something to save him. He is innocent, of course; but that will not help him with a man like Giraud, who has his reputation to think of. He must arrest someone, and that someone will be Jack.'

'The facts will tell against him,' said Poirot. 'You realize that?'

She faced him squarely.

'I am not a child, monsieur. I can be brave and look facts in the face. He is innocent, and we must save him.'

She spoke with a kind of desperate energy, then was silent, frowning as she thought.

'Mademoiselle,' said Poirot, observing her keenly, 'is there not something that you are keeping back that you could tell us?'

She nodded perplexedly.

'Yes, there is something, but I hardly know whether you will believe it – it seems so absurd.'

'At any rate, tell us, mademoiselle.'

'It is this. M. Giraud sent for me, as an afterthought, to see if I could identify the man in there.' She signed with her head towards the shed. 'I could not. At least I could not at the moment. But since I have been thinking –'

'Well?'

'It seems so queer, and yet I am almost sure. I will tell you. On the morning of the day Monsieur Renauld was murdered, I was walking in the garden here, when I heard a sound of men's voices quarrelling. I pushed aside the bushes and looked through. One of the men was Monsieur Renauld and the other was a tramp, a dreadful-looking creature in filthy rags. He was alternately whining and threatening. I gathered he was asking for money, but at that moment *maman* called me from the house, and I had to go. That is all, only – I am almost sure that the tramp and the dead man in the shed are one and the same.'

Poirot uttered an exclamation.

'But why did you not say at the time, mademoiselle?'

'Because at first it only struck me that the face was vaguely familiar in some way. The man was differently dressed, and apparently belonged to a superior station in life.'

A voice called from the house.

'*Maman*,' whispered Marthe: 'I must go.' And she slipped away through the trees.

'Come,' said Poirot and, taking my arm, turned in the direction of the villa.

'What do you really think?' I asked in some curiosity. 'Was that story true, or did the girl make it up in order to divert suspicion from her lover?'

'It is a curious tale,' said Poirot, 'but I believe it to be the absolute truth. Unwittingly, Mademoiselle Marthe told us the truth on another point – and incidentally gave Jack Renauld the lie. Did you notice his hesitation when I asked him if he saw Marthe Daubreuil on the night of the crime? He paused and then said "Yes". I suspected that he was lying. It was necessary for me to see Mademoiselle Marthe before he could put her on her guard. Three little words gave me the information I wanted. When I asked her if she knew that Jack Renauld was here that night, she answered, "He *told* me". Now, Hastings, what was Jack Renauld doing here on that eventful evening, and if he did not see Mademoiselle Marthe whom did he see?'

'Surely, Poirot,' I cried, aghast, 'you cannot believe that a boy like that would murder his own father!'

'*Mon ami*,' said Poirot. 'You continue to be of a sentimentality unbelievable! I have seen mothers who murdered their little children for the sake of the insurance money! After that, one can believe anything.'

'And the motive?'

'Money of course. Remember that Jack Renauld thought that he would come into half his father's fortune at the latter's death.'

'But the tramp. Where does he come in?'

Poirot shrugged his shoulders.

'Giraud would say that he was an accomplice – an apache who helped young Renauld to commit the crime, and who was conveniently put out of the way afterwards.'

'But the hair round the dagger? The woman's hair?'

'Ah!' said Poirot, smiling broadly. 'That is the cream of Giraud's little jest. According to him, it is not a woman's hair at all. Remember that the youths of today wear their hair brushed straight back from the forehead with pomade or hair wash to make it lie flat. Consequently some of the hairs are of considerable length.'

'And you believe that too?'

'No,' said Poirot, with a curious smile. 'For I know it to be the hair of a woman – and more, which woman!'

'Madame Daubreuil,' I announced positively.

'Perhaps,' said Poirot, regarding me quizzically. But I refused to allow myself to get annoyed.

'What are we going to do now?' I asked, as we entered the hall of the Villa Geneviève.

'I wish to make a search among the effects of M. Jack Renauld. That is why I had to get him out of the way for a few hours.'

Neatly and methodically, Poirot opened each drawer in turn, examined the contents, and returned them exactly to their places. It was a singularly dull and uninteresting proceeding. Poirot waded on through collars, pyjamas, and socks. A purring noise outside drew me to the window. Instantly I became galvanized into life.

'Poirot!' I cried. 'A car has just driven up. Giraud is in it, and Jack Renauld, and two gendarmes.'

'*Sacré tonnerre!*' growled Poirot. 'That animal of a Giraud, could he not wait? I shall not be able to replace the things in this last drawer with the proper method. Let us be quick.'

Unceremoniously he tumbled out the things on the floor, mostly ties and handkerchiefs. Suddenly with a cry of triumph Poirot pounced on something, à small square of cardboard, evidently a photograph. Thrusting it into his pocket, he returned the things pell-mell to the drawer, and seizing me by the arm dragged me out of the room and down the stairs. In the hall stood Giraud, contemplating his prisoner.

'Good afternoon, Monsieur Giraud,' said Poirot. 'What have we here?'

Giraud nodded his head towards Jack.

'He was trying to make a getaway, but I was too sharp for him. He's under arrest for the murder of his father, Monsieur Paul Renauld.'

Poirot wheeled round to confront the boy, who was leaning limply against the door, his face ashy pale.

'What do you say to that, *jeune homme*?'

Jack Renauld stared at him stonily.

'Nothing,' he said.

CHAPTER 19

I USE MY GREY CELLS

I was dumbfounded. Up to the last, I had not been able to bring myself to believe Jack Renauld guilty. I had expected a ringing proclamation of his innocence when Poirot challenged him. But now, watching him as he stood, white and limp against the wall, and hearing the damning admission fall from his lips, I doubted no longer.

But Poirot had turned to Giraud.

'What are your grounds for arresting him?'

'Do you expect me to give them to you?'

'As a matter of courtesy, yes.'

Giraud looked at him doubtfully. He was torn between a desire to refuse rudely and the pleasure of triumphing over his adversary.

'You think I have made a mistake, I suppose?' he sneered.

'It would not surprise me,' replied Poirot, with a soupçon of malice.

Giraud's face took on a deeper tinge of red.

'*Eh bien*, come in here. You shall judge for yourself.'

He flung open the door of the salon, and we passed in, leaving Jack Renauld in the care of the two other men.

'Now, Monsieur Poirot,' said Giraud, laying his hat on the table, and speaking with the utmost sarcasm, 'I will treat you to a little lecture on detective work. I will show how we moderns work.'

'*Bien!*' said Poirot, composing himself to listen. 'I will show you how admirably the Old Guard can listen.' And he leaned back and closed his eyes, opening them for a moment to remark: 'Do not fear that I shall sleep. I will attend most carefully.'

'Of course,' began Giraud, 'I soon saw through all that Chilean tomfoolery. Two men were in it – but they were not mysterious foreigners! All that was a blind.'

'Very creditable so far, my dear Giraud,' murmured Poirot. 'Especially after that clever trick of theirs with the match and cigarette end.'

Giraud glared, but continued.

'A man must have been connected with the case, in order to dig the grave. There is no man who actually benefits by the crime, but there was a man who *thought* he would benefit. I heard of Jack Renauld's quarrel with his father, and of the threats that he had used. The motive was established. Now as to means. Jack Renauld was in Merlinville that night. He concealed the fact – which turned suspicion into certainty. Then we found a second victim – *stabbed with the same dagger*. We know when that dagger was stolen. Captain Hastings here can fix the time. Jack Renauld, arriving from Cherbourg, was the only person who could have taken it. I have accounted for all the other members of the household.'

Poirot interrupted.

'You are wrong. There is one other person who could have taken the dagger.'

'You refer to Monsieur Stonor? He arrived at the front door, in an automobile which had brought him straight from Calais. Ah! believe me, I have looked into everything. Monsieur Jack Renauld arrived by train. An hour elapsed between his arrival and the moment when he presented himself at the house. Without doubt, he saw Captain Hastings and his companion leave the shed, slipped in himself and took the dagger, stabbed his accomplice in the shed –'

'Who was already dead!'

Giraud shrugged his shoulders.

'Possibly he did not observe that. He may have judged him to be sleeping. Without doubt they had a rendezvous. In any case he knew this apparent second murder would greatly complicate the case. It did.'

'But it could not deceive Monsieur Giraud,' murmured Poirot.

'You mock at me! But I will give you one last irrefutable proof. Madame Renauld's story was false – a fabrication from beginning to end. We believe Madame Renauld to have loved her husband – *yet she lied to shield his murderer*. For whom will a woman lie? Sometimes for herself, usually for the man she loves, *always* for her children. That is the last – the irrefutable proof. You cannot get round it.'

Giraud paused, flushed and triumphant. Poirot regarded him steadily.

'That is my case,' said Giraud. 'What have you to say to it?'

'Only that there is one thing you have failed to take into account.'

'What is that?'

'Jack Renauld was presumably acquainted with the planning out of the golf course. He knew that the body would be discovered almost at once, when they started to dig the bunker.'

Giraud laughed out loud.

'But it is idiotic what you say there! He wanted the body to be found! Until it was found, he could not presume death, and would have been unable to enter into his inheritance.'

I saw a quick flash of green in Poirot's eyes as he rose to his feet.

'Then why bury it?' he asked very softly. 'Reflect, Giraud. Since it was to Jack Renauld's advantage that the body should be found without delay, *why dig a grave at all?*'

Giraud did not reply. The question found him unprepared. He shrugged his shoulders as though to intimate that it was of no importance.

Poirot moved towards the door. I followed him.

'There is one more thing that you have failed to take into account,' he said over his shoulder.

'What is that?'

'The piece of lead piping,' said Poirot, and left the room.

Jack Renauld still stood in the hall, with a white dumb face, but as we came out of the salon he looked up sharply. At the same moment there was the sound of a footfall on the staircase. Mrs Renauld was descending it. At the sight of her son, standing between the two myrmidons of the law, she stopped as though petrified.

'Jack,' she faltered. 'Jack, what is this?'

He looked up at her, his face set.

'They have arrested me, mother.'

'What?'

She uttered a piercing cry, and before anyone could get to her, swayed, and fell heavily. We both ran to her and lifted her up. In a minute Poirot stood up again.

'She has cut her head badly, on the corner of the stairs. I fancy there is slight concussion also. If Giraud wants a statement from her, he will have to wait. She will probably be unconscious for at least a week.'

Denise and Françoise had run to their mistress, and leaving her in their charge Poirot left the house. He walked with his head down, frowning thoughtfully. For some time I did not speak, but at last I ventured to put a question to him:

'Do you believe then, in spite of all appearances to the contrary, that Jack Renauld may not be guilty?'

Poirot did not answer at once, but after a long wait he said gravely:

'I do not know, Hastings. There is just a chance of it. Of course Giraud is all wrong – wrong from beginning to end. If Jack Renauld is guilty, it is in spite of Giraud's arguments, not *because* of them. And the gravest indictment against him is known only to me.'

'What is that?' I asked, impressed.

'If you would use your grey cells, and see the whole case clearly as I do, you too would perceive it, my friend.'

This was what I called one of Poirot's irritating answers. He went on, without waiting for me to speak:

'Let us walk this way to the sea. We will sit on that little mound there, overlooking the beach, and review the case. You shall know all that I know, but I would prefer that you should come at the truth by your own efforts – not by my leading you by the hand.'

We established ourselves on the grassy knoll as Poirot had suggested, looking out to sea.

'Think, my friend,' said Poirot's voice encouragingly. 'Arrange your ideas. Be methodical. Be orderly. There is the secret of success.'

I endeavoured to obey him, casting my mind back over all the details of the case. And suddenly I started as an idea of bewildering luminosity shot into my brain. Tremblingly I built up my hypothesis.

'You have a little idea, I see, *mon ami!* Capital. We progress.'

I sat up, and lit a pipe.

'Poirot,' I said, 'it seems to me we have been strangely remiss. I say *we* – although I dare say *I* would be nearer the mark. But you must pay the penalty of your determined secrecy. So I say again we have been strangely remiss. There is someone we have forgotten.'

'And who is that?' inquired Poirot, with twinkling eyes.

'Georges Conneau!'

CHAPTER 20

AN AMAZING STATEMENT

The next moment Poirot embraced me warmly on the cheek.

'*Enfin!* You have arrived! And all by yourself. It is superb! Continue your reasoning. You are right. Decidedly we have done wrong to forget Georges Conneau.'

I was so flattered by the little man's approval that I could hardly continue. But at last I collected my thoughts and went on.

'Georges Conneau disappeared twenty years ago, but we have no reason to believe that he is dead.'

'*Aucunement,*' agreed Poirot. 'Proceed.'

'Therefore we will assume that he is alive.'

'Exactly.'

'Or that he was alive until recently.'

'*De mieux en mieux!*'

'We will presume,' I continued, my enthusiasm rising, 'that he has fallen on evil days. He has become a criminal, an apache, a tramp – a what you will. He chances to come to Merlinville. There he finds the woman he has never ceased to love.'

'Eh eh! The sentimentality,' warned Poirot.

'Where one hates one also loves,' I quoted or misquoted. 'At any rate he finds her there, living under an assumed name. But she has a new lover, the Englishman, Renauld. Georges Conneau, the memory of old wrongs rising in him, quarrels with this Renauld. He lies in wait for him as he comes to visit his mistress, and stabs him in the back. Then, terrified at what he has done, he starts to dig a grave. I imagine it likely that Madame Daubreuil comes out to look for her lover. She and Conneau have a terrible scene. He drags her into the shed, and there suddenly falls down in an epileptic fit. Now supposing Jack Renauld to appear. Madame Daubreuil tells him all, points out to him the dreadful consequences to her daughter if this scandal of the past is revived. His father's murderer is dead – let them do their best to hush it up. Jack Renauld consents – goes to the house and has an interview with his mother, winning her over to his point of view. Primed with the story that Madame Daubreuil has suggested to him, she permits herself to be gagged and bound. There, Poirot, what do you think of that?' I leaned back, flushed with the pride of successful reconstruction.

Poirot looked at me thoughtfully.

'I think that you should write for the Kinema, *mon ami*,' he remarked at last.

'You mean –'

'It would mean a good film, the story that you have recounted to me there – but it bears no sort of resemblance to everyday life.'

'I admit that I haven't gone into all the details, but –'

'You have gone farther – you have ignored them magnificently. What about the way the two men were dressed? Do you suggest that after stabbing his victim, Conneau removed his suit of clothes, donned it himself, and replaced the dagger?'

'I don't see that that matters,' I objected rather huffily. 'He may have obtained clothes and money from Madame Daubreuil by threats earlier in the day.'

'By threats – eh? You seriously advance that supposition?'

'Certainly. He could have threatened to reveal her identity to the Renaulds, which would probably have put an end to all hopes of her daughter's marriage.'

'You are wrong, Hastings. He could not blackmail her, for she had the whip-hand. Georges Conneau, remember, is still wanted for murder. A word from her and he is in danger of the guillotine.'

I was forced, rather reluctantly, to admit the truth of this.

'*Your* theory,' I remarked acidly, 'is doubtless correct as to all the details?'

'My theory is the truth,' said Poirot quietly. 'And the truth is necessarily correct. In your theory you made a fundamental error. You permitted your imagination to lead you astray with midnight assignations and passionate love scenes. But in investigating crime we must take our stand upon the commonplace. Shall I demonstrate my methods to you?'

'Oh, by all means let us have a demonstration!'

Poirot sat very upright and began, wagging his forefinger emphatically to emphasize his points:

'I will start as you started from the basic fact of Georges Conneau. Now the story told by Madame Beroldy in court as to the "Russians" was admittedly a fabrication. If she was innocent of connivance in the crime, it was concocted by her, and by her only as she stated. If, on the other hand, she was *not* innocent, it might have been invented by either her or Georges Conneau.

'Now, in this case we are investigating, we meet the same tale. As I pointed out to you, the facts render it very unlikely that Madame Daubreuil inspired it. So we turn to the hypothesis that the story had its origin in the brain of Georges Conneau. Very good. Georges Conneau, therefore, planned the crime, with Mrs Renauld as his accomplice. She is in the limelight, and behind her is a shadowy figure whose present *alias* is unknown to us.

'Now let us go carefully over the Renauld Case from the beginning, setting down each significant point in its chronological order. You have a notebook and pencil? Good. Now what is the earliest point to note down?'

'The letter to you?'

'That was the first we knew of it, but it is not the proper beginning of the case. The first point of any significance, I should say, is the change that came over Monsieur Renauld shortly after arriving in Merlinville, and which is attested to by several witnesses. We have also to consider his friendship with Madame Daubreuil, and the large sums of money paid over to her. From thence we can come directly to the 23rd May.'

Poirot paused, cleared his throat, and signed to me to write:

'*23rd May.* M. Renauld quarrels with his son over latter's wish to marry Marthe Daubreuil. Son leaves for Paris.

'*24th May.* M. Renauld alters his will, leaving entire control of his fortune in his wife's hands.

'*7th June.* Quarrel with tramp in garden, witnessed by Marthe Daubreuil.

'Letter written to M. Hercule Poirot, imploring assistance.

'Telegram sent to M. Jack Renauld, bidding him proceed by the *Anzora* to Buenos Aires.

'Chauffeur, Masters, sent off on a holiday.

'Visit of a lady that evening. As he is seeing her out, his words are "Yes, yes – but for God's sake go now . . ."'

Poirot paused.

'There, Hastings, take each of those facts one by one, consider them carefully by themselves and in relation to the whole, and see if you do not get new light on the matter.'

I endeavoured conscientiously to do as he had said. After a moment or two, I said rather doubtfully:

'As to the first points, the question seems to be whether we adopt the theory of blackmail, or of an infatuation for this woman.'

'Blackmail, decidedly. You heard what Stonor said as to his character and habits.'

'Mrs Renauld did not confirm his view,' I argued.

'We have already seen that Madame Renauld's testimony cannot be relied upon in any way. We must trust to Stonor on that point.'

'Still, if Renauld had an affair with a woman called Bella, there seems no inherent improbability in his having another with Madame Daubreuil.'

'None whatever, I grant you, Hastings. But did he?'

'The letter, Poirot. You forget the letter.'

'No, I do not forget. But what makes you think that letter was written to Monsieur Renauld?'

'Why, it was found in his pocket, and – and –'

'And that is all!' cut in Poirot. 'There was no mention of any name to show to whom the letter was addressed. We assumed it was to the dead man because it was in the pocket of his overcoat. Now, *mon ami*, something about that overcoat struck me as unusual. I measured it, and made the remark that he wore his overcoat very long. That remark should have given you to think.'

'I thought you were just saying it for the sake of saying something,' I confessed.

'Ah, *quelle idée!* Later you observed me measuring the overcoat of Monsieur Jack Renauld. *Eh bien*, Monsieur Jack Renauld wears his overcoat very short. Put those two facts together with a third, namely, that Monsieur Jack Renauld flung out of the house in a hurry on his departure for Paris, and tell me what you make of it!'

'I see,' I said slowly, as the meaning of Poirot's remarks bore in upon me. 'That letter was written to Jack Renauld – not to his father. He caught up the wrong overcoat in his haste and agitation.'

Poirot nodded.

'*Précisément!* We can return to this point later. For the moment let us content ourselves with accepting the letter as having nothing to do with Monsieur Renauld *père*, and pass to the next chronological event.'

'"*23rd May*."' I read: '"M. Renauld quarrels with his son over latter's wish to marry Marthe Daubreuil. Son leaves for Paris." I don't see anything much to remark upon there, and the altering of the will the following day seems straightforward enough. It was the direct result of the quarrel.'

'We agree, *mon ami* – at least as to the cause. But what exact motive underlay this procedure of Monsieur Renauld's?'

I opened my eyes in surprise.

'Anger against his son of course.'

'Yet he wrote him affectionate letters to Paris?'

'So Jack Renauld says, but he cannot produce them.'

'Well, let us pass from that.'

'Now we come to the day of the tragedy. You have placed the events of the morning in a certain order. Have you any justification for that?'

'I have ascertained that the letter to me was posted at the same time as the telegram was dispatched. Masters was informed he could take a holiday shortly afterwards. In my opinion the quarrel with the tramp took place anterior to these happenings.'

'I do not see that you can fix that definitely unless you question Madame Daubreuil again.'

'There is no need. I am sure of it. And if you do not see that, you see nothing, Hastings!'

I looked at him for a moment.

'Of course! I am an idiot. If the tramp was Georges Conneau, it was after the stormy interview with him that Mr Renauld apprehended danger. He sent away the chauffeur, Masters, whom he suspected of being in the other's pay, he wired to his son, and sent for you.'

A faint smile crossed Poirot's lips.

'You do not think it strange that he should use exactly the same expressions in his letter as Madame Renauld used, later in her story? If the mention of Santiago was a blind, why should Renauld speak of it, and – what is more – send his son there?'

'It is puzzling, I admit, but perhaps we shall find some explanation later. We come now to the evening, and the visit of the mysterious lady. I confess that that fairly baffles me, unless it was indeed Madame Daubreuil, as Françoise all along maintained.'

Poirot shook his head.

'My friend, my friend, where are your wits wandering? Remember the fragment of cheque, and the fact that the name Bella Duveen was faintly familiar to Stonor, and I think we may take it for granted that Bella Duveen is the full name of Jack's unknown correspondent, and that it was she who came to the Villa Geneviève that night. Whether she intended to see Jack, or whether she meant all along to appeal to his father, we cannot be certain, but I think we may assume that this is what occurred. She produced her claim upon Jack, probably showed letters that he had written her, and the older man tried to buy her off by writing a cheque. This she indignantly tore up. The terms of her letter are those of a woman genuinely in love, and she would probably deeply resent being offered money. In the end he got rid of her, and here the words that he used are significant.'

'"Yes, yes, but for God's sake go now",' I repeated. 'They seem to me a little vehement, perhaps, that is all.'

'That is enough. He was desperately anxious for the girl to go. Why? Not because the interview was unpleasant. No, it was the time that was slipping by, and for some reason time was precious.'

'Why should it be?' I asked bewildered.

'That is what we ask ourselves. Why should it be? But later we have the incident of the wristwatch – which again shows us that time plays a very important part in the crime. We are now fast approaching the actual drama. It is half past ten when Bella Duveen leaves, and by the evidence of the wristwatch we know that the crime was committed, or at any rate that it was staged, before twelve o'clock. We have reviewed all the events anterior to the murder, there remains only one unplaced. By the doctor's evidence, the tramp, when found, had been dead at least forty-eight hours – with a possible margin of twenty-four hours more. Now, with no other facts to help me than those we have discussed, I place the death as having occurred on the morning of 7th June.'

I stared at him, stupefied.

'But how? Why? How can you possibly know?'

'Because only in that way can the sequence of events be logically explained. *Mon ami*, I have taken you step by step along the way. Do you not now see what is so glaringly plain?'

'My dear Poirot, I can't see anything glaring about it. I did think I was beginning to see my way before, but I'm now hopelessly fogged. For goodness' sake, get on, and tell me who killed Mr Renauld.'

'That is just what I am not sure of as yet.'

'But you said it was glaringly clear!'

'We talk at cross-purposes, my friend. Remember, it is *two* crimes we are investigating – for which, as I pointed out to you, we have the necessary two bodies. There, there, *ne vous impatientez pas!* I explain all. To begin with, we apply our psychology. We find three points at which Monsieur Renauld displays a distinct change of view and action – three psychological points therefore. The first occurs immediately after arriving in Merlinville, the second after quarrelling with his son on a certain subject, the third on the morning of 7th June. Now for the three causes. We can attribute No 1 to meeting Madame Daubreuil. No 2 is indirectly connected with her, since it concerns a marriage between Monsieur Renauld's son and her daughter. But the cause of No 3 is hidden from us. We had to deduce it. Now, *mon ami*, let me ask you a question: whom do we believe to have planned this crime?'

'Georges Conneau,' I said doubtfully, eyeing Poirot warily.

'Exactly. Now Giraud laid it down as an axiom that a woman lies to save herself, the man she loves, and her child. Since we are satisfied that it was Georges Conneau who dictated the lie to her, and as Georges Conneau is not Jack Renauld, it follows that the third case is put out of court. And, still attributing the crime to Georges Conneau, the first is equally so. So we are forced to the second – that Madame Renauld lied for the sake of the man she loved – or in other words, for the sake of Georges Conneau. You agree to that?'

'Yes,' I admitted. 'It seems logical enough.'

'*Bien!* Madame Renauld loves Georges Conneau. Who, then, is Georges Conneau?'

'The tramp.'

'Have we any evidence to show that Madame Renauld loved the tramp?'

'No, but –'

'Very well then. Do not cling to theories where facts no longer support them. Ask yourself instead whom Madame Renauld *did* love.'

I shook my head perplexed.

'*Mais oui*, you know perfectly. Whom did Madame Renauld love so dearly that when she saw his dead body she fell down in a swoon?'

I stared dumbfounded.

'Her husband?' I gasped.

Poirot nodded.

'Her husband – or Georges Conneau, whichever you like to call him.'

I rallied myself.

'But it's impossible.'

'How "impossible"? Did we not agree just now that Madame Daubreuil was in a position to blackmail Georges Conneau?'

'Yes, but –'

'And did she not very effectively blackmail Monsieur Renauld?'

'That may be true enough, but –'

'And is it not a fact that we know nothing of Monsieur Renauld's youth and upbringing? That he springs suddenly into existence as a French-Canadian exactly twenty-two years ago?'

'All that is so,' I said more firmly, 'but you seem to me to be overlooking one salient point.'

'What is that, my friend?'

'Why, we have admitted that Georges planned the crime. That brings us to the ridiculous statement *that he planned his own murder!*'

'*Eh bien, mon ami*,' said Poirot placidly, 'that is just what he did do!'

CHAPTER 21

HERCULE POIROT ON THE CASE

In a measured voice Poirot began his exposition.

'It seems strange to you, *mon ami*, that a man should plan his own death? So strange, that you prefer to reject the truth as fantastic, and to revert to a story that is in reality ten times more impossible. Yes, Monsieur Renauld planned his own death, but there is one detail that perhaps escapes you – he did not intend to die.'

I shook my head, bewildered.

'But no, it is all most simple really,' said Poirot kindly. 'For the crime that Monsieur Renauld proposed a murderer was not necessary, as I told you, but a body was. Let us reconstruct, seeing events this time from a different angle.

'Georges Conneau flies from justice – to Canada. There, under an assumed name, he marries, and finally acquires a vast fortune in South America. But there is a nostalgia upon him for his own country. Twenty years have elapsed, he is considerably changed in appearance, besides being a man of such eminence that no one is likely to connect him with a fugitive from justice many years ago. He deems it quite safe to return. He takes up his headquarters in England, but intends to spend the summers in France. And ill fortune, or that obscure justice which shapes men's ends and will not allow them to evade the consequences of their acts, takes him to Merlinville. There, in the whole of France, is the one person who is capable of recognizing him. It is, of course, a gold mine to Madame Daubreuil, and a gold mine of which she is not slow to take advantage. He is helpless, absolutely in her power. And she bleeds him heavily.

'And then the inevitable happens. Jack Renauld falls in love with the beautiful girl he sees almost daily, and wishes to marry her. That rouses his father. At all costs, he will prevent his son marrying the daughter of this evil woman. Jack Renauld knows nothing of his father's past, but Madame Renauld knows everything. She is a woman of great force of character and passionately devoted to her husband. They take counsel together. Renauld sees only one way of escape – death. He must appear to die, in reality escaping to another country where he will start again under an assumed name and where Madame Renauld, having played the widow's part for a while, can join him. It is essential that she should have control of the money, so he alters his will. How they meant to manage the body business originally, I do not know – possibly an art student's skeleton and a fire – or something of the kind, but long before their plans have matured an event occurs which plays into their hands. A rough tramp, violent and abusive, finds his way into the garden. There is a struggle, Renauld seeks to eject him, and suddenly the tramp, an epileptic, falls down in a fit. He is dead. Renauld calls his wife. Together they drag him into the shed – as we know the event had occurred just outside – and they realize the marvellous opportunity that has been vouchsafed them. The man bears no resemblance to Renauld but he is middle-aged, of a usual French type. That is sufficient.

'I rather fancy that they sat on the bench up there, out of earshot from the house, discussing matters. Their plan was quickly made. The identification must rest solely on Madame Renauld's evidence. Jack Renauld and the chauffeur (who had been with his master two years) must be got out of the way. It was unlikely that the French women servants would go near the body, and in any case Renauld intended to take measures to deceive anyone not likely to appreciate details. Masters was sent off, a telegram dispatched to Jack, Buenos Aires being selected to give credence to the story that Renauld had decided upon. Having heard of me as a rather obscure elderly detective, he wrote his appeal for help, knowing that when I arrived, the production of the letter would have a profound effect upon the examining magistrate – which, of course, it did.

'They dressed the body of the tramp in a suit of Renauld's and left his ragged coat and trousers by the door of the shed, not daring to take them into the house. And then, to give credence to the tale Madame Renauld was to tell, they drove the aeroplane dagger through his heart. That night Renauld will first bind and gag his wife, and then, taking a spade, will dig a grave in that particular plot of ground where he knows a – how do you call it? – bunkair? is to be made. It is essential that the body should be found – Madame Daubreuil must have no suspicions. On the other hand, if a little time elapses, any dangers as to identity will be greatly lessened. Then, Renauld will don the tramp's rags, and shuffle off to the station, where he will leave, unnoticed, by the 12.10 train. Since the crime will be supposed to have taken place two hours later, no suspicion can possibly attach to him.

'You see now his annoyance at the inopportune visit of the girl, Bella. Every moment of delay is fatal to his plans. He gets rid of her as soon as he can, however. Then, to work! He leaves the front door slightly ajar to create the impression that assassins left that way. He binds and gags Madame Renauld, correcting his mistake of twenty-two years ago, when the looseness of the bonds caused suspicion to fall upon his accomplice, but leaving her primed with essentially the same story as he had invented before, proving the unconscious recoil of the mind against originality. The night is chilly, and he slips on an overcoat over his under-clothing, intending to cast it into the grave with the dead man. He goes out by the window, smoothing over the flower-bed carefully, and thereby furnishing the most positive evidence against himself. He goes out on to the lonely golf links, and he digs – And then –'

'Yes?'

'And then,' said Poirot gravely, 'the justice that he has so long eluded overtakes him. An unknown hand stabs him in the back . . . Now, Hastings, you understand what I mean when I talk of *two* crimes. The first crime, the crime that Monsieur Renauld, in his arrogance, asked us to investigate, is solved. But behind it lies a deeper riddle. And to solve that will be difficult – since the criminal, in his wisdom, has been content to avail himself of the devices prepared by Renauld. It has been a particularly perplexing and baffling mystery to solve.'

'You're marvellous, Poirot,' I said, with admiration. 'Absolutely marvellous. No one on earth but you would have done it!'

I think my praise pleased him. For once in his life he looked almost embarrassed.

'That poor Giraud,' said Poirot, trying unsuccessfully to look modest. 'Without doubt it is not all stupidity. He has had *la mauvaise chance* once or twice. That dark hair coiled round the dagger, for instance. To say the least, it was misleading.'

'To tell you the truth, Poirot,' I said slowly, 'even now I don't quite see – whose hair was it?'

'Madame Renauld's, of course. That is where *la mauvaise*

chance came in. Her hair, dark originally, is almost completely silvered. It might just as easily have been a grey hair – and then, by no conceivable effort could Giraud have persuaded himself it came from the head of Jack Renauld! But it is all of a piece. Always the facts must be twisted to fit the theory!

'Without doubt, when Madame Renauld recovers, she will speak. The possibility of her son being accused of the murder never occurred to her. How should it, when she believed him safely at sea on board the *Anzora? Ah! voilà une femme*, Hastings! What force, what self-command! She only made one slip. On his unexpected return: "It does not matter – *now*." And no one noticed – no one realized the significance of those words. What a terrible part she has had to play, poor woman. Imagine the shock when she goes to identify the body and, instead of what she expects, sees the actual lifeless form of the husband she has believed miles away by now. No wonder she fainted! But since then, despite her grief and her despair, how resolutely she has played her part and how the anguish of it must wring her. She cannot say a word to set us on the track of the real murderers. For her son's sake, no one must know that Paul Renauld was Georges Conneau, the criminal. Final and most bitter blow, she has admitted publicly that Madame Daubreuil was her husband's mistress – for a hint of blackmail might be fatal to her secret. How cleverly she dealt with the examining magistrate when he asked her if there was any mystery in her husband's past life. "Nothing so romantic, I am sure, monsieur." It was perfect, the indulgent tone, the soupçon of sad mockery. At once Monsieur Hautet felt himself foolish and melodramatic. Yes, she is a great woman! If she loved a criminal, she loved him royally!'

Poirot lost himself in contemplation.

'One thing more, Poirot, what about the piece of lead-piping?'

'You do not see? To disfigure the victim's face so that it would be unrecognizable. It was that which first set me on the right track. And that imbecile of a Giraud, swarming all over it to look for match ends! Did I not tell you that a clue of two foot long was quite as good as a clue of two inches? You see, Hastings, we must now start again. Who killed Monsieur Renauld? Someone who was near the villa just before twelve o'clock that night, someone who would benefit by his death – the description fits Jack Renauld only too well. The crime need not have been premeditated. And then the dagger!'

I started, I had not realized that point.

'Of course,' I said, 'Mrs Renauld's dagger was the second one we found in the tramp. There *were* two, then?'

'Certainly, and since they were duplicates, it stands to reason that Jack Renauld was the owner. But that would not trouble me so much. In fact, I had a little idea as to that. No, the worst indictment against him is again psychological – heredity, *mon ami*, heredity! Like father, like son – Jack Renauld, when all is said or done, is the son of Georges Conneau.'

His tone was grave and earnest, and I was impressed in spite of myself.

'What is your little idea that you mentioned just now?' I asked.

For answer, Poirot consulted his turnip-faced watch, and then asked:

'What time is the afternoon boat from Calais?'

'About five, I believe.'

'That will do very well. We shall just have time.'

'You are going to England?'

'Yes, my friend.'

'Why?'

'To find a possible – witness.'

'Who?'

With a rather peculiar smile upon his face, Poirot replied:

'Miss Bella Duveen.'

'But how will you find her – what do you know about her?'

'I know nothing about her – but I can guess a good deal. We may take it for granted that her name *is* Bella Duveen, and since that name was faintly familiar to Monsieur Stonor, though evidently not in connexion with the Renauld family, it is probable that she is on the stage. Jack Renauld was a young man with plenty of money, and twenty years of age. The stage is sure to have been the home of his first love. It tallies, too, with Monsieur Renauld's attempt to placate her with a cheque. I think I shall find her all right – especially with the help of *this*.'

And he brought out the photograph I had seen him take from Jack Renauld's drawer. 'With love from Bella' was scrawled across the corner, but it was not that which held my eyes fascinated. The likeness was not first rate – but for all that it was unmistakable to me. I felt a cold sinking, as though some unutterable calamity had befallen me.

It was the face of Cinderella.

CHAPTER 22
I FIND LOVE

For a moment or two I sat as though frozen, the photograph still in my hand. Then summoning all my courage to appear unmoved, I handed it back. At the same time I stole a quick glance at Poirot. Had he noticed anything? But to my relief he did not seem to be observing me. Anything unusual in my manner had certainly escaped him.

He rose briskly to his feet.

'We have no time to lose. We must make our departure with all dispatch. All is well – the sea it will be calm!'

In the bustle of departure, I had no time for thinking, but once on board the boat, secure from Poirot's observation, I pulled myself together, and attacked the facts dispassionately. How much did Poirot know, and why was he bent on finding this girl? Did he suspect her of having seen Jack Renauld commit the crime? Or did he suspect – But that was impossible! The girl had no grudge against the elder Renauld, no possible motive for wishing his death. What had brought her back to the scene of the murder? I went over the facts carefully. She must have left the train at Calais where I parted from her that day. No wonder I had been unable to find her on the boat. If she had dined in Calais, and then taken a train out to Merlinville, she would have arrived at the Villa Geneviève just about the time that Françoise said. What had she done when she left the house just after ten? Presumably either gone to an hotel, or returned to Calais. And then? The crime had been committed on Tuesday night. On Thursday morning she was once more in Merlinville. Had she ever left France at all? I doubted it very much. What kept her there – the hope of seeing Jack Renauld? I had told her (as at the time we believed) that he was on the high seas *en route* to Buenos Aires. Possibly she was aware that the *Anzora* had not sailed. But to know that she must have seen Jack. Was that what Poirot was after? Had Jack Renauld, returning to see Marthe Daubreuil, come face to face instead with Bella Duveen, the girl he had heartlessly thrown over?

I began to see daylight. If that were indeed the case, it might furnish Jack with the alibi he needed. Yet under those circumstances his silence seemed difficult to explain. Why could he not have spoken out boldly? Did he fear for this former entanglement of his to come to the ears of Marthe Daubreuil? I shook my head, dissatisfied. The thing had been harmless enough, a foolish boy-and-girl affair, and I reflected cynically that the son of a millionaire was not likely to be thrown over by a penniless French girl, who moreover loved him devotedly, without a much graver cause.

Poirot reappeared brisk and smiling at Dover, and our journey to London was uneventful. It was past nine o'clock when we arrived, and I supposed that we should return straight away to our rooms and do nothing till the morning.

But Poirot had other plans.

'We must lose no time, *mon ami*. The news of the arrest will not be in the English papers until the day after tomorrow, but still we must lose no time.'

I did not quite follow his reasoning, but I merely asked how he proposed to find the girl.

'You remember Joseph Aarons, the theatrical agent? No? I assisted him in a little matter of a Japanese wrestler. A pretty little problem, I must recount it to you one day. He, without doubt, will be able to put us in the way of finding out what we want to know.'

It took us some time to run Mr Aarons to earth, and it was after midnight when we finally managed it. He greeted Poirot with every evidence of warmth, and professed himself ready to be of service to us in any way.

'There's not much about the profession I don't know,' he said, beaming genially.

'*Eh bien*, Monsieur Aarons, I desire to find a young girl called Bella Duveen.'

'Bella Duveen. I know the name, but for a moment I can't place it. What's her line?'

'That I do not know – but here is her photograph.'

Mr Aarons studied it for a moment, then his face lighted.

'Got it!' He slapped his thigh. 'The Dulcibella Kids, by the Lord!'

'The Dulcibella Kids?'

'That's it. They're sisters. Acrobats, dancers, and singers. Give quite a good little turn. They're in the provinces, somewhere, I believe – if they're not resting. They've been on in Paris for the last two or three weeks.'

'Can you find out for me exactly where they are?'

'Easy as a bird. You go home, and I'll send you round the dope in the morning.'

With this promise we took leave of him. He was as good as his word. About eleven o'clock the following day, a scribbled note reached us.

'The Dulcibella Sisters are on at the Palace in Coventry. Good luck to you.'

Without more ado, we started for Coventry. Poirot made no inquiries at the theatre, but contented himself with booking stalls for the variety performance that evening.

The show was wearisome beyond words – or perhaps it was only my mood that made it seem so. Japanese families balanced themselves precariously, would-be fashionable men, in greenish evening dress and exquisitely slicked hair, reeled off society patter and danced marvellously. Stout prima donnas sang at the top of the human register, a comic comedian endeavoured to be Mr George Robey and failed signally.

At last the number went up which announced the Dulcibella Kids. My heart beat sickeningly. There she was – there they both were, the pair of them, one flaxen-haired, one dark, matching as to size, with short fluffy skirts and immense 'Buster Brown' bows. They looked a pair of extremely piquant children. They began to sing. Their voices were fresh and true, rather thin and music-hally, but attractive.

It was quite a pretty little turn. They danced neatly, and did some clever little acrobatic feats. The words of their songs were crisp and catchy. When the curtain fell, there was a full meed of applause. Evidently the Dulcibella Kids were a success.

Suddenly I felt that I could remain no longer. I must get out into the air. I suggested leaving to Poirot.

'Go by all means, *mon ami*. I amuse myself, and will stay to the end. I will rejoin you later.'

It was only a few steps from the theatre to the hotel. I went up to the sitting-room, ordered a whisky and soda, and sat drinking it, staring meditatively into the empty grate. I heard the door open, and turned my head, thinking it was Poirot. Then I jumped to my feet. It was Cinderella who stood in the doorway. She spoke haltingly, her breath coming in little gasps.

'I saw you in front. You and your friend. When you got up to go, I was waiting outside and followed you. Why are you here – in Coventry? What were you doing there tonight? Is the man who was with you the – the detective?'

She stood there, the cloak she had wrapped round her stage dress slipping from her shoulders. I saw the whiteness of her cheeks under the rouge, and heard the terror in her voice. And in that moment I understood everything – understood why Poirot was seeking her, and what she feared, and understood at last my own heart . . .

'Yes,' I said gently.

'Is he looking for – me?' she half whispered.

Then, as I did not answer for a moment, she slipped down by the big chair, and burst into violent bitter weeping.

I knelt down by her, holding her in my arms, and smoothing the hair back from her face.

'Don't cry, child, don't cry, for God's sake. You're safe here. I'll take care of you. Don't cry, darling. Don't cry. I know – I know everything.'

'Oh, but you don't!'

'I think I do.' And after a moment, as her sobs grew quieter, I asked: 'It was you who took the dagger, wasn't it?'

'Yes.'

'That was why you wanted me to show you round? And why you pretended to faint?'

Again she nodded.

'Why did you take the dagger?' I asked presently.

She replied as simply as a child:

'I was afraid there might be finger-marks on it.'

'But didn't you remember that you had worn gloves?'

She shook her head as though bewildered, and then said slowly:

'Are you going to give me up to – to the police?'

'Good God! no.'

Her eyes sought mine long and earnestly, and then she asked in a little quiet voice that sounded afraid of itself:

'Why not?'

It seemed a strange place and a strange time for a declaration of love – and God knows, in all my imagining, I had never pictured love coming to me in such a guise. But I answered simply and naturally enough:

'Because I love you, Cinderella.'

She bent her head down, as though ashamed, and muttered in a broken voice:

'You can't – you can't – not if you knew –' And then, as though rallying herself, she faced me squarely, and asked, 'What do you know, then?'

'I know that you came to see Mr Renauld that night. He offered you a cheque and you tore it up indignantly. Then you left the house –' I paused.

'Go on – what next?'

'I don't know whether you knew Jack Renauld would be coming that night, or whether you just waited about on the chance of seeing him, but you did wait about. Perhaps you were just miserable and walked aimlessly – but at any rate just before twelve you were still near there, and you saw a man on the golf links –'

Again I paused. I had leapt to the truth in a flash as she entered the room, but now the picture rose before me even more convincingly. I saw vividly the peculiar pattern of the overcoat on the dead body of Mr Renauld, and I remembered the amazing likeness that had startled me into believing for one instant that the dead man had risen from the dead when his son burst into our conclave in the salon.

'Go on,' repeated the girl steadily.

'I fancy his back was to you – but you recognized him, or thought you recognized him. The gait and the carriage were familiar to you, and the pattern of his overcoat.' I paused. 'You used a threat in one of your letters to Jack Renauld. When you saw him there, your anger and jealousy drove you mad – and you struck! I don't believe for a minute that you meant to kill him. But you did kill him, Cinderella.'

She had flung up her hands to cover her face, and in a choked voice she said:

'You're right . . . you're right . . . I can see it all as you tell it.' Then she turned on me almost savagely. 'And you love me? Knowing what you do, how can you love me?'

'I don't know,' I said a little wearily. 'I think love is like that – a thing one cannot help. I have tried, I know – ever since the first day I met you. And love has been too strong for me.'

And then suddenly, when I least expected it, she broke down again, casting herself down on the floor and sobbing wildly.

'Oh, I can't!' she cried. 'I don't know what to do. I don't know which way to turn. Oh, pity me, pity me, someone, and tell me what to do!'

Again I knelt by her, soothing her as best I could.

'Don't be afraid of me, Bella. For God's sake don't be afraid of me. I love you, that's true – but I don't want anything in return. Only let me help you. Love him still if you have to, but let me help you, as he can't.'

It was as though she had been turned to stone by my words. She raised her head from her hands and stared at me.

'You think that?' she whispered. 'You think that I love Jack Renauld?'

Then, half laughing, half crying, she flung her arms passionately round my neck, and pressed her sweet wet face to mine.

'Not as I love you,' she whispered. 'Never as I love you!'

Her lips brushed my cheek, and then, seeking my mouth, kissed me again and again with a sweetness and fire beyond belief. The wildness of it – and the wonder, I shall not forget – no, not as long as I live!

It was a sound in the doorway that made us look up. Poirot was standing there looking at us.

I did not hesitate. With a bound I reached him and pinioned his arms to his sides.

'Quick,' I said to the girl. 'Get out of here. As fast as you can. I'll hold him.'

With one look at me, she fled out of the room past us. I held Poirot in a grip of iron.

'*Mon ami*,' observed the latter mildly, 'you do this sort of thing very well. The strong man holds me in his grasp and I am helpless as a child. But all this is uncomfortable and slightly ridiculous. Let us sit down and be calm.'

'You won't pursue her?'

'*Mon Dieu!* no. Am I Giraud? Release me, my friend.'

Keeping a suspicious eye upon him, for I paid Poirot the compliment of knowing that I was no match for him in astuteness, I relaxed my grip, and he sank into an armchair, feeling his arms tenderly.

'It is that you have the strength of a bull when you are roused, Hastings! *Eh bien*, and do you think you have behaved well to your old friend? I show you the girl's photograph and you recognize it, but you never say a word.'

'There was no need if you knew that I recognized it,' I said rather bitterly. So Poirot had known all along! I had not deceived him for an instant.

'Ta-ta! You did not know that I knew that. And tonight you help the girl to escape when we have found her with so much trouble. *Eh bien!* it comes to this – are you going to work with me or against me, Hastings?'

For a moment or two I did not answer. To break with my old friend gave me great pain. Yet I must definitely range myself against him. Would he ever forgive me, I wondered? He had been strangely calm so far, but I knew him to possess marvellous self-command.

'Poirot,' I said, 'I'm sorry. I admit I've behaved badly to you over this. But sometimes one has no choice. And in future I must take my own line.'

Poirot nodded his head several times.

'I understand,' he said. The mocking light had quite died out of his eyes, and he spoke with a sincerity and kindness that surprised me. 'It is that, my friend, is it not? It is love that has come – not as you imagined it, all cock-a-hoop with fine feathers, but sadly, with bleeding feet. Well, well – I warned you. When I realized that this girl must have taken the dagger, I warned you. Perhaps you remember. But already it was too late. But, tell me, how much do you know?'

I met his eyes squarely.

'Nothing that you could tell me would be any surprise to me, Poirot. Understand that. But in case you think of resuming your search for Miss Duveen, I should like you to know one thing clearly. If you have any idea that she was concerned in the crime, or was the mysterious lady who called upon Mr Renauld that night, you are wrong. I travelled home from France with her that day, and parted from her at Victoria that evening, so that it is clearly impossible for her to have been in Merlinville.'

'Ah!' Poirot looked at me thoughtfully. 'And you would swear to that in a court of law?'

'Most certainly I would.'

Poirot rose and bowed.

'*Mon ami! Vive l'amour!* It can perform miracles. It is decidedly ingenious what you have thought of there. It defeats even Hercule Poirot!'

CHAPTER 23
DIFFICULTIES AHEAD

After a moment of stress, such as I have just described, reaction is bound to set in. I retired to rest that night on a note of triumph, but I awoke to realize that I was by no means out of the wood. True, I could see no flaw in the alibi I had so suddenly conceived. I had but to stick to my story, and I failed to see how Bella could be convicted in face of it.

But I felt the need of treading warily. Poirot would not take defeat lying down. Somehow or other, he would endeavour to turn the tables on me, and that in the way, and at the moment, when I least expected it.

We met at breakfast the following morning as though nothing had happened. Poirot's good temper was imperturbable, yet I thought I detected a film of reserve in his manner which was new. After breakfast, I announced my intention of going out for a stroll. A malicious gleam shot through Poirot's eyes.

'If it is information you seek, you need not be at the pains of deranging yourself. I can tell you all you wish to know. The Dulcibella Sisters have cancelled their contract, and have left Coventry for an unknown destination.'

'Is that really so, Poirot?'

'You can take it from me, Hastings. I made inquiries the first thing this morning. After all, what else did you expect?'

True enough, nothing else could be expected under the circumstances. Cinderella had profited by the slight start I had been able to secure her, and would certainly not lose a moment in removing herself from the reach of the pursuer. It was what I had intended and planned. Nevertheless, I was aware of being plunged into a network of fresh difficulties.

I had absolutely no means of communicating with the girl, and it was vital that she should know the line of defence that had occurred to me, and which I was prepared to carry out. Of course it was possible that she might try to send word to me in some way or another, but I hardly thought it likely. She would know the risk she ran of a message being intercepted by Poirot, thus setting him on her track once more. Clearly her only course was to disappear utterly for the time being.

But, in the meantime, what was Poirot doing? I studied him attentively. He was wearing his most innocent air, and staring meditatively into the far distance. He looked altogether too placid and supine to give me reassurance. I had learned, with Poirot, that the less dangerous he looked, the more dangerous he was. His quiescence alarmed me. Observing a troubled quality in my glance, he smiled benignantly.

'You are puzzled, Hastings? You ask yourself why I do not launch myself in pursuit?'

'Well – something of the kind.'

'It is what you would do, were you in my place. I understand that. But I am not of those who enjoy rushing up and down a country seeking a needle in a haystack, as you English say. No – let Mademoiselle Bella Duveen go. Without doubt, I shall be able to find her when the time comes. Until then, I am content to wait.'

I stared at him doubtfully. Was he seeking to mislead me? I had an irritating feeling that, even now, he was master of the situation.

My sense of superiority was gradually waning. I had contrived the girl's escape, and evolved a brilliant scheme for saving her from the consequences of her rash act – but I could not rest easy in my mind. Poirot's perfect calm awakened a thousand apprehensions.

'I suppose, Poirot,' I said rather diffidently, 'I mustn't ask what your plans are? I've forfeited the right.'

'But not at all. There is no secret about them. We return to France without delay.'

'*We?*'

'Precisely – "*we*"! You know very well that you cannot afford to let Papa Poirot out of your sight. Eh? is it not so, my friend? But remain in England by all means if you wish –'

I shook my head. He had hit the nail on the head. I could not afford to let him out of my sight. Although I could not expect his confidence after what had happened, I could still check his actions. The only danger to Bella lay with him. Giraud and the French police were indifferent to her existence. At all costs I must keep near Poirot.

Poirot observed me attentively as these reflections passed through my mind, and gave me a nod of satisfaction.

'I am right, am I not? And as you are quite capable of trying to follow me, disguised with some absurdity such as a false beard – which everyone would perceive, *bien entendu* – I much prefer that we should voyage together. It would annoy me greatly that anyone should mock themselves at you.'

'Very well, then. But it's only fair to warn you –'

'I know – I know all. You are my enemy! Be my enemy, then. It does not worry me at all.'

'So long as it's all fair and above-board, I don't mind.'

'You have to the full the English passion for "fair play"! Now your scruples are satisfied, let us depart immediately. There is no time to be lost. Our stay in England has been short but sufficient. I know – what I wanted to know.'

The tone was light, but I read a veiled menace into the words.

'Still –' I began, and stopped.

'Still – as you say! Without doubt you are satisfied with the part you are playing. Me, I preoccupy myself with Jack Renauld.'

Jack Renauld! The words gave me a start. I had completely forgotten that aspect of the case. Jack Renauld, in prison, with the shadow of the guillotine looming over him. I saw the part I was playing in a more sinister light. I could save Bella – yes, but in doing so I ran the risk of sending an innocent man to his death.

I pushed the thought from me with horror. It could not be. He would be acquitted. Certainly he would be acquitted. But the cold fear came back. Suppose he were not? What then? Could I have it on my conscience – horrible thought! Would it come to that in the end? A decision. Bella or Jack Renauld? The promptings of my heart were to save the girl I loved at any cost to myself. But, if the cost were to another, the problem was altered.

What would the girl herself say? I remembered that no word of Jack Renauld's arrest had passed my lips. As yet she was in total ignorance of the fact that her former lover was in prison charged with a hideous crime which he had not committed. When she knew, how would she act? Would she permit her life to be saved at the expense of his? Certainly she must do nothing rash. Jack Renauld might, and probably would, be acquitted without any intervention on her part. If so, good. But if he was not! That was the terrible, the unanswerable problem. I fancied that she ran no risk of the extreme penalty. The circumstances of the crime were quite different in her case. She could plead jealousy and extreme provocation, and her youth and beauty would go for much. The fact that by a tragic mistake it was Mr Renauld, and not his son, who paid the penalty would not alter the motive of the crime. But in any case, however lenient the sentence of the Court, it must mean a long term of imprisonment.

No, Bella must be protected. And, at the same time, Jack Renauld must be saved. How this was to be accomplished I did not see clearly. But I pinned my faith to Poirot. He *knew*. Come what might, he would manage to save an innocent man. He must find some pretext other than the real one. It might be difficult, but he would manage it somehow. And with Bella unsuspected, and Jack Renauld acquitted, all would end satisfactorily.

So I told myself repeatedly, but at the bottom of my heart there still remained a cold fear.

CHAPTER 24

'SAVE HIM!'

We crossed from England by the evening boat, and the following morning saw us in St Omer, whither Jack Renauld had been taken. Poirot lost no time in visiting M. Hautet. As he did not seem disposed to make any objections to my accompanying him, I bore him company.

After various formalities and preliminaries, we were conducted to the examining magistrate's room. He greeted us cordially.

'I was told that you had returned to England, Monsieur Poirot. I am glad to find that such is not the case.'

'It is true I went there, monsieur, but it was only for a flying visit. A side issue, but one that I fancied might repay investigation.'

'And it did – eh?'

Poirot shrugged his shoulders. M. Hautet nodded, sighing.

'We must resign ourselves, I fear. That animal Giraud, his manners are abominable, but he is undoubtedly clever! Not much chance of that one making a mistake.'

'You think not?'

It was the examining magistrate's turn to shrug his shoulders.

'Oh, well, speaking frankly – in confidence, of course – can you come to any other conclusion?'

'Frankly, there seem to me to be many points that are obscure.'

'Such as –?'

But Poirot was not to be drawn.

'I have not yet tabulated them,' he remarked. 'It was a general reflection that I was making. I liked the young man, and should be sorry to believe him guilty of such a hideous crime. By the way, what has he to say for himself on the matter?'

The magistrate frowned.

'I cannot understand him. He seems incapable of putting up any sort of defence. It has been most difficult to get him to answer questions. He contents himself with a general denial, and beyond that takes refuge in a most obstinate silence. I am interrogating him again tomorrow, perhaps you would like to be present?'

We accepted the invitation with *empressement*.

'A distressing case,' said the magistrate with a sigh. 'My sympathy for Madame Renauld is profound.'

'How is Madame Renauld?'

'She has not yet recovered consciousness. It is merciful in a way, poor woman, she is being spared much. The doctors say that there is no danger, but that when she comes to herself she must be kept as quiet as possible. It was, I understand, quite as much the shock as the fall which caused her present state. It would be terrible if her brain became unhinged; but I should not wonder at all – no, really, not at all.'

M. Hautet leaned back, shaking his head, with a sort of mournful enjoyment, as he envisaged the gloomy prospect.

He roused himself at length, and observed with a start:

'That reminds me. I have here a letter for you, Monsieur Poirot. Let me see, where did I put it?'

He proceeded to rummage among his papers. At last he found the missive, and handed it to Poirot.

'It was sent under cover to me in order that I might forward it to you,' he explained. 'But as you left no address I could not do so.'

Poirot studied the letter curiously. It was addressed in a long, sloping, foreign hand, and the writing was decidedly a woman's. Poirot did not open it. Instead he put it in his pocket and rose to his feet.

'Till tomorrow then. Many thanks for your courtesy and amiability.'

'But not at all. I am always at your service.'

We were just leaving the building when we came face to face with Giraud, looking more dandified than ever, and thoroughly pleased with himself.

'Aha! Monsieur Poirot,' he cried airily. 'You have returned from England then?'

'As you see,' said Poirot.

'The end of the case is not far off now, I fancy.'

'I agree with you, Monsieur Giraud.'

Poirot spoke in a subdued tone. His crestfallen manner seemed to delight the other.

'Of all the milk-and-water criminals! Not an idea of defending himself. It is extraordinary!'

'So extraordinary that it gives one to think, does it not?' suggested Poirot mildly.

But Giraud was not even listening. He twirled his cane amicably.

'Well, good day, Monsieur Poirot. I am glad you're satisfied of young Renauld's guilt at last.'

'*Pardon!* But I am not in the least satisfied. Jack Renauld is innocent.'

Giraud stared for a moment – then burst out laughing, tapping his head significantly with the brief remark: '*Toqué!*'

Poirot drew himself up. A dangerous light showed in his eyes.

'Monsieur Giraud, throughout the case your manner to me has been deliberately insulting. You need teaching a lesson. I am prepared to wager you five hundred francs that I find the murderer of Monsieur Renauld before you do. Is it agreed?'

Giraud stared helplessly at him, and murmured again: '*Toqué!*'

'Come now,' urged Poirot, 'is it agreed?'

'I have no wish to take your money from you.'

'Make your mind easy – you will not!'

'Oh, well then, I agree! You speak of my manner to you being insulting. Well, once or twice, *your* manner has annoyed *me*.'

'I am enchanted to hear it,' said Poirot. 'Good morning, Monsieur Giraud. Come, Hastings.'

I said no word as we walked along the street. My heart was heavy. Poirot had displayed his intentions only too plainly. I doubted more than ever my powers of saving Bella from the consequences of her act. This unlucky encounter with Giraud had roused Poirot and put him on his mettle.

Suddenly I felt a hand laid on my shoulder, and turned to face Gabriel Stonor. We stopped and greeted him, and he proposed strolling with us back to our hotel.

'And what are you doing here, Monsieur Stonor?' inquired Poirot.

'One must stand by one's friends,' replied the other dryly. 'Especially when they are unjustly accused.'

'Then you do not believe that Jack Renauld committed the crime?' I asked eagerly.

'Certainly I don't. I know the lad. I admit that there have been one or two things in this business that have staggered me completely, but none the less, in spite of his fool way of taking it, I'll never believe that Jack Renauld is a murderer.'

My heart warmed to the secretary. His words seemed to lift a secret weight from my heart.

'I have no doubt that many people feel as you do,' I exclaimed. 'There is really absurdly little evidence against him. I should say that there was no doubt of his acquittal – no doubt whatever.'

But Stonor hardly responded as I could have wished.

'I'd give a lot to think as you do,' he said gravely. He turned to Poirot. 'What's your opinion, monsieur?'

'I think that things look very black against him,' said Poirot quietly.

'You believe him guilty?' said Stonor sharply.

'No. But I think he will find it hard to prove his innocence.'

'He's behaving so damned queerly,' muttered Stonor. 'Of course, I realize that there's a lot more in this affair than meets the eye. Giraud's not wise to that because he's an outsider, but the whole thing has been damned odd. As to that, least said soonest mended. If Mrs Renauld wants to hush anything up, I'll take my cue from her. It's her show, and I've too much respect for her judgement to shove my oar in, but I can't get behind this attitude of Jack's. Anyone would think he *wanted* to be thought guilty.'

'But it's absurd,' I cried, bursting in. 'For one thing, the dagger –' I paused, uncertain as to how much Poirot would wish me to reveal. I continued, choosing my words carefully, 'We know that the dagger could not have been in Jack Renauld's possession that evening. Mrs Renauld knows that.'

'True,' said Stonor. 'When she recovers, she will doubtless say all this and more. Well, I must be leaving you.'

'One moment.' Poirot's hand arrested his departure. 'Can you arrange for word to be sent to me at once should Mrs Renauld recover consciousness?'

'Certainly. That's easily done.'

'That point about the dagger is good, Poirot,' I urged as we went upstairs. 'I couldn't speak very plainly before Stonor.'

'That was quite right of you. We might as well keep the knowledge to ourselves as long as we can. As to the dagger, your point hardly helps Jack Renauld. You remember that I was absent for an hour this morning, before we started from London?'

'Yes?'

'Well, I was employed in trying to find the firm Jack Renauld employed to convert his souvenirs. It was not very difficult. *Eh bien*, Hastings, they made to his order not *two* paper knives, but *three*.'

'So that –'

'So that, after giving one to his mother and one to Bella Duveen, there was a third which he doubtless retained for his own use. No, Hastings, I fear the dagger question will not help us to save him from the guillotine.'

'It won't come to that,' I cried, stung.

Poirot shook his head uncertainly.

'You will save him,' I cried positively.

Poirot glanced at me dryly.

'Have you not rendered it impossible, *mon ami*?'

'Some other way,' I muttered.

'Ah! *Sapristi!* But it is miracles you ask from me. No – say no more. Let us instead see what is in this letter.'

And he drew out the envelope from his breast pocket.

His face contracted as he read, then he handed the one flimsy sheet to me.

'There are other women in the world who suffer, Hastings.'

The writing was blurred and the note had evidently been written in great agitation.

Dear M. Poirot – If you get this, I beg of you to come to my aid. I have no one to turn to, and at all costs Jack must be saved. I implore of you on my knees to help us.

Marthe Daubreuil

I handed it back, moved.

'You will go?'

'At once. We will command an auto.'

Half an hour later saw us at the Villa Marguerite. Marthe was at the door to meet us, and let Poirot in, clinging with both hands to one of his.

'Ah, you have come – it is good of you. I have been in despair, not knowing what to do. They will not let me go to see him in prison even. I suffer horribly. I am nearly mad.

'Is it true what they say, that he does not deny the crime? But that is madness. It is impossible that he should have done it! Never for one minute will I believe it.'

'Neither do I believe it, mademoiselle,' said Poirot gently.

'But then why does he not speak? I do not understand.'

'Perhaps because he is screening someone,' suggested Poirot, watching her.

Marthe frowned.

'Screening someone? Do you mean his mother? Ah, from the beginning I have suspected her. Who inherits all that vast fortune? She does. It is easy to wear widow's weeds and play the hypocrite. And they say that when he was arrested she fell down like *that!*' She made a dramatic gesture. 'And without doubt, Monsieur Stonor, the secretary, he helped her. They are thick as thieves, those two. It is true she is older than he – but what do men care – if a woman is rich!'

There was a hint of bitterness in her tone.

'Stonor was in England,' I put in.

'He says so – but who knows?'

'Mademoiselle,' said Poirot quietly, 'if we are to work together, you and I, we must have things clear. First, I will ask you a question.'

'Yes, monsieur?'

'Are you aware of your mother's real name?'

Marthe looked at him for a minute, then, letting her head fall forward on her arms, she burst into tears.

'There, there,' said Poirot, patting her on the shoulder. 'Calm yourself, *petite*, I see that you know. Now a second question – did you know who Monsieur Renauld was?'

'Monsieur Renauld,' she raised her head from her hands and gazed at him wonderingly.

'Ah, I see you do not know that. Now listen to me carefully.'

Step by step, he went over the case, much as he had done to me on the day of our departure for England. Marthe listened spellbound. When he had finished, she drew a long breath.

'But you are wonderful – magnificent! You are the greatest detective in the world.'

With a swift gesture she slipped off her chair and knelt before him with an abandonment that was wholly French.

'Save him, monsieur,' she cried. 'I love him so. Oh, save him, save him – save him!'

CHAPTER 25

AN UNEXPECTED DÉNOUEMENT

We were present the following morning at the examination of Jack Renauld. Short as the time had been, I was shocked at the change that had taken place in the young prisoner. His cheeks had fallen in, there were deep black circles round his eyes, and he looked haggard and distraught, as one who had wooed sleep in vain for several nights. He betrayed no emotion at seeing us.

'Renauld,' began the magistrate, 'do you deny that you were in Merlinville on the night of the crime?'

Jack did not reply at once, then he said with a hesitancy of manner which was piteous:

'I – I – told you that I was in Cherbourg.'

The magistrate turned sharply.

'Send in the station witnesses.'

In a moment or two the door opened to admit a man whom I recognized as being a porter at Merlinville station.

'You were on duty on the night of 7th June?'

'Yes, monsieur.'

'You witnessed the arrival of the 11.40 train?'

'Yes, monsieur.'

'Look at the prisoner. Do you recognize him as having been one of the passengers to alight?'

'Yes, monsieur.'

'There is no possibility of your being mistaken?'

'No, monsieur. I know Monsieur Jack Renauld well.'

'Nor of your being mistaken as to the date?'

'No, monsieur. Because it was the following morning, 8th June, that we heard of the murder.'

Another railway official was brought in, and confirmed the first one's evidence. The magistrate looked at Jack Renauld.

'These men have identified you positively. What have you to say?'

Jack shrugged his shoulders.

'Nothing.'

'Renauld,' continued the magistrate, 'do you recognize this?'

He took something from the table by his side and held it out to the prisoner. I shuddered as I recognized the aeroplane dagger.

'Pardon,' cried Jack's counsel, Maître Grosier. 'I demand to speak to my client before he answers that question.'

But Jack Renauld had no consideration for the feelings of the wretched Grosier. He waved him aside, and replied quietly:

'Certainly I recognize it. It was a present given by me to my mother, as a souvenir of the war.'

'Is there, as far as you know, any duplicate of that dagger in existence?'

Again Maître Grosier burst out, and again Jack overrode him.

'Not that I know of. The setting was my own design.'

Even the magistrate almost gasped at the boldness of the reply. It did, in very truth, seem as though Jack was rushing on his fate. I realized, of course, the vital necessity he was under of concealing, for Bella's sake, the fact that there was a duplicate dagger in the case. So long as there was supposed to be only one weapon, no suspicion was likely to attach to the girl who had had the second paper-knife in her possession. He was valiantly shielding the woman he had once loved – but at what cost to himself! I began to realize the magnitude of the task I had so lightly set Poirot. It would not be easy to secure the acquittal of Jack Renauld by anything short of the truth.

M. Hautet spoke again, with a peculiarly biting inflection:

'Madame Renauld told us that this dagger was on her dressing-table on the night of the crime. But Madame Renauld is a mother! It will doubtless astonish you, Renauld, but I consider it highly likely that Madame Renauld was mistaken, and that, by inadvertence perhaps, you had taken it with you to Paris. Doubtless you will contradict me –'

I saw the lad's handcuffed hands clench themselves. The

perspiration stood out in beads upon his brow, as with a supreme effort he interrupted M. Hautet in a hoarse voice:

'I shall not contradict you. It is possible.'

It was a stupefying moment. Maître Grosier rose to his feet, protesting:

'My client has undergone a considerable nervous strain. I should wish it put on record that I do not consider him answerable for what he says.'

The magistrate quelled him angrily. For a moment a doubt seemed to arise in his own mind. Jack Renauld had almost overdone his part. He leaned forward, and gazed at the prisoner searchingly.

'Do you fully understand, Renauld, that on the answers you have given me I shall have no alternative but to commit you for trial?'

Jack's pale face flushed. He looked steadily back.

'Monsieur Hautet, I swear that I did not kill my father.'

But the magistrate's brief moment of doubt was over. He laughed a short unpleasant laugh.

'Without doubt, without doubt – they are always innocent, our prisoners! By your own mouth you are condemned. You can offer no defence, no alibi – only a mere assertion which would not deceive a babe! – that you are not guilty. You killed your father, Renauld – a cruel and cowardly murder – for the sake of the money which you believed would come to you at his death. Your mother was an accessory after the fact. Doubtless, in view of the fact that she acted as a mother, the courts will extend an indulgence to her that they will not accord to you. And rightly so! Your crime was a horrible one – to be held in abhorrence by gods and men!'

M. Hautet was interrupted – to his intense annoyance. The door was pushed open.

'Monsieur le juge, Monsieur le juge,' stammered the attendant, 'there is a lady who says – who says –'

'Who says what?' cried the justly incensed magistrate. 'This is highly irregular. I forbid it – I absolutely forbid it.'

But a slender figure pushed the stammering gendarme aside. Dressed all in black, with a long veil that hid her face, she advanced into the room.

My heart gave a sickening throb. She had come then! All my efforts were in vain. Yet I could not but admire the courage that had led her to take this step so unfalteringly.

She raised her veil – and I gasped. For, though as like her as two peas, this girl was not Cinderella! On the other hand, now that I saw her without the fair wig she had worn on the stage, I recognized her as the girl of the photograph in Jack Renauld's room.

'You are the Juge d'Instruction, Monsieur Hautet?' she queried.

'Yes, but I forbid –'

'My name is Bella Duveen. I wish to give myself up for the murder of Mr Renauld.'

CHAPTER 26
I RECEIVE A LETTER

'My friend, – You will know all when you get this. Nothing that I can say will move Bella. She has gone out to give herself up. I am tired out with struggling.

'You will know now that I deceived you, that where you gave me trust I repaid you with lies. It will seem, perhaps, indefensible to you, but I should like, before I go out of your life for ever, to show you just how it all came about. If I knew that you forgave me, it would make life easier for me. It wasn't for myself I did it – that's the only thing I can put forward to say for myself.

'I'll begin from the day I met you in the boat train from Paris. I was uneasy then about Bella. She was just desperate about Jack Renauld, she'd have lain down on the ground for him to walk on, and when he began to change, and to stop writing so often, she began getting in a state. She got it into her head that he was keen on another girl – and of course, as it turned out afterwards, she was quite right there. She'd made up her mind to go to their villa at Merlinville, and try and see Jack. She knew I was against it, and tried to give me the slip. I found she was not on the train at Calais, and determined I would not go on to England without her. I'd an uneasy feeling that something awful was going to happen if I couldn't prevent it.

'I met the next train from Paris. She was on it, and set upon going out then and there to Merlinville. I argued with her for all I was worth, but it wasn't any good. She was all strung up and set upon having her own way. Well, I washed my hands of it. I'd done all I could. It was getting late. I went to an hotel, and Bella started for Merlinville. I still couldn't shake off my feeling of what the books call "impending disaster".

'The next day came – but no Bella. She'd made a date with me to meet at the hotel, but she didn't keep it. No sign of her all day. I got more and more anxious. Then came an evening paper with the news.

'It was awful! I couldn't be sure, of course – but I was terribly afraid. I figured it out that Bella had met Papa Renauld and told him about her and Jack, and that he'd insulted her or something like that. We've both got terribly quick tempers.

'Then all the masked foreigner business came out, and I began to feel more at ease. But it still worried me that Bella hadn't kept her date with me.

'By the next morning I was so rattled that I'd just got to go and see what I could. First thing, I ran up against you. You know all that ... When I saw the dead man, looking so like Jack, and wearing Jack's fancy overcoat, I knew! And there was the identical paper-knife – wicked little thing! – that Jack had given Bella! Ten to one it had her fingermarks on it. I can't hope to explain to you the sort of helpless horror of that moment. I only saw one thing clearly – I must get hold of that dagger, and get right away with it before they found out it was gone. I pretended to faint, and while you were away getting water I took the thing and hid it away in my dress.

'I told you that I was staying at the Hôtel du Phare, but of course really I made a bee-line back to Calais, and then on to England by the first boat. When we were in mid-Channel I dropped that little devil of a dagger into the sea. Then I felt I could breathe again.

'Bella was in our digs in London. She looked like nothing on God's earth. I told her what I'd done, and that she was pretty safe for the time being. She stared at me, and then began laughing ... laughing ... laughing ... it was horrible to hear her! I felt that the best thing to do was to keep busy. She'd go mad if she had time to brood on what she'd done. Luckily we got an engagement at once.

'And then, I saw you and your friend watching us that night . . . I was frantic. You must suspect, or you wouldn't have tracked us down. I had to know the worst, so I followed you. I was desperate. And then, before I'd had time to say anything, I tumbled to it that it was me you suspected, not Bella! Or at least that you thought I *was* Bella, since I'd stolen the dagger.

'I wish, honey, that you could see back into my mind at that moment . . . you'd forgive me, perhaps . . . I was so frightened, and muddled, and desperate . . . All I could get clearly was that you would try and save me – I didn't know whether you'd be willing to save her . . . I thought very likely not – It wasn't the same thing! And I couldn't risk it! Bella's my twin – I'd got to do the best for her. So I went on lying. I felt mean – I feel mean still . . . That's all – enough too, you'll say, I expect. I ought to have trusted you . . . If I had –

'As soon as the news was in the paper that Jack Renauld had been arrested, it was all up. Bella wouldn't even wait to see how things went . . .

'I'm very tired. I can't write any more.'

She had begun to sign herself Cinderella, but had crossed that out and written instead 'Dulcie Duveen.'

It was an ill-written, blurred epistle – but I have kept it to this day.

Poirot was with me when I read it. The sheets fell from my hand, and I looked across at him.

'Did you know all the time that it was – the other?'

'Yes, my friend.'

'Why did you not tell me?'

'To begin with, I could hardly believe it conceivable that you could make such a mistake. You had seen the photograph. The sisters are very alike, but by no means incapable of distinguishment.'

'But the fair hair?'

'A wig, worn for the sake of a piquant contrast on the stage. Is it conceivable that with twins one should be fair and one dark?'

'Why didn't you tell me that night at the hotel in Coventry?'

'You were rather high-handed in your methods, *mon ami*,' said Poirot dryly. 'You did not give me a chance.'

'But afterwards?'

'Ah, afterwards! Well, to begin with, I was hurt at your want of faith in me. And then, I wanted to see whether your – feelings would stand the test of time. In fact, whether it was love, or a flash in the pan, with you. I should not have left you long in your error.'

I nodded. His tone was too affectionate for me to bear resentment. I looked down on the sheets of the letter. Suddenly I picked them up from the floor, and pushed them across to him.

'Read that,' I said. 'I'd like you to.'

He read it through in silence, then he looked up at me.

'What is it that worries you, Hastings?'

This was quite a new mood in Poirot. His mocking manner seemed laid quite aside. I was able to say what I wanted without too much difficulty.

'She doesn't say – she doesn't say – well, not whether she cares for me or not?'

Poirot turned back the pages.

'I think you are mistaken, Hastings.'

'Where?' I cried, leaning forward eagerly.

Poirot smiled.

'She tells you that in every line of the letter, *mon ami*.'

'But where am I to find her? There's no address on the letter. There's a French stamp, that's all.'

'Excite yourself not! Leave it to Papa Poirot. I can find her for you as soon as I have five little minutes!'

CHAPTER 27

JACK RENAULD'S STORY

'Congratulations, Monsieur Jack,' said Poirot, wringing the lad warmly by the hand.

Young Renauld had come to us as soon as he was liberated – before starting for Merlinville to rejoin Marthe and his mother. Stonor accompanied him. His heartiness was in strong contrast to the lad's wan looks. It was plain that the boy was on the verge of a nervous breakdown. He smiled mournfully at Poirot, and said in a low voice:

'I went through it to protect her, and now it's all no use.'

'You could hardly expect the girl to accept the price of your life,' remarked Stonor dryly. 'She was bound to come forward when she saw you heading straight for the guillotine.'

'*Eh ma foi!* and you were heading for it too!' added Poirot, with a slight twinkle. 'You would have had Maître Grosier's death from rage on your conscience if you had gone on.'

'He was a well meaning ass, I suppose,' said Jack. 'But he worried me horribly. You see, I couldn't very well take him into my confidence. But, my God! what's going to happen about Bella?'

'If I were you,' said Poirot frankly, 'I should not distress myself unduly. The French Courts are very lenient to youth and beauty, and the *crime passionnel!* A clever lawyer will make out a great case of extenuating circumstances. It will not be pleasant for you –'

'I don't care about that. You see, Monsieur Poirot, in a way I *do* feel guilty of my father's murder. But for me, and my entanglement with this girl, he would be alive and well today. And then my cursed carelessness in taking away the wrong overcoat. I can't help feeling responsible for his death. It will haunt me for ever!'

'No, no,' I said soothingly.

'Of course it's horrible to me to think that Bella killed my father,' resumed Jack. 'But I'd treated her shamefully. After I met Marthe, and realized I'd made a mistake, I ought to have written and told her so honestly. But I was so terrified of a row, and of its coming to Marthe's ears, and her thinking there was more in it than there ever had been, that – well, I was a coward, and went on hoping the thing would die down of itself. I just drifted, in fact – not realizing that I was driving the poor kid desperate. If she'd really knifed me, as she meant to, I should have got no more than my deserts. And the way she's come forward now is downright plucky. I'd have stood the racket, you know – up to the end.'

He was silent for a moment or two, and then burst out on another tack:

'What gets me is why the Governor should be wandering about in underclothes and my overcoat at that time of night. I suppose he'd just given the foreign johnnies the slip, and my mother must have made a mistake about its being two o'clock when they came.

Or – or, it wasn't all a frame-up, was it? I mean, my mother didn't think – couldn't think – that – that it was *me*?'

Poirot reassured him quickly.

'No, no, Monsieur Jack. Have no fears on that score. As for the rest, I will explain it to you one of these days. It is rather curious. But will you recount to us exactly what did occur on that terrible evening?'

'There's very little to tell. I came from Cherbourg, as I told you, in order to see Marthe before going to the other end of the world. The train was late, and I decided to take the short cut across the golf links. I could easily get into the grounds of the Villa Marguerite from there. I had nearly reached the place when –'

He paused and swallowed.

'Yes?'

'I heard a terrible cry. It wasn't loud – a sort of choke and gasp – but it frightened me. For a moment I stood rooted to the spot. Then I came round the corner of a bush. There was moonlight. I saw the grave, and a figure lying face downwards with a dagger sticking in the back. And then – and then – I looked up and saw *her*. She was looking at me as though she saw a ghost – it's what she must have thought me at first – all expression seemed frozen out of her face by horror. And then she gave a cry, and turned and ran.'

He stopped, trying to master his emotion.

'And afterwards?' asked Poirot gently.

'I really don't know. I stayed there for a time, dazed. And then I realized I'd better get away as fast as I could. It didn't occur to me that they would suspect me, but I was afraid of being called upon to give evidence against her. I walked to St Beauvais as I told you, and got a car from there back to Cherbourg.'

A knock came at the door, and a page entered with a telegram which he delivered to Stonor. He tore it open. Then he got up from his seat.

'Mrs Renauld has regained consciousness,' he said.

'Ah!' Poirot sprang to his feet. 'Let us all go to Merlinville at once!'

A hurried departure was made forthwith. Stonor, at Jack's insistence, agreed to stay behind and do all that could be done for Bella Duveen. Poirot, Jack Renauld, and I set off in the Renauld car.

The run took just over forty minutes. As we approached the doorway of the Villa Marguerite Jack Renauld shot a questioning glance at Poirot.

'How would it be if you went on first – to break the news to my mother that I am free –'

'While you break it in person to Mademoiselle Marthe, eh?' finished Poirot, with a twinkle. 'But yes, by all means, I was about to propose such an arrangement myself.'

Jack Renauld did not wait for more. Stopping the car, he swung himself out, and ran up the path to the front door. We went on in the car to the Villa Geneviève.

'Poirot,' I said, 'do you remember how we arrived here that first day? And were met by the news of Mr Renauld's murder?'

'Ah, yes, truly. Not so long ago either. But what a lot of things have happened since then – especially for *you, mon ami!*'

'Yes, indeed,' I sighed.

'You are regarding it from the sentimental standpoint, Hastings. That was not my meaning. We will hope that Mademoiselle Bella will be dealt with leniently, and after all Jack Renauld cannot marry both the girls! I spoke from a professional standpoint. This is not a crime well ordered and regular, such as a detective delights in. The *mise en scène* designed by Georges Conneau, that indeed is perfect, but the *dénouement* – ah, no! A man killed by accident in a girl's fit of anger – ah, indeed, what order or method is there in that?'

And in the midst of a fit of laughter on my part at Poirot's peculiarities, the door was opened by Françoise.

Poirot explained that he must see Mrs Renauld at once, and the old woman conducted him upstairs. I remained in the salon. It was some time before Poirot reappeared. He was looking unusually grave.

'*Vous voilà*, Hastings! *Sacré tonnerre!* but there are squalls ahead!'

'What do you mean?' I cried.

'I would hardly have credited it,' said Poirot thoughtfully, 'but women are very unexpected.'

'Here are Jack and Marthe Daubreuil,' I exclaimed, looking out of the window.

Poirot bounded out of the room, and met the young couple on the steps outside.

'Do not enter. It is better not. Your mother is very upset.'

'I know, I know,' said Jack Renauld. 'I must go up to her at once.'

'But no, I tell you. It is better not.'

'But Marthe and I –'

'In any case, do not take Mademoiselle with you. Mount, if you must, but you would be wise to be guided by me.'

A voice on the stairs behind made us all start.

'I thank you for your good offices, Monsieur Poirot, but I will make my own wishes clear.'

We stared in astonishment. Descending the stairs, leaning on Léonie's arm, was Mrs Renauld, her head still bandaged. The French girl was weeping, and imploring her mistress to return to bed.

'Madame will kill herself. It is contrary to all the doctor's orders!'

But Mrs Renauld came on.

'Mother,' cried Jack, starting forward.

But with a gesture she drove him back.

'I am no mother of yours! You are no son of mine! From this day and hour I renounce you.'

'Mother!' cried the lad, stupefied.

For a moment she seemed to waver, to falter before the anguish in his voice. Poirot made a mediating gesture. But instantly she regained command of herself.

'Your father's blood is on your head. You are morally guilty of his death. You thwarted and defied him over this girl, and by your heartless treatment of another girl, you brought about his death. Go out from my house. Tomorrow I intend to take such steps as shall make it certain that you shall never touch a penny of his money. Make your way in the world as best you can with the help of the girl who is the daughter of your father's bitterest enemy!'

And slowly, painfully, she retraced her way upstairs.

We were all dumbfounded – totally unprepared for such a demonstration. Jack Renauld, worn out with all he had already gone through, swayed and nearly fell. Poirot and I went quickly to his assistance.

'He is overdone,' murmured Poirot to Marthe. 'Where can we take him?'

'But home! To the Villa Marguerite. We will nurse him, my mother and I. My poor Jack!'

We got the lad to the villa, where he dropped limply on to a chair in a semi-dazed condition. Poirot felt his head and hands.

'He has fever. The long strain begins to tell. And now this shock on top of it. Get him to bed, and Hastings and I will summon a doctor.'

A doctor was soon procured. After examining the patient, he gave it as his opinion that it was simply a case of nerve strain. With perfect rest and quiet, the lad might be almost restored by the next day, but, if excited, there was a chance of brain fever. It would be advisable for someone to sit up all night with him.

Finally, having done all we could, we left him in the charge of Marthe and her mother, and set out for the town. It was past our usual hour of dining, and we were both famished. The first restaurant we came to assuaged the pangs of hunger with an excellent omelette, and an equally excellent entrecôte to follow.

'And now for quarters for the night,' said Poirot, when at length *café noir* had completed the meal. 'Shall we try our old friend, the Hôtel de Bains?'

We traced our steps there without more ado. Yes, Messieurs could be accommodated with two good rooms overlooking the sea. Then Poirot asked a question which surprised me:

'Has an English lady, Miss Robinson, arrived?'

'Yes, Monsieur. She is in the little salon.'

'Ah!'

'Poirot,' I cried, keeping pace with him, as he walked along the corridor, 'who on earth is Miss Robinson?'

Poirot beamed kindly on me.

'It is that I have arranged you a marriage, Hastings.'

'But I say –'

'Bah!' said Poirot, giving me a friendly push over the threshold of the door. 'Do you think I wish to trumpet aloud in Merlinville the name of Duveen?'

It was indeed Cinderella who rose to greet us. I took her hand in both of mine. My eyes said the rest.

Poirot cleared his throat.

'*Mes enfants,*' he said, 'for the moment we have no time for sentiment. There is work ahead of us. Mademoiselle, were you able to do what I asked you?'

In response, Cinderella took from her bag an object wrapped up in paper, and handed it silently to Poirot. The latter unwrapped it. I gave a start – for it was the aeroplane dagger which I understood she had cast into the sea. Strange, how reluctant women always are to destroy the most compromising of objects and documents!

'*Très bien, mon enfant,*' said Poirot. 'I am pleased with you. Go now and rest yourself. Hastings here and I have work to do. You shall see him tomorrow.'

'Where are you going?' asked the girl, her eyes widening.

'You shall hear all about it tomorrow.'

'Because wherever you're going, I'm coming too.'

'But, mademoiselle –'

'I'm coming too, I tell you.'

Poirot realized that it was futile to argue. He gave in.

'Come then, mademoiselle. But it will not be amusing. In all probability nothing will happen.'

The girl made no reply.

Twenty minutes later we set forth. It was quite dark now, a close oppressive evening. Poirot led the way out of the town in the direction of the Villa Geneviève. But when he reached the Villa Marguerite he paused.

'I should like to assure myself that all goes well with Jack Renauld. Come with me, Hastings. Mademoiselle will perhaps remain outside. Madame Daubreuil might say something which would wound her.'

We unlatched the gate, and walked up the path. As we went round to the side of the house, I drew Poirot's attention to a window on the first floor. Thrown sharply on the blind was the profile of Marthe Daubreuil.

'Ah!' said Poirot. 'I figure to myself that that is the room where we shall find Jack Renauld.'

Madame Daubreuil opened the door to us. She explained that

Jack was much the same, but perhaps we would like to see for ourselves. She led us upstairs and into the bedroom. Marthe Daubreuil was sitting by a table with a lamp on it, working. She put her finger to her lips as we entered.

Jack Renauld was sleeping an uneasy, fitful sleep, his head turning from side to side, and his face still unduly flushed.

'Is the doctor coming again?' asked Poirot in a whisper.

'Not unless we send. He is sleeping – that is the great thing. *Maman* made him a tisane.'

She sat down again with her embroidery as we left the room. Madame Daubreuil accompanied us down the stairs. Since I had learned of her past history, I viewed this woman with increased interest. She stood there with her eyes cast down, the same very faint enigmatical smile that I remembered on her lips. And suddenly I felt afraid of her, as one might feel afraid of a beautiful poisonous snake.

'I hope we have not deranged you, madame,' said Poirot politely, as she opened the door for us to pass out.

'Not at all, monsieur.'

'By the way,' said Poirot, as though struck by an afterthought, 'Monsieur Stonor has not been in Merlinville today, has he?'

I could not at all fathom the point of this question, which I well knew to be meaningless as far as Poirot was concerned.

Madame Daubreuil replied quite composedly:

'Not that I know of.'

'He has not had an interview with Madame Renauld?'

'How should I know that, monsieur?'

'True,' said Poirot. 'I thought you might have seen him coming or going, that is all. Goodnight, madame.'

'Why –' I began.

'No whys, Hastings. There will be time for that later.'

We rejoined Cinderella and made our way rapidly in the direction of the Villa Geneviève. Poirot looked over his shoulder once at the lighted window and the profile of Marthe as she bent over her work.

'He is being guarded at all events,' he muttered.

Arrived at the Villa Geneviève, Poirot took up his stand behind some bushes to the left of the drive, where, while enjoying a good view ourselves, we were completely hidden from sight. The villa itself was in total darkness, everybody was without doubt in bed and asleep. We were almost immediately under the window of Mrs Renauld's bedroom, which window, I noticed, was open. It seemed to me that it was upon this spot that Poirot's eyes were fixed.

'What are we going to do?' I whispered.

'Watch.'

'But –'

'I do not expect anything to happen for at least an hour, probably two hours, but the –'

His words were interrupted by a long, thin drawn cry:

'Help!'

A light flashed up in the first-floor room on the right-hand side of the front door. The cry came from there. And even as we watched there came a shadow on the blind as of two people struggling.

'*Mille tonnerres!*' cried Poirot. 'She must have changed her room.'

Dashing forward, he battered wildly on the front door. Then rushing to the tree in the flower-bed, he swarmed up it with the agility of a cat. I followed him, as with a bound he sprang in through the open window. Looking over my shoulder, I saw Dulcie reaching the branch behind me.

'Take care,' I exclaimed.

'Take care of your grandmother!' retorted the girl. 'This is child's play to me.'

Poirot had rushed through the empty room and was pounding on the door.

'Locked and bolted on the outside,' he growled. 'And it will take time to burst it open.'

The cries for help were getting noticeably fainter. I saw despair in Poirot's eyes. He and I together put our shoulders to the door.

Cinderella's voice, calm and dispassionate, came from the window:

'You'll be too late. I guess I'm the only one who can do anything.'

Before I could move a hand to stop her, she appeared to leap from the window into space. I rushed and looked out.

To my horror, I saw her hanging by her hands from the roof, propelling herself along by jerks in the direction of the lighted window.

'Good heavens! She'll be killed,' I cried.

'You forget. She's a professional acrobat, Hastings. It was the providence of the good God that made her insist on coming with us tonight. I only pray that she may be in time. Ah!'

A cry of absolute terror floated out on to the night, as the girl disappeared through the window, and then in Cinderella's clear tones came the words:

'No, you don't! I've got you – and my wrists are just like steel.'

At the same moment the door of our prison was opened cautiously by Françoise. Poirot brushed her aside unceremoniously and rushed down the passage to where the other maids were grouped round the farther door.

'It's locked on the inside, monsieur.'

There was the sound of a heavy fall within. After a moment or two the key turned and the door swung slowly open. Cinderella, very pale, beckoned us in.

'She is safe?' demanded Poirot.

'Yes, I was just in time. She was exhausted.'

Mrs Renauld was half sitting, half lying on the bed. She was gasping for breath.

'Nearly strangled me,' she murmured painfully.

The girl picked up something from the floor and handed it to Poirot. It was a rolled-up ladder of silk rope, very fine but quite strong.

'A getaway,' said Poirot. 'By the window, while we were battering at the door. Where is – the other?'

The girl stood aside a little and pointed. On the ground lay a figure wrapped in some dark material, a fold of which hid the face.

'Dead?'

She nodded.

'I think so. Head must have struck the marble fender.'

'But who is it?' I cried.

'The murderer of Renauld, Hastings. And the would-be murderer of Madame Renauld.'

Puzzled and uncomprehending, I knelt down, and lifting the fold of cloth, looked into the dead beautiful face of Marthe Daubreuil!

CHAPTER 28

JOURNEY'S END

I have confused memories of the further events of that night. Poirot seemed deaf to my repeated questions. He was engaged in overwhelming Françoise with reproaches for not having told him of Mrs Renauld's change of sleeping quarters.

I caught him by the shoulder, determined to attract his attention, and make myself heard.

'But you *must* have known,' I expostulated. 'You were taken up to see her this afternoon.'

Poirot deigned to attend to me for a brief moment.

'She had been wheeled on a sofa into the middle room – her boudoir,' he explained.

'But, monsieur,' cried Françoise, 'Madame changed her room almost immediately after the crimes. The associations – they were too distressing!'

'Then why was I not told?' vociferated Poirot, striking the table, and working himself into a first-class passion. 'I demand of you – why – was – I – not – told? You are an old woman completely imbecile! And Léonie and Denise are no better. All of you are triple idiots! Your stupidity has nearly caused the death of your mistress. But for this courageous child –'

He broke off, and, darting across the room to where the girl was bending over ministering to Mrs Renauld, he embraced her with Gallic fervour – slightly to my annoyance.

I was aroused from my condition of mental fog by a sharp command from Poirot to fetch the doctor immediately on Mrs Renauld's behalf. After that, I might summon the police. And he added, to complete my dudgeon:

'It will hardly be worth your while to return here. I shall be too busy to attend to you, and of Mademoiselle here I make a *garde-malade*.'

I retired with what dignity I could command. Having done my

errands, I returned to the hotel. I understood next to nothing of what had occurred. The events of the night seemed fantastic and impossible. Nobody would answer my questions. Nobody had seemed to hear them. Angrily, I flung myself into bed, and slept the sleep of the bewildered and utterly exhausted.

I awoke to find the sun pouring in through the open windows and Poirot, neat and smiling, sitting beside the bed.

'*Enfin*, you wake! But it is that you are a famous sleeper, Hastings! Do you know that it is nearly eleven o'clock?'

I groaned and put a hand to my head.

'I must have been dreaming,' I said. 'Do you know, I actually dreamt that we found Marthe Daubreuil's body in Mrs Renauld's room, and that you declared her to have murdered Mr Renauld?'

'You were not dreaming. All that is quite true.'

'But Bella Duveen killed Mr Renauld?'

'Oh no, Hastings, she did not! She said she did – yes – but that was to save the man she loved from the guillotine.'

'What?'

'Remember Jack Renauld's story. They both arrived on the scene on the same instant, and each took the other to be the perpetrator of the crime. The girl stares at him in horror, and then with a cry rushes away. But, when she hears that the crime has been brought home to him, she cannot bear it, and comes forward to accuse herself and save him from certain death.'

Poirot leaned back in his chair, and brought the tips of his fingers together in familiar style.

'The case was not quite satisfactory to me,' he observed judicially. 'All along I was strongly under the impression that we were dealing with a cold-blooded and premeditated crime committed by someone who had contented themselves (very cleverly) with using Monsieur Renauld's own plans for throwing the police off the track. The great criminal (as you may remember my remarking to you once) is always supremely simple.'

I nodded.

'Now, to support this theory, the criminal must have been fully cognizant of Monsieur Renauld's plans. That leads us to Mrs Renauld. But facts fail to support any theory of her guilt. Is there anyone else who might have known of them? Yes. From Marthe

Daubreuil's own lips we have the admission that she overheard Mr Renauld's quarrel with the tramp. If she could overhear that, there is no reason why she should not have heard everything else, especially if Mr and Madame Renauld were imprudent enough to discuss their plans sitting on the bench. Remember how easily you overheard Marthe's conversation with Jack Renauld from that spot.'

'But what possible motive could Marthe have for murdering Mr Renauld?' I argued.

'What motive! Money! Renauld was a millionaire several times over, and at his death (or so she and Jack believed) half that vast fortune would pass to his son. Let us reconstruct the scene from the standpoint of Marthe Daubreuil.

'Marthe Daubreuil overhears what passes between Renauld and his wife. So far he has been a nice little source of income to the Daubreuil mother and daughter, but now he proposes to escape from their toils. At first, possibly, her idea is to prevent that escape. But a bolder idea takes its place, and one that fails to horrify the daughter of Jeanne Beroldy! At present Renauld stands inexorably in the way of her marriage with Jack. If the latter defies his father, he will be a pauper – which is not at all to the mind of Mademoiselle Marthe. In fact, I doubt if she has ever cared a straw for Jack Renauld. She can simulate emotion but in reality she is of the same cold, calculating type as her mother. I doubt, too, whether she was really very sure of her hold over the boy's affections. She had dazzled and captivated him, but separated from her, as his father could so easily manage to separate him, she might lose him. But with Renauld dead, and Jack the heir to half his millions, the marriage can take place at once, and at a stroke she will attain wealth – not the beggarly thousands that have been extracted from him so far. And her clever brain takes in the simplicity of the thing. It is all so easy. Renauld is planning all the circumstances of his death – she has only to step in at the right moment and turn the farce into a grim reality. And here comes in the second point which led me infallibly to Marthe Daubreuil – the dagger! Jack Renauld had *three* souvenirs made. One he gave to his mother, one to Bella Duveen – was it not highly probable that he had given the third one to Marthe Daubreuil?

'So, then, to sum up, there were four points of note against Marthe Daubreuil:

'1. Marthe Daubreuil could have overheard Renauld's plans.
'2. Marthe Daubreuil had a direct interest in causing Renauld's death.
'3. Marthe Daubreuil was the daughter of the notorious Madame Beroldy who in my opinion was morally and virtually the murderess of her husband, although it may have been Georges Conneau's hand which struck the actual blow.
'4. Marthe Daubreuil was the only person, besides Jack Renauld, likely to have the third dagger in her possession.'

Poirot paused and cleared his throat.

'Of course, when I learned of the existence of the other girl, Bella Duveen, I realized that it was quite possible that *she* might have killed Renauld. The solution did not commend itself to me, because, as I pointed out to you, Hastings, an expert, such as I am, likes to meet a foeman worthy of his steel. Still, one must take crimes as one finds them, not as one would like them to be. It did not seem very likely that Bella Duveen would be wandering about carrying a souvenir paper-knife in her hand, but of course she might have had some idea all the time of revenging herself on Jack Renauld. When she actually came forward and confessed to the murder, it seemed that all was over. And yet – I was not satisfied, *mon ami. I was not satisfied* . . .

'I went over the case again minutely, and I came to the same conclusion as before. If it was *not* Bella Duveen, the only other person who could have committed the crime was Marthe Daubreuil. But I had not one single proof against her!

'And then you showed me that letter from Mademoiselle Dulcie, and I saw a chance of settling the matter once for all. The original dagger was stolen by Dulcie Duveen and thrown into the sea – since, as she thought, it belonged to her sister. But if, by any chance, it was *not* her sister's, but the one given by Jack to Marthe Daubreuil – why then, Bella Duveen's dagger would be still intact! I said no word to you, Hastings (it was no time for romance), but I sought out Mademoiselle Dulcie, told her as much as I deemed needful, and set her to search among the effects of her sister. Imagine my elation, when she sought me out (according to my instructions) as Miss Robinson, with the precious souvenir in her possession!

'In the meantime I had taken steps to force Mademoiselle Marthe into the open. By my orders, Madame Renauld repulsed her son, and declared her intention of making a will on the morrow which should cut him off from ever enjoying even a portion of his father's fortune. It was a desperate step, but a necessary one, and Madame Renauld was fully prepared to take the risk – though unfortunately she also never thought of mentioning her change of room. I suppose she took it for granted that I knew. All happened as I thought. Marthe Daubreuil made a last bold bid for the Renauld millions – and failed!'

'What absolutely bewilders me,' I said, 'is how she ever got into the house without our seeing her. It seems an absolute miracle. We left her behind at the Villa Marguerite, we go straight to the Villa Geneviève – and yet she is there before us!'

'Ah, but we did not leave her behind. She was out of the Villa Marguerite by the back way while we were talking to her mother in the hall. That is where, as the Americans say, she "put it over" on Hercule Poirot!'

'But the shadow on the blind? We saw it from the road.'

'*Eh bien*, when we looked up, Madame Daubreuil had just had time to run upstairs and take her place.'

'Madame Daubreuil?'

'Yes. One is old, and one is young, one dark, and one fair, but, for the purpose of a silhouette on a blind, their profiles are singularly alike. Even I did not suspect – triple imbecile that I was! I thought I had plenty of time before me – that she would not try to gain admission to the villa until much later. She had brains, that beautiful Mademoiselle Marthe.'

'And her object was to murder Mrs Renauld?'

'Yes. The whole fortune would then pass to her son. But it would have been suicide, *mon ami!* On the floor by Marthe Daubreuil's body, I found a pad and a little bottle of chloroform and a hypodermic syringe containing a fatal dose of morphine. You understand? The chloroform first – then when the victim is unconscious the prick of the needle. By the morning the smell of the chloroform has quite disappeared, and the syringe lies where it has fallen from Madame Renauld's hand. What would he say, the excellent Monsieur Hautet? "Poor woman! What did I tell you? The shock of joy, it was too much on top of the rest! Did I not say that I should not be surprised if her brain became unhinged. Altogether a most tragic case, the Renauld Case!"

'However, Hastings, things did not go quite as Mademoiselle Marthe had planned. To begin with, Madame Renauld was awake and waiting for her. There is a struggle. But Madame Renauld is terribly weak still. There is a last chance for Marthe Daubreuil. The idea of suicide is at an end, but if she can silence Madame Renauld with her strong hands, make a getaway with her little silk ladder while we are still battering on the inside of the farther door, and be back at the Villa Marguerite before we return there, it will be hard to prove anything against her. But she was checkmated, not by Hercule Poirot, but by *la petite acrobate* with her wrists of steel.'

I mused over the whole story.

'When did you first begin to suspect Marthe Daubreuil, Poirot? When she told us she had overheard the quarrel in the garden?'

Poirot smiled.

'My friend, do you remember when we drove into Merlinville that first day? And the beautiful girl we saw standing at the gate? You asked me if I had noticed a young goddess, and I replied to you that I had seen only a girl with anxious eyes. That is how I have thought of Marthe Daubreuil from the beginning. *The girl with the anxious eyes!* Why was she anxious? Not on Jack Renauld's behalf, for she did not know then that he had been in Merlinville the previous evening.'

'By the way,' I exclaimed, 'how is Jack Renauld?'

'Much better. He is still at the Villa Marguerite. But Madame Daubreuil has disappeared. The police are looking for her.'

'Was she in with her daughter, do you think?'

'We shall never know. Madame is a lady who can keep her secrets. And I doubt very much if the police will ever find her.'

'Has Jack Renauld been – told?'

'Not yet.'

'It will be a terrible shock to him.'

'Naturally. And yet, do you know, Hastings, I doubt if his heart was ever seriously engaged? So far we have looked upon Bella Duveen as a siren, and Marthe Daubreuil as the girl he really loved. But I think that if we reversed the terms we should come nearer to the truth. Marthe Daubreuil was very beautiful. She set herself to fascinate Jack, and she succeeded, but remember his curious reluctance to break with the other girl. And see how he was willing to go to the guillotine rather than implicate her. I have a little idea that when he learns the truth, he will be horrified – revolted, and his false love will wither away.'

'What about Giraud?'

'He has a *crise* of the nerves, that one! He has been obliged to return to Paris.'

We both smiled.

Poirot proved a fairly true prophet. When at length the doctor pronounced Jack Renauld strong enough to hear the truth, it was Poirot who broke it to him. The shock was indeed terrific. Yet Jack rallied better than I could have supposed possible. His mother's devotion helped him to live through those difficult days. The mother and son were inseparable now.

There was a further revelation to come. Poirot had acquainted Mrs Renauld with the fact that he knew her secret, and had represented to her that Jack should not be left in ignorance of his father's past.

'To hide the truth, never does it avail, madame! Be brave and tell him everything.'

With a heavy heart Mrs Renauld consented, and her son learned that the father he had loved had been in actual fact a fugitive from justice. A halting question was promptly answered by Poirot.

'Reassure yourself, Monsieur Jack. The world knows nothing. As far as I can see, there is no obligation for me to take the police into my confidence. Throughout the case I have acted, not for them, but for your father. Justice overtook him at last, but no one need ever know that he and Georges Conneau were one and the same.'

There were, of course, various points in the case that remained puzzling to the police, but Poirot explained things in so plausible a fashion that all query about them was gradually stilled.

Shortly after we got back to London, I noticed a magnificent model of a foxhound adorning Poirot's mantelpiece. In answer to my inquiring glance, Poirot nodded.

'*Mais oui!* I got my five hundred francs! Is he not a splendid fellow? I call him Giraud!'

A few days later Jack Renauld came to see us with a resolute expression on his face.

'Monsieur Poirot, I've come to say goodbye. I'm sailing for South America almost immediately. My father had large interests over the continent, and I mean to start a new life out there.'

'You go alone, Monsieur Jack?'

'My mother comes with me – and I shall keep Stonor on as my secretary. He likes out-of-the-way parts of the world.'

'No one else goes with you?'

Jack flushed.

'You mean –?'

'A girl who loves you very dearly – who has been willing to lay down her life for you.'

'How could I ask her?' muttered the boy. 'After all that has happened, could I go to her and – Oh, what sort of a lame story could I tell?'

'*Les femmes* – they have a wonderful genius for manufacturing crutches for stories like that.'

'Yes, but – I've been such a damned fool.'

'So have all of us, one time and another,' observed Poirot philosophically.

But Jack's face had hardened.

'There's something else. I'm my father's son. Would anyone marry me, knowing that?'

'You are your father's son, you say. Hastings here will tell you that I believe in heredity –'

'Well, then –'

'Wait. I know a woman, a woman of courage and endurance, capable of great love, of supreme self-sacrifice –'

The boy looked up. His eyes softened.

'My mother!'

'Yes. You are your mother's son as well as your father's. Then go to Mademoiselle Bella. Tell her everything. Keep nothing back – and see what she will say!'

Jack looked irresolute.

'Go to her as a boy no longer, but a man – a man bowed by the fate of the Past, and the fate of Today, but looking forward to a new and wonderful life. Ask her to share it with you. You may not realize it, but your love for each other has been tested in the fire and not found wanting. You have both been willing to lay down your lives for each other.'

And what of Captain Arthur Hastings, humble chronicler of these pages?

There is some talk of his joining the Renaulds on a ranch across the seas, but for the end of this story I prefer to go back to a morning in the garden of the Villa Geneviève.

'I can't call you Bella,' I said, 'since it isn't your name. And Dulcie seems so unfamiliar. So it's got to be Cinderella. Cinderella married the Prince, you remember. I'm not a Prince, but –'

She interrupted me.

'Cinderella warned him, I'm sure. You see, she couldn't promise to turn into a princess. She was only a little scullion after all –'

'It's the Prince's turn to interrupt,' I interpolated. 'Do you know what he said?'

'No?'

'"Hell!" said the Prince – and kissed her!'

And I suited the action to the word.

THE BIG FOUR

CONTENTS

CHAPTER I

THE UNEXPECTED GUEST

I have met people who enjoy a channel crossing; men who can sit calmly in their deckchairs and, on arrival, wait until the boat is moored, then gather their belongings together without fuss and disembark. Personally, I can never manage this. From the moment I get on board I feel that the time is too short to settle down to anything. I move my suitcases from one spot to another, and if I go down to the saloon for a meal, I bolt my food with an uneasy feeling that the boat may arrive unexpectedly whilst I am below. Perhaps all this is merely a legacy from one's short leaves in the war, when it seemed a matter of such importance to secure a place near the gangway, and to be amongst the first to disembark lest one should waste precious minutes of one's three or five days' leave.

On this particular July morning, as I stood by the rail and watched the white cliffs of Dover drawing nearer, I marvelled at the passengers who could sit calmly in their chairs and never even raise their eyes for the first sight of their native land. Yet perhaps their case was different from mine. Doubtless many of them had only crossed to Paris for the weekend, whereas I had spent the last year and a half on a ranch in the Argentine. I had prospered there, and my wife and I had both enjoyed the free and easy life of the South American continent, nevertheless it was with a lump in my throat that I watched the familiar shore draw nearer and nearer.

I had landed in France two days before, transacted some necessary business, and was now en route for London. I should be there some months – time enough to look up old friends, and one old friend in particular. A little man with an egg-shaped head and green eyes – Hercule Poirot! I proposed to take him completely by surprise. My last letter from the Argentine had given no hint of my intended voyage – indeed, that had been decided upon hurriedly as a result of certain business complications – and I spent many amused moments picturing to myself his delight and stupefaction on beholding me.

He, I knew, was not likely to be far from his headquarters. The time when his cases had drawn him from one end of England to the other was past. His fame had spread, and no longer would he allow one case to absorb all his time. He aimed more and more, as time went on, at being considered a 'consulting detective' – as much a specialist as a Harley Street physician. He had always scoffed at the popular idea of the human bloodhound who assumed wonderful disguises to track criminals, and who paused at every footprint to measure it.

'No, my friend Hastings,' he would say, 'we leave that to Giraud and his friends. Hercule Poirot's methods are his own. Order and method, and "the little grey cells". Sitting at ease in our own armchairs we see the things that these others overlook, and we do not jump to the conclusion like the worthy Japp.'

No; there was little fear of finding Hercule Poirot far afield. On arrival in London, I deposited my luggage at an hotel and drove straight on to the old address. What poignant memories it brought back to me! I hardly waited to greet my old landlady, but hurried up the stairs two at a time and rapped on Poirot's door.

'Enter, then,' cried a familiar voice from within.

I strode in. Poirot stood facing me. In his arms he carried a small valise, which he dropped with a crash on beholding me.

'*Mon ami*, Hastings!' he cried. '*Mon ami*, Hastings!'

And, rushing forward, he enveloped me in a capacious embrace. Our conversation was incoherent and inconsequent. Ejaculations, eager questions, incomplete answers, messages from my wife, explanations as to my journey, were all jumbled up together.

'I suppose there's someone in my old rooms?' I asked at last, when we had calmed down somewhat. 'I'd love to put up here again with you.'

Poirot's face changed with startling suddenness.

'*Mon Dieu!* but what a *chance épouvantable*. Regard around you, my friend.'

For the first time I took note of my surroundings. Against the wall stood a vast ark of a trunk of prehistoric design. Near to it were placed a number of suitcases, ranged neatly in order of size from large to small. The inference was unmistakable.

'You are going away?'

'Yes.'

'Where to?'

'South America.'

'*What?*'

'Yes, it is a droll farce, is it not? It is to Rio I go, and every day I say to myself, I will write nothing in my letters – but oh! the surprise of the good Hastings when he beholds me!'

'But when are you going?'

Poirot looked at his watch.

'In an hour's time.'

'I thought you always said nothing would induce you to make a long sea voyage?'

Poirot closed his eyes and shuddered.

'Speak not of it to me, my friend. My doctor, he assures me that one dies not of it – and it is for the one time only; you understand, that never – never shall I return.'

He pushed me into a chair.

'Come, I will tell you how it all came about. Do you know who is the richest man in the world? Richer even than Rockefeller? Abe Ryland.'

'The American Soap King?'

'Precisely. One of his secretaries approached me. There is some very considerable, as you would call it, hocus-pocus going on in connection with a big company in Rio. He wished me to investigate matters on the spot. I refused. I told him that if the facts were laid before me, I would give him my expert opinion. But that he professed himself unable to do. I was to be put in possession of the facts only on my arrival out there. Normally, that would have closed the matter. To dictate to Hercule Poirot is sheer impertinence. But the sum offered was so stupendous that for the first time in my life I was tempted by mere money. It was a competence – a fortune! And there was a second attraction – *you*, my friend. For this last year and a half I have been a very lonely old man. I thought to myself, Why not? I am beginning to weary of this unending solving of foolish problems. I have achieved sufficient fame. Let me take this money and settle down somewhere near my old friend.'

I was quite affected by this token of Poirot's regard.

'So I accepted,' he continued, 'and in an hour's time I must leave to catch the boat train. One of life's little ironies, is it not? But I will admit to you, Hastings, that had not the money offered been so big, I might have hesitated, for just lately I have begun a little investigation of my own. Tell me, what is commonly meant by the phrase, "The Big Four"?'

'I suppose it had its origin at the Versailles Conference, and then there's the famous "Big Four" in the film world, and the term is used by hosts of smaller fry.'

'I see,' said Poirot thoughtfully. 'I have come across the phrase, you understand, under certain circumstances where none of those explanations would apply. It seems to refer to a gang of international criminals or something of that kind; only –'

'Only what?' I asked, as he hesitated.

'Only that I fancy that it is something on a large scale. Just a little idea of mine, nothing more. Ah, but I must complete my packing. The time advances.'

'Don't go,' I urged. 'Cancel your package and come out on the same boat with me.'

Poirot drew himself up and glanced at me reproachfully.

'Ah, is it that you don't understand! I have passed my word, you comprehend – the word of Hercule Poirot. Nothing but a matter of life or death could detain me now.'

'And that's not likely to occur,' I murmured ruefully. 'Unless at the eleventh hour "the door opens and the unexpected guest comes in".'

I quoted the old saw with a slight laugh, and then, in the pause that succeeded it, we both started as a sound came from the inner room.

'What's that?' I cried.

'*Ma foi!*' retorted Poirot. 'It sounds very like your "unexpected guest" in my bedroom.'

'But how can anyone be in there? There's no door except into this room.'

'Your memory is excellent, Hastings. Now for the deductions.'

'The window! But it's a burglar, then? He must have had a stiff climb of it – I should say it was almost impossible.'

I had risen to my feet and was striding in the direction of the door when the sound of fumbling at the handle from the other side arrested me.

The door swung slowly open. Framed in the doorway stood a man. He was coated from head to foot with dust and mud; his face was thin and emaciated. He stared at us for a moment, and then swayed and fell. Poirot hurried to his side, then he looked up and spoke to me.

'Brandy – quickly.'

I dashed some brandy into a glass and brought it. Poirot managed to administer a little, and together we raised him and carried him to the couch. In a few minutes he opened his eyes and looked round him with an almost vacant stare.

'What is it you want, monsieur?' asked Poirot.

The man opened his lips and spoke in a queer mechanical voice.

'M. Hercule Poirot, 14 Farraway Street.'

'Yes, yes; I am he.'

The man did not seem to understand, and merely repeated in exactly the same tone:

'M. Hercule Poirot, 14 Farraway Street.'

Poirot tried him with several questions. Sometimes the man did not answer at all; sometimes he repeated the same phrase. Poirot made a sign to me to ring up on the telephone.

'Get Dr Ridgeway to come round.'

The doctor was in, luckily; and as his house was only just round the corner, few minutes elapsed before he came bustling in.

'What's all this, eh?'

Poirot gave him a brief explanation, and the doctor started examining our strange visitor, who seemed quite unconscious of his presence or ours.

'H'm!' said Dr Ridgeway, when he had finished. 'Curious case.'

'Brain fever?' I suggested.

The doctor immediately snorted with contempt.

'Brain fever! Brain fever! No such thing as brain fever. An invention of novelists. No; the man's had a shock of some kind. He's come here under the force of a persistent idea – to find M. Hercule Poirot, 14 Farraway Street – and he repeats those words mechanically without in the least knowing what they mean.'

'Aphasia?' I said eagerly.

This suggestion did not cause the doctor to snort quite as violently as my last one had done. He made no answer, but handed the man a sheet of paper and a pencil.

'Let's see what he'll do with that,' he remarked.

The man did nothing with it for some moments, then he suddenly began to write feverishly. With equal suddenness he stopped and let both paper and pencil fall to the ground. The doctor picked it up, and shook his head.

'Nothing here. Only the figure 4 scrawled a dozen times, each one bigger than the last. Wants to write 14 Farraway Street, I expect. It's an interesting case – very interesting. Can you possibly keep him here until this afternoon? I'm due at the hospital now, but I'll come back this afternoon and make all arrangements about him. It's too interesting a case to be lost sight of.'

I explained Poirot's departure and the fact that I proposed to accompany him to Southampton.

'That's all right. Leave the man here. He won't get into mischief. He's suffering from complete exhaustion. Will probably sleep for eight hours on end. I'll have a word with that excellent Mrs Funnyface of yours, and tell her to keep an eye on him.'

And Dr Ridgeway bustled out with his usual celerity. Poirot himself completed his packing, with one eye on the clock.

'The time, it marches with a rapidity unbelievable. Come now, Hastings, you cannot say that I have left you with nothing to do. A most sensational problem. The man from the unknown. Who is he? What is he? Ah, *sapristi*, but I would give two years of my life to have this boat go tomorrow instead of today. There is something here very curious – very interesting. But one must have time – *time*. It may be days – or even months – before he will be able to tell us what he came to tell.'

'I'll do my best, Poirot,' I assured him. 'I'll try to be an efficient substitute.'

'Ye-es.'

His rejoinder struck me as being a shade doubtful. I picked up the sheet of paper.

'If I were writing a story,' I said lightly, 'I should weave this in with your latest idiosyncrasy and call it *The Mystery of the Big Four*.' I tapped the pencilled figures as I spoke.

And then I started, for our invalid, roused suddenly from his stupor, sat up in his chair and said clearly and distinctly:

'Li Chang Yen.'

He had the look of a man suddenly awakened from sleep. Poirot made a sign to me not to speak. The man went on. He spoke in a clear, high voice, and something in his enunciation made me feel that he was quoting from some written report or lecture.

'Li Chang Yen may be regarded as representing the brains of the Big Four. He is the controlling and motive force. I have designated him, therefore, as Number One. Number Two is seldom mentioned by name. He is represented by an "S" with two lines through it – the sign for a dollar; also by two stripes and a star. It may be conjectured, therefore, that he is an American subject, and that he represents the power of wealth. There seems no doubt that Number Three is a woman, and her nationality French. It is possible that she may be one of the sirens of the *demi-monde*, but nothing is known definitely. Number Four –'

His voice faltered and broke. Poirot leant forward.

'Yes,' he prompted eagerly, 'Number Four?'

His eyes were fastened on the man's face. Some overmastering terror seemed to be gaining the day; the features were distorted and twisted.

'The *destroyer*,' gasped the man. Then, with a final convulsed movement, he fell back in a dead faint.

'*Mon Dieu!*' whispered Poirot, 'I was right then. I was right.'

'You think –?'

He interrupted me.

'Carry him on to the bed in my room. I have not a minute to lose if I would catch my train. Not that I want to catch it. Oh, that I could miss it with a clear conscience! But I gave my word. Come, Hastings!'

Leaving our mysterious visitor in the charge of Mrs Pearson, we drove away, and duly caught the train by the skin of our teeth. Poirot was alternately silent and loquacious. He would sit staring out of the window like a man lost in a dream, apparently not hearing a word that I said to him. Then, reverting to animation suddenly, he would shower injunctions and commands upon me, and urge the necessity of constant marconigrams.

We had a long fit of silence just after we passed Woking. The train, of course, did not stop anywhere until Southampton; but just here it happened to be held up by a signal.

'Ah! *Sacré mille tonnerres!*' cried Poirot suddenly. 'But I have been an imbecile. I see clearly at last. It is undoubtedly the blessed saints who stopped the train. Jump, Hastings, but jump, I tell you.'

In an instant he had unfastened the carriage door, and jumped out on the line.

'Throw out the suitcases and jump yourself.'

I obeyed him. Just in time. As I alighted beside him, the train moved on.

'And now, Poirot,' I said, in some exasperation, 'perhaps you will tell me what all this is about.'

'It is, my friend, that I have seen the light.'

'That,' I said, 'is very illuminating to me.'

'It should be,' said Poirot, 'but I fear – I very much fear that it is not. If you can carry two of these valises, I think I can manage the rest.'

CHAPTER 2

THE MAN FROM THE ASYLUM

Fortunately the train had stopped near a station. A short walk brought us to a garage where we were able to obtain a car, and half an hour later we were spinning rapidly back to London. Then, and not till then, did Poirot deign to satisfy my curiosity.

'You do not see? No more did I. But I see now. Hastings, *I was being got out of the way.*'

'What!'

'Yes. Very cleverly. Both the place and the method were chosen with great knowledge and acumen. They were afraid of me.'

'Who were?'

'Those four geniuses who have banded themselves together to work outside the law. A Chinaman, an American, a Frenchwoman, and – another. Pray the good God we arrive back in time, Hastings.'

'You think there is danger to our visitor?'

'I am sure of it.'

Mrs Pearson greeted us on arrival. Brushing aside her ecstasies of astonishment on beholding Poirot, we asked for information. It was reassuring. No one had called, and our guest had not made any sign.

With a sigh of relief we went up to the rooms. Poirot crossed the outer one and went through to the inner one. Then he called me, his voice strangely agitated.

'Hastings, he's dead.'

I came running to join him. The man was lying as we had left him, but he was dead, and had been dead some time. I rushed out for a doctor. Ridgeway, I knew, would not have returned yet. I found one almost immediately, and brought him back with me.

'He's dead right enough, poor chap. Tramp you've been befriending, eh?'

'Something of the kind,' said Poirot evasively. 'What was the cause of death, doctor?'

'Hard to say. Might have been some kind of fit. There are signs of asphyxiation. No gas laid on, is there?'

'No, electric light – nothing else.'

'And both windows wide open, too. Been dead about two hours, I should say. You'll notify the proper people, won't you?'

He took his departure. Poirot did some necessary telephoning. Finally, somewhat to my surprise, he rang up our old friend Inspector Japp, and asked him if he could possibly come round.

No sooner were these proceedings completed than Mrs Pearson appeared, her eyes as round as saucers.

'There's a man here from 'Anwell – from the 'Sylum. Did you ever? Shall I show him up?'

We signified assent, and a big burly man in uniform was ushered in.

''Morning, gentlemen,' he said cheerfully. 'I've got reason to believe you've got one of my birds here. Escaped last night, he did.'

'He *was* here,' said Poirot quietly.

'Not got away again, has he?' asked the keeper, with some concern.

'He is dead.'

The man looked more relieved than otherwise.

'You don't say so. Well, I dare say it's best for all parties.'

'Was he – dangerous?'

''Omicidal, d'you mean? Oh, no. 'Armless enough. Persecution mania very acute. Full of secret societies from China that had got him shut up. They're all the same.'

I shuddered.

'How long has he been shut up?' asked Poirot.

'A matter of two years now.'

'I see,' said Poirot quietly. 'It never occurred to anybody that he might – be sane?'

The keeper permitted himself to laugh.

'If he was sane, what would he be doing in a lunatic asylum? They all *say* they're sane, you know.'

Poirot said no more. He took the man in to see the body. The identification came immediately.

'That's him – right enough,' said the keeper callously: 'funny sort of bloke, ain't he? Well, gentlemen, I had best go off now and make arrangements under the circumstances. We won't trouble you with the corpse much longer. If there's a hinquest, you will have to appear at it, I dare say. Good morning, sir.'

With a rather uncouth bow he shambled out of the room.

A few minutes later Japp arrived. The Scotland Yard inspector was jaunty and dapper as usual.

'Here I am, Moosior Poirot. What can I do for you? Thought you were off to the coral strands of somewhere or other today?'

'My good Japp, I want to know if you have ever seen this man before.'

He led Japp into the bedroom. The inspector stared down at the figure on the bed with a puzzled face.

'Let me see now – he seems sort of familiar – and I pride myself on my memory, too. Why, God bless my soul, it's Mayerling!'

'Secret Service chap – not one of our people. Went to Russia five years ago. Never heard of again. Always thought the Bolshies had done him in.'

'It all fits in,' said Poirot, when Japp had taken his leave, 'except for the fact that he seems to have died a natural death.'

He stood looking down on the motionless figure with a dissatisfied frown. A puff of wind set the window-curtains flying out, and he looked up sharply.

'I suppose you opened the windows when you laid him down on the bed, Hastings?'

'No, I didn't,' I replied. 'As far as I remember, they were shut.'

Poirot lifted his head suddenly.

'Shut – and now they are open. What can that mean?'

'Somebody came in that way,' I suggested.

'Possibly,' agreed Poirot, but he spoke absently and without conviction. After a minute or two he said:

'That is not exactly the point I had in mind, Hastings. If only one window was open it would not intrigue me so much. It is both windows being open that strikes me as curious.'

He hurried into the other room.

'The sitting-room window is open, too. That also we left shut. Ah!'

He bent over the dead man, examining the corners of the mouth minutely. Then he looked up suddenly.

'He has been gagged, Hastings. Gagged and then poisoned.'

'Good heavens!' I exclaimed, shocked. 'I suppose we shall find out all about it from the post-mortem.'

'We shall find out nothing. He was killed by inhaling strong prussic acid. It was jammed right under his nose. Then the murderer went away again, first opening all the windows. Hydrocyanic acid is exceedingly volatile, but it has a pronounced smell of bitter almonds. With no trace of the smell to guide them, and no suspicion of foul play, death would be put down to some natural cause by the doctors. So this man was in the Secret Service, Hastings. And five years ago he disappeared in Russia.'

'The last two years he's been in the asylum,' I said. 'But what of the three years before that?'

Poirot shook his head, and then caught my arm.

'The clock, Hastings, look at the clock.'

I followed his gaze to the mantelpiece. The clock had stopped at four o'clock.

'*Mon ami*, someone has tampered with it. It had still three days to run. It is an eight-day clock, you comprehend?'

'But what should they want to do that for? Some idea of a false scent by making the crime appear to have taken place at four o'clock?'

'No, no; rearrange your ideas, *mon ami*. Exercise your little grey cells. You are Mayerling. You hear something perhaps – and you know well enough that your doom is sealed. You have just time to leave a sign. *Four* o'clock, Hastings. Number Four, the *destroyer*. Ah! an idea!'

He rushed into the other room and seized the telephone. He asked for Hanwell.

'You are the asylum, yes? I understand there has been an escape today? What is that you say? A little moment, if you please. Will you repeat that? Ah! *parfaitement*.'

He hung up the receiver, and turned to me.

'You heard, Hastings? *There has been no escape*.'

'But the man who came – the keeper?' I said.

'I wonder – I very much wonder.'

'You mean –?'

'Number Four – the destroyer.'

I gazed at Poirot dumbfounded. A minute or two after, on recovering my voice, I said:

'We shall know him again, anywhere, that's one thing. He was a man of very pronounced personality.'

'Was he, *mon ami*? I think not. He was burly and bluff and red-faced, with a thick moustache and a hoarse voice. He will be none of those things by this time, and for the rest, he has nondescript eyes, nondescript ears, and a perfect set of false teeth. Identification is not such an easy matter as you seem to think. Next time –'

'You think there will be a next time?' I interrupted.

Poirot's face grew very grave.

'It is a duel to the death, *mon ami*. You and I on the one side, the Big Four on the other. They have won the first trick; but they have failed in their plan to get me out of the way, and in the future they have to reckon with Hercule Poirot!'

CHAPTER 3

WE HEAR MORE ABOUT LI CHANG YEN

For a day or two after our visit from the fake asylum attendant I was in some hopes that he might return, and I refused to leave the flat even for a moment. As far as I could see, he had no reason to suspect that we had penetrated his disguise. He might, I thought, return and try to remove the body, but Poirot scoffed at my reasoning.

'*Mon ami*,' he said, 'if you wish you may wait in to put salt on the little bird's tail, but for me I do not waste my time so.'

'Well, then, Poirot,' I argued, 'why did he run the risk of coming at all? If he intended to return later for the body, I can see some point in his visit. He would at least be removing the evidence against himself; as it is, he does not seem to have gained anything.'

Poirot shrugged his most Gallic shrug. 'But you do not see with the eyes of Number Four, Hastings,' he said. 'You talk of evidence, but what evidence have we against him? True, we have a body, but we have no proof even that the man was murdered – prussic acid, when inhaled, leaves no trace. Again, we can find no one who saw anyone enter the flat during our absence, and we have found out nothing about the movements of our late friend, Mayerling . . .

'No, Hastings, Number Four has left no trace, and he knows it. His visit we may call a reconnaissance. Perhaps he wanted to make quite sure that Mayerling was dead, but more likely, I think, he came to see Hercule Poirot, and to have speech with the adversary whom alone he must fear.'

Poirot's reasoning appeared to be typically egotistical, but I forebore to argue.

'And what about the inquest?' I asked. 'I suppose you will explain things clearly there, and let the police have a full description of Number Four.'

'And to what end? Can we produce anything to impress a coroner's jury of your solid Britishers? Is our description of Number Four of any value? No; we shall allow them to call it "Accidental Death", and maybe, although I have not much hope, our clever murderer will pat himself on the back that he deceived Hercule Poirot in the first round.'

Poirot was right as usual. We saw no more of the man from the asylum, and the inquest, at which I gave evidence, but which Poirot did not even attend, aroused no public interest.

As, in view of his intended trip to South America, Poirot had wound up his affairs before my arrival, he had at this time no cases in hand, but although he spent most of his time in the flat

I could get little out of him. He remained buried in an armchair, and discouraged my attempts at conversation.

And then one morning, about a week after the murder, he asked me if I would care to accompany him on a visit he wished to make. I was pleased, for I felt he was making a mistake in trying to work things out so entirely on his own, and I wished to discuss the case with him. But I found he was not communicative. Even when I asked where we were going, he would not answer.

Poirot loves being mysterious. He will never part with a piece of information until the last possible moment. In this instance, having taken successively a bus and two trains, and arrived in the neighbourhood of one of London's most depressing southern suburbs, he consented at last to explain matters.

'We go, Hastings, to see the one man in England who knows most of the underground life of China.'

'Indeed! Who is he?'

'A man you have never heard of – a Mr John Ingles. To all intents and purposes, he is a retired Civil Servant of mediocre intellect, with a house full of Chinese curios with which he bores his friends and acquaintances. Nevertheless, I am assured by those who should know that the only man capable of giving me the information I seek is this same John Ingles.'

A few moments more saw us ascending the steps of The Laurels, as Mr Ingles's residence was called. Personally, I did not notice a laurel bush of any kind, so deduced that it had been named according to the usual obscure nomenclature of the suburbs.

We were admitted by an impassive-faced Chinese servant and ushered into the presence of his master. Mr Ingles was a squarely-built man, somewhat yellow of countenance, with deep-set eyes that were oddly reflective in character. He rose to greet us, setting aside an open letter which he had held in his hand. He referred to it after his greeting.

'Sit down, won't you? Hasley tells me that you want some information and that I may be useful to you in the matter.'

'That is so, monsieur. I ask of you if you have any knowledge of a man named Li Chang Yen?'

'That's rum – very rum indeed. How did you come to hear about the man?'

'You know him, then?'

'I've met him once. And I know something of him – not quite as much as I should like to. But it surprises me that anyone else in England should even have heard of him. He's a great man in his way – mandarin class and all that, you know – but that's not the crux of the matter. There's good reason to suppose that he's the man behind it all.'

'Behind what?'

'Everything. The world-wide unrest, the labour troubles that beset every nation, and the revolutions that break out in some. There are people, not scaremongers, who know what they are talking about, and they say that there is a force behind the scenes which aims at nothing less than the disintegration of civilization. In Russia, you know, there were many signs that Lenin and Trotsky were mere puppets whose every action was dictated by another's brain. I have no definite proof that would count with you, but I am quite convinced that this brain was Li Chang Yen's.'

'Oh, come,' I protested, 'isn't that a bit far-fetched? How would a Chinaman cut any ice in Russia?'

Poirot frowned at me irritably.

'For you, Hastings,' he said, 'everything is far-fetched that comes not from your own imagination; for me, I agree with this gentleman. But continue, I pray, monsieur.'

'What exactly he hopes to get out of it all I cannot pretend to say for certain,' went on Mr Ingles; 'but I assume his disease is one that has attacked great brains from the time of Akbar and Alexander to Napoleon – a lust for power and personal supremacy. Up to modern times armed force was necessary for conquest, but in this century of unrest a man like Li Chang Yen can use other means. I have evidence that he has unlimited money behind him for bribery and propaganda, and there are signs that he controls some scientific force more powerful than the world has dreamed of.'

Poirot was following Mr Ingles's words with the closest attention.

'And in China?' he asked. 'He moves there too?'

The other nodded in emphatic assent.

'There,' he said, 'although I can produce no proof that would count in a court of law, I speak from my own knowledge. I know personally every man who counts for anything in China today, and this I can tell you: the men who loom most largely in the public eye are men of little or no personality. They are marionettes who dance to the wires pulled by a master hand, and that hand is Li Chang Yen's. His is the controlling brain of the East today. We don't understand the East – we never shall; but Li Chang Yen is its moving spirit. Not that he comes out into the limelight – oh, not at all; he never moves from his palace in Peking. But he pulls strings – that's it, pulls strings – and things happen far away.'

'And there is no one to oppose him?' asked Poirot.

Mr Ingles leant forward in his chair.

'Four men have tried in the last four years,' he said slowly; 'men of character, and honesty, and brain power. Any one of them might in time have interfered with his plans.' He paused.

'Well?' I queried.

'Well, they are dead. One wrote an article, and mentioned Li Chang Yen's name in connection with the riots in Peking, and within two days he was stabbed in the street. His murderer was never caught. The offences of the other two were similar. In a speech or an article, or in conversation, each linked Li Chang Yen's name with rioting or revolution, and within a week of his indiscretion each was dead. One was poisoned; one died of cholera, an isolated case – not part of an epidemic; and one was found dead in his bed. The cause of the last death was never determined, but I was told by a doctor who saw the corpse that it was burnt and shrivelled as though a wave of electrical energy of incredible power had passed through it.'

'And Li Chang Yen?' inquired Poirot. 'Naturally nothing is traced to him, but there are signs, eh?'

Mr Ingles shrugged.

'Oh, signs – yes, certainly. And once I found a man who would talk, a brilliant young Chinese chemist who was a protégé of Li Chang Yen's. He came to me one day, this chemist, and I could see that he was on the verge of a nervous break-down. He hinted to me of experiments on which he'd been engaged in Li Chang Yen's palace under the mandarin's direction – experiments on coolies in which the most revolting disregard for human life and suffering had been shown. His nerve had completely broken, and he was in the most pitiable state of terror. I put him to bed in a top room of my own house, intending to question him the next day – and that, of course, was stupid of me.'

'How did they get him?' demanded Poirot.

'That I shall never know. I woke that night to find my house in flames, and was lucky to escape with my life. Investigation showed that a fire of amazing intensity had broken out on the top floor, and the remains of my young chemist friend were charred to a cinder.'

I could see from the earnestness with which he had been speaking that Mr Ingles was a man mounted on his hobby horse, and evidently he, too, realized that he had been carried away, for he laughed apologetically.

'But, of course,' he said, 'I have no proofs, and you, like the others, will merely tell me that I have a bee in my bonnet.'

'On the contrary,' said Poirot quietly, 'we have every reason to believe your story. We ourselves are more than a little interested in Li Chang Yen.'

'Very odd your knowing about him. Didn't fancy a soul in England had ever heard of him. I'd rather like to know how you did come to hear of him – if it's not indiscreet.'

'Not in the least, monsieur. A man took refuge in my rooms. He was suffering badly from shock, but he managed to tell us enough to interest us in this Li Chang Yen. He described four people – the Big Four – an organization hitherto undreamed of. Number One is Li Chang Yen, Number Two is an unknown American, Number Three an equally unknown Frenchwoman, Number Four may be called the executive of the organization – the *destroyer*. My informant died. Tell me, monsieur, is that phrase known to you at all? The Big Four.'

'Not in connection with Li Chang Yen. No, I can't say it is. But I've heard it, or read it, just lately – and in some unusual connection too. Ah, I've got it.'

He rose and went across to an inlaid lacquer cabinet – an exquisite thing, as even I could see. He returned with a letter in his hand.

'Here you are. Note from an old sea-faring man I ran against once in Shanghai. Hoary old reprobate – maudlin with drink by now, I should say. I took this to be the ravings of alcoholism.'

He read it aloud:

Dear Sir – You may not remember me, but you did me a good turn once in Shanghai. Do me another now. I must have money to get out of the country. I'm well hid here, I hope, but any day they may get me. The Big Four, I mean. It's life or death. I've plenty of money, but I daren't get at it, for fear of putting them wise. Send me a couple of hundred in notes. I'll repay it faithful – I swear to that. – Your servant, sir,

Jonathan Whalley.

'Dated from Granite Bungalow, Hoppaton, Dartmoor. I'm afraid I regarded it as rather a crude method of relieving me of a couple of hundred which I can ill spare. If it's any use to you –' He held it out.

'*Je vous remercie*, monsieur. I start for Hoppaton *à l'heure même.*'

'Dear me, this is very interesting. Supposing I came along too? Any objection?'

'I should be charmed to have your company, but we must start at once. We shall not reach Dartmoor until close on nightfall, as it is.'

John Ingles did not delay us more than a couple of minutes, and soon we were in the train moving out of Paddington bound for the West Country. Hoppaton was a small village clustering in a hollow right on the fringe of the moorland. It was reached by a nine-mile drive from Moretonhampstead. It was about eight o'clock when we arrived; but as the month was July, the daylight was still abundant.

We drove into the narrow street of the village and then stopped to ask our way of an old rustic.

'Granite Bungalow,' said the old man reflectively, 'it be Granite Bungalow you do want? Eh?'

We assured him that this was what we did want.

The old man pointed to a small grey cottage at the end of the street.

'There be t'Bungalow. Do yee want to see t'Inspector?'

'What Inspector?' asked Poirot sharply; 'what do you mean?'

'Haven't yee heard about t'murder, then? A shocking business t'was seemingly. Pools of blood, they do say.'

'*Mon Dieu!*' murmured Poirot. 'This Inspector of yours, I must see him at once.'

Five minutes later we were closeted with Inspector Meadows. The Inspector was inclined to be stiff at first, but at the magic name of Inspector Japp of Scotland Yard he unbent.

'Yes, sir; murdered this morning. A shocking business. They phoned to Moreton, and I came out at once. Looked a mysterious thing to begin with. The old man – he was about seventy, you know, and fond of his glass, from all I hear – was lying on the floor of the living-room. There was a bruise on his head and his throat was cut from ear to ear. Blood all over the place, as you can understand. The woman who cooks for him, Betsy Andrews, she told us that her master had several little Chinese jade figures, that he'd told her were very valuable, and these had disappeared. That, of course, looked like assault and robbery; but there were all sorts of difficulties in the way of that solution. The old fellow had two people in the house; Betsy Andrews, who is a Hoppaton woman, and a rough kind of manservant, Robert Grant. Grant had gone to the farm to fetch the milk, which he does every day, and Betsy had stepped out to have a chat with a neighbour. She was only away twenty minutes – between ten and half past – and the crime must have been done then. Grant returned to the house first. He went in by the back door, which was open – no one locks up doors round here – not in broad daylight, at all events – put the milk in the larder, and went into his own room to read the paper and have a smoke. He had no idea anything unusual had occurred – at least, that's what he says. Then Betsy comes in, goes into the living-room, sees what's happened, and lets out a screech to wake the dead. That's all fair and square. Someone got in whilst those two were out, and did the poor old man in. But it struck me at once that he must be a pretty cool customer. He'd have to come right up the village street, or creep through someone's back yard. Granite Bungalow has got houses all round it, as you can see. How was it that no one had seen him?'

The Inspector paused with a flourish.

'Aha, I perceive your point,' said Poirot. 'To continue?'

'Well, sir, fishy, I said to myself – fishy. And I began to look about me. Those jade figures, now. Would a common tramp ever suspect that they were valuable? Anyway, it was madness to try such a thing in broad daylight. Suppose the old man had yelled for help?'

'I suppose, Inspector,' said Mr Ingles, 'that the bruise on the head was inflicted before death?'

'Quite right, sir. First knocked him silly, the murderer did, and then cut his throat. That's clear enough. But how the dickens did he come or go? They notice strangers quick enough in a little place like this. It came to me all at once – nobody did come. I took a good look round. It had rained the night before, and there were footprints clear enough going in and out of the kitchen. In the living-room there were two sets of footprints only (Betsy Andrews's stopped at the door) – Mr Whalley's (he was wearing carpet slippers) and another man's. The other man had stepped in the bloodstains, and I traced his bloody footprints – I beg your pardon, sir.'

'Not at all,' said Mr Ingles, with a faint smile; 'the adjective is perfectly understood.'

'I traced them to the kitchen – but not beyond. Point Number One. On the lintel of Robert Grant's door was a faint smear – a smear of blood. That's point Number Two. Point Number Three was when I got hold of Grant's boots – which he had taken off – and fitted them to the marks. That settled it. It was an inside job. I warned Grant and took him into custody; and what do you think I found packed away in his port-manteau? The little jade figures and a ticket-of-leave. Robert Grant was also Abraham Biggs, convicted for felony and housebreaking five years ago.'

The Inspector paused triumphantly.

'What do you think of that, gentlemen?'

'I think,' said Poirot, 'that it appears a very clear case – of a surprising clearness, in fact. This Biggs, or Grant, he must be a man very foolish and uneducated, eh?'

'Oh, he is that – a rough, common sort of fellow. No idea of what a footprint may mean.'

'Clearly he reads not the detective fiction! Well, Inspector, I congratulate you. We may look at the scene of the crime. Yes?'

'I'll take you there myself this minute. I'd like you to see those footprints.'

'I, too, should like to see them. Yes, yes, very interesting, very ingenious.'

We set out forthwith. Mr Ingles and the Inspector forged ahead.

I drew Poirot back a little so as to be able to speak to him out of the Inspector's hearing.

'What do you really think, Poirot? Is there more in this than meets the eye?'

'That is just the question, *mon ami*. Whalley says plainly enough in his letter that the Big Four are on his track, and we know, you and I, that the Big Four is no bogey for the children. Yet everything seems to say that this man Grant committed the crime. Why did he do so? For the sake of the little jade figures? Or is he an agent of the Big Four? I confess that this last seems more likely. However valuable the jade, a man of that class was not likely to realize the fact – at any rate, not to the point of committing murder for them. (That, *par example*, ought to have struck the Inspector.) He could have stolen the jade and made off with it instead of committing a brutal murder. Ah, yes; I fear our Devonshire friend has not used his little grey cells. He has measured footprints, and has omitted to reflect and arrange his ideas with the necessary order and method.'

CHAPTER 4
THE IMPORTANCE OF A LEG OF MUTTON

The Inspector drew a key from his pocket and unlocked the door of Granite Bungalow. The day had been fine and dry, so our feet were not likely to leave any prints; nevertheless, we wiped them carefully on the mat before entering.

A woman came up out of the gloom and spoke to the Inspector, and he turned aside. Then he spoke over his shoulder.

'Have a good look round, Mr Poirot, and see all there is to be seen. I'll be back in about ten minutes. By the way, here's Grant's boot. I brought it along with me for you to compare the impressions.'

We went into the living-room, and the sound of the Inspector's footsteps died away outside. Ingles was attracted immediately by some Chinese curios on a table in the corner, and went over to examine them. He seemed to take no interest in Poirot's doings. I, on the other hand, watched him with breathless interest. The floor was covered with a dark-green linoleum which was ideal for showing up footprints. A door at the farther end led into the small kitchen. From there another door led into the scullery (where the back door was situated), and another into the bedroom which had been occupied by Robert Grant. Having explored the ground, Poirot commented upon it in a low running monologue.

'Here is where the body lay; that big dark stain and the splashes all around mark the spot. Traces of carpet slippers and "number nine" boots, you observe, but all very confused. Then two sets of tracks leading to and from the kitchen; whoever the murderer was, he came in that way. You have the boot, Hastings? Give it to me.' He compared it carefully with the prints. 'Yes, both made by the same man, Robert Grant. He came in that way, killed the old man, and went back to the kitchen. He had stepped in the blood; see the stains he left as he went out? Nothing to be seen in the kitchen – all the village has been walking about in it. He went into his own room – no, first he went back again to the scene of the crime – was that to get the little jade figures? Or had he forgotten something that might incriminate him?'

'Perhaps he killed the old man the second time he went in?' I suggested.

'*Mais non*, you do not observe. On one of the outgoing footmarks stained with blood there is superimposed an ingoing one. I wonder what he went back for – the little jade figures as an afterthought? It is all ridiculous – stupid.'

'Well, he's given himself away pretty hopelessly.'

'*N'est-ce pas*? I tell you, Hastings, it goes against reason. It offends my little grey cells. Let us go into his bedroom – ah, yes; there is the smear of blood on the lintel and just a trace of footmarks – bloodstained. Robert Grant's footmarks, and his only, near the body – Robert Grant the only man who went near the house. Yes, it must be so.'

'What about the old woman?' I said suddenly. 'She was in the house alone after Grant had gone for the milk. She might have killed him and then gone out. Her feet would leave no prints if she hadn't been outside.'

'Very good, Hastings. I wondered whether that hypothesis would occur to you. I had already thought of it and rejected it. Betsy Andrews is a local woman, well known hereabouts. She can have no connection with the Big Four; and, besides, old Whalley was a powerful fellow, by all accounts. This is a man's work – not a woman's.'

'I suppose the Big Four couldn't have had some diabolical contrivance concealed in the ceiling – something which descended automatically and cut the old man's throat and was afterwards drawn up again?'

'Like Jacob's ladder? I know, Hastings, that you have an imagination of the most fertile – but I implore of you to keep it within bounds.'

I subsided, abashed. Poirot continued to wander about, poking into rooms and cupboards with a profoundly dissatisfied expression on his face. Suddenly he uttered an excited yelp, reminiscent of a Pomeranian dog. I rushed to join him. He was standing in the larder in a dramatic attitude. In his hand he was brandishing a leg of mutton!

'My dear Poirot!' I cried. 'What is the matter? Have you suddenly gone mad?'

'Regard, I pray you, this mutton. But regard it closely!'

I regarded it as closely as I could, but could see nothing unusual about it. It seemed to me a very ordinary leg of mutton. I said as much. Poirot threw me a withering glance.

'But do you not see this – and this – and this –'

He illustrated each 'this' with a jab at the unoffending joint, dislodging small icicles as he did so.

Poirot had just accused me of being imaginative, but I now felt that he was far more wildly so than I had ever been. Did he seriously think these slivers of ice were crystals of a deadly poison? That was the only construction I could put upon his extraordinary agitation.

'It's frozen meat,' I explained gently. 'Imported, you know. New Zealand.'

He stared at me for a moment or two and then broke into a strange laugh.

'How marvellous is my friend Hastings! He knows everything – but everything! How do they say – Inquire Within Upon Everything. That is my friend Hastings.'

He flung down the leg of mutton on to its dish again and left the larder. Then he looked through the window.

'Here comes our friend the Inspector. It is well. I have seen all

I want to see here.' He drummed on the table absentmindedly, as though absorbed in calculation, and then asked suddenly, 'What is the day of the week, *mon ami?*'

'Monday,' I said, rather astonished. 'What –?'

'Ah! Monday, is it? A bad day of the week. To commit a murder on a Monday is a mistake.'

Passing back to the living-room, he tapped the glass on the wall and glanced at the thermometer.

'Set fair, and seventy degrees Fahrenheit. An orthodox English summer's day.'

Ingles was still examining various pieces of Chinese pottery.

'You do not take much interest in this inquiry, monsieur?' said Poirot.

The other gave a slow smile.

'It's not my job, you see. I'm a connoisseur of some things, but not of this. So I just stand back and keep out of the way. I've learnt patience in the East.'

The Inspector came bustling in, apologizing for having been so long away. He insisted on taking us over most of the ground again, but finally we got away.

'I must appreciate your thousand politenesses, Inspector,' said Poirot, as we were walking down the village street again.

'There is just one more request I should like to put to you.'

'You want to see the body, perhaps, sir?'

'Oh, dear me, no! I have not the least interest in the body. I want to see Robert Grant.'

'You'll have to drive back with me to Moreton to see him, sir.'

'Very well, I will do so. But I must see him and be able to speak to him alone.'

The Inspector caressed his upper lip.

'Well, I don't know about that, sir.'

'I assure you that if you can get through to Scotland Yard you will receive full authority.'

'I've heard of you, of course, sir, and I know you've done us a good turn now and again. But it's very irregular.'

'Nevertheless, it is necessary,' said Poirot calmly. 'It is necessary for this reason – Grant is not the murderer.'

'What? Who, is, then?'

'The murderer was, I should fancy, a youngish man. He drove

up to Granite Bungalow in a trap, which he left outside. He went in, committed the murder, came out, and drove away again. He was bareheaded, and his clothing was slightly bloodstained.'

'But – but the whole village would have seen him!'

'Not under certain circumstances.'

'Not if it was dark, perhaps; but the crime was committed in broad daylight.'

Poirot merely smiled.

'And the horse and trap, sir – how could you tell that? Any amount of wheeled vehicles have passed along outside. There's no mark of one in particular to be seen.'

'Not with the eyes of the body, perhaps; but with the eyes of the mind, yes.'

The Inspector touched his forehead significantly with a grin at me. I was utterly bewildered, but I had faith in Poirot. Further discussion ended in our all driving back to Moreton with the Inspector. Poirot and I were taken to Grant, but a constable was to be present during the interview. Poirot went straight to the point.

'Grant, I know you to be innocent of this crime. Relate to me in your own words exactly what happened.'

The prisoner was a man of medium height, with a somewhat unpleasing cast of features. He looked a jail-bird if ever a man did.

'Honest to God, I never did it,' he whined. 'Someone put those little glass figures amongst my traps. It was a frame-up, that's what it was. I went straight to my rooms when I came in, like I said. I never knew a thing till Betsy screeched out. S'welp me, God, I didn't.'

Poirot rose.

'If you can't tell me the truth, that is the end of it.'

'But, guv'nor –'

'You *did* go into the room – you *did* know your master was dead; and you were just preparing to make a bolt of it when the good Betsy made her terrible discovery.'

The man stared at Poirot with a dropped jaw.

'Come now, is it not so? I tell you solemnly – on my word of honour – that to be frank now is your only chance.'

'I'll risk it,' said the man suddenly. 'It was just as you say. I came in, and went straight to the master – and there he was, dead on the floor and blood all round. Then I got the wind up proper. They'd ferret out my record, and for a certainty they'd say it was me as had done him in. My only thought was to get away – at once – before he was found –'

'And the jade figures?'

The man hesitated.

'You see –'

'You took them by a kind of reversion to instinct, as it were? You had heard your master say that they were valuable, and you felt you might as well go the whole hog. That, I understand. Now, answer me this. Was it the second time that you went into the room that you took the figures?'

'I didn't go in a second time. Once was enough for me.'

'You are sure of that?'

'Absolutely certain.'

'Good. Now, when did you come out of prison?'

'Two months ago.'

'How did you obtain this job?'

'Through one of them Prisoners' Help Societies. Bloke met me when I came out.'

'What was he like?'

'Not exactly a parson, but looked like one. Soft black hat and mincing way of walking. Got a broken front tooth. Spectacled chap. Saunders his name was. Said he hoped I was repentant, and that he'd find me a good post. I went to old Whalley on his recommendation.'

Poirot rose once more.

'I thank you. I know all now. Have patience.' He paused in the doorway and added: 'Saunders gave you a pair of boots, didn't he?'

Grant looked very astonished.

'Why, yes, he did. But how did you know?'

'It is my business to know things,' said Poirot gravely.

After a word or two to the Inspector, the three of us went to the White Hart and discussed eggs and bacon and Devonshire cider.

'Any elucidations yet?' asked Ingles, with a smile.

'Yes, the case is clear enough now; but, see you, I shall have a good deal of difficulty in proving it. Whalley was killed by order of the Big Four – but not by Grant. A very clever man got Grant the post and deliberately planned to make him the scapegoat – an easy matter with Grant's prison record. He gave him a pair of boots, one of two duplicate pairs. The other he kept himself. It was all so simple. When Grant is out of the house, and Betsy is chatting in the village (which she probably did every day of her life), he drives up wearing the duplicate boots, enters the kitchen, goes through into the living-room, fells the old man with a blow, and then cuts his throat. Then he returns to the kitchen, removes the boots, puts on another pair, and, carrying the first pair, goes out to his trap and drives off again.'

Ingles looks steadily at Poirot.

'There's a catch in it still. Why did nobody see him?'

'Ah! That is where the cleverness of Number Four, I am convinced, comes in. Everybody saw him – and yet nobody saw him. You see, he drove up in a butcher's cart!'

I uttered an exclamation.

'The leg of mutton?'

'Exactly, Hastings, the leg of mutton. Everybody swore that no one had been to Granite Bungalow that morning, but, nevertheless, I found in the larder a leg of mutton, still frozen. It was Monday, so the meat must have been delivered that morning; for if on Saturday, in this hot weather, it would not have remained frozen over Sunday. So someone *had* been to the Bungalow, and a man on whom a trace of blood here and there would attract no attention.'

'Damned ingenious!' cried Ingles approvingly.

'Yes, he is clever, Number Four.'

'As clever as Hercule Poirot?' I murmured.

My friend threw me a glance of dignified reproach.

'There are some jests that you should not permit yourself, Hastings,' he said sententiously. 'Have I not saved an innocent man from being sent to the gallows? That is enough for one day.'

CHAPTER 5
DISAPPEARANCE OF A SCIENTIST

Personally, I don't think that, even when a jury had acquitted Robert Grant, alias Biggs, of the murder of Jonathan Whalley, Inspector Meadows was entirely convinced of his innocence. The case which he had built up against Grant – the man's record, the jade which he had stolen, the boots which fitted the footprints so exactly – was to his matter-of-fact mind too complete to be easily upset; but Poirot, compelled much against his inclination to give evidence, convinced the jury. Two witnesses were produced who had seen a butcher's cart drive up to the bungalow on that Monday morning, and the local butcher testified that his cart only called there on Wednesdays and Fridays.

A woman was actually found who, when questioned, remembered seeing the butcher's man leaving the bungalow, but she could furnish no useful description of him. The only impression he seemed to have left on her mind was that he was clean shaven, of medium height, and looked exactly like a butcher's man. At this description Poirot shrugged his shoulders philosophically.

'It is as I tell you, Hastings,' he said to me, after the trial. 'He is an artist, this one. He disguises himself not with the false beard and the blue spectacles. He alters his features, yes; but that is the least part. For the time being he *is* the man he would be. He lives in his part.'

Certainly I was compelled to admit that the man who had visited us from Hanwell had fitted in exactly with my idea of what an asylum attendant should look like. I should never for a moment have dreamt of doubting that he was genuine.

It was all a little discouraging, and our experience on Dartmoor did not seem to have helped us at all. I said as much to Poirot, but he would not admit that we had gained nothing.

'We progress,' he said; 'we progress. At every contact with this man we learn a little of his mind and his methods. Of us and our plans he knows nothing.'

'And there, Poirot,' I protested, 'he and I seem to be in the same boat. You don't seem to me to have any plans, you seem to sit and wait for him to do something.'

Poirot smiled.

'*Mon ami*, you do not change. Always the same Hastings, who would be up and at their throats. Perhaps,' he added, as a knock sounded on the door, 'you have here your chance; it may be our friend who enters.' And he laughed at my disappointment when Inspector Japp and another man entered the room.

'Good evening, moosior,' said the Inspector. 'Allow me to introduce Captain Kent of the United States Secret Service.'

Captain Kent was a tall, lean American, with a singularly impassive face which looked as though it had been carved out of wood.

'Pleased to meet you, gentlemen,' he murmured, as he shook hands jerkily.

Poirot threw an extra log on the fire, and brought forward more easy chairs. I brought out glasses and the whisky and soda. The captain took a deep draught, and expressed appreciation.

'Legislation in your country is still sound,' he observed.

'And now to business,' said Japp. 'Moosior Poirot here made a certain request to me. He was interested in some concern that went by the name of the Big Four, and he asked me to let him know at any time if I came across a mention of it in my official line of business. I didn't take much stock in the matter, but I remembered what he said, and when the captain here came over with rather a curious story, I said at once, "We'll go round to Moosior Poirot's."'

Poirot looked across at Captain Kent, and the American took up the tale.

'You may remember reading, M. Poirot, that a number of torpedo boats and destroyers were sunk by being dashed upon the rocks off the American coast. It was just after the Japanese earthquake, and the explanation given was that the disaster was the result of a tidal wave. Now, a short time ago, a roundup was made of certain crooks and gunmen, and with them were captured some papers which put an entirely new face upon the matter. They appeared to refer to some organization called the "Big Four", and gave an incomplete description of some powerful wireless installation – a concentration of wireless energy far beyond anything so far attempted, and capable of focusing a beam of great intensity upon some given spot. The claims made for this invention seemed manifestly absurd, but I turned them in to headquarters for what they were worth, and one of our highbrow professors got busy on them. Now it appears that one of your British scientists read a paper upon the subject before the British Association. His colleagues didn't think great shakes of it, by all accounts, thought it far-fetched and fanciful, but your scientist stuck to his guns, and declared that he himself was on the eve of success in his experiments.'

'*Eh bien?*' demanded Poirot, with interest.

'It was suggested that I should come over here and get an interview with this gentleman. Quite a young fellow, he is, Halliday by name. He is the leading authority on the subject, and I was to get from him whether the thing suggested was anyway possible.'

'And was it?' I asked eagerly.

'That's just what I don't know. I haven't seen Mr Halliday – and I'm not likely to, by all accounts.'

'The truth of the matter is,' said Japp shortly, 'Halliday's disappeared.'

'When?'

'Two months ago.'

'Was his disappearance reported?'

'Of course it was. His wife came to us in a great state. We did what we could, but I knew all along it would be no good.'

'Why not?'

'Never is – when a man disappears that way.' Japp winked.

'What way?'

'Paris.'

'So Halliday disappeared in Paris?'

'Yes. Went over there on scientific work – so he said. Of course, he'd have to say something like that. But you know what it means when a man disappears over there. Either it's Apache work, and that's the end of it – or else it's voluntary disappearance – and that's a great deal the commoner of the two, I can tell you. Gay Paree and all that, you know. Sick of home life. Halliday and his wife had had a tiff before he started, which all helps to make it a pretty clear case.'

'I wonder,' said Poirot thoughtfully.

The American was looking at him curiously.

'Say, mister,' he drawled, 'what's this Big Four idea?'

'The Big Four,' said Poirot, 'is an international organization which has at its head a Chinaman. He is known as Number One. Number Two is an American. Number Three is a Frenchwoman. Number Four, "the Destroyer", is an Englishman.'

'A Frenchwoman, eh?' The American whistled. 'And Halliday disappeared in France. Maybe there's something in this. What's her name?'

'I don't know. I know nothing about her.'

'But it's a mighty big proposition, eh?' suggested the other.

Poirot nodded, as he arranged the glasses in a neat row on the tray. His love of order was as great as ever.

'What was the idea in sinking those boats? Are the Big Four a German stunt?'

'The Big Four are for themselves – and for themselves only, M. le Capitaine. Their aim is world domination.'

The American burst out laughing, but broke off at the sight of Poirot's serious face.

'You laugh, monsieur,' said Poirot, shaking a finger at him. 'You reflect not – you use not the little grey cells of the brain. Who are these men who send a portion of your navy to destruction simply as a trial of their power? For that was all it was, Monsieur, a test of this new force of magnetical attraction which they hold.'

'Go on with you, moosior,' said Japp good-humouredly. 'I've read of super criminals many a time, but I've never come across them. Well, you've heard Captain Kent's story. Anything further I can do for you?'

'Yes, my good friend. You can give me the address of Mrs Halliday – and also a few words of introduction to her if you will be so kind.'

Thus it was that the following day saw us bound for Chetwynd Lodge, near the village of Chobham in Surrey.

Mrs Halliday received us at once, a tall, fair woman, nervous and eager in manner. With her was her little girl, a beautiful child of five.

Poirot explained the purpose of our visit.

'Oh! M. Poirot, I am so glad, so thankful. I have heard of you, of course. You will not be like these Scotland Yard people, who will not listen or try to understand. And the French police are just as bad – worse, I think. They are all convinced that my husband has gone off with some other woman. But he wasn't like that! All he thought of in life was his work. Half our quarrels came from that. He cared for it more than he did for me.'

'Englishmen, they are like that,' said Poirot soothingly. 'And if it is not work, it is the games, the sport. All those things they take *au grand sérieux*. Now, madame, recount to me exactly, in detail, and as methodically as you can, the exact circumstances of your husband's disappearance.'

'My husband went to Paris on Thursday, the 20th of July. He was to meet and visit various people there connected with his work, amongst them Madame Olivier.'

Poirot nodded at the mention of the famous French woman chemist, who had eclipsed even Madame Curie in the brilliance of her achievements. She had been decorated by the French Government, and was one of the most prominent personalities of the day.

'He arrived there in the evening and went at once to the Hotel Castiglione in the rue de Castiglione. On the following morning he had an appointment with Professor Bourgoneau, which he kept. His manner was normal and pleasant. The two men had a most interesting conversation, and it was arranged that he should witness some experiments in the professor's laboratory on the following day. He lunched alone at the Café Royal, went for a walk in the Bois, and then visited Madame Olivier at her house at Passy. There, also, his manner was perfectly normal. He left about six. Where he dined is not known, probably alone at some restaurant. He returned to the hotel about eleven o'clock and went straight up to his room, after inquiring if any letters had come for him. On the following morning, he walked out of the hotel, and has not been seen again.'

'At what time did he leave the hotel? At the hour when he would normally leave it to keep his appointment at Professor Bourgoneau's laboratory?'

'We do not know. He was not remarked leaving the hotel. But no *petit déjeuner* was served to him, which seems to indicate that he went out early.'

'Or he might, in fact, have gone out again after he came in the night before?'

'I do not think so. His bed had been slept in, and the night porter would have remembered anyone going out at that hour.'

'A very just observation, madame. We may take it, then, that he left early on the following morning – and that is reassuring from one point of view. He is not likely to have fallen a victim to any Apache assault at that hour. His baggage, now, was it all left behind?'

Mrs Halliday seemed rather reluctant to answer, but at last she said:

'No – he must have taken one small suitcase with him.'

'H'm,' said Poirot thoughtfully, 'I wonder where he was that evening. If we knew that, we should know a great deal. Whom did he meet? – there lies the mystery. Madame, myself, I do not of necessity accept the view of the police; with them is it always "*Cherchez la femme.*" Yet it is clear that something occurred that night to alter your husband's plans. You say he asked for letters on returning to the hotel. Did he receive any?'

'One only, and that must have been the one I wrote him on the day he left England.'

Poirot remained sunk in thought for a full minute, then he rose briskly to his feet.

'Well, madame, the solution of the mystery lies in Paris, and to find it I myself journey to Paris on the instant.'

'It is all a long time ago, monsieur.'

'Yes, yes. Nevertheless, it is there that we must seek.'

He turned to leave the room, but paused with his hand on the door.

'Tell me, madame, do you ever remember your husband mentioning the phrase, "The Big Four"?'

'The Big Four,' she repeated thoughtfully. 'No, I can't say I do.'

CHAPTER 6

THE WOMAN ON THE STAIRS

That was all that could be elicited from Mrs Halliday. We hurried back to London, and the following day saw us en route for the Continent. With rather a rueful smile, Poirot observed:

'This Big Four, they make me to bestir myself, *mon ami*. I run up and down, all over the ground, like our old friend "the human foxhound".'

'Perhaps you'll meet him in Paris,' I said, knowing that he referred to a certain Giraud, one of the most trusted detectives of the Sûreté, whom he had met on a previous occasion.

Poirot made a grimace. 'I devoutly hope not. He loved me not, that one.'

'Won't it be a very difficult task?' I asked. 'To find out what an unknown Englishman did on an evening two months ago?'

'Very difficult, *mon ami*. But as you know well, difficulties rejoice the heart of Hercule Poirot.'

'You think the Big Four kidnapped him?'

Poirot nodded.

Our inquiries necessarily went over old ground, and we learnt little to add to what Mrs Halliday had already told us. Poirot had a lengthy interview with Professor Bourgoneau, during which he sought to elicit whether Halliday had mentioned any plan of his own for the evening, but we drew a complete blank.

Our next source of information was the famous Madame Olivier. I was quite excited as we mounted the steps of her villa at Passy. It has always seemed to me extraordinary that a woman should go so far in the scientific world. I should have thought a purely masculine brain was needed for such work.

The door was opened by a young lad of seventeen or thereabouts, who reminded me vaguely of an acolyte, so ritualistic was his manner. Poirot had taken the trouble to arrange our interview beforehand, as he knew Madame Olivier never received anyone without an appointment, being immersed in research work most of the day.

We were shown into a small salon, and presently the mistress of the house came to us there. Madame Olivier was a very tall woman, her tallness accentuated by the long white overall she wore, and a coif like a nun's that shrouded her head. She had a long pale face, and wonderful dark eyes that burnt with a light almost fanatical. She looked more like a priestess of old than a modern Frenchwoman. One cheek was disfigured by a scar, and I remembered that her husband and co-worker had been killed in an explosion in the laboratory three years before, and that she herself had been terribly burned. Ever since then she had shut herself away from the world, and plunged with fiery energy into the work of scientific research. She received us with cold politeness.

'I have been interviewed by the police many times, messieurs. I think it hardly likely that I can help you, since I have not been able to help them.'

'Madame, it is possible that I shall not ask you quite the same questions. To begin with, of what did you talk together, you and M. Halliday?'

She looked a trifle surprised.

'But of his work! His work – and also mine.'

'Did he mention to you the theories he had embodied recently in his paper read before the British Association?'

'Certainly he did. It was chiefly of those we spoke.'

'His ideas were somewhat fantastic, were they not?' asked Poirot carelessly.

'Some people have thought so. I do not agree.'

'You consider them practicable?'

'Perfectly practicable. My own line of research has been somewhat similar, though not undertaken with the same end in view. I have been investigating the gamma rays emitted by the substance usually known as Radium C, a product of Radium emanation, and in doing so I have come across some very interesting magnetical phenomena. Indeed, I have a theory as to the actual nature of the force we call magnetism, but it is not yet time for my discoveries to be given to the world. Mr Halliday's experiments and views were exceedingly interesting to me.'

Poirot nodded. Then he asked a question which surprised me.

'Madame, where did you converse on these topics? In here?'

'No, monsieur. In the laboratory.'

'May I see it?'

'Certainly.'

She led the way to the door from which she had entered. It opened on a small passage. We passed through two doors and found ourselves in the big laboratory, with its array of beakers and crucibles and a hundred appliances of which I did not even know the names. There were two occupants, both busy with some experiment. Madame Olivier introduced them.

'Mademoiselle Claude, one of my assistants.' A tall, serious-faced young girl bowed to us. 'Monsieur Henri, an old and trusted friend.'

The young man, short and dark, bowed jerkily.

Poirot looked round him. There were two other doors besides the one by which we had entered. One, madame explained, led into the garden, the other into a smaller chamber also devoted to research. Poirot took all this in, then declared himself ready to return to the salon.

'Madame, were you alone with M. Halliday during your interview?'

'Yes, monsieur. My two assistants were in the smaller room next door.'

'Could your conversation be overheard – by them or anyone else?'

Madame reflected, then shook her head.

'I do not think so. I am almost sure it could not. The doors were all shut.'

'Could anyone have been concealed in the room?'

'There is the big cupboard in the corner – but the idea is absurd.'

'*Pas tout à fait*, madame. One thing more: did M. Halliday make any mention of his plans for the evening?'

'He said nothing whatever, monsieur.'

'I thank you, madame, and I apologize for disturbing you. Pray do not trouble – we can find our way out.'

We stepped out into the hall. A lady was just entering the front door as we did so. She ran quickly up the stairs, and I was left with an impression of the heavy mourning that denotes a French widow.

'A most unusual type of woman, that,' remarked Poirot, as we walked away.

'Madame Olivier? Yes, she –'

'*Mais non*, not Madame Olivier. *Cela va sans dire*! There are not many geniuses of her stamp in the world. No, I referred to the other lady – the lady on the stairs.'

'I didn't see her face,' I said, staring. 'And I hardly see how you could have done. She never looked at us.'

'That is why I said she was an unusual type,' said Poirot placidly. 'A woman who enters her home – for I presume that it is her home since she enters with a key – and runs straight upstairs without even looking at two strange visitors in the hall to see who they are, is a *very* unusual type of woman – quite unnatural, in fact. *Mille tonnerres*! what is that?'

He dragged me back – just in time. A tree had crashed down on to the sidewalk, just missing us. Poirot stared at it, pale and upset.

'It was a near thing that! But clumsy, all the same – for I had no suspicion – at least hardly any suspicion. Yes, but for my quick eyes, the eyes of a cat, Hercule Poirot might now be crushed out of existence – a terrible calamity for the world. And you, too, *mon ami* – though that would not be such a national catastrophe.'

'Thank you,' I said coldly. 'And what are we going to do now?'

'Do?' cried Poirot. 'We are going to think. Yes, here and now, we are going to exercise our little grey cells. This M. Halliday now, was he really in Paris? Yes, for Professor Bourgoneau, who knows him, saw and spoke to him.'

'What on earth are you driving at?' I cried.

'That was Friday morning. He was last seen at eleven Friday night – but *was* he seen then?'

'The porter –'

'A night porter – who had not previously seen Halliday. A man comes in, sufficiently like Halliday – we may trust Number Four for that – asks for letters, goes upstairs, packs a small suitcase, and slips out the next morning. Nobody saw Halliday all that evening – no, because he was already in the hands of his enemies. Was it Halliday whom Madame Olivier received? Yes, for though she did not know him by sight, an imposter could hardly deceive her on her own special subject. He came here, he had his interview, he left. What happened next?'

Seizing me by the arm, Poirot was fairly dragging me back to the villa.

'Now, *mon ami*, imagine that it is the day after the disappearance, and that we are tracking footprints. You love footprints, do you not? See – here they go, a man's, M. Halliday's . . . He turns to the right as we did, he walks briskly – ah! other footsteps following behind – very quickly – small footsteps, a woman's. See, she catches him up – a slim young woman, in a widow's veil. "Pardon, monsieur, Madame Olivier desires that I recall you." He stops, he turns. Now where would the young woman take him? Is it coincidence that she catches up with him just where a narrow alleyway opens, dividing two gardens? She leads him down it. "It is shorter this way, monsieur." On the right is the garden of Madame

Olivier's villa, on the left the garden of another villa – and from that garden, mark you, the tree fell – so nearly on us. Garden doors from both open on the alley. The ambush is there. Men pour out, overpower him, and carry him into the strange villa.'

'Good gracious, Poirot,' I cried, 'are you pretending to see all this?'

'I see it with the eyes of the mind, *mon ami*. So, and only so, could it have happened. Come, let us go back to the house.'

'You want to see Madame Olivier again?'

Poirot gave a curious smile.

'No, Hastings, I want to see the face of the lady on the stairs.'

'Who do you think she is, a relation of Madame Olivier's?'

'More probably a secretary – and a secretary engaged not very long ago.'

The same gentle acolyte opened the door to us.

'Can you tell me,' said Poirot, 'the name of the lady, the widow lady, who came in just now?'

'Madame Veroneau? Madame's secretary?'

'That is the lady. Would you be so kind as to ask her to speak to us for a moment.'

The youth disappeared. He soon reappeared.

'I am sorry. Madame Veroneau must have gone out again.'

'I think not,' said Poirot quietly. 'Will you give her my name, M. Hercule Poirot, and say that it is important I should see her at once, as I am just going to the Préfecture.'

Again our messenger departed. This time the lady descended. She walked into the salon. We followed her. She turned and raised her veil. To my astonishment I recognized our old antagonist, the Countess Rossakoff, a Russian countess, who had engineered a particularly smart jewel robbery in London.

'As soon as I caught sight of you in the hall, I feared the worst,' she observed plaintively.

'My dear Countess Rossakoff –'

She shook her head.

'Inez Veroneau now,' she murmured. 'A Spaniard, married to a Frenchman. What do you want of me, M. Poirot? You are a terrible man. You hunted me from London. Now, I suppose, you will tell our wonderful Madame Olivier about me, and hunt me from Paris? We poor Russians, we must live, you know.'

'It is more serious than that, madame,' said Poirot, watching her. 'I propose to enter the villa next door, and release M. Halliday, if he is still alive. I know everything, you see.'

I saw her sudden pallor. She bit her lip. Then she spoke with her usual decision.

'He is still alive – but he is not at the villa. Come, monsieur, I will make a bargain with you. Freedom for me – and M. Halliday, alive and well, for you.'

'I accept,' said Poirot. 'I was about to propose the same bargain myself. By the way, are the Big Four your employers, madame?'

Again I saw that deathly pallor creep over her face, but she left his question unanswered.

Instead, 'You permit me to telephone?' she asked, and crossing to the instrument she rang up a number. 'The number of the villa,' she explained, 'where our friend is now imprisoned. You may give it to the police – the nest will be empty when they arrive. Ah! I am through. Is that you, André? It is I, Inez. The little Belgian knows all. Send Halliday to the hotel, and clear out.'

She replaced the receiver, and came towards us, smiling.

'You will accompany us to the hotel, madame.'

'Naturally. I expected that.'

I got a taxi, and we drove off together. I could see by Poirot's face that he was perplexed. The thing was almost too easy. We arrived at the hotel. The porter came up to us.

'A gentleman has arrived. He is in your rooms. He seems very ill. A nurse came with him, but she has left.'

'That is all right,' said Poirot, 'he is a friend of mine.'

We went upstairs together. Sitting in a chair by the window was a haggard young fellow who looked in the last stages of exhaustion. Poirot went over to him.

'Are you John Halliday?' The man nodded. 'Show me your left arm. John Halliday has a mole just below the left elbow.'

The man stretched out his arm. The mole was there. Poirot bowed to the countess. She turned and left the room.

A glass of brandy revived Halliday somewhat.

'My God!' he muttered. 'I have been through hell – hell . . . Those fiends are devils incarnate. My wife, where is she? What does she think? They told me that she would believe – would believe –'

'She does not,' said Poirot firmly. 'Her faith in you has never wavered. She is waiting for you – she and the child.'

'Thank God for that. I can hardly believe that I am free once more.'

'Now that you are a little recovered, monsieur, I should like to hear the whole story from the beginning.'

Halliday looked at him with an indescribable expression.

'I remember – nothing,' he said.

'What?'

'Have you ever heard of the Big Four?'

'Something of them,' said Poirot dryly.

'You do not know what I know. They have unlimited power. If I remain silent, I shall be safe – if I say one word – not only I, but my nearest and dearest will suffer unspeakable things. It is no good arguing with me. *I know* . . . I remember – nothing.'

And, getting up, he walked from the room.

Poirot's face wore a baffled expression.

'So it is like that, is it?' he muttered. 'The Big Four win again. What is that you are holding in your hand, Hastings?'

I handed it to him.

'The countess scribbled it before she left,' I explained.

He read it.

'Au revoir. – I.V.'

'Signed with her initials – I.V. Just a coincidence, perhaps, that they also stand for *Four*. I wonder, Hastings, I wonder.'

CHAPTER 7

THE RADIUM THIEVES

On the night of his release, Halliday slept in the room next to ours at the hotel, and all night long I heard him moaning and protesting in his sleep. Undoubtedly his experience in the villa had broken his nerve, and in the morning we failed completely to extract any information from him. He would only repeat his statement about the unlimited power at the disposal of the Big Four, and his assurance of the vengeance which would follow if he talked.

After lunch he departed to rejoin his wife in England, but Poirot and I remained behind in Paris. I was all for energetic proceedings of some kind or other, and Poirot's quiescence annoyed me.

'For Heaven's sake, Poirot,' I urged, 'let us be up and at them.'

'Admirable, *mon ami*, admirable! Up where, and at whom? Be precise, I beg of you.'

'At the Big Four, of course.'

'*Cela va sans dire*. But how would you set about it?'

'The police,' I hazarded doubtfully.

Poirot smiled.

'They would accuse us of romancing. We have nothing to go upon – nothing whatever. We must wait.'

'Wait for what?'

'Wait for them to make a move. See now, in England you all comprehend and adore *la boxe*. If one man does not make a move, the other must, and by permitting the adversary to make the attack one learns something about him. That is our part – to let the other side make the attack.'

'You think they will?' I said doubtfully.

'I have no doubt whatever of it. To begin with, see, they try to get me out of England. That fails. Then, in the Dartmoor affair, we step in and save their victim from the gallows. And yesterday, once again, we interfere with their plans. Assuredly, they will not leave the matter there.'

As I reflected on this, there was a knock on the door. Without waiting for a reply, a man stepped into the room and closed the door behind him. He was a tall, thin man, with a slightly hooked nose and a sallow complexion. He wore an overcoat buttoned up to his chin, and a soft hat well pulled down over his eyes.

'Excuse me, gentlemen, for my somewhat unceremonious entry,' he said in a soft voice, 'but my business is of a rather unorthodox nature.'

Smiling, he advanced to the table and sat down by it. I was about to spring up, but Poirot restrained me with a gesture.

'As you say, monsieur, your entry is somewhat unceremonious. Will you kindly state your business?'

'My dear M. Poirot, it is very simple. You have been annoying my friends.'

'In what way?'

'Come, come, M. Poirot. You do not seriously ask me that? You know as well as I do.'

'It depends, monsieur, upon who these friends of yours are.'

Without a word, the man drew from his pocket a cigarette case, and, opening it, took out four cigarettes and tossed them on the table. Then he picked them up and returned them to his case, which he replaced in his pocket.

'Aha!' said Poirot, 'so it is like that, is it? And what do your friends suggest?'

'They suggest, monsieur, that you should employ your talents – your very considerable talents – in the detection of legitimate crime – return to your former avocations, and solve the problems of London society ladies.'

'A peaceful programme,' said Poirot. 'And supposing I do not agree?'

The man made an eloquent gesture.

'We should regret it, of course, exceedingly,' he said. 'So would all the friends and admirers of the great M. Hercule Poirot. But regrets, however poignant, do not bring a man to life again.'

'Put very delicately,' said Poirot, nodding his head. 'And supposing I – accept?'

'In that case I am empowered to offer you – compensation.'

He drew out a pocketbook, and threw ten notes on the table. They were for ten thousand francs each.

'That is merely a guarantee of our good faith,' he said. 'Ten times that amount will be paid you.'

'Good God,' I cried, springing up, 'you dare to think –'

'Sit down, Hastings,' said Poirot autocratically. 'Subdue your so beautiful and honest nature and sit down. To you, monsieur, I will say this. What is to prevent me ringing up the police and giving you into their custody, whilst my friend here prevents you from escaping?'

'By all means do so if you think it advisable,' said our visitor calmly.

'Oh! look here, Poirot,' I cried. 'I can't stand this. Ring up the police and have done with it.'

Rising swiftly, I strode to the door and stood with my back against it.

'It seems the obvious course,' murmured Poirot, as though debating with himself.

'But you distrust the obvious, eh?' said our visitor, smiling.

'Go on, Poirot,' I urged.

'It will be your responsibility, *mon ami*.'

As he lifted the receiver, the man made a sudden, cat-like jump at me. I was ready for him. In another minute we were locked together, staggering round the room. Suddenly I felt him slip and falter. I pressed my advantage. He went down before me. And then, in the very flush of victory, an extraordinary thing happened. I felt myself flying forwards. Head first, I crashed into the wall in a complicated heap. I was up in a minute, but the door was already closing behind my late adversary. I rushed to it and shook it, it was locked on the outside. I seized the telephone from Poirot.

'Is that the bureau? Stop a man who is coming out. A tall man, with a buttoned-up overcoat and a soft hat. He is wanted by the police.'

Very few minutes elapsed before we heard a noise in the corridor outside. The key was turned and the door flung open. The manager himself stood in the doorway.

'The man – you have got him?' I cried.

'No, monsieur. No one has descended.'

'You must have passed him.'

'We have passed no one, monsieur. It is incredible that he can have escaped.'

'You have passed someone, I think,' said Poirot, in his gentle voice. 'One of the hotel staff, perhaps?'

'Only a waiter carrying a tray, monsieur.'

'Ah!' said Poirot, in a tone that spoke infinities.

'So that was why he wore his overcoat buttoned up to his chin,' mused Poirot, when we had finally got rid of the excited hotel officials.

'I'm awfully sorry, Poirot,' I murmured, rather crestfallen. 'I thought I'd downed him all right.'

'Yes, that was a Japanese trick, I fancy. Do not distress yourself, *mon ami*. All went according to plan – his plan. That is what I wanted.'

'What's this?' I cried, pouncing on a brown object that lay on the floor.

It was a slim pocketbook of brown leather, and had evidently fallen from our visitor's pocket during his struggle with me. It contained two receipted bills in the name of M. Felix Laon, and a folded-up piece of paper which made my heart beat faster. It was a half sheet of notepaper on which a few words were scrawled in pencil, but they were words of supreme importance.

'The next meeting of the council will be on Friday at 34 rue des Echelles at 11 a.m.'

It was signed with a big figure 4.

And today was Friday, and the clock on the mantelpiece showed the hour to be 10.30.

'My God, what a chance!' I cried. 'Fate is playing into our hands. We must start at once, though. What stupendous luck.'

'So that was why he came,' murmured Poirot. 'I see it all now.'

'See what? Come on, Poirot, don't stay day-dreaming there.'

Poirot looked at me, and slowly shook his head, smiling as he did so.

'"Will you walk into my parlour, said the spider to the fly?" That is your little English nursery rhyme, is it not? No, no – they are subtle – but not so subtle as Hercule Poirot.'

'What on earth are you driving at, Poirot?'

'My friend, I have been asking myself the reason of this morning's visit. Did our visitor really hope to succeed in bribing me? Or, alternatively, in frightening me into abandoning my task? It seemed hardly credible. Why, then, did he come? And now I see the whole plan – very neat – very pretty – the ostensible reason to bribe or frighten me – the necessary struggle which he took no pains to avoid, and which should make the dropped pocketbook natural and reasonable – and finally – the pitfall! Rue des Echelles, 11 a.m.? I think not, *mon ami*! One does not catch Hercule Poirot as easily as that.'

'Good heavens,' I gasped.

Poirot was frowning to himself.

'There is still one thing I do not understand.'

'What is that?'

'The time, Hastings – the time. If they wanted to decoy me away, surely night time would be better? Why this early hour?

Is it possible that something is about to happen this morning? Something which they are anxious Hercule Poirot should not know about?'

He shook his head.

'We shall see. Here I sit, *mon ami*. We do not stir out this morning. We await events here.'

It was at half past eleven exactly that the summons came. A *petit bleu*. Poirot tore it open, then handed it to me. It was from Madame Olivier, the world-famous scientist, whom we had visited yesterday in connection with the Halliday case. It asked us to come out to Passy at once.

We obeyed the summons without an instant's delay. Madame Olivier received us in the same small salon. I was struck anew with the wonderful power of this woman, with her long nun's face and burning eyes – this brilliant successor of Becquerel and the Curies. She came to the point at once.

'Messieurs, you interviewed me yesterday about the disappearance of M. Halliday. I now learn that you returned to the house a second time, and asked to see my secretary, Inez Veroneau. She left the house with you, and has not returned here since.'

'Is that all, madame?'

'No, monsieur, it is not. Last night the laboratory was broken into, and several valuable papers and memoranda were stolen. The thieves had a try for something more precious still, but luckily they failed to open the big safe.'

'Madame, these are the facts of the case. Your late secretary, Madame Veroneau, was really the Countess Rossakoff, an expert thief, and it was she who was responsible for the disappearance of M. Halliday. How long had she been with you?'

'Five months, Monsieur. What you say amazes me.'

'It is true, nevertheless. These papers, were they easy to find? Or do you think an inside knowledge was shown?'

'It is rather curious that the thieves knew exactly where to look. You think Inez –'

'Yes, I have no doubt that it was upon her information that they acted. But what is this precious thing that the thieves failed to find? Jewels?'

Madame Olivier shook her head with a faint smile.

'Something much more precious than that, monsieur.' She

looked round her, then bent forward, lowering her voice. 'Radium, monsieur.'

'Radium?'

'Yes, monsieur. I am now at the crux of my experiments. I possess a small portion of radium myself – more has been lent to me for the process I am at work upon. Small though the actual quantity is, it comprises a large amount of the world's stock and represents a value of millions of francs.'

'And where is it?'

'In its leaden case in the big safe – the safe purposely appears to be of an old and worn-out pattern, but it is really a triumph of the safe-maker's art. That is probably why the thieves were unable to open it.'

'How long are you keeping this radium in your possession?'

'Only for two days more, monsieur. Then my experiments will be concluded.'

Poirot's eyes brightened.

'And Inez Veroneau is aware of the fact? Good – then our friends will come back. Not a word of me to anyone, madame. But rest assured, I will save your radium for you. You have a key of the door leading from the laboratory to the garden?'

'Yes, monsieur. Here it is. I have a duplicate for myself. And here is the key of the garden door leading out into the alleyway between this villa and the next one.'

'I thank you, madame. Tonight, go to bed as usual, have no fears, and leave all to me. But not a word to anyone – not to your two assistants – Mademoiselle Claude and Monsieur Henri, is it not? – particularly not a word to them.'

Poirot left the villa rubbing his hands in great satisfaction.

'What are we going to do now?' I asked.

'Now, Hastings, we are about to leave Paris – for England.'

'What?'

'We will pack our effects, have lunch, and drive to the Gare du Nord.'

'But the radium?'

'I said we were going to leave for England – I did not say we were going to arrive there. Reflect a moment, Hastings. It is quite certain that we are being watched and followed. Our enemies must believe that we are going back to England, and they certainly will not believe that unless they see us get on board the train and start.'

'Do you mean we are to slip off again at the last minute?'

'No, Hastings. Our enemies will be satisfied with nothing less than a *bona fide* departure.'

'But the train doesn't stop until Calais?'

'It will stop if it is paid to do so.'

'Oh, come now, Poirot – surely you can't pay an express to stop – they'd refuse.'

'My dear friend, have you never remarked the little handle – the *signal d'arrêt* – penalty for improper use, 100 francs, I think?'

'Oh! you are going to pull that?'

'Or rather a friend of mine, Pierre Combeau, will do so. Then, while he is arguing with the guard, and making a big scene, and all the train is agog with interest, you and I will fade quietly away.'

We duly carried out Poirot's plan. Pierre Combeau, an old crony of Poirot's, and who evidently knew my little friend's methods pretty well, fell in with the arrangements. The communication cord was pulled just as we got to the outskirts of Paris. Combeau 'made a scene' in the most approved French fashion, and Poirot and I were able to leave the train without anyone being interested in our departure. Our first proceeding was to make a considerable change in our appearance. Poirot had brought the materials for this with him in a small case. Two loafers in dirty blue blouses were the result. We had dinner in an obscure hostelry, and started back to Paris afterwards.

It was close on eleven o'clock when we found ourselves once more in the neighbourhood of Madame Olivier's villa. We looked up and down the road before slipping into the alleyway. The whole place appeared to be perfectly deserted. One thing we could be quite certain of, no one was following us.

'I do not expect them to be here yet,' whispered Poirot to me. 'Possibly they may not come until tomorrow night, but they know perfectly well that there are only two nights on which the radium will be there.'

Very cautiously we turned the key in the garden door. It opened noiselessly and we stepped into the garden.

And then, with complete unexpectedness, the blow fell. In a minute we were surrounded, gagged, and bound. At least ten men must have been waiting for us. Resistance was useless. Like two helpless bundles we were lifted up and carried along. To my intense astonishment, they took us *towards* the house and not away from it. With a key they opened the door into the laboratory and carried us into it. One of the men stooped down before a big safe. The door of it swung open. I felt an unpleasant sensation down my spine. Were they going to bundle us into it, and leave us there to asphyxiate slowly?

However, to my amazement, I saw that from the inside of the safe steps led down beneath the floor. We were thrust down this narrow way and eventually came out into a big subterranean chamber. A woman stood there, tall and imposing, with a black velvet mask covering her face. She was clearly in command of the situation by her gestures of authority. The men slung us down on the floor and left us – alone with the mysterious creature in the mask. I had no doubt who she was. This was the unknown Frenchwoman – Number Three of the Big Four.

She knelt down beside us and removed the gags, but left us bound, then rising and facing us, with a sudden swift gesture she removed her mask.

It was Madame Olivier!

'M. Poirot,' she said, in a low mocking tone. 'The great, the wonderful, the unique, M. Poirot. I sent a warning to you yesterday morning. You chose to disregard it – you thought you could pit your wits against US. And now, you are here!'

There was a cold malignity about her that froze me to the marrow. It was so at variance with the burning fire of her eyes. She was mad – mad – with the madness of genius!

Poirot said nothing. His jaw had dropped, and he was staring at her.

'Well,' she said softly, 'this is the end. We cannot permit our plans to be interfered with. Have you any last request to make?'

Never before, or since, have I felt so near death. Poirot was magnificent. He neither flinched nor paled, just stared at her with unabated interest.

'Your psychology interests me enormously, madame,' he said quietly. 'It is a pity that I have so short a time to devote to studying it. Yes, I have a request to make. A condemned man is always allowed a last smoke, I believe. I have my cigarette case on me. If you would permit –' He looked down at his bonds.

'Oh, yes!' she laughed. 'You would like me to untie your hands, would you not? You are clever, M. Hercule Poirot, I know that. I shall not untie your hands – but I will find you a cigarette.'

She knelt down by him, extracted his cigarette case, took out a cigarette, and placed it between his lips.

'And now a match,' she said, rising.

'It is not necessary, madame.' Something in his voice startled me. She, too, was arrested.

'Do not move, I pray of you, madame. You will regret it if you do. Are you acquainted at all with the properties of curare? The South American Indians use it as an arrow poison. A scratch with it means death. Some tribes use a little blow-pipe – I, too, have a little blow-pipe constructed so as to look exactly like a cigarette. I have only to blow . . . Ah! you start. Do not move, madame. The mechanism of this cigarette is most ingenious. One blows – and a tiny dart resembling a fishbone flies through the air – to find its mark. You do not wish to die, madame. Therefore, I beg of you to release my friend Hastings from his bonds. I cannot use my hands, but I can turn my head – so – you are still covered, madame. Make no mistake, I beg of you.'

Slowly, with shaking hands, and rage and hate convulsing her face, she bent down and did his bidding. I was free. Poirot's voice gave me instructions.

'Your bonds will now do for the lady, Hastings. That is right. Is she securely fastened? Then release me, I pray of you. It is a fortunate circumstance she sent away her henchmen. With a little luck we may hope to find the way out unobstructed.'

In another minute, Poirot stood by my side. He bowed to the lady.

'Hercule Poirot is not killed so easily, madame. I wish you good-night.'

The gag prevented her from replying, but the murderous gleam in her eyes frightened me. I hoped devoutly that we should never fall into her power again.

Three minutes later we were outside the villa, and hurriedly traversing the garden. The road outside was deserted, and we were soon clear of the neighbourhood.

Then Poirot broke out.

'I deserve all that that woman said to me. I am a triple imbecile, a miserable animal, thirty-six times an idiot. I was proud of myself for not falling into their trap. And it was not even meant as a trap – except exactly in the way in which I fell into it. They knew I would see through it – they counted on my seeing through it. This explains all – the ease with which they surrendered. Halliday – everything. Madame Olivier was the ruling spirit – Vera Rossakoff only her lieutenant. Madame needs Halliday's ideas – she herself had the necessary genius to supply the gaps that perplexed him. Yes, Hastings, we know now who Number Three is – the woman who is probably the greatest scientist in the world! Think of it. The brain of the East, the science of the West – and two others whose identities we do not yet know. But we must find out. Tomorrow we will return to London and set about it.'

'You are not going to denounce Madame Olivier to the police?'

'I should not be believed. The woman is one of the idols of France. And we can prove nothing. We are lucky if she does not denounce *us*.'

'What?'

'Think of it. We are found at night upon the premises with keys in our possession which she will swear she never gave us. She surprises us at the safe, and we gag and bind her and make away. Have no illusions, Hastings. The boot is not upon the right leg – is that how you say it?'

CHAPTER 8

IN THE HOUSE OF THE ENEMY

After our adventure in the villa at Passy, we returned post-haste to London. Several letters were awaiting Poirot. He read one of them with a curious smile, and then handed it to me.

'Read this, *mon ami*.'

I turned first to the signature, 'Abe Ryland', and recalled Poirot's words: 'the richest man in the world'. Mr Ryland's letter was curt and incisive. He expressed himself as profoundly dissatisfied with the reason Poirot had given for withdrawing from the South American proposition at the last moment.

'This gives one furiously to think, does it not?' said Poirot.

'I suppose it's only natural he should be a bit ratty.'

'No, no, you comprehend not. Remember the words of Mayerling, the man who took refuge here – only to die by the hands of his enemies. "Number Two is represented by an 'S' with two lines through it – the sign of a dollar; also by two stripes and a star. It may be conjectured therefore that he is an American subject, and that he represents the power of wealth." Add to those words the fact that Ryland offered me a huge sum to tempt me out of England – and – and what about it, Hastings?'

'You mean,' I said, staring, 'that you suspect Abe Ryland, the multi-millionaire, of being Number Two of the Big Four.'

'Your bright intellect has grasped the idea, Hastings. Yes, I do. The tone in which you said multi-millionaire was eloquent but let me impress upon you one fact – this thing is being run by men at the top – and Mr Ryland has the reputation of being no beauty in his business dealings. An able, unscrupulous man, a man who has all the wealth that he needs, and is out for unlimited power.'

There was undoubtedly something to be said for Poirot's view. I asked him when he had made up his mind definitely upon the point.

'That is just it. I am not sure. I cannot be sure. *Mon ami*, I would give anything to *know*. Let me but place Number Two definitely as Abe Ryland, and we draw nearer to our goal.'

'He has just arrived in London, I see by this,' I said, tapping the letter. 'Shall you call upon him, and make your apologies in person?'

'I might do so.'

Two days later, Poirot returned to our rooms in a state of boundless excitement. He grasped me by both hands in his most impulsive manner.

'My friend, an occasion stupendous, unprecedented, never to be repeated, has presented itself! But there is danger, grave danger. I should not even ask you to attempt it.'

If Poirot was trying to frighten me, he was going the wrong way to work, and so I told him. Becoming less incoherent, he unfolded his plan.

It seemed that Ryland was looking for an English secretary, one with a good social manner and presence. It was Poirot's suggestion that I should apply for the post.

'I would do it, myself, *mon ami*,' he explained apologetically. 'But, see you, it is almost impossible for me to disguise myself in the needful manner. I speak the English very well – except when I am excited – but hardly so as to deceive the ear; and even though I were to sacrifice my moustaches, I doubt not but that I should still be recognizable as Hercule Poirot.'

I doubted it also, and declared myself ready and willing to take up the part and penetrate into Ryland's household.

'Ten to one he won't engage me anyway,' I remarked.

'Oh, yes, he will. I will arrange for you such testimonials as shall make him lick his lips. The Home Secretary himself shall recommend you.'

This seemed to be carrying things a bit far, but Poirot waved aside my remonstrances.

'Oh, yes, he will do it. I investigated for him a little matter which might have caused a grave scandal. All was solved with discretion and delicacy, and now, as you would say, he perches upon my hand like the little bird and pecks the crumbs.'

Our first step was to engage the services of an artist in 'make up'. He was a little man, with a quaint bird-like turn of the head, not unlike Poirot's own. He considered me some time in silence, and then fell to work. When I looked at myself in the glass half an hour afterwards, I was amazed. Special shoes caused me to stand at least two inches taller, and the coat I wore was arranged so as to give me a long, lank, weedy look. My eyebrows had been cunningly altered, giving a totally different expression to my face, I wore pads in my cheeks, and the deep tan of my face was a thing of the past. My moustache had gone, and a gold tooth was prominent on one side of my mouth.

'Your name,' said Poirot, 'is Arthur Neville. God guard you, my friend – for I fear that you go into perilous places.'

It was with a beating heart that I presented myself at the Savoy, at an hour named by Mr Ryland, and asked to see the great man.

After being kept waiting a minute or two, I was shown upstairs to his suite.

Ryland was sitting at a table. Spread out in front of him was a letter which I could see out of the tail of my eye was in the Home

Secretary's handwriting. It was my first sight of the American millionaire, and, in spite of myself, I was impressed. He was tall and lean, with a jutting out chin and slightly hooked nose. His eyes glittered cold and grey behind penthouse brows. He had thick grizzled hair, and a long black cigar (without which, I learned later, he was never seen) protruded rakishly from the corner of his mouth.

'Siddown,' he grunted.

I sat. He tapped the letter in front of him.

'According to this piece here, you're the goods all right, and I don't need to look further. Say, are you well up in the social matters?'

I said that I thought I could satisfy him in that respect.

'I mean to say, if I have a lot of dooks and earls and viscounts and suchlike down to the country place I've gotten, you'll be able to sort them out all right and put them where they should be round the dining-table?'

'Oh! quite easily,' I replied, smiling.

We exchanged a few more preliminaries, and then I found myself engaged. What Mr Ryland wanted was a secretary conversant with English society, as he already had an American secretary and a stenographer with him.

Two days later I went down to Hatton Chase, the seat of the Duke of Loamshire, which the American millionaire had rented for a period of six months.

My duties gave me no difficulty whatever. At one period of my life I had been private secretary to a busy member of Parliament, so I was not called upon to assume a role unfamiliar to me. Mr Ryland usually entertained a large party over the weekend, but the middle of the week was comparatively quiet. I saw very little of Mr Appleby, the American secretary, but he seemed a pleasant, normal young American, very efficient in his work. Of Miss Martin, the stenographer, I saw rather more. She was a pretty girl of about twenty-three or four, with auburn hair and brown eyes that could look mischievous enough upon occasion, though they were usually cast demurely down. I had an idea that she both disliked and distrusted her employer, though, of course, she was careful never to hint at anything of the kind, but the time came when I was unexpectedly taken into her confidence.

I had, of course, carefully scrutinized all the members of the household. One or two of the servants had been newly engaged, one of the footmen, I think, and some of the housemaids. The butler, the house keeper, and the chef were the duke's own staff, who had consented to remain on in the establishment. The housemaids I dismissed as unimportant; I scrutinized James, the second footman, very carefully; but it was clear that he was an under-footman and an under-footman only. He had, indeed, been engaged by the butler. A person of whom I was far more suspicious was Deaves, Ryland's valet, whom he had brought over from New York with him. An Englishman by birth, with an irreproachable manner, I yet harboured vague suspicions about him.

I had been at Hatton Chase three weeks and not an incident of any kind had arisen which I could lay my finger on in support of our theory. There was no trace of the activities of the Big Four. Mr Ryland was a man of overpowering force and personality, but I was coming to believe that Poirot had made a mistake when he associated him with that dread organization. I even heard him mention Poirot in a casual way at dinner one night.

'Wonderful little man, they say. But he's a quitter. How do I know? I put him on a deal, and he turned me down the last minute. I'm not taking any more of your Monsieur Hercule Poirot.'

It was at moments such as these that I felt my cheek pads most wearisome!

And then Miss Martin told me a rather curious story. Ryland had gone to London for the day, taking Appleby with him. Miss Martin and I were strolling together in the garden after tea. I liked the girl very much, she was so unaffected and so natural. I could see that there was something on her mind, and at last out it came.

'Do you know, Major Neville,' she said, 'I am really thinking of resigning my post here.'

I looked somewhat astonished, and she went on hurriedly.

'Oh! I know it's a wonderful job to have got, in a way. I suppose most people would think me a fool to throw it up. But I can't stand abuse, Major Neville. To be sworn at like a trooper is more than I can bear. No gentleman would do such a thing.'

'Has Ryland been swearing at you?'

She nodded.

'Of course, he's always rather irritable and short tempered. That one expects. It's all in the day's work. But to fly into such an absolute fury – over nothing at all. He really looked as though he could have murdered me! And, as I say, over nothing at all!'

'Tell me about it?' I said, keenly interested.

'As you know, I open all Mr Ryland's letters. Some I hand on to Mr Appleby, others I deal with myself, but I do all the preliminary sorting. Now there are certain letters that come, written on blue paper, and with a tiny 4 marked on the corner – I beg your pardon, did you speak?'

I had been unable to repress a stifled exclamation, but I hurriedly shook my head, and begged her to continue.

'Well, as I was saying, these letters come, and there are strict orders that they are never to be opened, but to be handed over to Mr Ryland intact. And, of course, I always do so. But there was an unusually heavy mail yesterday morning, and I was opening these letters in a terrific hurry. By mistake I opened one of these letters. As soon as I saw what I had done, I took it to Mr Ryland and explained. To my utter amazement he flew into the most awful rage. As I tell you, I was quite frightened.'

'What was there in the letter, I wonder, to upset him so?'

'Absolutely nothing – that's just the curious part of it. I had read it before I discovered my mistake. It was quite short. I can still remember it word for word, and there was nothing in it that could possibly upset anyone.

'You can repeat it, you say?' I encouraged her.

'Yes.' She paused a minute and then repeated slowly, whilst I noted down the words unobtrusively, the following:

Dear Sir – The essential thing now, I should say, is to see the property. If you insist on the quarry being included, then seventeen thousand seems reasonable. 11 per cent commission too much, 4 per cent is ample.

Yours truly,
Arthur Leversham

Miss Martin went on:

'Evidently about some property Mr Ryland was thinking of buying. But really, I do feel that a man who can get into a rage over such a trifle is, well, dangerous. What do you think I ought to do, Major Neville? You've more experience of the world than I have.'

I soothed the girl down, pointed out to her that Mr Ryland had probably been suffering from the enemy of his race – dyspepsia. In the end I sent her away quite comforted. But I was not so easily satisfied myself. When the girl had gone, and I was alone, I took out my notebook, and ran over the letter which I had jotted down. What did it mean – this apparently innocent-sounding missive? Did it concern some business deal which Ryland was undertaking, and was he anxious that no details about it should leak out until it was carried through? That was a possible explanation. But I remembered the small figure 4 with which the envelopes were marked, and I felt that, at last, I was on the track of the thing we were seeking.

I puzzled over the letter all that evening, and most of the next day – and then suddenly the solution came to me. It was so simple, too. The figure 4 was the clue. Read every fourth word in the letter, and an entirely different message appeared. 'Essential should see you quarry seventeen eleven four.'

The solution of the figures was easy. Seventeen stood for the seventeenth of October – which was tomorrow, eleven was the time, and four was the signature – either referring to the mysterious Number Four himself – or else it was the 'trademark', so to speak, of the Big Four. The quarry was also intelligible. There was a big disused quarry on the estate about half a mile from the house – a lonely spot, ideal for a secret meeting.

For a moment or two I was tempted to run the show myself. It would be such a feather in my cap, for once, to have the pleasure of crowing over Poirot.

But in the end I overcame the temptation. This was a big business – I had no right to play a lone hand, and perhaps jeopardize our chances of success. For the first time, we had stolen a march upon our enemies. We must make good this time – and, disguise the fact as I might, Poirot had the better brain of the two.

I wrote off post-haste to him, laying the facts before him, and explaining how urgent it was that we should overhear what went on at the interview. If he liked to leave it to me, well and good, but

I gave him detailed instructions how to reach the quarry from the station in case he should deem it wise to be present himself.

I took the letter down to the village and posted it myself. I had been able to communicate with Poirot throughout my stay, but we agreed that he should not attempt to communicate with me in case my letters should be tampered with.

I was in a glow of excitement the following evening. No guests were staying in the house, and I was busy with Mr Ryland in his study all the evening. I had foreseen that this would be the case, which was why I had no hope of being able to meet Poirot at the station. I was, however, confident that I would be dismissed well before eleven o'clock.

Sure enough, just after ten-thirty, Mr Ryland glanced at the clock, and announced that he was 'through'. I took the hint and retired discreetly. I went upstairs as though going to bed, but slipped quietly down a side staircase and let myself out into the garden, having taken the precaution to don a dark overcoat to hide my white shirt-front.

I had gone some way down the garden when I chanced to look over my shoulder. Mr Ryland was just stepping out from his study window into the garden. He was starting to keep the appointment. I redoubled my pace, so as to get a clear start. I arrived at the quarry somewhat out of breath. There seemed no one about, and I crawled into a thick tangle of bushes and awaited developments.

Ten minutes later, just on the stroke of eleven, Ryland stalked up, his hat over his eyes and the inevitable cigar in his mouth. He gave a quick look round, and then plunged into the hollows of the quarry below. Presently I heard a low murmur of voices come up to me. Evidently the other man – or men – whoever they were, had arrived first at the rendezvous. I crawled cautiously out of the bushes, and inch by inch, using the utmost precaution against noise, I wormed myself down the steep path. Only a boulder now separated me from the talking men. Secure in the blackness, I peeped round the edge of it and found myself facing the muzzle of a black, murderous-looking automatic!

'Hands up!' said Mr Ryland succinctly. 'I've been waiting for you.'

He was seated in the shadow of the rock, so that I could not see his face, but the menace in his voice was unpleasant. Then I felt a ring of cold steel on the back of my neck, and Ryland lowered his own automatic.

'That's right, George,' he drawled. 'March him around here.'

Raging inwardly, I was conducted to a spot in the shadows, where the unseen George (whom I suspected of being the impeccable Deaves) gagged and bound me securely.

Ryland spoke again in a tone which I had difficulty in recognizing, so cold and menacing was it.

'This is going to be the end of you two. You've got in the way of the Big Four once too often. Ever heard of landslides? There was one about here two years ago. There's going to be another tonight. I've fixed that good and square. Say, that friend of yours doesn't keep his dates very punctually.'

A wave of horror swept over me. Poirot! In another minute he would walk straight into the trap. And I was powerless to warn him. I could only pray that he had elected to leave the matter in my hands, and had remained in London. Surely, if he had been coming, he would have been here by now.

With every minute that passed, my hopes rose.

Suddenly they were dashed to pieces. I heard footsteps – cautious footsteps, but footsteps nevertheless. I writhed in impotent agony. They came down the path, paused and then Poirot himself appeared, his head a little on one side, peering into the shadows.

I heard the growl of satisfaction Ryland gave as he raised the big automatic and shouted, 'Hands up.' Deaves sprang forward as he did so, and took Poirot in the rear. The ambush was complete.

'Pleased to meet you, Mr Hercule Poirot,' said the American grimly.

Poirot's self-possession was marvellous. He did not turn a hair. But I saw his eyes searching in the shadows.

'My friend? He is here?'

'Yes, you are both in the trap – the trap of the Big Four.'

He laughed.

'A trap?' queried Poirot.

'Say, haven't you tumbled to it yet?'

'I comprehend that there is a trap – yes,' said Poirot gently. 'But you are in error, monsieur. It is *you* who are in it – not I and my friend.'

'What?' Ryland raised the big automatic, but I saw his gaze falter.

'If you fire, you commit murder watched by ten pairs of eyes, and you will be hanged for it. This place is surrounded – has been for the last hour – by Scotland Yard men. It is checkmate, Mr Abe Ryland.'

He uttered a curious whistle, and, as though by magic, the place was alive with men. They seized Ryland and the valet and disarmed them. After speaking a few words to the officer in charge, Poirot took me by the arm, and led me away.

Once clear of the quarry he embraced me with vigour.

'You are alive – you are unhurt. It is magnificent. Often have I blamed myself for letting you go.'

'I'm perfectly all right,' I said, disengaging myself. 'But I'm just a bit fogged. You tumbled to their little scheme, did you?'

'But I was waiting for it! For what else did I permit you to go there? Your false name, your disguise, not for a moment was it intended to deceive!'

'What?' I cried. 'You never told me.'

'As I have frequently told you, Hastings, you have a nature so beautiful and so honest that unless you are yourself deceived, it is impossible for you to deceive others. Good, then, you are spotted from the first, and they do what I had counted on their doing – a mathematical certainty to anyone who uses his grey cells properly – use you as a decoy. They set the girl on – By the way, *mon ami*, as an interesting fact psychologically, had she got red hair?'

'If you mean Miss Martin,' I said coldly. 'Her hair is a delicate shade of auburn, but –'

'They are *épatants* – these people! They have even studied your psychology. Oh! yes, my friend, Miss Martin was in the plot – very much so. She repeats the letter to you, together with her tale of Mr Ryland's wrath, you write it down, you puzzle your brains – the cipher is nicely arranged, difficult, but not too difficult – you solve it, and you send for me.

'But what they do not know is that I am waiting for just this very thing to happen. I go post-haste to Japp and arrange things. And so, as you see, all is triumph!'

I was not particularly pleased with Poirot, and I told him so.

We went back to London on a milk train in the early hours of the morning, and a most uncomfortable journey it was.

I was just out of my bath and indulging in pleasurable thoughts of breakfast when I heard Japp's voice in the sitting-room. I threw on a bathrobe and hurried in.

'A pretty mare's nest you've got us into this time,' Japp was saying. 'It's too bad of you, M. Poirot. First time I've ever known you take a toss.'

Poirot's face was a study. Japp went on:

'There were we, taking all this Black Hand stuff seriously – and all the time it was the footman.'

'The footman?' I gasped.

'Yes, James, or whatever his name is. Seems he laid 'em a wager in the servants' hall that he could get taken for the old man by his nibs – that's you, Captain Hastings – and would hand him out a lot of spy stuff about a Big Four gang.'

'Impossible!' I cried.

'Don't you believe it. I marched our gentleman straight to Hatton Chase, and there was the real Ryland in bed and asleep, and the butler and the cook and God knows how many of them to swear to the wager. Just a silly hoax – that's all it was – and the valet is with him.'

'So that was why he kept in the shadow,' murmured Poirot.

After Japp had gone we looked at each other.

'We *know*, Hastings,' said Poirot at last. 'Number Two of the Big Four is Abe Ryland. The masquerading on the part of the footman was to ensure a way of retreat in case of emergencies. And the footman –'

'Yes,' I breathed.

'*Number Four,*' said Poirot gravely.

CHAPTER 9
THE YELLOW JASMINE MYSTERY

It was all very well for Poirot to say that we were acquiring information all the time and gaining an insight into our adversaries' minds – I felt myself that I required some more tangible success than this.

Since we had come into contact with the Big Four, they had committed two murders, abducted Halliday, and had been within an ace of killing Poirot and myself; whereas so far we had hardly scored a point in the game.

Poirot treated my complaints lightly.

'So far, Hastings,' he said, 'they laugh. That is true, but you have a proverb, have you not: "He laughs best who laughs at the end"? And at the end, *mon ami*, you shall see.

'You must remember, too,' he added, 'that we deal with no ordinary criminal, but with the second greatest brain in the world.'

I forebore to pander to his conceit by asking the obvious question. I knew the answer, at least I knew what Poirot's answer would be, and instead I tried without success to elicit some information as to what steps he was taking to track down the enemy. As usual he had kept me completely in the dark as to his movements, but I gathered that he was in touch with secret service agents in India, China, and Russia, and, from his occasional bursts of self-glorification, that he was at least progressing in his favourite game of gauging his enemy's mind.

He had abandoned his private practice almost entirely, and I know that at this time he refused some remarkably handsome fees. True, he would sometimes investigate cases which intrigued him, but he usually dropped them the moment he was convinced that they had no connection with the activities of the Big Four.

This attitude of his was remarkably profitable to our friend, Inspector Japp. Undeniably he gained much kudos for solving several problems in which his success was really due to a half-contemptuous hint from Poirot.

In return for such service Japp supplied full details of any case which he thought might interest the little Belgian, and when he was put in charge of what the newspapers called 'The Yellow Jasmine Mystery', he wired Poirot, asking him whether he would care to come down and look into the case.

It was in response to this wire that, about a month after my adventure in Abe Ryland's house, we found ourselves alone in a railway compartment whirling away from the smoke and dust of London, bound for the little town of Market Handford in Worcestershire, the seat of the mystery.

Poirot leant back in his corner.

'And what exactly is your opinion of the affair, Hastings?'

I did not at once reply to his question; I felt the need of going warily.

'It all seems so complicated,' I said cautiously.

'Does it not?' said Poirot delightedly.

'I suppose our rushing off like this is a pretty clear signal that you consider Mr Paynter's death to be murder – not suicide or the result of an accident?'

'No, no; you misunderstand me, Hastings. Granting that Mr Paynter died as a result of a particularly terrible accident, there are still a number of mysterious circumstances to be explained.'

'That was what I meant when I said it was all so complicated.'

'Let us go over all the main facts quietly and methodically. Recount them to me, Hastings, in an orderly and lucid fashion.'

I started forthwith, endeavouring to be as orderly and lucid as I could.

'We start,' I said, 'with Mr Paynter. A man of fifty-five, rich, cultured, and somewhat of a globe-trotter. For the last twelve years he has been little in England, but, suddenly tiring of incessant travelling, he bought a small place in Worcestershire, near Market Handford, and prepared to settle down. His first action was to write to his only relative, a nephew, Gerald Paynter, the son of his youngest brother, and to suggest to him that he should come and make his home at Croftlands (as the place is called) with his uncle. Gerald Paynter, who is an impecunious young artist, was glad enough to fall in with the arrangement, and had been living with his uncle for about seven months when the tragedy occurred.'

'Your narrative style is masterly,' murmured Poirot. 'I say to myself, it is a book that talks, not my friend Hastings.'

Paying no attention to Poirot, I went on, warming to the story.

'Mr Paynter kept up a fair staff at Croftlands – six servants as well as his own Chinese body servant – Ah Ling.'

'His Chinese servant, Ah Ling,' murmured Poirot.

'On Tuesday last, Mr Paynter complained of feeling unwell after dinner, and one of the servants was despatched to fetch the doctor. Mr Paynter received the doctor in his study, having refused to go to bed. What passed between them was not then known, but before Doctor Quentin left, he asked to see the housekeeper, and mentioned that he had given Mr Paynter a hypodermic injection as his heart was in a very weak state, recommended that he should not be disturbed, and then proceeded to ask some rather curious questions about the servants, how long they had been there, from whom they had come, etc.

'The housekeeper answered these questions as best she could, but was rather puzzled as to their purport. A terrible discovery was made on the following morning. One of the housemaids, on descending, was met by a sickening odour of burned flesh which seemed to come from her master's study. She tried the door, but it was locked on the inside. With the assistance of Gerald Paynter and the Chinaman, that was soon broken in, but a terrible sight greeted them. Mr Paynter had fallen forward into the gas fire, and his face and head were charred beyond recognition.

'Of course, at the moment, no suspicion was aroused as to its being anything but a ghastly accident. If blame attached to anyone, it was to Doctor Quentin for giving his patient a narcotic and leaving him in such a dangerous position. And then a rather curious discovery was made.

'There was a newspaper on the floor, lying where it had slipped from the old man's knees. On turning it over, words were found to be scrawled across it, feebly traced in ink. A writing-table stood close to the chair in which Mr Paynter had been sitting, and the forefinger of the victim's right hand was ink-stained up to the second joint. It was clear that, too weak to hold a pen, Mr Paynter had dipped his finger in the ink-pot and managed to scrawl these two words across the surface of the newspaper he held – but the words themselves seemed utterly fantastic: *Yellow Jasmine* – just that and nothing more.

'Croftlands has a large quantity of yellow jasmine growing up its walls, and it was thought that this dying message had some reference to them, showing that the poor old man's mind was wandering. Of course the newspapers, agog for anything out of the common, took up the story hotly, calling it the Mystery of the Yellow Jasmine – though in all probability the words are completely unimportant.'

'They are unimportant, you say?' said Poirot. 'Well, doubtless, since you say so, it must be so.'

I regarded him dubiously, but I could detect no mockery in his eye.

'And then,' I continued, 'there came the excitements of the inquest.'

'This is where you lick your lips, I perceive.'

'There was a certain amount of feeling evidenced against Dr Quentin. To begin with, he was not the regular doctor, only a locum, putting in a month's work, whilst Dr Bolitho was away on a well-earned holiday. Then it was felt that his carelessness was the direct cause of the accident. But his evidence was little short of sensational. Mr Paynter had been ailing in health since his arrival at Croftlands. Dr Bolitho had attended him for some time, but when Dr Quentin first saw his patient, he was mystified by some of the symptoms. He had only attended him once before the night when he was sent for after dinner. As soon as he was alone with Mr Paynter, the latter had unfolded a surprising tale. To begin with, he was not feeling ill at all, he explained, but the taste of some curry that he had been eating at dinner had struck him as peculiar. Making an excuse to get rid of Ah Ling for a few minutes, he had turned the contents of his plate into a bowl, and he now handed it over to the doctor with injunctions to find out if there were really anything wrong with it.

'In spite of his statement that he was not feeling ill, the doctor noted that the shock of his suspicions had evidently affected him, and that his heart was feeling it. Accordingly he administered an injection – not of a narcotic, but of strychnine.

'That, I think, completes the case – except for *the* crux of the whole thing – the fact that the uneaten curry, duly analysed, was found to contain enough powdered opium to have killed two men!'

I paused.

'And your conclusions, Hastings?' asked Poirot quietly.

'It's difficult to say. It *might* be an accident – the fact that someone attempted to poison him the same night might be merely a coincidence.'

'But you don't think so? You prefer to believe it – murder!'

'Don't you?'

'*Mon ami*, you and I do not reason in the same way. I am not trying to make up my mind between two opposite solutions –

murder or accident – that will come when we have solved the other problem – the mystery of the "Yellow Jasmine". By the way, you have left out something there.'

'You mean the two lines at right angles to each other faintly indicated under the words? I did not think they could be of any possible importance.'

'What you think is always so important to yourself, Hastings. But let us pass from the Mystery of the Yellow Jasmine to the Mystery of the Curry.'

'I know. Who poisoned it? Why? There are a hundred questions one can ask. Ah Ling, of course, prepared it. But why should he wish to kill his master? Is he a member of a *tong*, or something like that? One reads of such things. The *tong* of the Yellow Jasmine, perhaps. Then there is Gerald Paynter.'

I came to an abrupt pause.

'Yes,' said Poirot, nodding his head. 'There is Gerald Paynter, as you say. He is his uncle's heir. He was dining out that night, though.'

'He might have got at some of the ingredients of the curry,' I suggested. 'And he would take care to be out, so as not to have to partake of the dish.'

I think my reasoning rather impressed Poirot. He looked at me with a more respectful attention than he had given me so far.

'He returns late,' I mused, pursuing a hypothetical case. 'Sees the light in his uncle's study, enters, and, finding his plan has failed, thrusts the old man down into the fire.'

'Mr Paynter, who was a fairly hearty man of fifty-five, would not permit himself to be burnt to death without a struggle, Hastings. Such a reconstruction is not feasible.'

'Well, Poirot,' I cried, 'we're nearly there, I fancy. Let us hear what you think?'

Poirot threw me a smile, swelled out his chest, and began in a pompous manner.

'Assuming murder, the question at once arises, why choose that particular method? I can think of only one reason – to confuse identity, the face being charred beyond recognition.'

'What?' I cried. 'You think –'

'A moment's patience, Hastings. I was going on to say that I examine that theory. Is there any ground for believing that the body is not that of Mr Paynter? Is there anyone else whose body it possibly could be? I examine these two questions and finally I answer them both in the negative.'

'Oh!' I said, rather disappointed. 'And then?'

Poirot's eyes twinkled a little.

'And then I say to myself, "since there is here something that I do not understand, it would be well that I should investigate the matter. I must not permit myself to be wholly engrossed by the Big Four." Ah! We are just arriving. My little clothes brush, where does it hide itself? Here it is – brush me down, I pray you, my friend, and then I will perform the same service for you.

'Yes,' said Poirot thoughtfully, as he put away the brush, 'one must not permit oneself to be obsessed by one idea. I have been in danger of that. Figure to yourself, my friend, that even here, in this case, I am in danger of it. Those two lines you mentioned, a downstroke and a line at right angles to it, what are they but the beginning of a 4?'

'Good gracious, Poirot,' I cried, laughing.

'Is it not absurd? I see the hand of the Big Four everywhere, it is well to employ one's wits in a totally different *milieu*. Ah! There is Japp come to meet us.'

CHAPTER 10

WE INVESTIGATE AT CROFTLANDS

The Scotland Yard Inspector was, indeed, waiting on the platform, and greeted us warmly.

'Well, Moosior Poirot, this is good. Thought you'd like to be let in on this. Tip-top mystery, isn't it?'

I read this aright as showing Japp to be completely puzzled and hoping to pick up a pointer from Poirot.

Japp had a car waiting, and we drove up in it to Croftlands. It was a square, white house, quite unpretentious, and covered with creepers, including the starry yellow jasmine. Japp looked up at it as we did.

'Must have been balmy to go writing that, poor old cove,' he remarked. 'Hallucinations, perhaps, and thought he was outside.'

Poirot was smiling at him.

'Which was it, my good Japp?' he asked; 'accident or murder?'

The Inspector seemed a little embarrassed by the question.

'Well, if it weren't for that curry business, I'd be for accident every time. There's no sense in holding a live man's head in the fire – why, he'd scream the house down.'

'Ah!' said Poirot in a low voice. 'Fool that I have been. Triple imbecile! You are a cleverer man than I am, Japp.'

Japp was rather taken aback by the compliment – Poirot being usually given to exclusive self-praise. He reddened and muttered something about there being a lot of doubt about that.

He led the way through the house to the room where the tragedy had occurred – Mr Paynter's study. It was a wide, low room, with book-lined walls and big leather armchairs.

Poirot looked across at once to the window which gave upon a gravelled terrace.

'The window, was it unlatched?' he asked.

'That's the whole point, of course. When the doctor left this room, he merely closed the door behind him. The next morning it was found locked. Who locked it? Mr Paynter? Ah Ling declares that the window was closed and bolted. Dr Quentin, on the other hand, has an impression that it was closed, but not fastened, but he won't swear either way. If he could, it would make a great difference. If the man *was* murdered, someone entered the room either through the door or the window – if through the door, it was an inside job; if through the window, it might have been anyone. First thing when they had broken the door down, they flung the window open, and the housemaid who did it thinks that it wasn't fastened, but she's a precious bad witness – will remember anything you ask her to!'

'What about the key?'

'There you are again. It was on the floor among the wreck-age of the door. Might have fallen from the keyhole, might have been dropped there by one of the people who entered, might have been slipped underneath the door from the out-side.'

'In fact everything is "might have been"?'

'You've hit it, Moosior Poirot. That's just what it is.'

Poirot was looking around him, frowning unhappily.

'I cannot see light,' he murmured. 'Just now – yes, I got a

gleam, but now all is darkness once more. I have not the clue – the motive.'

'Young Gerald Paynter had a pretty good motive,' remarked Japp grimly. 'He's been wild enough in his time, I can tell you. *And* extravagant. You know what artists are, too – no morals at all.'

Poirot did not pay much attention to Japp's sweeping strictures on the artistic temperament. Instead he smiled knowingly.

'My good Japp, is it possible that you throw me the mud in my eyes? I know well enough that it is the Chinaman you suspect. But you are so artful. You want me to help you – and yet you drag the red kipper across the trail.'

Japp burst out laughing.

'That's you all over, Mr Poirot. Yes, I'd bet on the Chink, I'll admit it now. It stands to reason that it was he who doctored the curry, and if he'd try once in an evening to get his master out of the way, he'd try twice.'

'I wonder if he would,' said Poirot softly.

'But it's the motive that beats me. Some heathen revenge or other, I suppose.'

'I wonder,' said Poirot again. 'There has been no robbery? Nothing has disappeared? No jewellery, or money, or papers?'

'No – that is, not exactly.'

I pricked up my ears; so did Poirot.

'There's been no robbery, I mean,' explained Japp. 'But the old boy was writing a book of some sort. We only knew about it this morning when there was a letter from the publishers asking about the manuscript. It was just completed, it seems. Young Paynter and I have searched high and low, but can't find a trace of it – he must have hidden it away somewhere.'

Poirot's eyes were shining with the green light I knew so well.

'How was it called, this book?' he asked.

'*The Hidden Hand in China*, I think it was called.'

'Aha!' said Poirot, with almost a gasp. Then he said quickly, 'Let me see the Chinaman, Ah Ling.'

The Chinaman was sent for and appeared, shuffling along, with his eyes cast down, and his pigtail swinging. His impassive face showed no trace of any kind of emotion.

'Ah Ling,' said Poirot, 'are you sorry your master is dead?'

'I welly sorry. He good master.'

'You know who kill him?'

'I not know. I tell pleeceman if I know.'

The questions and answers went on. With the same impassive face, Ah Ling described how he had made the curry. The cook had had nothing to do with it, he declared, no hand had touched it but his own. I wondered if he saw where his admission was leading him. He stuck to it too, that the window to the garden was bolted that evening. If it was open in the morning, his master must have opened it himself. At last Poirot dismissed him.

'That will do, Ah Ling.' Just as the Chinaman had got to the door, Poirot recalled him. 'And you know nothing, you say, of the Yellow Jasmine?'

'No, what should I know?'

'Nor yet of the sign that was written underneath it?'

Poirot leaned forward as he spoke, and quickly traced something on the dust of a little table. I was near enough to see it before he rubbed it out. A down stroke, a line at right angles, and then a second line down which completed a big 4. The effect on the Chinaman was electrical. For one moment his face was a mask of terror. Then, as suddenly, it was impassive again, and repeating his grave disclaimer, he withdrew.

Japp departed in search of young Paynter, and Poirot and I were left alone together.

'The Big Four, Hastings,' cried Poirot. 'Once again, the Big Four. Paynter was a great traveller. In his book there was doubtless some vital information concerning the doings of Number One, Li Chang Yen, the head and brains of the Big Four.'

'But who – how –'

'Hush, here they come.'

Gerald Paynter was an amiable, rather weak-looking young man. He had a soft brown beard, and a peculiar flowing tie. He answered Poirot's questions readily enough.

'I dined out with some neighbours of ours, the Wycherleys,' he explained. 'What time did I get home? Oh, about eleven. I had a latchkey, you know. All the servants had gone to bed, and I naturally thought my uncle had done the same. As a matter of fact, I did think I caught sight of that soft-footed Chinese beggar, Ah Ling, just whisking round the corner of the hall, but I fancy I was mistaken.'

'When did you last see your uncle, Mr Paynter? I mean before you came to live with him?'

'Oh! not since I was a kid of ten. He and his brother (my father) quarrelled, you know.'

'But he found you again with very little trouble, did he not? In spite of all the years that had passed?'

'Yes, it was quite a bit of luck my seeing the lawyer's advertisement.'

Poirot asked no more questions.

Our next move was to visit Dr Quentin. His story was substantially the same as he had told at the inquest, and he had little to add to it. He received us in his surgery, having just come to the end of his consulting patients. He seemed an intelligent man. A certain primness of manner went well with his pince-nez, but I fancied that he would be thoroughly modern in his methods.

'I wish I could remember about the window,' he said frankly. 'But it's dangerous to think back, one becomes quite positive about something that never existed. That's psychology, isn't it, M. Poirot? You see, I've read all about your methods, and I may say I'm an enormous admirer of yours. No, I suppose it's pretty certain that the Chinaman put the powdered opium in the curry, but he'll never admit it, and we shall never know why. But holding a man down in a fire – that's not in keeping with our Chinese friend's character, it seems to me.'

I commented on this last point to Poirot as we walked down the main street of Market Handford.

'Do you think he let a confederate in?' I asked. 'By the way, I suppose Japp can be trusted to keep an eye on him?' (The Inspector had passed into the police station on some business or other.) 'The emissaries of the Big Four are pretty spry.'

'Japp is keeping an eye on both of them,' said Poirot grimly. 'They have been closely shadowed ever since the body was discovered.'

'Well, at any rate *we* know that Gerald Paynter had nothing to do with it.'

'You always know so much more than I do, Hastings, that it becomes quite fatiguing.'

'You old fox,' I laughed. 'You never will commit yourself.'

'To be honest, Hastings, the case is now quite clear to me – all but the words, *Yellow Jasmine* – and I am coming to agree with you that they have no bearing on the crime. In a case of this kind, you have got to make up your mind who is lying. I have done that. And yet –'

He suddenly darted from my side and entered an adjacent bookshop. He emerged a few minutes later, hugging a parcel. Then Japp rejoined us, and we all sought quarters at the inn.

I slept late the next morning. When I descended to the sitting-room reserved for us, I found Poirot already there, pacing up and down, his face contorted with agony.

'Do not converse with me,' he cried, waving an agitated hand. 'Not until I know that all is well – that the arrest is made. Ah! but my psychology has been weak. Hastings, if a man writes a dying message, it is because it is important. Everyone has said – "Yellow Jasmine? There is yellow jasmine growing up the house – it means nothing."'

'Well, what does it mean? Just what it says. Listen.' He held up a little book he was holding.

'My friend, it struck me that it would be well to inquire into the subject. What exactly is yellow jasmine? This little book has told me. Listen.'

He read.

'*Gelsemini Radix.* Yellow Jasmine. Composition: Alkaloids *gelseminine* $C_{22}H_{26}N_2O_3$, a potent poison acting like coniine; *gelsemine* $C_{12}H_{14}NO_2$, acting like strychnine; *gelsemic acid*, etc. Gelsemium is a powerful depressant to the central nervous system. At a late stage in its action it paralyses the motor nerve endings, and in large doses causes giddiness and loss of muscular power. Death is due to paralysis of the respiratory centre.

'You see, Hastings? At the beginning I had an inkling of the truth when Japp made his remark about a live man being forced into the fire. I realized then that it was a dead man who was burned.'

'But why? What was the point?'

'My friend, if you were to shoot a man, or stab a man after he were dead, or even knock him on the head, it would be apparent that the injuries were inflicted after death. But with his head charred to a cinder, no one is going to hunt about for obscure causes of death, and a man who has apparently just escaped being poisoned at dinner is not likely to be poisoned just afterwards.

Who is lying, that is always the question? I decided to believe Ah Ling –'

'What!' I exclaimed.

'You are surprised, Hastings? Ah Ling knew of the existence of the Big Four, that was evident – so evident that it was clear he knew nothing of their association with the crime until that moment. Had he been the murderer, he would have been able to retain his impassive face perfectly. So I decided, then, to believe Ah Ling, and I fixed my suspicions on Gerald Paynter. It seemed to me that Number Four would have found an impersonation of a long-lost nephew very easy.'

'What!' I cried. 'Number Four?'

'No, Hastings, *not* Number Four. As soon as I had read up the subject of yellow jasmine, I saw the truth. In fact, it leapt to the eye.'

'As always,' I said coldly, 'it doesn't leap to mine.'

'Because you will not use your little grey cells. Who had a chance to tamper with the curry?'

'Ah Ling. No one else.'

'No one else? *What about the doctor?*'

'But that was *afterwards.*'

'Of course it was afterwards. There was no trace of powdered opium in the curry served to Mr Paynter, but acting in obedience to the suspicions Dr Quentin had aroused, the old man eats none of it, and preserves it to give to his medical attendant, whom he summons according to plan. Dr Quentin arrives, takes charge of the curry, *and gives Mr Paynter an injection* – of strychnine, he says, but really of yellow jasmine – a poisonous dose. When the drug begins to take effect, he departs, after unlatching the window. Then, in the night, he returns by the window, finds the manuscript, and shoves Mr Paynter into the fire. He does not heed the newspaper that drops to the floor and is covered by the old man's body. Paynter knew what drug he had been given, and strove to accuse the Big Four of his murder. It is easy for Quentin to mix powdered opium with the curry before handing it over to be analysed. He gives his version of the conversation with the old man, and mentions the strychnine injection casually, in case the mark of the hypodermic needle is noticed. Suspicion at once is divided between accident and the guilt of Ah Ling owing to the poison of the curry.'

'But Dr Quentin cannot be Number Four?'

'I fancy he can. There is undoubtedly a real Dr Quentin who is probably abroad somewhere. Number Four has simply masqueraded as him for a short time. The arrangements with Dr Bolitho were all carried out by correspondence, the man who was to do locum orginally having been taken ill at the last minute.'

At that minute, Japp burst in, very red in the face.

'Have you got him?' cried Poirot anxiously.

Japp shook his head, very out of breath.

'Bolitho came back from his holiday this morning – recalled by telegram. No one knows who sent it. The other man left last night. We'll catch him yet, though.'

Poirot shook his head quietly.

'I think not,' he said, and absentmindedly he drew a big 4 on the table with a fork.

CHAPTER 11

A CHESS PROBLEM

Poirot and I often dined at a small restaurant in Soho. We were there one evening, when we observed a friend at an adjacent table. It was Inspector Japp, and as there was room at our table, he came and joined us. It was some time since either of us had seen him.

'Never do you drop in to see us nowadays,' declared Poirot reproachfully. 'Not since the affair of the Yellow Jasmine have we met, and that is nearly a month ago.'

'I've been up north – that's why. How are things with you? Big Four still going strong – eh?'

Poirot shook a finger at him reproachfully.

'Ah! You mock yourself at me – but the Big Four – they exist.'

'Oh! I don't doubt that – but they're not the hub of the universe, as you make out.'

'My friend, you are very much mistaken. The greatest power for evil in the world today is this "Big Four". To what end they are tending, no one knows, but there has never been another such criminal organization. The finest brain in China at the head of it, an American millionaire, and a French woman scientist as members, and for the fourth –'

Japp interrupted.

'I know – I know. Regular bee in your bonnet over it all. It's becoming your little mania, Moosior Poirot. Let's talk of something else for a change. Take any interest in chess?'

'I have played it, yes.'

'Did you see that curious business yesterday? Match between two players of world-wide reputation, and one died during the game?'

'I saw mention of it. Dr Savaronoff, the Russian champion, was one of the players, and the other, who succumbed to heart failure, was the brilliant young American, Gilmour Wilson.'

'Quite right. Savaronoff beat Rubinstein and became Russian champion some years ago. Wilson was said to be a second Capablanca.'

'A very curious occurrence,' mused Poirot. 'If I mistake not, you have a particular interest in the matter?'

Japp gave a rather embarrassed laugh.

'You've hit it, Moosior Poirot. I'm puzzled. Wilson was sound as a bell – no trace of heart trouble. His death is quite inexplicable.'

'You suspect Dr Savaronoff of putting him out of the way?' I cried.

'Hardly that,' said Japp dryly. 'I don't think even a Russian would murder another man in order not to be beaten at chess – and anyway, from all I can make out, the boot was likely to be on the other leg. The doctor is supposed to be very hot stuff – second to Lasker they say he is.'

Poirot nodded thoughtfully.

'Then what exactly is your little idea?' he asked. 'Why should Wilson be poisoned? For, I assume, of course, that it is poison you suspect.'

'Naturally. Heart failure means your heart stops beating – that's all there is to that. That's what a doctor says officially at the moment, but privately he tips us the wink that he's not satisfied.'

'When is the autopsy to take place?'

'Tonight. Wilson's death was extraordinarily sudden. He seemed quite as usual and was actually moving one of the pieces when he suddenly fell forward – dead!'

'There are very few poisons would act in such a fashion,' objected Poirot.

'I know. The autopsy will help us, I expect. But why should anyone want Gilmour Wilson out of the way – that's what I'd like to know? Harmless, unassuming young fellow. Just come over here from the States, and apparently hadn't an enemy in the world.'

'It seems incredible,' I mused.

'Not at all,' said Poirot, smiling. 'Japp has his theory, I can see.'

'I have, Moosior Poirot. I don't believe the poison was meant for Wilson – it was meant for the other man.'

'Savaronoff?'

'Yes. Savaronoff fell foul of the Bolsheviks at the outbreak of the Revolution. He was even reported killed. In reality he escaped, and for three years endured incredible hardships in the wilds of Siberia. His sufferings were so great that he is now a changed man. His friends and acquaintances declare they would hardly have recognized him. His hair is white, and his whole aspect that of a man terribly aged. He is a semi-invalid, and seldom goes out, living alone with a niece, Sonia Daviloff, and a Russian manservant in a flat down Westminster way. It is possible that he still considers himself a marked man. Certainly he was very unwilling to agree to this chess contest. He refused several times point blank, and it was only when the newspapers took it up and began making a fuss about the "unsportsmanlike refusal" that he gave in. Gilmour Wilson had gone on challenging him with real Yankee pertinacity, and in the end he got his way. Now I ask you, Moosior Poirot, why wasn't he willing? Because he didn't want attention drawn to him. Didn't want somebody or other to get on his track. That's my solution – Gilmour Wilson got pipped by mistake.'

'There is no one who has any private reason to gain by Savaronoff's death?'

'Well, his niece, I suppose. He's recently come into an immense fortune. Left him by Madame Gospoja whose husband was a sugar profiteer under the old regime. They had an affair together once, I believe, and she refused steadfastly to credit the reports of his death.'

'Where did the match take place?'

'In Savaronoff's own flat. He's an invalid, as I told you.'

'Many people there to watch it?'

'At least a dozen – probably more.'

Poirot made an expressive grimace.

'My poor Japp, your task is not an easy one.'

'Once I know definitely that Wilson was poisoned, I can get on.'

'Has it occurred to you that, in the meantime, supposing your assumption that Savaronoff was the intended victim to be correct, the murderer may try again?'

'Of course it has. Two men are watching Savaronoff's flat.'

'That will be very useful if anyone should call with a bomb under his arm,' said Poirot dryly.

'You're getting interested, Moosior Poirot,' said Japp, with a twinkle. 'Care to come round to the mortuary and see Wilson's body before the doctors start on it? Who knows, his tie pin may be askew, and that may give you a valuable clue that will solve the mystery.'

'My dear Japp, all through dinner my fingers have been itching to rearrange your own tie pin. You permit, yes? Ah! that is much more pleasing to the eye. Yes, by all means, let us go to the mortuary.'

I could see that Poirot's attention was completely captivated by this new problem. It was so long since he had shown any interest over any outside case that I was quite rejoiced to see him back in his old form.

For my own part, I felt a deep pity as I looked down upon the motionless form and convulsed face of the hapless young American who had come by his death in such a strange way. Poirot examined the body attentively. There was no mark on it anywhere, except a small scar on the left hand.

'And the doctor says that's a burn, not a cut,' explained Japp.

Poirot's attention shifted to the contents of the dead man's pockets which a constable spread out for our inspection. There was nothing much – a handkerchief, keys, notecase filled with notes, and some unimportant letters. But one object standing by itself filled Poirot with interest.

'A chessman!' he exclaimed. 'A white bishop. Was that in his pocket?'

'No, clasped in his hand. We had quite a difficulty to get it out of his fingers. It must be returned to Dr Savaronoff sometime. It's part of a very beautiful set of carved ivory chessmen.'

'Permit me to return it to him. It will make an excuse for my going there.'

'Aha!' cried Japp. 'So you want to come in on this case?'

'I admit it. So skilfully have you aroused my interest.'

'That's fine. Got you away from your brooding. Captain Hastings is pleased, too, I can see.'

'Quite right,' I said, laughing.

Poirot turned back towards the body.

'No other little detail you can tell me about – him?' he asked.

'I don't think so.'

'Not even – that he was left-handed?'

'You're a wizard, Moosior Poirot. How did you know that? He *was* left-handed. Not that it's anything to do with the case.'

'Nothing whatever,' agreed Poirot hastily, seeing that Japp was slightly ruffled. 'My little joke – that was all. I like to play you the trick, see you.'

We went out upon an amicable understanding.

The following morning saw us wending our way to Dr Savaronoff's flat in Westminster.

'Sonia Daviloff,' I mused. 'It's a pretty name.'

Poirot stopped, and threw me a look of despair.

'Always looking for romance! You are incorrigible. It would serve you right if Sonia Daviloff turned out to be our friend and enemy the Countess Vera Rossakoff.'

At the mention of the countess, my face clouded over.

'Surely, Poirot, you don't suspect –'

'But, no, no. It was a joke! I have not the Big Four on the brain to that extent, whatever Japp may say.'

The door of the flat was opened to us by a man-servant with a peculiarly wooden face. It seemed impossible to believe that that impassive countenance could ever display emotion.

Poirot presented a card on which Japp had scribbled a few words of introduction, and we were shown into a low, long room furnished with rich hangings and curios. One or two wonderful ikons hung upon the walls, and exquisite Persian rugs lay upon the floor. A samovar stood upon a table.

I was examining one of the ikons which I judged to be of considerable value, and turned to see Poirot prone upon the floor. Beautiful as the rug was, it hardly seemed to me to necessitate such close attention.

'Is it such a very wonderful specimen?' I asked.

'Eh? Oh! the rug? But no, it was not the rug I was remarking. But it *is* a beautiful specimen, far too beautiful to have a large nail wantonly driven through the middle of it. No, Hastings,' as I came forward, 'the nail is not there now. But the hole remains.'

A sudden sound behind us made me spin round, and Poirot sprang nimbly to his feet. A girl was standing in the doorway. Her eyes, full upon us, were dark with suspicion. She was of medium height, with a beautiful, rather sullen face, dark blue eyes, and very black hair which was cut short. Her voice, when she spoke, was rich and sonorous, and completely un-English.

'I fear my uncle will be unable to see you. He is a great invalid.'

'That is a pity, but perhaps you will kindly help me instead. You are Mademoiselle Daviloff, are you not?'

'Yes, I am Sonia Daviloff. What is it you want to know?'

'I am making some inquiries about that sad affair the night before last – the death of M. Gilmour Wilson. What can you tell me about it?'

The girl's eyes opened wide.

'He died of heart failure – as he was playing chess.'

'The police are not so sure that it was – heart failure, mademoiselle.'

The girl gave a terrified gesture.

'It was true then,' she cried. 'Ivan was right.'

'Who is Ivan, and why do you say he was right?'

'It was Ivan who opened the door to you – and he has already said to me that in his opinion Gilmour Wilson did not die a natural death – that he was poisoned by mistake.'

'By mistake.'

'Yes, the poison was meant for my uncle.'

She had quite forgotten her first distrust now, and was speaking eagerly.

'Why do you say that, mademoiselle? Who should wish to poison Dr Savaronoff?'

She shook her head.

'I do not know. I am in the dark. And my uncle, he will not trust me. It is natural, perhaps. You see, he hardly knows me. He saw me as a child, and not since till I came to live with him here in London. But this much I do know, he is in fear of something. We have many secret societies in Russia, and one day I overheard something which made me think it was of just such a society he went in fear. Tell me, monsieur' – she came a step nearer, and dropped her voice – 'have you ever heard of a society called the "Big Four"?'

Poirot jumped nearly out of his skin. His eyes positively bulged with astonishment.

'Why do you – what do you know of the Big Four, mademoiselle?'

'There is such an association, then! I overheard a reference to them, and asked my uncle about it afterwards. Never have I seen a man so afraid. He turned all white and shaking. He was in fear of them, monsieur, in great fear, I am sure of it. And, by mistake, they killed the American, Wilson.'

'The Big Four,' murmured Poirot. 'Always the Big Four! An astonishing coincidence, mademoiselle, your uncle is still in danger. I must save him. Now recount to me exactly the events of that fatal evening. Show me the chessboard, the table, how the two men sat – everything.'

She went to the side of the room and brought out a small table. The top of it was exquisite, inlaid with squares of silver and black to represent a chessboard.

'This was sent to my uncle a few weeks ago as a present, with the request that he would use it in the next match he played. It was in the middle of the room – so.'

Poirot examined the table with what seemed to me quite unnecessary attention. He was not conducting the inquiry at all as I would have done. Many of the questions seemed to me pointless, and upon really vital matters he seemed to have no questions to ask. I concluded that the unexpected mention of the Big Four had thrown him completely off his balance.

After a minute examination of the table and the exact position it had occupied, he asked to see the chessmen. Sonia Daviloff brought them to him in a box. He examined one or two of them in a perfunctory manner.

'An exquisite set,' he murmured absentmindedly.

Still not a question as to what refreshments there had been, or what people had been present.

I cleared my throat significantly.

'Don't you think, Poirot, that –'

He interrupted me peremptorily.

'Do not think, my friend. Leave all to me. Mademoiselle, is it quite impossible that I should see your uncle?'

A faint smile showed itself on her face.

'He will see you, yes. You understand, it is my part to interview all strangers first.'

She disappeared. I heard a murmur of voices in the next room, and a minute later she came back and motioned us to pass into the adjoining room.

The man who lay there on a couch was an imposing figure. Tall, gaunt, with huge bushy eyebrows and white beard, and a face haggard as the result of starvation and hardships, Dr Savaronoff was a distinct personality. I noted the peculiar formation of his head, its unusual height. A great chess player must have a great brain, I knew. I could easily understand Dr Savaronoff being the second greatest player in the world.

Poirot bowed.

'M. le Docteur, may I speak to you alone?'

Savaronoff turned to his niece.

'Leave us, Sonia.'

She disappeared obediently.

'Now, sir, what is it?'

'Dr Savaronoff, you have recently come into an enormous fortune. If you should – die unexpectedly, who inherits it?'

'I have made a will leaving everything to my niece, Sonia Daviloff. You do not suggest –'

'I suggest nothing, but you have not seen your niece since she was a child. It would have been easy for anyone to imperson-ate her.'

Savaronoff seemed thunderstruck by the suggestion. Poirot went on easily.

'Enough as to that: I give you the word of warning, that is all.

What I want you to do now is to describe to me the game of chess the other evening.'

'How do you mean – describe it?'

'Well, I do not play the chess myself, but I understand that there are various regular ways of beginning – the gambit, do they not call it?'

Dr Savaronoff smiled a little.

'Ah! I comprehend you now. Wilson opened Ruy Lopez – one of the soundest openings there is, and one frequently adopted in tournaments and matches.'

'And how long had you been playing when the tragedy happened?'

'It must have been about the third or fourth move when Wilson suddenly fell forward over the table, stone dead.'

Poirot rose to depart. He flung out his last question as though it was of absolutely no importance, but I knew better.

'Had he anything to eat or drink?'

'A whisky and soda, I think.'

'Thank you, Dr Savaronoff. I will disturb you no longer.'

Ivan was in the hall to show us out. Poirot lingered on the threshold.

'The flat below this, do you know who lives there?'

'Sir Charles Kingwell, a member of Parliament, sir. It has been let furnished lately, though.'

'Thank you.'

We went out into the bright winter sunlight.

'Well, really, Poirot,' I burst out. 'I don't think you've distinguished yourself this time. Surely your questions were very inadequate.'

'You think so, Hastings?' Poirot looked at me appealingly. 'I was *bouleversé*, yes. What would you have asked?'

I considered the question carefully, and then outlined my scheme to Poirot. He listened with what seemed to be close interest. My monologue lasted until we had nearly reached home.

'Very excellent, very searching, Hastings,' said Poirot, as he inserted his key in the door and preceded me up the stairs. 'But quite unnecessary.'

'Unnecessary!' I cried, amazed. 'If the man was poisoned –'

'Aha,' cried Poirot, pouncing upon a note which lay on the table.

'From Japp. Just as I thought.' He flung it over to me. It was brief and to the point. No traces of poison had been found, and there was nothing to show how the man came by his death.

'You see,' said Poirot, 'our questions would have been quite unnecessary.'

'You guessed this beforehand?'

'"Forecast the probable result of the deal,"' quoted Poirot from a recent Bridge problem on which I had spent much time. '*Mon ami*, when you do that successfully, you do not call it guessing.'

'Don't let's split hairs,' I said impatiently. 'You foresaw this?'

'I did.'

'Why?'

Poirot put his hand into his pocket and pulled out – a white bishop.

'Why,' I cried, 'you forgot to give it back to Dr Savaronoff.'

'You are in error, my friend. That bishop still reposes in my left-hand pocket. I took its fellow from the box of chessmen Mademoiselle Daviloff kindly permitted me to examine. The plural of one bishop is two bishops.'

He sounded the final 's' with a great hiss. I was completely mystified.

'But why did you take it?'

'*Parbleu*, I wanted to see if they were exactly alike.'

Poirot looked at them with his head on one side.

'They seem so, I admit. But one should take no fact for granted until it is proved. Bring me, I pray you, my little scales.'

With infinite care he weighed the two chessmen, then turned to me with a face alight with triumph.

'I was right. See you, I was right. Impossible to deceive Hercule Poirot!'

He rushed to the telephone – waited impatiently.

'Is that Japp? Ah! Japp, it is you. Hercule Poirot speaks. Watch the manservant. Ivan. On no account let him slip through your fingers. Yes, yes, it is as I say.'

He dashed down the receiver and turned to me.

'You see it not, Hastings? I will explain. Wilson was not poisoned, he was electrocuted. A thin metal rod passes up the middle of one of those chessmen. The table was prepared beforehand and set upon a certain spot on the floor. When the bishop was placed upon one of the silver squares, the current passed through Wilson's body, killing him instantly. The only mark was the electric burn upon his hand – his left hand, because he was left-handed. The "special table" was an extremely cunning piece of mechanism. The table I examined was a duplicate, perfectly innocent. It was substituted for the other immediately after the murder. The thing was worked from the flat below, which, if you remember, was let furnished. But one accomplice at least was in Savaronoff's flat. The girl is an agent of the Big Four, working to inherit Savaronoff's money.'

'And Ivan?'

'I strongly suspect that Ivan is none other than the famous Number Four.'

'*What?*'

'Yes. The man is a marvellous character actor. He can assume any part he pleases.'

I thought back over past adventures, the lunatic asylum keeper, the butcher's young man, the suave doctor, all the same man, and all totally unlike each other.

'It's amazing,' I said at last. 'Everything fits in. Savaronoff had an inkling of the plot, and that's why he was so averse to playing the match.'

Poirot looked at me without speaking. Then he turned abruptly away, and began pacing up and down.

'Have you a book on chess by any chance, *mon ami*?' he asked suddenly.

'I believe I have somewhere.'

It took me some time to ferret it out, but I found it at last, and brought it to Poirot, who sank down in a chair and started reading it with the greatest attention.

In about a quarter of an hour the telephone rang. I answered it. It was Japp. Ivan had left the flat, carrying a large bundle. He had sprung into a waiting taxi, and the chase had begun. He was evidently trying to lose his pursuers. In the end he seemed to fancy that he had done so, and had then driven to a big empty house at Hampstead. The house was surrounded.

I recounted all this to Poirot. He merely stared at me as though he scarcely took in what I was saying. He held out the chess book.

'Listen to this, my friend. This is the Ruy Lopez opening. 1 P-K4, P-K4; 2 Kt-KB3, K-QB3; 3 B-Kt5. Then there comes a question as to Black's best third move. He has the choice of various defences. It was White's third move that killed Gilmour Wilson, 3 B-Kt5. Only the third move – does that say nothing to you?'

I hadn't the least idea what he meant, and told him so.

'Suppose, Hastings, that, while you were sitting in this chair, you heard the front door being opened and shut, what would you think?'

'I should think someone had gone out, I suppose.'

'Yes – but there are always two ways of looking at things. Someone gone out – someone come *in* – two totally different things, Hastings. But if you assumed the wrong one, presently some little discrepancy would creep in and show you that you were on the wrong track.'

'What does all this mean, Poirot?'

Poirot sprang to his feet with sudden energy.

'It means that I have been a triple imbecile. Quick, quick, to the flat in Westminster. We may yet be in time.'

We tore off in a taxi. Poirot returned no answer to my excited questions. We raced up the stairs. Repeated rings and knocks brought no reply, but listening closely I could distinguish a hollow groan coming from within.

The hall porter proved to have a master key, and after a few difficulties he consented to use it.

Poirot went straight to the inner room. A whiff of chloroform met us. On the floor was Sonia Daviloff, gagged and bound, with a great wad of saturated cotton-wool over her nose and mouth. Poirot tore it off and began to take measures to restore her. Presently a doctor arrived, and Poirot handed her over to his charge and drew aside with me. There was no sign of Dr Savaronoff.

'What does it all mean?' I asked, bewildered.

'It means that before two equal deductions I chose the wrong one. You heard me say that it would be easy for anyone to impersonate Sonia Daviloff because her uncle had not seen her for so many years?'

'Yes?'

'Well, precisely the opposite held good also. It was equally easy for anyone to impersonate the uncle.'

'What?'

'Savaronoff *did* die at the outbreak of the Revolution. The man who pretended to have escaped with such terrible hardships, the man so changed "that his own friends could hardly recognize him", the man who successfully laid claim to an enormous fortune –'

'Yes. Who was he?'

'*Number Four*. No wonder he was frightened when Sonia let him know she had overheard one of his private conversations about the "Big Four". Again he has slipped through my fingers. He guessed I should get on the right track in the end, so he sent off the honest Ivan on a tortuous wild goose chase, chloroformed the girl, and got out, having by now doubtless realized most of the securities left by Madame Gospoja.'

'But – but who tried to kill him then?'

'Nobody tried to kill *him*. Wilson was the intended victim all along.'

'But why?'

'My friend, Savaronoff was the second greatest chess player in the world. In all probability Number Four did not even know the rudiments of the game. Certainly he could not sustain the fiction of a match. He tried all he knew to avoid the contest. When that failed, Wilson's doom was sealed. At all costs he must be prevented from discovering that the great Savaronoff did not even know how to play chess. Wilson was fond of the Ruy Lopez opening, and was certain to use it. Number Four arranged for death to come with the third move, before any complications of defence set in.'

'But, my dear Poirot,' I persisted, 'are we dealing with a lunatic? I quite follow your reasoning, and admit that you must be right, but to kill a man just to sustain his role! Surely there were simpler ways out of the difficulty than that? He could have said that his doctor forbade the strain of a match.'

Poirot wrinkled his forehead.

'*Certainement*, Hastings,' he said, 'there were other ways, but none so convincing. Besides, you are assuming that to kill a man is a thing to avoid, are you not? Number Four's mind, it does not act that way. I put myself in his place, a thing impossible for you. I picture his thoughts. He enjoys himself as the professor at that match, I doubt not he has visited the chess tourneys to study his part. He sits and frowns in thought; he gives the impression that he is thinking great plans, and all the time he laughs in himself. He is aware that two moves are all that he knows – and all that he *need know*. Again, it would appeal to his mind to foresee the time that suits Number Four . . . Oh, yes, Hastings, I begin to understand our friend and his psychology.'

I shrugged.

'Well, I suppose you're right, but I can't understand anyone running a risk he could so easily avoid.'

'Risk!' Poirot snorted. 'Where then lay the risk? Would Japp have solved the problem? No; if Number Four had not made one small mistake he would have run no risk.'

'And his mistake?' I asked, although I suspected the answer.

'*Mon ami*, he overlooked the little grey cells of Hercule Poirot.'

Poirot has his virtues, but modesty is not one of them.

CHAPTER 12

THE BAITED TRAP

It was mid-January – a typical English winter day in London, damp and dirty. Poirot and I were sitting in two chairs well drawn up to the fire. I was aware of my friend looking at me with a quizzical smile, the meaning of which I could not fathom.

'A penny for your thoughts,' I said lightly.

'I was thinking, my friend, that at midsummer, when you first arrived, you told me that you proposed to be in this country for a couple of months only.'

'Did I say that?' I asked, rather awkwardly. 'I don't remember.'

Poirot's smile broadened.

'You did, *mon ami*. Since then, you have changed your plan, is it not so?'

'Er – yes, I have.'

'And why is that?'

'Dash it all, Poirot, you don't think I'm going to leave you all alone when you're up against a thing like the "Big Four", do you?'

Poirot nodded gently.

'Just as I thought. You are a staunch friend, Hastings. It is to serve me that you remain on here. And your wife – little Cinderella as you call her, what does she say?'

'I haven't gone into details, of course, but she understands. She'd be the last one to wish me to turn my back on a pal.'

'Yes, yes, she, too, is a loyal friend. But it is going to be a long business, perhaps.'

I nodded, rather discouraged.

'Six months already,' I mused, 'and where are we? You know, Poirot, I can't help thinking that we ought to – well, to do something.'

'Always so energetic, Hastings! And what precisely would you have me do?'

This was somewhat of a poser, but I was not going to withdraw from my position.

'We ought to take the offensive,' I urged. 'What have we done all this time?'

'More than you think, my friend. After all, we have established the identity of Number Two and Number Three, and we have learnt more than a little about the ways and methods of Number Four.'

I brightened up a little. As Poirot put it, things didn't sound so bad.

'Oh! Yes, Hastings, we have done a great deal. It is true that I am not in a position to accuse either Ryland or Madame Olivier – who would believe me? You remember I thought once I had Ryland successfully cornered? Nevertheless I have made my suspicions known in certain quarters – the highest – Lord Aldington, who enlisted my help in the matter of the stolen submarine plans, is fully cognizant of all my information respecting the Big Four – and while others may doubt, he believes. Ryland and Madame Olivier, and Li Chang Yen himself may go their ways, but there is a searchlight turned on all their movements.'

'And Number Four?' I asked.

'As I said just now – I am beginning to know and understand his methods. You may smile, Hastings – but to penetrate a man's personality, to know exactly what he will do under any given circumstances – that is the beginning of success. It is a duel between us, and whilst he is constantly giving away his mentality to me, I endeavour to let him know little or nothing of mine. He is in the light, I in the shade. I tell you, Hastings, that every day they fear me the more for my chosen inactivity.'

'They've let us alone, anyway,' I observed. 'There have been no more attempts on your life, and no ambushes of any kind.'

'No,' said Poirot thoughtfully. 'On the whole, that rather surprises me. Especially as there are one or two fairly obvious ways of getting at us which I should have thought certain to have occurred to them. You catch my meaning, perhaps?'

'An infernal machine of some kind?' I hazarded.

Poirot made a sharp click with his tongue expressive of impatience.

'But no! I appeal to your imagination, and you can suggest nothing more subtle than bombs in the fireplace. Well, well, I have need of some matches, I will promenade myself despite the weather. Pardon, my friend, but it is possible that you read *The Future of the Argentine*, *Mirror of Society*, *Cattle Breeding*, *The Clue of Crimson* and *Sport in the Rockies* at one and the same time?'

I laughed, and admitted that *The Clue of Crimson* was at present engaging my sole attention. Poirot shook his head sadly.

'But replace then the others on the bookshelf! Never, never shall I see you embrace the order and the method. *Mon Dieu*, what then is a bookshelf for?'

I apologized humbly, and Poirot, after replacing the offending volumes, each in its appointed place, went out and left me to uninterrupted enjoyment of my selected book.

I must admit, however, that I was half asleep when Mrs Pearson's knock at the door aroused me.

'A telegram for you, captain.'

I tore the orange envelope open without much interest.

Then I sat as though turned to stone.

It was a cable from Bronsen, my manager out at the South American ranch, and it ran as follows:

Mrs Hastings disappeared yesterday, feared been kidnapped by some gang calling itself big four cable instructions have notified police but no clue as yet Bronsen.

I waved Mrs Pearson out of the room, and sat as though stunned, reading the words over and over again. Cinderella – kidnapped!

In the hands of the imfamous Big Four! God, what could I do?

Poirot! I must have Poirot. He would advise me. He would checkmate them somehow. In a few minutes now, he would be back. I must wait patiently until then. But Cinderella – in the hands of the Big Four!

Another knock. Mrs Pearson put her head in once more.

'A note for you, captain – brought by a heathen Chinaman. He's a-waiting downstairs.'

I seized it from her. It was brief and to the point.

'If you ever wish to see your wife again, go with the bearer of this note immediately. Leave no message for your friend or she will suffer.'

It was signed with a big 4.

What ought I to have done? What would you who read have done in my place?

I had no time to think. I saw only one thing – Cinderella in the power of those devils. I must obey – I dare not risk a hair of her head. I must go with this Chinaman and follow whither he led. It was a trap, yes, and it meant certain capture and possible death, but it was baited with the person dearest to me in the whole world, and I dared not hesitate.

What irked me most was to leave no word for Poirot. Once set him on my track, and all might yet be well! Dare I risk it? Apparently I was under no supervision, but yet I hesitated. It would have been so easy for the Chinaman to come up and assure himself that I was keeping to the letter of the command. Why didn't he? His very abstention made me more suspicious. I had seen so much of the omnipotence of the Big Four that I credited them with almost superhuman powers. For all I know, even the little bedraggled servant girl might be one of their agents.

No, I dared not risk it. But one thing I could do, leave the telegram. He would know then that Cinderella had disappeared, and who was responsible for her disappearance.

All this passed through my head in less time than it takes to tell, and I had clapped my hat on my head and was descending the stairs to where my guide waited, in a little over a minute.

The bearer of the message was a tall impassive Chinaman, neatly but rather shabbily dressed. He bowed and spoke to me.

His English was perfect, but he spoke with a slight sing-song intonation.

'You Captain Hastings?'

'Yes,' I said.

'You give me note, please.'

I had foreseen the request, and handed him over the scrap of paper without a word. But that was not all.

'You have a telegram today, yes? Come along just now? From South America, yes?'

I realized anew the excellence of their espionage system – or it might have been a shrewd guess. Bronsen was bound to cable me. They would wait until the cable was delivered and would strike hard upon it.

No good could come of denying what was palpably true.

'Yes,' I said. 'I did get a telegram.'

'You fetch him, yes? Fetch him now.'

I ground my teeth, but what could I do? I ran upstairs again. As I did so, I thought of confiding in Mrs Pearson, at any rate as far as Cinderella's disappearance went. She was on the landing, but close behind her was the little maidservant, and I hesitated. If she *was* a spy – the words of the note danced before my eyes: '. . . she will suffer . . .' I passed into the sitting-room without speaking.

I took up the telegram and was about to pass out again when an idea struck me. Could I not leave some sign which would mean nothing to my enemies but which Poirot himself would find significant. I hurried across to the bookcase and tumbled out four books on to the floor. No fear of Poirot's not seeing them. They would outrage his eyes immediately – and coming on top of his little lecture, surely he would find them unusual. Next I put a shovelful of coal on the fire and managed to spill four knobs into the grate. I had done all I could – pray Heaven Poirot would read the sign aright.

I hurried down again. The Chinaman took the telegram from me, read it, then placed it in his pocket and with a nod beckoned me to follow him.

It was a long weary march that he led me. Once we took a bus and once we went for some considerable way in a tram, and always our route led us steadily eastward. We went through strange districts, whose existence I had never dreamed of. We were down by the docks now, I knew, and I realized that I was being taken into the heart of Chinatown.

In spite of myself I shivered. Still my guide plodded on, turning and twisting through mean streets and byways, until at last he stopped at a dilapidated house and rapped four times upon the door.

It was opened immediately by another Chinaman who stood aside to let us pass in. The clanging to of the door behind me was the knell of my last hopes. I was indeed in the hands of the enemy.

I was now handed over to the second Chinaman. He led me down some rickety stairs and into a cellar which was filled with bales and casks and which exhaled a pungent odour, as of eastern spices. I felt wrapped all round with the atmosphere of the East, tortuous, cunning, sinister –

Suddenly my guide rolled aside two of the casks, and I saw a low tunnel-like opening in the wall. He motioned me to go ahead. The tunnel was of some length, and it was too low for me to stand upright. At last, however, it broadened out into a passage, and a few minutes later we stood in another cellar.

My Chinaman went forward, and rapped four times on one of the walls. A whole section of the wall swung out, leaving a narrow doorway. I passed through, and to my utter astonishment found myself in a kind of Arabian Nights' palace. A low long subterranean chamber hung with rich oriental silks, brilliantly lighted and fragrant with perfumes and spices. There were five or six silk-covered divans, and exquisite carpets of Chinese workmanship covered the ground. At the end of the room was a curtained recess. From behind these curtains came a voice.

'You have brought our honoured guest?'

'Excellency, he is here,' replied my guide.

'Let our guest enter,' was the answer.

At the same moment, the curtains were drawn aside by an unseen hand, and I was facing an immense cushioned divan on which sat a tall thin Oriental dressed in wonderfully embroidered robes, and clearly, by the length of his finger nails, a great man.

'Be seated, I pray you, Captain Hastings,' he said, with a wave of his hand. 'You acceded to my request to come immediately, I am glad to see.'

'Who are you?' I asked. 'Li Chang Yen?'

'Indeed no, I am but the humblest of the master's servants. I carry out his behests, that is all – as do other of his servants in other countries – in South America, for instance.'

I advanced a step.

'Where is she? What have you done with her out there?'

'She is in a place of safety – where none will find her. As yet, she is unharmed. You observe that I say – *as yet*!'

Cold shivers ran down my spine as I confronted this smiling devil.

'What do you want?' I cried. 'Money?'

'My dear Captain Hastings. We have no designs on your small savings, I can assure you. Not – pardon me – a very intelligent suggestion on your part. Your colleague would not have made it, I fancy.'

'I suppose,' I said heavily, 'you wanted to get me into your toils. Well, you have succeeded. I have come here with my eyes open. Do what you like with me, and let her go. She knows nothing, and she can be no possible use to you. You've used her to get hold of me – you've got me all right, and that settles it.'

The smiling Oriental caressed his smooth cheek, watching me obliquely out of his narrow eyes.

'You go too fast,' he said purringly. 'That does not quite – settle it. In fact, to "get hold of you" as you express it, is not really our objective. But through you, we hope to get hold of your friend, M. Hercule Poirot.'

'I'm afraid you won't do that,' I said, with a short laugh.

'What I suggest is this,' continued the other, his words running on as though he had not heard me. 'You will write M. Hercule Poirot a letter, such a letter as will induce him to hasten thither and join you.'

'I shall do no such thing,' I said angrily.

'The consequences of refusal will be disagreeable.'

'Damn your consequences.'

'The alternative might be death!'

A nasty shiver ran down my spine, but I endeavoured to put a bold face upon it.

'It's no good threatening me, and bullying me. Keep your threats for Chinese cowards.'

'My threats are very real ones, Captain Hastings. I ask you again, will you write this letter?'

'I will not, and what's more, you daren't kill me. You'd have the police on your tracks in no time.'

My interlocutor clapped his hands swiftly. Two Chinese attendants appeared as it were out of the blue, and pinioned me by both arms. Their master said something rapidly to them in Chinese, and they dragged me across the floor to a spot in one corner of the big chamber. One of them stooped, and suddenly, without the least warning, the flooring gave beneath my feet. But for the restraining hand of the other man I should have gone down the yawning gap beneath me. It was inky black, and I could hear the rushing of water.

'The river,' said my questioner from his place on the divan. 'Think well, Captain Hastings. If you refuse again, you go headlong to eternity, to meet your death in the dark waters below. For the last time, will you write that letter?'

I'm not braver than most men. I admit frankly that I was scared to death, and in a blue funk. That Chinese devil meant business, I was sure of that. It was goodbye to the good old world. In spite of myself, my voice wobbled a little as I answered.

'For the last time, no! To hell with your letter!'

Then involuntarily I closed my eyes and breathed a short prayer.

CHAPTER 13
THE MOUSE WALKS IN

Not often in a lifetime does a man stand on the edge of eternity, but when I spoke those words in that East End cellar I was perfectly certain that they were my last words on earth. I braced myself for the shock of those black, rushing waters beneath, and experienced in advance the horror of that breath-choking fall.

But to my surprise a low laugh fell on my ears. I opened my eyes. Obeying a sign from the man on the divan, my two jailers brought me back to my old seat facing him.

'You are a brave man, Captain Hastings,' he said. 'We of the East appreciate bravery. I may say that I expected you to act as you have done. That brings us to the appointed second act of your little drama. Death for yourself you have faced – will you face death for another?'

'What do you mean?' I asked hoarsely, a horrible fear creeping over me.

'Surely you have not forgotten the lady who is in our power – the Rose of the Garden.'

I stared at him in dumb agony.

'I think, Captain Hastings, that you will write that letter. See, I have a cable form here. The message I shall write on it depends on you, and means life or death for your wife.'

The sweat broke out on my brow. My tormentor continued, smiling amiably, and speaking with perfect sangfroid:

'There, captain, the pen is ready to your hand. You have only to write. If not –'

'If not?' I echoed.

'If not, that lady that you love dies – and dies slowly. My master, Li Chang Yen, amuses himself in his spare hours by devising new and ingenious methods of torture –'

'My God!' I cried. 'You fiend! Not that – you wouldn't do that –'

'Shall I recount to you some of his devices?'

Without heeding my cry of protest, his speech flowed on – evenly, serenely – till with a cry of horror I clapped my hands to my ears.

'It is enough, I see. Take up the pen and write.'

'You would not dare –'

'Your speech is foolishness, and you know it. Take up the pen and write.'

'If I do?'

'Your wife goes free. The cable shall be despatched immediately.'

'How do I know that you will keep faith with me?'

'I swear it to you on the sacred tombs of my ancestors. Moreover, judge for yourself – why should I wish to do her harm? Her detention will have answered its purpose.'

'And – and Poirot?'

'We will keep him in safe custody until we have concluded our operations. Then we will let him go.'

'Will you swear that also on the tombs of your ancestors?'

'I have sworn one oath to you. That should be sufficient.'

My heart sank. I was betraying my friend – to what? For a moment I hesitated – then the terrible alternative rose like a nightmare before my eyes. Cinderella – in the hands of these Chinese devils, dying by slow torture –

A groan rose to my lips. I seized the pen. Perhaps by careful wording of the letter I could convey a warning, and Poirot would be enabled to avoid the trap. It was the only hope.

But even that hope was not to remain. The Chinaman's voice rose, suave and courteous.

'Permit me to dictate to you.'

He paused, consulted a sheaf of notes that lay by his side, and then dictated as follows:

Dear Poirot, I think I'm on the track of Number Four. A Chinaman came this afternoon and lured me down here with a bogus message. Luckily I saw through his little game in time, and gave him the slip. Then I turned the tables on him, and managed to do a bit of shadowing on my own account – rather neatly too, I flatter myself. I'm getting a bright young lad to carry this to you. Give him half a crown, will you? That's what I promised him if it was delivered safely. I'm watching the house, and daren't leave. I shall wait for you until six o'clock, and if you haven't come then, I'll have a try at getting into the house on my own. It's too good a chance to miss, and, of course, the boy mightn't find you. But if he does, get him to bring you down here right away. And cover up those precious moustaches of yours in case anyone's watching out from the house and might recognize you.

Yours in haste,

A.H.

Every word that I wrote plunged me deeper in despair. The thing was diabolically clever. I realized how closely every detail of our life must be known. It was just such an epistle as I might have penned myself. The acknowledgement that the Chinaman who had called that afternoon had endeavoured to 'lure me away' discounted any good I might have done by leaving my 'sign' of four books. It *had* been a trap, and I had seen through it, that was what Poirot would think. The time, too, was cleverly planned. Poirot, on receiving the note, would have just time to rush off with his innocent-looking guide, and that he would do so I knew. My determination to make my way into the house would bring him post-haste. He always displayed a ridiculous distrust of my capacities. He would be convinced that I was running into danger without being equal to the situation, and would rush down to take command of the situation.

But there was nothing to be done. I wrote as bidden. My captor took the note from me, read it, then nodded his head approvingly and handed it to one of the silent attendants who disappeared with it behind one of the silken hangings on the wall which masked a doorway.

With a smile the man opposite me picked up a cable form and wrote. He handed it to me.

It read: 'Release the white bird with all despatch.'

I gave a sigh of relief.

'You will send it at once?' I urged.

He smiled, and shook his head.

'When M. Hercule Poirot is in my hands it shall be sent. Not until then.'

'But you promised –'

'If this device fails, I may have need of our white bird – to persuade you to further efforts.'

I grew white with anger.

'My God! If you –'

He waved a long, slim yellow hand.

'Be reassured, I do not think it will fail. And the moment M. Poirot is in our hands, I will keep my oath.'

'If you play me false –'

'I have sworn it by my honoured ancestors. Have no fear. Rest here awhile. My servants will see to your needs whilst I am absent.'

I was left alone in this strange underground nest of luxury. The second Chinese attendant had reappeared. One of them brought food and drink and offered it to me, but I waved them aside. I was sick – sick – at heart –

And then suddenly the master reappeared, tall and stately in his silken robes. He directed operations. By his orders I was hustled back through the cellar and tunnel into the original house I had entered. There they took me into a ground-floor room. The windows were shuttered, but one could see through the cracks into the street. An old ragged man was shuffling along the opposite side of the road, and when I saw him make a sign to the window, I understood that he was one of the gang on watch.

'It is well,' said my Chinese friend. 'Hercule Poirot has fallen into the trap. He approaches now – and alone except for the boy who guides him. Now, Captain Hastings, you have still one more part to play. Unless you show yourself he will not enter the house. When he arrives opposite, you must go out on the step and beckon him in.'

'What?' I cried, revolted.

'You play that part alone. Remember the price of failure. If Hercule Poirot suspects anything is amiss and does not enter the house, your wife dies by the Seventy lingering Deaths! Ah! Here he is.'

With a beating heart, and a feeling of deathly sickness, I looked through the crack in the shutters. In the figure walking along the opposite side of the street I recognized my friend at once, though his coat collar was turned up and an immense yellow muffler hid the bottom part of his face. But there was no mistaking that walk, and the pose of that egg-shaped head.

It was Poirot coming to my aid in all good faith, suspecting nothing amiss. By his side ran a typical London urchin, grimy of face and ragged of apparel.

Poirot paused, looking across at the house, whilst the boy spoke to him eagerly and pointed. It was the time for me to act. I went out into the hall. At a sign from the tall Chinaman, one of the servants unlatched the door.

'Remember the price of failure,' said my enemy in a low voice.

I was outside on the steps. I beckoned to Poirot. He hastened across.

'Aha! So all is well with you, my friend. I was beginning to be anxious. You managed to get inside? Is the house empty, then?'

'Yes,' I said, in a low voice I strove to make natural. 'There must be a secret way out of it somewhere. Come in and let us look for it.'

I stepped back across the threshold. In all innocence Poirot prepared to follow me.

And then something seemed to snap in my head. I saw only too clearly the part I was playing – the part of Judas.

'Back, Poirot!' I cried. 'Back for your life. It's a trap. Never mind me. Get away at once.'

Even as I spoke – or rather shouted my warning, hands gripped me like a vice. One of the Chinese servants sprang past me to grab Poirot.

I saw the latter spring back, his arm raised, then suddenly a dense volume of smoke was rising round me, choking me – killing me –

I felt myself falling – suffocating – this was death –

I came to myself slowly and painfully – all my senses dazed. The first thing I saw was Poirot's face. He was sitting opposite me watching me with an anxious face. He gave a cry of joy when he saw me looking at him.

'Ah, you revive – you return to yourself. All is well! My friend – my poor friend!'

'Where am I?' I said painfully.

'Where? But *chez vous*!'

I looked round me. True enough, I was in the old familiar surroundings. And in the grate were the identical four knobs of coal I had carefully spilt there.

Poirot had followed my glance.

'But yes, that was a famous idea of yours – that and the books. See you, if they should say to me any time, "That friend of yours, that Hastings, he has not the great brain, is it not so?" I shall reply to them: "You are in error." It was an idea magnificent and superb that occurred to you there.'

'You understood their meaning then?'

'Am I an imbecile? Of course I understood. It gave me just the warning I needed, and the time to mature my plans. Somehow or other the Big Four had carried you off. With what object? Clearly not for your *beaux yeux* – equally clearly not because they feared you and wanted to get you out of the way. No, their object was plain. You would be used as a decoy to get the great Hercule Poirot into their clutches. I have long been prepared for something of the kind. I make my little preparations, and presently, sure enough, the messenger arrives – such an innocent little street urchin. Me, I swallow everything, and hasten away with him, and, very fortunately, they permit you to come out on the doorstep. That was my one fear, that I should have to dispose of them before I had reached the place where you were concealed, and that I should have to search for you – perhaps in vain – afterwards.'

'Dispose of them, did you say?' I asked feebly. 'Singlehanded.'

'Oh, there is nothing very clever about that. If one is prepared in advance, all is simple – the motto of the Boy Scout, is it not? And a very fine one. Me, I was prepared. Not so long ago, I rendered a service to a very famous chemist, who did a lot of work in connection with poison gas during the war. He devised for me a little bomb – simple and easy to carry about – one has but to throw it and poof, the smoke – and then the unconsciousness. Immediately I blow a little whistle and straightway some of Japp's clever fellows who were watching the house here long before the boy arrived, and who managed to follow us all the way to Limehouse, came flying up and took charge of the situation.'

'But how was it you weren't unconscious too?'

'Another piece of luck. Our friend Number Four (who certainly composed that ingenious letter) permitted himself a little jest at my moustaches, which rendered it extremely easy for me to adjust my respirator under the guise of a yellow muffler.'

'I remember,' I cried eagerly, and then with the word 'remember' all the ghastly horror that I had temporarily forgotten came back to me. *Cinderella* –

I fell back with a groan.

I must have lost consciousness again for a minute or two. I awoke to find Poirot forcing some brandy between my lips.

'What is it, *mon ami*? But what is it – then? Tell me.' Word by word, I got the thing told, shuddering as I did so. Poirot uttered a cry.

'My friend! My friend! But what you must have suffered! And I who knew nothing of all this! But reassure yourself! All is well!'

'You will find her, you mean? But she is in South America. And by the time we get there – long before, she will be dead – and God knows how and in what horrible way she will have died.'

'No, no, you do not understand. She is safe and well. She has never been in their hands for one instant.'

'But I got a cable from Bronsen?'

'No, no, you did not. You may have got a cable from South America signed Bronsen – that is a very different matter. Tell me, has it never occurred to you that an organization of this kind, with ramifications all over the world, might easily strike at us through the little girl, Cinderella, whom you love so well?'

'No, never,' I replied.

'Well, it did to me. I said nothing to you because I did not want to upset you unnecessarily – but I took measures of my own. Your wife's letters all seem to have been written from the ranch, but in reality she has been in a place of safety devised by me for over three months.'

I looked at him for a long time.

'You are sure of that?'

'*Parbleu!* I know it. They tortured you with a lie!'

I turned my head aside. Poirot put his hand on my shoulder. There was something in his voice that I had never heard there before.

'You like not that I should embrace you or display the emotion, I know well. I will be very British. I will say nothing – but nothing at all. Only this – that in this last adventure of ours, the honours are all with you, and happy is the man who has such a friend as I have!'

CHAPTER 14

THE PEROXIDE BLONDE

I was very disappointed with the results of Poirot's bomb attack on the premises in Chinatown. To begin with, the leader of the gang had escaped. When Japp's men rushed up in response to Poirot's whistle they found four Chinamen unconscious in the hall, but the man who had threatened me with death was not among them. I remembered afterwards that when I was forced out on to the doorstep, to decoy Poirot into the house, this man had kept well in the background. Presumably he was out of the danger zone of the gas bomb, and made good his escape by one of the many exits which we afterwards discovered.

From the four who remained in our hands we learnt nothing. The fullest investigation by the police failed to bring to light anything to connect them with the Big Four. They were ordinary low-class residents of the district, and they professed bland ignorance of the name Li Chang Yen. A Chinese gentleman had hired them for service in the house by the waterside, and they knew nothing whatever of his private affairs.

By the next day I had, except for a slight headache, completely recovered from the effects of Poirot's gas bomb. We went down together to Chinatown and searched the house from which I had been rescued. The premises consisted of two ramshackle houses joined together by an underground passage. The ground floors and the upper storeys of each were unfurnished and deserted, the broken windows covered by decaying shutters. Japp had already been prying about in the cellars, and had discovered the secret of the entrance to the subterranean chamber where I had spent such an unpleasant half-hour. Closer investigation confirmed the impression that it had made on me the night before. The silks on the walls and divan and the carpets on the floor were of exquisite workmanship. Although I know very little about Chinese art, I could appreciate that every article in the room was perfect of its kind.

With the aid of Japp and some of his men we conducted a most thorough search of the apartment. I had cherished high hopes that we would find documents of importance. A list, perhaps, of some of the more important agents of the Big Four, or cipher notes of some of their plans, but we discovered nothing of the kind. The only papers we found in the whole place were the notes which the Chinaman had consulted whilst he was dictating the letter to Poirot. These consisted of a very complete record of each of our careers, an estimate of our characters, and suggestions about the weaknesses through which we might best be attacked.

Poirot was most childishly delighted with this discovery. Personally I could not see that it was of any value whatever, especially as whoever compiled the notes was ludicrously mistaken in some of his opinions. I pointed this out to my friend when we were back in our rooms.

'My dear Poirot,' I said, 'you know now what the enemy thinks of us. He appears to have a grossly exaggerated idea of your brain power, and to have absurdly underrated mine, but I do not see how we are better off for knowing this.'

Poirot chuckled in rather an offensive way.

'You do not see, Hastings, no? But surely now we can prepare ourselves for some of their methods of attack now that we are warned of some of our faults. For instance, my friend, we know that you should think before you act. Again, if you meet a red-haired young woman in trouble you should eye her – what you say – askance, is it not?'

Their notes had contained some absurd references to my supposed impulsiveness, and had suggested that I was susceptible to the charms of young women with hair of a certain shade. I thought Poirot's reference to be in the worst of taste, but fortunately I was able to counter him.

'And what about you?' I demanded. 'Are you going to try to cure your "overweening vanity"? Your "finicky tidiness"?'

I was quoting, and I could see that he was not pleased with my retort.

'Oh, without doubt, Hastings, in some things they deceive themselves – *tant mieux*! They will learn in due time. Meanwhile we have learnt something, and to know is to be prepared.'

This last was a favourite axiom of his lately; so much so that I had begun to hate the sound of it.

'We know something, Hastings,' he continued. 'Yes, we know something – and that is to the good – but we do not know nearly enough. We must know more.'

'In what way?'

Poirot settled himself back in his chair, straightened a box of matches which I had thrown carelessly down on the table, and assumed an attitude that I knew only too well. I saw that he was prepared to hold forth at some length.

'See you, Hastings, we have to contend against four adversaries, that is against four different personalities. With Number One we have never come into personal contact – we know him, as it were, only by the impress of his mind – and in passing, Hastings, I will tell you that I begin to understand that mind very well – a mind most subtle and Oriental – every scheme and plot that we have encountered has emanated from the brain of Li Chang Yen. Number Two and Number Three are so powerful, so high up, that they are for the present immune from our attacks. Nevertheless what is their safeguard is, by a perverse chance, our safeguard also. They are so much in the limelight that their movements must be carefully ordered. And so we come to the last member of the gang – we come to the man known as Number Four.'

Poirot's voice altered a little, as it always did when speaking of this particular individual.

'Number Two and Number Three are able to succeed, to go on their way unscathed, owing to their notoriety and their assured position. Number Four succeeds for the opposite reason – he succeeds by the way of obscurity. Who is he? Nobody knows. What does he look like? Again nobody knows. How many times have we seen him, you and I? Five times, is it not? And could either of us say truthfully that we could be sure of recognizing him again?'

I was forced to shake my head, as I ran back in my mind over those five different people who, incredible as it seemed, were one and the same man. The burly lunatic asylum keeper, the man in the buttoned-up overcoat in Paris, James, the footman, the quiet young medical man in the Yellow Jasmine case, and the Russian professor. In no way did any two of these people resemble each other.

'No,' I said hopelessly. 'We've nothing to go by whatsoever.'

Poirot smiled.

'Do not, I pray of you, give way to such enthusiastic despair. We know one or two things.'

'What kind of things?' I asked sceptically.

'We know that he is a man of medium height, and of medium or fair colouring. If he were a tall man of swarthy complexion he could never have passed himself off as the fair, stocky doctor. It is child's play, of course, to put on an additional inch or so for the part of James, or the Professor. In the same way he must have a short, straight nose. Additions can be built on to a nose by skilful make-up, but a large nose cannot be successfully reduced at a moment's notice. Then again, he must be a fairly young man, certainly not over thirty-five. You see, we are getting somewhere. A man between thirty and thirty-five, of medium height and colouring, an adept in the art of make-up, and with very few or any teeth of his own.'

'What?'

'Surely, Hastings. As the keeper, his teeth were broken and discoloured, in Paris they were even and white, as a doctor they protruded slightly, and as Savaronoff they had unusually long canines. Nothing alters the face so completely as a different set of teeth. You see where all this is leading us?'

'Not exactly,' I said cautiously.

'A man carries his profession written in his face, they say.'

'He's a criminal,' I cried.

'He is an adept in the art of making-up.'

'It's the same thing.'

'Rather a sweeping statement, Hastings, and one which would hardly be appreciated by the theatrical world. Do you not see that the man is, or has been, at one time or another, an actor?'

'An actor?'

'But certainly. He has the whole technique at his fingertips. Now there are two classes of actors, the one who sinks himself in his part, and the one who manages to impress his personality upon it. It is from the latter class that actor-managers usually spring. They seize a part and mould it to their own personality. The former class is quite likely to spend its days doing Mr Lloyd George at different music halls, or impersonating old men with beards in repertory plays. It is among that former class that we must look for our Number Four. He is a supreme artist in the way he sinks himself in each part he plays.'

I was growing interested.

'So you fancy you may be able to trace his identity through his connection with the stage?'

'Your reasoning is always brilliant, Hastings.'

'It might have been better,' I said coldly, 'if the idea had come to you sooner. We have wasted a lot of time.'

'You are in error, *mon ami*. No more time has been wasted than was unavoidable. For some months now my agents have been engaged on the task. Joseph Aarons is one of them. You remember him? They have compiled a list for me of men fulfilling the necessary qualifications – young men round about the age of thirty, of more or less nondescript appearance, and with a gift for playing character parts – men, moreover, who have definitely left the stage within the last three years.'

'Well?' I said, deeply interested.

'The list was, necessarily, rather a long one. For some time now, we have been engaged on the task of elimination. And finally we have boiled the whole thing down to four names. Here they are, my friend.'

He tossed me over a sheet of paper. I read its contents aloud.

'Ernest Luttrell. Son of a North Country parson. Always had a kink of some kind in his moral make-up. Was expelled from his public school. Went on the stage at the age of twenty-three. (Then followed a list of parts he had played, with dates and places.) Addicted to drugs. Supposed to have gone to Australia four years ago. Cannot be traced after leaving England. Age 32, height 5ft. 10½in., clean-shaven, hair brown, nose straight, complexion fair, eyes grey.

'John St Maur. Assumed name. Real name not known. Believed to be of cockney extraction. On stage since quite a child. Did music hall impersonations. Not been heard of for three years. Age, about 33, height 5ft. 10in., slim build, blue eyes, fair colouring.

'Austen Lee. Assumed name. Real name Austen Foly. Good family. Always had taste for acting and distinguished himself in that way at Oxford. Brilliant war record. Acted in – (The usual list followed. It included many repertory plays.) An enthusiast on criminology. Had bad nervous breakdown as the result of a motor accident three and a half years ago, and has not appeared on the stage since. No clue to his present whereabouts. Age 35, height 5ft. 9½in., complexion fair, eyes blue, hair brown.

'Claud Darrell. Supposed to be real name. Some mystery about his origin. Played at music halls, and also in repertory plays. Seems to have had no intimate friends. Was in China in 1919. Returned by way of America. Played a few parts in New York. Did not appear on stage one night, and has never been heard of since. New York police say most mysterious disappearance. Age about 33, hair brown, fair complexion, grey eyes. Height 5ft. 10½ in.

'Most interesting,' I said, as I laid down the paper. 'And so this is the result of the investigation of months? These four names. Which of them are you inclined to suspect?'

Poirot made an eloquent gesture.

'*Mon ami*, for the moment it is an open question. I would just point out to you that Claud Darrell has been in China and America – a fact not without significance, perhaps, but we must not allow ourselves to be unduly biased by that point. It may be a mere coincidence.'

'And the next step?' I asked eagerly.

'Affairs are already in train. Every day cautiously worded advertisements will appear. Friends and relatives of one or the other will be asked to communicate with my solicitor at his office. Even today we might – Aha, the telephone! Probably it is, as usual, the wrong number, and they will regret to have troubled us, but it may be – yes, it may be – that something has arisen.'

I crossed the room and picked up the receiver.

'Yes, yes. M. Poirot's rooms. Yes, Captain Hastings speaking. Oh, it's you, Mr McNeil! (McNeil and Hodgson were Poirot's solicitors.) I'll tell him. Yes, we'll come round at once.'

I replaced the receiver and turned to Poirot, my eyes dancing with excitement.

'I say, Poirot, there's a woman there. Friend of Claud Darrell's. Miss Flossie Monro. McNeil wants you to come round.'

'At the instant!' cried Poirot, disappearing into his bedroom, and reappearing with a hat.

A taxi soon took us to our destination, and we were ushered into Mr McNeil's private office. Sitting in the armchair facing the solicitor was a somewhat lurid-looking lady no longer in her first youth. Her hair was of an impossible yellow, and was prolific in curls over each ear, her eyelids were heavily blackened, and she had by no means forgotten the rouge and the lip salve.

'Ah, here is M. Poirot!' said Mr McNeil. 'M. Poirot, this is Miss – er – Monro, who has very kindly called to give us some information.'

'Ah, but that is most kind!' cried Poirot.

He came forward with great *empressement*, and shook the lady warmly by the hand.

'Mademoiselle blooms like a flower in this dry-as-dust old office,' he added, careless of the feelings of Mr McNeil.

This outrageous flattery was not without effect. Miss Monro blushed and simpered.

'Oh, go on now, Mr Poirot!' she exclaimed. 'I know what you Frenchmen are like.'

'Mademoiselle, we are not mute like Englishmen before beauty. Not that I am a Frenchman – I am a Belgian, you see.'

'I've been to Ostend myself,' said Miss Monro.

The whole affair, as Poirot would have said, was marching splendidly.

'And so you can tell us something about Mr Claud Darrell?' continued Poirot.

'I knew Mr Darrell very well at one time,' explained the lady. 'And I saw your advertisement, being out of a shop for the moment, and, my time being my own, I said to myself: There, they want to know about poor old Claudie – lawyers, too – maybe it's a fortune looking for the rightful heir. I'd better go round at once.'

Mr McNeil rose.

'Well, Monsieur Poirot, shall I leave you for a little conversation with Miss Monro?'

'You are too amiable. But stay – a little idea presents itself to me. The hour of the *déjeuner* approaches. Mademoiselle will perhaps honour me by coming out to luncheon with me?'

Miss Monro's eyes glistened. It struck me that she was in exceedingly low water, and that the chance of a square meal was not to be despised.

A few minutes later saw us all in a taxi, bound for one of London's most expensive restaurants. Once arrived there, Poirot ordered a most delectable lunch, and then turned to his guest.

'And for wine, mademoiselle? What do you say to champagne?'

Miss Monro said nothing – or everything.

The meal started pleasantly. Poirot replenished the lady's glass with thoughtful assiduity, and gradually slid on to the topic nearest his heart.

'The poor Mr Darrell. What a pity he is not with us.'

'Yes, indeed,' sighed Miss Monro. 'Poor boy, I do wonder what's become of him.'

'Is it a long time since you have seen him, yes?'

'Oh, simply ages – not since the war. He was a funny boy, Claudie, very close about things, never told you a word about himself. But, of course, that all fits in if he's a missing heir. Is it a title, Mr Poirot?'

'Alas, a mere heritage,' said Poirot unblushingly. 'But you see, it may be a question of identification. That is why it is necessary for us to find someone who knew him very well indeed. You knew him very well, did you not, mademoiselle?'

'I don't mind telling you, Mr Poirot. You're a gentleman. You know how to order a lunch for a lady – which is more than some of these young whippersnappers do nowadays. Downright mean, I call it. As I was saying, you being a Frenchman won't be shocked. Ah, you Frenchmen! Naughty, naughty!' She wagged her finger at him in an excess of archness. 'Well, there it was, me and Claudie, two young things – what else could you expect? And I've still a kindly feeling for him. Though, mind you, he didn't treat me well – no, he didn't – he didn't treat me well at all. Not as a lady should be treated. They're all the same when it comes to a question of money.'

'No, no, mademoiselle, do not say that,' protested Poirot, filling up her glass once more. 'Could you now describe this Mr Darrell to me?'

'He wasn't anything so very much to look at,' said Flossie Monro dreamily. 'Neither tall nor short, you know, but quite well set up. Spruce looking. Eyes a sort of blue-grey. And more or less fair-haired, I suppose. But oh, what an artist! *I* never saw anyone to touch him in the profession! He'd have made his name before now if it hadn't been for jealousy. Ah, Mr Poirot, jealousy – you wouldn't believe it, you really wouldn't, what we artists have to suffer through jealousy. Why, I remember once at Manchester –'

We displayed what patience we could in listening to a long complicated story about a pantomime, and the infamous conduct of the principal boy. Then Poirot led her gently back to the subject of Claud Darrell.

'It is very interesting, all this that you are able to tell us, mademoiselle, about Mr Darrell. Women are such wonderful observers – they see everything, they notice the little detail that escapes the mere man. I have seen a woman identify one man out of a dozen others – and why, do you think? She had observed that he had a trick of stroking his nose when he was agitated. Now would a man ever have thought of noticing a thing like that?'

'Did you ever!' cried Miss Monro. 'I suppose we do notice things. I remember Claudie, now I come to think of it, always fiddling with his bread at table. He'd get a little piece between his fingers and then dab it round to pick up crumbs. I've seen him do it a hundred times. Why, I'd know him anywhere by that one trick of his.'

'Is not that just what I say? The marvellous observation of a woman. And did you ever speak to him about this little habit of his, mademoiselle?'

'No, I didn't, Mr Poirot. You know what men are! They don't like you to notice things – especially if it should seem you were telling them off about it. I never said a word – but many's the time I smiled to myself. Bless you, he never knew he was doing it even.'

Poirot nodded gently. I noticed that his own hand was shaking a little as he stretched it out to his glass.

'Then there is always handwriting as a means of establishing identity,' he remarked. 'Without doubt you have preserved a letter written by Mr Darrell?'

Flossie Monro shook her head regretfully.

'He was never one for writing. Never wrote me a line in his life.'

'That is a pity,' said Poirot.

'I tell you what, though,' said Miss Monro suddenly. 'I've got a photograph if that would be any good?'

'You have a photograph?'

Poirot almost sprang from his seat with excitement.

'It's quite an old one – eight years old at least.'

'*Ça ne fait rien*! No matter how old and faded! Ah, *ma foi*, but what stupendous luck! You will permit me to inspect that photograph, mademoiselle?'

'Why, of course.'

'Perhaps you will even permit me to have a copy made? It would not take long.'

'Certainly if you like.'

Miss Monro rose.

'Well, I must run away,' she declared archly. 'Very glad to have met you and your friend, Mr Poirot.'

'And the photograph? When may I have it?'

'I'll look it out tonight. I think I know where to lay my hands upon it. And I'll send it to you right away.'

'A thousand thanks, mademoiselle. You are all that is of the most amiable. I hope that we shall soon be able to arrange another little lunch together.'

'As soon as you like,' said Miss Monro. 'I'm willing.'

'Let me see, I do not think that I have your address?'

With a grand air, Miss Monro drew a card from her handbag, and handed it to him. It was a somewhat dirty card, and the original address had been scratched out and another substituted in pencil.

Then, with a good many bows and gesticulations on Poirot's part, we bade farewell to the lady and got away.

'Do you really think this photograph so important?' I asked Poirot.

'Yes, *mon ami*. The camera does not lie. One can magnify a photograph, seize salient points that otherwise would remain unnoticed. And then there are a thousand details – such as the structure of the ears, which no one could ever describe to you in words. Oh, yes, it is a great chance, this, which has come our way! That is why I propose to take precautions.'

He went across to the telephone as he finished speaking, and gave a number which I knew to be that of a private detective agency which he sometimes employed. His instructions were clear and definite. Two men were to go to the address he gave, and, in general terms, were to watch over the safety of Miss Monro. They were to follow her wherever she went.

Poirot hung up the receiver and came back to me.

'Do you really think that necessary, Poirot?' I asked.

'It may be. There is no doubt that we are watched, you and I, and since that is so, they will soon know with whom we were lunching today. And it is possible that Number Four will scent danger.'

About twenty minutes later the telephone bell rang. I answered it. A curt voice spoke into the phone.

'Is that Mr Poirot? St James's Hospital speaking. A young woman was brought in ten minutes ago. Street accident. Miss Flossie Monro. She is asking very urgently for Mr Poirot. But he must come at once. She can't possibly last long.'

I repeated the words to Poirot. His face went white.

'Quick, Hastings. We must go like the wind.'

A taxi took us to the hospital in less than ten minutes. We asked for Miss Monro, and were taken immediately to the Accident Ward. But a white-capped sister met us in the doorway.

Poirot read the news in her face.

'It is over, eh?'

'She died six minutes ago.'

Poirot stood as though stunned.

The nurse, mistaking his emotion, began speaking gently.

'She did not suffer, and she was unconscious towards the last. She was run over by a motor, you know – and the driver of the car did not even stop. Wicked, isn't it? I hope someone took the number.'

'The stars fight against us,' said Poirot, in a low voice.

'You would like to see her?'

The nurse led the way, and we followed.

Poor Flossie Monro, with her rouge and her dyed hair. She lay there very peacefully, with a little smile on her lips.

'Yes,' murmured Poirot. 'The stars fight against us – but is it the stars?' He lifted his head as though struck by a sudden idea. 'Is it the stars, Hastings? If it is not – if it is not . . . Oh, I swear to you, my friend, standing here by this poor woman's body, that I will have no mercy when the time comes!'

'What do you mean?' I asked.

But Poirot had turned to the nurse and was eagerly demanding information. A list of the articles found in her handbag was finally obtained. Poirot gave a suppressed cry as he read it over.

'You see, Hastings, you see?'

'See what?'

'There is no mention of a latch-key. But she must have had a latch-key with her. No, she was run down in cold blood, and the first person who bent over her took the key from her bag. But we may yet be in time. He may not have been able to find at once what he sought.'

Another taxi took us to the address Flossie Monro had given us, a squalid block of Mansions in an unsavoury neighbourhood. It was some time before we could gain admission to Miss Monro's flat, but we had at least the satisfaction of knowing that no one could leave it whilst we were on guard outside.

Eventually we got in. It was plain that someone had been before us. The contents of drawers and cupboards were strewn all over the floor. Locks had been forced, and small tables had even been over-thrown, so violent had been the searcher's haste.

Poirot began to hunt through the débris. Suddenly he stood erect with a cry, holding out something. It was an old-fashioned photograph frame – empty.

He turned it slowly over. Affixed to the back was a small round label – a price label.

'It cost four shillings,' I commented.

'*Mon Dieu!* Hastings, use your eyes. That is a new clean label. It was stuck there by the man who took out the photograph, the man who was here before us, but knew that we should come, and so left this for us – Claud Darrell – alias Number Four.'

CHAPTER 15

THE TERRIBLE CATASTROPHE

It was after the tragic death of Miss Flossie Monro that I began to be aware of a change in Poirot. Up to now, his invincible confidence in himself had stood the test. But it seemed as though, at last, the long strain was beginning to tell. His manner was grave and brooding, and his nerves were on edge. In these days he was as jumpy as a cat. He avoided all discussion of the Big Four as far as possible, and seemed to throw himself into his ordinary work with almost his old ardour. Nevertheless, I knew that he was secretly active in the big matter. Extraordinary-looking Slavs were constantly calling to see him, and though he vouchsafed no explanation as to these mysterious activities, I realized that he was building some new defence or weapon of opposition with the help of these somewhat repulsive-looking foreigners. Once, purely by chance, I happened to see the entries in his passbook – he had asked me to verify some small item – and I noticed the paying out of a huge sum – a huge sum even for Poirot who was coining money nowadays – to some Russian with apparently every letter of the alphabet in his name.

But he gave no clue as to the line on which he proposed to operate. Only over and over again he gave utterance to one phrase.

'It is a mistake to underestimate your adversary. Remember that, *mon ami*.' And I realized that that was the pitfall he was striving at all costs to avoid.

So matters went on until the end of March, and then one morning Poirot made a remark which startled me considerably.

'This morning, my friend, I should recommend the best suit. We go to call upon the Home Secretary.'

'Indeed? That is very exciting. He has called you in to take up a case?'

'Not exactly. The interview is of my seeking. You may remember my saying that I once did him some small service? He is inclined to be foolishly enthusiastic over my capabilities in consequence, and I am about to trade on this attitude of his. As you know, the French Premier, M. Desjardeaux, is over in London, and at my request the Home Secretary has arranged for him to be present at our little conference this morning.'

The Right Honourable Sydney Crowther, His Majesty's Secretary of State for Home Affairs, was a well-known and popular figure. A man of some fifty years of age, with a quizzical expression and shrewd grey eyes, he received us with that delightful bonhomie of manner which was well-known to be one of his principal assets.

Standing with his back to the fireplace was a tall thin man with a pointed black beard and a sensitive face.

'M. Desjardeaux,' said Crowther. 'Allow me to introduce to you M. Hercule Poirot of whom you may, perhaps, already have heard.'

The Frenchman bowed and shook hands.

'I have indeed heard of M. Hercule Poirot,' he said pleasantly. 'Who has not?'

'You are too amiable, monsieur,' said Poirot, bowing, but his face flushed with pleasure.

'Any word for an old friend?' asked a quiet voice, and a man came forward from a corner by a tall bookcase.

It was our old acquaintance, Mr Ingles.

Poirot shook him warmly by the hand.

'And now, M. Poirot,' said Crowther. 'We are at your service. I understand you to say that you had a communication of the utmost importance to make to us.'

'That is so, monsieur. There is in the world today a vast organization – an organization of crime. It is controlled by four individuals, who are known and spoken of as the Big Four. Number One is a Chinaman, Li Chang Yen; Number Two is the American multi-millionaire, Abe Ryland; Number Three is a Frenchwoman; Number Four I have every reason to believe is an obscure English actor called Claud Darrell. These four are banded together to destroy the existing social order, and to replace it with an anarchy in which they would reign as dictators.'

'Incredible,' muttered the Frenchman. 'Ryland, mixed up with a thing of that kind? Surely the idea is too fantastic.'

'Listen, monsieur, whilst I recount to you some of the doings of this Big Four.'

It was an enthralling narrative which Poirot unfolded. Familiar as I was with all the details, they thrilled me anew as I heard the bald recital of our adventures and escapes.

M. Desjardeaux looked mutely at Mr Crowther as Poirot finished. The other answered the look.

'Yes, M. Desjardeaux, I think we must admit the existence of a "Big Four". Scotland Yard was inclined to jeer at first, but they have been forced to admit that M. Poirot was right in many of his claims. I cannot but feel that M. Poirot – er – exaggerates a little.'

For answer Poirot set forth ten salient points. I have been asked not to give them to the public even now, and so I refrain from doing so, but they included the extraordinary disasters to submarines which occurred in a certain month, and also a series of aeroplane accidents and forced landings. According to Poirot, these were all the work of the Big Four, and bore witness to the fact that they were in possession of various scientific secrets unknown to the world at large.

This brought us straight to the question which I had been waiting for the French premier to ask.

'You say that the third member of this organization is a Frenchwoman. Have you any idea of her name?'

'It is a well-known name, monsieur. An honoured name. Number Three is no less than the famous Madame Olivier.'

At the mention of the world-famous scientist, successor to the Curies, M. Desjardeaux positively bounded from his chair, his face purple with emotion.

'Madame Olivier! Impossible! Absurd! It is an insult what you say there!'

Poirot shook his head gently, but made no answer.

Desjardeaux looked at him in stupefaction for some moments. Then his face cleared, and he glanced at the Home Secretary and tapped his forehead significantly.

'M. Poirot is a great man,' he observed. 'But even the great man – sometimes he has his little mania, does he not? And seeks in high places for fancied conspiracies. It is well-known. You agree with me, do you not, Mr Crowther?'

The Home Secretary did not answer for some minutes. Then he spoke slowly and heavily.

'Upon my soul, I don't know,' he said at last. 'I have always had and still have the utmost belief in M. Poirot, but – well, this takes a bit of believing.'

'This Li Chang Yen, too,' continued M. Desjardeaux. 'Who has ever heard of him?'

'I have,' said the unexpected voice of Mr Ingles.

The Frenchman stared at him, and he stared placidly back again, looking more like a Chinese idol than ever. 'Mr Ingles,' explained the Home Secretary, 'is the greatest authority we have on the interior of China.'

'And you have heard of this Li Chang Yen?'

'Until M. Poirot here came to me, I imagined that I was the only man in England who had. Make no mistake, M. Desjardeaux, there is only one man in China who counts today – Li Chang Yen. He has, perhaps, I only say perhaps, the finest brain in the world at the present time.'

M. Desjardeaux sat as though stunned. Presently, however, he rallied.

'There may be something in what you say, M. Poirot,' he said coldly. 'But as regards Madame Olivier, you are most certainly mistaken. She is a true daughter of France, and devoted solely to the cause of science.'

Poirot shrugged his shoulders and did not answer.

There was a minute or two's pause, and then my little friend rose to his feet, with an air of dignity that sat rather oddly upon his quaint personality.

'That is all I have to say, messieurs – to warn you. I thought it likely that I should not be believed. But at least you will be on your guard. My words will sink in, and each fresh event that comes along will confirm your wavering faith. It was necessary for me to speak now – later I might not have been able to do so.'

'You mean –?' asked Crowther, impressed in spite of himself by the gravity of Poirot's tone.

'I mean, monsieur, that since I have penetrated the identity of Number Four, my life is not worth an hour's purchase. He will seek to destroy me at all costs – and not for nothing is he named "The Destroyer". Messieurs, I salute you. To you, M. Crowther, I deliver this key, and this sealed envelope. I have got together all my notes on the case, and my ideas as to how best to meet the menace that any day may break upon the world, and have placed them in a certain safe deposit. In the event of my death, M. Crowther, I authorize you to take charge of those papers and make what use you can of them. And now, messieurs, I wish you good day.'

Desjardeaux merely bowed coldly, but Crowther sprang up and held out his hand.

'You have converted me, M. Poirot. Fantastic as the whole thing seems, I believe utterly in the truth of what you have told us.'

Ingles left at the same time as we did.

'I am not disappointed with the interview,' said Poirot, as we walked along. 'I did not expect to convince Desjardeaux, but I have at least ensured that, if I die, my knowledge does not die with me. And I have made one or two converts. *Pas si mal!*'

'I'm with you, as you know,' said Ingles. 'By the way, I'm going out to China as soon as I can get off.'

'Is that wise?'

'No,' said Ingles drily. 'But it's necessary. One must do what one can.'

'Ah, you are a brave man!' cried Poirot with emotion. 'If we were not in the street, I would embrace you.'

I fancied that Ingles looked rather relieved.

'I don't suppose that I shall be in any more danger in China than you are in London,' he growled.

'That is possibly true enough,' admitted Poirot. 'I hope that they will not succeed in massacring Hastings also, that is all. That would annoy me greatly.'

I interrupted this cheerful conversation to remark that I had no intention of letting myself be massacred, and shortly afterwards Ingles parted from us.

For some time we went along in silence, which Poirot at length broke by uttering a totally unexpected remark.

'I think – I really think – that I shall have to bring my brother into this.'

'Your brother,' I cried, astonished. 'I never knew you had a brother?'

'You surprise me, Hastings. Do you not know that all celebrated detectives have brothers who would be even more celebrated than they are were it not for constitutional indolence?'

Poirot employs a peculiar manner sometimes which makes it wellnigh impossible to know whether he is jesting or in earnest. That manner was very evident at the moment.

'What is your brother's name?' I asked, trying to adjust myself to this new idea.

'Achille Poirot,' replied Poirot gravely. 'He lives near Spa in Belgium.'

'What does he do?' I asked with some curiosity, putting aside a half-formed wonder as to the character and disposition of the late Madame Poirot, and her classical taste in Christian names.

'He does nothing. He is, as I tell, of a singularly indolent disposition. But his abilities are hardly less than my own – which is saying a great deal.'

'Is he like you to look at?'

'Not unlike. But not nearly so handsome. And he wears no moustaches.'

'Is he older than you, or younger?'

'He happens to have been born on the same day.'

'A twin,' I cried.

'Exactly, Hastings. You jump to the right conclusion with unfailing accuracy. But here we are at home again. Let us at once get to work on that little affair of the Duchess's necklace.'

But the Duchess's necklace was doomed to wait awhile. A case of quite another description was waiting for us.

Our landlady, Mrs Pearson, at once informed us that a hospital nurse had called and was waiting to see Poirot.

We found her sitting in the big armchair facing the window, a pleasant-faced woman of middle age, in a dark blue uniform. She was a little reluctant to come to the point, but Poirot soon put her at her ease, and she embarked upon her story.

'You see, M. Poirot, I've never come across anything of the kind before. I was sent for, from the Lark Sisterhood, to go down to a case in Hertfordshire. An old gentleman, it is, Mr Templeton. Quite a pleasant house, and quite pleasant people. The wife, Mrs Templeton, is much younger than the husband, and he has a son by his first marriage who lives there. I don't know that the young man and the step-mother always get on together. He's not quite what you'd call normal – not "wanting" exactly, but decidedly dull in the intellect. Well, this illness of Mr Templeton's seemed to me from the first to be mysterious. At times there seemed really nothing the matter with him, and then he suddenly has one of these gastric attacks with pain and vomiting. But the doctor seemed quite satisfied, and it wasn't for me to say anything. But I couldn't help thinking about it. And then –' She paused, and became rather red.

'Something happened which aroused your suspicions?' suggested Poirot.

'Yes.'

But she still seemed to find it difficult to go on.

'I found the servants were passing remarks too.'

'About Mr Templeton's illness?'

'Oh, no! About – about this other thing –'

'Mrs Templeton?'

'Yes.'

'Mrs Templeton and the doctor, perhaps?'

Poirot had an uncanny flair in these things. The nurse threw him a grateful glance and went on.

'They *were* passing remarks. And then one day I happened to see them together myself – in the garden –'

It was left at that. Our client was in such an agony of outraged propriety that no one could feel it necessary to ask exactly what she had seen in the garden. She had evidently seen quite enough to make up her own mind on the situation.

'The attacks got worse and worse. Dr Treves said it was all perfectly natural and to be expected, and that Mr Templeton could not possibly live long, but I've never seen anything like it before myself – not in all my long experience of nursing. It seemed to me much more like some form of –'

She paused, hesitating.

'Arsenical poisoning?' said Poirot helpfully.

She nodded.

'And then, too, he, the patient, I mean, said something queer. "They'll do for me, the four of them. They'll do for me yet."'

'Eh?' said Poirot quickly.

'Those were his very words, M. Poirot. He was in great pain at the time, of course, and hardly knew what he was saying.'

'"They'll do for me, the four of them,"' repeated Poirot thoughtfully. 'What did he mean by "the four of them", do you think?'

'That I can't say, M. Poirot. I thought perhaps he meant his wife and son, and the doctor, and perhaps Miss Clark, Mrs Templeton's companion. That would make four, wouldn't it? He might think they were all in league against him.'

'Quite so, quite so,' said Poirot, in a preoccupied voice. 'What about food? Could you take no precautions about that?'

'I'm always doing what I can. But, of course, sometimes Mrs Templeton insists on bringing him his food herself, and then there are the times when I am off duty.'

'Exactly. And you are not sure enough of your ground to go to the police?'

The nurse's face showed her horror at the mere idea.

'What I have done, M. Poirot, is this. Mr Templeton had a very bad attack after partaking of a bowl of soup. I took a little from the bottom of the bowl afterwards, and have brought it up with me. I have been spared for the day to visit a sick mother, as Mr Templeton was well enough to be left.'

She drew out a little bottle of dark fluid and handed it to Poirot.

'Excellent, mademoiselle. We will have this analysed immediately. If you will return here in, say, an hour's time I think that we shall be able to dispose of your suspicions one way or another.'

First extracting from our visitor her name and qualifications, he ushered her out. Then he wrote a note and sent it off together with the bottle of soup. Whilst we waited to hear the result, Poirot amused himself by verifying the nurse's credentials, somewhat to my surprise.

'No, no, my friend,' he declared. 'I do well to be careful. Do not forget the Big Four are on our track.'

However, he soon elicited the information that a nurse of the name of Mabel Palmer was a member of the Lark Institute and had been sent to the case in question.

'So far, so good,' he said, with a twinkle. 'And now here comes Nurse Palmer back again, and here also is our analyst's report.'

'Is there arsenic in it?' she asked breathlessly.

Poirot shook his head, refolding the paper.

'No.'

We were both immeasurably surprised.

'There is no arsenic in it,' continued Poirot. 'But there is antimony, and that being the case, we will start immediately for Hertfordshire. Pray Heaven that we are not too late.'

It was decided that the simplest plan was for Poirot to represent himself truly as a detective, but that the ostensible reason of his visit should be to question Mrs Templeton about a servant formerly in her employment whose name he obtained from Nurse Palmer, and whom he could represent as being concerned in a jewel robbery.

It was late when we arrived at Elmstead, as the house was called. We had allowed Nurse Palmer to precede us by about twenty minutes, so that there should be no question of our all arriving together.

Mrs Templeton, a tall dark woman, with sinuous movements and uneasy eyes, received us. I noticed that as Poirot announced his profession, she drew in her breath with a sudden hiss, as though badly startled, but she answered his question about the maid-servant readily enough. And then, to test her, Poirot embarked upon a long history of a poisoning case in which a guilty wife had figured. His eyes never left her face as he talked, and try as she would, she could hardly conceal her rising agitation. Suddenly, with an incoherent word of excuse, she hurried from the room.

We were not long left alone. A squarely-built man with a small red moustache and pince-nez came in.

'Dr Treves,' he introduced himself. 'Mrs Templeton asked me to make her excuses to you. She's in a very bad state, you know. Nervous strain. Worry over her husband and all that. I've prescribed bed and bromide. But she hopes you'll stay and take pot luck, and I'm to do host. We've heard of you down here, M. Poirot, and we mean to make the most of you. Ah, here's Micky!'

A shambling young man entered the room. He had a very round face, and foolish-looking eyebrows raised as though in perpetual surprise. He grinned awkwardly as he shook hands. This was clearly the 'wanting' son.

Presently we all went in to dinner. Dr Treves left the room – to open some wine, I think – and suddenly the boy's physiognomy underwent a startling change. He leant forward, staring at Poirot.

'You've come about Father,' he said, nodding his head. '*I* know. I know lots of things – but nobody thinks I do. Mother will be glad when Father's dead and she can marry Dr Treves. She isn't my own mother, you know. I don't like her. She wants Father to die.'

It was all rather horrible. Luckily, before Poirot had time to reply, the doctor came back, and we had to carry on a forced conversation.

And then suddenly Poirot lay back in his chair with a hollow groan. His face was contorted with pain.

'My dear sir, what's the matter?' cried the doctor.

'A sudden spasm. I am used to them. No, no, I require no assistance from you, doctor. If I might lie down upstairs.'

His request was instantly acceded to, and I accompanied him upstairs, where he collapsed on the bed, groaning heavily.

For the first minute or two I had been taken in, but I had quickly realized that Poirot was – as he would have put it – playing the comedy, and that his object was to be left alone upstairs near the patient's room.

Hence I was quite prepared when, the instant we were alone, he sprang up.

'Quick, Hastings, the window. There is ivy outside. We can climb down before they begin to suspect.'

'Climb down?'

'Yes, we must get out of this house at once. You saw him at dinner?'

'The doctor?'

'No, young Templeton. His trick with his bread. Do you remember what Flossie Monro told us before she died? That

Claud Darrell had a habit of dabbing his bread on the table to pick up crumbs. Hastings, this is a vast plot, and that vacant-looking young man is our arch enemy – Number Four! Hurry.'

I did not wait to argue. Incredible as the whole thing seemed it was wiser not to delay. We scrambled down the ivy as quietly as we could and made a beeline for the small town and the railway station. We were just able to catch the last train, the 8.34 which would land us in town about eleven o'clock.

'A plot,' said Poirot thoughtfully. 'How many of them were in it, I wonder? I suspect that the whole Templeton family are just so many agents of the Big Four. Did they simply want to decoy us down there? Or was it more subtle than that? Did they intend to play the comedy down there and keep me interested until they had had time to do – what? I wonder now.'

He remained very thoughtful.

Arrived at our lodgings, he restrained me at the door of the sitting-room.

'Attention, Hastings. I have my suspicions. Let me enter first.'

He did so, and, to my slight amusement, took the precaution to press on the electric switch with an old galosh. Then he went round the room like a strange cat, cautiously, delicately, on the alert for danger. I watched him for some time, remaining obediently where I had been put by the wall.

'It seems all right, Poirot,' I said impatiently.

'It seems so, *mon ami*, it seems so. But let us make sure.'

'Rot,' I said. 'I shall light the fire, anyway, and have a pipe. I've caught you out for once. You had the matches last and you didn't put them back in the holder as usual – the very thing you're always cursing me for doing.'

I stretched out my hand. I heard Poirot's warning cry – saw him leaping towards me – my hand touched the matchbox.

Then – a flash of blue flame – an ear-rending crash – and darkness –

I came to myself to find the familiar face of our old friend Dr Ridgeway bending over me. An expression of relief passed over his features.

'Keep still,' he said soothingly. 'You're all right. There's been an accident, you know.'

'Poirot?' I murmured.

'You're in my digs. Everything's quite all right.'

A cold fear clutched at my heart. His evasion woke a horrible fear.

'Poirot?' I reiterated. 'What of Poirot?'

He saw that I had to know and that further evasions were useless.

'By a miracle you escaped – Poirot – did not!'

A cry burst from my lips.

'Not dead? Not dead?'

Ridgeway bowed his head, his features working with emotion.

With desperate energy I pulled myself to a sitting position.

'Poirot may be dead,' I said weakly. 'But his spirit lives on. I will carry on his work! Death to the Big Four!'

Then I fell back, fainting.

CHAPTER 16
THE DYING CHINAMAN

Even now I can hardly bear to write of those days in March.

Poirot – the unique, the inimitable Hercule Poirot – dead! There was a particularly diabolical touch in the disarranged match-box, which was certain to catch his eye, and which he would hasten to rearrange – and thereby touch off the explosion. That, as a matter of fact, it was I who actually precipitated the catastrophe never ceased to fill me with unavailing remorse. It was, Dr Ridgeway said, a perfect miracle that I had not been killed, but had escaped with a slight concussion.

Although it had seemed to me as though I regained consciousness almost immediately, it was in reality over twenty-four hours before I came back to life. It was not until the evening of the day following that I was able to stagger feebly into an adjoining room, and view with deep emotion the plain elm coffin which held the remains of one of the most marvellous men this world has ever known.

From the very first moment of regaining consciousness I had had only one purpose in mind – to avenge Poirot's death, and to hunt down the Big Four remorselessly.

I had thought that Ridgeway would have been of one mind with me about this, but to my surprise the good doctor seemed unaccountably lukewarm.

'Get back to South America,' was his advice, tendered on every occasion. Why attempt the impossible? Put as delicately as possible, his opinion amounted to this: If Poirot, the unique Poirot, had failed, was it likely that I should succeed?

But I was obstinate. Putting aside any question as to whether I had the necessary qualifications for the task (and I may say in passing that I did not entirely agree with his views on this point) I had worked so long with Poirot that I knew his methods by heart, and felt fully capable of taking up the work where he had laid it down; it was, with me, a question of feeling. My friend had been foully murdered. Was I to go tamely back to South America without an effort to bring his murderers to justice?

I said all this and more to Ridgeway, who listened attentively enough.

'All the same,' he said when I had finished, 'my advice does not vary. I am earnestly convinced that Poirot himself, if he were here, would urge you to return. In his name, I beg of you, Hastings, abandon these wild ideas and go back to your ranch.'

To that only one answer was possible, and, shaking his head sadly, he said no more.

It was a month before I was fully restored to health. Towards the end of April, I sought, and obtained, an interview with the Home Secretary.

Mr Crowther's manner was reminiscent of that of Dr Ridgeway. It was soothing and negative. Whilst appreciating the offer of my services, he gently and considerately declined them. The papers referred to by Poirot had passed into his keeping, and he assured me that all possible steps were being taken to deal with the approaching menace.

With that cold comfort I was forced to be satisfied. Mr Crowther ended the interview by urging me to return to South America. I found the whole thing profoundly unsatisfactory.

I should, I suppose, in its proper place, have described Poirot's funeral. It was a solemn and moving ceremony, and the extraordinary number of floral tributes passed belief. They came from high and low alike, and bore striking testimony to the place my friend had made for himself in the country of his adoption. For myself, I was frankly overcome by emotion as I stood by the graveside and thought of all our varied experiences and the happy days we had passed together.

By the beginning of May I had mapped out a plan of campaign. I felt that I could not do better than keep to Poirot's scheme of advertising for any information respecting Claud Darrell. I had an advertisement to this effect inserted in a number of morning newspapers, and I was sitting in a small restaurant in Soho, and judging of the effect of the advertisement, when a small paragraph in another part of the paper gave me a nasty shock.

Very briefly, it reported the mysterious disappearance of Mr John Ingles from the S.S. *Shanghai*, shortly after the latter had left Marseilles. Although the weather was perfectly smooth, it was feared that the unfortunate gentleman must have fallen overboard. The paragraph ended with a brief reference to Mr Ingles's long and distinguished service in China.

The news was unpleasant. I read into Ingles's death a sinister motive. Not for one moment did I believe the theory of an accident. Ingles had been murdered, and his death was only too clearly the handiwork of that accursed Big Four.

As I sat there, stunned by the blow, and turning the whole matter over in my mind, I was startled by the remarkable behaviour of the man sitting opposite me. So far I had not paid much attention to him. He was a thin, dark man of middle age, sallow of complexion, with a small pointed beard. He had sat down opposite me so quietly that I had hardly noticed his arrival.

But his actions now were decidedly peculiar, to say the least of them. Leaning forward, he deliberately helped me to salt, putting it in four little heaps round the edge of my plate.

'You will excuse me,' he said, in a melancholy voice. 'To help a stranger to salt is to help them to sorrow, they say. That may be an unavoidable necessity. I hope not, though. I hope that you will be reasonable.'

Then, with a certain significance, he repeated his operations with the salt on his own plate. The symbol 4 was too plain to be missed. I looked at him searchingly. In no way that I could see did he resemble the young Templeton, or James the footman, or any other of the various personalities we had come across.

Nevertheless, I was convinced that I had to do with no less than the redoubtable Number Four himself. In his voice there was certainly a faint resemblance to the buttoned-up stranger who had called upon us in Paris.

I looked round, undecided as to my course of action. Reading my thoughts, he smiled and gently shook his head.

'I should not advise it,' he remarked. 'Remember what came of your hasty action in Paris. Let me assure you that my way of retreat is well assured. Your ideas are inclined to be a little crude, Captain Hastings, if I may say so.'

'You devil,' I said, choking with rage, 'you incarnate devil!'

'Heated – just a trifle heated. Your late lamented friend would have told you that a man who keeps calm has always a great advantage.'

'You dare to speak of him,' I cried. 'The man you murdered so foully. And you come here –'

He interrupted me.

'I came here for an excellent and peaceful purpose. To advise you to return at once to South America. If you do so, that is the end of the matter as far as the Big Four are concerned. You and yours will not be molested in any way. I give you my word as to that.'

I laughed scornfully.

'And if I refuse to obey your autocratic command?'

'It is hardly a command. Shall we say that it is – a warning?'

There was a cold menace in his tone.

'The first warning,' he said softly. 'You will be well advised not to disregard it.'

Then, before I had any hint of his intention, he rose and slipped quickly away towards the door. I sprang to my feet and was after him in a second, but by bad luck I cannoned straight into an enormously fat man who blocked the way between me and the next table. By the time I had disentangled myself, my quarry was just passing through the doorway, and the next delay was from a waiter carrying a huge pile of plates who crashed into me without the least warning. By the time I got to the door there was no sign of the thin man with the dark beard.

The waiter was fulsome in apologies, the fat man was sitting placidly at a table ordering his lunch. There was nothing to show that both occurrences had not been a pure accident. Nevertheless,

I had my own opinion as to that. I knew well enough that the agents of the Big Four were everywhere.

Needless to say, I paid no heed to the warning given me. I would do or die in the good cause. I received in all only two answers to the advertisements. Neither of them gave me any information of value. They were both from actors who had played with Claud Darrell at one time or another. Neither of them knew him at all intimately, and no new light was thrown upon the problem of his identity and present whereabouts.

No further sign came from the Big Four until about ten days later. I was crossing Hyde Park, lost in thought, when a voice, rich with a persuasive foreign inflection, hailed me.

'Captain Hastings, is it not?'

A big limousine had just drawn up by the pavement. A woman was leaning out. Exquisitely dressed in black, with wonderful pearls, I recognized the lady first known to us as Countess Vera Rossakoff, and afterwards under a different alias as an agent of the Big Four. Poirot, for some reason or other, had always had a sneaking fondness for the countess. Something in her very flamboyance attracted the little man. She was, he was wont to declare in moments of enthusiasm, a woman in a thousand. That she was arrayed against us, on the side of our bitterest enemies, never seemed to weigh in his judgement.

'Ah, do not pass on!' said the countess. 'I have something most important to say to you. And do not try to have me arrested either, for that would be stupid. You were always a little stupid – yes, yes, it is so. You are stupid now, when you persist in disregarding the warning we sent you. It is the second warning I bring you. Leave England at once. You can do no good here – I tell you that frankly. You will never accomplish anything.'

'In that case,' I said stiffly, 'it seems rather extraordinary that you are all so anxious to get me out of the country.'

The countess shrugged her shoulders – magnificent shoulders, and a magnificent gesture.

'For my part, I think that, too, stupid. I would leave you here to play about happily. But the chiefs, you see, are fearful that some word of yours may give great help to those more intelligent than yourself. Hence – you are to be banished.'

The countess appeared to have a flattering idea of my abilities.

I concealed my annoyance. Doubtless this attitude of hers was assumed expressly to annoy me and to give me the idea that I was unimportant.

'It would, of course, be quite easy to – remove you,' she continued, 'but I am quite sentimental sometimes. I pleaded for you. You have a nice little wife somewhere, have you not? And it would please the poor little man who is dead to know that you were not to be killed. I always liked him, you know. He was clever – but clever! Had it not been a case of four against one I honestly believe he might have been too much for us. I confess it frankly – he was my master! I sent a wreath to the funeral as a token of my admiration – an enormous one of crimson roses. Crimson roses express my temperament.'

I listened in silence and a growing distaste.

'You have the look of a mule when it puts its ears back and kicks. Well, I have delivered my warning. Remember this, the third warning will come by the hand of the Destroyer –'

She made a sign, and the car whirled away rapidly. I noted the number mechanically, but without the hope that it would lead to anything. The Big Four were not apt to be careless in details.

I went home a little sobered. One fact had emerged from the countess's flood of volubility. I was in real danger of my life. Though I had no intention of abandoning the struggle, I saw that it behoved me to walk warily and adopt every possible precaution.

Whilst I was reviewing all these facts and seeking for the best line of action, the telephone bell rang. I crossed the room and picked up the receiver.

'Yes. Hallo. Who's speaking?'

A crisp voice answered me.

'This is St Giles's Hospital. We have a Chinaman here, knifed in the street and brought in. He can't last long. We rang you up because we found in his pockets a piece of paper with your name and address on it.'

I was very much astonished. Nevertheless, after a moment's reflection I said that I would come down at once. St Giles's Hospital, was, I knew, down by the docks, and it occurred to me that the Chinaman might have just come off some ship.

It was on my way down there that a sudden suspicion shot into my mind. Was the whole thing a trap? Wherever a Chinaman was, there might be the hand of Li Chang Yen. I remembered the adventure of the Baited Trap. Was the whole thing a ruse on the part of my enemies?

A little reflection convinced me that at any rate a visit to the hospital would do no harm. It was probable that the thing was not so much a plot as what is vulgarly known as a 'plant'. The dying Chinaman would make some revelation to me upon which I should act, and which would have the result of leading me into the hands of the Big Four. The thing to do was to preserve an open mind, and whilst feigning credulity be secretly on my guard.

On arriving at St Giles's Hospital, and making my business known, I was taken at once to the accident ward, to the bedside of the man in question. He lay absolutely still, his eyelids closed, and only a very faint movement of the chest showed that he still breathed. A doctor stood by the bed, his fingers on the Chinaman's pulse.

'He's almost gone,' he whispered to me. 'You know him, eh?'

I shook my head.

'I've never seen him before.'

'Then what was he doing with your name and address in his pocket? You are Captain Hastings, aren't you?'

'Yes, but I can't explain it any more than you can.'

'Curious thing. From his papers he seems to have been the servant of a man called Ingles – a retired Civil Servant. Ah, you know him, do you?' he added quickly, as I started at the name.

Ingles's servant! Then I *had* seen him before. Not that I had ever succeeded in being able to distinguish one Chinaman from another. He must have been with Ingles on his way to China, and after the catastrophe he had returned to England with a message, possibly, for me. It was vital, imperative that I should hear the message.

'Is he conscious?' I asked. 'Can he speak? Mr Ingles was an old friend of mine, and I think it possible that this poor fellow has brought me a message from him. Mr Ingles is believed to have gone overboard about ten days ago.'

'He's just conscious, but I doubt if he has the force to speak. He lost a terrible lot of blood, you know. I can administer a stimulant, of course, but we've already done all that is possible in that direction.'

Nevertheless, he administered a hypodermic injection, and I stayed by the bed, hoping against hope for a word – a sign – that might be of the utmost value to me in my work. But the minutes sped on and no sign came.

And suddenly a baleful idea shot across my mind. Was I not already falling into the trap? Suppose that this Chinaman had merely assumed the part of Ingles's servant, that he was in reality an agent of the Big Four? Had I not once read that certain Chinese priests were capable of simulating death? Or, to go further still, Li Chang Yen might command a little band of fanatics who would welcome death itself if it came at the command of their master. I must be on my guard.

Even as these thoughts flashed across my mind, the man in the bed stirred. His eyes opened. He murmured something incoherently. Then I saw his glance fasten upon me. He made no sign of recognition, but I was at once aware that he was trying to speak to me. Be he friend or foe, I must hear what he had to say.

I leaned over the bed, but the broken sounds conveyed no sort of meaning to me. I thought I caught the word 'hand', but in what connection it was used I could not tell. Then it came again, and this time I heard another word, the word 'Largo'. I stared in amazement, as the possible juxtaposition of the two suggested itself to me.

'Handel's Largo?' I queried.

The Chinaman's eyelids flickered rapidly, as though in assent, and he added another Italian word, the word '*carrozza*'. Two or three more words of murmured Italian came to my ears, and then he fell back abruptly.

The doctor pushed me aside. It was all over. The man was dead.

I went out into the air again thoroughly bewildered.

'Handel's Largo', and a '*carrozza*'. If I remembered rightly, a *carrozza* was a carriage. What possible meaning could lie behind those simple words? The man was a Chinaman, not an Italian, why should he speak in Italian? Surely, if he were indeed Ingles's servant, he must know English? The whole thing was profoundly mystifying. I puzzled over it all the way home. Oh, if only Poirot had been there to solve the problem with his lightning ingenuity!

I let myself in with my latch-key and went slowly up to my room.

A letter was lying on the table, and I tore it open carelessly enough. But in a minute I stood rooted to the ground whilst I read.

It was a communication from a firm of solicitors.

Dear Sir (it ran) – As instructed by our late client, M. Hercule Poirot, we forward you the enclosed letter. This letter was placed in our hands a week before his death, with instructions that in the event of his demise, it should be sent to you at a certain date after his death.

Yours faithfully, etc.

I turned the enclosed missive over and over. It was undoubtably from Poirot. I knew that familiar writing only too well. With a heavy heart, yet a certain eagerness, I tore it open.

Mon Cher Ami (it began) – When you receive this I shall be no more. Do not shed tears about me, but follow my orders. Immediately upon receipt of this, return to South America. Do not be pig-headed about this. It is not for sentimental reasons that I bid you undertake the journey. *It is necessary*. It is part of the plan of Hercule Poirot! To say more is unnecessary, to anyone who has the acute intelligence of my friend Hastings.

A bas the Big Four! I salute you, my friend, from beyond the grave.

Ever thine,
Hercule Poirot

I read and re-read this astonishing communication. One thing was evident. The amazing man had so provided for every eventuality that even his own death did not upset the sequence of his plans! Mine was to be the active part – his the directing genius. Doubtless I should find full instructions awaiting me beyond the seas. In the meantime my enemies, convinced that I was obeying their warning, would cease to trouble their heads about me. I could return, unsuspected, and work havoc in their midst.

There was now nothing to hinder my immediate departure. I sent off cables, booked my passage, and one week later found me embarking in the *Ansonia*, en route for Buenos Aires.

Just as the boat left the quay, a steward brought me a note. It had been given him, so he explained, by a big gentleman in a fur coat who had left the boat last thing before the gangway planks were lifted.

I opened it. It was terse and to the point.

'You are wise,' it ran. It was signed with a big figure 4.

I could afford to smile to myself!

The sea was not too choppy. I enjoyed a passable dinner, made up my mind as to the majority of my fellow passengers, and had a rubber or two of bridge. Then I turned in and slept like a log as I always do on board ship.

I was awakened by feeling myself persistently shaken. Dazed and bewildered, I saw that one of the ship's officers was standing over me. He gave a sigh of relief as I sat up.

'Thank the Lord I've got you awake at last. I've had no end of a job. Do you always sleep like that?'

'What's the matter?' I asked, still bewildered and not fully awake. 'Is there anything wrong with the ship?'

'I expect you know what's the matter better than I do,' he replied drily. 'Special instructions from the Admiralty. There's a destroyer waiting to take you off.'

'What?' I cried. 'In mid-ocean?'

'It seems a most mysterious affair, but that's not my business. They've sent a young fellow aboard who is to take your place, and we are all sworn to secrecy. Will you get up and dress?'

Utterly unable to conceal my amazement I did as I was told. A boat was lowered, and I was conveyed aboard the destroyer. There I was received courteously, but got no further information. The commander's instructions were to land me at a certain spot on the Belgian coast. There his knowledge and responsibility ended.

The whole thing was like a dream. The one idea I held to firmly was that all this must be part of Poirot's plan. I must simply go forward blindly, trusting in my dead friend.

I was duly landed at the spot indicated. There a motor was waiting, and soon I was rapidly whirling across the flat Flemish plains. I slept that night at a small hotel in Brussels. The next day we went on again. The country became wooded and hilly. I realized that we were penetrating into the Ardennes, and I suddenly remembered Poirot's saying that he had a brother who lived at Spa.

But we did not go to Spa itself. We left the main road and wound into the leafy fastnesses of the hills, till we reached a little hamlet, and an isolated white villa high on the hillside. Here the car stopped in front of the green door of the villa.

The door opened as I alighted. An elderly man-servant stood in the doorway bowing.

'M. le Capitaine Hastings?' he said in French. 'M. le Capitaine is expected. If he will follow me.'

He led the way across the hall, and flung open a door at the back, standing aside to let me pass in.

I blinked a little, for the room faced west and the afternoon sun was pouring in. Then my vision cleared and I saw a figure waiting to welcome me with outstretched hands.

It was – oh, impossible, it couldn't be – but yes!

'Poirot!' I cried, and for once did not attempt to evade the embrace with which he overwhelmed me.

'But yes, but yes, it is indeed I! Not so easy to kill Hercule Poirot!'

'But Poirot – *why*?'

'A *ruse de guerre*, my friend, a *ruse de guerre*. All is now ready for our grand *coup*.'

'But you might have told *me*!'

'No, Hastings, I could not. Never, never, in a thousand years, could you have acted the part at the funeral. As it was, it was perfect. It could not fail to carry conviction to the Big Four.'

'But what I've been through –'

'Do not think me too unfeeling. I carried out the deception partly for your sake. I was willing to risk my own life, but I had qualms about continually risking yours. So, after the explosion, I have an idea of great brilliancy. The good Ridgeway, he enables me to carry it out. I am dead, you will return to South America. But, *mon ami*, that is just what you would not do. In the end I have to arrange a solicitor's letter, and a long rigmarole. But, at all events, here you are – that is the great thing. And now we lie here – *perdus* – till the moment comes for the last grand *coup* – the final overthrowing of the Big Four.'

CHAPTER 17

NUMBER FOUR WINS A TRICK

From our quiet retreat in the Ardennes we watched the progress of affairs in the great world. We were plentifully supplied with newspapers, and every day Poirot received a bulky envelope, evidently containing some kind of report. He never showed these reports to me, but I could usually tell from his manner whether their contents had been satisfactory or otherwise. He never wavered in his belief that our present plan was the only one likely to be crowned by success.

'As a minor point, Hastings,' he remarked one day, 'I was in continual fear of your death lying at my door. And that rendered me nervous – like a cat upon the jumps, as you say. But now I am well satisfied. Even if they discover that the Captain Hastings who landed in South America is an impostor (and I do not think they will discover it, they are not likely to send an agent out there who knows you personally), they will only believe that you are trying to circumvent them in some clever manner of your own, and will pay no serious attention to discovering your whereabouts. Of the one vital fact, my supposed death, they are thoroughly convinced. They will go ahead and mature their plans.'

'And then?' I asked eagerly.

'And then, *mon ami*, grand resurrection of Hercule Poirot! At the eleventh hour I reappear, throw all into confusion, and achieve the supreme victory in my own unique manner!'

I realized that Poirot's vanity was of the case-hardened variety which could withstand all attacks. I reminded him that once or twice the honours of the game had lain with our adversaries. But I might have known that it was impossible to diminish Hercule Poirot's enthusiasm for his own methods.

'See you, Hastings, it is like the little trick that you play with the cards. You have seen it without doubt? You take the four knaves, you divide them, one on top of the pack, one underneath, and so on – you cut and you shuffle, and there they are all together again. That is my object. So far I have been contending, now against one of the Big Four, now against another. But let me get them all together, like the four knaves in the pack of cards, and then, with one *coup*, I destroy them all!'

'And how do you propose to get them all together?' I asked.

'By awaiting the supreme moment. By lying *perdu* until they are ready to strike.'

'That may mean a long wait,' I grumbled.

'Always impatient, the good Hastings! But no, it will not be so long. The one man they were afraid of – myself – is out of the way. I give them two or three months at most.'

His speaking of someone being got out of the way reminded me of Ingles and his tragic death, and I remembered that I had never told Poirot about the dying Chinaman in St Giles's Hospital.

He listened with keen attention to my story.

'Ingles's servant, eh? And the few words he uttered were in Italian? Curious.'

'That's why I suspected it might have been a plant on the part of the Big Four.'

'Your reasoning is at fault, Hastings. Employ the little grey cells. If your enemies wished to deceive you they would assuredly have seen to it that the Chinaman spoke in intelligible pidgin English. No, the message was genuine. Tell me again all that you heard?'

'First of all he made a reference to Handel's Largo, and then he said something that sounded like "*carrozza*" – that's a carriage, isn't it?'

'Nothing else?'

'Well, just at the end he murmured something like "*Cara*" somebody or other – some woman's name. Zia, I think. But I don't suppose that that had any bearing on the rest of it.'

'You would not suppose so, Hastings. Cara Zia is very important, very important indeed.'

'I don't see –'

'My dear friend, you *never* see – and anyway the English know no geography.'

'Geography?' I cried. 'What has geography got to do with it?'

'I dare say M. Thomas Cook would be more to the point.'

As usual, Poirot refused to say anything more – a most irritating trick of his. But I noticed that his manner became extremely cheerful, as though he had scored some point or other.

The days went on, pleasant if a trifle monotonous. There were plenty of books in the villa, and delightful rambles all around, but I chafed sometimes at the forced inactivity of our life, and marvelled at Poirot's state of placid content. Nothing occurred to ruffle our quiet existence, and it was not until the end of June, well within the limit that Poirot had given them, that we had our news of the Big Four.

A car drove up to the villa early one morning, such an unusual event in our peaceful life that I hurried down to satisfy my curiosity. I found Poirot talking to a pleasant-faced young fellow of about my own age.

He introduced me.

'This is Captain Harvey, Hastings, one of the most famous members of your Intelligence Service.'

'Not famous at all, I'm afraid,' said the young man, laughing pleasantly.

'Not famous except to those in the know, I should have said. Most of Captain Harvey's friends and acquaintances consider him an amiable but brainless young man – devoted only to the trot of the fox or whatever the dance is called.'

We both laughed.

'Well, well, to business,' said Poirot. 'You are of opinion the time has come, then?'

'We are sure of it, sir. China was isolated politically yesterday. What is going on out there, nobody knows. No news of any kind, wireless or otherwise, has come through – just a complete break – and silence!'

'Li Chang Yen has shown his hand. And the others?'

'Abe Ryland arrived in England a week ago, and left for the Continent yesterday.'

'And Madame Olivier?'

'Madame Olivier left Paris last night.'

'For Italy?'

'For Italy, sir. As far as we can judge, they are both making for the resort you indicated – though how you knew that –'

'Ah, that is not the cap with the feather for me! That was the work of Hastings here. He conceals his intelligence, you comprehend, but it is profound for all that.'

Harvey looked at me with due appreciation, and I felt rather uncomfortable.

'All is in train, then,' said Poirot. He was pale now, and completely serious. 'The time has come. The arrangements are all made?'

'Everything you ordered has been carried out. The governments of Italy, France, and England are behind you, and are all working harmoniously together.'

'It is, in fact, a new *Entente*,' observed Poirot drily. 'I am glad that Desjardeaux is convinced at last. *Eh bien*, then, we will start – or rather, I will start. You, Hastings, will remain here – yes, I pray of you. In verity, my friend, I am serious.'

I believed him, but it was not likely that I should consent to being left behind in that fashion. Our argument was short but decisive.

It was not until we were in the train, speeding towards Paris, that he admitted that he was secretly glad of my decision.

'For you have a part to play, Hastings. An important part! Without you, I might well fail. Nevertheless, I felt that it was my duty to urge you to remain behind –'

'There is danger, then?'

'*Mon ami*, where there is the Big Four there is always danger.'

On arrival in Paris, we drove across to the Gare de L'est, and Poirot at last announced our destination. We were bound for Bolzano and the Italian Tyrol.

During Harvey's absence from our carriage I took the opportunity of asking Poirot why he had said that the discovery of the rendezvous was my work.

'Because it was, my friend. How Ingles managed to get hold of the information I do not know, but he did, and he sent it to us by his servant. We are bound, *mon ami*, for Karersee, the new Italian name for which is Lago di Carrezza. You see now where your "*Cara Zia*" comes in and also your "Carrozza" and "Largo" – the Handel was supplied by your own imagination. Possibly some reference to the information coming from the "hand" of Mr Ingles started the train of association.'

'Karersee?' I queried. 'I never heard of it.'

'I always tell you that the English know no geography. But as a matter of fact it is a well known and very beautiful summer resort, four thousand feet up, in the heart of the Dolomites.'

'And it is in this out of the way spot that the Big Four have their rendezvous?'

'Say rather their headquarters. The signal has been given, and it is their intention to disappear from the world and issue orders from their mountain fastness. I have made the enquiries – a lot of quarrying of stone and mineral deposits is done there, and the company, apparently a small Italian firm, is in reality controlled by Abe Ryland. I am prepared to swear that a vast subterranean dwelling has been hollowed out in the very heart of the mountain, secret and inaccessible. From there the leaders of the organization will issue by wireless their orders to their followers who are numbered by thousands in every country. And from that crag in the Dolomites the dictators of the world will emerge. That is to say – they would emerge were it not for Hercule Poirot.'

'Do you seriously believe all this, Poirot? – What about the armies and general machinery of civilization?'

'What about it in Russia, Hastings? This will be Russia on an infinitely larger scale – and with this additional menace – that Madame Olivier's experiments have proceeded further than she has ever given out. I believe that she has, to a certain extent, succeeded in liberating atomic energy and harnessing it to her purpose. Her experiments with the nitrogen of the air have been very remarkable, and she has also experimented in the concentration of wireless energy, so that a beam of great intensity can be focused upon some given spot. Exactly how far she has progressed, nobody knows, but it is certain that it is much farther than has ever been given out. She is a genius, that woman – the Curies were as nothing to her. Add to her genius the powers of Ryland's almost unlimited wealth, and, with the brain of Li Chang Yen, the finest criminal brain ever known, to direct and plan – *eh bien*, it will not be, as you say, all jam for civilization.'

His words made me very thoughtful. Although Poirot was given at times to exaggeration of language, he was not really an alarmist. For the first time I realized what a desperate struggle it was upon which we were engaged.

Harvey soon rejoined us and the journey went on.

We arrived at Bolzano about midday. From there the journey on was by motor. Several big blue motor cars were waiting in the central square of the town, and we three got into one of them. Poirot, notwithstanding the heat of the day, was muffled to the eyes in greatcoat and scarf. His eyes and the tips of his ears were all that could be seen of him.

I did not know whether this was due to precaution or merely his exaggerated fear of catching a chill. The motor journey took a couple of hours. It was a really wonderful drive. For the first part of the way we wound in and out of huge cliffs, with a trickling waterfall on one hand. Then we emerged into a fertile valley, which continued for some miles, and then, still winding steadily upwards, the bare rock peaks began to show with dense clustering pinewoods at their base. The whole place was wild and lovely. Finally a series of abrupt curves, with the road running through the pinewoods on either side, and we came suddenly upon a big hotel and found we had arrived.

Our rooms had been reserved for us, and under Harvey's guidance we went straight up to them. They looked straight out over the rocky peaks and the long slopes of pinewoods leading up to them. Poirot made a gesture towards them.

'It is there?' he asked in a low voice.

'Yes,' replied Harvey. 'There is a place called the Felsenlabyrinth – all big boulders piled about in a most fantastic way – a path winds through them. The quarrying is to the right of that, but we think that the entrance is probably in the Felsenlabyrinth.'

Poirot nodded.

'Come, *mon ami*,' he said to me. 'Let us go down and sit upon the terrace and enjoy the sunlight.'

'You think that wise?' I asked.

He shrugged his shoulders.

The sunlight was marvellous – in fact the glare was almost too great for me. We had some creamy coffee instead of tea, then went upstairs and unpacked our few belongings. Poirot was in his most unapproachable mood, lost in a kind of reverie. Once or twice he shook his head and sighed.

I had been rather intrigued by a man who had got out of our train at Bolzano, and had been met by a private car. He was a small man, and one thing about him that attracted my attention was that he was almost as much muffled up as Poirot had been. More so, indeed, for in addition to greatcoat and muffler, he was wearing huge blue spectacles. I was convinced that here we had an emissary of the Big Four. Poirot did not seem very impressed by my idea. But when, leaning out of my bedroom window, I reported that the man in question was strolling about in the vicinity of the hotel, he admitted that there might be something in it.

I urged my friend not to go down to dinner, but he insisted on doing so. We entered the dining-room rather late, and were shown to a table by the window. As we sat down, our attention was attracted by an exclamation and a crash of falling china. A dish of haricots verts had been upset over a man who was sitting at the table next to ours.

The head waiter came up and was vociferous in apologies.

Presently, when the offending waiter was serving us with soup, Poirot spoke to him.

'An unfortunate accident, that. But it was not your fault.'

'Monsieur saw that? No, indeed it was not my fault. The gentleman half sprang up from his chair – I thought he was going to have an attack of some kind. I could not save the catastrophe.'

I saw Poirot's eyes shining with the green light I knew so well, and as the waiter departed he said to me in a low voice:

'You see, Hastings, the effect of Hercule Poirot – alive and in the flesh?'

'You think –'

I had not time to continue. I felt Poirot's hand on my knee, as he whispered excitedly:

'Look, Hastings, look. *His trick with the bread!* Number Four!'

Sure enough, the man at the next table to ours, his face unusually pale, was dabbing a small piece of bread mechanically about the table.

I studied him carefully. His face, clean-shaven and puffily fat, was of a pasty, unhealthy sallowness, with heavy pouches under the eyes and deep lines running from his nose to the corners of his mouth. His age might have been anything from thirty-five to forty-five. In no particular did he resemble any one of the characters which Number Four had previously assumed. Indeed, had it not been for his little trick with the bread, of which he was evidently quite unaware, I would have sworn readily enough that the man sitting there was someone whom I had never seen before.

'He has recognized you,' I murmured. 'You should not have come down.'

'My excellent Hastings, I have feigned death for three months for this one purpose.'

'To startle Number Four?'

'To startle him at a moment when he must act quickly or not at all. And we have this great advantage – he does not know that we recognize him. He thinks that he is safe in his new disguise. How I bless Flossie Monro for telling us of that little habit of his.'

'What will happen now?' I asked.

'What can happen? He recognizes the only man he fears, miraculously resurrected from the dead, at the very minute when the plans of the Big Four are in the balance. Madame Olivier and Abe Ryland lunched here today, and it is thought that they went to Cortina. Only we know that they have retired to their hiding-place. How much do we know? That is what Number Four is asking himself at this minute. He dare take no risks. I must be suppressed at all costs. *Eh bien*, let him try to suppress Hercule Poirot! I shall be ready for him.'

As he finished speaking, the man at the next table got up and went out.

'He has gone to make his little arrangements,' said Poirot placidly. 'Shall we have our coffee on the terrace, my friend? It would be pleasanter, I think. I will just go up and get a coat.'

I went out on to the terrace, a little disturbed in mind. Poirot's assurance did not quite content me. However, so long as we were on guard, nothing could happen to us. I resolved to keep thoroughly on the alert.

It was quite five minutes before Poirot joined me. With his usual precautions against cold, he was muffled up to the ears. He sat down beside me and sipped his coffee appreciatively.

'Only in England is the coffee so atrocious,' he remarked. 'On the Continent they understand how important it is for the digestion that it should be properly made.'

As he finished speaking, the man from the next table suddenly appeared on the terrace. Without any hesitation, he came over and drew up a third chair to our table.

'You do not mind my joining you, I hope,' he said in English.

'Not at all, monsieur,' said Poirot.

I felt very uneasy. It is true that we were on the terrace of the hotel, with people all around us, but nevertheless I was not satisfied. I sensed the presence of danger.

Meanwhile Number Four chatted away in a perfectly natural manner. It seemed impossible to believe that he was anything but a *bona fide* tourist. He described excursions and motor trips, and posed as quite an authority on the neighbourhood.

He took a pipe from his pocket and began to light it. Poirot drew out his case of tiny cigarettes. As he placed one between his lips, the stranger leant forward with a match.

'Let me give you a light.'

As he spoke, without the least warning, all the lights went out. There was a chink of glass, and something pungent under my nose, suffocating me –

CHAPTER 18

IN THE FELSENLABYRINTH

I could not have been unconscious more than a minute. I came to myself being hustled along between two men. They had me under each arm, supporting my weight, and there was a gag in my mouth. It was pitch dark, but I gathered that we were not outside, but passing through the hotel. All round I could hear people shouting and demanding in every known language what had happened to the lights. My captors swung me down some stairs. We passed along a basement passage, then through a door and out into the open again through a glass door at the back of the hotel. In another moment we had gained the shelter of the pine trees.

I had caught a glimpse of another figure in a similar plight to myself, and realized that Poirot, too, was a victim of this bold *coup*.

By sheer audacity, Number Four had won the day. He had employed, I gathered, an instant anaesthetic, probably ethyl chloride – breaking a small bulb of it under our noses. Then, in the confusion of the darkness, his accomplices, who had probably been guests sitting at the next table, had thrust gags in our mouths and hurried us away, taking us through the hotel to baffle pursuit.

I cannot describe the hour that followed. We were hurried

through the woods at a break-neck pace, going uphill the whole time. At last we emerged in the open, on the mountain-side, and I saw just in front of us an extraordinary conglomeration of fantastic rocks and boulders.

This must be the Felsenlabyrinth of which Harvey had spoken. Soon we were winding in and out of its recesses. The place was like a maze devised by some evil genie.

Suddenly we stopped. An enormous rock barred our path. One of the men stopped and seemed to push on something when, without a sound, the huge mass of rock turned on itself and disclosed a small tunnel-like opening leading into the mountain-side.

Into this we were hurried. For some time the tunnel was narrow, but presently it widened, and before very long we came out into a wide rocky chamber lighted by electricity. Then the gags were removed. At a sign from Number Four, who stood facing us with mocking triumph in his face, we were searched and every article was removed from our pockets, including Poirot's little automatic pistol.

A pang smote me as it was tossed down on the table. We were defeated – hopelessly defeated and out-numbered. It was the end.

'Welcome to the headquarters of the Big Four, M. Hercule Poirot,' said Number Four in a mocking tone. 'To meet you again is an unexpected pleasure. But was it worth while returning from the grave only for this?'

Poirot did not reply. I dared not look at him.

'Come this way,' continued Number Four. 'Your arrival will be somewhat of a surprise to my colleagues.'

He indicated a narrow doorway in the wall. We passed through and found ourselves in another chamber. At the very end of it was a table behind which four chairs were placed. The end chair was empty, but it was draped with a mandarin's cape. On the second, smoking a cigar, sat Mr Abe Ryland. Leaning back on the third chair, with her burning eyes and her nun's face, was Madame Olivier. Number Four took his seat on the fourth chair.

We were in the presence of the Big Four.

Never before had I felt so fully the reality and the presence of Li Chang Yen as I did now when confronting his empty seat.

Far away in China, he yet controlled and directed this malign organization.

Madame Olivier gave a faint cry on seeing us. Ryland, more self-controlled, only shifted his cigar, and raised his grizzled eyebrows.

'M. Hercule Poirot,' said Ryland slowly. 'This is a pleasant surprise. You put it over on us all right. We thought you were good and buried. No matter, the game is up now.'

There was a ring as of steel in his voice. Madame Olivier said nothing, but her eyes burned, and I disliked the slow way she smiled.

'Madame and messieurs, I wish you good evening,' said Poirot quietly.

Something unexpected, something I had not been prepared to hear in his voice made me look at him. He seemed quite composed. Yet there was something about his whole appearance that was different.

Then there was a stir of draperies behind us, and the Countess Vera Rossakoff came in.

'Ah!' said Number Four. 'Our valued and trusted lieutenant. An old friend of yours is here, my dear lady.'

The countess whirled round with her usual vehemence of movement.

'God in Heaven!' she cried. 'It is the little man! Ah! but he has the nine lives of a cat! Oh, little man, little man! Why did you mix yourself up in this?'

'Madame,' said Poirot with a bow. 'Me, like the great Napoleon, I am on the side of the big battalions.'

As he spoke I saw a sudden suspicion flash into her eyes, and at the same moment I knew the truth which subconsciously I already sensed.

The man beside me was not Hercule Poirot.

He was very like him, extraordinarily like him. There was the same egg-shaped head, the same strutting figure, delicately plump. But the voice was different, and the eyes instead of being green were dark, and surely the moustaches – those famous moustaches –?

My reflections were cut short by the countess's voice. She stepped forward, her voice ringing with excitement.

'You have been deceived. This man is not Hercule Poirot!'

Number Four uttered an incredulous exclamation, but the countess leant forward and snatched at Poirot's moustaches. They came off in her hand, and then, indeed, the truth was plain. For this man's upper lip was disfigured by a small scar which completely altered the expression of the face.

'Not Hercule Poirot,' muttered Number Four. 'But who can he be then?'

'I know,' I cried suddenly, and then stopped dead, afraid I had ruined everything.

But the man I will still refer to as Poirot had turned to me encouragingly.

'Say it if you will. It makes no matter now. The trick has succeeded.'

'This is Achille Poirot,' I said slowly. 'Hercule Poirot's twin brother.'

'Impossible,' said Ryland sharply, but he was shaken.

'Hercule's plan has succeeded to a marvel,' said Achille placidly.

Number Four leapt forward, his voice harsh and menacing.

'Succeeded, has it?' he snarled. 'Do you realize that before many minutes have passed you will be dead – dead?'

'Yes,' said Achille Poirot gravely. 'I realize that. It is you who do not realize that a man may be willing to purchase success by his life. There were men who laid down their lives for their country in the war. I am prepared to lay down mine in the same way for the world.'

It struck me just then that although perfectly willing to lay down my life I might have been consulted in the matter. Then I remembered how Poirot had urged me to stay behind and I felt appeased.

'And in what way will your laying down your life benefit the world?' asked Ryland sardonically.

'I see that you do not perceive the true inwardness of Hercule's plan. To begin with, your place of retreat was known some months ago, and practically all the visitors, hotel assistants and others are detectives or Secret Service men. A cordon has been drawn round the mountain. You may have more than one means of egress, but even so you cannot escape. Poirot himself is directing the operations outside. My boots were smeared with a preparation of aniseed tonight, before I came down to the terrace in my brother's place. Hounds are following the trail. It will lead them infallibly to the rock in the Felsenlabyrinth where the entrance is situated. You see, do what you will to us, the net is drawn tightly round you. You cannot escape.'

Madame Olivier laughed suddenly.

'You are wrong. There is one way we can escape, and, like Samson, of old, destroy our enemies at the same time. What do you say, my friends?'

Ryland was staring at Achille Poirot.

'Suppose he's lying,' he said hoarsely.

The other shrugged his shoulders.

'In an hour it will be dawn. Then you can see for yourself the truth of my words. Already they should have traced me to the entrance in the Felsenlabyrinth.'

Even as he spoke, there was a far-off reverberation, and a man ran in shouting incoherently. Ryland sprang up and went out. Madame Olivier moved to the end of the room and opened a door that I had not noticed. Inside I caught a glimpse of a perfectly equipped laboratory which reminded me of the one in Paris. Number Four also sprang up and went out. He returned with Poirot's revolver which he gave to the countess.

'There is no danger of their escaping,' he said grimly. 'But still you had better have this.'

Then he went out again.

The countess came over to us and surveyed my companion attentively for some time. Suddenly she laughed.

'You are very clever, M. Achille Poirot,' she said mockingly.

'Madame, let us talk business. It is fortunate that they have left us alone together. What is your price?'

'I do not understand. What price?'

'Madame, you can aid us to escape. You know the secret way out of this retreat. I ask you, what is your price?'

She laughed again.

'More than you could pay, little man! Why, all the money in the world would not buy me!'

'Madame, I did not speak of money. I am a man of intelligence.

Nevertheless, this is a true fact – *everyone has his price!* In exchange for life and liberty, I offer you your heart's desire.'

'So you are a magician!'

'You can call me so if you like.'

The countess suddenly dropped her jesting manner. She spoke with passionate bitterness.

'Fool! My heart's desire! Can you give me revenge upon my enemies? Can you give me back youth and beauty and a gay heart? Can you bring the dead to life again?'

Achille Poirot was watching her very curiously.

'Which of the three, Madame? Make your choice.'

She laughed sardonically.

'You will send me the Elixir of Life, perhaps? Come, I will make a bargain with you. Once, I had a child. Find my child for me – and you shall go free.'

'Madame, I agree. It is a bargain. Your child shall be restored to you. On the faith of – on the faith of Hercule Poirot himself.'

Again that strange woman laughed – this time long and unrestrainedly.

'My dear M. Poirot, I am afraid I laid a little trap for you. It is very kind of you to promise to find my child for me, but, you see, I happen to know that you would not succeed, and so that would be a very one-sided bargain, would it not?'

'Madame, I swear to you by the Holy Angels that I will restore your child to you.'

'I asked you before, M. Poirot, could you restore the dead to life?'

'Then the child is –'

'Dead? Yes.'

He stepped forward and took her wrist.

'Madame, I – I who speak to you, swear once more. *I will bring the dead back to life.*'

She stared at him as though fascinated.

'You do not believe me. I will prove my words. Get my pocketbook which they took from me.'

She went out of the room, and returned with it in her hand. Throughout all she retained her grip on the revolver. I felt that Achille Poirot's chances of bluffing her were very slight. The Countess Vera Rossakoff was no fool.

'Open it, madame. The flap on the left-hand side. That is right. Now take out that photograph and look at it.'

Wonderingly, she took out what seemed to be a small snapshot. No sooner had she looked at it than she uttered a cry and swayed as though about to fall. Then she almost flew at my companion.

'Where? Where? You shall tell me. Where?'

'Remember your bargain, madame.'

'Yes, yes, I will trust you. Quick, before they come back.'

Catching him by the hand, she drew him quickly and silently out of the room. I followed. From the outer room she led us into the tunnel by which we had first entered, but a short way along this forked, and she turned off to the right. Again and again the passage divided, but she led us on, never faltering or seeming to doubt her way, and with increasing speed.

'If only we are in time,' she panted. 'We must be out in the open before the explosion occurs.'

Still we went on. I understood that this tunnel led right through the mountain and that we should finally emerge on the other side, facing a different valley. The sweat streamed down my face, but I raced on.

And then, far away, I saw a gleam of daylight. Nearer and nearer. I saw green bushes growing. We forced them aside, pushed our way through. We were in the open again, with the faint light of dawn making everything rosy.

Poirot's cordon was a reality. Even as we emerged, three men fell upon us, but released us again with a cry of astonishment.

'Quick,' cried my companion. 'Quick – there is no time to lose –'

But he was not destined to finish. The earth shook and trembled under our feet, there was a terrific roar and the whole mountain seemed to dissolve. We were flung headlong through the air.

I came to myself at last. I was in a strange bed and a strange room. Someone was sitting by the window. He turned and came and stood by me.

It was Achille Poirot – or, stay, was it –

The well-known ironical voice dispelled any doubts I might have had.

'But yes, my friend, it is. Brother Achille has gone home again

– to the land of myths. It was I all the time. It is not only Number Four who can act a part. Belladonna in the eyes, the sacrifice of the moustaches, and a real scar the inflicting of which caused me much pain two months ago – but I could not risk a fake beneath the eagle eyes of Number Four. And the final touch, your own knowledge and belief that there was such a person as Achille Poirot! It was invaluable, the assistance you rendered me, half the success of the *coup* is due to you! The whole crux of the affair was to make them believe that Hercule Poirot was still at large directing operations. Otherwise, everything was true, the aniseed, the cordon, etc.'

'But why not really send a substitute?'

'And let you go into danger without me by your side. You have a pretty idea of me there! Besides, I always had a hope of finding a way out through the countess.'

'How on earth did you manage to convince her? It was a pretty thin story to make her swallow – all that about a dead child.'

'The countess has a great deal more perspicacity than you have, my dear Hastings. She was taken in at first by my disguise; but she soon saw through it. When she said, "You are very clever, M. Achille Poirot," I knew that she had guessed the truth. It was then or never to play my trump card.'

'All that rigmarole about bringing the dead to life?'

'Exactly – but then, you see, I had the child all along.'

'*What?*'

'But yes! You know my motto – Be prepared. As soon as I found that the Countess Rossakoff was mixed up with the Big Four, I had every possible inquiry made as to her antecedents. I learnt that she had had a child who was reported to have been killed, and I also found that there were discrepancies in the story which led me to wonder whether it might not, after all, be alive. In the end, I succeeded in tracing the boy, and by paying out a big sum I obtained possession of the child's person. The poor little fellow was nearly dead of starvation. I placed him in a safe place, with kindly people, and took a snapshot of him in his new surroundings. And so, when the time came, I had my little *coup de théâtre* all ready!'

'You are wonderful, Poirot; absolutely wonderful!'

'I was glad to do it, too. For I had admired the countess. I should have been sorry if she had perished in the explosion.'

'I've been half afraid to ask you – what of the Big Four?'

'All the bodies have now been recovered. That of Number Four was quite unrecognizable, the head blown to pieces. I wish – I rather wish it had not been so. I should have liked to be *sure* – but no more of that. Look at this.'

He handed me a newspaper in which a paragraph was marked. It reported the death, by suicide, of Li Chang Yen, who had engineered the recent revolution which had failed so disastrously.

'My great opponent,' said Poirot gravely. 'It was fated that he and I should never meet in the flesh. When he received the news of the disaster here, he took the simplest way out. A great brain, my friend, a great brain. But I wish I had seen the face of the man who was Number Four . . . Supposing that, after all – but I romance. He is dead. Yes, *mon ami*, together we have faced and routed the Big Four; and now you will return to your charming wife, and I – I shall retire. The great case of my life is over. Anything else will seem tame after this. No, I shall retire. Possibly I shall grow vegetable marrows! I might even marry and arrange myself!'

He laughed heartily at the idea, but with a touch of embarrassment. I hope . . . small men always admire big, flamboyant women –

'Marry and arrange myself,' he said again. 'Who knows?'

PERIL AT END HOUSE

To Eden Philpotts
To whom I shall always be grateful
for his friendship and the encouragement
he gave me many years ago

CONTENTS

CHAPTER I

THE MAJESTIC HOTEL

No seaside town in the south of England is, I think, as attractive as St Loo. It is well named the Queen of Watering Places and reminds one forcibly of the Riviera. The Cornish coast is to my mind every bit as fascinating as that of the south of France.

I remarked as much to my friend, Hercule Poirot. 'So it said on our menu in the restaurant car yesterday, *mon ami*. Your remark is not original.'

'But don't you agree?'

He was smiling to himself and did not at once answer my question. I repeated it.

'A thousand pardons, Hastings. My thoughts were wandering. Wandering indeed to that part of the world you mentioned just now.'

'The south of France?'

'Yes. I was thinking of that last winter that I spent there and of the events which occurred.'

I remembered. A murder had been committed on the Blue Train, and the mystery – a complicated and baffling one – had been solved by Poirot with his usual unerring acumen.

'How I wish I had been with you,' I said with deep regret.

'I too,' said Poirot. 'Your experience would have been invaluable to me.'

I looked at him sideways. As a result of long habit, I distrust his compliments, but he appeared perfectly serious. And after all, why not? I have a very long experience of the methods he employs.

'What I particularly missed was your vivid imagination, Hastings,' he went on dreamily. 'One needs a certain amount of light relief. My valet, Georges, an admirable man with whom I sometimes permitted myself to discuss a point, has no imagination whatever.' This remark seemed to me quite irrelevant.

'Tell me, Poirot,' I said. 'Are you never tempted to renew your activities? This passive life –'

'Suits me admirably, my friend. To sit in the sun – what could be more charming? To step from your pedestal at the zenith of your fame – what could be a grander gesture? They say of me: *"That is Hercule Poirot! – The great – the unique! – There was never any one like him, there never will be!"* *Eh bien* – I am satisfied. I ask no more. I am modest.'

I should not myself have used the word modest. It seemed to me that my little friend's egotism had certainly not declined with his years. He leaned back in his chair, caressing his moustache and almost purring with self-satisfaction.

We were sitting on one of the terraces of the Majestic Hotel. It is the biggest hotel in St Loo and stands in its own grounds on a headland overlooking thé sea. The gardens of the hotel lay below us freely interspersed with palm trees. The sea was of a deep and lovely blue, the sky clear and the sun shining with all the single-hearted fervour an August sun should (but in England so often does not) have. There was a vigorous humming of bees, a pleasant sound – and altogether nothing could have been more ideal.

We had only arrived last night, and this was the first morning of what we proposed should be a week's stay. If only these weather conditions continued, we should indeed have a perfect holiday.

I picked up the morning paper which had fallen from my hand and resumed my perusal of the morning's news. The political situation seemed unsatisfactory, but uninteresting, there was trouble in China, there was a long account of a rumoured City swindle, but on the whole there was no news of a very thrilling order.

'Curious thing this parrot disease,' I remarked, as I turned the sheet.

'Very curious.'

'Two more deaths at Leeds, I see.'

'Most regrettable.'

I turned a page.

'Still no news of that flying fellow, Seton, in his round-the-world flight. Pretty plucky, these fellows. That amphibian machine of his, the *Albatross*, must be a great invention. Too bad if he's gone west. Not that they've given up hope yet. He may have made one of the Pacific islands.'

'The Solomon islanders are still cannibals, are they not?' inquired Poirot pleasantly.

'Must be a fine fellow. That sort of thing makes one feel it's a good thing to be an Englishman after all.'

'It consoles for the defeats at Wimbledon,' said Poirot.

'I – I didn't mean,' I began.

My friend waved my attempted apology aside gracefully.

'Me,' he announced. 'I am not amphibian, like the machine of the poor Captain Seton, but I am cosmopolitan. And for the English I have always had, as you know, a great admiration. The thorough way, for instance, in which they read the daily paper.'

My attention had strayed to political news.

'They seem to be giving the Home Secretary a pretty bad time of it,' I remarked with a chuckle.

'The poor man. He has his troubles, that one. Ah! yes. So much so that he seeks for help in the most improbable quarters.'

I stared at him.

With a slight smile, Poirot drew from his pocket his morning's correspondence, neatly secured by a rubber band. From this he selected one letter which he tossed across to me.

'It must have missed us yesterday,' he said.

I read the letter with a pleasurable feeling of excitement.

'But, Poirot,' I cried. 'This is most flattering!'

'You think so, my friend?'

'He speaks in the warmest terms of your ability.'

'He is right,' said Poirot, modestly averting his eyes.

'He begs you to investigate this matter for him – puts it as a personal favour.'

'Quite so. It is unnecessary to repeat all this to me. You understand, my dear Hastings. I have read the letter myself.'

'It is too bad,' I cried. 'This will put an end to our holiday.'

'No, no, *calmez vous* – there is no question of that.'

'But the Home Secretary says the matter is urgent.'

'He may be right – or again he may not. These politicians, they are easily excited. I have seen myself, in the Chambre des Deputés in Paris –'

'Yes, yes, but Poirot, surely we ought to be making arrangements? The express to London has gone – it leaves at twelve o'clock. The next –'

'Calm yourself, Hastings, calm yourself, I pray of you! Always the excitement, the agitation. We are not going to London today – nor yet tomorrow.'

'But this summons –'

'Does not concern me. I do not belong to your police force, Hastings. I am asked to undertake a case as a private investigator. I refuse.'

'You *refuse?*'

'Certainly. I write with perfect politeness, tender my regrets, my apologies, explain that I am completely desolated – but what will you? I have retired – I am finished.'

'You are not finished,' I exclaimed warmly.

Poirot patted my knee.

'There speaks the good friend – the faithful dog. And you have reason, too. The grey cells, they still function – the order, the method – it is still there. But when I have retired, my friend, I have retired! It is finished! I am not a stage favourite who gives the world a dozen farewells. In all generosity I say: let the young men have a chance. They may possibly do something creditable. I doubt it, but they may. Anyway they will do well enough for this doubtless tiresome affair of the Home Secretary's.'

'But, Poirot, the compliment!'

'Me, I am above compliments. The Home Secretary, being a man of sense, realizes that if he can only obtain my services all will be successful. What will you? He is unlucky. Hercule Poirot has solved his last case.'

I looked at him. In my heart of hearts I deplored his obstinacy. The solving of such a case as was indicated might add still further lustre to his already world-wide reputation. Nevertheless I could not but admire his unyielding attitude.

Suddenly a thought struck me and I smiled.

'I wonder,' I said, 'that you are not afraid. Such an emphatic pronouncement will surely tempt the gods.'

'Impossible,' he replied, 'that anyone should shake the decision of Hercule Poirot.'

'*Impossible*, Poirot?'

'You are right, *mon ami*, one should not use such a word. *Eh, ma foi*, I do not say that if a bullet should strike the wall by my head, I would not investigate the matter! One is human after all!'

I smiled. A little pebble had just struck the terrace beside us, and Poirot's fanciful analogy from it tickled my fancy. He stooped now and picked up the pebble as he went on.

'Yes – one is human. One is the sleeping dog – well and good, but the sleeping dog can be roused. There is a proverb in your language that says so.'

'In fact,' I said, 'if you find a dagger planted by your pillow tomorrow morning – let the criminal who put it there beware!'

He nodded, but rather absently.

Suddenly, to my surprise, he rose and descended the couple of steps that led from the terrace to the garden. As he did so, a girl came into sight hurrying up towards us.

I had just registered the impression that she was a decidedly pretty girl when my attention was drawn to Poirot who, not looking where he was going, had stumbled over a root and fallen heavily. He was just abreast of the girl at the time and she and I between us helped him to his feet. My attention was naturally on my friend, but I was conscious of an impression of dark hair, an impish face and big dark-blue eyes.

'A thousand pardons,' stammered Poirot. 'Mademoiselle, you are most kind. I regret exceedingly – ouch! – my foot he pains me considerably. No, no, it is nothing really – the turned ankle, that is all. In a few minutes all will be well. But if you could help me, Hastings – you and Mademoiselle between you, if she will be so very kind. I am ashamed to ask it of her.'

With me on the one side and the girl on the other we soon got Poirot on to a chair on the terrace. I then suggested fetching a doctor, but this my friend negatived sharply.

'It is nothing, I tell you. The ankle turned, that is all. Painful for the moment, but soon over.' He made a grimace. 'See, in a little minute I shall have forgotten. Mademoiselle, I thank you a thousand times. You were most kind. Sit down, I beg of you.'

The girl took a chair.

'It's nothing,' she said. 'But I wish you would let it be seen to.'

'Mademoiselle, I assure you, it is a *bagatelle*! In the pleasure of your society the pain passes already.'

The girl laughed.

'That's good.'

'What about a cocktail?' I suggested. 'It's just about the time.'

'Well –' She hesitated. 'Thanks very much.'

'Martini?'

'Yes, please – dry Martini.'

I went off. On my return, after having ordered the drinks, I found Poirot and the girl engaged in animated conversation.

'Imagine, Hastings,' he said, 'that house there – the one on the point – that we have admired so much, it belongs to Mademoiselle here.'

'Indeed?' I said, though I was unable to recall having expressed any admiration. In fact I had hardly noticed the house. 'It looks rather eerie and imposing standing there by itself far from anything.'

'It's called End House,' said the girl. 'I love it – but it's a tumble-down old place. Going to rack and ruin.'

'You are the last of an old family, Mademoiselle?'

'Oh! we're nothing important. But there have been Buckleys here for two or three hundred years. My brother died three years ago, so I'm the last of the family.'

'That is sad. You live there alone, Mademoiselle?'

'Oh! I'm away a good deal and when I'm at home there's usually a cheery crowd coming and going.'

'That is so modern. Me, I was picturing you in a dark mysterious mansion, haunted by a family curse.'

'How marvellous! What a picturesque imagination you must have. No, it's not haunted. Or if so, the ghost is a beneficent one. I've had three escapes from sudden death in as many days, so I must bear a charmed life.'

Poirot sat up alertly.

'Escapes from death? That sounds interesting, Mademoiselle.'

'Oh! they weren't very thrilling. Just accidents you know.' She jerked her head sharply as a wasp flew past. 'Curse these wasps. There must be a nest of them round here.'

'The bees and the wasps – you do not like them, Mademoiselle? You have been stung – yes?'

'No – but I hate the way they come right past your face.'

'The bee in the bonnet,' said Poirot. 'Your English phrase.'

At that moment the cocktails arrived. We all held up our glasses and made the usual inane observations.

'I'm due in the hotel for cocktails, really,' said Miss Buckley. 'I expect they're wondering what has become of me.'

Poirot cleared his throat and set down his glass.

'Ah! for a cup of good rich chocolate,' he murmured. 'But in England they make it not. Still, in England you have some very pleasing customs. The young girls, their hats come on and off – so prettily – so easily –'

The girl stared at him.

'What do you mean? Why shouldn't they?'

'You ask that because you are young – so young, Mademoiselle. But to me the natural thing seems to have a coiffure high and rigid – so – and the hat attached with many hat pins – *là* – *là* – *là* – *et là.*'

He executed four vicious jabs in the air.

'But how frightfully uncomfortable!'

'Ah! I should think so,' said Poirot. No martyred lady could have spoken with more feeling. 'When the wind blew it was the agony – it gave you the *migraine.*'

Miss Buckley dragged off the simple wide-brimmed felt she was wearing and cast it down beside her.

'And now we do this,' she laughed.

'Which is sensible and charming,' said Poirot, with a little bow.

I looked at her with interest. Her dark hair was ruffled and gave her an elfin look. There was something elfin about her altogether. The small, vivid face, pansy shaped, the enormous dark-blue eyes, and something else – something haunting and arresting. Was it a hint of recklessness? There were dark shadows under the eyes.

The terrace on which we were sitting was a little-used one. The main terrace where most people sat was just round the corner at a point where the cliff shelved directly down to the sea.

From round this corner now there appeared a man, a red-faced man with a rolling carriage who carried his hands half clenched by his side. There was something breezy and carefree about him – a typical sailor.

'I can't think where the girl's got to,' he was saying in tones that easily carried to where we sat. 'Nick – Nick.'

Miss Buckley rose.

'I knew they'd be getting in a state. Attaboy – George – here I am.'

'Freddie's frantic for a drink. Come on, girl.'

He cast a glance of frank curiosity at Poirot, who must have differed considerably from most of Nick's friends.

The girl performed a wave of introduction.

'This is Commander Challenger – er –'

But to my surprise Poirot did not supply the name for which she was waiting. Instead he rose, bowed very ceremoniously and murmured:

'Of the English Navy. I have a great regard for the English Navy.'

This type of remark is not one that an Englishman acclaims most readily. Commander Challenger flushed and Nick Buckley took command of the situation.

'Come on, George. Don't gape. Let's find Freddie and Jim.'

She smiled at Poirot.

'Thanks for the cocktail. I hope the ankle will be all right.'

With a nod to me she slipped her hand through the sailor's arm and they disappeared round the corner together.

'So that is one of Mademoiselle's friends,' murmured Poirot thoughtfully. 'One of her cheery crowd. What about him? Give me your expert judgement, Hastings. Is he what you call a good fellow – yes?'

Pausing for a moment to try and decide exactly what Poirot thought I should mean by a 'good fellow', I gave a doubtful assent.

'He seems all right – yes,' I said. 'So far as one can tell by a cursory glance.'

'I wonder,' said Poirot.

The girl had left her hat behind. Poirot stooped to pick it up and twirled it round absent-mindedly on his finger.

'Has he a *tendresse* for her? What do you think, Hastings?'

'My dear Poirot! How *can* I tell? Here – give me that hat. The lady will want it. I'll take it to her.'

Poirot paid no attention to my request. He continued to revolve the hat slowly on his finger.

'*Pas encore. Ça m'amuse.*'

'Really, Poirot!'

'Yes, my friend, I grow old and childish, do I not?'

This was so exactly what I was feeling that I was somewhat disconcerted to have it put into words. Poirot gave a little chuckle, then leaning forward he laid a finger against the side of his nose.

'But no – I am not so completely imbecile as you think! We will return the hat – but assuredly – but later! We will return it to End House and thus we shall have the opportunity of seeing the charming Miss Nick again.'

'Poirot,' I said. 'I believe you have fallen in love.'

'She is a pretty girl – eh?'

'Well – you saw for yourself. Why ask me?'

'Because, alas! I cannot judge. To me, nowadays, anything young is beautiful. *Jeunesse – jeunesse* . . . It is the tragedy of my years. But you – I appeal to you! Your judgement is not up-to-date, naturally, having lived in the Argentine so long. You admire the figure of five years ago, but you are at any rate more modern than I am. She is pretty – yes? She has the appeal to the sexes?'

'One sex is sufficient, Poirot. The answer, I should say, is very much in the affirmative. Why are you so interested in the lady?'

'Am I interested?'

'Well – look at what you've just been saying.'

'You are under a misapprehension, *mon ami*. I may be interested in the lady – yes – but I am much more interested in her hat.'

I stared at him, but he appeared perfectly serious.

He nodded his head at me.

'Yes, Hastings, this very hat.' He held it towards me. 'You see the reason for my interest?'

'It's a nice hat,' I said, bewildered. 'But quite an ordinary hat. Lots of girls have hats like it.'

'Not like this one.'

I looked at it more closely.

'You see, Hastings?'

'A perfectly plain fawn felt. Good style –'

'I did not ask you to describe the hat. It is plain that you do *not* see. Almost incredible, my poor Hastings, how you hardly ever *do* see! It amazes me every time anew! But regard, my dear old imbecile – it is not necessary to employ the grey cells – the eyes will do. Regard – regard –'

And then at last I saw to what he had been trying to draw my attention. The slowly turning hat was revolving on his finger, and that finger was stuck neatly through a hole in the brim of the hat. When he saw that I had realized his meaning, he drew his finger out and held the hat towards me. It was a small neat hole, quite round, and I could not imagine its purpose, if purpose it had.

'Did you observe the way Mademoiselle Nick flinched when a bee flew past? The bee in the bonnet – the hole in the hat.'

'But a bee couldn't make a hole like that.'

'Exactly, Hastings! What acumen! It could not. *But a bullet could, mon cher!*'

'*A bullet?*'

'*Mais oui!* A bullet like *this*.'

He held out his hand with a small object in the palm of it.

'A spent bullet, *mon ami*. It was that which hit the terrace just now when we were talking. A spent bullet!'

'You mean –'

'*I mean that one inch of a difference and that hole would not be through the hat but through the head.* Now do you see why I am interested, Hastings? You were right, my friend, when you told me not to use the word "impossible". Yes – one is human! Ah! but he made a grave mistake, that would-be murderer, when he shot at his victim within a dozen yards of Hercule Poirot! For him, it is indeed *la mauvaise chance*. But you see now why we must make our entry into End House and get into touch with Mademoiselle? *Three near escapes from death in three days.* That is what she said. We must act quickly, Hastings. The peril is very close at hand.'

CHAPTER 2
END HOUSE

'Poirot,' I said. 'I have been thinking.'

'An admirable exercise, my friend. Continue it.'

We were sitting facing each other at lunch at a small table in the window.

'This shot must have been fired quite close to us. And yet we did not hear it.'

'And you think that in the peaceful stillness, with the rippling waves the only sound, we should have done so?'

'Well, it's odd.'

'No, it is not odd. Some sounds – you get used to them so soon that you hardly notice they are there. All this morning, my friend, speedboats have been making trips in the bay. You complained at first – soon, you did not even notice. But, *ma foi*, you could fire a machine gun almost and not notice it when one of those boats is on the sea.'

'Yes, that's true.'

'Ah! *voilà*,' murmured Poirot. 'Mademoiselle and her friends. They are to lunch here, it seems. And therefore I must return the hat. But no matter. The affair is sufficiently serious to warrant a visit all on its own.'

He leaped up nimbly from his seat, hurried across the room, and presented the hat with a bow just as Miss Buckley and her companions were seating themselves at table.

They were a party of four, Nick Buckley, Commander Challenger, another man and another girl. From where we sat we had a very imperfect view of them. From time to time the naval man's laugh boomed out. He seemed a simple, likeable soul, and I had already taken a fancy to him.

My friend was silent and distrait during our meal. He crumbled his bread, made strange little ejaculations to himself and straightened everything on the table. I tried to talk, but meeting with no encouragement soon gave up.

He continued to sit on at the table long after he had finished his cheese. As soon as the other party had left the room, however, he too rose to his feet. They were just settling themselves at a table in the lounge when Poirot marched up to them in his most military fashion, and addressed Nick directly.

'Mademoiselle, may I crave one little word with you.'

The girl frowned. I realized her feelings clearly enough. She was afraid that this queer little foreigner was going to be a nuisance. I could not but sympathize with her, knowing how it must appear in her eyes. Rather unwillingly, she moved a few steps aside.

Almost immediately I saw an expression of surprise pass over her face at the low hurried words Poirot was uttering.

In the meantime, I was feeling rather awkward and ill at ease. Challenger with ready tact came to my rescue, offering me a cigarette and making some commonplace observation. We had taken each other's measure and were inclined to be sympathetic to each other. I fancied that I was more his own kind than the man with whom he had been lunching. I now had the opportunity of observing the latter. A tall, fair, rather exquisite young man, with a rather fleshy nose and over-emphasized good looks. He had a supercilious manner and a tired drawl. There was a sleekness about him that I especially disliked.

Then I looked at the woman. She was sitting straight opposite me in a big chair and had just thrown off her hat. She was an unusual type – a weary Madonna describes it best. She had fair, almost colourless hair, parted in the middle and drawn straight down over her ears to a knot in the neck. Her face was dead white and emaciated – yet curiously attractive. Her eyes were very light grey with large pupils. She had a curious look of detachment. She was staring at me. Suddenly she spoke.

'Sit down – till your friend has finished with Nick.'

She had an affected voice, languid and artificial – yet which had a curious attraction – a kind of resonant lingering beauty. She impressed me, I think, as the most tired person I had ever met. Tired in mind, not in body, as though she had found everything in the world to be empty and valueless.

'Miss Buckley very kindly helped my friend when he twisted his ankle this morning,' I explained as I accepted her offer.

'So Nick said.' Her eyes considered me, still detachedly. 'Nothing wrong with his ankle now, is there?'

I felt myself blushing.

'Just a momentary sprain,' I explained.

'Oh! well – I'm glad to hear Nick didn't invent the whole thing. She's the most heaven-sent little liar that ever existed, you know. Amazing – it's quite a gift.'

I hardly knew what to say. My discomfiture seemed to amuse her.

'She's one of my oldest friends,' she said, 'and I always think loyalty's such a tiresome virtue, don't you? Principally practised by the Scots – like thrift and keeping the Sabbath. But Nick is a liar, isn't she, Jim? That marvellous story about the brakes of the car – and Jim says there was nothing in it at all.'

The fair man said in a soft rich voice:

'I know something about cars.'

He half turned his head. Outside amongst other cars was a long, red car. It seemed longer and redder than any car could be. It had a long gleaming bonnet of polished metal. A super car!

'Is that your car?' I asked on a sudden impulse.

He nodded.

'Yes.'

I had an insane desire to say, 'It would be!'

Poirot rejoined us at that moment. I rose, he took me by the arm, gave a quick bow to the party, and drew me rapidly away.

'It is arranged, my friend. We are to call on Mademoiselle at End House at half-past six. She will be returned from the motoring by then. Yes, yes, surely she will have returned – in safety.'

His face was anxious and his tone was worried.

'What did you say to her?'

'I asked her to accord me an interview – as soon as possible. She was a little unwilling – naturally. She thinks – I can see the thoughts passing through her mind: "Who is he – this little man? Is he the bounder, the upstart, the Moving Picture director?" If she could have refused she would – but it is difficult – asked like that on the spur of the moment it is easier to consent. She admits that she will be back by six-thirty. *Ça y est!*'

I remarked that that seemed to be all right then, but my remark met with little favour. Indeed Poirot was as jumpy as the proverbial cat. He walked about our sitting-room all the afternoon, murmuring to himself and ceaselessly rearranging and straightening the ornaments. When I spoke to him, he waved his hands and shook his head.

In the end we started out from the hotel at barely six o'clock.

'It seems incredible,' I remarked, as we descended the steps of the terrace. 'To attempt to shoot anyone in a hotel garden. Only a madman would do such a thing.'

'I disagree with you. Given one condition, it would be quite a reasonably safe affair. To begin with the garden is deserted. The people who come to hotels are like a flock of sheep. It is customary to sit on the terrace overlooking the bay – *eh bien*, so everyone sits on the terrace. Only, I who am an original, sit overlooking the garden. And even then, I *saw* nothing. There is plenty of cover, you observe – trees, groups of palms, flowering shrubs. Anyone could hide himself comfortably and be unobserved whilst he waited for Mademoiselle to pass this way. And she would come this way. To come round by the road from End House would be much longer. Mademoiselle Nick Buckley, she would be of those who are always late and taking the short cut!'

'All the same, the risk was enormous. He might have been seen – and you can't make shooting look like an accident.'

'Not like an *accident* – no.'

'What do you mean?'

'Nothing – a little idea. I may or may not be justified. Leaving it aside for a moment, there is what I mentioned just now – an essential *condition*.'

'Which is?'

'Surely you can tell me, Hastings.'

'I wouldn't like to deprive you of the pleasure of being clever at my expense!'

'Oh! the sarcasm! The irony! Well, what leaps to the eye is this: *the motive cannot be obvious*. If it *were* – why, then, truly the risk would indeed be too great to be taken! People would say: "I wonder if it were So-and-So. Where was So-and-So when the shot was fired?" No, the murderer – the would-be murderer, I should say – cannot be obvious. And that, Hastings is why I am afraid! Yes, at this minute I am afraid. I reassure myself. I say: "There are four of them." I say: "Nothing can happen when they are all together." I say: "It would be madness!" And all the time I am afraid. These "accidents" – I want to hear about them!'

He turned back abruptly.

'It is still early. We will go the other way by the road. The garden has nothing to tell us. Let us inspect the orthodox approach to End House.'

Our way led out of the front gate of the hotel and up a sharp hill to the right. At the top of it was a small lane with a notice on the wall: 'TO END HOUSE ONLY.'

We followed it and after a few hundred yards the lane gave an abrupt turn and ended in a pair of dilapidated entrance gates, which would have been the better for a coat of paint.

Inside the gates, to the right, was a small lodge. This lodge presented a piquant contrast to the gates and to the condition of the grass-grown drive. The small garden round it was spick and span, the window frames and sashes had been lately painted and there were clean bright curtains at the windows.

Bending over a flower-bed was a man in a faded Norfolk jacket. He straightened up as the gate creaked and turned to look at us. He was a man of about sixty, six foot at least, with a powerful frame and a weather-beaten face. His head was almost completely bald. His eyes were a vivid blue and twinkled. He seemed a genial soul.

'Good-afternoon,' he observed as we passed.

I responded in kind and as we went on up the drive I was conscious of those blue eyes raking our backs inquisitively.

'I wonder,' said Poirot, thoughtfully.

He left it at that without vouchsafing any explanation of what it was that he wondered.

The house itself was large and rather dreary looking. It was shut in by trees, the branches of which actually touched the roof. It was clearly in bad repair. Poirot swept it with an appraising glance before ringing the bell – an old-fashioned bell that needed a Herculean pull to produce any effect and which once started, echoed mournfully on and on.

The door was opened by a middle-aged woman – 'a decent woman in black' – so I felt she should be described. Very respectable, rather mournful, completely uninterested.

Miss Buckley, she said, had not yet returned. Poirot explained that we had an appointment. He had some little difficulty in gaining his point, she was the type that is apt to be suspicious of foreigners. Indeed I flatter myself that it was *my* appearance which turned the scale. We were admitted and ushered into the drawing-room to await Miss Buckley's return.

There was no mournful note here. The room gave on the sea and was full of sunshine. It was shabby and betrayed conflicting styles – ultra modern of a cheap variety superimposed on solid Victorian. The curtains were of faded brocade, but the covers were new and gay and the cushions were positively hectic. On the walls were hung family portraits. Some of them, I thought, looked remarkably good. There was a gramophone and there were some records lying idly about. There were a portable wireless, practically no books, and one newspaper flung open on the end of the sofa. Poirot picked it up – then laid it down with a grimace. It was the St Loo *Weekly Herald and Directory*. Something impelled him to pick it up a second time, and he was glancing at a column when the door opened and Nick Buckley came into the room.

'Bring the ice, Ellen,' she called over her shoulder, then addressed herself to us.

'Well, here I am – and I've shaken off the others. I'm devoured with curiosity. Am I the long-lost heroine that is badly wanted for the Talkies? You were so very solemn' – she addressed herself to Poirot – 'that I feel it can't be anything else. Do make me a handsome offer.'

'Alas! Mademoiselle –' began Poirot.

'Don't say it's the opposite,' she begged him. 'Don't say you paint miniatures and want me to buy one. But no – with that moustache and staying at the Majestic, which has the nastiest food and the highest prices in England – no, it simply can't be.'

The woman who had opened the door to us came into the room with ice and a tray of bottles. Nick mixed cocktails expertly, continuing to talk. I think at last Poirot's silence (so unlike him) impressed itself upon her. She stopped in the very act of filling the glasses and said sharply:

'Well?'

'That is what I wish it to be – well, Mademoiselle.' He took the cocktail from her hand. 'To your good health, Mademoiselle – to your continued good health.'

The girl was no fool. The significance of his tone was not lost on her.

'Is – anything the matter?'

'Yes, Mademoiselle. This . . .'

He held out his hand to her with the bullet on the palm of it. She picked it up with a puzzled frown.

'You know what that is?'

'Yes, of course I know. It's a bullet.'

'Exactly. Mademoiselle – it was not a wasp that flew past your face this morning – it was this bullet.'

'Do you mean – was some criminal idiot shooting bullets in a hotel garden?'

'It would seem so.'

'Well, I'm damned,' said Nick frankly. 'I do seem to bear a charmed life. That's number four.'

'Yes,' said Poirot. 'That is number four. I want, Mademoiselle, to hear about the other three – accidents.'

She stared at him.

'I want to be very sure, Mademoiselle, that they were – *accidents*.'

'Why, of course! What else could they be?'

'Mademoiselle, prepare yourself, I beg, for a great shock. What if someone is attempting your life?'

All Nick's response to this was a burst of laughter. The idea seemed to amuse her hugely.

'What a marvellous idea! My dear man, who on earth do you think would attempt my life? I'm not the beautiful young heiress whose death releases millions. I wish somebody *was* trying to kill me – that *would* be a thrill, if you like – but I'm afraid there's not a hope!'

'Will you tell me, Mademoiselle, about those accidents?'

'Of course – but there's nothing in it. They were just stupid things. There's a heavy picture hangs over my bed. It fell in the night. Just by pure chance I had happened to hear a door banging somewhere in the house and went down to find it and shut it – and so I escaped. It would probably have bashed my head in. That's No. 1.'

Poirot did not smile.

'Continue, Mademoiselle. Let us pass to No. 2.'

'Oh, that's weaker still. There's a scrambly cliff path down to the sea. I go down that way to bathe. There's a rock you can dive off. A boulder got dislodged somehow and came roaring down just missing me. The third thing was quite different. Something went wrong with the brakes of the car – I don't know quite what – the garage man explained, but I didn't follow it. Anyway if I'd gone through the gate and down the hill, they wouldn't have held and I suppose I'd have gone slap into the Town Hall and there would have been the devil of a smash. Slight defacement of the Town Hall, complete obliteration of me. But owing to my *always* leaving something behind, I turned back and merely ran into the laurel hedge.'

'And you cannot tell me what the trouble was?'

'You can go and ask them at Mott's Garage. They'll know. It was something quite simple and mechanical that had been unscrewed, I think. I wondered if Ellen's boy (my stand-by who opened the door to you, has got a small boy) had tinkered with it. Boys do like messing about with cars. Of course Ellen swore he'd never been near the car. I think something must just have worked loose in spite of what Mott said.'

'Where is your garage, Mademoiselle?'

'Round the other side of the house.'

'Is it kept locked?'

Nick's eyes widened in surprise.

'Oh! *no*. Of course not.'

'Anyone could tamper with the car unobserved?'

'Well – yes – I suppose so. But it's so silly.'

'No, Mademoiselle. It is not silly. You do not understand. You are in danger – grave danger. I tell it to you. I! And you do not know who I am?'

'No,' said Nick, breathlessly.

'I am Hercule Poirot.'

'Oh!' said Nick, in rather a flat tone. 'Oh, yes.'

'You know my name, eh?'

'Oh, yes.'

She wriggled uncomfortably. A hunted look came into her eyes. Poirot observed her keenly.

'You are not at ease. That means, I suppose, that you have not read my books.'

'Well – no – not all of them. But I know the name, of course.'

'Mademoiselle, you are a polite little liar.' (I started, remembering the words spoken at the Majestic Hotel that day after lunch.) 'I forget – you are only a child – you would not have heard. So quickly does fame pass. My friend there – he will tell you.'

Nick looked at me. I cleared my throat, somewhat embarrassed.

'Monsieur Poirot is – er – was – a great detective,' I explained.

'Ah! my friend,' cried Poirot. 'Is that all you can find to say?

Mais dis donc! Say then to Mademoiselle that I am a detective unique, unsurpassed, the greatest that ever lived!'

'That is now unnecessary,' I said coldly. 'You have told her yourself.'

'Ah, yes, but it is more agreeable to have been able to preserve the modesty. One should not sing one's own praises.'

'One should not keep a dog and have to bark oneself,' agreed Nick, with mock sympathy. 'Who is the dog, by the way? Dr Watson, I presume.'

'My name is Hastings,' I said coldly.

'Battle of – 1066,' said Nick. 'Who said I wasn't educated? Well, this is all too, *too* marvellous! Do you think someone really wants to do away with me? It would be thrilling. But, of course, that sort of thing doesn't really happen. Only in books. I expect Monsieur Poirot is like a surgeon who's invented an operation or a doctor who's found an obscure disease and wants everyone to have it.'

'*Sacré tonnerre!*' thundered Poirot. 'Will you be serious? You young people of today, will nothing make you serious? It would not have been a joke, Mademoiselle, if you had been lying in the hotel garden a pretty little corpse with a nice little hole through your head instead of your hat. You would not have laughed then – eh?'

'Unearthly laughter heard at a *séance*,' said Nick. 'But seriously, M. Poirot – it's very kind of you and all that – but the whole thing *must* be an accident.'

'You are as obstinate as the devil!'

'That's where I got my name from. My grandfather was popularly supposed to have sold his soul to the devil. Everyone round here called him Old Nick. He was a wicked old man – but great fun. I adored him. I went everywhere with him and so they called us Old Nick and Young Nick. My real name is Magdala.'

'That is an uncommon name.'

'Yes, it's a kind of family one. There have been lots of Magdalas in the Buckley family. There's one up there.'

She nodded at a picture on the wall.

'Ah!' said Poirot. Then looking at a portrait hanging over the mantelpiece, he said:

'Is that your grandfather, Mademoiselle?'

'Yes, rather an arresting portrait, isn't it? Jim Lazarus offered to buy it, I wouldn't sell. I've got an affection for Old Nick.'

'Ah!' Poirot was silent for a minute, then he said very earnestly:

'*Revenons à nos moutons*. Listen, Mademoiselle. I implore you to be serious. You are in danger. Today, somebody shot at you with a Mauser pistol –'

'A Mauser pistol? –'

For a moment she was startled.

'Yes, why? Do you know of anyone who has a Mauser pistol?' She smiled.

'I've got one myself.'

'You have?'

'Yes – it was Dad's. He brought it back from the War. It's been knocking round here ever since. I saw it only the other day in that drawer.'

She indicated an old-fashioned bureau. Now, as though suddenly struck by an idea, she crossed to it and pulled the drawer open. She turned rather blankly. Her voice held a new note.

'Oh!' she said. 'It's – it's gone.'

CHAPTER 3
ACCIDENTS?

It was from that moment that the conversation took on a different tone. Up to now, Poirot and the girl had been at cross-purposes. They were separated by a gulf of years. His fame and reputation meant nothing to her – she was of the generation that knows only the great names of the immediate moment. She was, therefore, unimpressed by his warnings. He was to her only a rather comic elderly foreigner with an amusingly melodramatic mind.

And this attitude baffled Poirot. To begin with, his vanity suffered. It was his constant dictum that all the world knew Hercule Poirot. Here was someone who did not. Very good for him, I could not but feel – but not precisely helpful to the object in view!

With the discovery of the missing pistol, however, the affair took on a new phase. Nick ceased to treat it as a mildly amusing joke. She still treated the matter lightly, because it was her habit and her creed to treat all occurrences lightly, but there was a distinct difference in her manner.

She came back and sat down on the arm of a chair, frowning thoughtfully.

'That's odd,' she said.

Poirot whirled round on me.

'You remember, Hastings, the little idea I mentioned? Well, it was correct, my little idea! Supposing Mademoiselle had been found shot lying in the hotel garden? She might not have been found for some hours – few people pass that way. And *beside her hand* – just fallen from it – *is her own pistol*. Doubtless the good Madame Ellen would identify it. There would be suggestions, no doubt, of worry or of sleeplessness –'

Nick moved uneasily.

'That's true. I have been worried to death. Everybody's been telling me I'm nervy. Yes – they'd say all that . . .'

'And bring in a verdict of suicide. Mademoiselle's fingerprints conveniently on the pistol and nobody else's – but yes, it would be very simple and convincing.'

'How terribly amusing!' said Nick, but not, I was glad to note, as though she were terribly amused.

Poirot accepted her words in the conventional sense in which they were uttered.

'*N'est ce pas*? But you understand, Mademoiselle, there must be no more of this. Four failures – yes – but the fifth time there may be a success.'

'Bring out your rubber-tyred hearses,' murmured Nick.

'But we are here, my friend and I, to obviate all that!' I felt grateful for the 'we'. Poirot has a habit of sometimes ignoring my existence.

'Yes,' I put in. 'You mustn't be alarmed, Miss Buckley. We will protect you.'

'How frightfully nice of you,' said Nick. 'I think the whole thing is perfectly marvellous. Too, too thrilling.'

She still preserved her airy detached manner, but her eyes, I thought, looked troubled.

'And the first thing to do,' said Poirot, 'is to have the consultation.'

He sat down and beamed upon her in a friendly manner.

'To begin with, Mademoiselle, a conventional question – but – have you any enemies?'

Nick shook her head rather regretfully.

'I'm afraid not,' she said apologetically.

'*Bon*. We will dismiss that possibility then. And now we ask the question of the cinema, of the detective novel – Who profits by your death, Mademoiselle?'

'I can't imagine,' said Nick. 'That's why it all seems such nonsense. There's this beastly old barn, of course, but it's mortgaged up to the hilt, the roof leaks and there can't be a coal mine or anything exciting like that hidden in the cliff.'

'It is mortgaged – *hein*?'

'Yes. I had to mortgage it. You see there were two lots of death duties – quite soon after each other. First my grandfather died – just six years ago, and then my brother. That just about put the lid on the financial position.'

'And your father?'

'He was invalided home from the War, then got pneumonia and died in 1919. My mother died when I was a baby. I lived here with grandfather. He and Dad didn't get on (I don't wonder), so Dad found it convenient to park me and go roaming the world on his own account. Gerald – that was my brother – didn't get on with grandfather either. I dare say I shouldn't have got on with him if I'd been a boy. Being a girl saved me. Grandfather used to say I was a chip off the old block and had inherited his spirit.' She laughed. 'He was an awful old rip, I believe. But frightfully lucky. There was a saying round here that everything he touched turned to gold. He was a gambler, though, and gambled it away again. When he died he left hardly anything beside the house and land. I was sixteen when he died and Gerald was twenty-two. Gerald was killed in a motor accident just three years ago and the place came to me.'

'And after you, Mademoiselle? Who is your nearest relation?'

'My cousin, Charles. Charles Vyse. He's a lawyer down here. Quite good and worthy but very dull. He gives me good advice and tries to restrain my extravagant tastes.'

'He manages your affairs for you – eh?'

'Well – yes, if you like to put it that way. I haven't many affairs to manage. He arranged the mortgage for me and made me let the lodge.'

'Ah! – the lodge. I was going to ask you about that. It is let?'

'Yes – to some Australians. Croft their name is. Very hearty, you know – and all that sort of thing. Simply oppressively kind. Always bringing up sticks of celery and early peas and things like that. They're shocked at the way I let the garden go. They're rather a nuisance, really – at least he is. Too terribly friendly for words. She's a cripple, poor thing, and lies on a sofa all day. Anyway they pay the rent and that's the great thing.'

'How long have they been here?'

'Oh! about six months.'

'I see. Now, beyond this cousin of yours – on your father's side or your mother's, by the way?'

'Mother's. My mother was Amy Vyse.'

'*Bien!* Now, beyond this cousin, as I was saying, have you any other relatives?'

'Some very distant cousins in Yorkshire – Buckleys.'

'No one else?'

'No.'

'That is lonely.'

Nick stared at him.

'Lonely? What a funny idea. I'm not down here much, you know. I'm usually in London. Relations are too devastating as a rule. They fuss and interfere. It's much more fun to be on one's own.'

'I will not waste the sympathy. You are a modern, I see, Mademoiselle. Now – your household.'

'How grand that sounds! Ellen's the household. And her husband, who's a sort of gardener – not a very good one. I pay them frightfully little because I let them have the child here. Ellen does for me when I'm down here and if I have a party we get in who and what we can to help. I'm giving a party on Monday. It's Regatta week, you know.'

'Monday – and today is Saturday. Yes. Yes. And now, Mademoiselle, your friends – the ones with whom you were lunching today, for instance?'

'Well, Freddie Rice – the fair girl – is practically my greatest friend. She's had a rotten life. Married to a beast – a man who drank and drugged and was altogether a queer of the worst description. She had to leave him a year or two ago. Since then she's drifted round. I wish to goodness she'd get a divorce and marry Jim Lazarus.'

'Lazarus? The art dealer in Bond Street?'

'Yes. Jim's the only son. Rolling in money, of course. Did you see that car of his? He's a Jew, of course, but a frightfully decent one. And he's devoted to Freddie. They go about everywhere together. They are staying at the Majestic over the week-end and are coming to me on Monday.'

'And Mrs Rice's husband?'

'The mess? Oh! he's dropped out of everything. Nobody knows where he is. It makes it horribly awkward for Freddie. You can't divorce a man when you don't know where he is.'

'*Évidemment!*'

'Poor Freddie,' said Nick, pensively. 'She's had rotten luck. The thing was all fixed once. She got hold of him and put it to him, and he said he was perfectly willing, but he simply hadn't got the cash to take a woman to a hotel. So the end of it all was she forked out – and he took it and off he went and has never been heard of from that day to this. Pretty mean, I call it.'

'Good heavens,' I exclaimed.

'My friend Hastings is shocked,' remarked Poirot. 'You must be more careful, Mademoiselle. He is out of date, you comprehend. He has just returned from those great clear open spaces, etc., and he has yet to learn the language of nowadays.'

'Well, there's nothing to get shocked about,' said Nick, opening her eyes very wide. 'I mean, everybody knows, don't they, that there are such people. But I call it a low-down trick all the same. Poor old Freddie was so damned hard up at the time that she didn't know where to turn.'

'Yes, yes, not a very pretty affair. And your other friend, Mademoiselle. The good Commander Challenger?'

'George? I've known George all my life – well, for the last five years anyway. He's a good scout, George.'

'He wishes you to marry him – eh?'

'He does mention it now and again. In the small hours of the morning or after the second glass of port.'

'But you remain hard-hearted.'

'What would be the use of George and me marrying one another? We've neither of us got a bean. And one would get terribly bored with George. That "playing for one's side", "good old school" manner. After all, he's forty if he's a day.'

The remark made me wince slightly.

'In fact he has one foot in the grave,' said Poirot. 'Oh! do not mind me, Mademoiselle. I am a grandpapa – a nobody. And now tell me more about these accidents. The picture, for instance?'

'It's been hung up again – on a new cord. You can come and see it if you like.'

She led the way out of the room and we followed her. The picture in question was an oil painting in a heavy frame. It hung directly over the bed-head.

With a murmured, 'You permit, Mademoiselle,' Poirot removed his shoes and mounted upon the bed. He examined the picture and the cord, and gingerly tested the weight of the painting. With an elegant grimace he descended.

'To have that descend on one's head – no, it would not be pretty. The cord by which it was hung, Mademoiselle, was it, like this one, a wire cable?'

'Yes, but not so thick. I got a thicker one this time.'

'That is comprehensible. And you examined the break – the edges were frayed?'

'I think so – but I didn't notice particularly. Why should I?'

'Exactly. As you say, why should you? All the same, I should much like to look at that piece of wire. Is it about the house anywhere?'

'It was still on the picture. I expect the man who put the new wire on just threw the old one away.'

'A pity. I should like to have seen it.'

'You don't think it was just an accident after all? Surely it couldn't have been anything else.'

'It may have been an accident. It is impossible to say. But the damage to the brakes of your car – that was not an accident. And the stone that rolled down the cliff – I should like to see the spot where that accident occurred.'

Nick took us out in the garden and led us to the cliff edge. The sea glittered blue below us. A rough path led down the face of the rock. Nick described just where the accident occurred and Poirot nodded thoughtfully. Then he asked:

'How many ways are there into your garden, Mademoiselle?'

'There's the front way – past the lodge. And a tradesman's entrance – a door in the wall half-way up that lane. Then there's a gate just along here on the cliff edge. It leads out on to a zig zag path that leads up from that beach to the Majestic Hotel. And then, of course, you can go straight through a gap in the hedge into the Majestic garden – that's the way I went this morning. To go through the Majestic garden is a short cut to the town anyway.'

'And your gardener – where does he usually work?'

'Well, he usually potters round the kitchen garden, or else he sits in the potting-shed and pretends to be sharpening the shears.'

'Round the other side of the house, that is to say?'

'So that if anyone were to come in here and dislodge a boulder he would be very unlikely to be noticed.'

Nick gave a sudden little shiver.

'Do you – do you really think that is what happened?' she asked. 'I can't believe it somehow. It seems so perfectly futile.'

Poirot drew the bullet from his pocket again and looked at it.

'That was not futile, Mademoiselle,' he said gently.

'It must have been some madman.'

'Possibly. It is an interesting subject of after-dinner conversation – are all criminals really madmen? There may be a malformation in their little grey cells – yes, it is very likely. That, it is the affair of the doctor. For me – I have different work to perform. I have the innocent to think of, not the guilty – the victim, not the criminal. It is you I am considering now, Mademoiselle, not your unknown assailant. You are young and beautiful, and the sun shines and the world is pleasant, and there is life and love ahead of you. It is all that of which I think, Mademoiselle. Tell me, these friends of yours, Mrs Rice and Mr Lazarus – they have been down here, how long?'

'Freddie came down on Wednesday to this part of the world. She stopped with some people near Tavistock for a couple of nights. She came on here yesterday. Jim has been touring round about, I believe.'

'And Commander Challenger?'

'He's at Devonport. He comes over in his car whenever he can – week-ends mostly.'

Poirot nodded. We were walking back to the house. There was a silence, and then he said suddenly:

'Have you a friend whom you can trust, Mademoiselle?'

'There's Freddie.'

'Other than Mrs Rice.'

'Well, I don't know. I suppose I have. Why?'

'Because I want you to have a friend to stay with you – immediately.'

'Oh!'

Nick seemed rather taken aback. She was silent a moment or two, thinking. Then she said doubtfully:

'There's Maggie. I could get hold of her, I expect.'

'Who is Maggie?'

'One of my Yorkshire cousins. There's a large family of them. He's a clergyman, you know. Maggie's about my age, and I usually have her to stay sometime or other in the summer. She's no fun, though – one of those painfully pure girls, with the kind of hair that has just become fashionable by accident. I was hoping to get out of having her this year.'

'Not at all. Your cousin, Mademoiselle, will do admirably. Just the type of person I had in mind.'

'All right,' said Nick, with a sigh. 'I'll wire her. I certainly don't know who else I could get hold of just now. Everyone's fixed up. But if it isn't the Choirboys' Outing or the Mothers' Beanfeast she'll come all right. Though what you expect her to *do* . . .'

'Could you arrange for her to sleep in your room?'

'I suppose so.'

'She would not think that an odd request?'

'Oh, no, Maggie never thinks. She just *does* – earnestly, you know. Christian works – with faith and perseverance. All right, I'll wire her to come on Monday.'

'Why not tomorrow?'

'With Sunday trains? She'll think I'm dying if I suggest that. No, I'll say Monday. Are you going to tell her about the awful fate hanging over me?'

'*Nous verrons*. You still make a jest of it? You have courage, I am glad to see.'

'It makes a diversion anyway,' said Nick.

Something in her tone struck me and I glanced at her curiously. I had a feeling that there was something she had left untold. We had re-entered the drawing-room. Poirot was fingering the newspaper on the sofa.

'You read this, Mademoiselle?' he asked, suddenly.

'The St Loo *Herald*? Not seriously. I opened it to see the tides. It gives them every week.'

'I see. By the way, Mademoiselle, have you ever made a will?'

'Yes, I did. About six months ago. Just before my op.'

'*Qu'est ce que vous dites*? Your *op*?'

'Operation. For appendicitis. Someone said I ought to make a will, so I did. It made me feel quite important.'

'And the terms of that will?'

'I left End House to Charles. I hadn't much else to leave, but what there was I left to Freddie. I should think probably the – what do you call them – liabilities would have exceeded the assets, really.'

Poirot nodded absently.

'I will take my leave now. *Au revoir, Mademoiselle*. Be careful.'

'What of?' asked Nick.

'You are intelligent. Yes, that is the weak point – in which direction are you to be careful? Who can say? But have confidence, Mademoiselle. In a few days I shall have discovered the truth.'

'Until then beware of poison, bombs, revolver shots, motor accidents and arrows dipped in the secret poison of the South American Indians,' finished Nick glibly.

'Do not mock yourself, Mademoiselle,' said Poirot gravely.

He paused as he reached the door.

'By the way,' he said. 'What price did M. Lazarus offer you for the portrait of your grandfather?'

'Fifty pounds.'

'Ah!' said Poirot.

He looked earnestly back at the dark saturnine face above the mantelpiece.

'But, as I told you, I don't want to sell the old boy.'

'No,' said Poirot, thoughtfully. 'No, I understand.'

CHAPTER 4

THERE MUST BE SOMETHING!

'Poirot,' I said, as soon as we were out upon the road. 'There is one thing I think you ought to know.'

'And what is that, *mon ami*?'

I told him of Mrs Rice's version of the trouble with the motor.

'*Tiens! C'est intéressant, ça.* There is, of course, a type, vain, hysterical, that seeks to make itself interesting by having marvellous escapes from death and which will recount to you surprising histories that never happened! Yes, it is well known, that type there. Such people will even do themselves grave bodily injury to sustain the fiction.'

'You don't think that –'

'That Mademoiselle Nick is of that type? No, indeed. You observed, Hastings, that we had great difficulty in convincing her of her danger. And right to the end she kept up the farce of a half-mocking disbelief. She is of her generation, that little one. All the same, it is interesting – what Madame Rice said. Why should she say it? Why say it even if it were true? It was unnecessary – almost *gauche*.'

'Yes,' I said. 'That's true. She dragged it into the conversation neck and crop – for no earthly reason that I could see.'

'That is curious. Yes, that is curious. The little facts that are curious, I like to see them appear. They are significant. They point the way.'

'The way – where?'

'You put your finger on the weak spot, my excellent Hastings. Where? Where indeed! Alas, we shall not know till we get there.'

'Tell me, Poirot,' I said. 'Why did you insist on her getting this cousin to stay?'

Poirot stopped and waved an excited forefinger at me.

'Consider,' he cried. 'Consider for one little moment, Hastings. How we are handicapped! How are our hands tied! To hunt down a murderer after a crime has been committed – *c'est tout simple!* Or at least it is simple to one of my ability. The murderer has, so to speak, signed his name by committing the crime. But here there is no crime – and what is more we do not want a crime. To detect a crime before it has been committed – that is indeed of a rare difficulty.

'What is our first aim? The safety of Mademoiselle. And that is not easy. No, it is not easy, Hastings. We cannot watch over her day and night – we cannot even send a policeman in big boots to watch over her. We cannot pass the night in a young lady's sleeping chamber. The affair bristles with difficulties.

'But we can do one thing. We can make it more difficult for our assassin. We can put Mademoiselle upon her guard and we can introduce a perfectly impartial witness. It will take a very clever man to get round those two circumstances.'

He paused, and then said in an entirely different tone of voice:

'But what I am afraid of, Hastings –'

'Yes?'

'What I am afraid of is – that he *is* a very clever man. And I am not easy in my mind. No, I am not easy at all.'

'Poirot,' I said. 'You're making me feel quite nervous.'

'So am I nervous. Listen, my friend, that paper, the St Loo *Weekly Herald*. It was open and folded back at – where do you think? A little paragraph which said, "*Among the guests staying at the Majestic Hotel are M. Hercule Poirot and Captain Hastings.*" Supposing – just supposing that someone had read that paragraph. They know my name – everyone knows my name –'

'Miss Buckley didn't,' I said, with a grin.

'She is a scatterbrain – she does not count. A serious man – a criminal – would know my name. And he would be afraid! He would wonder! He would ask himself questions. Three times he has attempted the life of Mademoiselle and now Hercule Poirot arrives in the neighbourhood. "Is that coincidence?" he would ask himself. And he would fear that it might *not* be coincidence. What would he do then?'

'Lie low and hide his tracks,' I suggested.

'Yes – yes – or else – if he had real audacity, he would strike *quickly* – without loss of time. Before I had time to make inquiries – *pouf*, Mademoiselle is dead. That is what a man of audacity would do.'

'But why do you think that somebody read that paragraph other than Miss Buckley?'

'It was not Miss Buckley who read that paragraph. When I mentioned my name it meant nothing to her. It was not even familiar. Her face did not change. Besides she told us – she opened the paper to look at the tides – nothing else. Well, there was no tide table on that page.'

'You think someone in the house –'

'Someone in the house or who has access to it. And that last is easy – the window stands open. Without doubt Miss Buckley's friends pass in and out.'

'Have you any idea? Any suspicion?'

Poirot flung out his hands.

'Nothing. Whatever the motive, it is, as I predicted, not an obvious one. That is the would-be murderer's security – that is why he could act so daringly this morning. On the face of it, no one seems to have any reason for desiring the little Nick's death. The property? End House? That passes to the cousin – but does he particularly want a heavily mortgaged and very dilapidated old house? It is not even a family place so far as he is concerned. He is not a Buckley, remember. We must see this Charles Vyse, certainly, but the idea seems fantastic.

'Then there is Madame – the bosom friend – with her strange eyes and her air of a lost Madonna –'

'You felt that too?' I asked, startled.

'What is her concern in the business? She tells you that her friend is a liar. *C'est gentil, ça!* Why does she tell you? Is she afraid of something that Nick may say? Is that something connected with the car? Or did she use that as an instance, and was her real fear of something else? Did anyone tamper with the car, and if so, who? And does she know about it?

'Then the handsome blond, M. Lazarus. Where does he fit in? With his marvellous automobile and his money. Can he possibly be concerned in any way? Commander Challenger –'

'He's all right,' I put in quickly. 'I'm sure of that. A real *pukka sahib.*'

'Doubtless he has been to what you consider the right school. Happily, being a foreigner, I am free from these prejudices, and can make investigations unhampered by them. But I will admit that I find it hard to connect Commander Challenger with the case. In fact, I do not see that he can be connected.'

'Of course he can't,' I said warmly.

Poirot looked at me meditatively.

'You have an extraordinary effect on me, Hastings. You have so strongly the *flair* in the wrong direction that I am almost tempted to go by it! You are that wholly admirable type of man, honest, credulous, honourable, who is invariably taken in by any scoundrel. You are the type of man who invests in doubtful oil fields, and non-existent gold mines. From hundreds like you, the swindler makes his daily bread. Ah, well – I shall study this Commander Challenger. You have awakened my doubts.'

'My dear Poirot,' I cried, angrily. 'You are perfectly absurd. A man who has knocked about the world like I have –'

'Never learns,' said Poirot, sadly. 'It is amazing – but there it is.'

'Do you suppose I'd have made a success of my ranch out in the Argentine if I were the kind of credulous fool you make out?'

'Do not enrage yourself, *mon ami*. You have made a great success of it – you and your wife.'

'Bella,' I said, 'always goes by my judgement.'

'She is as wise as she is charming,' said Poirot. 'Let us not quarrel, my friend. See, there ahead of us, it says Mott's Garage. That, I think, is the garage mentioned by Mademoiselle Buckley. A few inquiries will soon give us the truth of that little matter.'

We duly entered the place and Poirot introduced himself by explaining that he had been recommended there by Miss Buckley. He made some inquiries about hiring a car for some afternoon drives and from there slid easily into the topic of the damage sustained by Miss Buckley's car not long ago.

Immediately the garage proprietor waxed voluble. Most extra-ordinary thing he'd ever seen. He proceeded to be technical. I, alas, am not mechanically minded. Poirot, I should imagine, is even less so. But certain facts did emerge unmistakably. The car had been tampered with. And the damage had been something quite easily done, occupying very little time.

'So that is that,' said Poirot, as we strolled away. 'The little Nick was right, and the rich M. Lazarus was wrong. Hastings, my friend, all this is very interesting.'

'What do we do now?'

'We visit the post office and send off a telegram if it is not too late.'

'A telegram?' I said hopefully.

'Yes,' said Poirot thoughtfully. 'A telegram.'

The post office was still open. Poirot wrote out his telegram and despatched it. He vouchsafed me no information as to its contents. Feeling that he wanted me to ask him, I carefully refrained from doing so.

'It is annoying that tomorrow is Sunday,' he remarked, as we strolled back to the hotel. 'We cannot now call upon M. Vyse till Monday morning.'

'You could get hold of him at his private address.'

'Naturally. But that is just what I am anxious not to do. I would prefer, in the first place, to consult him professionally and to form my judgement of him from that aspect.'

'Yes,' I said thoughtfully. 'I suppose that would be best.'

'The answer to one simple little question, for instance, might make a great difference. If M. Charles Vyse was in his office at twelve-thirty this morning, then it was not he who fired that shot in the garden of the Majestic Hotel.'

'Ought we not to examine the *alibis* of the three at the hotel?'

'That is much more difficult. It would be easy enough for one of them to leave the others for a few minutes, a hasty egress from one of the innumerable windows – lounge, smoking-room, drawing-room, writing-room, quickly under cover to the spot where the girl must pass – the shot fired and a rapid retreat. But as yet, *mon ami*, we are not even sure that we have arrived at all the *dramatis personae* in the drama. There is the respectable Ellen – and her so far unseen husband. Both inmates of the house and possibly, for all we know, with a grudge against our little Mademoiselle. There are even the unknown Australians at the lodge. And there may be others, friends and intimates of Miss Buckley's whom she has no reason for suspecting and consequently has not mentioned. I cannot help feeling, Hastings, that there is something *behind* this – *something* that has not yet come to light. I have a little idea that Miss Buckley knows more than she told us.'

'You think she is keeping something back?'

'Yes.'

'Possibly with an idea of shielding whoever it is?'

Poirot shook his head with the utmost energy.

'No, no. As far as that goes, she gave me the impression of being utterly frank. I am convinced that as regards these attempts on her life, she was telling all she knew. But there is something else – something that she believes has nothing to do with that at all. And I should like to know what that something is. For I – I say it in all modesty – am a great deal more intelligent than *une petite comme ça*. I, Hercule Poirot, might see a connection where she sees none. It might give me the clue I am seeking. For I announce to you, Hastings, quite frankly and humbly, that I am as you express it, all on the sea. Until I can get some glimmering of the *reason* behind all this, I am in the dark. There must be *something* – some factor in the case that I do not grasp. What is it? *Je me demande ça sans cesse. Qu'est-ce que c'est?*'

'You will find out,' I said, soothingly.

'So long,' he said sombrely, 'as I do not find out too late.'

CHAPTER 5

MR AND MRS CROFT

There was dancing that evening at the hotel. Nick Buckley dined there with her friends and waved a gay greeting to us.

She was dressed that evening in floating scarlet chiffon that dragged on the floor. Out of it rose her white neck and shoulders and her small impudent dark head.

'An engaging young devil,' I remarked.

'A contrast to her friend – eh?'

Frederica Rice was in white. She danced with a languorous weary grace that was as far removed from Nick's animation as anything could be.

'She is very beautiful,' said Poirot suddenly.

'Who? Our Nick?'

'No – the other. Is she evil? Is she good? Is she merely unhappy? One cannot tell. She is a mystery. She is, perhaps, nothing at all. But I tell you, my friend, she is an *allumeuse*.'

'What do you mean?' I asked curiously.

He shook his head, smiling.

'You will feel it sooner or later. Remember my words.'

Presently to my surprise, he rose. Nick was dancing with George Challenger. Frederica and Lazarus had just stopped and had sat down at their table. Then Lazarus got up and went away. Mrs Rice was alone. Poirot went straight to her table. I followed him.

His methods were direct and to the point.

'You permit?' He laid a hand on the back of a chair, then slid into it. 'I am anxious to have a word with you while your friend is dancing.'

'Yes?' Her voice sounded cool, uninterested.

'Madame, I do not know whether your friend has told you. If not, I will. Today her life has been attempted.'

Her great grey eyes widened in horror and surprise. The pupils, dilated black pupils, widened too.

'What do you mean?'

'Mademoiselle Buckley was shot at in the garden of this hotel.'

She smiled suddenly – a gentle, pitying, incredulous smile.

'Did Nick tell you so?'

'No, Madame, I happened to see it with my own eyes. Here is the bullet.'

He held it out to her and she drew back a little.

'But, then – but, then –'

'It is no fantasy of Mademoiselle's imagination, you understand. I vouch for that. And there is more. Several very curious accidents have happened in the last few days. You will have heard – no, perhaps you will not. You only arrived yesterday, did you not?'

'Yes – yesterday.'

'Before that you were staying with friends, I understand. At Tavistock.'

'Yes.'

'I wonder, Madame, what were the names of the friends with whom you were staying.'

She raised her eyebrows.

'Is there any reason why I should tell you that?' she asked coldly.

Poirot was immediately all innocent surprise.

'A thousand pardons, Madame. I was most *maladroit*. But I myself, having friends at Tavistock, fancied that you might have met them there . . . Buchanan – that is the name of my friends.'

Mrs Rice shook her head.

'I don't remember them. I don't think I can have met them.' Her tone now was quite cordial. 'Don't let us talk about boring people. Go on about Nick. Who shot at her? Why?'

'I do not know who – *as yet*,' said Poirot. 'But I shall find out. Oh! yes, I shall find out. I am, you know, a detective. Hercule Poirot is my name.'

'A very famous name.'

'Madame is too kind.'

She said slowly:

'What do you want me to do?'

I think she surprised us both there. We had not expected just that.

'I will ask you, Madame, to watch over your friend.'

'I will.'

'That is all.'

He got up, made a quick bow, and we returned to our own table.

'Poirot,' I said, 'aren't you showing your hand very plainly?'

'*Mon ami*, what else can I do? It lacks subtlety, perhaps, but it makes for safety. *I can take no chances*. At any rate one thing emerges plain to see.'

'What is that?'

'*Mrs Rice was not at Tavistock*. Where was she? Ah! but I will find out. Impossible to keep information from Hercule Poirot. See – the handsome Lazarus has returned. She is telling him. He looks over at us. He is clever, that one. Note the shape of his head. Ah! I wish I knew –'

'What?' I asked, as he came to a stop.

'What I shall know on Monday,' he returned, ambiguously.

I looked at him but said nothing. He sighed.

'You have no longer the curiosity, my friend. In the old days –'

'There are some pleasures,' I said, coldly, 'that it is good for you to do without.'

'You mean –?'

'The pleasure of refusing to answer questions.'

'*Ah c'est malin.*'

'Quite so.'

'Ah, well, well,' murmured Poirot. 'The strong silent man beloved of novelists in the Edwardian age.'

His eyes twinkled with their old glint.

Nick passed our table shortly afterwards. She detached herself from her partner and swooped down on us like a gaily-coloured bird.

'Dancing on the edge of death,' she said lightly.

'It is a new sensation, Mademoiselle?'

'Yes. Rather fun.'

She was off again, with a wave of her hand.

'I wish she hadn't said that,' I said, slowly.

'Dancing on the edge of death. I don't like it.'

'I know. It is too near the truth. She has courage, that little one. Yes, she has courage. But unfortunately it is not courage that is needed at this moment. Caution, not courage – *voilà ce qu'il nous faut!*'

The following day was Sunday. We were sitting on the terrace in front of the hotel, and it was about half-past eleven when Poirot suddenly rose to his feet.

'Come, my friend. We will try a little experiment. I have ascertained that M. Lazarus and Madame have gone out in the car and Mademoiselle with them. The coast is clear.'

'Clear for what?'

'You shall see.'

We walked down the steps and across a short stretch of grass to the sea. A couple of bathers were coming up it. They passed us laughing and talking.

When they had gone, Poirot walked to the point where an inconspicuous small gate, rather rusty on its hinges, bore the words in half obliterated letters, 'End House. Private.' There was no one in sight. We passed quietly through.

In another minute we came out on the stretch of lawn in front of the house. There was no one about. Poirot strolled to the edge of the cliff and looked over. Then he walked towards the house itself. The French windows on to the verandah were open and we passed straight into the drawing-room. Poirot wasted no time there. He opened the door and went out into the hall. From there he mounted the stairs, I at his heels. He went straight to Nick's bedroom – sat down on the edge of the bed and nodded to me with a twinkle.

'You see, my friend, how easy it is. No one has seen us come. No one will see us go. We could do any little affair we had to do in perfect safety. We could, for instance, fray through a picture wire so that it would be bound to snap before many hours had passed. And supposing that by chance anyone did happen to be in front of the house and see us coming. Then we would have a perfectly natural excuse – providing that we were known as friends of the house.'

'You mean that we can rule out a stranger?'

'That is what I mean, Hastings. It is no stray lunatic who is at the bottom of this. We must look nearer home than that.'

He turned to leave the room and I followed him. We neither of us spoke. We were both, I think, troubled in mind.

And then, at the bend of the staircase, we both stopped abruptly. A man was coming up.

He too stopped. His face was in shadow but his attitude was one of one completely taken aback. He was the first to speak, in a loud, rather bullying voice.

'What the hell are you doing here, I'd like to know?'

'Ah!' said Poirot. 'Monsieur – Croft, I think?'

'That's my name, but what –'

'Shall we go into the drawing-room to converse? It would be better, I think.'

The other gave way, turned abruptly and descended, we following close on his heels. In the drawing-room, with the door shut, Poirot made a little bow.

'I will introduce myself. Hercule Poirot at your service.'

The other's face cleared a little.

'Oh!' he said slowly. 'You're the detective chap. I've read about you.'

'In the St Loo *Herald*?'

'Eh? I've read about you way back in Australia. French, aren't you?'

'Belgian. It makes no matter. This is my friend, Captain Hastings.'

'Glad to meet you. But look, what's the big idea? What are you doing here? Anything – wrong?'

'It depends what you call – wrong.'

The Australian nodded. He was a fine-looking man in spite of his bald head and advancing years. His physique was magnificent. He had a heavy, rather underhung face – a crude face, I called it to myself. The piercing blue of his eyes was the most noticeable thing about him.

'See here,' he said. 'I came round to bring little Miss Buckley a handful of tomatoes and a cucumber. That man of hers is no good – bone idle – doesn't grow a thing. Lazy hound. Mother and I – why, it makes us mad, and we feel it's only neighbourly to do what we can! We've got a lot more tomatoes than we can eat. Neighbours should be matey, don't you think? I came in, as usual, through the window and dumped the basket down. I was just going off again when I heard footsteps and men's voices overhead. That struck me as odd. We don't deal much in burglars round here – but after all it was possible. I thought I'd just make sure everything was all right. Then I met you two on the stairs coming down. It gave me a bit of a surprise. And now you tell me you're a bonza detective. What's it all about?'

'It is very simple,' said Poirot, smiling. 'Mademoiselle had a rather alarming experience the other night. A picture fell above her bed. She may have told you of it?'

'She did. A mighty fine escape.'

'To make all secure I promised to bring her some special chain – it will not do to repeat the occurrence, eh? She tells me she is going out this morning, but I may come and measure what amount of chain will be needed. *Voilà* – it is simple.'

He flung out his hands with a childlike simplicity and his most engaging smile.

Croft drew a deep breath.

'So that's all it is?'

'Yes – you have had the scare for nothing. We are very law-abiding citizens, my friend and I.'

'Didn't I see you yesterday?' said Croft, slowly. 'Yesterday evening it was. You passed our little place.'

'Ah! yes, you were working in the garden and were so polite as to say good-afternoon when we passed.'

'That's right. Well – well. And you're the Monsieur Hercule Poirot I've heard so much about. Tell me, are you busy, Mr Poirot? Because if not, I wish you'd come back with me now – have a cup of morning tea, Australian fashion, and meet my old lady. She's read all about you in the newspapers.'

'You are too kind, M. Croft. We have nothing to do and shall be delighted.'

'That's fine.'

'You have the measurements correctly, Hastings?' asked Poirot, turning to me.

I assured him that I had the measurements correctly and we accompanied our new friend.

Croft was a talker; we soon realized that. He told us of his home near Melbourne, of his early struggles, of his meeting with his wife, of their combined efforts and of his final good fortune and success.

'Right away we made up our minds to travel,' he said. 'We'd always wanted to come to the old country. Well, we did. We came down to this part of the world – tried to look up some of my wife's people – they came from round about here. But we couldn't trace any of them. Then we took a trip on the Continent – Paris, Rome, the Italian Lakes, Florence – all those places. It was while we were in Italy that we had the train accident. My poor wife was badly smashed up. Cruel, wasn't it? I've taken her to the best doctors and they all say the same – there's nothing for it but time – time and lying up. It's an injury to the spine.'

'What a misfortune!'

'Hard luck, isn't it? Well, there it was. And she'd only got one kind of fancy – to come down here. She kind of felt if we had a little place of our own – something small – it would make all the difference. We saw a lot of messy-looking shacks, and then by good luck we found this. Nice and quiet and tucked away – no cars passing, or gramophones next door. I took it right away.'

With the last words we had come to the lodge itself. He sent his voice echoing forth in a loud 'Cooee,' to which came an answering 'Cooee.'

'Come in,' said Mr Croft. He passed through the open door and up the short flight of stairs to a pleasant bedroom. There, on a sofa, was a stout middle-aged woman with pretty grey hair and a very sweet smile.

'Who do you think this is, mother?' said Mr Croft. 'The extra-special, world-celebrated detective, Mr Hercule Poirot. I brought him right along to have a chat with you.'

'If that isn't too exciting for words,' cried Mrs Croft, shaking Poirot warmly by the hand. 'Read about that Blue Train business, I did, and you just happening to be on it, and a lot about your other cases. Since this trouble with my back, I've read all the detective stories that ever were, I should think. Nothing else seems to pass the time away so quick. Bert, dear, call out to Edith to bring the tea along.'

'Right you are, mother.'

'She's a kind of nurse attendant, Edith is,' Mrs Croft explained. 'She comes along each morning to fix me up. We're not bothering with servants. Bert's as good a cook and a house-parlourman as you'd find anywhere, and it gives him occupation – that and the garden.'

'Here we are,' cried Mr Croft, reappearing with a tray. 'Here's the tea. This is a great day in our lives, mother.'

'I suppose you're staying down here, Mr Poirot?' Mrs Croft asked, as she leaned over a little and wielded the teapot.

'Why, yes, Madame, I take the holiday.'

'But surely I read that you had retired – that you'd taken a holiday for good and all.'

'Ah! Madame, you must not believe everything you read in the papers.'

'Well, that's true enough. So you still carry on business?'

'When I find a case that interests me.'

'Sure you're not down here on work?' inquired Mr Croft, shrewdly. 'Calling it a holiday might be all part of the game.'

'You mustn't ask him embarrassing questions, Bert,' said Mrs Croft. 'Or he won't come again. We're simple people, Mr Poirot, and you're giving us a great treat coming here today – you and your friend. You really don't know the pleasure you're giving us.'

She was so natural and so frank in her gratification that my heart quite warmed to her.

'That was a bad business about that picture,' said Mr Croft.

'That poor little girl might have been killed,' said Mrs Croft, with deep feeling. 'She *is* a live wire. Livens the place up when she comes down here. Not much liked in the neighbourhood, so I've heard. But that's the way in these stuck English places. They don't like life and gaiety in a girl. I don't wonder she doesn't spend much time down here, and that long-nosed cousin of hers has no more chance of persuading her to settle down here for good and all than – than – well, I don't know what.'

'Don't gossip, Milly,' said her husband.

'Aha!' said Poirot. 'The wind is in that quarter. Trust the instinct of Madame! So M. Charles Vyse is in love with our little friend?'

'He's silly about her,' said Mrs Croft. 'But she won't marry a country lawyer. And I don't blame her. He's a poor stick, anyway. I'd like her to marry that nice sailor – what's his name, Challenger. Many a smart marriage might be worse than that. He's older than she is, but what of that? Steadying – that's what she needs. Flying about all over the place, the Continent even, all alone or with that queer-looking Mrs Rice. She's a sweet girl, Mr Poirot – I know that well enough. But I'm worried about her. She's looked none too happy lately. She's had what I call a haunted kind of look. And that worries me! I've got my reasons for being interested in that girl, haven't I, Bert?'

Mr Croft got up from his chair rather suddenly.

'No need to go into that, Milly,' he said. 'I wonder, Mr Poirot, if you'd care to see some snapshots of Australia?'

The rest of our visit passed uneventfully. Ten minutes later we took our leave.

'Nice people,' I said. 'So simple and unassuming. Typical Australians.'

'You liked them?'

'Didn't you?'

'They were very pleasant – very friendly.'

'Well, what is it, then? There's something, I can see.'

'They were, perhaps, just a shade too "typical",' said Poirot, thoughtfully. 'That cry of Cooee – that insistence on show-ing us snapshots – was it not playing a part just a little too thoroughly?'

'What a suspicious old devil you are!'

'You are right, *mon ami*. I am suspicious of everyone – of everything. I am afraid, Hastings – afraid.'

CHAPTER 6

A CALL UPON MR VYSE

Poirot clung firmly to the Continental breakfast. To see me consuming eggs and bacon upset and distressed him – so he always said. Consequently he breakfasted in bed upon coffee and rolls and I was free to start the day with the traditional Englishman's breakfast of bacon and eggs and marmalade.

I looked into his room on Monday morning as I went downstairs. He was sitting up in bed arrayed in a very marvellous dressing-gown.

'*Bonjour*, Hastings. I was just about to ring. This note that I have written, will you be so good as to get it taken over to End House and delivered to Mademoiselle at once.'

I held out my hand for it. Poirot looked at me and sighed.

'If only – if only, Hastings, you would part your hair in the middle instead of at the side! What a difference it would make to the symmetry of your appearance. And your moustache. If you *must* have a moustache, let it be a real moustache – a thing of beauty such as mine.'

Repressing a shudder at the thought, I took the note firmly from Poirot's hand and left the room.

I had rejoined him in our sitting-room when word was sent up to say Miss Buckley had called. Poirot gave the order for her to be shown up.

She came in gaily enough, but I fancied that the circles under her eyes were darker than usual. In her hand she held a telegram which she handed to Poirot.

'There,' she said. 'I hope that will please you!'

Poirot read it aloud.

'Arrive 5.30 today. Maggie.'

'My nurse and guardian!' said Nick. 'But you're wrong, you know. Maggie's got no kind of brains. Good works is about all she's fit for. That and never seeing the point of jokes. Freddie would be ten times better at spotting hidden assassins. And Jim

Lazarus would be better still. I never feel one has got to the bottom of Jim.'

'And the Commander Challenger?'

'Oh! George! He'd never see anything till it was under his nose. But he'd let them have it when he did see. Very useful when it came to a show-down, George would be.'

She tossed off her hat and went on:

'I gave orders for the man you wrote about to be let in. It sounds mysterious. Is he installing a dictaphone or something like that?'

Poirot shook his head.

'No, no, nothing scientific. A very simple little matter of opinion, Mademoiselle. Something I wanted to know.'

'Oh, well,' said Nick. 'It's all great fun, isn't it?'

'Is it, Mademoiselle?' asked Poirot, gently.

She stood for a minute with her back to us, looking out of the window. Then she turned. All the brave defiance had gone out of her face. It was childishly twisted awry, as she struggled to keep back the tears.

'No,' she said. 'It – it isn't, really. I'm afraid – I'm afraid. Hideously afraid. And I always thought I was brave.'

'So you are, *mon enfant*, so you are. Both Hastings and I, we have both admired your courage.'

'Yes, indeed,' I put in warmly.

'No,' said Nick, shaking her head. 'I'm not brave. It's – it's the *waiting*. Wondering the whole time if anything more's going to happen. And *how* it'll happen! And *expecting* it to happen.'

'Yes, yes – it is the strain.'

'Last night I pulled my bed out into the middle of the room. And fastened my window and bolted my door. When I came here this morning, I came round by the road. I couldn't – I simply couldn't come through the garden. It's as though my nerve had gone all of a sudden. It's this thing coming on top of everything else.'

'What do you mean exactly by that, Mademoiselle? On top of everything else?'

There was a momentary pause before she replied.

'I don't mean anything particular. What the newspapers call "the strain of modern life", I suppose. Too many cocktails, too many cigarettes – all that sort of thing. It's just that I've got into a ridiculous – sort of – of state.'

She had sunk into a chair and was sitting there, her small fingers curling and uncurling themselves nervously.

'You are not being frank with me, Mademoiselle. There is something.'

'There isn't – there really isn't.'

'There is something you have not told me.'

'I've told you every single smallest thing.'

She spoke sincerely and earnestly.

'About these accidents – about the attacks upon you, yes.'

'Well – then?'

'But you have not told me everything that is in your heart – in your life . . .'

She said slowly:

'Can anyone do that . . . ?'

'Ah! then,' said Poirot, with triumph. 'You admit it!'

She shook her head. He watched her keenly.

'Perhaps,' he suggested, shrewdly. 'It is not *your* secret?'

I thought I saw a momentary flicker of her eyelids. But almost immediately she jumped up.

'Really and truly, M. Poirot, I've told you every single thing I know about this stupid business. If you think I know something about someone else, or have suspicions, you are wrong. It's having *no* suspicions that's driving me mad! Because I'm not a fool. I can see that if those "accidents" weren't accidents, they must have been engineered by somebody very near at hand – somebody who – knows me. And that's what is so awful. Because I haven't the least idea – not the very least – who that somebody might be.'

She went over once more to the window and stood looking out. Poirot signed to me not to speak. I think he was hoping for some further revelation, now that the girl's self-control had broken down.

When she spoke, it was in a different tone of voice, a dreamy far-away voice.

'Do you know a queer wish I've always had? I love End House. I've always wanted to produce a play there. It's got an – an atmosphere of drama about it. I've seen all sorts of plays staged there in my mind. And now it's as though a drama were being acted there. Only I'm not producing it . . . I'm *in* it! I'm *right* in it! I am, perhaps, the person who – dies in the first act.'

Her voice broke.

'Now, now, Mademoiselle.' Poirot's voice was resolutely brisk and cheerful. 'This will not do. This is hysteria.'

She turned and looked at him sharply.

'Did Freddie tell you I was hysterical?' she asked. 'She says I am, sometimes. But you mustn't always believe what Freddie says. There are times, you know when – when she isn't quite herself.'

There was a pause, then Poirot asked a totally irrelevant question:

'Tell me, Mademoiselle,' he said. 'Have you ever received an offer for End House?'

'To sell it, do you mean?'

'That is what I meant.'

'No.'

'Would you consider selling it if you got a good offer?'

Nick considered for a moment.

'No, I don't think so. Not, I mean, unless it was such a ridiculously good offer that it would be perfectly foolish not to.'

'*Précisément.*'

'I don't want to sell it, you know, because I'm fond of it.'

'Quite so. I understand.'

Nick moved slowly towards the door.

'By the way, there are fireworks tonight. Will you come? Dinner at eight o'clock. The fireworks begin at nine-thirty. You can see them splendidly from the garden where it overlooks the harbour.'

'I shall be enchanted.'

'Both of you, of course,' said Nick.

'Many thanks,' I said.

'Nothing like a party for reviving the drooping spirits,' remarked Nick. And with a little laugh she went out.

'*Pauvre enfant,*' said Poirot.

He reached for his hat and carefully flicked an infinitesimal speck of dust from its surface.

'We are going out?' I asked.

'*Mais oui,* we have legal business to transact, *mon ami.*'

'Of course. I understand.'

'One of your brilliant mentality could not fail to do so, Hastings.'

The offices of Messrs Vyse, Trevannion & Wynnard were situated in the main street of the town. We mounted the stairs to the first floor and entered a room where three clerks were busily writing. Poirot asked to see Mr Charles Vyse.

A clerk murmured a few words down a telephone, received, apparently, an affirmative reply, and remarking that Mr Vyse would see us now, he led us across the passage, tapped on a door and stood aside for us to pass in.

From behind a large desk covered with legal papers, Mr Vyse rose up to greet us.

He was a tall young man, rather pale, with impassive features. He was going a little bald on either temple and wore glasses. His colouring was fair and indeterminate.

Poirot had come prepared for the encounter. Fortunately he had with him an agreement, as yet unsigned, and so on some technical points in connection with this, he wanted Mr Vyse's advice.

Mr Vyse, speaking carefully and correctly, was soon able to allay Poirot's alleged doubts, and to clear up some obscure points of the wording.

'I am very much obliged to you,' murmured Poirot. 'As a foreigner, you comprehend, these legal matters and phrasing are most difficult.'

It was then that Mr Vyse asked who had sent Poirot to him.

'Miss Buckley,' said Poirot, promptly. 'Your cousin, is she not? A most charming young lady. I happened to mention that I was in perplexity and she told me to come to you. I tried to see you on Saturday morning – about half-past twelve – but you were out.'

'Yes, I remember. I left early on Saturday.'

'Mademoiselle your cousin must find that large house very lonely? She lives there alone, I understand.'

'Quite so.'

'Tell me, Mr Vyse, if I may ask, is there any chance of that property being in the market?'

'Not the least, I should say.'

'You understand, I do not ask idly. I have a reason! I am in search, myself, of just such a property. The climate of St Loo enchants me. It is true that the house appears to be in bad repair, there has not been, I gather, much money to spend upon it. Under those circumstances, is it not possible that Mademoiselle would consider an offer?'

'Not the least likelihood of it.' Charles Vyse shook his head with the utmost decision. 'My cousin is absolutely devoted to the place. Nothing would induce her to sell, I know. It is, you understand, a family place.'

'I comprehend that, but –'

'It is absolutely out of the question. I know my cousin. She has a fanatical devotion to the house.'

A few minutes later we were out in the street again.

'Well, my friend,' said Poirot. 'And what impression did this M. Charles Vyse make upon you?'

I considered.

'A very negative one,' I said at last. 'He is a curiously negative person.'

'Not a strong personality, you would say?'

'No, indeed. The kind of man you would never remember on meeting him again. A mediocre person.'

'His appearance is certainly not striking. Did you notice any discrepancy in the course of our conversation with him?'

'Yes,' I said slowly, 'I did. With regard to the selling of End House.'

'Exactly. Would you have described Mademoiselle Buckley's attitude towards End House as one of "fanatical devotion"?'

'It is a very strong term.'

'Yes – and Mr Vyse is not given to using strong terms. His normal attitude – a legal attitude – is to under, rather than over, state. Yet he says that Mademoiselle has a fanatical devotion to the home of her ancestors.'

'She did not convey that impression this morning,' I said. 'She spoke about it very sensibly, I thought. She's obviously fond of the place – just as anyone in her position would be – but certainly nothing more.'

'So, in fact, one of the two is lying,' said Poirot, thoughtfully.

'One would not suspect Vyse of lying.'

'Clearly a great asset if one has any lying to do,' remarked

Poirot. 'Yes, he has quite the air of a George Washington, that one. Did you notice another thing, Hastings?'

'What was that?'

'*He was not in his office at half-past twelve on Saturday.*'

CHAPTER 7

TRAGEDY

The first person we saw when we arrived at End House that evening was Nick. She was dancing about the hall wrapped in a marvellous kimono covered with dragons.

'Oh! it's only you!'

'Mademoiselle – I am desolated!'

'I know. It did sound rude. But you see, I'm waiting for my dress to arrive. They promised – the brutes – promised faithfully!'

'Ah! if it is a matter of *la toilette*! There is a dance tonight, is there not?'

'Yes. We are all going on to it after the fireworks. That is, I suppose we are.'

There was a sudden drop in her voice. But the next minute she was laughing.

'Never give in! That's my motto. Don't think of trouble and trouble won't come! I've got my nerve back tonight. I'm going to be gay and enjoy myself.'

There was a footfall on the stairs. Nick turned.

'Oh! here's Maggie. Maggie, here are the sleuths that are protecting me from the secret assassin. Take them into the drawing-room and let them tell you about it.'

In turn we shook hands with Maggie Buckley, and, as requested, she took us into the drawing-room. I formed an immediate favourable opinion of her.

It was, I think, her appearance of calm good sense that so attracted me. A quiet girl, pretty in the old-fashioned sense – certainly not smart. Her face was innocent of make-up and she wore a simple, rather shabby, black evening dress. She had frank blue eyes, and a pleasant slow voice.

'Nick has been telling me the most amazing things,' she said.

'Surely she must be exaggerating? Who ever would want to harm Nick? She can't have an enemy in the world.'

Incredulity showed strongly in her voice. She was looking at Poirot in a somewhat unflattering fashion. I realized that to a girl like Maggie Buckley, foreigners were always suspicious.

'Nevertheless, Miss Buckley, I assure you that it is the truth,' said Poirot quietly.

She made no reply, but her face remained unbelieving.

'Nick seems quite fey tonight,' she remarked. 'I don't know what's the matter with her. She seems in the wildest spirits.'

That word – fey! It sent a shiver through me. Also, something in the intonation of her voice had set me wondering.

'Are you Scotch, Miss Buckley?' I asked, abruptly.

'My mother was Scottish,' she explained.

She viewed me, I noticed, with more approval than she viewed Poirot. I felt that my statement of the case would carry more weight with her than Poirot's would.

'Your cousin is behaving with great bravery,' I said. 'She's determined to carry on as usual.'

'It's the only way, isn't it?' said Maggie. 'I mean – whatever one's inward feelings are – it is no good making a fuss about them. That's only uncomfortable for everyone else.' She paused and then added in a soft voice: 'I'm very fond of Nick. She's been good to me always.'

We could say nothing more for at that moment Frederica Rice drifted into the room. She was wearing a gown of Madonna blue and looked very fragile and ethereal. Lazarus soon followed her and then Nick danced in. She was wearing a black frock, and round her was wrapped a marvellous old Chinese shawl of vivid lacquer red.

'Hello, people,' she said. 'Cocktails?'

We all drank, and Lazarus raised his glass to her.

'That's a marvellous shawl, Nick,' he said. 'It's an old one, isn't it?'

'Yes – brought back by Great-Great-Great-Uncle Timothy from his travels.'

'It's a beauty – a real beauty. You wouldn't find another to match it if you tried.'

'It's warm,' said Nick. 'It'll be nice when we're watching the fireworks. And it's gay. I – I hate black.'

'Yes,' said Frederica. 'I don't believe I've ever seen you in a black dress before, Nick. Why did you get it?'

'Oh! I don't know.' The girl flung aside with a petulant gesture, but I had caught a curious curl of her lips as though of pain. 'Why does one do anything?'

We went in to dinner. A mysterious manservant had appeared – hired, I presume, for the occasion. The food was indifferent. The champagne, on the other hand, was good.

'George hasn't turned up,' said Nick. 'A nuisance his having to go back to Plymouth last night. He'll get over this evening sometime or other, I expect. In time for the dance anyway. I've got a man for Maggie. Presentable, if not passionately interesting.'

A faint roaring sound drifted in through the window.

'Oh! curse that speedboat,' said Lazarus. 'I get so tired of it.'

'That's not the speedboat,' said Nick. 'That's a seaplane.'

'I believe you're right.'

'Of course I'm right. The sound's quite different.'

'When are you going to get your Moth, Nick?'

'When I can raise the money,' laughed Nick.

'And then, I suppose you'll be off to Australia like that girl – what's her name?'

'I'd love to –'

'I admire her enormously,' said Mrs Rice, in her tired voice. 'What marvellous nerve! All by herself too.'

'I admire all these flying people,' said Lazarus. 'If Michael Seton had succeeded in his flight round the world he'd have been the hero of the day – and rightly so. A thousand pities he's come to grief. He's the kind of man England can't afford to lose.'

'He may still be all right,' said Nick.

'Hardly. It's a thousand to one against by now. Poor Mad Seton.'

'They always called him Mad Seton, didn't they?' asked Frederica.

Lazarus nodded.

'He comes of rather a mad family,' he said. 'His uncle, Sir Matthew Seton, who died about a week ago – he was as mad as a hatter.'

'He was the mad millionaire who ran bird sanctuaries, wasn't he?' asked Frederica.

'Yes. Used to buy up islands. He was a great woman-hater. Some girl chucked him once, I believe, and he took to Natural History by way of consoling himself.'

'Why do you say Michael Seton is dead?' persisted Nick. 'I don't see any reason for giving up hope – yet.'

'Of course, you knew him, didn't you?' said Lazarus. 'I forgot.'

'Freddie and I met him at Le Touquet last year,' said Nick. 'He was too marvellous, wasn't he, Freddie?'

'Don't ask me, darling. He was your conquest, not mine. He took you up once, didn't he?'

'Yes – at Scarborough. It was simply too wonderful.'

'Have you done any flying, Captain Hastings?' Maggie asked of me in polite conversational tones.

I had to confess that a trip to Paris and back was the extent of my acquaintance with air travel.

Suddenly, with an exclamation, Nick sprang up.

'There's the telephone. Don't wait for me. It's getting late. And I've asked lots of people.'

She left the room. I glanced at my watch. It was just nine o'clock. Dessert was brought, and port. Poirot and Lazarus were talking Art. Pictures, Lazarus was saying, were a great drug in the market just now. They went on to discuss new ideas in furniture and decoration.

I endeavoured to do my duty by talking to Maggie Buckley, but I had to admit that the girl was heavy in hand. She answered pleasantly, but without throwing the ball back. It was uphill work.

Frederica Rice sat dreamily silent, her elbows on the table and the smoke from her cigarette curling round her fair head. She looked like a meditative angel.

It was just twenty past nine when Nick put her head round the door.

'Come out of it, all of you! The animals are coming in two by two.'

We rose obediently. Nick was busy greeting arrivals. About a dozen people had been asked. Most of them were rather uninteresting. Nick, I noticed, made a good hostess. She sank her modernisms and made everyone welcome in an old-fashioned way. Among the guests I noticed Charles Vyse.

Presently we all moved out into the garden to a place overlooking the sea and the harbour. A few chairs had been placed there for the elderly people, but most of us stood. The first rocket flamed to Heaven.

At that moment I heard a loud familiar voice, and turned my head to see Nick greeting Mr Croft.

'It's too bad,' she was saying, 'that Mrs Croft can't be here too. We ought to have carried her on a stretcher or something.'

'It's bad luck on poor mother altogether. But she never complains – that woman's got the sweetest nature – Ha! that's a good one.' This as a shower of golden rain showed up in the sky.

The night was a dark one – there was no moon – the new moon being due in three days' time. It was also, like most summer evenings, cold. Maggie Buckley, who was next to me, shivered.

'I'll just run in and get a coat,' she murmured.

'Let me.'

'No, you wouldn't know where to find it.'

She turned towards the house. At that moment Frederica Rice's voice called:

'Oh, Maggie, get mine too. It's in my room.'

'She didn't hear,' said Nick. 'I'll get it, Freddie. I want my fur one – this shawl isn't nearly hot enough. It's this wind.'

There was, indeed, a sharp breeze blowing off the sea.

Some set pieces started down on the quay. I fell into conversation with an elderly lady standing next to me who put me through a rigorous catechism as to life, career, tastes and probable length of stay.

Bang! A shower of green stars filled the sky. They changed to blue, then red, then silver.

Another and yet another.

'"Oh!" and then "Ah!" that is what one says,' observed Poirot suddenly close to my ear. 'At the end it becomes monotonous, do you not find? Brrr! The grass, it is damp to the feet! I shall suffer for this – a chill. And no possibility of obtaining a proper *tisane*!'

'A chill? On a lovely night like this?'

'A lovely night! A lovely night! You say that, because the rain it does not pour down in sheets! Always when the rain does not fall, it is a lovely night. But I tell you, my friend, if there were a little thermometer to consult you would see.'

'Well,' I admitted, 'I wouldn't mind putting on a coat myself.'

'You are very sensible. You have come from a hot climate.'

'I'll bring yours.'

Poirot lifted first one, then the other foot from the ground with a cat-like motion.

'It is the dampness of the feet I fear. Would it, think you, be possible to lay hands on a pair of goloshes?'

I repressed a smile.

'Not a hope,' I said. 'You understand, Poirot, that it is no longer done.'

'Then I shall sit in the house,' he declared. 'Just for the Guy Fawkes show, shall I want only *enrhumer* myself? And catch, perhaps, a *fluxion de poitrine*?'

Poirot still murmuring indignantly, we bent our footsteps towards the house. Loud clapping drifted up to us from the quay below where another set piece was being shown – a ship, I believe, with *Welcome to Our Visitors* displayed across it.

'We are all children at heart,' said Poirot, thoughtfully. '*Les Feux D'Artifices*, the party, the games with balls – yes, and even the conjurer, the man who deceives the eye, however carefully it watches – *mais qu'est-ce que vous avez?*'

I had caught him by the arm, and was clutching him with one hand, while with the other I pointed.

We were within a hundred yards of the house, and just in front of us, between us and the open French window, *there lay a huddled figure wrapped in a scarlet Chinese shawl* . . .

'*Mon Dieu!*' whispered Poirot. '*Mon Dieu* . . .'

CHAPTER 8
THE FATAL SHAWL

I suppose it was not more than forty seconds that we stood there, frozen with horror, unable to move, but it seemed like an hour. Then Poirot moved forward, shaking off my hand. He moved stiffly like an automaton.

'It has happened,' he murmured, and I can hardly describe the anguished bitterness of his voice. 'In spite of everything – in spite of my precautions, it has happened. Ah! miserable criminal that I am, why did I not guard her better. I should have foreseen. Not for one instant should I have left her side.'

'You mustn't blame yourself,' I said.

My tongue stuck to the roof of my mouth, and I could hardly articulate.

Poirot only responded with a sorrowful shake of his head. He knelt down by the body.

And at that moment we received a second shock.

For Nick's voice rang out, clear and gay, and a moment later Nick appeared in the square of the window silhouetted against the lighted room behind.

'Sorry I've been so long, Maggie,' she said. 'But –'

Then she broke off – staring at the scene before her.

With a sharp exclamation, Poirot turned over the body on the lawn and I pressed forward to see.

I looked down into the dead face of Maggie Buckley.

In another minute Nick was beside us. She gave a sharp cry.

'Maggie – Oh! Maggie – it – it can't –'

Poirot was still examining the girl's body. At last very slowly he rose to his feet.

'Is she – is –' Nick's voice broke off.

'Yes, Mademoiselle. She is dead.'

'But why? But why? Who could have wanted to kill *her*?'

Poirot's reply came quickly and firmly.

'It was not her they meant to kill, Mademoiselle! It was *you*! They were misled by the shawl.'

A great cry broke from Nick.

'Why couldn't it have been me?' she wailed. 'Oh! why couldn't it have been me? I'd so much rather. I don't want to live – *now*. I'd be glad – willing – happy – to die.'

She flung up her arms wildly and then staggered slightly. I passed an arm round her quickly to support her.

'Take her into the house, Hastings,' said Poirot. 'Then ring up the police.'

'The police?'

'*Mais oui!* Tell them someone has been shot. And afterwards stay with Mademoiselle Nick. *On no account leave her.*'

I nodded comprehension of these instructions, and supporting the half-fainting girl, made my way through the drawing-room window. I laid the girl on the sofa there, with a cushion under her head, and then hurried out into the hall in search of the telephone.

I gave a slight start on almost running into Ellen. She was standing there with a most peculiar expression on her meek, respectable face. Her eyes were glittering and she was passing her tongue repeatedly over her dry lips. Her hands were trembling, as though with excitement. As soon as she saw me, she spoke.

'Has – has anything happened, sir?'

'Yes,' I said curtly. 'Where's the telephone?'

'Nothing – nothing wrong, sir?'

'There's been an accident,' I said evasively. 'Somebody hurt. I must telephone.'

'Who has been hurt, sir?'

There was a positive eagerness in her face.

'Miss Buckley. Miss Maggie Buckley.'

'Miss Maggie? Miss *Maggie*? Are you sure, sir – I mean are you sure that – that it's Miss Maggie?'

'I'm quite sure,' I said. 'Why?'

'Oh! – nothing. I – I thought it might be one of the other ladies. I thought perhaps it might be – Mrs Rice.'

'Look here,' I said. 'Where's the telephone?'

'It's in the little room here, sir.' She opened the door for me and indicated the instrument.

'Thanks,' I said. And, as she seemed disposed to linger, I added: 'That's all I want, thank you.'

'If you want Dr Graham –'

'No, no,' I said. 'That's all. Go, please.'

She withdrew reluctantly, as slowly as she dared. In all probability she would listen outside the door, but I could not help that. After all, she would soon know all there was to be known.

I got the police station and made my report. Then, on my own initiative, I rang up the Dr Graham Ellen had mentioned. I found his number in the book. Nick, at any rate, should have medical attention, I felt – even though a doctor could do nothing for that poor girl lying out there. He promised to come at once and I hung up the receiver and came out into the hall again.

If Ellen had been listening outside the door she had managed to disappear very swiftly. There was no one in sight when I came out. I went back into the drawing-room. Nick was trying to sit up.

'Do you think – could you get me – some brandy?'

'Of course.'

I hurried into the dining-room, found what I wanted and came back. A few sips of the spirit revived the girl. The colour began to come back into her cheeks. I rearranged the cushion for her head.

'It's all – so awful.' She shivered. 'Everything – everywhere.'

'I know, my dear, I know.'

'No, you don't! You can't. And it's all such a *waste*. If it were only me. It would be all over . . .'

'You mustn't,' I said, '"be morbid".'

She only shook her head, reiterating: 'You don't know! You don't *know*!'

Then, suddenly, she began to cry. A quiet, hopeless sobbing like a child. That, I thought, was probably the best thing for her, so I made no effort to stem her tears.

When their first violence had died down a little, I stole across to the window and looked out. I had heard an outcry of voices a few minutes before. They were all there by now, a semi-circle round the scene of the tragedy, with Poirot like a fantastical sentinel, keeping them back.

As I watched, two uniformed figures came striding across the grass. The police had arrived.

I went quietly back to my place by the sofa. Nick lifted her tear-stained face.

'Oughtn't I to be doing something?'

'No, my dear. Poirot will see to it. Leave it to him.' Nick was silent for a minute or two, then she said:

'Poor Maggie. Poor dear old Maggie. Such a good sort who never harmed a soul in her life. That this should happen to *her*. I feel as though I'd killed her – bringing her down in the way that I did.'

I shook my head sadly. How little one can foresee the future. When Poirot insisted on Nick's inviting a friend, how little did he think that he was signing an unknown girl's death warrant.

We sat in silence. I longed to know what was going on outside, but I loyally fulfilled Poirot's instructions and stuck to my post.

It seemed hours later when the door opened and Poirot and a police inspector entered the room. With them came a man who was evidently Dr Graham. He came over at once to Nick.

'And how are you feeling, Miss Buckley? This must have been a terrible shock.' His fingers were on her pulse.

'Not too bad.'

He turned to me.

'Has she had anything?'

'Some brandy,' I said.

'I'm all right,' said Nick, bravely.

'Able to answer a few questions, eh?'

'Of course.'

The police inspector moved forward with a preliminary cough. Nick greeted him with the ghost of a smile.

'Not impeding the traffic this time,' she said.

I gathered they were not strangers to each other.

'This is a terrible business, Miss Buckley,' said the inspector. 'I'm very sorry about it. Now Mr Poirot here, whose name I'm very familiar with (and proud we are to have him with us, I'm sure), tells me that to the best of his belief you were shot at in the grounds of the Majestic Hotel the other morning?'

Nick nodded.

'I thought it was just a wasp,' she explained. 'But it wasn't.'

'And you'd had some rather peculiar accidents before that?'

'Yes – at least it was odd their happening so close together.'

She gave a brief account of the various circumstances.

'Just so. Now how came it that your cousin was wearing your shawl tonight?'

'We came in to fetch her coat – it was rather cold watching the fireworks. I flung off the shawl on the sofa here. Then I went upstairs and put on the coat I'm wearing now – a light nutria one. I also got a wrap for my friend Mrs Rice out of her room. There it is on the floor by the window. Then Maggie called out that she couldn't find her coat. I said it must be downstairs. She went down and called up she still couldn't find it. I said it must have been left in the car – it was a tweed coat she was looking for – she hasn't got an evening furry one – and I said I'd bring her down something of mine. But she said it didn't matter – she'd take my shawl if I didn't want it. And I said of course but would that be enough? And she said Oh, yes, because she really didn't feel it particularly cold after Yorkshire. She just wanted *something*. And I said all right, I'd be out in a minute. And when I did – did come out –'

She stopped, her voice breaking . . .

'Now, don't distress yourself, Miss Buckley. Just tell me this. Did you hear a shot – or two shots?'

Nick shook her head.

'No – only just the fireworks popping and the squibs going off.'

'That's just it,' said the inspector. 'You'd never notice a shot with all that going on. It's no good asking you, I suppose, if you've any clue to who it is making these attacks upon you?'

'I haven't the least idea,' said Nick. 'I can't imagine.'

'And you wouldn't be likely to,' said the inspector. 'Some homicidal maniac – that's what it looks like to me. Nasty business. Well, I won't need to ask you any more questions to-night, miss. I'm more sorry about this than I can say.'

Dr Graham stepped forward.

'I'm going to suggest, Miss Buckley, that you don't stay here. I've been talking it over with M. Poirot. I know of an excellent nursing home. You've had a shock, you know. What you need is complete rest –'

Nick was not looking at him. Her eyes had gone to Poirot.

'Is it – because of the shock?' she asked.

He came forward.

'I want you to feel safe, *mon enfant*. And *I* want to feel, too, that you *are* safe. There will be a nurse there – a nice practical unimaginative nurse. She will be near you all night. When you wake up and cry out – she will be there, close at hand. You understand?'

'Yes,' said Nick, 'I understand. But *you* don't. I'm not afraid any longer. I don't care one way or another. If anyone wants to murder me, they can.'

'Hush, hush,' I said. 'You're over-strung.'

'You don't know. None of you know!'

'I really think M. Poirot's plan is a good one,' the doctor broke in soothingly. 'I will take you in my car. And we will give you a little something to ensure a good night's rest. Now what do you say?'

'I don't mind,' said Nick. 'Anything you like. It doesn't matter.'

Poirot laid his hand on hers.

'I know, Mademoiselle. I know what you must feel. I stand before you ashamed and stricken to the heart. I, who promised protection, have not been able to protect. I have failed. I am a miserable. But believe me, Mademoiselle, my heart is in agony because of that failure. If you know what I am suffering you would forgive, I am sure.'

'That's all right,' said Nick, still in the same dull voice. 'You mustn't blame yourself. I'm sure you did the best you could. Nobody could have helped it – or done more, I'm sure. Please don't be unhappy.'

'You are very generous, Mademoiselle.'

'No, I –'

There was an interruption. The door flew open and George Challenger rushed into the room.

'What's all this?' he cried. 'I've just arrived. To find a policeman at the gate and a rumour that somebody's dead. What is it all about? For God's sake, tell me. Is it – is it – Nick?'

The anguish in his tone was dreadful to hear. I suddenly realized that Poirot and the doctor between them completely blotted out Nick from his sight.

Before anyone had time to answer, he repeated his question.

'Tell me – it can't be true – Nick isn't *dead*?'

'No, *mon ami*,' said Poirot, gently. 'She is alive.'

And he drew back so that Challenger could see the little figure on the sofa.

For a moment or two Challenger stared at her incredulously. Then, staggering a little, like a drunken man, he muttered:

'Nick – Nick.'

And suddenly dropping on his knees beside the sofa and hiding his head in his hands, he cried in a muffled voice:

'Nick – my darling – I thought that you were dead.'

Nick tried to sit up.

'It's all right, George. Don't be an idiot. I'm quite safe.'

He raised his head and looked round wildly.

'But *somebody's* dead? The policeman said so.'

'Yes,' said Nick. 'Maggie. Poor old Maggie. Oh! –'

A spasm twisted her face. The doctor and Poirot came forward. Graham helped her to her feet. He and Poirot, one on each side, helped her from the room.

'The sooner you get to your bed the better,' remarked the doctor. 'I'll take you along at once in my car. I've asked Mrs Rice to pack a few things ready for you to take.'

They disappeared through the door. Challenger caught my arm.

'I don't understand. Where are they taking her?'

I explained.

'Oh! I see. Now, then, Hastings, for God's sake give me the hang of this thing. What a ghastly tragedy! That poor girl.'

'Come and have a drink,' I said. 'You're all to pieces.'

'I don't mind if I do.'

We adjourned to the dining-room.

'You see,' he explained, as he put away a stiff whisky and soda, 'I thought it was Nick.'

There was very little doubt as to the feelings of Commander George Challenger. A more transparent lover never lived.

<hr>

CHAPTER 9
A. TO J.

I doubt if I shall ever forget the night that followed. Poirot was a prey to such an agony of self-reproach that I was really alarmed. Ceaselessly he strode up and down the room heaping anathemas on his own head and deaf to my well-meant remonstrances.

'What it is to have too good an opinion of oneself. I am punished – yes, I am punished. I, Hercule Poirot. I was too sure of myself.'

'No, no,' I interpolated.

'But who would imagine – who could imagine – such unparalleled audacity? I had taken, as I thought, all possible precautions. I had warned the murderer –'

'Warned the murderer?'

'*Mais oui.* I had drawn attention to myself. I had let him see that I suspected – someone. I had made it, or so I thought, too dangerous for him to dare to repeat his attempts at murder. I had drawn a cordon round Mademoiselle. And he slips through it! Boldly – under our very eyes almost, he slips through it! In spite of us all – of everyone being on the alert, he achieves his object.'

'Only he doesn't,' I reminded him.

'That is the chance only! From my point of view, it is the same. A human life has been taken, Hastings – whose life is non-essential.'

'Of course,' I said. 'I didn't mean that.'

'But on the other hand, what you say is true. And that makes it worse – ten times worse. For the murderer is still as far as ever from achieving his object. Do you understand, my friend? The position is changed – for the worse. It may mean that not one life – but two – will be sacrificed.'

'Not while you're about,' I said stoutly.

He stopped and wrung my hand.

'*Merci, mon ami! Merci!* You still have confidence in the old one – you still have the faith. You put new courage into me. Hercule Poirot will not fail again. No second life shall be taken. I will rectify my error – for, see you, there must have been an error! Somewhere there has been a lack of order and method in my usually so well arranged ideas. I will start again. Yes, I will start at the beginning. And this time – I will not fail.'

'You really think then,' I said, 'that Nick Buckley's life is still in danger?'

'My friend, for what other reason did I send her to this nursing home?'

'Then it wasn't the shock –'

'The shock! Pah! One can recover from shock as well in one's own home as in a nursing home – better, for that matter. It is not amusing there, the floors of green linoleum, the conversation of the nurses – the meals on trays, the ceaseless washing. No, no, it is for safety and safety only. I take the doctor into my confidence. He agrees. He will make all arrangements. No one, *mon ami, not even her dearest friend*, will be admitted to see Miss Buckley. You and I are the only ones permitted. *Pour les autres – eh bien!* "Doctor's orders," they will be told. A phrase very convenient and one not to be gainsayed.'

'Yes,' I said. 'Only –'

'Only what, Hastings?'

'That can't go on for ever.'

'A very true observation. But it gives us a little breathing space. And you realize, do you not, that the character of our operations has changed.'

'In what way?'

'Our original task was to ensure the safety of Mademoiselle. Our task now is a much simpler one – a task with which we are well acquainted. It is neither more nor less than the hunting down of a murderer.'

'You call that simpler?'

'Certainly it is simpler. The murderer has, as I said the other day, *signed his name to the crime*. He has come out into the open.'

'You don't think –' I hesitated, then went on. 'You don't think that the police are right? That this is the work of a madman, some wandering lunatic with homicidal mania?'

'I am more than ever convinced that such is not the case.'

'You really think that –'

I stopped. Poirot took up my sentence, speaking very gravely.

'That the murderer is someone in Mademoiselle's own circle? Yes, *mon ami*, I do.'

'But surely last night must almost rule out that possibility. We were all together and –'

He interrupted.

'Could you swear, Hastings, that any particular person had never left our little company there on the edge of the cliff? Is there any one person there whom you could swear you had seen *all* the time?'

'No,' I said slowly, struck by his words. 'I don't think I could. It was dark. We all moved about, more or less. On different occasions I noticed Mrs Rice, Lazarus, you, Croft, Vyse – but all the time – no.'

Poirot nodded his head.

'Exactly. It would be a matter of a very few minutes. The two girls go to the house. The murderer slips away unnoticed, hides behind that sycamore tree in the middle of the lawn. Nick Buckley, or so he thinks, comes out of the window, passes within a foot of him, he fires three shots in rapid succession –'

'Three?' I interjected.

'Yes. He was taking no chances this time. We found three bullets in the body.'

'That was risky, wasn't it?'

'Less risky in all probability than one shot would have been. A Mauser pistol does not make a great deal of noise. It would resemble more or less the popping of the fireworks and blend in very well with the noise of them.'

'Did you find the pistol?' I asked.

'No. And there, Hastings, lies to my mind the indisputable proof that no stranger is responsible for this. We agree, do we not, that Miss Buckley's own pistol was taken in the first place for one reason only – to give her death the appearance of suicide.'

'Yes.'

'That is the only possible reason, is it not? But now, you observe, there is no pretence of suicide. *The murderer knows that we should not any longer be deceived by it.* He knows, in fact, what we know!'

I reflected, admitting to myself the logic of Poirot's deduction.

'What did he do with the pistol do you think?'

Poirot shrugged his shoulders.

'For that, it is difficult to say. But the sea was exceedingly handy. A good toss of the arm, and the pistol sinks, never to be recovered. We cannot, of course, be absolutely sure – but that is what *I* should have done.'

His matter-of-fact tone made me shiver a little.

'Do you think – do you think he realized that he'd killed the wrong person?'

'I am quite sure he did not,' said Poirot, grimly. 'Yes, that must have been an unpleasant little surprise for him when he learnt the truth. To keep his face and betray nothing – it cannot have been easy.'

At that moment I bethought me of the strange attitude of the maid, Ellen. I gave Poirot an account of her peculiar demeanour. He seemed very interested.

'She betrayed surprise, did she, that it was Maggie who was dead?'

'Great surprise.'

'That is curious. And yet, the fact of a tragedy was clearly *not* a surprise to her. Yes, there is something there that must be looked into. Who is she, this Ellen? So quiet, so respectable in the English manner? Could it be she who –?' He broke off.

'If you're going to include the accidents,' I said, 'surely it would take a man to have rolled that heavy boulder down the cliff.'

'Not necessarily. It is very largely a question of leverage. Oh, yes, it could be done.'

He continued his slow pacing up and down the room.

'Anyone who was at End House last night comes under suspicion. But those guests – no, I do not think it was one of them. For the most part, I should say, they were mere acquaintances. There was no intimacy between them and the young mistress of the house.'

'Charles Vyse was there,' I remarked.

'Yes, we must not forget him. He is, logically, our strongest suspect.' He made a gesture of despair and threw himself into a chair opposite mine. '*Voilà* – it is always that we come back to! Motive! We must find the motive if we are to understand this crime. And it is there, Hastings, that I am continually baffled. Who can possibly have a motive for doing away with Mademoiselle Nick? I have let myself go to the most absurd suppositions. I, Hercule Poirot, have descended to the most ignominious flights of fancy. I have adopted the mentality of the cheap thriller. The grandfather – the "Old Nick" – he who is supposed to have gambled his money away. Did he really do so, I have asked myself? Did he, on the contrary, hide it away? Is it hidden somewhere in End House? Buried somewhere in the grounds? With that end in view (I am ashamed to say it) I inquired of Mademoiselle Nick whether there had ever been any offers to buy the house.'

'Do you know, Poirot,' I said, 'I call that rather a bright idea. There may be something in it.'

Poirot groaned.

'You would say that! It would appeal, I knew, to your romantic but slightly mediocre mind. Buried treasure – yes, you would enjoy that idea.'

'Well – I don't see why not –'

'Because, my friend, the more prosaic explanation is nearly always more probable. Then Mademoiselle's father – I have played with even more degrading ideas concerning him. He was a traveller. Supposing, I say to myself, that he has stolen a jewel – the eye of a God. Jealous priests are on his tracks. Yes, I, Hercule Poirot, have descended to depths such as these.

'I have had other ideas concerning this father,' he went on. 'Ideas at once more dignified and more probable. Did he, in the course of his wanderings, contract a second marriage? Is there a nearer heir than M. Charles Vyse? But again, that leads nowhere, for we are up against the same difficulty – that there is really nothing of value to inherit.

'I have neglected no possibility. Even that chance reference of Mademoiselle Nick's to the offer made her by M. Lazarus. You remember? The offer to purchase her grandfather's portrait. I telegraphed on Saturday for an expert to come down and examine that picture. He was the man about whom I wrote to Mademoiselle this morning. Supposing, for instance, it were worth several thousand pounds?'

'You surely don't think a rich man like young Lazarus –?'

'Is he rich? Appearances are not everything. Even an old-established firm with palatial showrooms and every appearance of prosperity may rest on a rotten basis. And what does one do then? Does one run about crying out that times are hard? No, one buys a new and luxurious car. One spends a little more money than usual. One lives a little more ostentatiously. For credit, see you, is everything! But sometimes a monumental business has crashed – for no more than a few thousand pounds – *of ready money*.

'Oh! I know,' he continued, forestalling my protests. 'It is far-fetched – but it is not so bad as revengeful priests or buried treasure. It bears, at any rate, some relationship to things as they happen. And we can neglect nothing – nothing that might bring us nearer the truth.'

With careful fingers he straightened the objects on the table in front of him. When he spoke, his voice was grave and, for the first time, calm.

'*Motive!*' he said. 'Let us come back to that, and regard this problem calmly and methodically. To begin with, how many kinds of motive are there for murder? What are the motives which lead one human being to take another human being's life?

'We exclude for the moment homicidal mania. Because I am absolutely convinced that the solution of our problem does not lie there. We also exclude killing done on the spur of the moment under the impulse of an ungovernable temper. This is cold-blooded deliberate murder. What are the motives that actuate such a murder as that?

'There is, first, *Gain*. Who stood to gain by Mademoiselle Buckley's death? Directly or indirectly? Well, we can put down Charles Vyse. He inherits a property that, from the financial point of view, is probably not worth inheriting. He might, perhaps, pay off the mortgage, build small villas on the land and eventually make a small profit. It is possible. The place might be worth something to him if he had any deeply cherished love of it – if, it were, for instance, a family place. That is, undoubtedly, an instinct very deeply implanted in some human beings, and it has, in cases I have known, actually led to crime. But I cannot see any such motive in M. Vyse's case.

'The only other person who would benefit at all by Mademoiselle Buckley's death is her friend, Madame Rice. But the amount would clearly be a very small one. Nobody else, as far as I can see, *gains* by Mademoiselle Buckley's death.

'What is another motive? Hate – or love that has turned to hate. The *crime passionnel*. Well, there again we have the word of the observant Madame Croft that both Charles Vyse and Commander Challenger are in love with the young lady.'

'I think we can say that we have observed the latter phenomenon for ourselves,' I remarked, with a smile.

'Yes – he tends to wear his heart on his sleeve, the honest sailor. For the other, we rely on the word of Madame Croft. Now, if Charles Vyse felt that he were supplanted, would he be so powerfully affected that he would kill his cousin rather than let her become the wife of another man?'

'It sounds very melodramatic,' I said, doubtfully.

'It sounds, you would say, un-English. I agree. But even the English have emotions. And a type such as Charles Vyse, is the most likely to have them. He is a repressed young man. One who does not show his feelings easily. Such often have the most violent feelings. I would never suspect the Commander Challenger of murder for emotional reasons. No, no, he is not the type. But with Charles Vyse – yes, it is possible. But it does not entirely satisfy me.

'Another motive for crime – Jealousy. I separate it from the last, because jealousy may not, necessarily, be a sexual emotion. There is envy – envy of possession – of supremacy. Such a jealousy as drove the Iago of your great Shakespeare to one of the cleverest crimes (speaking from the professional point of view) that has ever been committed.'

'Why was it so clever?' I asked, momentarily diverted.

'*Parbleu* – because he got others to execute it. Imagine a criminal nowadays on whom one was unable to put the handcuffs because he had never done anything himself. But this is not the subject we were discussing. Can jealousy, of any kind, be responsible for this crime? Who has reason to envy Mademoiselle? Another woman? There is only Madame Rice, and as far as we can see, there was no rivalry between the two women. But again, that is only "as far as we can see". There may be something there.

'Lastly – Fear. Does Mademoiselle Nick, by any chance, hold somebody's secret in her power? Does she know something which, if it were known, might ruin another life? If so, I think we can say very definitely, *that she herself is unaware of it*. But that might be, you know. That might be. And if so, it makes it very difficult. Because, whilst she holds the clue in her hands, she holds it unconsciously and will be quite unable to tell us what it is.'

'You really think that is possible?'

'It is a hypothesis. I am driven to it by the difficulty of finding a reasonable theory elsewhere. When you have eliminated other possibilities you turn to the one that is left and say – since the other is not – *this must be so . . .*'

He was silent a long time.

At last, rousing himself from his absorption, he drew a sheet of paper towards him and began to write.

'What are you writing?' I asked, curiously.

'*Mon ami*, I am composing a list. It is a list of people surrounding Mademoiselle Buckley. Within that list, if my theory is correct, there must be the name of the murderer.'

He continued to write for perhaps twenty minutes – then shoved the sheets of paper across to me.

'*Voilà, mon ami*. See what you make of it.'

The following is a reproduction of the paper:

A. Ellen.
B. Her gardener husband.
C. Their child.
D. Mr Croft.
E. Mrs Croft.
F. Mrs Rice.
G. Mr Lazarus.
H. Commander Challenger.
I. Mr Charles Vyse.
J.

Remarks:

A. *Ellen*. – Suspicious circumstances. Her attitude and words on hearing of the crime. Best opportunity of anyone to have staged accidents and to have known of pistol, *but* unlikely to have tampered with car, and general mentality of crime seems above her level.

   Motive. – None – unless hate arising out of some incident unknown.

   Note. – Further inquiries as to her antecedents and general relations with N. B.

B. *Her Husband*. – Same as above. More likely to have tampered with car.

   Note. – Should be interviewed.

C. *Child*. – Can be ruled out.

   Note. – Should be interviewed. Might give valuable information.

D. *Mr Croft*. – Only suspicious circumstance the fact that we met him mounting the stair to bedroom floor. Had ready explanation which may be true. But it may not!
Nothing known of antecedents.
Motive. – None.

E. *Mrs Croft*. – Suspicious circumstances. – None.
Motive. – None.

F. *Mrs Rice*. – Suspicious circumstances. Full opportunity. Asked N. B. to fetch wrap. Has deliberately tried to create impression that N. B. is a liar and her account of 'accidents' not to be relied on. Was not at Tavistock when accidents occurred. Where was she?
Motive. – *Gain?* Very slight. *Jealousy?* Possible, but nothing known. *Fear?* Also possible, but nothing known.
Note. – Converse with N. B. on subject. See if any light is thrown upon matter. Possibly something to do with F. R.'s marriage.

G. *Mr Lazarus*. – Suspicious circumstances. General opportunity. Offer to buy picture. Said brakes of car were quite all right (according to F. R.). May have been in neighbourhood prior to Friday.
Motive. – None – unless profit on picture. *Fear?* – unlikely.
Note. – Find out where J. L. was before arriving at St Loo. Find out financial position of Aaron Lazarus & Son.

H. *Commander Challenger*. – Suspicious circumstances. None. Was in neighbourhood all last week, so opportunity for 'accidents' good. Arrived half an hour after murder.
Motive. – None.

I. *Mr Vyse*. – Suspicious circumstances. Was absent from office at time when shot was fired in garden of hotel. Opportunity good. Statement about selling of End House open to doubt. Of a repressed temperament. Would probably know about pistol.
Motive. – *Gain?* (slight) *Love or Hate?* Possible with one of his temperament. *Fear?* Unlikely.
Note. – Find out who held mortgage. Find out position of Vyse's firm.

J. ? – There *could* be a J., *e.g.* an outsider. *But* with a link in the form of one of the foregoing. If so, probably connected with

A. D. and E. or F. The existence of J. would explain (1) Ellen's lack of surprise at crime and her pleasurable satisfaction. (But that might be due to natural pleasurable excitement of her class over deaths.) (2) The reason for Croft and his wife coming to live in lodge. (3) Might supply motive for F. R.'s *fear* of secret being revealed or for *jealousy*.

Poirot watched me as I read.

'It is very English, is it not?' he remarked, with pride. 'I am more English when I write than when I speak.'

'It's an excellent piece of work,' I said, warmly. 'It sets all the possibilities out most clearly.'

'Yes,' he said, thoughtfully, as he took it back from me. 'And one name leaps to the eye, my friend. *Charles Vyse.* He has the best opportunities. We have given him the choice of two motives. *Ma foi* – if that was a list of racehorses, he would start favourite, *n'est-ce pas?*'

'He is certainly the most likely suspect.'

'You have a tendency, Hastings, to prefer the least likely. That, no doubt, is from reading too many detective stories. In real life, nine times out of ten, it is the most likely and the most obvious person who commits the crime.'

'But you don't really think that is so this time?'

'There is only one thing that is against it. The boldness of the crime! That has stood out from the first. Because of that, as I say, the motive *cannot be obvious.*'

'Yes, that is what you said at first.'

'And that is what I say again.'

With a sudden brusque gesture he crumpled the sheets of paper and threw them on the floor.

'No,' he said, as I uttered an exclamation of protest. 'That list has been in vain. Still, it has cleared my mind. *Order and method!* That is the first stage. To arrange the facts with neatness and precision. The next stage –'

'Yes.'

'The next stage is that of the psychology. The correct employment of the little grey cells! I advise you, Hastings, to go to bed.'

'No,' I said. 'Not unless you do. I'm not going to leave you.'

'Most faithful of dogs! But see you, Hastings, you cannot assist me to think. That is all I am going to do – think.'

I still shook my head.

'You might want to discuss some point with me.'

'Well – well – you are a loyal friend. Take at least, I beg of you, the easy-chair.'

That proposal I did accept. Presently the room began to swim and dip. The last thing I remember was seeing Poirot carefully retrieving the crumpled sheets of paper from the floor and putting them away tidily in the waste-paper basket.

Then I must have fallen asleep.

CHAPTER 10
NICK'S SECRET

It was daylight when I awoke.

Poirot was still sitting where he had been the night before. His attitude was the same, but in his face was a difference. His eyes were shining with that queer cat-like green light that I knew so well.

I struggled to an upright position, feeling very stiff and uncomfortable. Sleeping in a chair is a proceeding not to be recommended at my time of life. Yet one thing at least resulted from it – I awoke not in that pleasant state of lazy somnolence but with a mind and brain as active as when I fell asleep.

'Poirot,' I cried. 'You have thought of something.'

He nodded. He leaned forward, tapping the table in front of him.

'Tell me, Hastings, the answer to these three questions. *Why has Mademoiselle Nick been sleeping badly lately? Why did she buy a black evening dress – she never wears black? Why did she say last night, "I have nothing to live for – now"?*'

I stared. The questions seemed beside the point.

'Answer those questions, Hastings, answer them.'

'Well – as to the first – she said she had been worried lately.'

'Precisely. What has she been worried about?'

'And the black dress – well, everybody wants a change sometimes.'

'For a married man, you have very little appreciation of feminine psychology. If a woman thinks she does not look well in a colour, she refuses to wear it.'

'And the last – well, it was a natural thing to say after that awful shock.'

'No, *mon ami*, it was *not* a natural thing to say. To be horror-struck by her cousin's death, to reproach herself for it – yes, all that is natural enough. But the other, no. She spoke of life with weariness – as of a thing no longer dear to her. Never before had she displayed that attitude. She had been defiant – yes – she had snapped the fingers, yes – and then, when that broke down, she was afraid. Afraid, mark you, because life was sweet and she did not wish to die. But weary of life – no! That never! Even before dinner that was not so. We have there, Hastings, a *psychological change*. And that is interesting. What was it caused her point of view to change?'

'The shock of her cousin's death.'

'I wonder. It was the shock that loosed her tongue. But suppose the change was before that. Is there anything else could account for it?'

'I don't know of anything.'

'Think, Hastings. Use your little grey cells.'

'Really –'

'What was the last moment we had the opportunity of observing her?'

'Well, actually, I suppose, at dinner.'

'Exactly. After that, we only saw her receiving guests, making them welcome – purely a formal attitude. What happened at the end of dinner, Hastings?'

'She went to telephone,' I said, slowly.

'*A la bonne heure*. You have got there at last. She went to telephone. And she was absent a long time. Twenty minutes at least. That is a long time for a telephone call. Who spoke to her over the telephone? What did they say? Did she really telephone? We have to find out, Hastings, what happened in that twenty minutes. For there, or so I fully believe, we shall find the clue we seek.'

'You really think so?'

'*Mais oui, mais oui!* All along, Hastings, I have told you that

Mademoiselle has been keeping something back. She doesn't think it has any connection with the murder – but I, Hercule Poirot, know better! It *must* have a connection. For, all along, I have been conscious that there is a factor lacking. If there were not a factor lacking – why then, the whole thing would be plain to me! And as it is not plain to me – *eh bien* – then the missing factor is the keystone of the mystery! I know I am right, Hastings.

'I must know the answer to those three questions. And, then – and then – I shall begin *to see* . . .'

'Well,' I said, stretching my stiffened limbs, 'I think a bath and a shave are indicated.'

By the time I had had a bath and changed into day clothing I felt better. The stiffness and weariness of a night passed in uncomfortable conditions passed off. I arrived at the breakfast table feeling that one drink of hot coffee would restore me to my normal self.

I glanced at the paper, but there was little news in it beyond the fact that Michael Seton's death was now definitely confirmed. The intrepid airman had perished. I wondered whether, tomorrow, new headlines would have sprung into being: 'GIRL MURDERED DURING FIREWORK PARTY. MYSTERIOUS TRAGEDY.' Something like that.

I had just finished breakfast when Frederica Rice came up to my table. She was wearing a plain little frock of black marocain with a little soft pleated white collar. Her fairness was more evident than ever.

'I want to see M. Poirot, Captain Hastings. Is he up yet, do you know?'

'I will take you up with me now,' I said. 'We shall find him in the sitting-room.'

'Thank you.'

'I hope,' I said, as we left the dining-room together, 'that you didn't sleep too badly?'

'It was a shock,' she said, in a meditative voice. 'But, of course, I didn't know the poor girl. It's not as though it had been Nick.'

'I suppose you'd never met this girl before?'

'Once – at Scarborough. She came over to lunch with Nick.'

'It will be a terrible blow to her father and mother,' I said.

'Dreadful.'

But she said it very impersonally. She was, I fancied, an egoist. Nothing was very real to her that did not concern herself.

Poirot had finished his breakfast and was sitting reading the morning paper. He rose and greeted Frederica with all his customary Gallic politeness.

'Madame,' he said. '*Enchanté!*'

He drew forward a chair.

She thanked him with a very faint smile and sat down. Her two hands rested on the arms of the chair. She sat there very upright, looking straight in front of her. She did not rush into speech. There was something a little frightening about her stillness and aloofness.

'M. Poirot,' she said at last. 'I suppose there is no doubt that this – sad business last night was all part and parcel of the same thing? I mean – that the intended victim was really Nick?'

'I should say, Madame, that there was no doubt at all.'

Frederica frowned a little.

'Nick bears a charmed life,' she said.

There was some curious undercurrent in her voice that I could not understand.

'Luck, they say, goes in cycles,' remarked Poirot.

'Perhaps. It is certainly useless to fight against it.'

Now there was only weariness in her tone. After a moment or two, she went on.

'I must beg your pardon, M. Poirot. Nick's pardon, too. Up till last night I did not believe. I never dreamed that the danger was – serious.'

'Is that so, Madame?'

'I see now that everything will have to be gone into – carefully. And I imagine that Nick's immediate circle of friends will not be immune from suspicion. Ridiculous, of course, but there it is. Am I right, M. Poirot?'

'You are very intelligent, Madame.'

'You asked me some questions about Tavistock the other day, M. Poirot. As you will find out sooner or later, I might as well tell you the truth now. I was not at Tavistock.'

'No, Madame?'

'I motored down to this part of the world with Mr Lazarus

early last weeek. We did not wish to arouse more comment than necessary. We stayed at a little place called Shellacombe.'

'That is, I think, about seven miles from here, Madame?'

'About that – yes.'

Still that quiet far-away weariness.

'May I be impertinent, Madame?'

'Is there such a thing – in these days?'

'Perhaps you are right, Madame. How long have you and M. Lazarus been friends?'

'I met him six months ago.'

'And you – care for him, Madame?'

Frederica shrugged her shoulders.

'He is – rich.'

'Oh! *là là*,' cried Poirot. 'That is an ugly thing to say.'

She seemed faintly amused.

'Isn't it better to say it myself – than to have you say it for me?'

'Well – there is always that, of course. May I repeat, Madame, that you are *very* intelligent.'

'You will give me a diploma soon,' said Frederica, and rose.

'There is nothing more you wish to tell me, Madame?'

'I do not think so – no. I am going to take some flowers round to Nick and see how she is.'

'Ah, that is very *aimable* of you. Thank you, Madame, for your frankness.'

She glanced at him sharply, seemed about to speak, then thought better of it and went out of the room, smiling faintly at me as I held the door open for her.

'She is intelligent,' said Poirot. 'Yes, but so is Hercule Poirot!'

'What do you mean?'

'That it is all very well and very pretty to force the richness of M. Lazarus down my throat –'

'I must say that rather disgusted me.'

'*Mon cher*, always you have the right reaction in the wrong place. It is not, for the moment, a question of good taste or otherwise. If Madame Rice has a devoted friend who is rich and can give her all she needs – why then obviously Madame Rice would not need to murder her dearest friend for a mere pittance.'

'Oh!' I said.

'*Précisément!* "Oh!"'

'Why didn't you stop her going to the nursing home?'

'Why should I show my hand? Is it Hercule Poirot who prevents Mademoiselle Nick from seeing her friends? *Quelle idée!* It is the doctors and the nurses. Those tiresome nurses! So full of rules and regulations and "doctor's' orders".'

'You're not afraid that they may let her in after all? Nick may insist.'

'Nobody will be let in, my dear Hastings, but you and me. And for that matter, the sooner we make our way there, the better.'

The sitting-room door flew open and George Challenger barged in. His tanned face was alive with indignation.

'Look here, M. Poirot,' he said. 'What's the meaning of this? I rang up that damned nursing home where Nick is. Asked how she was and what time I could come round and see her. And they say the doctor won't allow any visitors. I want to know the meaning of that. To put it plainly, is this your work? Or is Nick really ill from shock?'

'I assure you, Monsieur, that I do not lay down rules for nursing homes. I would not dare. Why not ring up the good doctor – what was his name now? – Ah, yes, Graham.'

'I have. He says she's going on as well as could be expected – usual stuff. But I know all the tricks – my uncle's a doctor. Harley Street. Nerve specialist. Psychoanalysis – all the rest of it. Putting relations and friends off with soothing words. I've heard about it all. I don't believe Nick isn't up to seeing any one. I believe you're at the bottom of this, M. Poirot.'

Poirot smiled at him in a very kindly fashion. Indeed, I have always observed that Poirot has a kindly feeling for a lover.

'Now listen to me, *mon ami*,' he said. 'If one guest is admitted, others cannot be kept out. You comprehend? It must be all or none. We want Mademoiselle's safety, you and I, do we not? Exactly. Then, you understand – it must be *none*.'

'I get you,' said Challenger, slowly. 'But then –'

'*Chut!* We will say no more. We will forget even what we have said. The prudence, the extreme prudence, is what is needed at present.'

'I can hold my tongue,' said the sailor quietly.

He turned away to the door, pausing as he went out to say:

'No embargo on flowers, is there? So long as they are not white ones.'

Poirot smiled.

'And now,' he said, as the door shut behind the impetuous Challenger, 'whilst M. Challenger and Madame and perhaps M. Lazarus all encounter each other in the flower shop, you and I will drive quietly to our destination.'

'And ask for the answer to the three questions?' I said.

'Yes. We will ask. Though, as a matter of fact, I know the answer.'

'What?' I exclaimed.

'Yes.'

'But when did you find out?'

'Whilst I was eating my breakfast, Hastings. It stared me in the face.'

'Tell me.'

'No, I will leave you to hear it from Mademoiselle.'

Then, as if to distract my mind, he pushed an open letter across to me.

It was a report by the expert Poirot had sent to examine the picture of old Nicholas Buckley. It stated definitely that the picture was worth at most twenty pounds.

'So that is one matter cleared up,' said Poirot.

'No mouse in that mousehole,' I said, remembering a metaphor of Poirot's on one past occasion.

'Ah! you remember that? No, as you say, no mouse in that mousehole. Twenty pounds and M. Lazarus offered fifty. What an error of judgement for a seemingly astute young man. But there, there, we must start on our errand.'

The nursing home was set high on a hill overlooking the bay. A white-coated orderly received us. We were put into a little room downstairs and presently a brisk-looking nurse came to us.

One glance at Poirot seemed to be enough. She had clearly received her instructions from Dr Graham together with a minute description of the little detective. She even concealed a smile.

'Miss Buckley has passed a very fair night,' she said. 'Come up, will you?'

In a pleasant room with the sun streaming into it, we found Nick. In the narrow iron bed, she looked like a tired child. Her face was white and her eyes were suspiciously red, and she seemed listless and weary.

'It's good of you to come,' she said in a flat voice.

Poirot took her hand in both of his.

'Courage, Mademoiselle. There is always something to live for.'

The words startled her. She looked up in his face.

'Oh!' she said. 'Oh!'

'Will you not tell me now, Mademoiselle, what it was that has been worrying you lately? Or shall I guess? And may I offer you, Mademoiselle, my very deepest sympathy.'

Her face flushed.

'So you know. Oh, well, it doesn't matter who knows now. Now that it's all over. Now that I shall never see him again.'

Her voice broke.

'Courage, Mademoiselle.'

'I haven't got any courage left. I've used up every bit in these last weeks. Hoping and hoping and – just lately – hoping against hope.'

I stared. I could not understand one word.

'Regard the poor Hastings,' said Poirot. 'He does not know what we are talking about.'

Her unhappy eyes met mine.

'Michael Seton, the airman,' she said. 'I was engaged to him – and he's dead.'

CHAPTER 11

THE MOTIVE

I was dumbfounded.

I turned on Poirot.

'Is this what you meant?'

'Yes, *mon ami*. This morning – I knew.'

'How did you know? How did you guess? You said it stared you in the face at breakfast.'

'So it did, my friend. From the front page of the newspaper.

I remembered the conversation at dinner last night – and I saw everything.'

He turned to Nick again.

'You heard the news last night?'

'Yes. On the wireless. I made an excuse about the telephone. I wanted to hear the news alone – in case . . .' She swallowed hard. 'And I heard it . . .'

'I know, I know.' He took her hand in both of his.

'It was – pretty ghastly. And all the people arriving. I don't know how I got through it. It all felt like a dream. I could see myself from outside – behaving just as usual. It was queer somehow.'

'Yes, yes, I understand.'

'And then, when I went to fetch Freddie's wrap – I broke down for a minute. I pulled myself together quite quickly. But Maggie kept calling up about her coat. And then at last she took my shawl and went, and I put on some powder and some rouge and followed her out. And there she was – dead . . .'

'Yes, yes, it must have been a terrible shock.'

'You don't understand. I was angry! I wished it had been *me!* I wanted to be dead – and there I was – alive and perhaps to live for years! And Michael dead – drowned far away in the Pacific.'

'*Pauvre enfant.*'

'I don't want to be alive. I don't want to live, I tell you!' she cried, rebelliously.

'I know – I know. To all of us, Mademoiselle, there comes a time when death is preferable to life. But it passes – sorrow passes and grief. You cannot believe that now, I know. It is useless for an old man like me to talk. Idle words – that is what you think – idle words.'

'You think I'll forget – and marry someone else? Never!'

She looked rather lovely as she sat up in bed, her two hands clenched and her cheeks burning.

Poirot said gently:

'No, no. I am not thinking anything of the kind. You are very lucky, Mademoiselle. You have been loved by a brave man – a hero. How did you come to meet him?'

'It was at Le Touquet – last September. Nearly a year ago.'

'And you became engaged – when?'

'Just after Christmas. But it had to be a secret.'

'Why was that?'

'Michael's uncle – old Sir Matthew Seton. He loved birds and hated women.'

'*Ah! ce n'est pas raisonnable!*'

'Well – I don't mean quite that. He was a complete crank. Thought women ruined a man's life. And Michael was absolutely dependent on him. He was frightfully proud of Michael and it was he who financed the building of the *Albatross* and the expenses of the round-the-world flight. It was the dearest dream of his life as well as of Michael's. If Michael had pulled it off – well, then he could have asked his uncle anything. And even if old Sir Matthew had still cut up rough, well, it wouldn't have really mattered. Michael would have been made – a kind of world hero. His uncle would have come round in the end.'

'Yes, yes, I see.'

'But Michael said it would be fatal if anything leaked out. We must keep it a dead secret. And I did. I never told anyone – not even Freddie.'

Poirot groaned.

'If only you had told me, Mademoiselle.'

Nick stared at him.

'But what difference would it have made? It couldn't have anything to do with these mysterious attacks on me? No, I'd promised Michael – and I kept my word. But it was awful – the anxiety, wondering and getting in a state the whole time. And everyone saying one was so nervy. And being unable to explain.'

'Yes, I comprehend all that.'

'He was missing once before, you know. Crossing the desert on the way to India. That was pretty awful, and then after all, it was all right. His machine was damaged, but it was put right, and he went on. And I kept saying to myself that it would be the same this time. Everyone said he must be dead – and I kept telling myself that he must be all right, really. And then – last night . . .'

Her voice trailed away.

'You had hoped up till then?'

'I don't know. I think it was more that I refused to believe. It was awful never being able to talk to anyone.'

'Yes, I can imagine that. Were you never tempted to tell Madame Rice, for instance?'

'Sometimes I wanted to frightfully.'

'You do not think she – guessed?'

'I don't think so.' Nick considered the idea carefully. 'She never said anything. Of course she used to hint things sometimes. About our being great friends and all that.'

'You never considered telling her when M. Seton's uncle died? You know that he died about a week ago?'

'I know. He had an operation or something. I suppose I might have told anybody then. But it wouldn't have been a nice way of doing it, would it? I mean, it would have seemed rather boastful – to do it just then – when all the papers were full of Michael. And reporters would have come and interviewed me. It would all have been rather cheap. And Michael would have hated it.'

'I agree with you, Mademoiselle. You could not have announced it publicly. I only meant that you could have spoken of it privately to a friend.'

'I did sort of hint to one person,' said Nick. 'I – thought it was only fair. But I don't know how much he – the person took in.'

Poirot nodded.

'Are you on good terms with your cousin M. Vyse?' he asked, with a rather abrupt change of subject.

'Charles? What put him into your head?'

'I was just wondering – that was all.'

'Charles means well,' said Nick. 'He's a frightful stick, of course. Never moves out of this place. He disapproves of me, I think.'

'Oh! Mademoiselle, Mademoiselle. And I hear that he has laid all his devotion at your feet!'

'Disapproving of a person doesn't keep you from having a pash for them. Charles thinks my mode of life is reprehensible and he disapproves of my cocktails, my complexion, my friends and my conversation. But he still feels my fatal fascination. He always hopes to reform me, I think.'

She paused and then said, with a ghost of a twinkle:

'Who have you been pumping to get the local information?'

'You must not give me away, Mademoiselle. I had a little conversation with the Australian lady, Madame Croft.'

'She's rather an old dear – when one has time for her. Terribly sentimental. Love and home and children – you know the sort of thing.'

'I am old-fashioned and sentimental myself, Mademoiselle.'

'Are you? I should have said that Captain Hastings was the sentimental one of you two.'

I blushed indignantly.

'He is furious,' said Poirot, eying my discomfiture with a good deal of pleasure. 'But you are right, Mademoiselle. Yes, you are right.'

'Not at all,' I said, angrily.

'Hastings has a singularly beautiful nature. It has been the greatest hindrance to me at times.'

'Don't be absurd, Poirot.'

'He is, to begin with, reluctant to see evil anywhere, and when he does see it his righteous indignation is so great that he is incapable of dissembling. Altogether a rare and beautiful nature. No, *mon ami*, I will not permit you to contradict me. It is as I say.'

'You've both been very kind to me,' said Nick, gently.

'*Là, là*, Mademoiselle. That is nothing. We have much more to do. To begin with, you will remain here. You will obey orders. You will do what I tell you. At this juncture I must not be hampered.'

Nick sighed wearily.

'I'll do anything you like. I don't care what I do.'

'You will see no friends for the present.'

'I don't care. I don't want to see anyone.'

'For you the passive part – for us the active one. Now, Mademoiselle, I am going to leave you. I will not intrude longer upon your sorrow.'

He moved towards the door, pausing with his hand on the handle to say over his shoulder:

'By the way, you once mentioned a will you made. Where is it, this will?'

'Oh! it's knocking round somewhere.'

'At End House?'

'Yes.'

'In a safe? Locked up in your desk?'

'Well, I really don't know. It's somewhere about.' She frowned. 'I'm frightfully untidy, you know. Papers and things like that would be mostly in the writing-table in the library. That's where most of the bills are. The will is probably with them. Or it might be in my bedroom.'

'You permit me to make the search – yes?'

'If you want to – yes. Look at anything you like.'

'*Merci*, Mademoiselle. I will avail myself of your permission.'

CHAPTER 12

ELLEN

Poirot said no word till we had emerged from the nursing home into the outer air. Then he caught me by the arm.

'You see, Hastings? You see? Ah! *Sacré tonnerre!* I was right! I was right! Always I knew there was something lacking – some piece of the puzzle that was not there. And without that missing piece the whole thing was meaningless.'

His almost despairing triumph was double-Dutch to me. I could not see that anything very epoch-making had occurred.

'It was there all the time. And I could not see it. But how should I? To know there is *something* – that, yes – but to know what that something is. *Ah! Ça c'est bien plus difficile.*'

'Do you mean that this has some direct bearing on the crime?'

'*Ma foi*, do you not see?'

'As a matter of fact, I don't.'

'Is it possible? Why, it gives us what we have been looking for – the motive – the hidden obscure motive!'

'I may be very dense, but I can't see it. Do you mean jealousy of some kind?'

'Jealousy? No, no, my friend. The usual motive – the inevitable motive. Money, my friend, money!'

I stared. He went on, speaking more calmly.

'Listen, *mon ami*. Just over a week ago Sir Matthew Seton dies. And Sir Matthew Seton was a millionaire – one of the richest men in England.'

'Yes, but –'

'*Attendez*. One step at a time. He has a nephew whom he

idolizes and to whom, we may safely assume, he has left his vast fortune.'

'But –'

'*Mais oui* – legacies, yes, an endowment to do with his hobby, yes, but the bulk of the money would go to Michael Seton. Last Tuesday, Michael Seton is reported missing – *and on Wednesday the attacks on Mademoiselle's life begin*. Supposing, Hastings, that Michael Seton made a will before he started on his flight, and that in that will he left all he had to his fiancée.'

'That's pure supposition.'

'It is supposition – yes. *But it must be so*. Because, if it is not so, there is no meaning in anything that has happened. It is no paltry inheritance that is at stake. It is an enormous fortune.'

I was silent for some minutes, turning the matter over in my mind. It seemed to me that Poirot was leaping to conclusions in a most reckless manner, and yet I was secretly convinced that he was right. It was his extraordinary flair for being right that influenced me. Yet it seemed to me that there was a good deal to be proved still.

'But if nobody knew of the engagement,' I argued.

'Pah! Somebody *did* know. For the matter of that, somebody always *does* know. If they do not know, they guess. Madame Rice suspected. Mademoiselle Nick admitted as much. She may have had means of turning those suspicions into certainties.'

'How?'

'Well, for one thing, there must have been letters from Michael Seton to Mademoiselle Nick. They had been engaged some time. And her best friend could not call that young lady anything but careless. She leaves things here and there, and everywhere. I doubt if she has ever locked up anything in her life. Oh, yes, there would be means of making sure.'

'And Frederica Rice would know about the will that her friend had made?'

'Doubtless. Oh, yes, it narrows down now. You remember my list – a list of persons numbered from A. to J. It has narrowed down to only two persons. I dismiss the servants. I dismiss the Commander Challenger – even though he did take one hour and a half to reach here from Plymouth – and the distance is only thirty miles. I dismiss the long-nosed M. Lazarus who offered fifty pounds for a picture that was only worth twenty (it is odd, that, when you come to think of it. Most uncharacteristic of his race). I dismiss the Australians – so hearty and so pleasant. I keep two people on my list still.'

'One is Frederica Rice,' I said slowly.

I had a vision of her face, the golden hair, the white fragility of the features.

'Yes. She is indicated very clearly. However carelessly worded Mademoiselle's will may have been, she would be plainly indi-cated as residuary legatee. Apart from End House, everything was to go to her. If Mademoiselle Nick instead of Mademoiselle Maggie had been shot last night, Madame Rice would be a rich woman today.'

'I can hardly believe it!'

'You mean that you can hardly believe that a beautiful woman can be a murderess? One often has a little difficulty with members of a jury on that account. But you may be right. There is still another suspect.'

'Who?'

'Charles Vyse.'

'But he only inherits the house.'

'Yes – but he may not know that. Did he make Mademoiselle's will for her? I think not. If so, it would be in his keeping, not "knocking around somewhere", or whatever the phrase was that Mademoiselle used. So, you see, Hastings, *it is quite probable that he knows nothing about that will.* He may believe that she has never made a will and that, in that case, he will inherit as next of kin.'

'You know,' I said, 'that really seems to me much more probable.'

'That is your romantic mind, Hastings. The wicked solicitor. A familiar figure in fiction. If as well as being a solicitor he has an impassive face, it makes the matter almost certain. It is true that, in some ways, he is more in the picture than Madame. He would be more likely to know about the pistol and more likely to use one.'

'And to send the boulder crashing down.'

'Perhaps. Though, as I have told you, much can be done by leverage. And the fact that the boulder was dislodged at the wrong minute, and consequently missed Mademoiselle, is more suggestive of feminine agency. The idea of tampering with the interior of a car seems masculine in conception – though many women are as good mechanics as men nowadays. On the other hand, there are one or two gaps in the theory against M. Vyse.'

'Such as –?'

'He is less likely to have known of the engagement than Madame. And there is another point. His action was rather precipitate.'

'What do you mean?'

'Well, until last night there was no *certitude* that Seton was dead. To act rashly, without due assurance, seems very uncharacteristic of the legal mind.'

'Yes,' I said. 'A woman would jump to conclusions.'

'Exactly. *Ce que femme veut, Dieu veut.* That is the attitude.'

'It's really amazing the way Nick has escaped. It seems almost incredible.'

And suddenly I remembered the tone in Frederica's voice as she had said: 'Nick bears a charmed life.'

I shivered a little.

'Yes,' said Poirot, thoughtfully. 'And I can take no credit to myself. Which is humiliating.'

'Providence,' I murmured.

'Ah! *mon ami*, I would not put on the shoulders of the good God the burden of men's wrongdoing. You say that in your Sunday morning voice of thankfulness – without reflecting that what you are really saying is that *le bon Dieu* has killed Miss Maggie Buckley.'

'Really, Poirot!'

'Really, my friend! But I will not sit back and say "*le bon Dieu* has arranged everything, I will not interfere". Because I am convinced that *le bon Dieu* created Hercule Poirot for the express purpose of interfering. It is my *métier*.'

We had been slowly ascending the zig-zag path up the cliff. It was at this juncture that we passed through the little gate into the grounds of End House.

'Pouf!' said Poirot. 'That ascent is a steep one. I am hot. My moustaches are limp. Yes, as I was saying just now, I am on the side of the innocent. I am on the side of Mademoiselle Nick because she was attacked. I am on the side of Mademoiselle Maggie because she has been killed.'

'And you are against Frederica Rice and Charles Vyse.'

'No, no, Hastings. I keep an open mind. I say only that at the moment one of those two is indicated. Chut!'

We had come out on the strip of lawn by the house, and a man was driving a mowing machine. He had a long, stupid face and lack-lustre eyes. Beside him was a small boy of about ten, ugly but intelligent-looking.

It crossed my mind that we had not heard the mowing machine in action, but I presumed that the gardener was not overworking himself. He had probably been resting from his labours, and had sprung into action on hearing our voices approaching.

'Good morning,' said Poirot.

'Good morning, sir.'

'You are the gardener, I suppose. The husband of Madame who works in the house.'

'He's my Dad,' said the small boy.

'That's right, sir,' said the man. 'You'll be the foreign gentleman, I take it, that's really a detective. Is there any news of the young mistress, sir?'

'I come from seeing her at the immediate moment. She has passed a satisfactory night.'

'We've had policemen here,' said the small boy. 'That's where the lady was killed. Here by the steps. I seen a pig killed once, haven't I, Dad?'

'Ah!' said his father, unemotionally.

'Dad used to kill pigs when he worked on a farm. Didn't you, Dad? I seen a pig killed. I liked it.'

'Young 'uns like to see pigs killed,' said the man, as though stating one of the unalterable facts of nature.

'Shot with a pistol, the lady was,' continued the boy. 'She didn't have her throat cut. No!'

We passed on to the house, and I felt thankful to get away from the ghoulish child.

Poirot entered the drawing-room, the windows of which were open, and rang the bell. Ellen, neatly attired in black, came in answer to the bell. She showed no surprise at seeing us.

Poirot explained that we were here by permission of Miss Buckley to make a search of the house.

'Very good, sir.'

'The police have finished?'

'They said they had seen everything they wanted, sir. They've been about the garden since very early in the morning. I don't know whether they've found anything.'

She was about to leave the room when Poirot stopped her with a question.

'Were you very surprised last night when you heard Miss Buckley had been shot?'

'Yes, sir, very surprised. Miss Maggie was a nice young lady, sir. I can't imagine anyone being so wicked as to want to harm her.'

'If it had been anyone else, you would not have been so surprised – eh?'

'I don't know what you mean, sir?'

'When I came into the hall last night,' he said, 'you asked at once whether anyone had been hurt. Were you expecting anything of the kind?'

She was silent. Her fingers pleated a corner of her apron. She shook her head and murmured:

'You gentlemen wouldn't understand.'

'Yes, yes,' said Poirot, 'I would understand. However fantastic what you may say, I would understand.'

She looked at him doubtfully, then seemed to make up her mind to trust him.

'You see, sir,' she said, 'this isn't a good house.'

I was surprised and a little contemptuous. Poirot, however, seemed to find the remark not in the least unusual.

'You mean it is an old house.'

'Yes, sir, not a good house.'

'You have been here long?'

'Six years, sir. But I was here as a girl. In the kitchen as kitchen-maid. That was in the time of old Sir Nicholas. It was the same then.'

Poirot looked at her attentively.

'In an old house,' he said, 'there is sometimes an atmosphere of evil.'

'That's it, sir,' said Ellen, eagerly. 'Evil. Bad thoughts and bad deeds too. It's like dry rot in a house, sir, you can't get it out. It's a sort of feeling in the air. I always knew something bad would happen in this house, some day.'

'Well, you have been proved right.'

'Yes, sir.'

There was a very slight underlying satisfaction in her tone, the satisfaction of one whose gloomy prognostications have been shown to be correct.

'But you didn't think it would be Miss Maggie.'

'No, indeed, I didn't, sir. Nobody hated *her* – I'm sure of it.'

It seemed to me that in those words was a clue. I expected Poirot to follow it up, but to my surprise he shifted to quite a different subject.

'You didn't hear the shots fired?'

'I couldn't have told with the fireworks going on. Very noisy they were.'

'You weren't out watching them?'

'No, I hadn't finished clearing up dinner.'

'Was the waiter helping you?'

'No, sir, he'd gone out into the garden to have a look at the fireworks.'

'But you didn't go.'

'No, sir.'

'Why was that?'

'I wanted to get finished.'

'You don't care for fireworks?'

'Oh, yes, sir, it wasn't that. But you see, there's two nights of them, and William and I get the evening off tomorrow and go down into the town and see them from there.'

'I comprehend. And you heard Mademoiselle Maggie asking for her coat and unable to find it?'

'I heard Miss Nick run upstairs, sir, and Miss Buckley call up from the front hall saying she couldn't find something and I heard her say, "All right – I'll take the shawl –"'

'Pardon,' Poirot interrupted. 'You did not endeavour to search for the coat for her – or get it from the car where it had been left?'

'I had my work to do, sir.'

'Quite so – and doubtless neither of the two young ladies asked you because they thought you were out looking at the fireworks?'

'Yes, sir.'

'So that, other years, you *have* been out looking at the fire-works?'

A sudden flush came into her pale cheeks.

'I don't know what you mean, sir. We're always allowed to go out into the garden. If I didn't feel like it this year, and would rather get on with my work and go to bed, well, that's my business, I imagine.'

'*Mais oui. Mais oui.* I did not intend to offend you. Why should you not do as you prefer. To make a change, it is pleasant.'

He paused and then added:

'Now another little matter in which I wonder whether you can help me. This is an old house. Are there, do you know, any secret chambers in it?'

'Well – there's a kind of sliding panel – in this very room. I remember being shown it as a girl. Only I can't remember just now where it is. Or was it in the library? I can't say, I'm sure.'

'Big enough for a person to hide in?'

'Oh, no indeed, sir! A little cupboard place – a kind of niche. About a foot square, sir, not more than that.'

'Oh! that is not what I mean at all.'

The blush rose to her face again.

'If you think I was hiding anywhere – I wasn't! I heard Miss Nick run down the stairs and out and I heard her cry out – and I came into the hall to see if – if anything was the matter. And that's the gospel truth, sir. That's the gospel truth.'

CHAPTER 13
LETTERS

Having successfully got rid of Ellen, Poirot turned a somewhat thoughtful face towards me.

'I wonder now – did she hear those shots? I think she did. She heard them, she opened the kitchen door. She heard Nick rush down the stairs and out, and she herself came into the hall to find out what had happened. That is natural enough. But why did she not go out and watch the fireworks that evening? That is what I should like to know, Hastings.'

'What was your idea in asking about a secret hiding place?'

'A mere fanciful idea that, after all, we might not have disposed of J.'

'J?'

'Yes. The last person on my list. The problematical outsider. Supposing for some reason connected with Ellen, that J. had come to the house last night. He (I assume a he) conceals himself in a secret chamber in this room. A girl passes through whom he takes to be Nick. He follows her out – and shoots her. *Non – c'est idiot!* And anyway, we know that there is no hiding place. Ellen's decision to remain in the kitchen last night was a pure hazard. Come, let us search for the will of Mademoiselle Nick.'

There were no papers in the drawing-room. We adjourned to the library, a rather dark room looking out on the drive. Here there was a large old-fashioned walnut bureau-writing-table.

It took us some time to go through it. Everything was in complete confusion. Bills and receipts were mixed up together. Letters of invitation, letters pressing for payment of accounts, letters from friends.

'We will arrange these papers,' said Poirot, sternly, 'with order and method.'

He was as good as his word. Half an hour later, he sat back with a pleased expression on his face. Everything was neatly sorted, docketed and filed.

'*C'est bien, ça.* One thing is at least to the good. We have had to go through everything so thoroughly that there is no possibility of our having missed anything.'

'No, indeed. Not that there's been much to find.'

'Except possibly this.'

He tossed across a letter. It was written in large sprawling handwriting, almost indecipherable.

'Darling, – Party was too too marvellous. Feel rather a worm today. You were wise not to touch that stuff – don't ever start, darling. It's too damned hard to give up. I'm writing the boy friend to hurry up the supply. What Hell life is!

'Yours,

'Freddie.'

'Dated last February,' said Poirot thoughtfully. 'She takes drugs, of course, I knew that as soon as I looked at her.'

'Really? I never suspected such a thing.'

'It is fairly obvious. You have only to look at her eyes. And then there are her extraordinary variations of mood. Sometimes she is all on edge, strung up – sometimes she is lifeless – inert.'

'Drug-taking affects the moral sense, does it not?'

'Inevitably. But I do not think Madame Rice is a real addict. She is at the beginning – not the end.'

'And Nick?'

'There are no signs of it. She may have attended a dope party now and then for fun, but she is no taker of drugs.'

'I'm glad of that.'

I remembered suddenly what Nick had said about Frederica: that she was not always herself. Poirot nodded and tapped the letter he held.

'This is what she was referring to, undoubtedly. Well, we have drawn the blank, as you say, here. Let us go up to Mademoiselle's room.'

There was a desk in Nick's room also, but comparatively little was kept in it. Here again, there was no sign of a will. We found the registration book of her car and a perfectly good dividend warrant of a month back. Otherwise there was nothing of importance.

Poirot sighed in an exasperated fashion.

'The young girls – they are not properly trained nowadays. The order, the method, it is left out of their bringing up. She is charming, Mademoiselle Nick, but she is a feather-head. Decidedly, she is a feather-head.'

He was now going through the contents of a chest of drawers.

'Surely, Poirot,' I said, with some embarrassment, 'those are underclothes.'

He paused in surprise.

'And why not, my friend?'

'Don't you think – I mean – we can hardly –'

He broke into a roar of laughter.

'Decidedly, my poor Hastings, you belong to the Victorian era. Mademoiselle Nick would tell you so if she were here. In all probability she would say that you had the mind like the sink! Young ladies are not ashamed of their underclothes nowadays.

The camisole, the camiknicker, it is no longer a shameful secret. Every day, on the beach, all these garments will be discarded within a few feet of you. And why not?'

'I don't see any need for what you are doing.'

'*Ecoutez*, my friend. Clearly, she does not lock up her treasures, Mademoiselle Nick. If she wished to hide anything from sight – where would she hide it? Underneath the stockings and the petticoats. Ah! what have we here?'

He held up a packet of letters tied with a faded pink ribbon.

'The love letters of M. Michael Seton, if I mistake not.'

Quite calmly he untied the ribbon and began to open out the letters.

'Poirot,' I cried, scandalized. 'You really can't do that. It isn't playing the game.'

'I am not playing a game, *mon ami*.' His voice rang out suddenly harsh and stern. 'I am hunting down a murderer.'

'Yes, but private letters –'

'May have nothing to tell me – on the other hand, they may. I must take every chance, my friend. Come, you might as well read them with me. Two pairs of eyes are no worse than one pair. Console yourself with the thought that the staunch Ellen probably knows them by heart.'

I did not like it. Still I realized that in Poirot's position he could not afford to be squeamish, and I consoled myself by the quibble that Nick's last word had been, 'Look at anything you like.'

The letters spread over several dates, beginning last winter.

New Year's Day.
'*Darling, – The New Year is in and I'm making good resolutions. It seems too wonderful to be true – that you should actually love me. You've made all the difference to my life. I believe we both knew – from the very first moment we met. Happy New Year, my lovely girl.*

'*Yours for ever,*
Michael.'

February 8th.
'*Dearest Love, – How I wish I could see you more often. This is pretty rotten, isn't it? I hate all this beastly concealment, but I*

explained to you how things are. I know how much you hate lies and concealment. I do too. But honestly, it might upset the whole apple cart. Uncle Matthew has got an absolute bee in his bonnet about early marriages and the way they wreck a man's career. As though you could wreck mine, you dear angel!

'*Cheer up, darling. Everything will come right.*
'*Yours,*
'*Michael.*'

March 2nd.

'*I oughtn't to write to you two days running, I know. But I must. When I was up yesterday I thought of you. I flew over Scarborough. Blessed, blessed, blessed Scarborough – the most wonderful place in the world. Darling, you don't know how I love you!*
'*Yours,*
'*Michael.*'

April 18th.

'*Dearest, – The whole thing is fixed up. Definitely. If I pull this off (and I shall pull it off) I shall be able to take a firm line with Uncle Matthew – and if he doesn't like it – well, what do I care? It's adorable of you to be so interested in my long technical descriptions of the* Albatross. *How I long to take you up in her. Some day! Don't, for goodness' sake, worry about me. The thing isn't half so risky as it sounds. I simply couldn't get killed now that I know you care for me. Everything will be all right, sweetheart. Trust your Michael.*'

April 20th.

'*You Angel, – Every word you say is true and I shall treasure that letter always. I'm not half good enough for you. You are so different from everybody else. I adore you.*
'*Your*
'*Michael.*'

The last was undated.

'Dearest, – Well – I'm off tomorrow. Feeling tremendously keen and excited and absolutely certain of success. The old Albatross is all tuned up. She won't let me down.

'Cheer up, sweetheart, and don't worry. There's a risk, of course, but all life's a risk really. By the way, somebody said I ought to make a will (tactful fellow – but he meant well), so I have – on a half sheet of notepaper – and sent it to old Whitfield. I'd no time to go round there. Somebody once told me that a man made a will of three words, "All to Mother", and it was legal all right. My will was rather like that – I remembered your name was really Magdala, which was clever of me! A couple of the fellows witnessed it.

'Don't take all this solemn talk about wills to heart, will you? (I didn't mean that pun. An accident.) I shall be as right as rain. I'll send you telegrams from India and Australia and so on. And keep up heart. It's going to be all right. See?

'Good night and God bless you,
'Michael.'

Poirot folded the letters together again.

'You see, Hastings? I had to read them – to make sure. It is as I told you.'

'Surely you could have found out some other way?'

'No, mon cher, that is just what I could not do. It had to be this way. We have now some very valuable evidence.'

'In what way?'

'We now know that the fact of Michael's having made a will in favour of Mademoiselle Nick is actually recorded in writing. Anyone who had read those letters would know the fact. And with letters carelessly hidden like that, anyone could read them.'

'Ellen?'

'Ellen, almost certainly, I should say. We will try a little experiment on her before passing out.'

'There is no sign of the will.'

'No, that is curious. But in all probability it is thrown on top of a bookcase, or inside a china jar. We must try to awaken Mademoiselle's memory on that point. At any rate, there is nothing more to be found here.'

Ellen was dusting the hall as we descended.

Poirot wished her good morning very pleasantly as we passed. He turned back from the front door to say:

'You knew, I suppose, that Miss Buckley was engaged to the airman, Michael Seton?'

She stared.

'What? The one there's all the fuss in the papers about?'

'Yes.'

'Well, I never. To think of that. Engaged to Miss Nick.'

'Complete and absolute surprise registered very convincingly,' I remarked, as we got outside.

'Yes. It really seemed genuine.'

'Perhaps it was,' I suggested.

'And that packet of letters reclining for months under the *lingerie*? No, *mon ami*.'

'All very well,' I thought to myself. 'But we are not all Hercule Poirots. We do not all go nosing into what does not concern us.'

But I said nothing.

'This Ellen – she is an enigma,' said Poirot. 'I do not like it. There is something here that I do not understand.'

CHAPTER 14

THE MYSTERY OF THE MISSING WILL

We went straight back to the nursing home.

Nick looked rather surprised to see us.

'Yes, Mademoiselle,' said Poirot, answering her look. 'I am like the Jack in the Case. I pop up again. To begin with I will tell you that I have put the order in your affairs. Everything is now neatly arranged.'

'Well, I expect it was about time,' said Nick, unable to help smiling. 'Are you *very* tidy, M. Poirot?'

'Ask my friend Hastings here.'

The girl turned an inquiring gaze on me.

I detailed some of Poirot's minor peculiarities – toast that had to be made from a square loaf – eggs matching in size – his objection to golf as a game 'shapeless and haphazard', whose only redeeming feature was the tee boxes! I ended by telling her the famous case which Poirot had solved by his habit of straightening ornaments on the mantelpiece.

Poirot sat by smiling.

'He makes the good tale of it, yes,' he said, when I had finished. 'But on the whole it is true. Figure to yourself, Mademoiselle, that I never cease trying to persuade Hastings to part his hair in the middle instead of on the side. See what an air, lop-sided and unsymmetrical, it gives him.'

'Then you must disapprove of me, M. Poirot,' said Nick. 'I wear a side parting. And you must approve of Freddie who parts her hair in the middle.'

'He was certainly admiring her the other evening,' I put in maliciously. 'Now I know the reason.'

'*C'est assez*,' said Poirot. 'I am here on serious business. Mademoiselle, this will of yours, I find it not.'

'Oh!' She wrinkled her brows. 'But does it matter so much? After all, I'm not dead. And wills aren't really important till you are dead, are they?'

'That is correct. All the same, I interest myself in this will of yours. I have various little ideas concerning it. Think Mademoiselle. Try to remember where you placed it – where you saw it last?'

'I don't suppose I put it anywhere particular,' said Nick. 'I never do put things in places. I probably shoved it into a drawer.'

'You did not put it in the secret panel by any chance?'

'The secret *what?*'

'Your maid, Ellen, says that there is a secret panel in the drawing-room or the library.'

'Nonsense,' said Nick. 'I've never heard of such a thing. *Ellen* said so?'

'*Mais oui.* It seems she was in service at End House as a young girl. The cook showed it to her.'

'It's the first I've ever heard of it. I suppose Grandfather must have known about it, but, if so, he didn't tell me. And I'm sure he *would* have told me. M. Poirot, are you sure Ellen isn't making it all up?'

'No, Mademoiselle, I am not at all sure! *Il me semble* that there is something – odd about this Ellen of yours.'

'Oh! I wouldn't call her odd. William's a half-wit, and the

child is a nasty little brute, but Ellen's all right. The essence of respectability.'

'Did you give her leave to go out and see the fireworks last night, Mademoiselle?'

'Of course. They always do. They clear up afterwards.'

'Yet she did not go out.'

'Oh, yes, she did.'

'How do you know, Mademoiselle?'

'Well – well – I suppose`I don't know. I told her to go and she thanked me – and so, of course, I assumed that she did go.'

'On the contrary – she remained in the house.'

'But – how very odd!'

'You think it odd?'

'Yes, I do. I'm sure she's never done such a thing before. Did she say why?'

'She did not tell me the real reason – of that I am sure.'

Nick looked at him questioningly.

'Is it – important?'

Poirot flung out his hands.

'That is just what I cannot say, Mademoiselle. *C'est curieux.* I leave it like that.'

'This panel business too,' said Nick, reflectively. 'I can't help thinking that's frightfully queer – and unconvincing. Did she show you where it was?'

'She said she couldn't remember.'

'I don't believe there is such a thing.'

'It certainly looks like it.'

'She must be going batty, poor thing.'

'She certainly recounts the histories! She said also that End House was not a good house to live in.'

Nick gave a little shiver.

'Perhaps she's right there,' she said slowly. 'Sometimes I've felt that way myself. There's a queer feeling in that house . . .'

Her eyes grew large and dark. They had a fated look. Poirot hastened to recall her to other topics.

'We have wandered from our subject, Mademoiselle. The will. The last will and testament of Magdala Buckley.'

'I put that,' said Nick, with some pride. 'I remember putting that, and I said pay all debts and testamentary expenses. I remembered that out of a book I'd read.'

'You did not use a will form, then?'

'No, there wasn't time for that. I was just going off to the nursing home, and besides Mr Croft said will forms were very dangerous. It was better to make a simple will and not try to be too legal.'

'M. Croft? He was there?'

'Yes. It was he who asked me if I'd made one. I'd never have thought of it myself. He said if you died in – in –'

'Intestate,' I said.

'Yes, that's it. He said if you died intestate, the Crown pinched a lot and that would be a pity.'

'Very helpful, the excellent M. Croft!'

'Oh, he was,' said Nick warmly. 'He got Ellen in and her husband to witness it. Oh! of course! What an idiot I've been!'

We looked at her inquiringly.

'I've been a perfect idiot. Letting you hunt round End House. Charles has got it, of course! My cousin, Charles Vyse.'

'Ah! so that is the explanation.'

'Mr Croft said a lawyer was the proper person to have charge of it.'

'*Très correct, ce bon M. Croft.*'

'Men are useful sometimes,' said Nick. 'A lawyer or the Bank – that's what he said. And I said Charles would be best. So we stuck it in an envelope and sent it off to him straight away.'

She lay back on her pillows with a sigh.

'I'm sorry I've been so frightfully stupid. But it is all right now. Charles has got it, and if you really want to see it, of course he'll show it to you.'

'Not without an authorization from you,' said Poirot, smiling.

'How silly.'

'No, Mademoiselle. Merely prudent.'

'Well, I think it's silly.' She took a piece of paper from a little stack that lay beside her bed. 'What shall I say? Let the dog see the rabbit?'

'*Comment?*'

I laughed at his startled face.

He dictated a form of words, and Nick wrote obediently.

'Thank you, Mademoiselle,' said Poirot, as he took it.

'I'm sorry to have given you such a lot of trouble. But I really had forgotten. You know how one forgets things almost at once?'

'With order and method in the mind one does not forget.'

'I'll have to have a course of some kind,' said Nick. 'You're giving me quite an inferiority complex.'

'That is impossible. *Au revoir, Mademoiselle.*' He looked round the room. 'Your flowers are lovely.'

'Aren't they? The carnations are from Freddie and the roses from George and the lilies from Jim Lazarus. And look here –'

She pulled the wrapping from a large basket of hothouse grapes by her side.

Poirot's face changed. He stepped forward sharply.

'You have not eaten any of them?'

'No. Not yet.'

'Do not do so. You must eat nothing, Mademoiselle, that comes in from outside. *Nothing.* You comprehend?'

'Oh!'

She stared at him, the colour ebbing slowly from her face.

'I see. You think – you think it isn't over yet. You think they're still trying?' she whispered.

He took her hand.

'Do not think of it. You are safe here. But remember – nothing that comes in from outside.'

I was conscious of that white frightened face on the pillow as we left the room.

Poirot looked at his watch.

'*Bon.* We have just time to catch M. Vyse at his office before he leaves it for lunch.'

On arrival we were shown into Charles Vyse's office after the briefest of delays.

The young lawyer rose to greet us. He was as formal and unemotional as ever.

'Good morning, M. Poirot. What can I do for you?'

Without more ado Poirot presented the letter Nick had written. He took it and read it, then gazed over the top of it in a perplexed manner.

'I beg your pardon. I really am at a loss to understand?'

'Has not Mademoiselle Buckley made her meaning clear?'

'In this letter,' he tapped it with his finger-nail, 'she asks me to hand over to you a will made by her and entrusted to my keeping in February last.'

'Yes, Monsieur.'

'But, my dear sir, no will has been entrusted to my keeping!'

'*Comment?*'

'As far as I know my cousin never made a will. I certainly never made one for her.'

'She wrote this herself, I understand, on a sheet of notepaper and posted it to you.'

The lawyer shook his head.

'In that case all I can say is that I never received it.'

'Really, M. Vyse –'

'I never received anything of the kind, M. Poirot.'

There was a pause, then Poirot rose to his feet.

'In that case, M. Vyse, there is nothing more to be said. There must be some mistake.'

'Certainly there must be some mistake.'

He rose also.

'Good day, M. Vyse.'

'Good day, M. Poirot.'

'And that is that,' I remarked, when we were out in the street once more.

'*Précisément.*'

'Is he lying, do you think?'

'Impossible to tell. He has the good poker face, M. Vyse, besides looking as though he had swallowed one. One thing is clear, he will not budge from the position he has taken up. *He never received the will.* That is his point.'

'Surely Nick will have a written acknowledgment of its receipt.'

'*Cette petite*, she would never bother her head about a thing like that. She despatched it. It was off her mind. *Voilà.* Besides, on that very day, she went into a nursing home to have her appendix out. She had her emotions, in all probability.'

'Well, what do we do now?'

'*Parbleu*, we go and see M. Croft. Let us see what he can remember about this business. It seems to have been very much his doing.'

'He didn't profit by it in any way,' I said, thoughtfully.

'No. No, I cannot see anything in it from his point of view. He is probably merely the busybody – the man who likes to arrange his neighbour's affairs.'

Such an attitude was indeed typical of Mr Croft, I felt. He was the kindly knowall who causes so much exasperation in this world of ours.

We found him busy in his shirt sleeves over a steaming pot in the kitchen. A most savoury smell pervaded the little lodge.

He relinquished his cookery with enthusiasm, being clearly eager to talk about the murder.

'Half a jiffy,' he said. 'Walk upstairs. Mother will want to be in on this. She'd never forgive us for talking down here. Cooee – Milly. Two friends coming up.'

Mrs Croft greeted us warmly and was eager for news of Nick. I liked her much better than her husband.

'That poor dear girl,' she said. 'In a nursing home, you say? Had a complete breakdown, I shouldn't wonder. A dreadful business, M. Poirot – perfectly dreadful. An innocent girl like that shot dead. It doesn't bear thinking about – it doesn't indeed. And no lawless wild part of the world either. Right here in the heart of the old country. Kept me awake all night, it did.'

'It's made me nervous about going out and leaving you, old lady,' said her husband, who had put on his coat and joined us. 'I don't like to think of your having been left all alone here yesterday evening. It gives me the shivers.'

'You're not going to leave me again, I can tell you,' said Mrs Croft. 'Not after dark, anyway. And I'm thinking I'd like to leave this part of the world as soon as possible. I shall never feel the same about it. I shouldn't think poor Nicky Buckley could ever bear to sleep in that house again.'

It was a little difficult to reach the object of our visit. Both Mr and Mrs Croft talked so much and were so anxious to know all about everything. Were the poor dead girl's relations coming down? When was the funeral? Was there to be an inquest? What did the police think? Had they any clue yet? Was it true that a man had been arrested in Plymouth?

Then, having answered all these questions, they were insistent on offering us lunch. Only Poirot's mendacious statement that we were obliged to hurry back to lunch with the Chief Constable saved us.

At last a momentary pause occurred and Poirot got in the question he had been waiting to ask.

'Why, of course,' said Mr Croft. He pulled the blind cord up and down twice, frowning at it abstractedly. 'I remember all about it. Must have been when we first came here. I remember. Appendicitis – that's what the doctor said –'

'And probably not appendicitis at all,' interrupted Mrs Croft. 'These doctors – they always like cutting you up if they can. It wasn't the kind you *have* to operate on anyhow. She'd had indigestion and one thing and another, and they'd X-rayed her and they said out it had better come. And there she was, poor little soul, just going off to one of those nasty Homes.'

'I just asked her,' said Mr Croft, 'if she'd made a will. More as a joke than anything else.'

'Yes?'

'And she wrote it out then and there. Talked about getting a will form at the post office – but I advised her not to. Lot of trouble they cause sometimes, so a man told me. Anyway, her cousin is a lawyer. He could draw her out a proper one afterwards if everything was all right – as, of course, I knew it would be. This was just a precautionary matter.'

'Who witnessed it?'

'Oh! Ellen, the maid, and her husband.'

'And afterwards? What was done with it?'

'Oh! we posted it to Vyse. The lawyer, you know.'

'You know that it was posted?'

'My dear M. Poirot, I posted it myself. Right in this box here by the gate.'

'So if M. Vyse says he never got it –'

Croft stared.

'Do you mean that it got lost in the post? Oh! but surely that's impossible.'

'Anyway, you are certain that you posted it.'

'Certain sure,' said Mr Croft, heartily. 'I'll take my oath on that any day.'

'Ah! well,' said Poirot. 'Fortunately it does not matter. Mademoiselle is not likely to die just yet awhile.'

'*Et voilà!*' said Poirot, when we were out of earshot and walking down to the hotel. 'Who is lying? M. Croft? Or M. Charles Vyse? I must confess I see no reason why M. Croft should be lying. To suppress the will would be of no advantage to him – especially when he had been instrumental in getting it made. No, his statement seems clear enough and tallies exactly with what was told us by Mademoiselle Nick. But all the same –'

'Yes?'

'All the same, I am glad that M. Croft was doing the cooking when we arrived. He left an excellent impression of a greasy thumb and first finger on a corner of the newspaper that covered the kitchen table. I managed to tear it off unseen by him. We will send it to our good friend Inspector Japp of Scotland Yard. There is just a chance that he might know something about it.'

'Yes?'

'You know, Hastings, I cannot help feeling that our genial M. Croft is a little too good to be genuine.'

'And now,' he added. '*Le déjeuner.* I faint with hunger.'

CHAPTER 15
STRANGE BEHAVIOUR OF FREDERICA

Poirot's inventions about the Chief Constable were proved not to have been so mendacious after all. Colonel Weston called upon us soon after lunch.

He was a tall man of military carriage with considerable good-looks. He had a suitable reverence for Poirot's achievements, with which he seemed to be well acquainted.

'Marvellous piece of luck for us having you down here, M. Poirot,' he said again and again.

His one fear was that he should be compelled to call in the assistance of Scotland Yard. He was anxious to solve the mystery and catch the criminal without their aid. Hence his delight at Poirot's presence in the neighbourhood.

Poirot, so far as I could judge, took him completely into his confidence.

'Deuced odd business,' said the Colonel. 'Never heard of

anything like it. Well, the girl ought to be safe enough in a nursing home. Still, you can't keep her there for ever!'

'That, M. le Colonel, is just the difficulty. There is only one way of dealing with it.'

'And that is?'

'We must lay our hands on the person responsible.'

'If what you suspect is true, that isn't going to be so easy.'

'*Ah! je le sais bien.*'

'Evidence! Getting evidence is going to be the devil.'

He frowned abstractedly.

'Always difficult, these cases, where there's no routine work. If we could get hold of the pistol –'

'In all probability it is at the bottom of the sea. That is, if the murderer had any sense.'

'Ah!' said Colonel Weston. 'But often they haven't. You'd be surprised at the fool things people do. I'm not talking of murders – we don't have many murders down in these parts, I'm glad to say – but in ordinary police court cases. The sheer damn foolishness of these people would surprise you.'

'They are of a different mentality, though.'

'Yes – perhaps. If Vyse is the chap, well, we'll have our work cut out. He's a cautious man and a sound lawyer. He'll not give himself away. The woman – well, there would be more hope there. Ten to one she'll try again. Women have no patience.'

He rose.

'Inquest tomorrow morning. Coroner will work in with us and give away as little as possible. We want to keep things dark at present.'

He was turning towards the door when he suddenly came back.

'Upon my soul, I'd forgotten the very thing that will interest you most, and that I want your opinion about.'

Sitting down again, he drew from his pocket a torn scrap of paper with writing on it and handed it to Poirot.

'My police found this when they were searching the grounds. Not far from where you were all watching the fireworks. It's the only suggestive thing they did find.'

Poirot smoothed it out. The writing was large and straggling.

'... *must have money at once. If not you ... what will happen.*
I'm warning you.'

Poirot frowned. He read and re-read it.

'This is interesting,' he said. 'I may keep it?'

'Certainly. There are no finger-prints on it. I'll be glad if you can make anything of it.'

Colonel Weston got to his feet again.

'I really must be off. Inquest tomorrow, as I said. By the way, you are not being called as witness – only Captain Hastings. Don't want the newspaper people to get wise to your being on the job.'

'I comprehend. What of the relations of the poor young lady?'

'The father and mother are coming from Yorkshire today. They'll arrive about half-past five. Poor souls. I'm heartily sorry for them. They are taking the body back with them the following day.'

He shook his head.

'Unpleasant business. I'm not enjoying this, M. Poirot.'

'Who could, M. le Colonel? It is, as you say, an unpleasant business.'

When he had gone, Poirot examined the scrap of paper once more.

'An important clue?' I asked.

He shrugged his shoulders.

'How can one tell? There is a hint of blackmail about it! Someone of our party that night was being pressed for money in a very unpleasant way. Of course, it is possible that it was one of the strangers.'

He looked at the writing through a little magnifying glass.

'Does this writing look at all familiar to you, Hastings?'

'It reminds me a little of something – Ah! I have it – that note of Mrs Rice's.'

'Yes,' said Poirot, slowly. 'There are resemblances. Decidedly there are resemblances. It is curious. Yet I do not think that this is the writing of Madame Rice. Come in,' he said, as a knock came at the door.

It was Commander Challenger.

'Just looked in,' he explained. 'Wanted to know if you were any further forward.'

'*Parbleu*,' said Poirot. 'At this moment I am feeling that I am considerably further back. I seem to progress *en reculant*.'

'That's bad. But I don't really believe it, M. Poirot. I've been hearing all about you and what a wonderful chap you are. Never had a failure, they say.'

'That is not true,' said Poirot. 'I had a bad failure in Belgium in 1893. You recollect, Hastings? I recounted it to you. The affair of the box of chocolates.'

'I remember,' I said.

And I smiled, for at the time that Poirot told me that tale, he had instructed me to say 'chocolate box' to him if ever I should fancy he was growing conceited! He was then bitterly offended when I used the magical words only a minute and a quarter later.

'Oh, well,' said Challenger, 'that is such a long time ago it hardly counts. You are going to get to the bottom of this, aren't you?'

'That I swear. On the word of Hercule Poirot. I am the dog who stays on the scent and does not leave it.'

'Good. Got any ideas?'

'I have suspicions of two people.'

'I suppose I mustn't ask you who they are?'

'I should not tell you! You see, I might possibly be in error.'

'My *alibi* is satisfactory, I trust,' said Challenger, with a faint twinkle.

Poirot smiled indulgently at the bronzed face in front of him. 'You left Devonport at a few minutes past 8.30. You arrived here at five minutes past ten – twenty minutes after the crime had been committed. But the distance from Devonport is only just over thirty miles, and you have often done it in an hour since the road is good. So, you see, your alibi is not good at all!'

'Well, I'm –'

'You comprehend, I inquire into everything. Your *alibi*, as I say, is not good. But there are other things beside alibis. You would like, I think, to marry Mademoiselle Nick?'

The sailor's face flushed.

'I've always wanted to marry her,' he said huskily.

'Precisely. *Eh bien* – Mademoiselle Nick was engaged to another man. A reason, perhaps, for killing the other man. But that is unnecessary – he dies the death of a hero.'

'So it *is* true – that Nick was engaged to Michael Seton? There's a rumour to that effect all over the town this morning.'

'Yes – it is interesting how soon news spreads. You never suspected it before?'

'I knew Nick was engaged to someone – she told me so two days ago. But she didn't give me a clue as to whom it was.'

'It was Michael Seton. *Entre nous*, he has left her, I fancy, a very pretty fortune. Ah! assuredly, it is not a moment for killing Mademoiselle Nick – from your point of view. She weeps for her lover now, but the heart consoles itself. She is young. And I think, Monsieur, that she is very fond of you . . .'

Challenger was silent for a moment or two.

'If it should be . . .' he murmured.

There was a tap on the door.

It was Frederica Rice.

'I've been looking for you,' she said to Challenger. 'They told me you were here. I wanted to know if you'd got my wrist-watch back yet.'

'Oh, yes, I called for it this morning.'

He took it from his pocket and handed it to her. It was a watch of rather an unusual shape – round, like a globe, set on a strap of plain black moiré. I remembered that I had seen one much the same shape on Nick Buckley's wrist.

'I hope it will keep better time now.'

'It's rather a bore. Something is always going wrong with it.'

'It is for beauty, Madame, and not for utility,' said Poirot.

'Can't one have both?' She looked from one to the other of us. 'Am I interrupting a conference?'

'No, indeed, Madame. We were talking gossip – not the crime. We were saying how quickly news spreads – how that everyone now knows that Mademoiselle Nick was engaged to that brave airman who perished.'

'So Nick *was* engaged to Michael Seton!' exclaimed Frederica.

'It surprises you, Madame?'

'It does a little. I don't know why. Certainly I did think he was very taken with her last autumn. They went about a lot together.

And then, after Christmas, they both seemed to cool off. As far as I know, they hardly met.'

'The secret, they kept it very well.'

'That was because of old Sir Matthew, I suppose. He was really a little off his head, I think.'

'You had no suspicion, Madame? And yet Mademoiselle was such an intimate friend.'

'Nick's a close little devil when she likes,' murmured Frederica. 'But I understand now why she's been so nervy lately. Oh! and I ought to have guessed from something she said only the other day.'

'Your little friend is very attractive, Madame.'

'Old Jim Lazarus used to think so at one time,' said Challenger, with his loud, rather tactless laugh.

'Oh! Jim –' She shrugged her shoulders, but I thought she was annoyed.

She turned to Poirot.

'Tell me, M. Poirot, did you –'

She stopped. Her tall figure swayed and her face turned whiter still. Her eyes were fixed on the centre of the table.

'You are not well, Madame.'

I pushed forward a chair, helped her to sink into it. She shook her head, murmured, 'I'm all right,' and leaned forward, her face between her hands. We watched her awkwardly.

She sat up in a minute.

'How absurd! George, darling, don't look so worried. Let's talk about murders. Something exciting. I want to know if M. Poirot is on the track.'

'It is early to say, Madame,' said Poirot, non-committally.

'But you have ideas – yes?'

'Perhaps. But I need a great deal more evidence.'

'Oh!' She sounded uncertain.

Suddenly she rose.

'I've got a head. I think I'll go and lie down. Perhaps tomorrow they'll let me see Nick.'

She left the room abruptly. Challenger frowned.

'You never know what that woman's up to. Nick may have been fond of her, but I don't believe she was fond of Nick. But there, you can't tell with women. It's darling – darling – darling

– all the time – and "damn you" would probably express it much better. Are you going out, M. Poirot?' For Poirot had risen and was carefully brushing a speck off his hat.

'Yes, I am going into the town.'

'I've got nothing to do. May I come with you.'

'Assuredly. It will be a pleasure.'

We left the room. Poirot, with an apology, went back.

'My stick,' he explained, as he rejoined us.

Challenger winced slightly. And indeed the stick, with its embossed gold band, was somewhat ornate.

Poirot's first visit was to a florist.

'I must send some flowers to Mademoiselle Nick,' he explained.

He proved difficult to suit.

In the end he chose an ornate gold basket to be filled with orange carnations. The whole to be tied up with a large blue bow.

The shopwoman gave him a card and he wrote on it with a flourish: 'With the Compliments of Hercule Poirot.'

'I sent her some flowers this morning,' said Challenger. 'I might send her some fruit.'

'*Inutile!*' said Poirot.

'What?'

'I said it was useless. The eatable – it is not permitted.'

'Who says so?'

'I say so. I have made the rule. It has already been impressed on Mademoiselle Nick. She understands.'

'Good Lord!' said Challenger.

He looked thoroughly startled. He stared at Poirot curiously.

'So that's it, is it?' he said. 'You're still – afraid.'

CHAPTER 16

INTERVIEW WITH MR WHITFIELD

The inquest was a dry proceeding – mere bare bones. There was evidence of identification, then I gave evidence of the finding of the body. Medical evidence followed.

The inquest was adjourned for a week.

The St Loo murder had jumped into prominence in the daily

press. It had, in fact, succeeded 'Seton Still Missing. Unknown Fate of Missing Airman.'

Now that Seton was dead and due tribute had been paid to his memory, a new sensation was due. The St Loo Mystery was a godsend to papers at their wits' end for news in the month of August.

After the inquest, having successfully dodged reporters, I met Poirot, and we had an interview with the Rev. Giles Buckley and his wife.

Maggie's father and mother were a charming pair, completely unworldly and unsophisticated.

Mrs Buckley was a woman of character, tall and fair and showing very plainly her northern ancestry. Her husband was a small man, grey-haired, with a diffident appealing manner.

Poor souls, they were completely dazed by the misfortune that had overtaken them and robbed them of a well-beloved daughter. 'Our Maggie', as they called her.

'I can scarcely realize it even now,' said Mr Buckley. 'Such a dear child, M. Poirot. So quiet and unselfish – always thinking of others. Who could wish to harm her?'

'I could hardly understand the telegram,' said Mrs Buckley. 'Why it was only the morning before that we had seen her off.'

'In the midst of life we are in death,' murmured her husband.

'Colonel Weston has been very kind,' said Mrs Buckley. 'He assures us that everything is being done to find the man who did this thing. He must be a madman. No other explanation is possible.'

'Madame, I cannot tell you how I sympathize with you in your loss – and how I admire your bravery!'

'Breaking down would not bring Maggie back to us,' said Mrs Buckley, sadly.

'My wife is wonderful,' said the clergyman. 'Her faith and courage are greater than mine. It is all so – so bewildering, M. Poirot.'

'I know – I know, Monsieur.'

'You are a great detective, M. Poirot?' said Mrs Buckley.

'It has been said, Madame.'

'Oh! I know. Even in our remote country village we have heard of you. You are going to find out the truth, M. Poirot?'

'I shall not rest until I do, Madame.'

'It will be revealed to you, M. Poirot,' quavered the clergyman. 'Evil cannot go unpunished.'

'Evil never goes unpunished, Monsieur. But the punishment is sometimes secret.'

'What do you mean by that, M. Poirot?'

Poirot only shook his head.

'Poor little Nick,' said Mrs Buckley. 'I am really sorriest of all for her. I had a most pathetic letter. She says she feels she asked Maggie down here to her death.'

'That is morbid,' said Mr Buckley.

'Yes, but I know how she feels. I wish they would let me see her. It seems so extraordinary not to let her own family visit her.'

'Doctors and nurses are very strict,' said Poirot, evasively. 'They make the rules – so – and nothing will change them. And doubtless they fear for her the emotion – the natural emotion – she would experience on seeing you.'

'Perhaps,' said Mrs Buckley, doubtfully. 'But I don't hold with nursing homes. Nick would do much better if they let her come back with me – right away from this place.'

'It is possible – but I fear they will not agree. It is long since you have seen Mademoiselle Buckley?'

'I haven't seen her since last autumn. She was at Scarborough. Maggie went over and spent the day with her and then she came back and spent a night with us. She's a pretty creature – though I can't say I like her friends. And the life she leads – well, it's hardly her fault, poor child. She's had no upbringing of any kind.'

'It is a strange house – End House,' said Poirot thoughtfully.

'I don't like it,' said Mrs Buckley. 'I never have. There's something all wrong about that house. I disliked old Sir Nicholas intensely. He made me shiver.'

'Not a good man, I'm afraid,' said her husband. 'But he had a curious charm.'

'*I* never felt it,' said Mrs Buckley. 'There's an evil feeling about that house. I wish we'd never let our Maggie go there.'

'Ah! wishing,' said Mr Buckley, and shook his head.

'Well,' said Poirot. 'I must not intrude upon you any longer. I only wished to proffer to you my deep sympathy.'

'You have been very kind, M. Poirot. And we are indeed grateful for all you are doing.'

'You return to Yorkshire – when?'

'Tomorrow. A sad journey. Goodbye, M. Poirot, and thank you again.'

'Very simple delightful people,' I said, after we had left.

Poirot nodded.

'It makes the heart ache, does it not, *mon ami*? A tragedy so useless – so purposeless. *Cette jeune fille* – Ah! but I reproach myself bitterly. I, Hercule Poirot, was on the spot and I did not prevent the crime!'

'Nobody could have prevented it.'

'You speak without reflection, Hastings. No ordinary person could have prevented it – but of what good is it to be Hercule Poirot with grey cells of a finer quality than other people's, if you do not manage to do what ordinary people cannot?'

'Well, of course,' I said. 'If you are going to put it like that –'

'Yes, indeed. I am abased, downhearted – completely abased.'

I reflected that Poirot's abasement was strangely like other people's conceit, but I prudently forebore from making any remark.

'And now,' he said, '*en avant. To London.*'

'London?'

'*Mais oui.* We shall catch the two o'clock train very comfortably. All is peaceful here. Mademoiselle is safe in the nursing home. No one can harm her. The watchdogs, therefore, can take leave of absence. There are one or two little pieces of information that I require.'

Our first proceeding on arriving in London was to call upon the late Captain Seton's solicitors, Messrs Whitfield, Pargiter & Whitfield.

Poirot had arranged for an appointment beforehand, and although it was past six o'clock, we were soon closeted with Mr Whitfield, the head of the firm.

He was a very urbane and impressive person. He had in front of him a letter from the Chief Constable and another from some high official at Scotland Yard.

'This is all very irregular and unusual, M. – ah – Poirot,' he said, as he polished his eyeglasses.

'Quite so, M. Whitfield. But then murder is also irregular – and, I am glad to say, sufficiently unusual.'

'True. True. But rather far-fetched – to make a connection between this murder and my late client's bequest – eh?'

'I think not.'

'Ah! you think not. Well – under the circumstances – and I must admit that Sir Henry puts it very strongly in his letter – I shall be – er – happy to do anything that is in my power.'

'You acted as legal adviser to the late Captain Seton?'

'To all the Seton family, my dear sir. We have done so – our firm have done so, I mean – for the last hundred years.'

'*Parfaitement*. The late Sir Matthew Seton made a will?'

'We made it for him.'

'And he left his fortune – how?'

'There were several bequests – one to the Natural History Museum – but the bulk of his large – his, I may say, *very large fortune* – he left to Captain Michael Seton absolutely. He had no other near relations.'

'A very large fortune, you say?'

'The late Sir Matthew was the second richest man in England,' replied Mr Whitfield, composedly.

'He had somewhat peculiar views, had he not?' Mr Whitfield looked at him severely.

'A millionaire, M. Poirot, is allowed to be eccentric. It is almost expected of him.'

Poirot received his correction meekly and asked another question.

'His death was unexpected, I understand?'

'*Most* unexpected. Sir Matthew enjoyed remarkably good health. He had an internal growth, however, which no one had suspected. It reached a vital tissue and an immediate operation was necessary. The operation was, as always on these occasions, completely successful. But Sir Matthew died.'

'And his fortune passed to Captain Seton.'

'That is so.'

'Captain Seton had, I understand, made a will before leaving England?'

'If you can call it a will – yes,' said Mr Whitfield, with strong distaste.

'It is legal?'

'It is perfectly legal. The intention of the testator is plain and it is properly witnessed. Oh, yes, it is legal.'

'But you do not approve of it?'

'My dear sir, what are *we* for?'

I had often wondered. Having once had occasion to make a perfectly simple will myself. I had been appalled at the length and verbiage that resulted from my solicitor's office.

'The truth of the matter was,' continued Mr Whitfield, 'that at the time Captain Seton had little or nothing to leave. He was dependent on the allowance he received from his uncle. He felt, I suppose, that anything would do.'

And had thought correctly, I whispered to myself.

'And the terms of this will?' asked Poirot.

'He leaves everything of which he dies possessed to his affianced wife, Miss Magdala Buckley absolutely. He names me as his executor.

'Then Miss Buckley inherits?'

'Certainly Miss Buckley inherits.'

'And if Miss Buckley had happened to die last Monday?'

'Captain Seton having predeceased her, the money would go to whomever she had named in her will as residuary legatee – or failing a will to her next of kin.

'I may say,' added Mr Whitfield, with an air of enjoyment, 'that death duties would have been enormous. Enormous! Three deaths, remember, in rapid succession.' He shook his head. 'Enormous!'

'But there would have been something left?' murmured Poirot, meekly.

'My dear sir, as I told you, Sir Matthew was the second richest man in England.'

Poirot rose.

'Thank you, Mr Whitfield, very much for the information that you have given me.'

'Not at all. Not at all. I may say that I shall be in communication with Miss Buckley – indeed, I believe the letter has already gone. I shall be happy to be of any service I can to her.'

'She is a young lady,' said Poirot, 'who could do with some sound legal advice.'

'There will be fortune hunters, I am afraid,' said Mr Whitfield, shaking his head.

'It seems indicated,' agreed Poirot. 'Good day, Monsieur.'

'Goodbye, M. Poirot. Glad to have been of service to you. Your name is – ah! – familiar to me.'

He said this kindly – with an air of one making a valuable admission.

'It is all exactly as you thought, Poirot,' I said, when we were outside.

'*Mon ami*, it was bound to be. *It could not be any other way*. We will go now to the Cheshire Cheese where Japp meets us for an early dinner.'

We found Inspector Japp of Scotland Yard awaiting us at the chosen rendezvous. He greeted Poirot with every sign of warmth.

'Years since I've seen you, Moosior Poirot. Thought you were growing vegetable marrows in the country.'

'I tried, Japp, I tried. But even when you grow vegetable marrows you cannot get away from murder.'

He sighed. I knew of what he was thinking – that strange affair at Fernley Park. How I regretted that I had been far away at that time.

'And Captain Hastings too,' said Japp. 'How are you, sir?'

'Very fit, thanks,' I said.

'And now there are more murders?' continued Japp, facetiously.

'As you say – more murders.'

'Well, you mustn't be depressed, old cock,' said Japp. 'Even if you can't see your way clear – well – you can't go about at your time of life and expect to have the success you used to do. We all of us get stale as the years go by. Got to give the young 'uns a chance, you know.'

'And yet the old dog is the one who knows the tricks,' murmured Poirot. 'He is cunning. He does not leave the scent.'

'Oh! well – we're talking about human beings, not dogs.'

'Is there so much difference?'

'Well, it depends how you look at things. But you're a caution, isn't he, Captain Hastings? Always was. Looks much the same – hair a bit thinner on top but the face fungus fuller than ever.'

'Eh?' said Poirot. 'What is that?'

'He's congratulating you on your moustaches,' I said, soothingly.

'They are luxuriant, yes,' said Poirot, complacently caressing them.

Japp went off into a roar of laughter.

'Well,' he said, after a minute or two, 'I've done your bit of business. Those finger-prints you sent me –'

'Yes?' said Poirot, eagerly.

'Nothing doing. Whoever the gentleman may be – he hasn't passed through *our* hands. On the other hand, I wired to Melbourne and nobody of that description or name is known there.'

'Ah!'

'So there may be something fishy after all. But he's not one of the lads.

'As to the other business,' went on Japp.

'Yes?'

'Lazarus and Son have a good reputation. Quite straight and honourable in their dealings. Sharp, of course – but that's another matter. You've got to be sharp in business. But they're all right. They're in a bad way, though – financially, I mean.'

'Oh! – is that so?'

'Yes – the slump in pictures has hit them badly. And antique furniture too. All this modern continental stuff coming into fashion. They built new premises last year and – well – as I say, they're not far from Queer Street.'

'I am much obliged to you.'

'Not at all. That sort of thing isn't my line, as you know. But I made a point of finding out as you wanted to know. We can always get information.'

'My good Japp, what should I do without you?'

'Oh! that's all right. Always glad to oblige an old friend. I let you in on some pretty good cases in the old days, didn't I?'

This, I realized, was Japp's way of acknowledging indebtedness to Poirot, who had solved many a case which had baffled the inspector.

'They were the good days – yes.'

'I wouldn't mind having a chat with you now and again even in these days. Your methods may be old-fashioned but you've got your head screwed on the right way, M. Poirot.'

'What about my other question. The Dr MacAllister?'

'Oh, him! He's a woman's doctor. I don't mean a gynaecologist. I mean one of these nerve doctors – tell you to sleep in purple walls and orange ceiling – talk to you about your libido, whatever that is – tell you to let it rip. He's a bit of a quack, if you ask me – but he gets the women all right. They flock to him. Goes abroad a good deal – does some kind of medical work in Paris, I believe.'

'Why Dr MacAllister?' I asked, bewildered. I had never heard of the name. 'Where does he come in?'

'Dr MacAllister is the uncle of Commander Challenger,' explained Poirot. 'You remember he referred to an uncle who was a doctor?'

'How thorough you are,' I said. 'Did you think he had operated on Sir Matthew?'

'He's not a surgeon,' said Japp.

'*Mon ami,*' said Poirot, 'I like to inquire into everything. Hercule Poirot is a good dog. The good dog follows the scent, and if, regrettably, there is no scent to follow, he noses around – seeking always something that is not very nice. So also, does Hercule Poirot. And often – Oh! so often – does he find it!'

'It's not a nice profession, ours,' said Japp. 'Stilton, did you say? I don't mind if I do. No, it's not a nice profession. And yours is worse than mine – not official, you see, and therefore a lot more worming yourself into places in underhand ways.'

'I do not disguise myself, Japp. Never have I disguised myself.'

'You couldn't,' said Japp. 'You're unique. Once seen, never forgotten.'

Poirot looked at him rather doubtfully.

'Only my fun,' said Japp. 'Don't mind me. Glass of port? Well, if you say so.'

The evening became thoroughly harmonious. We were soon in the middle of reminiscences. This case, that case, and the other. I must say that I, too, enjoyed talking over the past. Those had been good days. How old and experienced I felt now!

Poor old Poirot. He was perplexed by this case – I could see that. His powers were not what they were. I had the feeling that he was going to fail – that the murderer of Maggie Buckley would never be brought to book.

'Courage, my friend,' said Poirot, slapping me on the shoulder. 'All is not lost. Do not pull the long face, I beg of you.'

'That's all right. I'm all right.'

'And so am I. And so is Japp.'

'We're all all right,' declared Japp, hilariously.

And on this pleasant note we parted.

The following morning we journeyed back to St Loo. On arrival at the hotel Poirot rang up the nursing home and asked to speak to Nick.

Suddenly I saw his face change – he almost dropped the instrument.

'*Comment?* What is that? Say it again, I beg.'

He waited for a minute or two listening. Then he said:

'Yes, yes, I will come at once.'

He turned a pale face to me.

'Why did I go away, Hastings? *Mon Dieu!* Why did I go away?'

'What has happened?'

'Mademoiselle Nick is dangerously ill. Cocaine poisoning. They have got at her after all. *Mon Dieu! Mon Dieu! Why did I go away?*'

CHAPTER 17

A BOX OF CHOCOLATES

All the way to the nursing home Poirot murmured and muttered to himself. He was full of self-reproach.

'I should have known,' he groaned. 'I should have known! And yet, what could I do? I took every precaution. It is impossible – impossible. *No one* could get to her! Who has disobeyed my orders?'

At the nursing home we were shown into a little room down-stairs, and after a few minutes Dr Graham came to us. He looked exhausted and white.

'She'll do,' he said. 'It's going to be all right. The trouble was knowing how much she'd taken of the damned stuff.'

'What was it?'

'Cocaine.'

'She will live?'

'Yes, yes, she'll live.'

'But how did it happen? How did they get at her? Who has been allowed in?' Poirot fairly danced with impotent excitement.

'Nobody has been allowed in.'

'Impossible.'

'It's true.'

'But then –'

'It was a box of chocolates.'

'Ah! *sacré*. And I told her to eat *nothing – nothing –* that came from outside.'

'I don't know about that. It's hard work keeping a girl from a box of chocolates. She only ate one, thank goodness.'

'Was the cocaine in all the chocolates?'

'No. The girl ate one. There were two others in the top layer. The rest were all right.'

'How was it done?'

'Quite clumsily. Chocolate cut in half – the cocaine mixed with the filling and the chocolate stuck together again. Amateurishly. What you might call a home-made job.'

Poirot groaned.

'Ah! if I knew – if I knew. Can I see Mademoiselle?'

'If you come back in an hour I think you can see her,' said the doctor. 'Pull yourself together, man. She isn't going to die.'

For another hour we walked the streets of St Loo. I did my best to distract Poirot's mind – pointing out to him that all was well, that, after all, no mischief had been done.

But he only shook his head, and repeated at intervals:

'*I am afraid, Hastings, I am afraid . . .*'

And the strange way he said it made me, too, feel afraid.

Once he caught me by the arm.

'Listen, my friend. *I am all wrong.* I have been all wrong from the beginning.'

'You mean it isn't the money –'

'No, no, I am right about that. Oh, yes. But those two – it is too simple – too easy, that. There is another twist still. Yes, there is something!'

And then in an outburst of indignation:

'*Ah! cette petite!* Did I not *forbid* her? Did I not say, "Do not touch anything from outside?" And she disobeys me – me, Hercule Poirot. Are not four escapes from death enough for her? Must she take a fifth chance? *Ah, c'est inoui!*'

At last we made our way back. After a brief wait we were conducted upstairs.

Nick was sitting up in bed. The pupils of her eyes were widely dilated. She looked feverish and her hands kept twitching violently.

'At it again,' she murmured.

Poirot experienced real emotion at the sight of her. He cleared his throat and took her hand in his.

'Ah! Mademoiselle – Mademoiselle.'

'I shouldn't care,' she said, defiantly, 'if they *had* got me this time. I'm sick of it all – sick of it!'

'*Pauvre petite!*'

'Something in me doesn't like to give them best!'

'That is the spirit – *le sport* – you must be the good sport, Mademoiselle.'

'Your old nursing home hasn't been so safe after all,' said Nick.

'If you had obeyed orders, Mademoiselle –'

She looked faintly astonished.

'But I have.'

'Did I not impress upon you that you were to eat nothing that came from outside?'

'No more I did.'

'But these chocolates –'

'Well, they were all right. *You* sent them.'

'What is that you say, Mademoiselle?'

'*You* sent them!'

'Me? Never. Never anything of the kind.'

'But you *did*. Your card was in the box.'

'What?'

Nick made a spasmodic gesture towards the table by the bed. The nurse came forward.

'You want the card that was in the box?'

'Yes, please, nurse.'

There was a moment's pause. The nurse returned to the room with it in her hand.

'Here it is.'

I gasped. So did Poirot. For on the card, in flourishing handwriting, were written the same words that I had seen Poirot inscribe on the card that accompanied the basket of flowers.

'With the Compliments of Hercule Poirot.'

'*Sacré tonnerre!*'

'You see,' said Nick, accusingly.

'I did not write this!' cried Poirot.

'What?'

'And yet,' murmured Poirot, 'and yet it is my handwriting.'

'I know. It's exactly the same as the card that came with the orange carnations. I never doubted that the chocolates came from you.'

Poirot shook his head.

'How should you doubt? Oh! the devil! The clever, cruel devil! To think of *that!* Ah! but he has genius, this man, genius! "*With the Compliments of Hercule Poirot.*" So simple. Yes, but one had to think of it. And I – I did not *think.* I omitted to foresee this move.'

Nick moved restlessly.

'Do not agitate yourself, Mademoiselle. You are blameless – blameless. It is I that am to blame, miserable imbecile that I am! I should have foreseen this move. Yes, I should have foreseen it.'

His chin dropped on his breast. He looked the picture of misery.

'I really think –' said the nurse.

She had been hovering nearby, a disapproving expression on her face.

'Eh? Yes, yes, I will go. Courage, Mademoiselle. This is the last mistake I will make. I am ashamed, desolated – I have been tricked, outwitted – as though I were a little schoolboy. *But it shall not happen again.* No. I promise you. Come, Hastings.'

Poirot's first proceeding was to interview the matron. She was, naturally, terribly upset over the whole business.

'It seems incredible to me, M. Poirot, absolutely incredible. That a thing like that should happen in my nursing home.'

Poirot was sympathetic and tactful. Having soothed her sufficiently, he began to inquire into the circumstance of the arrival of the fatal packet. Here, the matron declared, he would do best to interview the orderly who had been on duty at the time of its arrival.

The man in question, whose name was Hood, was a stupid but honest-looking young fellow of about twenty-two. He looked nervous and frightened. Poirot put him at his ease, however.

'No blame can be attached to you,' he said kindly. 'But I want you to tell me exactly when and how this parcel arrived.'

The orderly looked puzzled.

'It's difficult to say, sir,' he said, slowly. 'Lots of people come and inquire and leave things for the different patients.'

'The nurse says this came last night,' I said. 'About six o'clock.'

The lad's face brightened.

'I do remember, now, sir. A gentleman brought it.'

'A thin-faced gentleman – fair-haired?'

'He was fair-haired – but I don't know about thin-faced.'

'Would Charles Vyse bring it himself?' I murmured to Poirot. I had forgotten that the lad would know a local name.

'It wasn't Mr Vyse,' he said. 'I know him. It was a bigger gentleman – handsome-looking – came in a big car.'

'Lazarus,' I exclaimed.

Poirot shot me a warning glance and I regretted my precipitance.

'He came in a large car and he left this parcel. It was addressed to Miss Buckley?'

'Yes, sir.'

'And what did you do with it?'

'I didn't touch it, sir. Nurse took it up.'

'Quite so, but you touched it when you took it from the gentleman, n'est ce pas?'

'Oh! that, yes, of course, sir. I took it from him and put it on the table.'

'Which table? Show me, if you please.'

The orderly led us into the hall. The front door was open. Close to it, in the hall, was a long marble-topped table on which lay letters and parcels.

'Everything that comes is put on here, sir. Then the nurses take things up to the patients.'

'Do you remember what time this parcel was left?'

'Must have been about five-thirty, or a little after. I know the post had just been, and that's usually at about half-past five. It was a pretty busy afternoon, a lot of people leaving flowers and coming to see patients.'

'Thank you. Now, I think, we will see the nurse who took up the parcel.'

This proved to be one of the probationers, a fluffy little person all agog with excitement. She remembered taking the parcel up at six o'clock when she came on duty.

'Six o'clock,' murmured Poirot. 'Then it must have been twenty minutes or so that the parcel was lying on the table downstairs.'

'Pardon?'

'Nothing, Mademoiselle. Continue. You took the parcel to Miss Buckley?'

'Yes, there were several things for her. There was this box and some flowers also – sweet peas – from a Mr and Mrs Croft, I think. I took them up at the same time. And there was a parcel that had come by post – and curiously enough *that* was a box of Fuller's chocolates also.'

'*Comment?* A second box?'

'Yes, rather a coincidence. Miss Buckley opened them both. She said: "Oh! what a shame. I'm not allowed to eat them." Then she opened the lids to look inside and see if they were both just the same, and your card was in one and she said, "Take the other impure box away, nurse. I might have got them mixed up." Oh! dear, whoever would have thought of such a thing? Seems like an Edgar Wallace, doesn't it?'

Poirot cut short this flood of speech.

'Two boxes, you say? From whom was the other box?'

'There was no name inside.'

'And which was the one that came – that had the appearance of coming – from me? The one by post or the other?'

'I declare now – I can't remember. Shall I go up and ask Miss Buckley?'

'If you would be so amiable.'

She ran up the stairs.

'Two boxes,' murmured Poirot. 'There is confusion for you.'

The nurse returned breathless.

'Miss Buckley isn't sure. She unwrapped them both before she looked inside. But she thinks it wasn't the box that came by post.'

'Eh?' said Poirot, a little confused.

'The box from you was the one that didn't come by post. At least she thinks so, but she isn't quite sure.'

'*Diable!*' said Poirot, as we walked away. 'Is no one ever quite sure? In detective books – yes. But life – real life – is always full of muddle. Am I sure, myself, about anything at all? No, no – a thousand times, no.'

'Lazarus,' I said.

'Yes, that is a surprise, is it not?'

'Shall you say anything to him about it?'

'Assuredly. I shall be interested to see how he takes it. By the way, we might as well exaggerate the serious condition of Mademoiselle. It will do no harm to let it be assumed that she is at death's door. You comprehend? The solemn face – yes, admirable. You resemble closely an undertaker. *C'est tout à fait bien.*'

We were lucky in finding Lazarus. He was bending over the bonnet of his car outside the hotel.

Poirot went straight up to him.

'Yesterday evening, Monsieur Lazarus, you left a box of chocolates for Mademoiselle,' he began without preamble.

Lazarus looked rather surprised.

'Yes?'

'That was very amiable of you.'

'As a matter of fact they were from Freddie, from Mrs Rice. She asked me to get them.'

'Oh! I see.'

'I took them round in the car.'

'I comprehend.'

He was silent for a minute or two and then said:

'Madame Rice, where is she?'

'I think she's in the lounge.'

We found Frederica having tea. She looked up at us with an anxious face.

'What is this I hear about Nick being taken ill?'

'It is a most mysterious affair, Madame. Tell me, did you send her a box of chocolates yesterday?'

'Yes. At least she asked me to get them for her.'

'*She* asked you to get them for her?'

'Yes.'

'But she was not allowed to see anyone. How did you see her?'

'I didn't. She telephoned.'

'Ah! And she said – what?'

'Would I get her a two-pound box of Fuller's chocolates.'

'How did her voice sound – weak?'

'No – not at all. Quite strong. But different somehow. I didn't realize it was she speaking at first.'

'Until she told you who she was?'

'Yes.'

'Are you sure, Madame, that it *was* your friend?'

Frederica looked startled.

'I – I – why, of course it was. Who else could it have been?'

'That is an interesting question, Madame.'

'You don't mean –'

'*Could you swear*, Madame, that it was your friend's voice – apart from what she said?'

'No,' said Frederica, slowly, 'I couldn't. Her voice was certainly different. I thought it was the phone – or perhaps being ill . . .'

'If she had not told you who she was, you would not have recognized it?'

'No, no, I don't think I should. Who was it, M. Poirot? Who was it?'

'That is what I mean to know, Madame.'

The graveness of his face seemed to awaken her suspicions.

'Is Nick – has anything happened?' she asked, breathlessly.

Poirot nodded.

'She is ill – dangerously ill. Those chocolates, Madame – were poisoned.'

'The chocolates *I* sent her? But that's impossible – impossible!'

'Not impossible, Madame, since Mademoiselle is at death's door.'

'Oh, my God.' She hid her face in her hands, then raised it white and quivering. 'I don't understand – I don't understand. The other, yes, but not this. They couldn't be poisoned. Nobody ever touched them but me and Jim. You're making some dreadful mistake, M. Poirot.'

'It is not I that make a mistake – even though my name was in the box.'

She stared at him blankly.

'If Mademoiselle Nick dies –' he said, and made a threatening gesture with his hand.

She gave a low cry.

He turned away, and taking me by the arm, went up to the sitting-room.

He flung his hat on the table.

'I understand nothing – but nothing! I am in the dark. I am a little child. Who stands to gain by Mademoiselle's death? Madame Rice. Who buys the chocolates and admits it and tells a story of being rung up on the telephone that cannot hold water for a minute? Madame Rice. It is too simple – too stupid. And she is not stupid – no.'

'Well, then –'

'But she takes cocaine, Hastings. I am certain she takes cocaine. There is no mistaking it. And there was cocaine in those chocolates. And what did she mean when she said, "*The other, yes, but not this.*" It needs explaining, that! And the sleek M. Lazarus – what is *he* doing in all this? What does she know, Madame Rice? She knows something. But I cannot make her speak. She is not of those you can frighten into speech. But she knows something, Hastings. Is her tale of the telephone true, or did she invent it? If it is true whose voice was it?

'I tell you, Hastings. This is all very black – very black.'

'Always darkest before dawn,' I said reassuringly.

He shook his head.

'Then the other box – that came by post. Can we rule that out? No, we cannot, because Mademoiselle is not sure. It is an annoyance, that!'

He groaned.

I was about to speak when he stopped me.

'No, no. Not another proverb. I cannot bear it. If you would be the good friend – the good helpful friend –'

'Yes,' I said eagerly.

'Go out, I beg of you, and buy me some playing cards.'

I stared.

'Very well,' I said coldly.

I could not but suspect that he was making a deliberate excuse to get rid of me.

Here, however, I misjudged him. That night, when I came into the sitting-room about ten o'clock, I found Poirot carefully building card houses – and I remembered!

It was an old trick of his – soothing his nerves. He smiled at me.

'Yes – you remember. One needs the precision. One card on another – so – in exactly the right place and that supports the weight of the card on top and so on, up and up. Go to bed, Hastings. Leave me here, with my house of cards. I clear the mind.'

It was about five in the morning when I was shaken awake.

Poirot was standing by my bedside. He looked pleased and happy.

'It was very just what you said, *mon ami*. Oh! it was very just. More, it was *spirituel*!'

I blinked at him, being imperfectly awake.

'Always darkest before dawn – that is what you said. It has been very dark – and now it is dawn.'

I looked at the window. He was perfectly right.

'No, no, Hastings. In the head! The mind! The little grey cells!'

He paused and then said quietly:

'You see, Hastings, Mademoiselle is dead.'

'What?' I cried, suddenly wide awake.

'Hush – hush. It is as I say. Not really – *bien entendu* – but it can be arranged. Yes, for twenty-four hours it can be arranged. I arrange it with the doctor, with the nurses.

'You comprehend, Hastings? *The murderer has been success-ful*. Four times he has tried and failed. The fifth time he has succeeded.

'*And now, we shall see what happens next* . . .

'It will be very interesting.'

CHAPTER 18

THE FACE AT THE WINDOW

The events of the next day are completely hazy in my memory. I was unfortunate enough to awake with fever on me. I have been liable to these bouts of fever at inconvenient times ever since I once contracted malaria.

In consequence, the events of that day take on in my memory the semblance of a nightmare – with Poirot coming and going as a kind of fantastic clown, making a periodic appearance in a circus.

He was, I fancy, enjoying himself to the full. His poise of baffled despair was admirable. How he achieved the end he had in view and which he had disclosed to me in the early hours of the morning, I cannot say. But achieve it he did.

It cannot have been easy. The amount of deception and subterfuge involved must have been colossal. The English character is averse to lying on a wholesale scale and that, no less, was what Poirot's plan required. He had, first, to get Dr Graham converted to the scheme. With Dr Graham on his side, he had to persuade the Matron and some members of the staff of the nursing home to conform to the plan. There again, the difficulties must have been immense. It was probably Dr Graham's influence that turned the scale.

Then there was the Chief Constable and the police. Here, Poirot would be up against officialdom. Nevertheless he wrung at last an unwilling consent out of Colonel Weston. The Colonel made it clear that it was in no way his responsibility. Poirot and Poirot alone was responsible for the spreading abroad of these lying reports. Poirot agreed. He would have agreed to anything so long as he was permitted to carry out his plan.

I spent most of the day dozing in a large armchair with a rug over my knees. Every two or three hours or so, Poirot would burst in and report progress.

'*Comment ça va, mon ami?* How I commiserate you. But it is as well, perhaps. The farce, you do not play it as well as I do. I come this moment from ordering a wreath – a wreath immense – stupendous. Lilies, my friend – large quantities of lilies. "*With heartfelt regret. From Hercule Poirot.*" Ah! what a comedy.'

He departed again.

'I come from a most poignant conversation with Madame Rice,' was his next piece of information. 'Very well dressed in black, that one. Her poor friend – what a tragedy! I groan sympathetically. Nick, she says, was so joyous, so full of life. Impossible to think of her as dead. I agree. "It is," I say, "the irony of death that it takes one like that. The old and useless are left." Oh! *là là!* I groan again.'

'How you are enjoying this,' I murmured feebly.

'*Du tout.* It is part of my plan, that is all. To play the comedy successfully, you must put the heart into it. Well, then, the conventional expressions of regret over, Madame comes to matters nearer home. All night she has lain awake wondering about those sweets. It is impossible – impossible. "Madame," I say, "it is not impossible. You can see the analyst's report." Then she says, and her voice is far from steady, "It was – *cocaine*, you say?" I assent. And she says, "Oh, my God. I don't understand."'

'Perhaps that's true.'

'She understands well enough that she is in danger. She is intelligent. I told you that before. Yes, she is in danger, and she knows it.'

'And yet it seems to me that for the first time you don't believe her guilty.'

Poirot frowned. The excitement of his manner abated.

'It is profound what you say there, Hastings. No – it seems to me that – somehow – the facts no longer fit. These crimes – so far what has marked them most – the subtlety, is it not? And here is no subtlety at all – only the crudity, pure and simple. No, it does not fit.'

He sat down at the table.

'*Voilà* – let us examine the facts. There are three possibilities. There are the sweets bought by Madame and delivered by M. Lazarus. And in that case the guilt rests with one or the other or *both.* And the telephone call, supposedly from Mademoiselle Nick, that is an invention pure and simple. That is the straightforward – the obvious solution.

'Solution 2: The *other* box of sweets – that which came by post.

Anyone may have sent those. Any of the suspects on our list from A. to J. (You remember? A very wide field.) But, if that were the guilty box, *what is the point of the telephone call?* Why complicate matters with a second box?'

I shook my head feebly. With a temperature of 102, any complication seemed to me quite unnecessary and absurd.

'Solution 3: A poisoned box was substituted for the innocent box bought by Madame. In that case the telephone call is ingenious and understandable. Madame is to be what you call the kitten's paw. She is to pull the roasting chestnuts out of the fire. So Solution 3 is the most logical – but, alas, it is also the most difficult. How be sure of substituting a box at the right moment? The orderly might take the box straight upstairs – a hundred and one possibilities might prevent the substitution being effected. No, it does not seem sense.'

'Unless it were Lazarus,' I said.

Poirot looked at me.

'You have the fever, my friend. It mounts, does it not?'

I nodded.

'Curious how a few degrees of heat should stimulate the intellect. You have uttered there an observation of profound simplicity. So simple, was it, that I had failed to consider it. But it would suppose a very curious state of affairs. M. Lazarus, the dear friend of Madame, doing his best to get her hanged. It opens up possibilities of a very curious nature. But complex – very complex.'

I closed my eyes. I was glad I had been brilliant, but I did not want to think of anything complex. I wanted to go to sleep.

Poirot, I think, went on talking, but I did not listen. His voice was vaguely soothing . . .

It was late afternoon when I saw him next.

'My little plan, it has made the fortune of flower shops,' he announced. 'Everybody orders wreaths. M. Croft, M. Vyse, Commander Challenger –'

The last name awoke a chord of compunction in my mind.

'Look here, Poirot,' I said. 'You must let him in on this. Poor fellow, he will be distracted with grief. It isn't fair.'

'You have always the tenderness for him, Hastings.'

'I like him. He's a thoroughly decent chap. You've got to take him into the secret.'

Poirot shook his head.

'No, *mon ami*. I do not make the exceptions.'

'But you don't suspect him to have anything to do with it?'

'I do not make the exceptions.'

'Think how he must be suffering.'

'On the contrary, I prefer to think of what a joyful surprise I prepare for him. To think the loved one dead – and find her alive! It is a sensation unique – stupendous.'

'What a pig-headed old devil you are. He'd keep the secret all right.'

'I am not so sure.'

'He's the soul of honour. I'm certain of it.'

'That makes it all the more difficult to keep a secret. Keeping a secret is an art that requires many lies magnificently told, and a great aptitude for playing the comedy and enjoying it. Could he dissemble, the Commander Challenger? If he is what you say he is, he certainly could *not*.'

'Then you won't tell him?'

'I certainly refuse to imperil my little idea for the sake of the sentiment. It is life and death we play with, *mon cher*. Anyway, the suffering, it is good for the character. Many of your famous clergymen have said so – even a Bishop if I am not mistaken.'

I made no further attempt to shake his decision. His mind, I could see, was made up.

'I shall not dress for dinner,' he murmured. 'I am too much the broken old man. That is my part, you understand. All my self-confidence has crashed – I am broken. I have failed. I shall eat hardly any dinner – the food untasted on the plate. That is the attitude, I think. In my own apartment I will consume some brioches and some chocolate *éclairs* (so called) which I had the foresight to buy at a confectioners. *Et vous?*'

'Some more quinine, I think,' I said, sadly.

'Alas, my poor Hastings. But courage, all will be well to-morrow.'

'Very likely. These attacks often last only twenty-four hours.'

I did not hear him return to the room. I must have been asleep.

When I awoke, he was sitting at the table writing. In front of him was a crumpled sheet of paper smoothed out. I recognized it for the paper on which he had written that list of people – A. to J. – which he had afterwards crumpled up and thrown away.

He nodded in answer to my unspoken thought.

'Yes, my friend. I have resurrected it. I am at work upon it from a different angle. I compile a list of questions concerning each person. The questions may have no bearing on the crime – they are just things that I do not know – things that remain unexplained, and for which I seek to supply the answer from my own brain.'

'How far have you got?'

'I have finished. You would like to hear? You are strong enough?'

'Yes, as a matter of fact, I am feeling a great deal better.'

'*A la bonne heure!* Very well, I will read them to you. Some of them, no doubt, you will consider puerile.'

He cleared his throat.

'A. *Ellen.* – Why did she remain in the house and not go out to see fireworks? (Unusual, as Mademoiselle's evidence and surprise make clear.) What did she think or suspect might happen? Did she admit anyone (J. for instance) to the house? Is she speaking the truth about the secret panel? If there is such a thing why is she unable to remember where it is? (Mademoiselle seems very certain there is no such thing – and she would surely know.) If she invented it, why did she invent it? Had she read Michael Seton's love letters or was her surprise at Mademoiselle Nick's engagement genuine?

'B. *Her Husband.* – Is he as stupid as he seems? Does he share Ellen's knowledge, whatever it is, or does he not? Is he, in any respect, a mental case?

'C. *The Child.* – Is his delight in blood a natural instinct common to his age and development, or is it morbid, and is that morbidity inherited from either parent? Has he ever shot with a toy pistol?

'D. *Who is Mr Croft?* – Where does he really come from? Did he post the will as he swears he did? What motive could he have in *not* posting it?

'E. *Mrs Croft. Same as above.* – Who *are* Mr and Mrs Croft? Are they in hiding for some reason – and if so, what reason? Have they any connection with the Buckley family?

'F. *Mrs Rice.* – Was she really aware of the engagement between Nick and Michael Seton? Did she merely guess it, or had she actually read the letters which passed between them? (In that case she would know Mademoiselle was Seton's heir.) Did she know that she herself was Mademoiselle's residuary legatee? (This, I think, is likely. Mademoiselle would probably tell her so, adding perhaps that she would not get much out of it.) Is there any truth in Commander Challenger's suggestion that Lazarus was attracted by Mademoiselle Nick? (This might explain a certain lack of cordiality between the two friends which seems to have shown itself in the last few months.) Who is the "boy friend" mentioned in her note as supplying the drug? *Could this possibly be J.?* Why did she turn faint one day in this room? Was it something that had been said – or was it something she *saw?* Is her account of the telephone message asking her to buy chocolates correct – or is it a deliberate lie? What did she mean by "I can understand the other – but not this"? If she is not herself guilty, what knowledge has she got that she is keeping to herself?

'You perceive,' said Poirot, suddenly breaking off, 'that the questions concerning Madame Rice are almost innumerable. From beginning to end, she is an enigma. And that forces me to a conclusion. Either Madame Rice is guilty – or she knows – or shall we say, thinks she knows – who *is* guilty. But is she right? Does she know or does she merely suspect? And how is it possible to make her speak?'

He sighed.

'Well, I will go on with my list of questions.

'G. *Mr. Lazarus.* – Curious – there are practically no questions to ask concerning him – except the crude one, "Did he substitute the poisoned sweets?" Otherwise I find only one totally irrelevant question. But I have put it down. "Why did M. Lazarus offer fifty pounds for a picture that was only worth twenty?"'

'He wanted to do Nick a good turn,' I suggested.

'He would not do it that way. He is a dealer. He does not buy to sell at a loss. If he wished to be amiable he would lend her money as a private individual.'

'It can't have any bearing on the crime, anyway.'

'No, that is true – but all the same, I should like to know. I am a student of the psychology, you understand.

'Now we come to H.'

'H. *Commander Challenger*. – Why did Mademoiselle Nick tell him she was engaged to someone else? What necessitated her having to tell him that? She told no one else. Had he proposed to her? What are his relations with his uncle?'

'His uncle, Poirot?'

'Yes, the doctor. That rather questionable character. Did any private news of Michael Seton's death come through to the Admiralty before it was announced publicly?'

'I don't quite see what you're driving at Poirot. Even if Challenger knew beforehand about Seton's death, it does not seem to get us anywhere. It provides no earthly motive for killing the girl he loved.'

'I quite agree. What you say is perfectly reasonable. But these are just things I should like to know. I am still the dog, you see, nosing about for the things that are not very nice!

'I. *M. Vyse*. – Why did he say what he did about his cousin's fanatical devotion to End House? What possible motive could he have in saying that? Did he, or did he not, receive the will? Is he, in fact, an honest man – or is he not an honest man?

'And now *J*. – Eh bien, J. is what I put down before – a giant question mark. Is there such a person, or is there not –

'*Mon Dieu!* my friend, what have you?'

I had started from my chair with a sudden shriek. With a shaking hand I pointed at the window.

'A face, Poirot!' I cried. 'A face pressed against the glass. A dreadful face! It's gone now – but I saw it.'

Poirot strode to the window and pushed it open. He leant out.

'There is no one there now,' he said, thoughtfully. 'You are sure you did not imagine it, Hastings?'

'Quite sure. It was a horrible face.'

'There is a balcony, of course. Anyone could reach there quite easily if they wanted to hear what we were saying. When you say a dreadful face, Hastings, just what do you mean?'

'A white, staring face, hardly human.'

'*Mon ami*, that is the fever. A face, yes. An unpleasant face, yes. But a face hardly human – *no*. What you saw was the effect of a face pressed closely against the glass – that allied to the shock of seeing it there at all.'

'It was a dreadful face,' I said, obstinately.

'It was not the face of – anyone you know?'

'No, indeed.'

'H'm – it might have been, though! I doubt if you would recognize it under these circumstances. I wonder now – yes, I very much wonder . . .'

He gathered up his papers thoughtfully.

'One thing at least is to the good. If the owner of that face overheard our conversation we did not mention that Mademoiselle Nick was alive and well. Whatever else our visitor may have heard, that at least escaped him.'

'But surely,' I said, 'the results of this – eh – brilliant manoeuvre of yours have been slightly disappointing up to date. Nick is dead and no startling developments have occurred!'

'I did not expect them yet awhile. Twenty-four hours, I said. *Mon ami, tomorrow, if I am not mistaken, certain things will arise. Otherwise* – otherwise I am wrong from start to finish. There is the post, you see. I have hopes of tomorrow's post.'

I awoke in the morning feeling weak but with the fever abated. I also felt hungry. Poirot and I had breakfast served in our sitting-room.

'Well?' I said, maliciously, as he sorted his letters. 'Has the post done what you expected of it?'

Poirot, who had just opened two envelopes which patently contained bills, did not reply. I thought he looked rather cast down and not his usual cock-a-hoop self.

I opened my own mail. The first was a notice of a spiritualist meeting.

'If all else fails, we must go to the spiritualists,' I remarked. 'I often wonder that more tests of this kind aren't made. The spirit of the victim comes back and names the murderer. That would be a proof.'

'It would hardly help us,' said Poirot, absently. 'I doubt if Maggie Buckley knew whose hand it was shot her down. Even if she could speak she would have nothing of value to tell us. *Tiens!* that is odd.'

'What is?'

'You talk of the dead speaking, and at that moment I open this letter.'

He tossed it across to me. It was from Mrs Buckley and ran as follows:

Langley Rectory.

'*Dear Monsieur Poirot, – On my return here I found a letter written by my poor child on her arrival at St Loo. There is nothing in it of interest to you, I'm afraid, but I thought perhaps you would care to see it.*

'*Thanking you for your kindness,*

'*Yours sincerely,*

'*Jean Buckley.*'

The enclosure brought a lump to my throat. It was so terribly commonplace and so completely untouched by any apprehension of tragedy:

'*Dear Mother, – I arrived safely. Quite a comfortable journey. Only two people in the carriage all the way to Exeter.*

'*It is lovely weather here. Nick seems very well and gay – a little restless, perhaps, but I cannot see why she should have telegraphed for me in the way she did. Tuesday would have done just as well.*

'*No more now. We are going to have tea with some neighbours. They are Australians and have rented the lodge. Nick says they are kind but rather awful. Mrs Rice and Mr Lazarus are coming to stay. He is the art dealer. I will post this in the box by the gate, then it will catch the post. Will write to-morrow.*

'*Your loving daughter,*
'*Maggie.*'

'*P.S. – Nick says there* is *a reason for her wire. She will tell me after tea. She is very queer and jumpy.*'

'The voice of the dead,' said Poirot, quietly. 'And it tells us – nothing.'

'The box by the gate,' I remarked idly. 'That's where Croft said he posted the will.'

'Said so – yes. I wonder. How I wonder!'

'There is nothing else of interest among your letters?'

'Nothing. Hastings, I am very unhappy. I am in the dark. Still in the dark. I comprehend nothing.'

At that moment the telephone rang. Poirot went to it.

Immediately I saw a change come over his face. His manner was very restrained, nevertheless he could not disguise from my eyes his intense excitement.

His own contributions to the conversation were entirely non-committal so that I could not gather what it was all about.

Presently, however, with a '*Très bien. Je vous remercie,*' he put back the receiver and came back to where I was sitting. His eyes were sparkling with excitement.

'*Mon ami,*' he said. '*What did I tell you?* Things have begun to happen.'

'What was it?'

'That was M. Charles Vyse on the telephone. He informs me that this morning, through the post, he has received a will signed by his cousin, Miss Buckley, and dated the 25th February last.'

'What? *The* will?'

'*Evidemment.*'

'It has turned up?'

'Just at the right moment, *n'est-ce pas?*'

'Do you think he is speaking the truth?'

'Or do I think he has had the will all along? Is that what you would say? Well, it is all a little curious. But one thing is certain; I told you that, if Mademoiselle Nick were supposed to be dead, we should have developments – and sure enough here they are!'

'Extraordinary,' I said. 'You were right. I suppose this is the will making Frederica Rice residuary legatee?'

'M. Vyse said nothing about the contents of the will. He was far too correct. But there seems very little reason to doubt that this is the same will. It is witnessed, he tells me, by Ellen Wilson and her husband.'

'So we are back at the old problem,' I said. 'Frederica Rice.'

'The enigma!'

'Frederica Rice,' I murmured, inconsequently. 'It's a pretty name.'

'Prettier than what her friends call her. Freddie' – he made a face – '*ce n'est pas joli* – for a young lady.'

'There aren't many abbreviations of Frederica,' I said. 'It's not like Margaret where you can have half a dozen – Maggie, Margot, Madge, Peggie –'

'True. Well, Hastings, are you happier now? That things have begun to happen?'

'Yes, of course. Tell me – did you expect *this* to happen?'

'No – not exactly. I had formulated nothing very precise to myself. All I had said was that given a certain result, the causes of that result must make themselves evident.'

'Yes,' I said, respectfully.

'What was it that I was going to say just as that telephone rang?' mused Poirot. 'Oh, yes, that letter from Mademoiselle Maggie. I wanted to look at it once again. I have an idea in the back of my mind that something in it struck me as rather curious.'

I picked it up from where I had tossed it, and handed it to him.

He read it over to himself. I moved about the room, looking out of the window and observing the yachts racing on the bay.

Suddenly an exclamation startled me. I turned round. Poirot was holding his head in his hands and rocking himself to and fro, apparently in an agony of woe.

'Oh!' he groaned. 'But I have been blind – blind.'

'What's the matter?'

'Complex, I have said? Complicated? *Mais non.* Of a simplicity extreme – extreme. And miserable one that I am, I saw nothing – nothing.'

'Good gracious, Poirot, what is this light that has suddenly burst upon you?'

'Wait – wait – do not speak! I must arrange my ideas. Rearrange them in the light of this discovery so stupendous.'

Seizing his list of questions, he ran over them silently, his lips moving busily. Once or twice he nodded his head emphatically.

Then he laid them down and leaning back in his chair he shut his eyes. I thought at last that he had gone to sleep.

Suddenly he sighed and opened his eyes.

'But yes!' he said. 'It all fits in! All the things that have puzzled me. All the things that have seemed to me a little unnatural. They all have their place.'

'You mean – you know everything?'

'Nearly everything. All that matters. In some respects I have been right in my deductions. In other ways ludicrously far from the truth. But now it is all clear. I shall send today a telegram asking two questions – but the answers to them I know already – I know *here*!' He tapped his forehead.

'And when you receive the answers?' I asked, curiously.

He sprang to his feet.

'My friend, do you remember that Mademoiselle Nick said she wanted to stage a play at End House? Tonight, we stage such a play in End House. But it will be a play produced by Hercule Poirot. Mademoiselle Nick will have a part to play in it.' He grinned suddenly. 'You comprehend, Hastings, *there will be a ghost in this play*. Yes, a ghost. End House has never seen a ghost. It will have one tonight. No' – as I tried to ask a question – 'I will say no more. Tonight, Hastings, we will produce our comedy – and reveal the truth. But now, there is much to do – much to do.'

He hurried from the room.

CHAPTER 19
POIROT PRODUCES A PLAY

It was a curious gathering that met that night at End House.

I had hardly seen Poirot all day. He had been out for dinner but had left me a message that I was to be at End House at nine o'clock. Evening dress, he had added, was not necessary.

The whole thing was like a rather ridiculous dream.

On arrival I was ushered into the dining-room and when I looked round I realized that every person on Poirot's list from A. to I. (J. was necessarily excluded, being in the Mrs Harris-like position of 'there ain't no such person') was present.

Even Mrs Croft was there in a kind of invalid chair. She smiled and nodded at me.

'This is a surprise, isn't it?' she said, cheerfully. 'It makes a change for me, I must say. I think I shall try and get out now and again. All M. Poirot's idea. Come and sit by me, Captain Hastings. Somehow I feel this is rather a gruesome business – but Mr Vyse made a point of it.'

'Mr Vyse?' I said, rather surprised.

Charles Vyse was standing by the mantelpiece. Poirot was beside him talking earnestly to him in an undertone.

I looked round the room. Yes, they were all there. After showing me in (I had been a minute or two late) Ellen had taken her place on a chair just beside the door. On another chair, sitting painfully straight and breathing hard, was her husband. The child, Alfred, squirmed uneasily between his father and mother.

The rest sat round the dining-table. Frederica in her black dress, Lazarus beside her, George Challenger and Croft on the other side of the table. I sat a little away from it near Mrs Croft. And now Charles Vyse, a final nod of the head, took his place at the head of the table, and Poirot slipped unobtrusively into a seat next to Lazarus.

Clearly the producer, as Poirot had styled himself, did not propose to take a prominent part in the play. Charles Vyse was apparently in charge of the proceedings. I wondered what surprises Poirot had in store for him.

The young lawyer cleared his throat and stood up. He looked just the same as ever, impassive, formal and unemotional.

'This is rather an unconventional gathering we have here tonight,' he said. 'But the circumstances are very peculiar. I refer, of course, to the circumstances surrounding the death of my cousin, Miss Buckley. There will have, of course, to be an autopsy – there seems to be no doubt that she met her death by poison, and that that poison was administered with the intent to kill. This is police business and I need not go into it. The police would doubtless prefer me not to do so.

'In an ordinary case, the will of a deceased person is read after the funeral, but in deference to M. Poirot's special wish, I am proposing to read it before the funeral takes place. In fact, I am proposing to read it here and now. That is why everyone has been asked to come here. As I said just now, the circumstances are unusual and justify a departure from precedent.

'The will itself came into my possession in a somewhat unusual manner. Although dated last February, it only reached me by post this morning. However, it is undoubtedly in the handwriting of my cousin – I have no doubt on that point, and though a most informal document, it is properly attested.'

He paused and cleared his throat once more.

Every eye was upon his face.

From a long envelope in his hand, he drew out an enclosure. It was, as we could see, an ordinary piece of End House notepaper with writing on it.

'It is quite short,' said Vyse. He made a suitable pause, then began to read:

> 'This is the last Will and Testament of Magdala Buckley. I direct that all my funeral expenses should be paid and I appoint my cousin Charles Vyse as my executor. I leave everything of which I die possessed to Mildred Croft in grateful recognition of the services rendered by her to my father, Philip Buckley, which services nothing can ever repay.
>
> 'Signed – Magdala Buckley,
> 'Witnesses – Ellen Wilson, William Wilson.'

I was dumbfounded! So I think was everyone else. Only Mrs Croft nodded her head in quiet understanding.

'It's true,' she said, quietly. 'Not that I ever meant to let on about it. Philip Buckley was out in Australia, and if it hadn't been for me – well, I'm not going into that. A secret it's been and a secret it had better remain. She knew about it, though. Nick did, I mean. Her father must have told her. We came down here because we wanted to have a look at the place. I'd always been curious about this End House Philip Buckley talked of. And that dear girl knew all about it, and couldn't do enough for us. Wanted us to come and live with her, she did. But we wouldn't do that. And so she insisted on our having the lodge – and not a penny of rent would she take. We pretended to pay it, of course, so as not to cause talk, but she handed it back to us. And now – this! Well, if anyone says there is no gratitude in the world, I'll tell them they're wrong! This proves it.'

There was still an amazed silence. Poirot looked at Vyse.

'Had you any idea of this?'

Vyse shook his head.

'I knew Philip Buckley had been in Australia. But I never heard any rumours of a scandal there.'

He looked inquiringly at Mrs Croft.

She shook her head.

'No, you won't get a word out of me. I never have said a word and I never shall. The secret goes to the grave with me.'

Vyse said nothing. He sat quietly tapping the table with a pencil.

'I presume, M. Vyse' – Poirot leaned forward – 'that as next of kin you could contest that will? There is, I understand, a vast fortune at stake which was not the case when the will was made.'

Vyse looked at him coldly.

'The will is perfectly valid. I should not dream of contesting my cousin's disposal of her property.'

'You're an honest fellow,' said Mrs Croft, approvingly. 'And I'll see you don't lose by it.'

Charles sank a little from this well-meant but slightly embarrassing remark.

'Well, Mother,' said Mr Croft, with an elation he could not quite keep out of his voice. 'This *is* a surprise! Nick didn't tell *me* what she was doing.'

'The dear sweet girl,' murmured Mrs Croft, putting her handkerchief to her eyes. 'I wish she could look down and see us now. Perhaps she does – who knows?'

'Perhaps,' agreed Poirot.

Suddenly an idea seemed to strike him. He looked round.

'An idea! We are all here seated round a table. Let us hold a *séance*.'

'A *séance?*' said Mrs Croft, somewhat shocked. 'But surely –'

'Yes, yes, it will be most interesting. Hastings, here, has pronounced mediumistic powers.' (Why fix on *me*, I thought.) 'To get through a message from the other world – the opportunity is unique! I feel the conditions are propitious. You feel the same, Hastings.'

'Yes,' I said resolutely, playing up.

'Good. I knew it. Quick, the lights.'

In another minute he had risen and switched them off. The whole thing had been rushed on the company before they had had the energy to protest had they wanted to do so. As a matter of fact they were, I think, still dazed with astonishment over the will.

The room was not quite dark. The curtains were drawn back and the window was open for it was a hot night, and through those windows came a faint light. After a minute or two, as we sat in silence, I began to be able to make out the faint outlines of the furniture. I wondered very much what I was supposed to do and cursed Poirot heartily for not having given me my instructions beforehand.

However, I closed my eyes and breathed in a rather stertorous manner.

Presently Poirot rose and tiptoed to my chair. Then returning to his own, he murmured:

'Yes, he is already in a trance. Soon – things will begin to happen.'

There is something about sitting in the dark, waiting, that fills one with unbearable apprehension. I know that I myself was a prey to nerves and so, I was sure, was everyone else. And yet I had at least an idea of what was about to happen. I knew the one vital fact that no one else knew.

And yet, in spite of all that, my heart leapt into my mouth as I saw the dining-room door slowly opening.

It did so quite soundlessly (it must have been oiled) and the effect was horribly grisly. It swung slowly open and for a minute or two that was all. With its opening a cold blast of air seemed to enter the room. It was, I suppose, a common or garden draught owing to the open window, but it *felt* like the icy chill mentioned in all the ghost stories I have ever read.

And then we all saw it! Framed in the doorway was a white shadowy figure. Nick Buckley . . .

She advanced slowly and noiselessly – with a kind of floating ethereal motion that certainly conveyed the impression of nothing human . . .

I realized then what an actress the world had missed. Nick had wanted to play a part at End House. Now she was playing it, and I felt convinced that she was enjoying herself to the core. She did it perfectly.

She floated forward into the room – and the silence was broken.

There was a gasping cry from the invalid chair beside me. A kind of gurgle from Mr Croft. A startled oath from Challenger. Charles Vyse drew back his chair, I think. Lazarus leaned forward. Frederica alone made no sound or movement.

And then a scream rent the room. Ellen sprang up from her chair.

'It's her!' she shrieked. 'She's come back. She's walking! Them that's murdered always walks. It's her! It's her!'

And then, with a click the lights went on.

I saw Poirot standing by them, the smile of the ringmaster on his face. Nick stood in the middle of the room in her white draperies.

It was Frederica who spoke first. She stretched out an unbelieving hand – touched her friend.

'Nick,' she said. 'You're – you're *real*!'

It was almost a whisper.

Nick laughed. She advanced.

'Yes,' she said. 'I'm real enough. Thank you so much for what you did for my father, Mrs Croft. But I'm afraid you won't be able to enjoy the benefit of that will just yet.'

'Oh, my God,' gasped Mrs Croft. 'Oh, my God.' She twisted to and fro in her chair. 'Take me away, Bert. Take me away. It was all a joke, my dear – all a joke, that's all it was. Honest.'

'A queer sort of joke,' said Nick.

The door had opened again and a man had entered so quietly that I had not heard him. To my surprise I saw that it was Japp. He exchanged a quick nod with Poirot as though satisfying him of something. Then his face suddenly lit up and he took a step forward towards the squirming figure in the invalid chair.

'Hello-ello-ello,' he said. 'What's this? An old friend! Milly Merton, I declare! And at your old tricks again, my dear.'

He turned round in an explanatory way to the company disregarding Mrs Croft's shrill protests.

'Cleverest forger we've ever had, Milly Merton. We knew there had been an accident to the car they made their last getaway in. But there! Even an injury to the spine wouldn't keep Milly from her tricks. She's an artist, she is!'

'Was that will a forgery?' said Vyse.

He spoke in tones of amazement.

'Of course it was a forgery,' said Nick scornfully. 'You don't think I'd make a silly will like that, do you? I left you End House, Charles, and everything else to Frederica.'

She crossed as she spoke and stood by her friend, and just at that moment *it happened!*

A spurt of flame from the window and the hiss of a bullet. Then another and the sound of a groan and a fall outside . . .

And Frederica on her feet with a thin trickle of blood running down her arm . . .

CHAPTER 20

J.

It was all so sudden that for a moment no one knew what had happened.

Then, with a violent exclamation, Poirot ran to the window. Challenger was with him.

A moment later they reappeared, carrying with them the limp body of a man. As they lowered him carefully into a big leather armchair and his face came into view, I uttered a cry.

'*The face* – the face at the window . . .'

It was the man I had seen looking in on us the previous evening. I recognized him at once. I realized that when I had said he was hardly human I had exaggerated as Poirot had accused me of doing.

Yet there was something about his face that justified my

impression. It was a lost face – the face of one removed from ordinary humanity.

White, weak, depraved – it seemed a mere mask – as though the spirit within had fled long ago.

Down the side of it there trickled a stream of blood.

Frederica came slowly forward till she stood by the chair.

Poirot intercepted her.

'You are hurt, Madame?'

She shook her head.

'The bullet grazed my shoulder – that is all.'

She put him aside with a gentle hand and bent down.

The man's eyes opened and he saw her looking down at him.

'I've done for you this time, I hope,' he said in a low vicious snarl, and then, his voice changing suddenly till it sounded like a child's, 'Oh! Freddie, I didn't mean it. I didn't mean it. You've always been so decent to me . . .'

'It's all right –'

She knelt down beside him.

'I didn't mean –'

His head dropped. The sentence was never finished.

Frederica looked up at Poirot.

'Yes, Madame, he is dead,' he said, gently.

She rose slowly from her knees and stood looking down at him. With one hand she touched his forehead – pitifully, it seemed. Then she sighed and turned to the rest of us.

'He was my husband,' she said, quietly.

'J.,' I murmured.

Poirot caught my remark, and nodded a quick assent.

'Yes,' he said softly. 'Always I felt that there was a J. I said so from the beginning, did I not?'

'He was my husband,' said Frederica again. Her voice was terribly tired. She sank into a chair that Lazarus brought for her. 'I might as well tell you everything – now.

'He was – completely debased. He was a drug fiend. He taught me to take drugs. I have been fighting the habit ever since I left him. I think – at last – I am nearly cured. But it has been difficult. Oh! so horribly difficult. Nobody knows how difficult!

'I could never escape from him. He used to turn up and demand money – with threats. A kind of blackmail. If I did not give him money he would shoot himself. That was always his threat. Then he took to threatening to shoot *me*. He was not responsible. He was mad – crazy . . .

'I suppose it was he who shot Maggie Buckley. He didn't mean to shoot her, of course. He must have thought it was me.

'I ought to have said, I suppose. But, after all, I wasn't *sure*. And those queer accidents Nick had – that made me feel that perhaps it wasn't him after all. It might have been someone quite different.

'And then – one day – I saw a bit of his handwriting on a torn piece of paper on M. Poirot's table. It was part of a letter he had sent me. I knew then that M. Poirot was on the track.

'Since then I have felt that it was only a matter of time . . .'

'But I don't understand about the sweets. He wouldn't have wanted to poison *Nick*. And anyway, I don't see how he *could* have had anything to do with that. I've puzzled and puzzled.'

She put both hands to her face, then took them away and said with a queer pathetic finality:

'That's all . . .'

CHAPTER 21
THE PERSON – K.

Lazarus came quickly to her side.

'My dear,' he said. 'My dear.'

Poirot went to the sideboard, poured out a glass of wine and brought it to her, standing over her while she drank it.

She handed the glass back to him and smiled.

'I'm all right now,' she said. 'What – what had we better do next?'

She looked at Japp, but the Inspector shook his head. 'I'm on a holiday, Mrs Rice. Just obliging an old friend – that's all I'm doing. The St Loo police are in charge of the case.'

She looked at Poirot.

'And M. Poirot is in charge of the St Loo Police?'

'Oh! *quelle idée, Madame!* I am a mere humble adviser.'

'M. Poirot,' said Nick. 'Can't we hush it up?'

'You wish that, Mademoiselle?'

'Yes. After all – I'm the person most concerned. And there will be no more attacks on me – now.'

'No, that is true. There will be no more attacks on you now.'

'You're thinking of Maggie. But, M. Poirot, nothing will bring Maggie back to life again! If you make all this public, you'll only bring a terrible lot of suffering and publicity on Frederica – and she hasn't deserved it.'

'You say she has not deserved it?'

'Of course she hasn't! I told you right at the beginning that she had a brute of a husband. You've seen to-night – what he was. Well, he's dead. Let that be the end of things. Let the police go on looking for the man who shot Maggie. They just won't find him, that's all.'

'So that is what you say, Mademoiselle? *Hush it all up.*'

'Yes. Please. Oh! *Please.* Please, *dear* M. Poirot.'

Poirot looked slowly round.

'What do you all say?'

Each spoke in turn.

'I agree,' I said, as Poirot looked at me.

'I, too,' said Lazarus.

'Best thing to do,' from Challenger.

'Let's forget everything that's passed in this room tonight.' This very determinedly from Croft.

'You *would* say that!' interpolated Japp.

'Don't be hard on me, dearie,' his wife sniffed to Nick, who looked at her scornfully but made no reply.

'Ellen?'

'Me and William won't say a word, sir. Least said, soonest mended.'

'And you, M. Vyse?'

'A thing like this can't be hushed up,' said Charles Vyse. 'The facts must be made known in the proper quarter.'

'Charles!' cried Nick.

'I'm sorry, dear. I look at it from the legal aspect.'

Poirot gave a sudden laugh.

'So you are seven to one. The good Japp is neutral.'

'I'm on holiday,' said Japp, with a grin. 'I don't count.'

'Seven to one. Only M. Vyse holds out – on the side of law and order! You know, M. Vyse, you are a man of character!'

Vyse shrugged his shoulders.

'The position is quite clear. There is only one thing to do.'

'Yes – you are an honest man. *Eh bien* – I, too, range myself on the side of the minority. *I, too, am for the truth.*'

'M. Poirot!' cried Nick.

'Mademoiselle – you dragged me into the case. I came into it at your wish. You cannot silence me now.'

He raised a threatening forefinger in a gesture that I knew well.

'Sit down – all of you, and I will tell you – the truth.'

Silenced by his imperious attitude, we sat down meekly and turned attentive faces towards him.

'*Ecoutez!* I have a list here – a list of persons connected with the crime. I numbered them with the letters of the alphabet including the letter J. J. stood for a person unknown – linked to the crime by one of the others. I did not know who J. was until tonight, *but I knew that there was such a person.* The events of tonight have proved that I was right.

'But yesterday, I suddenly realized that I had made a grave error. I had made an omission. I added another letter to my list. The letter K.'

'Another person unknown?' asked Vyse, with a slight sneer.

'Not exactly. I adopted J. as the symbol for a person unknown. Another person unknown would be merely another J. K. has a different significance. *It stands for a person who should have been included in the original list, but who was overlooked.*'

He bent over Frederica.

'Reassure yourself, Madame. *Your husband was not guilty of murder.* It was the person K. who shot Mademoiselle Maggie.'

She stared.

'But who is K.?'

Poirot nodded to Japp. He stepped forward and spoke in tones reminiscent of the days when he had given evidence in police courts.

'Acting on information received, I took up a position here early in the evening, having been introduced secretly into the house by M. Poirot. I was concealed behind the curtains in the drawing-room. When everyone was assembled in this room, a young lady entered the drawing-room and switched on the light.

She made her way to the fireplace and opened a small recess in the panelling that appeared to be operated with a spring. She took from the recess a pistol. With this in her hand she left the room. I followed her and opening the door a crack I was able to observe her further movements. Coats and wraps had been left in the hall by the visitors on arrival. The young lady carefully wiped the pistol with a handkerchief and then placed it in the pocket of a grey wrap, the property of Mrs Rice –'

A cry burst from Nick.

'This is untrue – every word of it!'

Poirot pointed a hand at her.

'*Voilà!*' he said. '*The person K.! It was Mademoiselle Nick who shot her cousin, Maggie Buckley.*'

'Are you mad?' cried Nick. 'Why should I kill Maggie?'

'In order to inherit the money left to her by Michael Seton! Her name too was Magdala Buckley – and it was to her he was engaged – not you.'

'You – you –'

She stood there trembling – unable to speak. Poirot turned to Japp.

'You telephoned to the police?'

'Yes, they are waiting in the hall now. They've got the warrant.'

'You're all mad!' cried Nick, contemptuously. She moved swiftly to Frederica's side. 'Freddie, give me your wrist-watch as – as a souvenir, will you?'

Slowly Frederica unclasped the jewelled watch from her wrist and handed it to Nick.

'Thanks. And now – I suppose we must go through with this perfectly ridiculous comedy.'

'The comedy you planned and produced in End House. Yes – but you should not have given the star part to Hercule Poirot. That, Mademoiselle, was your mistake – your very grave mistake.'

CHAPTER 22
THE END OF THE STORY

'You want me to explain?'

Poirot looked round with a gratified smile and the air of mock humility I knew so well.

We had moved into the drawing-room and our numbers had lessened. The domestics had withdrawn tactfully, and the Crofts had been asked to accompany the police. Frederica, Lazarus, Challenger, Vyse and I remained.

'*Eh bien* – I confess it – I was fooled – fooled completely and absolutely. The little Nick, she had me where she wanted me, as your idiom so well expresses it. Ah! Madame, when you said that your friend was a clever little liar – how right you were! How right!'

'Nick always told lies,' said Frederica, composedly. 'That's why I didn't really believe in these marvellous escapes of hers.'

'And I – imbecile that I was – did!'

'Didn't they really happen?' I asked. I was, I admit, still hopelessly confused.

'They were invented – very cleverly – to give just the impression they did.'

'What was that?'

'They gave the impression that Mademoiselle Nick's life was in danger. But I will begin earlier than that. I will tell you the story as I have pieced it out – not as it came to me imperfectly and in flashes.

'At the beginning of the business then, we have this girl, this Nick Buckley, young and beautiful, unscrupulous, and passionately and fanatically devoted to her home.'

Charles Vyse nodded.

'I told you that.'

'And you were right. Mademoiselle Nick loved End House. But she had no money. The house was mortgaged. She wanted money – she wanted it feverishly – and she could not get it. She meets this young Seton at Le Touquet, he is attracted by her. She knows that in all probability he is his uncle's heir and that that uncle is worth millions. Good, her star is in the ascendant, she thinks. But he is not really seriously attracted. He thinks her good fun, that is all. They meet at Scarborough, he takes her up in his machine and then – the catastrophe occurs. He meets Maggie and falls in love with her at first sight.

'Mademoiselle Nick is dumbfounded. Her cousin Maggie whom she has never considered pretty! But to young Seton she is "different". The one girl in the world for him. They become secretly engaged. Only one person knows – has to know. That person is Mademoiselle Nick. The poor Maggie – she is glad that there is one person she can talk to. Doubtless she reads to her cousin parts of her fiancé's letters. So it is that Mademoiselle gets to hear of the will. She pays no attention to it at the time. But it remains in her mind.

'Then comes the sudden and unexpected death of Sir Matthew Seton, and hard upon that the rumours of Michael Seton's being missing. And straightaway an outrageous plan comes into our young lady's head. Seton does not know that her name is Magdala also. He only knows her as Nick. His will is clearly quite informal – a mere mention of a name. But in the eyes of the world Seton is her friend! It is with *her* that his name has been coupled. If she were to claim to be engaged to him, no one would be surprised. *But to do that successfully Maggie must be out of the way.*

'Time is short. She arranges for Maggie to come and stay in a few days' time. Then she has her escapes from death. The picture whose cord she cuts through. The brake of the car that she tampers with. The boulder – that perhaps was natural and she merely invented the story of being underneath on the path.

'And then – she sees *my* name in the paper. (I told you, Hastings, everyone knew Hercule Poirot!) and she has the audacity to make *me* an accomplice! The bullet through the hat that falls at my feet. Oh! the pretty comedy. And I am taken in! I believe in the peril that menaces her! *Bon!* She has got a valuable witness on her side. I play into her hands by asking her to send for a friend.

'She seizes the chance and sends for Maggie to come a day earlier.

'How easy the crime is actually! She leaves us at the dinner table and after hearing on the wireless that Seton's death is a fact, she starts to put her plan into action. She has plenty of time, then, to take Seton's letters to Maggie – look through them and select the few that will answer her purpose. These she places in her own room. Then, later, she and Maggie leave the fireworks and go back to the house. She tells her cousin to put on her shawl. Then stealing out after her, she shoots her. Quick, into the house, the pistol concealed in the secret panel (of whose existence she thinks nobody knows). Then upstairs. There she waits till voices are heard. The body is discovered. It is her cue.

'Down she rushes and out through the window.

'How well she played her part! Magnificently! Oh, yes, she staged a fine drama here. The maid, Ellen, said this was an evil house. I am inclined to agree with her. It was from the house that Mademoiselle Nick took her inspiration.'

'But those poisoned sweets,' said Frederica. 'I still don't understand about that.'

'It was all part of the same scheme. Do you not see that if Nick's life was attempted *after* Maggie was dead that absolutely settled the question that Maggie's death had been a mistake.

'When she thought the time was ripe she rang up Madame Rice and asked her to get her a box of chocolates.'

'Then it *was* her voice?'

'But, yes! How often the simple explanation is the true one! *N'est ce pas?* She made her voice sound a little different – that was all. So that you might be in doubt when questioned. Then, when the box arrived – again how simple. She fills three of the chocolates with cocaine (she had cocaine with her, cleverly concealed), eats one of them and is ill – but not *too* ill. She knows very well how much cocaine to take and just what symptoms to exaggerate.

'And the card – *my* card! *Ah! Sapristi* – she has a nerve! It *was* my card – the one I sent with the flowers. Simple, was it not? Yes, but it had to be thought of . . .'

There was a pause and then Frederica asked:

'Why did she put the pistol in my coat?'

'I thought you would ask me that, Madame. It was bound to occur to you in time. Tell me – had it ever entered your head that Mademoiselle Nick no longer liked you? Did you ever feel that she might – hate you?'

'It's difficult to say,' said Frederica, slowly. 'We lived an insincere life. She *used* to be fond of me.'

'Tell me, M. Lazarus – it is not a time for false modesty, you understand – was there ever anything between you and her?'

'No.' Lazarus shook his head. 'I was attracted to her at one time. And then – I don't know why – I went off her.'

'Ah!' said Poirot, nodding his head sagely. 'That was her tragedy. She attracted people – and then they "went off her". Instead of liking her better and better you fell in love with her friend. She began to hate Madame – Madame who had a rich friend behind her. Last winter when she made a will, she was fond of Madame. Later it was different.

'She remembered that will. She did not know that Croft had suppressed it – that it had never reached its destination. Madame (or so the world would say) had got a motive for desiring her death. So it was to Madame she telephoned asking her to get the chocolates. Tonight, the will would have been read, naming Madame her residuary legatee – and then the pistol would be found in her coat – *the pistol with which Maggie Buckley was shot*. If Madame found it, she might incriminate herself by trying to get rid of it.'

'She must have hated me,' murmured Frederica.

'Yes, Madame. You had what she had not – the knack of winning love, and *keeping* it.'

'I'm rather dense,' said Challenger, 'but I haven't quite fathomed the will business yet.'

'No? That's a different business altogether – a very simple one. The Crofts are lying low down here. Mademoiselle Nick has to have an operation. She has made no will. The Crofts see a chance. They persuade her to make one and take charge of it for the post. Then, if anything happens to her – if she dies – they produce a cleverly forged will – leaving the money to Mrs Croft with a reference to Australia and Philip Buckley whom they know once visited the country.

'But Mademoiselle Nick has her appendix removed quite satisfactorily so the forged will is no good. For the moment, that is. Then the attempts on her life begin. The Crofts are hopeful once more. Finally, I announce her death. The chance is too good to be missed. The forged will is immediately posted to M. Vyse. Of course, to begin with, they naturally thought her much richer than she is. They knew nothing about the mortgage.'

'What I really want to know, M. Poirot,' said Lazarus, 'is how you actually got wise to all this. When did you begin to suspect?'

'Ah! there I am ashamed. I was so long – so long. There were things that worried me – yes. Things that seemed not quite right. Discrepancies between what Mademoiselle Nick told me and what other people told me. Unfortunately, I always believed Mademoiselle Nick.

'And then, suddenly, I got a revelation. Mademoiselle Nick made one mistake. She was too clever. When I urged her to send for a friend she promised to do so – and suppressed the fact that she had already sent for Mademoiselle Maggie. It seemed to her less suspicious – *but it was a mistake.*

'For Maggie Buckley wrote a letter home immediately on arrival, and in it she used one innocent phrase that puzzled me: "*I don't see why Nick should have telegraphed for me the way she did. Tuesday would have done just as well.*" What did that mention of Tuesday mean? *It could only mean one thing.* Maggie had been coming to stay on Tuesday anyway. But in that case Mademoiselle Nick had lied – or had at any rate suppressed the truth.

'And for the first time I looked at her in a different light. I criticized her statements. Instead of believing them, I said, "Suppose this were not true." I remembered the discrepancies. "How would it be if every time it was Mademoiselle Nick who was lying and not the other person?"

'I said to myself: "Let us be simple. What has *really* happened?"

'And I saw that what had really happened was that *Maggie Buckley* had been killed. Just that! But who could want Maggie Buckley dead?

'And then I thought of something else – a few foolish remarks that Hastings had made not five minutes before. He had said that there were plenty of abbreviations for Margaret – Maggie, Margot, etc. And it suddenly occurred to me to wonder what was Mademoiselle Maggie's real name?

'Then, *tout d'un coup*, it came to me! Supposing her name was *Magdala*! It was a Buckley name, Mademoiselle Nick had told me so. Two Magdala Buckleys. Supposing . . .

'In my mind I ran over the letters of Michael Seton's that I had read. Yes – there was nothing impossible. There was a mention of Scarborough – but Maggie had been in Scarborough with Nick – her mother had told me so.

'And it explained one thing which had worried me. Why were there so *few* letters? If a girl keeps her love letters at all, she keeps *all* of them. Why these select few? Was there any peculiarity about them?

'And I remembered that there was no *name* mentioned in them. They all began differently – but they began with a term of endearment. Nowhere in them was there the name – *Nick.*

'And there was something else, something that I ought to have seen at once – that cried the truth aloud.'

'What was that?'

'Why – this. Mademoiselle Nick underwent an operation for appendicitis on February 27th last. There is a letter of Michael Seton's dated March 2nd, and no mention of anxiety, of illness or anything unusual. That ought to have shown me that the letters were written to a *different person altogether.*

'Then I went through a list of questions that I had made. And I answered them in the light of my new idea.

'In all but a few isolated questions the result was simple and convincing. And I answered, too, another question which I had asked myself earlier. *Why did Mademoiselle Nick buy a black dress?* The answer was that she and her cousin had to be dressed alike, with the scarlet shawl as an additional touch. That was the true and convincing answer, *not* the other. A girl would not buy mourning before she knew her lover was dead. She would be unreal – unnatural.

'And so I, in turn, staged my little drama. And the thing I hoped for happened! Nick Buckley had been very vehement about the question of a secret panel. She had declared there was no such thing. But if there were – and I did not see why Ellen should have invented it – *Nick must know of it.* Why was she so vehement? Was it possible that she had hidden the pistol there? With the secret intention of using it to throw suspicion on somebody later?

'I let her see that appearances were very black against Madame. That was as she had planned. As I foresaw, she was unable to resist the crowning proof. Besides it was safer for herself. That secret panel might be found by Ellen and the pistol in it!

'We are all safely in here. She is waiting outside for her cue. It is absolutely safe, she thinks, to take the pistol from its hiding place and put it in Madame's coat . . .'

'And so – at the last – she failed . . .'

Frederica shivered.

'All the same,' she said. 'I'm glad I gave her my watch.'

'Yes, Madame.'

She looked up at him quickly.

'You know about that too?'

'What about Ellen?' I asked, breaking in. 'Did she know or suspect anything?'

'No. I asked her. She told me that she decided to stay in the house that night because in her own phrase she "thought something was up". Apparently Nick urged her to see the fireworks rather too decisively. She had fathomed Nick's dislike of Madame. She told me that "she felt in her bones something was going to happen", but she thought it was going to happen to Madame. She knew Miss Nick's temper, she said, and she was always a queer little girl.'

'Yes,' murmured Frederica. 'Yes, let us think of her like that. A queer little girl. A queer little girl who couldn't help herself . . . I shall – anyway.'

Poirot took her hand and raised it gently to his lips.

Charles Vyse stirred uneasily.

'It's going to be a very unpleasant business,' he said, quietly. 'I must see about some kind of defence for her, I suppose.'

'There will be no need, I think,' said Poirot, gently. 'Not if I am correct in my assumptions.'

He turned suddenly on Challenger.

'That's where you put the stuff, isn't it?' he said. 'In those wrist-watches.'

'I – I –' The sailor stammered – at a loss.

'Do not try and deceive me – with your hearty good-fellow manner. It has deceived Hastings – but it does not deceive *me*. You make a good thing out of it, do you not – the traffic in drugs – you and your uncle in Harley Street.'

'M. Poirot.'

Challenger rose to his feet.

My little friend blinked up at him placidly.

'You are the useful "boy friend". Deny it, if you like. But I advise you, if you do not want the facts put in the hands of the police – to go.'

And to my utter amazement, Challenger did go. He went from the room like a flash. I stared after him open-mouthed.

Poirot laughed.

'I told you so, *mon ami*. Your instincts are always wrong. *C'est épatant!*'

'Cocaine was in the wrist-watch –' I began.

'Yes, yes. That is how Mademoiselle Nick had it with her so conveniently at the nursing home. And having finished her supply in the chocolate box she asked Madame just now for hers *which was full.*'

'You mean she can't do without it?'

'*Non, non.* Mademoiselle Nick is not an addict. Sometimes – for fun – that is all. But tonight she needed it for a different purpose. It will be a full dose this time.'

'You mean –?' I gasped.

'It is the best way. Better than the hangman's rope. But pst! we must not say so before M. Vyse who is all for law and order. Officially I know nothing. The contents of the wrist-watch – it is the merest guess on my part.'

'Your guesses are always right, M. Poirot,' said Frederica.

'I must be going,' said Charles Vyse, cold disapproval in his attitude as he left the room.

Poirot looked from Frederica to Lazarus.

'You are going to get married – eh?'

'As soon as we can.'

'And indeed, M. Poirot,' said Frederica. 'I am not the drug-taker you think. I have cut myself down to a tiny dose. I think now – with happiness in front of me – I shall not need a wrist-watch any more.'

'I hope you will have happiness, Madame,' said Poirot, gently. 'You have suffered a great deal. And in spite of everything you have suffered, you have still the quality of mercy in your heart . . .'

'I will look after her,' said Lazarus. 'My business is in a bad way, but I believe I shall pull through. And if I don't – well, Frederica does not mind being poor – with me.'

She shook her head, smiling.

'It is late,' said Poirot, looking at the clock.

We all rose.

'We have spent a strange night in this strange house,' Poirot went on. 'It is, I think, as Ellen says, an evil house . . .'

He looked up at the picture of old Sir Nicholas.

Then, with a sudden gesture, he drew Lazarus aside.

'I ask your pardon, but, of all my questions, there is one still unanswered. Tell me, why did you offer fifty pounds for that picture? It would give me much pleasure to know – so as, you comprehend, to leave nothing unanswered.'

Lazarus looked at him with an impassive face for a minute or two. Then he smiled.

'You see, M. Poirot,' he said. 'I am a dealer.'

'Exactly.'

'That picture is not worth a penny more than twenty pounds. I knew that if I offered Nick fifty, she would immediately suspect it was worth more and would get it valued elsewhere. Then she would find that I had offered her far more than it was worth. The next time I offered to buy a picture she would not have got it valued.'

'Yes, and then?'

'The picture on the far wall is worth at least five thousand pounds,' said Lazarus drily.

'Ah!' Poirot drew a long breath.

'Now I know everything,' he said happily.